Strangers

Dean R. Koontz

A STAR BOOK
published by
the Paperback Division of
W.H. Allen & Co. Plc

A Star Book
Published in 1986
by the Paperback Division of
W.H. Allen & Co. Plc
44 Hill Street, London W1X 8LB

First published in Great Britain by W.H. Allen & Co. Plc
in 1986

Copyright © Dean R. Koontz, 1986

Printed and bound in Great Britain by
Anchor Brendon Ltd, Tiptree, Essex

ISBN 0 352 31986 0

To Bob Tanner, whose enthusiasm at a crucial stage was more important than he can know.

PART ONE

A Time of Trouble

A faithful friend is a strong defence.
A faithful friend is the medicine of life.

– The Apocrypha

A terrible darkness has fallen upon us, but we must not surrender to it. We shall lift lamps of courage and find our way through to the morning.

– Anonymous member of the French Resistance, 1943

ONE

November 7 – December 2

1.

LAGUNA BEACH, CALIFORNIA

Dominick Corvaisis went to sleep under a light wool blanket and a crisp white sheet, sprawled alone in his bed, but he woke elsewhere – in the darkness at the back of the large foyer closet, behind concealing coats and jackets. He was curled in a fetal position. His hands were squeezed into tight fists. The muscles in his neck and arms ached from the tension of a bad though unremembered dream.

He could not recall leaving the comfort of his mattress during the night, but he was not surprised to find that he had travelled in the dark hours. It had happened on two other occasions, and recently.

Somnambulism, a potentially dangerous practice commonly referred to as sleepwalking, has fascinated people throughout history. It fascinated Dom, too, from the moment he became a baffled victim of it. He had found references to sleepwalkers in writings dating as far back as 1000 BC. The ancient Persians believed that the wandering body of a sleepwalker was seeking his spirit, which had detached itself and drifted away during the night. Europeans of the grim Medieval period favoured demonic possession or lycanthropy as an explanation.

Dom Corvaisis did not worry about his affliction, though he was discomfited and somewhat embarrassed by it. As a novelist, he was intrigued by these new nocturnal ramblings, for he viewed all new experiences as material for his fiction.

Nevertheless, though he might eventually make art and a

profit from creative use of his own somnambulism, it *was* an affliction. He crawled out of the closet, wincing as the pain in his neck spread up across his scalp and down into his shoulders. He had difficulty getting to his feet because his legs were cramped.

As always, he felt sheepish. He now knew that somnambulism was a condition to which adults were vulnerable, but he still considered it a childhood problem. Like bed-wetting.

Wearing blue pyjama bottoms, bare-chested, slipperless, he shuffled across the living room, down the short hall, into the master bedroom, and into the bath. In the mirror, he looked dissipated, a libertine surfacing from a shameless week of indulgence in a wide variety of sins.

In fact, he was a man of remarkably few vices. He did not smoke, overeat, or take drugs. He drank little. He liked women, but he was not promiscuous; he believed in commitment in a relationship. Indeed, he had not slept with anyone in – what was it now? – almost four months.

He only looked this bad – dissipated, wrung-out – when he woke and discovered that he had taken one of his unscheduled nocturnal trips to a makeshift bed. Each time he had been exhausted. Though asleep, he got no rest on the nights he walked.

He sat down on the edge of the bathtub, bent his leg up to look at the bottom of his left foot, then checked the bottom of his right foot. Neither was cut, scratched, or particularly dirty, so he had not left the house while sleepwalking. He had awakened in closets twice before, once last week and once twelve days prior to that, and he had not had dirty feet on those occasions, either. As before, he felt as if he had travelled miles while unconscious, but if he actually had gone that far, he had done it by making countless circuits of his own small house.

A long, hot shower soaked away a lot of his muscle discomfort. He was lean and fit, thirty-five years old, with recuperative powers commensurate with his age. By the time he finished breakfast, he felt almost human.

After lingering with a cup of coffee on his patio, studying the pleasant geography of Laguna Beach, which shelved down the hills toward the sea, he went to his study, sure that his work was the cause of his sleepwalking. Not the work itself as much as the amazing success of his first novel, *Twilight in Babylon*, which he had finished last February.

The first agent he approached had accepted him as a client. *Twilight* was put up for auction, and to Dom's astonishment a deal was made with Random House, which paid a remarkably large advance for a first novel. Within a month, movie rights were sold (providing the downpayment on his house), and the Literary Guild took *Twilight* as a main selection. He had spent seven laborious months of sixty-, seventy, and eighty-hour weeks in the writing of that story, not to mention a decade getting himself *ready* to write it, but he still felt like an overnight success, up from genteel poverty in one great leap.

The once-poor Dominick Corvaisis occasionally caught a glimpse of the now-rich Dominick Corvaisis in a mirror or a sun-silvered window, saw himself unguarded, and wondered if he really deserved what had come his way. Sometimes he worried that he was heading for a great fall. With such triumph and acclaim came considerable tension.

When *Twilight* was published next February, would it be well-received and justify Random House's investment, or would it fail and humiliate him? Could he do it again – or was *Twilight* a fluke?

Every hour of his waking day, those and other questions circled his mind with vulturine persistence, and he supposed the same damn questions still swooped through his mind while he slept. That was why he walked in his sleep: he was trying to escape those relentless concerns, seeking a secret place to rest, where his worries could not find him.

Now, at his desk, he switched on the IBM Displaywriter and called up chapter eighteen on the first disk of his new book, as yet untitled. He had stopped yesterday in the middle of the sixth page of the chapter, but when he summoned the document, intending to begin where he had left off, he saw a full page where there had been half. Unfamiliar green lines of text glowed on the word-processor's video display.

For a moment he blinked stupidly at the neat letters of light, then shook his head in pointless denial of what lay before him.

The back of his neck was suddenly cool and damp.

The existence of those unremembered lines on page six was not what gave him the creeps; it was what the lines *said*.

11

Furthermore, there should not have been a page seven in the chapter, for he had not yet created one, but it was there. He also found an eighth page.

As he scrolled through the material on the disk, his hands became clammy. The startling addition to his work-in-progress was only a two-word sentence repeated hundreds of times:

I'm scared. I'm scared. I'm scared. I'm scared.

Double-spacing, quadruple-indentation, four sentences to a line, thirteen lines on page six, twenty-seven lines on page seven, another twenty-seven on page eight – that made 268 repetitions of the sentence. The machine had not created them by itself, for it was merely an obedient slave that did precisely what it was told. And it made no sense to speculate that someone had broken into the house during the night to tamper with his electronically stored manuscript. There were no signs of a break-in, and he could not think of anyone who would play such a prank. Clearly, he had come to the word processor while sleepwalking and had obsessively typed in this sentence 268 times, though he had absolutely no recollection of having done it.

I'm scared.

Scared of what – sleepwalking? It was a disorienting experience, at least on the morning-end, but it was not an ordeal that would cause such terror as this.

He was frightened by the quickness of his literary ascent and by the possibility of an equally swift descent into oblivion. Yet he could not completely dismiss the nagging thought that this had nothing to do with his career, that the threat hanging over him was something else altogether, something strange, something his conscious mind did not yet see but which his subconscious perceived and which it had tried to convey to him by means of that message left while he was sleeping.

No. Nonsense. That was only the novelist's overactive imagination at work. Work. That was the best medicine for him.

Besides, from his research into the subject, he knew that most adult sleepwalkers made short careers of it. Few experienced more than half a dozen episodes, usually contained within a time span of six months or less. Chances were good that his sleep would never again be complicated by midnight ramblings and that he would never again wake huddled and tense in the back of a closet.

He deleted the unwanted words from the disk and went to work on chapter eighteen.

When he next looked at the clock, he was surprised to see that it was past one and that he had laboured through the lunch hour.

Even for southern California, the day was warm for early November, so he ate lunch on the patio. The palm trees rustled in a mild breeze, and the air was scented with autumn flowers. With style and grace, Laguna sloped down to the shores of the Pacific, and the ocean was spangled with sunlight.

Finishing his last sip of Coke, he suddenly tilted his head back, looked straight up into the brilliantly blue sky, and laughed. 'You see – no falling safe. No plummeting piano. No sword of Damocles.'

It was November 7.

2.

BOSTON, MASSACHUSETTS

Dr Ginger Marie Weiss never expected trouble in Bernstein's Delicatessen, but that was where it started, with the incident of the black gloves.

Usually, Ginger could deal with any problems that came her way. She relished every challenge life presented, thrived on trouble. She would have been bored if her path had been always easy, unobstructed. However, it had never occurred to her that she might eventually be confronted with trouble she could not handle.

As well as challenges, life provides lessons, and some are more welcome than others. Some lessons are easy, some difficult.

Some are devastating.

Ginger was intelligent, pretty, ambitious, hard-working, and an excellent cook, but her primary advantage in life was

13

that no one took her seriously on first encounter. She was slender, a wisp, a graceful sprite who seemed as insubstantial as she was lovely. Most people underestimated her for weeks or months, only gradually realising that she was a formidable competitor, colleague – or adversary.

The story of Ginger's mugging was legend at Columbia Presbyterian Hospital, in New York, where she served her internship four years prior to the trouble at Bernstein's Delicatessen. Like all interns, she had often worked sixteen-hour shifts and longer, day after day, and had left the hospital with barely enough energy to drag herself home. One hot, humid Saturday night in July, after completing an especially gruelling tour of duty, she headed for home shortly after ten o'clock – and was accosted by a hulking Neanderthal with hands as big as shovel blades, huge arms, no neck, and a sloped forehead.

'You scream,' he said, launching himself at her with jack-in-the-box suddenness, 'and I'll bust your goddamned teeth out.' He seized her arm and twisted it behind her back. 'You understand me, bitch?'

No other pedestrians were close, and the nearest cars were two blocks away, stopped at a traffic light. No help in sight.

He shoved her into a narrow night-mantled serviceway between two buildings, into a trash-strewn passage with only one dim light. She slammed into a garbage bin, hurting her knee and shoulder, stumbled but did not fall. Many-armed shadows embraced her.

With ineffectual whimpers and breathless protests, she made her assailant feel confident because at first she thought he had a gun.

Humour a gunman, she thought. Don't resist. Resisters get shot.

'Move!' he said between clenched teeth, and he shoved her again.

When he pushed her into a recessed doorway three-quarters of the way along the passage, not far from the single faint bulb at the end, he started talking filthy, telling her what he was going to do with her after he took her money, and even in the poor light she could see he held no weapon. Suddenly she had hope. His vocabulary of obscenities was blood-curdling, but his sexual threats were so stupidly repetitive that they were almost funny. She realised he was just a big dumb loser who relied on his size to get what he wanted. Men of his type seldom carried guns. His muscles gave him a false sense of invulnerability, so he probably had no fighting skill, either.

While he was emptying the purse that she willingly relinquished, Ginger summoned all her courage and kicked him squarely in the crotch. He doubled over from the blow. She moved fast, seized one of his hands, and bent the index finger backwards, savagely, until the pain must have been as excruciating as the throbbing in his bruised privates.

Radical, violent, backward extension of the index finger could quickly incapacitate any man, regardless of his size and strength. By this action she was straining the digital nerve on the front of his hand while simultaneously pinching the highly sensitive median and radial nerves on the back. The intense pain also travelled into the acromial nerves in his shoulder, into his neck.

He grabbed her hair with his free hand and pulled. That counter-attack hurt, made her cry out, blurred her vision, but she gritted her teeth, endured the agony, and bent his captive finger even farther. Her relentless pressure quickly banished all thought of resistance from his mind. Involuntary tears burst from his eyes, and he dropped to his knees, squealing and cursing and helpless.

'Let go of me! Let go of me, you *bitch*!'

Blinking sweat out of her eyes, tasting the same salty effluence at the corners of her mouth, Ginger gripped his index finger with both hands. She shuffled cautiously backwards and led him out of the passage in an awkward three-point crawl, as if dragging a dangerous dog on a tightened choke-chain.

Scuttling, scraping, hitching, and humping himself along on one hand and two knees, he glared up at her with eyes muddied by a murderous urge. His mean, lumpish face became less visible as they moved away from the light, but she could see that it was so contorted by pain and fury and humiliation that it did not seem human, a goblin face. And in a shrill goblin voice he squealed a chilling array of dire imprecations.

By the time they had clumsily negotiated fifteen yards of the

15

serviceway, he was overwhelmed by the agony in his hand and by the sickening waves of pain that must have been rushing outward through his body from his injured testicles. He gagged, choked, and vomited on himself.

She still did not dare let go of him. Now, given the opportunity, he would not merely beat her senseless: he would kill her. Disgusted and terrified, she urged him along even faster than before.

Reaching the sidewalk with the befouled and chastened mugger in tow, she saw no pedestrians who could call the police for her, so she forced her humbled assailant into the middle of the street, where passing traffic came to a standstill at this unexpected spectacle.

When the cops finally arrived, Ginger's relief was exceeded by that of the thug who had attacked her.

*   *   *

In part, people underestimated Ginger because she was small: five-two, a hundred and two pounds, not physically imposing, certainly not intimidating. Likewise, she was shapely but not a blonde bombshell. She *was* blonde, however, and the particular silvery shade of her hair was what caught a man's eye, whether he was seeing her for the first time or the hundredth. Even in bright sunshine her hair recalled moonlight. That ethereally pale and radiant hair, her delicate features, blue eyes that were the very definition of gentleness, an Audrey Hepburn neck, slender shoulders, thin wrists, long-fingered hands, and her tiny waist – all contributed to an impression of fragility that was misleading. Furthermore, she was quiet and watchful by nature, two qualities that might be mistaken for timidity. Her voice was so soft and musical that anyone could easily fail to apprehend the self-assurance and underlying authority in those dulcet tones.

Ginger had inherited her silver-blonde mane, cerulean eyes, beauty, and ambition from her mother, Anna, a five-foot-ten Swede.

'You're my golden girl,' Anna said when Ginger graduated from sixth grade at the age of nine, two years ahead of schedule, after being promoted twice in advance of her peers.

Ginger had been the best student in her class, receiving a

gilt-edged scroll in honour of her academic excellence. Also, as one of three student performers who had provided entertainment before the graduation ceremony, she had played two pieces on the piano – Mozart, followed by a ragtime tune – and had brought the surprised audience to its feet.

'Golden girl,' Anna said, hugging her all the way home in the car.

Jacob drove, blinking back tears of pride. Jacob was an emotional man, easily moved. Somewhat embarrassed by the frequency with which his eyes moistened, he usually tried to conceal the depth of his feelings by blaming his tears or reddened eyes on a never-specified allergy. 'Must be unusual pollens in the air today,' he said twice on the way home from graduation. 'Irritating pollens.'

Anna said, 'It's all come together in you, *bubeleh*. My best features and your father's best, and you're going places, by God, you just wait and see if you aren't. High school, then college, then maybe law school or medical school, anything you want to do. Anything.'

The only people who *never* underestimated Ginger were her parents.

They reached home, turned into the driveway. Jacob stopped short of the garage and said, in surprise, 'What are we doing? Our only child graduates from sixth grade, our child who – since she can do absolutely *anything* – will probably marry the King of Siam and ride a giraffe to the moon, our child wears her first cap and gown and we aren't celebrating? Should we drive into Manhattan, have maybe champagne at the Plaza? Dinner at the Waldorf? No. Something better. Only the best for our giraffe-riding astronaut. We'll go to the soda fountain at Walgreen's!'

'Yeah!' Ginger said.

At Walgreen's, they must have been as odd a family as the soda jerk had ever seen: the Jewish father, not much bigger than a jockey, with a Germanic name but a Sephardic complexion; the Swedish mother, blonde and gloriously feminine, five inches taller than her husband; and the child, a wraith, an elf, petite though her mother was not, fair though her father was dark, with a beauty altogether different from her mother's, a more subtle beauty with a fey quality. Even as

17

a child, Ginger knew that strangers, seeing her with her parents, must think she was adopted.

From her father, Ginger had inherited her slight stature, soft voice, intellect, and gentleness.

She loved them both so completely and intensely that, as a child, her vocabulary had been insufficient to convey her feelings. Even as an adult, she could not find the words to express what they had meant to her. They were both gone now, to early graves.

When Anna died in a traffic accident, shortly after Ginger's twelfth birthday, the common wisdom among Jacob's relatives was that both Ginger and her father would be adrift without the Swede, whom the Weiss clan had long ago ceased to regard as an interloping gentile and for whom they had developed both respect and love. Everyone knew how close the three had been, but more importantly everyone knew that Anna had been the engine powering the family's success. It was Anna who had taken the least ambitious of the Weiss brothers – Jacob the dreamer, Jacob the meek, Jacob with his nose always in a detective novel or a science fiction story – and had made something of him. He had been an employee in a jewellery store when she married him, but by the time she died he owned two shops of his own.

After the funeral, the family gathered at Aunt Rachel's big house in Brooklyn Heights. As soon as she could slip away, Ginger sought solace in the dark solitude of the pantry. Sitting on a stool, with the aroma of many spices heavy in the air of that narrow place, praying to God to bring her mother back, she heard Aunt Francine talking to Rachel in the kitchen. Fran was bemoaning the grim future awaiting Jacob and his little girl in a world without Anna:

'He won't be able to keep the business going, you know he won't, not even once the grief has passed and he goes back to work. The poor *luftmensch*. Anna was his common sense and his motivation and his best adviser, and without her in five years he'll be lost.'

They were underestimating Ginger.

To be fair, Ginger was only twelve, and even though she was already in tenth grade, she was still a child in most people's eyes. No one could have foreseen that she would fill

18

Anna's shoes so quickly. She shared her mother's love of cooking, so in the weeks following the funeral she pored through cookbooks and, with the amazing diligence and perseverance that were her trademarks, she acquired what culinary skills she had not already learned. The first time relatives came for dinner after Anna's death, they exclaimed over the food. Homemade potato rolls and cheese kolacky. Vegetable soup with plump cheese and beef kreplachs floating in it. Schrafe fish as an appetiser. Braised veal paprika, tzimmes with prunes and potatoes, creamy macaroni patties fried in hot fat and served in tomato sauce. A choice of baked peach pudding or apple schalet for dessert. Francine and Rachel thought Jacob was hiding a marvellous new housekeeper in the kitchen. They were disbelieving when he pointed to his daughter. Ginger did not think she had done anything remarkable. A cook was needed, so she became a cook.

She had to take care of her father now, and she applied herself to that responsibility with vigour and enthusiasm. She cleaned house swiftly, efficiently, and with a thoroughness that defied her Aunt Francine's *sub rosa* inspections for dust and grime. Although she was only twelve, she learned to plan a budget, and before she was thirteen she was in charge of all the household accounts.

At fourteen, three years younger than her classmates, Ginger was the valedictorian of her high school class. When it became known that she had been accepted by several universities but had chosen Barnard, everyone began to wonder whether, at the tender age of fourteen, she had finally taken too big a bite and would choke trying to swallow it.

Barnard *was* more difficult than high school. She no longer learned faster than other kids, but she learned as well as the best of them, and her grade average was frequently 4.0, never less than 3.8 – and *that* was the semester in her junior year when Jacob was sick with his first bout of pancreatitis, when she spent every evening at the hospital.

Jacob lived to see her get her first degree, was sallow and weak when she received her medical degree, even hung on tenaciously until she had served six months of her internship. But after three bouts of recurring pancreatitis, he developed pancreatic cancer, and he died before Ginger had finally made up her mind to go for a surgical residency at Boston Memorial instead of pursuing a career in research.

Because she had been given more years with Jacob than she had been given with her mother, her feelings for him were understandably more profound, and the loss of him was even more devastating than the loss of Anna had been. Yet she dealt with that time of trouble as she dealt with every challenge that came her way, and she finished her internship with excellent reports and superb recommendations.

She delayed her residency by going to Stanford, in California, for a unique and arduous two-year programme of additional study in cardio-vascular pathology. Thereafter, following a one-month vacation (by far the longest rest she had ever taken), she moved East again, to Boston, acquired a mentor in Dr George Hannaby (chief of surgery at Memorial and renowned for his pioneering achievements in various cardio-vascular surgical procedures), and served the first three-quarters of her two-year residency without a hitch.

Then, on a Tuesday morning in November, she went into Bernstein's Deli to buy a few items, and terrible things began happening. The incident of the black gloves. That was the start of it.

*   *   *

Tuesday was her day off, and unless one of her patients had a life-threatening crisis, she was neither needed nor expected at the hospital. During her first two months at Memorial, with her usual enthusiasm and tireless drive, she had gone to work on most of her days off, for there had been nothing else that she would rather have done. But George Hannaby had put an end to that habit as soon as he learned of it. George said that the practice of medicine was high-pressure work, and that every physician needed time off, even Ginger Weiss.

'If you drive yourself too hard, too fast, too relentlessly,' he said, 'it's not only you that suffers but the patient, as well.'

So every Tuesday she slept an extra hour, showered, and had two cups of coffee while she read the morning paper at the kitchen table by the window that looked out on Mount Vernon Street. By ten o'clock she dressed, walked several blocks to Bernstein's on Charles Street, and bought pastrami, corned beef, homemade rolls or sweet pumpernickel, potato salad, blintzes, maybe some lox, maybe some smoked sturgeon, sometimes cottage cheese vareniki to be reheated at home. Then she walked home with her bag of goodies and ate shamelessly all day while she read Christie, Dick Francis, John D. MacDonald, Elmore Leonard, sometimes a Heinlein. While she had not yet begun to like relaxation half as much as she liked work, she had gradually begun to enjoy her time off, and Tuesday had ceased to be the dreaded day it had been when she had first begun her reluctant observance of the six-day week.

That bad Tuesday in November started out fine, cold with a grey winter sky, brisk and invigorating rather than frigid, and her routine brought her to Bernstein's (crowded, as usual) at 10:21. Ginger drifted from one end of the long counter to the other, peering into cabinets full of baked goods, looking through the cold glass of the refrigerated display cases, choosing from the array of delicacies with gluttonous pleasure. The room was a stewpot of wonderful smells and happy sounds: hot dough, cinnamon; laughter; garlic, cloves; rapid conversations in which the English was spiced with everything from Yiddish to Boston accents to current rock-and-roll slang; roasted hazelnuts, sauerkraut, pickles, coffee; the *clink-clank* of silverware. When Ginger had everything she wanted, had paid for it, had pulled on her blue knit gloves, and had hefted the bag, she went past the small tables at which a dozen people were having a late breakfast, and headed for the door.

She held the grocery bag in her left arm, and with her free hand she tried to put her wallet back in the purse that was slung over her right shoulder. She was looking down at the purse as she reached the door, and a man in a grey tweed topcoat and a black Russian hat entered the deli at that moment, his attention as distracted as hers, and they collided. As cold air swept in from outside, she stumbled backwards a step. He grabbed at her bag of groceries to keep it from falling, then steadied her with one hand on her arm.

'Sorry,' he said. 'That was stupid of me.'

'My fault,' she said.

'Daydreaming,' he said.

'I wasn't looking where I was going,' she said.

21

'You all right?'

'Fine. Really.'

He held the bag of groceries towards her.

She thanked him, took the bag – and noticed his black gloves. They were obviously expensive, of genuine high-grade leather, so neatly and tightly stitched that the seams were hardly visible, but there was nothing about those gloves that could explain her instant and powerful reaction to them, nothing unusual, nothing strange, nothing threatening. Yet she *did* feel threatened. Not by the man. He was ordinary, pale, doughy-faced, with kind eyes behind thick tortoise-shell glasses. Inexplicably, unreasonably, the gloves themselves were what abruptly terrified her. Her breath caught in her throat, and her heart hammered.

The most bizarre thing was the way every object and all the people in the deli began to fade as if they were not real but merely figments of a dream that was dissolving as the dreamer woke. The customers having breakfast at the small tables, the shelves laden with canned and packaged food, the display cases, the wall clock with the Manischewitz logo, the pickle barrel, the tables and chairs all seemed to shimmer and slip away into a niveous haze, as if a fog was rising from some realm beneath the floor. Only the portentous gloves did not fade, and in fact, as she stared at them, they grew more detailed, strangely more vivid, more *real*, and increasingly threatening.

'Miss?' the doughy faced man said, and his voice seemed to come from a great distance, from the far end of a long tunnel.

Although the shapes and colours of the delicatessen bleached towards white on all sides of Ginger, the sounds did not dwindle as well but, instead, grew louder, louder, until her ears filled with a roar of meaningless jabber and with the jarring clatter of silverware, until the clinking of dishes and the soft chatter of the electronic cash register were thunderous, unbearable.

She could not take her eyes off the gloves.

'Is something wrong?' the man asked, holding up one leather-clad hand, half reaching toward her in an inquisitive gesture.

Black, tight, shiny . . . with a barely visible grain to the leather,

22

neat little stitches along the fingers . . . taut across the knuckles . . .

Dizzy, disoriented, with a tremendous weight of undefinable fear pressing down on her, she suddenly knew that she must run or die. Run or die. She did not know why. She did not understand the danger. But she *knew* she must run or perish where she stood.

Her heartbeat, already fast, became frantic. The breath that was snagged in her throat now flew free with a feeble cry, and she lunged forward as if in pursuit of the pathetic sound that had escaped her. Amazed by her response to the gloves but unable to be objective about it, confused by her own behaviour even as she acted, clutching the grocery bag to her breast, she shouldered past the man who had collided with her. She was only vaguely aware that she almost knocked him off his feet. She must have wrenched open the door, though she could not remember having done so, and then she was outside, in the crisp November air. The traffic on Charles Street – car horns, rumbling engines, the hiss-sigh-crunch of tyres – was on her right, and the deli windows flashed past on her left as she ran.

Thereafter she was oblivious of everything, for the world around her faded completely away, and she was plunging through a featureless greyness, legs pumping hard, coattails flapping, as if fleeing across an amorphous dreamscape, struck dumb by fear. There must have been many other people on the sidewalk, people whom she dodged or shoved aside, but she was not cognisant of them. She was aware only of the need to escape. She ran deer-swift though no one pursued her, with her lips peeled back in a grimace of pure terror though she could not identify the danger from which she fled.

Running. Running like crazy.

Temporarily blind, deaf.

Lost.

Minutes later, when the mists cleared, she found herself on Mount Vernon Street, part of the way up the hill, leaning against a wrought-iron railing beside the front steps of a stately red-brick town house. She was gripping two of the iron balusters, with her hands curled so tightly around them that her knuckles ached, with her forehead on the heavy metal balustrade, as if she were a melancholy prisoner slumped against the door of her cell. She was sweating and gasping for breath. Her mouth was dry, sour. Her throat burned, and her chest ached. She was bewildered, unable to recall how she had arrived at this place, as if washed onto an alien shore by moon-timed tides and waves of amnesia.

Something had frightened her.

She could not remember what it had been.

Gradually the fear subsided, and her breathing regained an almost regular rhythm, and her heartbeat slowed slightly.

She raised her head, blinked her eyes, looking around warily and in bafflement as her tear-blurred vision slowly cleared. She turned her face up until she saw the bare black branches of a linden and a low, ominous grey November sky beyond the skeletal tree. Antique iron gas lamps glowed softly, activated by solenoids that had mistaken the wintry morning for the onset of dusk. At the top of the hill stood the Massachusetts State House, and at the bottom the traffic was heavy where Mount Vernon intersected Charles Street.

Bernstein's Delicatessen. Yes, of course. It was Tuesday, and she had been at Bernstein's when . . . when something happened.

What? What had happened at Bernstein's?

And where was the deli bag?

She let go of the iron railing, raised her hands, and blotted her eyes on her blue knit gloves.

Gloves. Not hers, not *these* gloves. The myopic man in the Russian hat. His black leather gloves. That was what had frightened her.

But why had she been gripped by hysteria, overwhelmed by dread at the sight of them? What was so frightening about black gloves?

Across the street, an elderly couple watched her intently, and she wondered what she had done to draw their attention. Though she strained to remember, she could not summon the faintest recollection of her journey up the hill. The past three minutes – perhaps longer? – were utterly blank. She must have run up Mount Vernon Street in a panic. Evidently, judging by the expressions on the faces of those observing her, she had made quite a spectacle of herself.

Embarrassed, she turned away from them and started hesitantly down Mount Vernon Street, back the way she had come. At the bottom, just around the corner, she found her bag of groceries, which was on its side on the pavement. She stood over it for long seconds, staring at the crumpled brown bundle, trying to recall the moment when she had dropped it. But where that moment should have been, her memory contained only greyness, nothingness.

What's wrong with me?

A few items had spilled from the fallen parcel, but none was torn open, so she put them back in the paper sack.

Unsettled by her baffling loss of control, weak in the knees, she headed home, her breath pluming in the frosty air. After a few steps she halted. Hesitated. Finally she turned toward Bernstein's.

She stopped just outside the deli and had to wait only a minute or two before the man in the Russian hat and the tortoise-shell glasses came out with a grocery bag of his own.

'Oh.' He blinked in surprise, 'Uh . . . listen, did I say I'm sorry? The way you stormed out of there, I thought maybe I'd only *meant* to say it, you know –'

She stared at his leather-sheathed right hand where it gripped his brown paper bag. He gestured with his other hand as he spoke, and she followed it as it described a brief small pattern in the chilly air. The gloves did not frighten her now. She could not imagine why the sight of them had thrown her into a panic.

'It's all right. I was here waiting to apologise. I was startled and . . . and it's been an unusual morning,' she said, quickly turning away from him. Over her shoulder, she called out: 'Have a nice day.'

Although her apartment was not far away, the walk home seemed like an epic journey over vast expanses of grey pavement.

What's wrong with me?

She felt colder than the November day could explain.

She lived on Beacon Hill, on the second floor of a four-storey house that had once been the home of a 19th-century banker. She'd chosen the place because she liked the carefully preserved period detail: elaborate ceiling mouldings, medallions above the doorways, mahogany doors, bay windows with French panes, two fireplaces (living room, bedroom) with ornately carved and highly polished marble mantels. The rooms had a feeling of permanence, continuity, stability.

Ginger prized constancy and stability more than anything, perhaps as a reaction to having lost her mother when she was only twelve.

Still shivering even though the apartment was warm, she put away the groceries in the breadbox and refrigerator, then went into the bathroom to look closely at herself in the mirror. She was very pale. She did not like the hunted, haunted look in her eyes.

To her reflection, she said, 'What happened out there, *shnook*? You were a real *meshuggene*, let me tell you. Totally *farfufket*. But why? Huh? You're the bigshot doctor, so tell me. Why?'

Listening to her voice as it echoed off the high ceiling of the bathroom, she knew she was in serious trouble. Jacob, her father, had been a Jew by virtue of his genes and heritage, and proud of it, but he had not been a Jew by virtue of his religious practices. He had seldom gone to synagogue and had observed holidays in the same secular spirit with which many fallen-away Christians celebrated Easter and Christmas. And Ginger was one step farther removed from the faith than Jacob had been, for she called herself an agnostic. Furthermore, while Jacob's Jewishness was integral, evident in everything he did and said, that was not true of Ginger. If asked to define herself, she would have said, 'Woman, physician, workaholic, political dropout,' and other things before finally remembering to add, 'Jew.' The only time Yiddish peppered her speech was when she was in trouble, when she was deeply worried or scared, as if on a subconscious level she felt those words possessed talismanic value, charms against misfortune and catastrophe.

'Running through the streets, dropping your groceries, forgetting where you are, afraid when there's no reason to be afraid, acting like a regular *farmishteh*,' she said disdainfully to her reflection. 'People see you behaving like that, and they'll think for sure you're a *shikker*, and people don't go to doctors who're drunkards. *Nu?*'

The talismanic power of the old words worked a little magic, not much but enough to bring colour to her cheeks and soften

26

the stark look in her eyes. She stopped shivering, but she still felt chilled.

She washed her face, brushed her silver-blonde hair, and changed into pyjamas and a robe, which was her usual ensemble for a typically self-indulgent Tuesday. She went into the small spare bedroom that she used as a home office, took the well-thumbed *Taber's Cyclopedic Medical Dictionary* from the bookshelf, and opened it to the F listings.

Fugue.

She knew what the word meant, though she did not know why she had come in here to consult the dictionary when it could tell her nothing new. Maybe the dictionary was another talisman. If she looked at the word in cold print, it would cease to have any power over her. Sure. Voodoo for the over-educated. Nevertheless, she read the entry:

> fugue (fyug) [L. *fuga*, flight]. Serious personality dissociation. Leaving home or surroundings on impulse. Upon recovering from the fugue state there usually is loss of memory for actions occurring while in the state.

She closed the dictionary and returned it to the shelf.

She had other reference volumes that could provide more detailed information about fugues, their causes and significance, but she decided not to pursue the matter. She simply could not believe her transient attack had been a symptom of a serious medical problem.

Maybe she was under too much stress, working too hard, and maybe the overload had led to that one, isolated, transient fugue. A two- or three-minute blank. A little warning. So she would continue taking off every Tuesday, and would try to knock off work an hour earlier each day, and she would have no more problems.

She had worked very hard to be the doctor that her mother had hoped she would be, to make something special of herself and thereby honour her sweet father and the long-dead but well-remembered and desperately missed Swede. She had made many sacrifices to come this far. She had worked more weekends than not, had foregone vacations and most other pleasures. Now, in only six months, she would finish her residency and establish a practice of her own, and nothing

27

would be allowed to interfere with her plans. Nothing was going to rob her of her dream.

Nothing.

It was November 12.

3.

ELKO COUNTY, NEVADA

Ernie Block was afraid of the dark. Indoor darkness was bad, but the darkness of the outdoors, the vast blackness of night here in northern Nevada, was what most terrified Ernie. During the day he favoured rooms with several lamps and lots of windows, but at night he preferred rooms with few windows or even no windows at all because sometimes it seemed to him that the night was pressing against the glass, as if it were a living creature that wanted to get in at him and gobble him up. He obtained no relief from drawing the drapes, for he still knew the night was out there, waiting for its chance.

He was deeply ashamed of himself. He did not know why he had recently become afraid of the dark. He just *was*.

Millions of people shared his phobia, of course, but nearly all of them were children. Ernie was fifty-two.

On Friday afternoon, the day after Thanksgiving, he worked alone in the motel office because Faye had flown to Wisconsin to visit Lucy, Frank, and the grandkids. She would not be back until Tuesday. Come December, they intended to close up for a week and both go to Milwaukee for Christmas with the kids; but this time Faye had gone by herself.

Ernie missed her terribly. He missed her because she was his wife of thirty-one years *and* his best friend. He missed her because he loved her more now than he had on their wedding day. And because . . . without Faye, the nights alone seemed longer, deeper, darker than ever.

By two-thirty Friday afternoon, he had cleaned all the rooms and changed the linen, and the Tranquillity Motel was ready for its next wave of journeyers. It was the only lodging within twelve miles, perched on a knoll north of the superhighway, a neat little way station on a vast expanse of sagebrush-strewn plains that sloped up into grassy meadows. Elko lay over thirty miles to the east, Battle Mountain forty miles to the west. The town of Carlin and the tiny village of Beowawe were closer, though from the Tranquillity Motel Ernie had not a glimpse of either settlement. In fact, from the parking lot, no other building was visible in any direction, and there was probably no motel in the world more aptly named than this one.

Ernie was now in the office, working with a can of wood stain, touching up a few scratches on the oak counter where guests signed in and checked out. The counter was not really in bad shape. He was just keeping busy until customers started pulling in from Interstate 80 in the late afternoon. If he did not keep his mind occupied, he would start thinking about how early dusk arrived in November, and he would begin to worry about nightfall, and then by the time darkness actually came, he would be as jumpy as a cat with a can tied to its tail.

The motel office was a shrine to light. From the moment he had opened at six-thirty this morning, every lamp had been burning. A squat fluorescent lamp with a flexible neck stood on the oak desk in the work areas behind the check-in counter, casting a pale rectangle on the green felt blotter. A brass floor lamp glowed in the corner by the file cabinets. On the public side of the counter was a carousel of post cards, a wall rack holding about forty paperbacks, another rack full of free travel brochures, a single slot machine by the door, and a beige sofa flanked by end tables and ginger-jar lamps equipped with three-way bulbs – 75, 100, and 150 watts – which were turned up all the way. There was a frosted-glass ceiling fixture, too, with two bulbs, and of course most of the front wall of the office featured a large window. The motel faced south-southwest, so at this time of day the declining sun's honey-coloured beams angled through the enormous pane, giving an amber tint to the white wall behind the sofa, fracturing into hundreds of bright erratic lines in the crackled glaze of the ginger-jar lamps, and leaving blazing reflections in the brass medallions that ornamented the tables.

When Faye was here, Ernie left some of the lamps off

29

because she was sure to remark on the waste of electricity and extinguish a few of them. Leaving a lamp unlit made him uneasy, but he endured the sight of dead bulbs in order to keep his secret. As far as he knew, Faye was not aware of the phobia that had been creeping up on him during the past four months, and he did not want her to know because he was ashamed of this sudden strangeness in himself and because he did not want to worry her. He did not know the cause of his irrational fear, but he knew he would conquer it, sooner or later, so there was no sense in humiliating himself and causing Faye unnecessary anxiety over a temporary condition.

He refused to believe that it was serious. He had been ill only rarely in his fifty-two years. He had only been laid up in the hospital once, after taking a bullet in the butt and another one in the back during his second tour of duty in Vietnam. There had never been mental illness in his family, and Ernest Eugene Block was absolutely-sure-as-hell-and-without-a-doubt *not* going to be the first one of his clan to go crawling and whimpering to a psychiatrist's couch. You could bet your ass on that and never have to worry what you would sit on. He would tough this out, weird as it was, unsettling as it was.

It had begun in September, a vague uneasiness that built in him as nightfall approached and that remained until dawn. At first he was not troubled every night, but it got steadily worse, and by the middle of October, dusk always brought with it an inexplicable spiritual distress. By early November the distress became fear, and during the past two weeks his anxiety grew until now his days were measured – and almost totally defined – by this perplexing fear of the night to come. For the past ten days, he'd avoided going out after darkfall, and thus far Faye had not noticed, though she could not remain oblivious much longer.

Ernie Block was so big that it was ridiculous for him to be afraid of *anything*. He was six feet tall and so solidly and squarely built that his surname was equally suitable as a one-word description of him. His wiry grey hair was brush-cut, revealing slabs of skull bone, and his facial features were clean and appealing, though so squared-off that he looked as if he had been carved out of granite. His thick neck, massive shoulders, and barrel chest gave him a top-heavy appearance.

When he had been a high-school football star, other players called him 'Bull,' and during his twenty-eight-year career in the Marines, from which he had been retired for six years, most people called him 'sir,' even some who were of equal rank. They would be astonished to learn that, lately, Ernie Block's palms got sweaty every day when sunset drew near.

Now, intent upon keeping his thoughts far from sunset, he dawdled over the repairs to the counter and finally finished at 3:45. The quality of the daylight had changed. It was no longer honey-coloured but amber-orange, and the sun was drawing down toward the west.

At four o'clock he got his first check-in, a couple his own age, Mr and Mrs Gilney, who were heading home to Salt Lake City after spending a week in Reno, visiting their son. He chatted with them and was disappointed when they took their key and left.

The sunlight was completely orange now, burnt orange, no yellow in it at all. The high, scattered clouds had been transformed from white sailing ships to gold and scarlet galleons gliding eastward above the Great Basin in which almost the entire state of Nevada lay.

Ten minutes later a cadaverous man, visiting the area on special assignment for the Bureau of Land Management, took a room for two days.

Alone again, Ernie tried not to look at his watch.

He tried not to look at the windows, either, for beyond the glass the day was bleeding away.

I'm not going to panic, he told himself. I've been to war, seen the worst a man can see, and by God I'm still *here*, still as big and ugly as ever, so I won't come unglued just because night is coming.

By four-fifty the sunlight was no longer orange but bloody red.

His heart was speeding up, and he began to feel as if his rib cage had become a vice that was squeezing his vital organs between its jaws.

He went to the desk, sat down in the chair, closed his eyes, and did some deep-breathing exercises to calm himself.

He turned on the radio. Sometimes music helped. Kenny Rogers was singing about loneliness.

The sun touched the horizon and slowly sank out of sight. The crimson afternoon faded to electric blue, then to a luminous purple that reminded Ernie of day's end in Singapore, where he had been stationed for two years as an embassy guard when he had been a young recruit.

It came. The twilight.

Then worse. Night.

The outside lights, including the blue and green neon sign that could be seen clearly from the freeway, had blinked on automatically as dusk crept in, but that had not made Ernie feel any better. Dawn was an eternity away. Night ruled.

With the dying of the light, the outside temperature fell below freezing. To cut the chill in the office, the oil furnace kicked in more frequently. In spite of the chill, Ernie Block was sweating.

At six o'clock, Sandy Sarver dashed over from the Tranquillity Grille, which stood west of the motel. It was a small sandwich shop with a limited menu, serving only lunch and dinner to the guests and to hungry truckers who swung in from the highway for a bite. (Breakfast for guests was complimentary sweet rolls and coffee delivered to their rooms, if they asked for it the night before.) Sandy, thirty-two, and her husband, Ned, ran the restaurant for Ernie and Faye; Sandy waited tables, and Ned cooked. They lived in a trailer up near Beowawe and drove in every day in their battered Ford pickup.

Ernie winced when Sandy entered, for when she opened the door he had the irrational feeling that the darkness outside would spring panther-like into the office.

'Brought supper,' Sandy said, shivering in the gust of cold air that entered with her. She set a small, lidless, cardboard box on the counter. It held a cheeseburger, French fries, a plastic container of coleslaw, and a can of Coors. 'Figured you'd need a Coors to sluice all this cholesterol out of your system.'

'Thanks, Sandy.'

Sandy Sarver was not much to look at, plain and washed-out, even drab, though she had more potential than she realised. Her legs were too thin but not unattractive. She was under-weight, but if she put on fifteen or even twenty pounds, she would have a reasonably good shape. She was flat-chested, though an appealing suppleness compensated for her lack of amplitude, and she had a charming feminine delicateness most apparent in her small bones, slender arms, and swanlike neck. Also, she possessed an infrequently seen but arresting gracefulness that was usually disguised by her habit of shuffling when she walked and slumping round-shouldered when she sat. Her brown hair was lustreless and limp, probably because she washed it with soap instead of shampoo. She never wore make-up, not even lipstick. Her nails were bitten and neglected. However, she was good-hearted, with a generous spirit, which was why Ernie and Faye wished she could look better and get more out of life.

Sometimes Ernie worried about her, the same way he used to worry about Lucy, his own daughter, before Lucy found and married Frank and became so obviously, perfectly happy. He sensed that something bad had happened to Sandy Sarver a long time ago, that she had taken a very hard blow which had not broken her but had taught her to keep a low profile, to keep her head tucked down, to harbour only meagre expectations in order to protect herself from disappointment, pain, and human cruelty.

Relishing the aroma of the food, popping the tab on the Coors, Ernie said, 'Ned makes the best darned cheeseburgers I've ever eaten.'

Sandy smiled shyly. 'It's a blessing having a man who cooks.' Her voice was soft, meek. 'Especially in my case 'cause I'm no good at it.'

'Oh, I'll bet you're a fine cook, too,' Ernie said.

'No, no, not me, not even a little bit. Never was, never will be.'

He looked at her bare, goose-pimpled arms, exposed by her short-sleeved uniform. 'You shouldn't come out on a night like this without a sweater. You'll catch your death.'

'Not me,' she said, 'I . . . I got used to the cold a long time ago.'

That seemed an odd thing to say, and the tone of voice in which she said it was even odder. But before Ernie could think of a way to draw her out and discover her meaning, she headed toward the door.

33

'See you later, Ernie.'

'Uh . . . much business?'

'Some. And the truckers'll be pulling in for supper soon.' She paused with the door open. 'You sure keep it bright in here.'

A bite of cheeseburger stuck in his throat when she opened the door. She was exposing him to the dangers of the darkness.

Cold air swept in.

'You could get a tan in here,' she said.

'I . . . I like it bright. People come into a motel office that's dimly lit . . . well, the impression is it's dirty.'

'Oh! I would've never thought of that. Guess that's why you're the boss. I was in charge, I'd never think of little things like that. I'm no good at details. Gotta scoot.'

He held his breath while the door was open, sighed with relief when she pulled it shut behind her. He watched her scurry past the windows and out of sight. He could not remember ever hearing Sandy admit to a virtue. Likewise, she never hesitated to point out her faults and shortcomings, both real and imagined. The kid was sweet, but she was sometimes dreary company. Tonight, of course, even dreary company was welcome. He was sorry to see her go.

At the counter, eating while standing up, Ernie concentrated intently on his food, not once lifting his eyes from it until he was done, using it to take his mind off the irrational fear that made his scalp prickle and kept the cold sweat trickling down from his armpits.

By 6:50, eight of the motel's twenty rooms were occupied. Because it was the second of a four-day holiday weekend, with more than the usual number of travellers, he would rent out at least another eight units if he stayed open until nine o'clock.

He could not do it. He was a Marine, retired but still a Marine, to whom the words 'duty' and 'courage' were sacred, and he had never failed to do his duty, not even in Vietnam, not even with bullets flying and bombs bursting and people dying on all sides, but he was incapable of the simple task of manning the motel desk until nine o'clock. There were no drapes at the big office windows, no blind over the glass door, no way to escape the sight of darkness. Each time the door opened, he was sick with dread because no barrier lay between him and the night.

He looked at his big strong hands. They were trembling. His sour stomach churned. He was so jumpy he could not keep still. He paced the small work area. He fiddled with this and that.

Finally, at a quarter past seven, surrendering to his irrational anxiety, he used a switch under the counter to turn on the NO VACANCY sign outside, and he locked the front door. He clicked off the lamps, one at a time, edging away from the shadows that rushed in where light had ruled, and he quickly retreated to the rear of the room. Steps led up to the owner's apartment on the second floor. He intended to climb them at an ordinary pace, telling himself that it was silly and stupid to be afraid, telling himself that nothing was coming after him from the dark corners of the office behind, nothing – such a *ridiculous* thought – nothing, absolutely nothing. But reassurances of that sort did him no good whatsoever, for it was not something *in* the dark that scared him; he was, instead, terrified by the darkness itself, by the mere absence of light. He started moving faster, grabbing at the handrail. To his chagrin, he quickly panicked and bounded up the steps two at a time. At the top, heart pounding, Ernie stumbled into the living room, fumbled for the wall switch, snapped off the last of the lights below, slammed the door so hard that the whole wall seemed to shake, locked it, and leaned with his broad back against it.

He could not stop gasping. He could not stop shaking, either. He could smell his own rank sweat.

Several lights had been burning in the apartment during the day, but a few were unlit. He hurried from room to room, clicking on every lamp and ceiling fixture. The drapes and shades were all drawn tight from his previous nocturnal ordeal, so he had not a single glimpse of the blackness beyond the windows.

When he had regained control of himself, he phoned the Tranquillity Grille, told Sandy that he was not feeling well and that he had shut down early. He asked them to keep the day's receipts until tomorrow morning rather than bother him tonight when they closed the restaurant.

Sickened by his pungent perspiration odour – not so much by the smell itself as by the total loss of control that the smell represented – Ernie showered. After he had towelled himself dry, he put on fresh underwear, belted himself into a thick warm robe, and stepped into slippers.

Heretofore, in spite of his bewilderingly unfocussed apprehension, he had been able to sleep in a dark room, though not without anxiety, and not without the aid of a couple of beers. Then, two nights ago, with Faye in Wisconsin, when he was alone, he was able to nod off only with the constant companionship of the nightstand lamp. He knew he would need that luminous comfort tonight, as well.

And when Faye returned on Tuesday? Would he be able to go back to sleeping without a light?

What if Faye turned off the light . . . and he started screaming like a badly frightened child?

The thought of that impending humiliation made him grind his teeth with anger and drove him to the nearest window.

He put one beefy hand on the tightly drawn drapes. Hesitated. His heart did an imitation of muffled machine gun fire.

He had always been strong for Faye, a rock on which she could depend. That was what a man was supposed to be: a rock. He must not let Faye down. He had to overcome this bizarre affliction before she returned from Wisconsin.

His mouth went dry and a chill returned when he thought about what lay beyond the now-concealed glass, but he knew the only way to beat this thing was to confront it. That was the lesson life had taught him: be bold, confront the enemy, engage in battle. That philosophy of action had always worked for him. It would work again. This window looked out from the back of the motel, across the vast meadows and hills of the uninhabited uplands, and the only light out there was what fell from the stars. He must pull the drapes aside, come face to face with that tenebrous landscape, stand fast, endure it. Confrontation would be a purgative, flushing the poison from his system.

Ernie pulled open the drape. He peered out at the night and told himself that this perfect blackness was not so bad – deep and pure, vast and cold, but not malevolent, and in no way a personal threat.

However, as he watched, unmoving and unmovable,

portions of the darkness seemed to . . . well, to shift, to *coalesce*, forming into not-quite-visible but nonetheless solid shapes, lumps of pulsing and denser blackness within the greater blackness, lurking phantoms that at any moment might launch themselves toward the fragile window.

He clenched his jaws, put his forehead against the ice-cold glass.

The Nevada barrens, a huge emptiness to begin with, now seemed to expand even farther. He could not see the night-cloaked mountains, but he sensed that they were magically receding, that the plains between him and the mountains were growing larger, extending outwards hundreds of miles, thousands, expanding swiftly towards infinity, until suddenly he was at the centre of a void so immense that it defied description. On all sides of him, there was emptiness and lightlessness beyond man's ability to measure, beyond the limits of his own feeble imagination, a terrible emptiness, to the left and right, front and back, above and below, and suddenly he could not *breathe*.

This was considerably worse than anything he had known before. A deeper-reaching fear. Profound. Shocking in its power. And it was in total control of him.

Abruptly he was aware of all the *weight* of that enormous darkness, and it seemed to be sliding inexorably in upon him, sliding and sliding, incalculably high walls of heavy darkness, collapsing, pressing down, squeezing the breath out of him –

He screamed and threw himself back from the window.

He fell to his knees as the drapes dropped into place with a soft rustle. The window was hidden again. The darkness was concealed. All round him was light, blessed light. He hung his head, shuddered, and took great gulps of air.

He crawled to the bed and hoisted himself onto the mattress, where he lay for a long time, listening to his heartbeat, which was like footfalls, sprinting then running then just walking fast inside him. Instead of solving his problem, bold confrontation had made it worse.

'What's happening here?' he said aloud, staring at the ceiling. 'What's wrong with me? Dear God, what's *wrong* with me?'

It was November 22.

LAGUNA BEACH, CALIFORNIA

Saturday, in desperate reaction to yet another troubling episode of somnambulism, Dom Corvaisis thoroughly, methodically exhausted himself. By nightfall, he intended to be so wrung-out that he'd sleep as still as a stone locked immemorially in the bosom of the earth. At seven o'clock in the morning, with the night's cool mist lingering in the canyons and bearding the trees, he performed half an hour of vigorous calisthenics on the patio overlooking the ocean, then put on his running shoes and did seven arduous miles on Laguna's sloped streets. He spent the next five hours doing heavy gardening. Then, because it was a warm day, he put on his swimsuit, put towels in his Firebird, and went to the beach. He sunbathed a little and swam a lot. After dinner at Picasso's, he walked for another hour along shop-lined streets sparsely populated by off-season tourists. At last he drove home.

Undressing in his bedroom, Dom felt as if he were in the land of Lilliput, where a thousand tiny people were pulling him down with grappling lines. He rarely drank, but now he tossed back a shot of Remy Martin. In bed, he fell asleep even as he clicked off the lamp.

*   *   *

The incidents of somnambulism were growing more frequent, and the problem was now the central issue of his life. It was interfering with his work. The new book, which had been going well, which contained the best writing he had ever done, was stalled. In the past two weeks, he had awakened in a closet on nine occasions, four times in the last four nights. The affliction had ceased to be amusing and intriguing. He was afraid to go to sleep because, asleep, he was not in control of himself.

Yesterday, Friday, he had finally gone to his physician, Dr Paul Cobletz, in Newport Beach. Haltingly, he told Cobletz all about his sleepwalking, but he found himself unwilling and unable to express the true depth and seriousness of his concern. Dom had always been a very private person, made so by a childhood spent in a dozen foster homes and under the care of surrogate parents, some of whom were indifferent or even hostile, all of whom were dismayingly temporary presences in his life. He was reluctant to share his most important and personal thoughts except through the mouths of imaginary characters in his fiction.

As a result, Cobletz was not unduly worried. After a full physical examination, he pronounced Dom exceptionally fit. He attributed the somnambulism to stress, to the upcoming publication of the novel.

'You don't think we should do any tests?' Dom asked.

Cobletz said, 'You're a writer, so of course your imagination is running away with you. Brain tumour, you're thinking. Am I right?'

'Well . . . yes.'

'Any headaches? Dizziness? Blurred vision?'

'No.'

'I've examined your eyes. There's no change in your retinas, no indication of intracranial pressure. Any inexplicable vomiting?'

'No. Nothing like that.'

'Giddy spells? Giggling or periods of euphoria without apparent reason? Anything of that nature?'

'No.'

'Then I see no reason for tests at this stage.'

'Do you think I need . . . psychotherapy?'

'Good heavens, no! I'm sure this will pass soon.'

Finished dressing, Dom watched Cobletz close the file. He said, 'I thought perhaps sleeping pills –'

'No, no,' Cobletz said. 'Not yet. I don't believe in drugs as a treatment of first resort. Here's what you do, Dom. Get away from the writing for a few weeks. Don't do anything cerebral. Get plenty of physical exercise. Go to bed tired every night, so tired that you can't even bother to think about the book you've been working on. A few days of that, and you'll be cured. I'm convinced of it.'

*   *   *

Saturday, Dom began the treatment Dr Cobletz prescribed, devoting himself to physical activity, though with more single-mindedness and flagellant persistence than the doctor had suggested. Consequently, he plummeted into a deep sleep the moment he put his head upon the pillow, and in the morning he did not wake in a closet.

He did not wake in bed, either. This time, he was in the garage.

He regained consciousness in a breathless state of terror, gasping, heart hammering so hard it seemed capable of shattering his ribs with its furious blows. His mouth was dry, his hands curled into fists. He was cramped and sore, partly from Saturday's excess of exercise, but partly from the unnatural and uncomfortable position in which he had been sleeping. During the night he evidently had taken two folded canvas dropcloths from a shelf above the workbench, and had squirrelled into a narrow service space behind the furnace. That was where he lay now, concealed beneath the tarps.

'Concealed' was the right word. He had not dragged the tarpaulins over himself merely for warmth. He had taken refuge behind the furnace and beneath the canvas because he had been hiding from something.

From what?

Even now, as Dominick pushed the tarps aside and struggled to sit up, as sleep receded and as his bleary eyes adjusted to the shadow-filled garage, the intense anxiety that had accompanied him up from sleep still clung tenaciously. His pulse pounded.

Fear of what?

Dreaming. In his nightmare he must have been running and hiding from some monster. Yes. Of course. His peril in the nightmare caused him to sleepwalk, and when, in the dream, he sought a place to hide, he also hid in reality, creeping behind the furnace.

His white Firebird loomed ghostlike in the vague light from the wall vents and the single window above the work bench. Shuffling across the garage, he felt as if he were a revenant himself.

In the house, he went directly to his office. Morning light filled the room, making him squint. He sat at the desk in his filthy pyjama bottoms, switched on the word processor, and studied the documents on the diskette that he had left in the machine. The diskette was as he had left it on Thursday; it contained no new material.

Dom had hoped that, in his sleep, he might have left a message that would help him understand the source of his anxiety. That knowledge was obviously held by his subconscious but thus far denied to his conscious mind. When sleepwalking, his subconscious was in control, and possibly it would try to explain things to his conscious mind by way of the Displaywriter. But as yet, it had not.

He switched off the machine. He sat for a long time, staring out the window, towards the ocean. Wondering . . .

Later, in the bedroom, as he was on his way to the master bath, he found something strange. Nails were scattered across the carpet, and he had to be careful where he walked. He stooped, picked up several of them. They were all alike: 1.5-inch steel finishing nails. At the far side of the room, he saw two objects that drew him there. Beneath the window, from which the drapes had been drawn aside, a box of nails lay on the floor by the baseboard; it was only half full because part of its contents had spilled from it. Beside the box was a hammer.

He lifted the hammer, hefted it, frowned.

What had he been doing in those lonely hours of the night?

He raised his eyes to the windowsill and saw three loose nails that he had laid there. They gleamed in the sunlight.

Judging from the evidence, he'd been preparing to nail the windows shut. Jesus. Something had so frightened him that he had intended to nail the windows shut and make a fortress of his house, but before he could set himself to the task, he had been suddenly *overwhelmed* by fear and had fled to the garage, where he had hidden behind the furnace.

He dropped the hammer, stood, looked out the window. Beyond lay only bloom-laden rose bushes, a small strip of lawn, and an ivy-covered slope that led up to another house. A lovely landscape. Peaceful. He could not believe that it had been any different last night, that something more threatening had been crouching out there in the darkness.

And yet . . .

For a while Dom Corvaisis watched the day grow brighter, watched the bees visit the roses, then began to pick up the nails.

It was November 24.

BOSTON, MASSACHUSETTS

After the incident of the black gloves, two weeks passed without another attack.

For a few days following the embarrassing scene at Bernstein's Delicatessen, Ginger Weiss remained on edge, expecting another seizure. She was unusually self-aware, acutely conscious of her physiological and psychological conditions, searching for subtle symptoms of serious disorder, alert for the slightest sign of another impending fugue, but she noticed nothing worrisome. She had no headaches, no attacks of nausea, no joint or muscle pain. Gradually, her confidence rose to its usual high level. She became convinced that her wild flight had been entirely stress-related, a never-to-be-repeated aberration.

Her days at Memorial were busier than ever. George Hannaby, chief of surgery – a tall burly bear of a man who talked slow, walked slow, and looked deceptively lazy – maintained a heavy schedule, and though Ginger was not the only resident working under him, she was the only one who currently worked *exclusively* with him. She assisted in many – perhaps a majority – of his procedures: aortal grafts, amputations, popliteal bypasses, embolectomies, portocaval shunts, thoracotomies, arteriograms, the installation of temporary and permanent pacemakers, and more.

George observed her every move, was quick to note the slightest flaw in her skill and techniques. Although he looked like a friendly bear, he was a tough taskmaster and had no patience for laziness, ineptitude, or carelessness. He could be scathing in his criticism, and he made all the young doctors sweat. His scorn was not merely withering; it was dehydrating, searing, a nuclear heat.

Some residents considered George tyrannical, but Ginger enjoyed assisting him precisely because his standards were so high. She knew that his criticisms, though sometimes blisteringly delivered, were motivated solely by his concern for the patient, and she never took them personally. When she finally earned Hannaby's unqualified blessing . . . well, that would be almost as good as God's own seal of approval.

On the last Monday in November, thirteen days after her strange seizure, Ginger assisted in a triple heart bypass operation on Johnny O'Day, a fifty-three-year-old Boston police officer who had been forced into early retirement by cardiovascular disease. Johnny was stocky, rubber-faced, tousle-haired, with merry blue eyes, unassuming, quick to laugh in spite of his troubles. Ginger was especially drawn to him because, although he looked nothing whatsoever like the late Jacob Weiss, he nevertheless reminded her of her father.

She was afraid Johnny O'Day was going to die – and that it was going to be, in part, her fault.

She had no reason to believe that he was more vulnerable than other cardiac patients. In fact, Johnny was in comparatively little danger. He was ten years younger than the average recipient of bypass surgery, with greater resources for recuperation. His cardiac ailment was not complicated by any other debilitating condition, such as phlebitis or excessively high blood pressure. His prospects were encouraging.

But Ginger could not twist free of the dread in which she found herself increasingly tangled. On Monday afternoon, as the hour of surgery drew near, she grew tense, and her stomach turned sour. For the first time since she had sat a lonely vigil beside her father's hospital bed and had helplessly watched him die, Ginger was filled with doubt.

Perhaps her apprehension grew from the unjustified but inescapable notion that if she somehow failed this patient she would in a sense be failing Jacob yet again. Or perhaps her fear was utterly unwarranted and would seem foolish and laughable in hindsight. Perhaps.

Nevertheless, entering the operating theater at George's side, she wondered if her hands would shake. A surgeon's hands must never shake.

The operating room was all white and aqua tile, filled with gleaming chrome-plated and stainless-steel equipment. Nurses and an anaesthesiologist were preparing the patient.

Johnny O'Day lay on the cruciform operating table, arms extended, palms up and wrists exposed for the intravenous spikes.

43

Agatha Tandy, a private surgical technician who was employed by George rather than by the hospital, stretched thin latex gloves over her boss's freshly scrubbed hands, then over Ginger's hands, as well.

The patient hade been anaesthetised. He was orange with iodine from the neck to the waist, swathed in neatly tucked and folded layers of green cloth from the hips down. His eyes were taped shut to keep them from drying out. His breathing was slow but regular.

A portable tape deck with stereo speakers was on a stool in one corner. George preferred to cut to the accompaniment of Bach, and that calming music now filled the room.

It may have calmed the others, but today it did not calm Ginger. A secret scurrying something spun a web of ice in her stomach.

Hannaby positioned himself at the table. Agatha stood at his right side with an elaborately ordered tray of instruments. The circulating nurse waited to fetch whatever might be required from the cabinets along one wall. An assisting nurse with large grey eyes noticed an errant flap of green sheeting and quickly tucked it into place around the patient's body. The anaesthesiologist and his nurse were at the head of the table, monitoring the IV and the EKG. Ginger moved into position. The team was ready.

Ginger looked at her hands. They were not shaking.

Inside, though, she was all aquiver.

In spite of her sense of impending disaster, the surgery went smoothly. George Hannaby operated with quickness, sureness, dexterity, and skill that were even more impressive than usual. Twice, he stepped aside and requested that Ginger complete a part of the procedure.

Ginger surprised herself by functioning with her customary sureness and speed, her fear and tension revealed only by a tendency to perspire more than usual. However, the nurse was always there to blot her brow.

Afterwards, at the scrub sink, George said, 'Like clockwork.'

Soaping her hands under the hot water, she said, 'You always seem so relaxed, as if . . . as if you weren't a surgeon at all . . . as if you were just a tailor altering a suit of clothes.'

44

'I may seem that way,' he said, 'but I'm always tense. That's why I play Bach.' He finished washing up. 'You were very tense today.'

'Yes,' she admitted.

'Exceptionally tense. It happens.' Big as he was, he sometimes seemed to have the eyes of a sweet, gentle child. 'The important thing is that it didn't affect your skill. You were as smooth as ever. First rate. That's the key. You've got to use tension to your advantage.'

'I guess I'm learning.'

He grinned. 'As usual, you're being too hard on yourself. I'm proud of you, kid. For a while there, I thought maybe you'd have to give up medicine and earn your living as a meat cutter in a supermarket, but now I know you'll make it.'

She grinned back at him, but the grin was counterfeit. She had been more than tense. She had been seized by a cold, black fear that might easily have overwhelmed her, and that was much different from a healthy tension. That fear was something she had never felt before, something that she knew George Hannaby had never felt in his life, not in an operating room. If it continued, if the fear became a constant companion during surgery and would not be dispelled . . . what then?

*   *   *

At ten-thirty that evening, when she was reading in bed, the phone rang. It was George Hannaby. If the call had come earlier, she'd have panicked and assumed that Johnny O'Day had taken a serious turn for the worse, but now she had regained her perspective. 'So sorry. Missy Weiss not home. I no speak the English. Call back next April, please.'

'If that's supposed to be a Spanish accent,' George said, 'it's atrocious. If it's supposed to be Oriental, it's merely terrible. Be thankful you chose medicine as a career instead of acting.'

'You, on the other hand, would've done well as a drama critic.'

'I do have the refined and sensitive perspective, the cool judgment and unerring insight, of a first-rate critic, don't I? Now shut up and listen: I've got good news. I think you're ready, smartass.'

'Ready? For what?'

45

'The big time. An aortal graft,' he said.

'You mean . . . I wouldn't just assist you? Do it entirely myself?'

'Chief surgeon for the entire procedure.'

'Aortal graft?'

'Sure. You didn't specialise in cardio-vascular surgery just to perform appendectomies for the rest of your life.'

She was sitting straight up in bed now. Her heart was beating faster, and she was flushed with excitement. 'When?'

'Next week. There's a patient checking in this Thursday or Friday. Name's Fletcher. We'll go over her file together on Wednesday. If things proceed according to schedule, I would think we'd be ready to cut on Monday morning. Of course, you'll be responsible for scheduling all the final tests and making the decision to go ahead.'

'Oh, God.'

'You'll do fine.'

'You'll be with me.'

'I'll assist you . . . if you feel you need me for anything.'

'And you'll take over if I start to screw up.'

'Don't be silly. You won't screw up.'

She thought about it for a moment, then said, 'No, I won't screw up.'

'That's my Ginger. You can do whatever you set your mind to.'

'Even ride a giraffe to the moon.'

'What?'

'Private joke.'

'Listen, I know you came close to panic this afternoon, but don't worry. All residents experience that. Most have to deal with it early, when they begin to assist in the surgery. They call it The Clutch. But you've been cool and collected from the start, and I'd finally decided you'd never clutch up like the rest of them. Today, at last you did. The Clutch just came later for you than for most. And though I imagine you're still worried about it, I think you should be glad it happened. The Clutch is a seasoning experience. The important thing is that you dealt with it superbly.'

'Thanks, George. Even better than a drama critic, you'd have made a good baseball coach.'

Minutes later, when they concluded their conversation and hung up, she fell back against the pillows again and hugged herself and felt so fine that she actually giggled. After a while she went to the closet and dug around in there until she located the Weiss family photograph album. She brought it back to bed and sat for a time, paging through the pictures of Jacob and Anna, for although she could not share her triumphs with them any more, she needed to feel that they were close.

Later still, in the dark bedroom, as she lay balanced on the thin edge of wakefulness, she finally understood why she had been frightened this afternoon. She had not been seized by The Clutch. Although she had not been able to admit it until now, she had been afraid that, in the midst of surgery, she would black out, plummet into a state of fugue, as she had done that Tuesday, two weeks ago. If an attack came while she held a scalpel, while she was doing delicate cutting, or while stitching in a vascular graft . . .

That thought brought her eyes open wide. The creeping form of sleep retreated like a thief caught in the middle of a burglary. For a long time she lay there, stiff, staring at the dark and newly ominous shapes of the bedroom furniture and at the window, where incompletely drawn draperies revealed a band of glass silvered by a fall of moonlight and by the rising beams of streetlamps below.

Could she accept the responsibility of chief surgeon on an aortal graft? Her seizure had surely been a one-time occurrence. It would never happen again. Surely not. But did she dare test that theory?

Sleep crept back again and claimed her, though not for hours.

*   *   *

Tuesday, after a successful trip to Bernstein's Delicatessen, much food, and several lazy hours in an easy chair with a good book, her self-confidence was knitted up again, and she began to look forward to the challenge ahead, with only an ordinary degree and kind of apprehension.

On Wednesday, Johnny O'Day continued to recover from his triple bypass and was in high spirits. *This* was what made the years of study and hard work worthwhile: preserving life, relieving suffering, bringing hope and happiness to those who had known despair.

She assisted in a pacemaker implantation that went without a hitch, and she performed an aortogram, a dye test on a patient's circulation. She also sat in with George while he examined seven people who had been referred to him by other physicians.

When all the new patients had been seen, George and Ginger huddled for half an hour over the file of the candidate for the aortal graft – a fifty-eight-year-old woman, Viola Fletcher. After studying the file, Ginger decided she wanted Mrs Fletcher admitted to Memorial on Thursday for testing and preparation. If there were no counter-indications, surgery could take place first thing Monday morning. George agreed, and all the necessary arrangements were made.

Thus Wednesday progressed, always busy, never dull. By 6:30, she had put in a twelve-hour day, but she was not tired. In fact, although she had nothing to keep her at the hospital, she was reluctant to leave. George Hannaby was home already. But Ginger hung around, chatting with patients, double-checking charts, until at last she went to George's office, where she intended to look again at Viola Fletcher's file.

The professional offices were in the back wing of the building, separate from the hospital itself. At that hour the corridors were virtually deserted. Ginger's rubber-soled shoes squeaked on the highly polished tile floors. The air smelled of pine-scented disinfectant.

George Hannaby's waiting room, examining rooms, and private office were dark and quiet, and Ginger did not switch on all the lights as she moved through the outer rooms into the inner sanctum. There, she snapped on only the desk lamp as she passed it on her way to the file room door, which was locked. George had given her keys to everything, and in a minute she had withdrawn Viola Fletcher's records from the cabinet and had returned with them to George's desk.

She sat down in the big leather chair, opened the folder in the pool of light from the desk lamp – and only then noticed an object that riveted her attention and caused her breath to catch in her throat. It lay on the green blotter, along the curvature of light: a hand-held ophthalmoscope, an instrument used to examine the interior of the eye. There was nothing unusual – certainly nothing ominous – about the ophthalmoscope. Every doctor used such an instrument during a routine physical examination. Yet the sight of this one not only inhibited her breathing but filled her with a sudden sense of terrible danger.

She had broken out in a cold sweat.

Her heart was hammering so hard, so loud, that the sound of it seemed to come not from within but without, as if a parade drum was thumping in the street beyond the window.

She could not take her eyes off the ophthalmoscope. As with the black gloves in Bernstein's Delicatessen more than two weeks ago, all other objects in George's office began to fade, until the shining instrument was the only thing that she could see in any detail. She was aware of every tiny scratch and minute nick on its handle. Every humble feature of its design seemed abruptly and enormously important, as if this were not a doctor's ordinary tool but the lynchpin of the universe, an arcane instrument with the potential for catastrophic destruction.

Disorientated, suddenly made claustrophobic by a heavy, insistent, pressing mantle of irrational fear that had descended over her like a great sodden cloak, she pushed the chair away from the desk and stood up. Gasping, whimpering, she felt suffocated yet chilled to the bone at the same time.

The shank of the ophthalmoscope glistened as if made of ice.

The lens shone like an iridescent and chillingly alien eye.

Her resolve to stand fast now swiftly melted, even as her heart seemed to freeze under the cold breath of terror.

Run or die, a voice said within her. *Run or die*.

A cry escaped her, and it sounded like the tortured appeal of a lost and frightened child.

She turned from the desk, stumbled around it, almost fell over a chair. She crossed the room, burst into the outer office, fled into the deserted corridor, keening shrilly, seeking safety, finding none. She wanted help, a friendly face, but she was the only person on the floor, and the danger was closing in. The unknown threat that was somehow embodied in the harmless ophthalmoscope was drawing nearer, so she ran fast as she could, her footsteps booming along the hallway.

Run or die.

The mist descended.

*   *   *

Minutes later, when the mist cleared, when she was again aware of her surroundings, she found herself in the emergency stairwell at the end of the office wing, on a concrete landing between floors. She could not remember leaving the office corridor and taking to the stairs. She was sitting on the landing, squeezed into the corner, her back pressed to the cinderblock wall, staring out at the railing along the far side of the steps. A single bare bulb burned behind a wire basket overhead. To her left and right, flights of stairs led up and down into shadow before coming to other lighted landings. The air was musty and cool. If not for her ragged breathing, silence would have ruled.

It was a lonely place, especially when your life was coming apart at the seams and you needed the reassurance of bright places and people. The grey walls, stark light, looming shadows, the metal railing . . . The place seemed a reflection of her own despair.

Her wild flight and whatever other bizarre behaviour she exhibited in her inexplicable fugue had evidently not been seen, or she would not now be alone. At least that was a blessing. At least no one knew.

She knew, however, and that was bad enough.

She shivered, not entirely from fear, for the mindless terror that had gripped her was gone. She shivered because she was cold, and she was cold because her clothes clung to her, damp, soaked with sweat.

She raised one hand, wiped her face.

She rose, looked up the stairwell then down. She did not know whether she was above or below the floor on which George Hannaby had his office. After a moment she decided to go up.

Her footsteps echoed eerily.

For some reason, she thought of tombs.

'*Meshugge*,' she said shakily.

It was November 27.

50

6

CHICAGO, ILLINOIS

The first Sunday morning in December was cold under a low grey sky that promised snow. By afternoon the first scattered flakes would begin to fall, and by early evening the city's grimy face and soiled skirts would be temporarily concealed beneath the white pancake make-up and pristine cloaks of snow. This night, from the Gold Coast to the slum tenements, everywhere in the city, the number one topic of conversation would be the storm. Everywhere, that is, but in the Roman Catholic homes throughout the parish of Saint Bernadette's, where they would still be talking about the shocking thing Father Brendan Cronin had done during the early Mass that morning.

Father Cronin rose at 5:30 a.m., said prayers, showered, shaved, dressed in cassock and biretta, picked up his breviary, and left the parish house without bothering to put on a coat. He stood for a moment on the rear porch, breathing deeply of the crisp December air.

He was thirty years old, but with his direct green eyes and unruly auburn hair and freckled face, he looked younger than he was. He was fifty or sixty pounds overweight, though not particularly thick in the middle. On him, fat distributed evenly, filling him out equally in face, arms, torso, and legs. From childhood through college, until his second year at the seminary, his nickname had been 'Pudge.'

Regardless of his emotional state, Father Cronin nearly always looked happy. His face had a natural cherubic aspect, and the round lines of it were not designed for the clear and easy expression of anger, melancholy, or grief. This morning he looked mildly pleased with himself and with the world, though he was deeply troubled.

He followed a flagstone path across the yard, past denuded flower beds where the bare earth lay in frozen clumps. He unlocked the door of the sacristy and let himself in. Myrrh and spikenard blended with the scent of the lemon-oil furniture polish with which the old church's oak panelling, pews, and other wooden objects were anointed.

Without switching on the lights, with only the flickering ruby glow of the sacristy lamp to guide him, Father Cronin knelt at the *prie-dieu* and bowed his head. In silence, he petitioned the Divine Father to make him a worthy priest. In the past, this private devotion, before the arrival of the sexton and the altar boy, had sent his spirits soaring and had filled him with exultation at the prospect of celebrating Mass. But now, as on most other mornings during the last four months, joy eluded him. He felt only a leaden bleakness, an emptiness that made his heart ache dully and that induced a cold, sick trembling in his belly.

Clenching his jaws, gritting his teeth, as if he could *will* himself into a state of spiritual ecstasy, he repeated his petition, elaborated upon his initial prayers, but still he felt unmoved, hollow.

After washing his hands and murmuring, '*Da Domine*,' Father Cronin laid his biretta on the *prie-dieu* and went to the vesting bench to attire himself for the sacred celebration ahead. He was a sensitive man with an artist's soul, and in the great beauty of the ceremony he perceived a pleasing pattern of divine order, a subtle echo of God's grace. Usually, when placing the linen amice over his shoulders, when arranging the white alb so that it fell evenly to his ankles, a shiver of awe passed through him, awe that *he*, Brendan Cronin, should have achieved this sacred office.

Usually. But not today. And not for weeks of days before this.

Even as he lifted the maniple, kissed the cross in the centre of it, and placed it on his left forearm, he felt nothing. There was just that cold, throbbing, hollow ache where belief and joy had once existed.

Four months ago, in early August, Father Brendan Cronin had begun to lose his faith. A small but relentless fire of doubt burned within him, unquenchable, gradually consuming all of his long-held beliefs.

For any priest, the loss of faith is a devastating process. But it was worse for Brendan Cronin than it would have been for most others. He had never even briefly entertained the thought of being anything *but* a priest. His parents were devout, and they fostered in him a devotion to the Church.

52

However, he had not become a priest to please them. Simply, as trite as it might sound to others in this age of agnosticism, he had been *called* to the priesthood at a very young age. Now, though faith was gone, his holy office continued to be the essential part of his self-image; yet he knew he could not go on saying Mass and praying and comforting the afflicted when it was nothing but a charade to him.

As Brendan Cronin placed the stole around his neck and crossed it over his breast, the courtyard door to the sacristy was flung open, and a young boy burst into the room, switching on the electric lights that the priest had preferred to do without. 'Morning, Father!'

'Good morning, Kerry. How're you this fine morning?'

Except that his hair was much redder than Father Cronin's, Kerry McDevit might have been the priest's blood relative. He was slightly plump, freckled, with green eyes full of mischief. 'I'm fine, Father. But it's sure cold out there this morning. Cold as a witch's . . .'

'Oh, yes? Cold as a witch's what?'

'Refrigerator,' the boy said, embarrassed. 'Cold as a witch's refrigerator, Father. And that's *cold*.'

If his mood had not been so bleak, Brendan would have been amused by the boy's narrow avoidance of an innocent obscenity, but in his current state of mind he could not summon even a shadow of a smile. Undoubtedly, his silence was interpreted as stern disapproval, for Kerry averted his eyes and went quickly to the closet, where he stowed his coat, scarf, and gloves, and took his surplice from a hanger.

Father Cronin put on the chasuble, passed the strings around his back, tied them against his breast with no more emotion than a welder getting dressed for work in a factory. As his hands were occupied with that task, his mind drifted back to a melancholy recollection of the exuberance with which he had once approached every priestly duty.

Until last August, he never doubted the wisdom of his commitment to the Church. He had been such a bright and hard-working student of both mundane subjects and religion that he had been chosen to complete his Catholic education at the North American College in Rome. He loved the Holy City – the architecture, the history, and the friendly people. Upon ordination and acceptance into the Society of Jesus, he had spent two years at the Vatican, as an assistant to Monsignor Giuseppi Orbella, chief speech writer and doctrinal adviser to His Holiness, the Pope. That honour could have been followed by a prized assignment to the staff of the Cardinal of the Chicago Archdiocese, but Father Cronin had requested, instead, a curacy at a small or medium-size parish, like any young priest. Thus, after a visit to Bishop Santefiore in San Francisco (an old friend of Monsignor Orbella's), and after a vacation during which he drove from San Francisco to Chicago, he had come to St Bernadette's, where he'd taken great pleasure in even the most ordinary day-to-day chores of a curate's life. And never a regret or doubt.

Now, as he watched his altar boy slip into a surplice, Father Cronin longed for the simple faith that had for so long comforted and sustained him. Was it gone only temporarily, or had he lost it forever?

When Kerry was dressed, he led the way through the inner sacristy door, into the sanctuary of the church. Several steps beyond the door, he evidently sensed that Father Cronin was not coming after him, for he glanced back, a puzzled look upon his face.

Brendan Cronin hesitated. Through the door he had a side-view of the towering crucifix on the back wall and the altar platform straight ahead. This holiest part of the church was dismayingly strange, as if he were seeing it objectively for the first time. And he could not imagine why he had ever thought of it as sacred territory. It was just a *place*. A place like any other. If he walked out there now, if he went through the familiar rituals and litanies, he would be a hypocrite. He would be defrauding everyone in the congregation.

The puzzlement on Kerry McDevit's face had turned to worry. The boy glanced out toward the pews that Brendan Cronin could not see, then looked again at his priest.

How can I say Mass when I no longer believe? Brendan wondered.

But there was nothing else to be done.

Holding the chalice in his left hand, with his right hand over the burse and veil, he kept the sacred vessel close to his breast and followed Kerry, at last, into the sanctuary, where the face of Christ upon the cross seemed, for a moment, to gaze at him accusingly.

As usual, less than a hundred people were in attendance for the early service. Their faces were unusually pale and radiant, as if God had not allowed real worshippers to attend this morning but had sent a deputation of judgmental angels to witness the sacrilege of a doubting priest who dared to offer Mass in spite of his fallen condition.

As the Mass progressed, Father Cronin's despair deepened. From the moment he spoke the *Introibo ad altare Dei*, each step of the ceremony compounded the priest's misery. By the time Kerry McDevit transferred the missal from the Epistle to the Gospel side of the altar, Father Cronin's despondency was so heavy that he felt crushed beneath it. His spiritual and emotional exhaustion were so profound that he could barely lift his arms, could hardly find strength to focus on the Gospel and mutter the lines from the sacred text. The faces of the worshippers blurred into featureless blobs. By the time he reached the Canon of the Mass, Father Cronin could barely whisper. He knew that Kerry was gaping at him openly now, and he was sure that the congregation was aware that something was wrong. He was sweating and shaking. The awful greyness in him grew darker now, swiftly turning to black, and he felt as if he were spiralling down into a frighteningly dark void.

Then, as he held the Host in his hands and elevated it, speaking the five words that signified the mystery of transubstantiation, he was suddenly angry with himself for being unable to believe, angry with the Church for failing to provide him with better armour against doubt, angry that his entire life seemed misdirected, wasted, expended in pursuit of idiotic myths. His anger churned, heated up, reached the boiling point, was transformed into a steam of fury, a blistering vapour of *rage*.

To his astonishment, a wretched cry burst from him, and he pitched the chalice across the sanctuary. With a loud *clank*, it struck the sanctuary wall, spraying wine, rebounded, bounced off a statue of the Blessed Virgin, and clattered to a stop against the foot of the podium at which he had not long ago read from the Gospels.

55

Kerry McDevit stumbled back in shock, and in the nave a hundred people gasped as one, but that response had no effect on Brendan Cronin. In a rage that was his only protection against suicidal despair, he flung one arm wide and swept a tray of communion wafers to the floor. With another wild cry, half anger and half grief, he tore off the stole that lay around his neck and across his breast, threw it down, turned from the altar, and raced into the sacristy. There, the anger departed as suddenly as it had come, and he stopped, stood swaying in confusion.

It was December 1.

7.

LAGUNA BEACH, CALIFORNIA

That first Sunday in December, Dom Corvaisis had lunch with Parker Faine on the terrace at Las Brisas, in the shade of an umbrella-table, overlooking the sun-dappled sea. The good weather was holding well this year. While the breeze brought them the cries of gulls, the tang of the sea, and the sweet scent of star jasmine that was growing nearby, Dominick told Parker every embarrassing and distressing detail of his escalating battle with somnambulism.

Parker Faine was his best friend, perhaps the only person in the world with whom he could open up like this, though on the surface they seemed to have little in common. Dom was a slender, lean-muscled man, but Parker Faine was squat, burly, beefy. Beardless, Dom went to the barber for a haircut every three weeks; but Parker's hair was shaggy, and his beard was shaggy, and his eyebrows bristled. He looked like a cross between a professional wrestler and a beatnik from the 1950s. Dom drank little and was easily intoxicated, while Parker's thirst was legendary and his capacity prodigious. Although Dom was solitary by nature and slow to make friends, Parker had the gift of seeming like an old acquaintance just an hour after you first met him. At fifty, Parker Faine was fifteen years older than Dom. He had been rich and famous for almost a quarter of a century, and he was comfortable with both his wealth and fame, utterly unable to understand Dom's uneasiness over the money and notoriety that was beginning to come his way because of *Twilight in Babylon*. Dom had come to lunch at Las Brisas in Bally loafers, dark brown slacks, and a lighter brown-checkered shirt with a button-down collar, but Parker had arrived in blue tennis shoes, heavily crinkled white cotton pants, and a white-and-blue flowered shirt worn over his belt, which made it seem as if they had dressed for entirely different engagements, had met outside the restaurant sheerly by chance, and had decided to have lunch together on a whim.

In spite of all the ways they differed from each other, they had become fast friends because in several important ways they were alike. Both were artists, not by choice or inclination but by compulsion. Dom painted with words; Parker painted with paint; and they approached their different arts with identical high standards, commitment, craftsmanship. Furthermore, though Parker made friends more easily than Dom did, each placed enormous value on friendship and nurtured it.

They had met six years ago, when Parker had moved to Oregon for eighteen months, in search of new subject matter for a series of landscapes done in his unique style, which successfully married supra-realism with a surreal imagination. While there, he had signed to give one lecture a month at the University of Portland, where Dom held a position in the Department of English.

Now, while Parker hunched over the table, munching on nachos that were dripping with cheese and guacamole and sour cream, Dom sipped slowly at a bottle of Negra Modello and recounted his unconscious nocturnal adventures. He spoke softly, though discretion was probably unnecessary; the other diners on the terrace were noisily involved in their own conversations. He did not touch the nachos. This morning, for the fourth time, he had awakened behind the furnace in the garage, in a state of undiluted terror, and his continued inability to get control of himself had left him dispirited and without an appetite. By the time he finished his tale, he had drunk only half the beer, for even that rich dark Mexican brew tasted flat and stale today.

Parker, on the other hand, had poured down three double-shot margaritas and had ordered a fourth. However, the painter's attention was not dulled by the alcohol he consumed. 'Jesus, buddy, why didn't you tell me about this sooner, *weeks* ago?'

'I felt sort of . . . foolish.'

'Nonsense. Bullshit,' the painter insisted, gesturing expansively with one huge hand, but keeping his voice low.

The Mexican waiter, a diminutive Wayne Newton look-alike, arrived with a margarita for Parker and inquired if they wished to order lunch.

'No, no. Sunday lunch is an excuse to have too many margaritas, and I'm a long way from having too many. What a sad waste to order lunch after only four margaritas! That'd leave most of the afternoon unfilled, and we'd find ourselves on the street with nothing to occupy us, and then without doubt we'd get into trouble, attract the attention of the police. God knows what might happen. No, no. To avoid jail and protect our reputations, we must not order lunch sooner than three o'clock. In fact, bring me *another* margarita. And another order of these magnificent nachos, please. More salsa, hotter if you've got it. A dish of chopped onions, too, please. And another beer for my dismayingly restrained friend.'

'No,' Dom said. 'I'm only half-finished with this one.'

'That's what I meant by "dismayingly restrained," you hopeless Puritan. You've sucked at that one so long it must be warm.'

Ordinarily, Dominick would have leaned back and enjoyed Parker Faine's energetic performance. The painter's ebullience, his unfailing enthusiasm for life, was invigorating and amusing. Today, however, Dom was so troubled that he was not amused.

As the waiter turned away, a small cloud passed over the sun, and Parker leaned in farther under the suddenly deeper shadow beneath the umbrella, returning his attention to Dominick, as if he had read his companion's mind. 'All right, let's brainstorm. Let's find some sort of explanation and figure out what to do. You don't think the problem's just related to stress . . . the upcoming publication of your book?'

'I did. But not any more. I mean, if the problem was just a

58

mild one, I might be able to accept that career worries lay behind it. But, Jesus, my concerns about *Twilight* just aren't great enough to generate behaviour this unusual, this obsessive . . . this *crazy*. I go walking almost every night now, and it's not just the walking that's weird. The depth of my trance is incredible. Few sleepwalkers are as utterly comatose as I am, and few of them engage in such elaborate tasks as I do. I mean, I was attempting to nail the windows shut! And you don't attempt to nail your windows shut just to keep out your worries about your career.'

'You may be more deeply worried about *Twilight* than you realise.'

'No. It doesn't make sense. In fact, when the new book continued to go well, my anxiety about *Twilight* started fading. You can't sit there and honestly tell me you think all this middle-of-the-night lunacy springs just from a few career worries.'

'No, I can't,' Parker agreed.

'I crawl into the backs of those closets to *hide*. And when I wake up behind the furnace, when I'm still half-asleep, I have the feeling that something's stalking me, searching for me, something that'll kill me if it finds my hidey-hole. A couple of mornings I woke up trying to scream but unable to get it out. Yesterday, I woke up shouting, 'Stay away, stay away, stay away!' And this morning, the knife . . .'

'Knife?' Parker said. 'You didn't tell me about a knife.'

'Woke up behind the furnace, hiding again. Had a butcher's knife. I'd removed it from the rack in the kitchen while I was sleeping.'

'For protection? From what?'

'From whatever . . . from whoever's stalking me.'

'And who *is* stalking you?'

Dom shrugged. 'Nobody that I'm aware of.'

'I don't like this. You could've cut yourself, maybe badly.'

'That's not what scares me the most.'

'So what scares you the most?'

Dom looked around at the other people on the terrace. Though some had followed Parker Faine's bit of theatre with the waiter, no one was now paying the least attention to him or Dominick.

'What scares you the most?' Parker repeated.

'That I might . . . might cut someone else.'

Incredulous, Faine said, 'You mean take a butcher's knife and . . . go on a murdering rampage in your sleep? No chance.' He gulped his margarita. 'Good heavens, what a melodramatic notion! Thankfully, your fiction is not quite so sloppily imagined. Relax, my friend. You're not the homicidal type.'

'I didn't think I was the sleepwalking type, either.'

'Oh, bullshit. There's an explanation for this. You're not mad. Madmen never doubt their sanity.'

'I think I'm going to have to see a psychiatrist, a counsellor of some kind. And have a few medical tests.'

'The medical tests, yes. But put a hold on the psychiatrist. That's a waste of time. You're no more neurotic than psychotic.'

The waiter returned with more nachos, salsa, a dish of chopped onions, a beer, and a fifth margarita.

Parker surrendered his empty glass, took the full one. He scooped up some of the corn chips with generous globs of guacamole and sour cream, spooned some onions on top, and ate with an appreciation only one step removed from manic glee.

'I wonder if this problem of yours is somehow related to the changes you underwent two summers ago.'

Puzzled, Dom said, 'What changes?'

'You know what I'm talking about. When I first met you in Portland six years ago, you were a pale, retiring, unadventurous slug.'

'Slug?'

'It's true, and you know it. You were bright, talented, but a slug nonetheless. You know why you were a slug? I'll tell you why. You had all those brains and all that talent, but you were afraid to use them. You were afraid of competition, failure, success, *life*. You just wanted to plod along, unnoticed. You dressed drably, spoke almost inaudibly, dreaded calling attention to yourself. You took refuge in the academic world because there was less competition there. God, man, you were a timid rabbit burrowing in the earth and curling up in its den.'

'Oh, yeah? If I was all that disgusting, why on earth did you ever go out of your way to strike up a friendship with me?'

'Because, you thick-headed booby, I saw through your masquerade. I saw beyond the timidity, saw through the practised dullness and the mask of insipidness. I sensed something

60

special in you, saw glimpses and glimmers of it. That's what I *do*, you know. I see what other people can't. That's what any good artist does. He *sees* what most cannot.'

'And *you* called *me* insipid?'

'It's true – about what an artist does and about you being a rabbit. Remember how long you knew me before you found enough confidence to admit being a writer? Three months!'

'Well, in those days, I wasn't really a writer.'

'You had drawers full of stories! More than a hundred short stories, not *one* of which had ever been submitted to any publication anywhere! Not just because you were afraid of rejection. You were afraid of acceptance, too. Afraid of success. How many months did I have to hammer at you till you finally sent a couple to market?'

'I don't remember.'

'*I* do. Six months! I wheedled and cajoled and demanded and pushed and nagged until you broke down and started submitting stories. I'm a persuasive character, but prying you out of your rabbit hole was almost beyond even my formidable talent for persuasion.'

With an almost obscene enthusiasm, Parker scooped up dripping masses of nachos and stuffed himself. After slurping his margarita, he said, 'Even when your short stories started selling, you wanted to stop. I had to push you constantly. And after I left Oregon and came back here, when I left you on your own again, you only continued to submit stories for a few months. Then you crawled back into your rabbit hole.'

Dom did not argue because everything the painter said was true. After leaving Oregon and returning to his home in Laguna, Parker continued to encourage Dom through letters and phone calls, but long-distance encouragement was insufficient to motivate him. He'd convinced himself that, after all, he was not a writer worthy of publication, in spite of more than a score of sales he'd racked up in less than a year. He stopped sending his stories to magazines and quickly fabricated another shell to replace the one Parker had helped him break out of. Though he was still compelled to produce stories, he reverted to his previous habit of consigning them to his deepest desk drawer, with no thought of marketing them. Parker had continued to urge him to write a novel, but Dom had been certain that his talent was too humble and that he was too lacking in self-discipline to tackle such a large and complex project. He tucked his head down once more, spoke softly, walked softly, and tried to live a life that was largely beneath notice.

'But the summer before last, all of that changed,' Parker said. 'Suddenly you throw away your teaching career. You take the plunge and become a full-time writer. Almost overnight, you change from an accountant type to a risk-taker, a Bohemian. Why? You've never been clear about that. *Why*?'

Dominick frowned, considered the question for a moment, and was surprised that he had not thought about it much before this. 'I don't know why. I really don't know.'

At the University of Portland, he had been up for tenure, had felt that he would not be given it, and had grown panicky at the prospect of being cast loose from his sheltered moorings. Obsessed with keeping a low profile, he had faded *too* completely from the notice of the campus movers-and-shakers, and when the time arrived for the tenure board to consider him, they had begun to question whether he had embraced the University with sufficient enthusiasm to warrant a grant of lifetime employment. Dom was enough of a realist to see that, if the board refused tenure, he would find it difficult to obtain a position at another university, for the hiring committee would want to know why he had been turned down at Portland. In an uncharacteristic burst of self-promotion, hoping to slip out from under the university's axe before it fell, he applied for positions at institutions in several Western states, emphasising his published stories because that was the *only* thing worth emphasising.

Mountainview College in Utah, with a student body of only four thousand, had been so impressed by the list of magazines in which he had published that they flew him from Portland for an interview. Dom made a considerable effort to be more outgoing than he had ever been before. He was offered a contract to teach English and creative writing with guaranteed tenure. He had accepted, if not with enormous delight then at least with enormous relief.

Now, on the terrace of Las Brisas, as the California sun slid out from behind a band of white jewelled clouds, he took a sip

62

of his beer, sighed, and said, 'I left Portland late in June that year. I had a U-Haul trailer hooked to the car, just a small one, filled mostly with books and clothes. I was in a good mood. Didn't feel as if I'd failed at Portland. Not at all. I just felt . . . well, that I was getting a fresh start. I was really looking forward to life at Mountainview. In fact, I don't remember ever being happier than the day I hit the road.'

Parker Faine nodded knowingly. 'Of course you were happy! You had tenure in a hick school, where not much would be expected of you, where your introversion would be excused as an artist's temperament.'

'A perfect rabbit hole, huh?'

'Exactly. So why didn't you wind up teaching in Mountainview?'

'I told you before . . . at the last minute, when I got there the second week in July, I just couldn't bear the idea of going on with the kind of life I'd had before. I was tired of being a mouse, a rabbit.'

'Just like that, you were repelled by the low-key life. Why?'

'It wasn't very fulfilling.'

'But why were you tired of it *all of a sudden*?'

'I don't know.'

'You must have some idea. Haven't you thought about it a lot?'

'Surprisingly, I haven't,' Dom said. He stared out to sea for a long moment, watching a dozen sailboats and a large yacht as they moved majestically along the coast. 'I just now realised how amazingly *little* I've thought about it. Strange . . . I'm usually too self-analytical for my own good, but in this case I've never probed very deeply.'

'Ah ha!' Parker exclaimed. 'I knew I was on the right trail! The changes you went through *then* are somehow related to the problems you're having *now*. So go on. So you told the people at Mountainview that you didn't want their job any more?'

'They weren't happy.'

'And you took a tiny apartment in town.'

'One room, plus kitchen and bath. Not much of a place. Nice view of the mountains, though.'

'Decided to live on your savings while you wrote a novel?'

'There wasn't a *lot* in the bank, but I'd always been frugal.'

'Impulsive behaviour. Risky. And not a damn bit *like* you,' Parker said. 'So why did you do it? What changed you?'

'I guess it was building for a long time. By the time I got to Mountainview, my dissatisfaction was so great that I *had* to change.'

Parker leaned back in his chair. 'No good, my friend. There must be more to it than that. Listen, by your own admission, you were as happy as a pig in shit when you left Portland with your U-Haul. You had a job with a liveable salary, guaranteed tenure, in a place where no one was ever going to demand too much of you. All you had to do was settle down in Mountainview and disappear. But by the time you got there, you couldn't wait to throw it all over, move into a garret, and risk eventual starvation, all for your art. What the hell happened to you during that long drive to Utah? Something must've given you a real jolt, something big enough to knock you out of your complacency.'

'Nope. It was an uneventful trip.'

'Not inside your head, it wasn't.'

Dominick shrugged. 'As far as I remember, I just relaxed, enjoyed the drive, took my time, looked at the scenery. . . .'

'*Amigo!*' Parker roared, startling their waiter, who was passing by. '*Uno* margarita! And another *cerveza* for my friend.'

'No, no,' Dom said. 'I –'

'You haven't finished *that* beer,' Parker said. 'I know, I know. But you are going to finish it and drink another, and gradually you're going to loosen up, and we're going to get to the bottom of this sleepwalking. I'm sure it's related to the changes you underwent the summer before last. You know why I'm so sure? I'll tell you why I'm so sure. Nobody undergoes *two* personality crises in two years for utterly unrelated reasons. The two have to be tied together somehow.'

Dom grimaced. 'I wouldn't exactly call this a personality *crisis*.'

'Oh, wouldn't you?' Leaning forward, lowering his shaggy head, putting all the force of his powerful personality behind the question, Parker said, 'Wouldn't you really call it a crisis, my friend?'

Dom sighed. 'Well . . . yeah. I guess maybe I would. A crisis.'

*　　　*　　　*

They left Las Brisas late that afternoon, without arriving at any answers. That night, when he went to bed, he was filled with dread, wondering where he would find himself in the morning.

And in the morning, he virtually exploded out of sleep with a shrill scream and found himself in total, claustrophobic darkness. Something had hold of him, something cold and clammy and strange and *alive*. He struck out blindly, flailed and clawed, twisted and kicked, freed himself, scrambled away in panic, through the cloying blackness, on his hands and knees, until he collided with a wall. The lightless room reverberated with thunderous pounding and shouting, an unnerving cacophony, the source of which he could not identify. He scrambled along the baseboard until he came to a junction of walls, where he put his back into the corner and faced out upon the lightless chamber, certain that the clammy creature would leap on him from the gloom.

What was in the room with him?

The noise grew louder: shouting, hammering, a crash followed by a clatter-rattle of wood, more shouting, and another crash.

Still groggy from sleep, senses distorted by hysteria and excess adrenalin, Dom was convinced that the thing from which he had been hiding had at last come for him. He had tried to fool it by sleeping in closets and behind the furnace. But tonight it would not be deceived; it meant to have him; he could hide no longer; the end had come.

From the darkness, someone or something shouted his name – '*Dom!*' – and he realised that someone had been calling to him for the last minute or two, maybe longer. '*Dominick, answer me!*'

Another shuddering crash. The brittle crack of splintering wood.

Huddling in the corner, Dom finally woke completely. The clammy creature had not been real. A figment of a dream. He recognised the voice calling to him as that of Parker Faine.

Even as the residual hysteria of his nightmare subsided, another crash, the loudest of all, generated a chain-reaction of destruction, a cracking-sliding-scraping-toppling-crashing-booming-clattering-rattling that culminated with the opening of a door and the intrusion of light into the darkness.

Dom squinted against the glare and saw Parker silhouetted like some hulking troll in the bedroom door, the hall light behind him. The door had been locked, and Parker had forced it, had thrown himself against it until the lock disintegrated.

'Dominick, buddy, are you okay?'

The door had been barricaded as well, which had made entrance even more difficult. Dom saw that, in his sleep, he had evidently moved the dresser in front of the door, had stacked the two nightstands atop the dresser, and had put the bedroom armchair in front of it. Those overturned pieces of furniture now lay on the floor in a jumbled heap.

Parker stepped into the room. 'Buddy? Are you all right? You were screaming. I could hear you clear out in the driveway.'

'A dream.'

'Must've been a lulu.'

'I can't remember what it was,' Dom said, remaining on the floor, in the corner, too exhausted and weak-kneed to get up. 'You're a sight for sore eyes, Parker. But . . . what on earth are you doing here?'

Parker blinked. 'Don't you know? You phoned me. Not more than ten minutes ago. You were shouting for help. You said *they* were here and were going to get you. Then you hung up.'

Dom felt humiliation settle over him as if it were a painful burn.

'Ah, so you *did* make the call in your sleep,' the painter said. 'Thought as much. You sounded . . . not yourself. Maybe I should've called the police, but I suspected this sleepwalking thing. Knew you wouldn't want it brought into the open in front of strangers, a bunch of cops.'

'I'm out of control, Parker. Something's . . . snapping inside me.'

'That's enough of that crap. I won't listen to any more of it.'

Dom felt like a helpless child. He was afraid he was going to

66

cry. He bit his tongue, squeezed back the tears, cleared his throat, and said, 'What time is it?'

'A few minutes after four. Middle of the night.' Parker looked toward the window and frowned.

Following the other man's gaze, Dom saw that the draperies were drawn tight shut and that the highboy had been moved in front of the window, barring entrance by that route. He had been busy in his sleep.

'Oh, Christ,' Parker said, moving to the bed, where he stopped, a vivid expression of shock on his broad face. 'This is no good, my friend. This is no good at all.'

Holding on to the wall, Dom rose shakily to his feet to see what Parker was talking about, but when he saw it, he wished he had remained on the floor. An arsenal was laid out on the bed: the .22 automatic that he usually kept in his nightstand; a butcher's knife; two other meat knives; a cleaver; a hammer; the axe he used for splitting firewood and which, the last he remembered, had been in the garage.

Parker said, 'What were you expecting – a Soviet invasion? What frightens you so?'

'I don't know. Something in my nightmares.'

'So what do you dream about?'

'I don't know.'

'You can't remember any of it?'

'No.' He shivered again, violently.

Parker came to him, put a hand on his shoulder. 'You better take a shower, get dressed. I'll start rustling up some breakfast. Okay? Then I . . . I think we'd better pay a visit to that doctor of yours as soon as his office opens. I think he's got to take a second look at you.'

Dominick nodded.

It was December 2.

TWO
December 2 – December 16

1.

BOSTON, MASSACHUSETTS

Viola Fletcher, a fifty-eight-year-old elementary-school teacher, mother of two daughters, wife of a devoted husband, a wry and witty woman with an infectious laugh, was silent now, and still, lying on the operating table, unconscious, her life in Dr Ginger Weiss's hands.

Ginger's entire life had been a funnel, focusing on this moment: for the first time, she was assuming the senior surgeon's role in a major and complicated procedure. Years of arduous education, an immeasurable weight of hopes and dreams, lay behind her ascension to this moment. She had a prideful yet humbling sense of just how great a distance her journey had covered.

And she was half sick with dread.

Mrs Fletcher had been anaesthetised and draped in cool green sheets. None of the patient's body was visible except that portion of her torso on which surgery would be performed, a neat square of flesh painted with iodine and framed by lime-coloured cloth. Even her face was out of sight beneath tented sheeting, as an added precaution against airborne contamination of the wound that would shortly be made in her abdomen. The effect was to depersonalise the patient, and perhaps that was in part the *intent* of the draping, as well, thereby sparing the surgeon the need to look upon the human face of agony and death if, God forbid, his skill and education should fail him.

On Ginger's right, Agatha Tandy, the surgical technician, stood ready with spreaders, rakes, haemostats, scalpels, and other instruments. On her left, a scrub nurse was prepared to assist. Another scrub nurse, the circulating nurse, the anaesthesiologist and his nurse also waited for the procedure to begin.

George Hannaby stood on the other side of the table, looking less like a doctor than 'ike the former star fullback on a pro football team. His wife, Rita, had once talked him into playing Paul Bunyan in a comedy sketch for a hospital charity show, and he had appeared at home in woodsman's boots, jeans, and a red plaid shirt. He brought with him an aura of strength, calmness, and competency that was most reassuring.

Ginger held out her right hand.

Agatha put a scalpel in it.

A keen, thin, bright curve of light outlined the razor-sharp edge of the instrument.

Hand poised over the score lines on the patient's torso, Ginger hesitated and took a deep breath.

George's stereo tape deck stood on a small table in the corner, and familiar strains of Bach issued from the speakers.

She was remembering the ophthalmoscope, the shiny black gloves. . . .

However, as frightening as those incidents had been, they had not utterly destroyed her self-confidence. She had felt fine ever since the most recent attack: strong, alert, energetic. If she had noticed the slightest weariness or fuzzy-mindedness, she would have cancelled this procedure. On the other hand, she had not acquired her education, had not worked seven days a week all these years, only to throw away her future because of two aberrant moments of stress-related hysteria. Everything was going to be fine, just fine.

The wall clock said 7:42. Time to get on with it.

She made the first cut. With haemostats and clamps and a faultless skill that always surprised her, she moved deeper, constructing a shaft through skin, fat, and muscle, into the centre of that patient's belly. Soon the incision was large enough to accommodate both her hands and those of her assisting physician, George Hannaby, if his help should be required. The scrub nurses moved close to the table, one on each side, grasped the sculpted handles of the retractors, and pulled back gently on them, drawing apart the walls of the wound.

Agatha Tandy picked up a fluffy, absorbent cloth and quickly blotted Ginger's forehead, careful to avoid the jeweller's lenses that protruded from her operating glasses.

Above his mask, George's eyes squinted in a smile. *He* was not sweating. He seldom did.

Ginger swiftly tied off bleeders and removed clamps, and Agatha ordered new supplies from the circulating nurse.

In the brief blank spaces between Bach's concertos and in the silence at the end of the tape before it was turned over, the loudest sounds in the tile-walled room were the sibilant exhalations and groaning inhalations of the artificial lung machine that breathed for Viola Fletcher. The patient could not breathe for herself because she was paralysed by a curare-derived muscle relaxant. Though entirely mechanical, those sounds possessed a haunting quality that made it impossible for Ginger to overcome her apprehension.

On other days, when George cut, there was more talk. He traded quips with the nurses and the assisting resident, using light banter to reduce the tension without also reducing concentration on the vital task at hand. Ginger was simply not up to that sort of dazzling performance, which seemed akin to playing basketball, chewing gum, and solving difficult mathematical problems at the same time.

Having completed the excursion into the belly, she ran the colon with both hands and determined that it was healthy. With damp gauze pads provided by Agatha, Ginger cradled the intestines, placed the hoe-like blades of the retractors against them, and turned them over to the scrub nurses, who held them out of the way, thus exposing the aorta, the main trunkline of the body's arterial system.

From the chest, the aorta entered the belly through the diaphragm, running parallel to the spine. Immediately above the groin, it split into two iliac arteries leading to the femoral arteries in the legs.

'There it is,' Ginger said. 'An aneurysm. Just like in the X-rays.' As if to confirm it, she glanced at the patient's X-ray that was fixed on the light screen, on the wall at the foot of the operating table. 'A dissecting aneurysm, just above the aortic saddle.'

Agatha blotted Ginger's forehead.

The aneurysm, a weakness in the wall of the aorta, had permitted the artery to bulge outward on both sides, forming a dumb-bell-shaped extrusion full of blood, which beat like a second heart. This condition caused difficulty in swallowing, extreme shortness of breath, severe coughing, and chest pains; and if the bulging vessel burst, death followed swiftly.

As Ginger stared at the pulsing aneurysm, an almost religious sense of mystery overcame her, a profound awe, as if she had stepped out of the real world into a mystic sphere, where the very meaning of life was soon to be revealed to her. Her feeling of power, of transcendence, rose from the realisation that she could do battle with death – and win. Death was lurking there in the body of her patient right now, in the form of the throbbing aneurysm, a dark bud waiting to flower, but she had the skill and training to banish it.

From a sterile package, Agatha Tandy had taken a section of artificial aorta – a thick, ribbed tube that split into two smaller tubes, the iliac arteries. It was woven entirely of Dacron. Ginger positioned it over the wound, trimmed it to fit with a pair of small sharp scissors, and returned it to the technician. Agatha put the white graft in a shallow stainless-steel tray that already contained some of the patient's blood, and swished it back and forth to wet it thoroughly.

The graft would be allowed to soak until it had clotted a bit. Once it was installed in the patient, Ginger would run some blood through it, clamp it, allow that blood to clot a bit more, then flush it out before actually sewing it in place. The thin layer of clotted blood would help prevent seepage, and in time the steady flow of blood would form a neointima, a leak-proof new lining virtually indistinguishable from that in a real artery. The amazing thing was that the Dacron vessel was not merely an adequate substitute for the damaged section of aorta but was, in fact, actually superior to what nature had provided; five hundred years from now, when nothing remained of Viola Fletcher but dust and time-worn bones, the Dacron graft would be still intact, still flexible and strong.

Agatha blotted Ginger's forehead.

'How do you feel?' George asked.

'Fine,' Ginger said.

'Tense?'

'Not really,' she lied.

He said, 'It's a genuine pleasure watching you work, Doctor.'

'I'll second that,' said one of the scrub nurses.

'Me too,' the other said.

'Thanks,' Ginger said, surprised and pleased.

George said, 'You have a certain grace in surgery, a lightness of touch, a splendid sensitivity of hand and eye that is, I'm sorry to say, not at all common in the profession.'

Ginger knew that he never gave voice to an insincere compliment, but coming from such a stern taskmaster, this bordered on excessive flattery. By God, George Hannaby was *proud* of her! That realisation flooded her with warm emotion. If she had been anywhere but in an operating room, tears would have come to her eyes, but here she kept a tighter rein on her feelings. However, the intensity of her reaction to his words made her aware of how completely he had filled the role of father-figure in her life; she took nearly as much satisfaction from his praise as she would have taken if it had come from Jacob Weiss himself.

Ginger proceeded with the operation in better spirits. The disturbing possibility of a seizure receded from her thoughts, and greater confidence allowed her to work with even more grace than before. Nothing could go wrong now.

She set about methodically controlling the flow of blood through the aorta, carefully exposing and temporarily clamping all branching vessels, using thin elastic loops of extremely pliable plastic tubing to valve off the smaller vessels, placing mosquito clamps and bulldog clamps on the larger arteries, including the iliacs and the aorta itself. In little less than an hour, she had stopped all bloodflow through the aorta to the patient's legs, and the throbbing aneurysm had ceased its mocking imitation of the heart.

With a small scalpel, she punctured the aneurysm, releasing a pool of blood; the aorta deflated. She sliced it open along its anterior wall. At that moment, the patient was without an aorta, more helpless and more dependent upon the surgeon than at any other time. There was no going back now. From this point on, the operation must be conducted not only with the greatest care but with the most prudent speed.

A hush had fallen on the surgical team. What little conversation there had been ceased. The Bach tape had reached the end again, and no one moved to turn it over. Time was measured by the wheezing and sucking of the artificial lung machine and by the beeping of the EKG.

Ginger removed the Dacron graft from the steel tray, where it had been soaking up blood and clotting precisely as desired. She sewed the top of it into the aortal trunk, using an extremely fine thread. Then, with the top of the graft sewn in place and the unattached bottom clamped off, Ginger filled it with blood to let it clot again.

Throughout these steps of the operation, it had not been necessary for Ginger to have the sweat blotted from her forehead. She hoped that George noticed her new dryness – and was sure he did.

Without needing to be told that it was once again time for music, the circulating nurse reset the Bach tape.

Hours of work lay ahead of Ginger, but she pressed on without the least weariness. She moved down the draped body, folding back the green sheets, revealing both of the patient's thighs. With the help of the circulating nurse, Agatha had replenished the instrument tray and was ready now with everything that Ginger needed to make two more incisions, one in each of the patient's legs, below the inguineal creases, where the legs attached to the body trunk. Clamping and tying off vessels, Ginger eventually exposed and separated the femoral arteries. As with the aorta before, she used thin elastic tubing and a variety of clamps to valve off the bloodflow through these vascular fields, then opened both arteries where the bifurcated legs of the graft would attach to them. A couple of times she caught herself humming along happily with the music, and the ease with which she worked made it seem almost as if she had been a surgeon in an earlier life, now reincarnated into the elite brotherhood of the caduceus, pre-destined for this labour.

But she should have remembered her father and his aphorisms, the bits of wisdom that he had collected and with which he had gently lectured or patiently admonished her on those rare occasions when she had been less than well behaved or when she had failed to do her very best in school. *Time waits for no man; God helps those who help themselves; a penny saved is a penny earned; resentment hurts only those who harbour it; judge not that ye be judged.* . . . He had a thousand of them, but there was none he liked better and none he repeated more often than this one: *Pride goeth before a great fall.*

She should have remembered those six words. The operation was going so well, and she was so happy with her work, so *proud* of her performance in this first major solo flight, that she forgot about the inevitable great fall.

Returning to the opened abdomen, she unclamped the bottom of the Dacron graft, flushed it out, then tunnelled the twin legs of it beneath the untouched flesh of the groin, beneath the inguineal creases, and into the incisions she had made in the femoral arteries. She stitched in both terminuses of the bifurcated graft, unclamped the restricted vascular network, and watched with delight as the pulse returned to the patched aorta. For twenty minutes, she searched for leaks and knitted them up with fine, strong thread. For another five minutes, she watched closely, in silence, as the graft throbbed like any normal, healthy arterial vessel, without any sign of chronic seepage.

At last she said, 'Time to close up.'

'Beautifully done,' George said.

Ginger was glad she was wearing a surgical mask, for beneath it her face was stretched by a smile so broad that she must have looked like the proverbial grinning idiot.

She closed the incisions in the patient's legs. She took the intestines from the nurses, who were clearly exhausted and eager to relinquish the retractors. She replaced the guts in the body and gently ran them once again, searching for irregularities but finding none. The rest was easy: laying fat and muscle back in place, closing up, layer by layer, until the original incision was drawn shut with heavy black cord.

The anaesthesiologist's nurse undraped Viola Fletcher's head.

The anaesthesiologist untaped her eyes, turned off the anaesthesia.

The circulating nurse cut Bach off in mid-passage.

Ginger looked at Mrs Fletcher's face, pale now but not unusually drawn. The mask of the respirator was still on her face, but she was getting only an oxygen mixture.

The nurses backed away and skinned off their rubber gloves.

Viola Fletcher's eyelids fluttered, and she groaned.

'Mrs Fletcher?' the anaesthesiologist said loudly.

The patient did not respond.

'Viola?' Ginger said. 'Can you hear me, Viola?'

The woman's eyes did not open, but though she was more asleep than awake, her lips moved, and in a fuzzy voice she said, 'Yes, Doctor.'

Ginger accepted congratulations from the team and left the room with George. As they stripped off their gloves, pulled off their masks, and removed their caps, she felt as if she were filled with helium, in danger of breaking loose of the bonds of gravity. But with each step toward the scrub sinks in the surgical hall, she became less buoyant. A tremendous exhaustion settled over her. Her neck and shoulders ached. Her back was sore. Her legs were stiff, and her feet were tired.

'My God,' she said, 'I'm pooped!'

'You should be,' George said. 'You started at seven-thirty, and it's past the lunch hour. An aortal graft is damned debilitating.'

'*You* feel this way when you've done one?'

'Of course.'

'But it hit me so suddenly. In there, I felt great. I felt I could go on for hours yet.'

'In there,' George said with evident affection and amusement, 'you were godlike, duelling with death and winning, and no god ever grows weary. Godwork is too much fun to ever get weary of it.'

At the sinks, they turned on the water, took off the surgical gowns they'd worn over their hospital greens, and broke open packets of soap.

As Ginger began to wash her hands, she leaned wearily against the sink and bent forward a bit, so she was looking straight down at the drain, at the water swirling around the stainless-steel basin, at the bubbles of soap whirling with the water, all of it funnelling into the drain, around and around and down into the drain, around and down, down and down. . . . This time, the irrational fear struck and overwhelmed her with even less warning than at Bernstein's Deli or in George's office last Wednesday. In an instant her attention had become entirely focused upon the drain, which appeared to throb and grow wider as if it were suddenly possessed of malignant life.

She dropped the soap and, with a bleat of terror, jumped back from the sink, collided with Agatha Tandy, cried out again. She vaguely heard George calling her name. But he was fading away in the manner of an image on a motion picture screen, retreating into a mist, as if he were part of a scene that was dissolving to a full-lens shot of steam or clouds or fog, and he no longer seemed real. Agatha Tandy and the hallway and the doors to the surgery were fading, too. *Everything* was fading but the sink, which appeared to grow larger and more solid, super-real. A sense of mortal danger settled over her. But it was just an ordinary scrub sink, for God's sake, and she had to hold on to that truth, clutch at the cliff of reality and resist the forces pulling her over the edge. Just a sink. Just an ordinary drain. Just –

She ran. From every side, the mist closed around her, and she lost all conscious awareness of her actions.

*   *   *

The first thing she became aware of was the snow. Large white flakes sifted past her face, gently turning, lazily eddying toward the ground in the manner of fluffy air-borne dandelion seeds, for there was no wind to drive them. She raised her head, looked up beyond the towering walls of the old highrise buildings that shouldered in around her, and saw a rectangular patch of low grey sky, from which the snow descended. As she stared into the winter heavens, momentarily confused as to her whereabouts and condition, her hair and eyebrows grew white. Flakes melted on her face, but she slowly realised that her cheeks were already wet with tears and that she was still weeping quietly.

Gradually, the cold impinged upon her. In spite of the absence of wind, the air was sharp-toothed; it bit her cheeks, nipped her chin, and her hands were numb from the cold

76

venom of countless bites. The chill penetrated her hospital greens, and she was shivering uncontrollably.

Next, she became aware of the freezing concrete beneath her and the ice-cold brick wall against her back. She was squeezed into a corner, facing out, knees drawn up to her chin, arms locked around her legs – a posture of defence and terror. Her body heat was being leeched away through every contact point with pavement and masonry, but she did not have the strength or will to get to her feet and go inside.

She remembered fixating upon the drain of the scrub sink. With unmitigated despair, she recalled the mindless panic, her collision with Agatha Tandy, the startled look on George Hannaby's face as he had reacted to her screams. Although the rest was a blank, she supposed she had then taken flight from imaginary dangers, like some madwoman, to the shock of her colleagues – and to the certain destruction of her career.

She pressed harder against the brick wall, wishing that it would suck away her body heat even faster.

She was sitting at the end of a wide alley, a blind serviceway that led into the core of the hospital complex. To her left, double metal doors led into the furnace room, and beyond those was the exit from the emergency stairs.

Inevitably, she was reminded of her encounter with a mugger during her internship at Columbia Presbyterian Hospital in New York. That night, he had dragged her into an alleyway much like this. However, in the New York alleyway, she had been in command, victorious – while here she was a loser, descendant rather than ascendant, weak and lost. She perceived a bleak irony and a frightening symmetry in having been brought to the lowest point of her life in such a place as this.

Pre-med, medical school, the long hours and hardships of her intern year, all the work and sacrifices, all the hopes and dreams had been for nothing. At the last minute, with a surgical career almost within her grasp, she had failed George, Anna, Jacob, and herself. She could no longer deny the truth or ignore the obvious: something was wrong with her, something so desperately wrong that it would surely preclude the resumption of a life in medicine. Psychosis? A brain tumour? Perhaps an aneurysm in the brain?

The door to the emergency stairs was flung open with a rattle and a screech of unoiled hinges, and George Hannaby came out into the snow, breathing hard. He took several quick steps into the alley, heedless of the risk posed by the quarter-inch skin of slippery new snow. The sight of her was sufficiently shocking to bring him to a lurching halt. A ghastly expression lined his face, and Ginger supposed he was regretting the extra time and attention and special guidance that he had given her. He had thought she was especially bright and good and worthy, but now she had proved him wrong. He had been so kind to her and so supportive that her betrayal of his trust, although beyond her control, filled her with self-loathing and brought more hot tears to her eyes.

'Ginger?' he said shakily. 'Ginger, what's wrong?'

She was able to respond only with a wretched, involuntary sob.

Seen through her tears, he shimmered, blurred. She wished he'd go away and leave her to stew in humiliation. Didn't he know how much worse it was to have him staring at her while she was in this condition?

The snow was falling harder. Other people appeared in the doorway through which he had come, but she could not identify them.

'Ginger, please talk to me,' George said as he drew near. 'What's wrong? Tell me what's wrong. Tell me what I can do.'

She bit her lip, tried to repress her tears, but instead she began to sob harder than ever. In a thin, blubbery voice that sickened her with proof of her own weakness, she said, 'S-Something's wrong with me.'

George stooped down in front of her. 'What? What's wrong?'

'I don't know.'

She had always been able to handle any trouble that came her way, unassisted. She was Ginger Weiss. She was different. She was a golden girl. She didn't know how to ask for help of this kind, of this degree.

Still stooping in front of her, George said, 'Whatever it is, we can work it out. I know you're fiercely proud of your self-reliance. You listening, kid? I've always stepped carefully when I'm with you because I know you resent being helped

78

along too much. You want to do it all yourself. But this time you simply can't handle it alone, and you don't have to. I'm here, and by God you're going to lean on me whether you like it or not. You hear?'

'I . . . I've ruined everything. I've d-disappointed you.'

He found a small smile. 'Not you, dear girl. Not ever. Rita and I have had all sons, but if we could've had a daughter, we would've hoped for one like you. Exactly like you. You're a special woman, Dr Weiss, a dear and special woman. Disappoint me? Impossible. I would consider it an honour and a pleasure if you would lean on me now, just as if you *were* my daughter, and let me help you through this as if I were the father you've lost.'

He held out a hand to her.

She grasped it and held on tightly.

It was Monday, December 2.

Many weeks would pass before she learned that other people in other places – all strangers – were living through eerie variations of her own nightmare.

2.

TRENTON, NEW JERSEY

A few minutes before midnight, Jack Twist opened the door and left the warehouse, stepping into the wind and sleet, and some guy was just getting out of a grey Ford van at the foot of the nearest loading ramp. The van's arrival had been masked by the rumble of a passing freight train. The night was deep around the warehouse, except for four meagre patches of murky yellow light from poorly maintained, grime-dimmed security lamps. Unfortunately, one of those lights was directly over the door through which Jack had exited, and its sickly glow reached precisely far enough to include the passenger's door of the van, out of which the unexpected visitor had appeared.

The guy had a face made for police mug books: heavy jaw, a

79

mouth that was hardly more than a slash, a nose that had been broken a couple of times, and hard little pig eyes. He was one of those obedient but pitiless sadists that the mob employed as enforcers, a man who, in other times, might have been a rape and pillage specialist in the armies of Genghis Khan, a grinning Nazi thug, a torture master in one of Stalin's death camps, or a Morlock from the future as imagined by H. G. Wells in *The Time Machine*. To Jack, the guy looked like serious trouble.

They startled each other, and Jack did not immediately raise his .38 and put a bullet in the bastard, which is what he should have done.

'Who the hell are you?' the Morlock asked. Then he saw the canvas bag that Jack was dragging with his left hand and the lowered pistol in Jack's right hand. His eyebrows shot up, and he shouted, 'Max!'

Max was probably the driver of the van, but Jack did not wait around for formal introductions. He did a quick reverse into the warehouse, slammed the door shut, and stepped to the side of it in case someone out there started using it for target practice.

The only light inside the warehouse came from the brightly lit office far at the back of the building and from an overhead bank of widely spaced, low-wattage bulbs set in tin shades, which were allowed to burn all night. But there was sufficient illumination for Jack to see the faces of his two companions – Mort Gersh and Tommy Sung – who had been following him. They did not look as happy as they had been only a couple of minutes ago.

They had been happy because they had successfully hit a major way station on the route of the Mafia cash train, a collection point for narcotics money from half the state of New Jersey. Suitcases and flight bags and cardboard boxes and styrofoam coolers full of cash arrived at the warehouse from a score of couriers, most of it on Sunday and Monday. Tuesdays, mob accountants in Pierre Cardin suits arrived to calculate the week's profits from the pharmaceutical division. Every Wednesday, suitcases full of tightly banded stacks of greenbacks went out to Miami, Vegas, Los Angeles, New York, and other centres of high finance, where investment advisers with Harvard or Columbia MBAs, on retainer to the mafia – or *fratellanza*, as the underworld referred to itself – wisely put it to work. Jack, Mort and Tommy had simply stepped in between the accountants and the investment advisers, and had taken four heavy bags full of cash for themselves. 'Just think of us as one more layer of middlemen,' Jack had told the three glowering thugs who were, even now, tied up in the warehouse office, and Mort and Tommy had laughed.

Mort was not laughing now. He was fifty years old, pot-bellied, slump-shouldered, balding. He wore a dark suit, porkpie hat, and grey overcoat. He always wore a dark suit and porkpie hat, though not always the overcoat. Jack had never seen him in anything else. Tonight, Jack and Tommy were wearing jeans and quilted vinyl jackets, but there was Mort looking like one of the guys in the background of an old Edward G. Robinson movie. The snapbrim of his hat had lost its sharp edge and gone slightly soft, rather like Mort himself, and the suit was rumpled. His voice was weary and dour. He said, 'Who's out there?' as Jack slammed the door and stepped away from it.

'At least two guys in a Ford van,' Jack said.

'Mob?'

'I only saw one of them,' Jack said, 'but he looked like one of Dr Frankenstein's experiments that *didn't* work out.'

'At least all the doors are locked.'

'They'll have keys.'

The three of them moved quickly away from the exit, back into the deep shadows in an aisle between piles of wooden crates and cardboard cartons that were stacked on pallets. The merchandise formed twenty-foot-high walls. The warehouse was immense, with a wide array of goods stored under its vaulted ceiling: hundreds of TV sets, microwave ovens, blenders and toasters by the thousand, tractor parts, plumbing supplies, Cuisinarts, and more. It was a clean, well-run establishment, but as with any giant industrial building at night, the place was eerie when all the workers were gone. Strange, whispery echoes floated along the maze of aisles. Outside, the sleet fell harder than before, rustling and ticking and tapping and hissing on the slate roof, as if a multitude of

81

unknown creatures moved through the rafters and inside the walls.

'I told you it was a mistake to hit the mob,' Tommy Sung said. He was a Chinese-American, about thirty, which made him seven years younger than Jack. 'Jewellery stores, armoured cars, even banks, okay, but not the mob, for God's sake. It's stupid to hit the mob. Might as well walk into a bar full of Marines and spit on the flag.'

'You're here,' Jack said.

'Yeah, well,' Tommy said, 'I don't always show good judgment.'

In a voice of doom and despair, Mort said, 'A van shows up at this hour, it means one thing. They're delivering one kind of shit or another, probably coke or horse. Which means there won't be just the driver and the ape you saw. There'll be two other guys in the back of the van with the merchandise, carrying converted Uzis or worse.'

Tommy said, 'Why aren't they already shooting their way in?'

'As far as they know,' Jack said, 'there's ten of us, and we have bazookas. They'll move cautiously.'

'A truck used on dope runs is sure to have radio communications,' Mort said. 'They'll have already called for back-up.'

Tommy said, 'You telling me the Mafia has a fleet of radio vans like the goddamned phone company or something?'

'These days, they're as organised as any business,' Mort said.

They listened for sounds of purposeful human movement in farther reaches of the building, but all they heard was sleet hitting the roof.

The .38 in Jack's hand suddenly felt like a toy. Mort was carrying a Smith & Wesson M39 9mm pistol, and Tommy had a Smith & Wesson Model 19 Combat Magnum that he had tucked inside his insulated jacket after the men in the office had been securely tied up, when it had seemed that the dangerous part of the job had been completed. They were well-armed, but they were not ready to face down Uzis. Jack remembered old television news films of hopelessly out-classed Hungarians trying to turn back invading Russian tanks with rocks and sticks. In times of trouble, Jack Twist had a tendency to melodramatise his plight and, regardless of the situation, to cast himself in the role of the noble underdog battling the forces of evil. He was aware of this tendency, and he thought it was one of his most endearing qualities. At the moment, however, their position was so tenuous that there was no way to melodramatise it.

Mort's thoughts had led him to precisely the same consideration, for he said, 'There's no use trying to get out by any of the back doors. They'll have split up by now – two in front, two in back.'

The front and rear exits – both the regular doors and roll-up cargo bay doors – were the only ways out. There were no openings, not even windows or vents, on the sides of the enormous building, no basement and therefore no basement exit, no way to get onto the roof. In preparation for the robbery, the three of them had studied detailed plans of the building, and now they knew they were trapped.

Tommy said, 'What are we going to do?'

The question was addressed to Jack Twist, not to Mort, because Jack organised any robbery he took part in. If unanticipated events required improvisation, Jack was expected to come up with the brilliant ideas.

'Hey,' Tommy said, taking a stab at brilliance himself, 'why don't we go out the same way we got in!'

They had entered the building with a variation on the Trojan Horse ploy, which was the only way to bypass the elaborate security systems that were in operation at night. The warehouse was a front for the illegal drug trade, but it was also a real, functioning, profitable warehouse that accepted regular shipments from legitimate businesses in need of temporary storage for excess inventory. Therefore, with the personal computer and modem in his apartment, Jack had tapped into the computers of both the warehouse and one of its reputable clients, and had created the file of electronic paperwork that would legitimise the delivery of a huge crate, which had arrived this morning and had been stored per instructions. He, Mort, and Tommy had been inside the crate, which had been designed and constructed with five concealed exits, so they could get out of it quietly even if it was blocked by other crates on four sides. A few minutes after eleven o'clock tonight, they had slipped out and had surprised the tough guys in the office, who had been quite confident that their multiple alarm systems and locked doors had transformed the warehouse into an inviolable fortress.

'We could get back in the crate,' Tommy said, 'and when they finally come in and don't find us, they'll go crazy trying to figure how we got away. By tomorrow night the heat'll be off. Then we can slip out and make our getaway.'

'No good,' Mort said sourly. 'They'll figure it out. They'll search this place until they find us.'

'No good, Tommy,' Jack agreed. 'Now, here's what I want you to do. . . .' He quickly improvised an escape plan, and they assented to it.

Tommy hurried to the master panel of light switches in the office, to kill every light in the warehouse.

Jack and Mort dragged the four heavy bags of money towards the south end of the long building, and the dry sound of canvas scraping along the concrete floor echoed and re-echoed through the chilly air. At that far end of the building, instead of more stacks of merchandise, there were several trucks that had been parked in the interior staging area, where, first thing in the morning, they would be loaded. Jack and Mort were less than halfway through the maze, still half a city block from the semis, when the dim lights winked out and the warehouse was plunged into unrelieved darkness. They paused long enough for Jack to switch on his Ever Ready before continuing through the gloom.

Bearing his own flashlight, Tommy rejoined them and took one of the bags from Jack, one from Mort.

The clicking impact and susurrant slide of sleet upon the roof began to subside slightly as the storm entered a lull, and Jack thought he heard the screech of brakes outside. Could reinforcements have arrived so soon?

The warehouse's interior loading zone contained four eighteen-wheelers: a Peterbilt, a White, and two Mack trucks. Each of them faced out towards a loading-bay door.

Jack went to the nearest Mack, dropped his sack of money, stepped up on the running board, opened the door, and shone his flashlight inside, along the dashboard. The keys dangled from the ignition. He had expected as much. Confident of their multi-layered security system, the warehouse employees did not believe there was any danger that one of these vehicles might be stolen during the night.

Jack and Mort went to the other three trucks, found the keys in all of them, and started the engines.

In the cab of the first Mack, there was a sleeping berth behind the seat, where one member of a long-distance driving team could catch a nap while his partner took the wheel. Tommy Sung stowed the four bags of money in that recess.

Jack returned to the Mack just as Tommy finished with the sacks. He settled in behind the wheel and switched off his flashlight. Mort got in on the passenger's side. Jack started the engine but did not switch on the headlights.

All four trucks were idling noisily now.

Carrying his flashlight, Tommy ran to the farthest of the four big roll-down doors of the interior loading zone and touched the control that started it moving laboriously upward on its track. Jack watched him tensely from the high seat of the big rig. Tommy hurried back along that outer wall, his progress marked by the bobbling beam of his flash, slapping his right hand against the door controls as he came to each of them. Then, snapping off his flashlight, he bolted toward the Mack as the four doors slowly lumbered open with much grating and clattering.

Outside, the Morlocks would know the doors were going up, would hear the trucks' engines. But they'd be looking into a dark building, and until they could throw some light in here, they couldn't know which rig was the intended escape vehicle. They might spray *all* of the trucks with submachine-gun fire, but Jack was counting on gaining a few precious seconds before they opted for that violent course of action.

Tommy clambered up into the cab of the Mack, pulling the door shut behind him, sandwiching Mort between himself and Jack.

'Damn rollers move too slow,' Mort said as the bay doors clattered toward the ceiling, gradually revealing the sleet-lashed night beyond.

'Drive through the sucker,' Tommy urged.

Fastening his seatbelt, Jack said, 'Can't risk getting hung up.'

The door was one-third open.

Gripping the wheel with both hands again, Jack saw movement in the murky, wintry world beyond, where the few dim exterior security lights did little to push back the darkness. Two men hurried across the wet and icy blacktop, from the left, slipping and skidding, both of them armed, one of them with what appeared to be an Uzi. They were trying to stay low to make poor targets of themselves and trying to stay on their feet at the same time, squinting into the black warehouse under the rising bay doors, and as yet they had not thought of meeting the crisis with an indiscriminate spray of bullets.

The first door, the one in front of Jack, was halfway up.

Abruptly, angling in from the left, the same direction from which the two hoods had come, the grey Ford van appeared, its tyres churning up silvery plumes of slush. It fish-tailed to a stop between the second and third ramps, blocking those exits. Its front wheels were up on the lower edge of the third ramp, so its headlights speared into the fourth bay, revealing that the cab of that truck was untenanted.

In front of Jack, the door was two-thirds up.

'Keep your heads down,' he said.

Mort and Tommy squeezed down as low as they could, and Jack hunched over the wheel. The heavy rolling panel was not all the way up, but he thought he could slip under it – with a little luck. In quick succession he released the brakes, popped the clutch, and hit the accelerator.

The instant he put the truck in gear, those outside knew that the break was being made from the first bay, and the night was shaken with the rattle of gunfire. Jack heard slugs slam into the truck as he reached the exit, drove through, and headed down the concrete ramp, but none penetrated the cab or shattered the windshield.

Below, another van, this one a Dodge, swept in at the foot of the incline, trying to block his path. Reinforcements had, indeed, arrived.

Instead of braking, Jack tramped down harder on the accelerator and grinned at the horrified expressions of the men in the Dodge as the massive grille of the Mack slammed into them. The rig rammed the van backwards so hard that the smaller vehicle tipped over on its side and slid fifteen or twenty feet across the macadam.

The impact jolted Jack, but his safety belt held him in check. Mort and Tommy were thrown forward, against the lower part of the dash and into the cramped space below. They protested with cries of pain.

To execute that manoeuvre, Jack had been forced to descend the ramp faster than he should have done, and now as he tried to wheel the truck to the left, towards the lane leading away from the warehouse, the rig lurched, swayed, threatened to either tear itself out of his control or tip over as the Dodge had done. Cursing, he held on to it, brought it around with an effort that made his arms feel as if they were pulling out of his shoulders, and then he was headed straight into the lane.

Ahead of him, three men stood around a midnight-blue Buick, and at least two of them were armed. They opened fire as he bore down on them. One man aimed too low, and bullets snapped off the top of the Mack's grille, sparking brightly where they struck. The other guy aimed too high; Jack heard slugs ricocheting off the brow of the cab, above the windshield. One of the two overhead-mounted air-horns was hit and torn loose; it fell down along the side of the cab, thumped against Tommy's window, hanging from its wires.

Jack was almost on top of the Buick, and the gunmen realised he meant to hit it, so they stopped shooting and scattered. Handling the huge rig as if it were a tank, he broadsided the car, shoving it out of the way. He kept going, past the end of the warehouse, towards another warehouse, past that one, still accelerating.

Mort and Tommy pushed themselves back onto the seat, groaning. Both were battered. Mort had a bloody nose, and Tommy was bleeding from a small cut over his right eye, but neither of them was seriously hurt.

'Why does every job go sour?' Mort asked morosely, his voice more nasal than usual because of his injured nose.

'It hasn't gone sour,' Jack said, switching on the windshield wipers to clear away the glimmering beads of sleet. 'It's just turned out to be a little more exciting than we expected.'

'I hate excitement,' Mort said, putting a handkerchief to his nose.

Jack glanced in the side mirror, back toward the *fratellanza's* warehouse, and he saw the Ford van turning around to follow him. He had put the Dodge and the Buick out of commission, and he only had the Ford to worry about. He had no hope of outrunning it. The roads were treacherously icy, and he had too little experience behind the wheel of a rig like this to risk pushing it to its limits in bad weather.

He was also worried about an unnerving chorus of small noises that had sprung up from the engine compartment following the ramming of the van and the Buick. Something rattled tinnily. Something else hissed. If the Mack broke down and left them stranded, they would very likely be killed in the ensuing shoot-out with the Morlocks.

They were in a vast industrial area of warehouses, packing plants, and factories, and the nearest major city street was more than a mile ahead of them. Though some of the factories had night shifts and were currently operating, the industrial park's main service road, along which they were speeding, was deserted.

Glancing at the mirror, Jack saw the Ford on their tail and gaining fast. He abruptly wheeled the rig to the right, into a branch road past a factory where a sign proclaimed HARK-WRIGHT CUSTOM FOAM PACKAGING.

'Where the hell you going?' Tommy asked.

'We can't outrun them,' Jack said.

'We can't face them down, either.' Mort said through his bloody handkerchief. 'Not handguns against Uzis.'

'Trust me,' Jack said.

Harkwright Custom Foam Packaging did not operate a late shift. The building itself was dark, but the road around it and the big truck lot behind were lit by sodium-vapour lamps that coloured the night yellow.

At the rear of the building, Jack turned left, into the truck lot, through drilling sleet that looked like molten gold under the big lamps. Two score of trailers, without cabs attached, stood in orderly ranks, like beheaded prehistoric beasts, all painted mustard by the fall of sodium light. He swung the rig in a wide circle, brought it in close to the back wall of the factory, doused the headlights, and drove parallel to the building, heading back towards the road that entered the lot and along which he had just come. He braked to a stop at the corner, close up against the factory wall, at a right angle to the branch road.

'Brace yourselves,' he said.

Mort and Tommy already knew what was coming. Their feet were pressed flat up against the dashboard and their backs were jammed against the back of the seat, as protection against the impact.

No sooner had Jack braked at the corner of the building – the Mack poised like a crouching cat anticipating a mouse – than a glow appeared on the passing road. The light approached from the right, from the front of the factory: the most out-reaching headlamp beams of the unseen but oncoming Ford van. The glow grew brighter, brighter still, and Jack tensed, trying to wait until the last best moment before pulling into the lane. Now the glow became two distinct parallel beams, lancing past the snout of the Mack, and the beams grew very bright. Finally Jack tramped hard on the accelerator, and the Mack lurched forward, but it was a big truck, not quick off the mark. The Ford, going faster than Jack had expected, shot past the corner, directly across the Mack's bow, and Jack surged forward in time to catch only the rear of it. But that was enough to send the small van into a spin. It whipped around 360 degrees, then again, on the icy surface of the parking lot, before crashing nose-first into one of the mustard-coloured cargo trailers.

Jack was sure that none of the men in the Ford was in any condition to come out of the wreck shooting, but he did not dawdle. He swung the Mack around and headed back past the side of Harkwright Custom Foam Packaging. When he reached the main service road, he turned right, away from the distant *fratellanza* warehouse, toward the entrance to the industrial park and the network of city streets beyond.

They were not followed.

He drove three miles by a direct route to an abandoned Texaco service station that they had scouted days ago. He pulled past the useless pumps and parked alongside the dilapidated little building.

The moment Jack halted the rig, Tommy Sung threw open the door on his side, jumped out, and walked away into the darkness. He was heading for a lower-middle-class residential

89

neighbourhood three blocks away, where, on Monday, they had parked a dirty, rusted, battered Volkswagen Rabbit. The car was newer under the hood than it was outside – and fast. It would get them back to Manhattan, where they would dump it.

They had also stashed an untraceable Pontiac in the industrial park on Monday, within a two-minute walk of the mob warehouse. They intended to hump the bags of money to the Pontiac, then drive the Pontiac here for the switch to the Rabbit. But alternative transportation had become essential, and the Pontiac had been left to rot where they stashed it.

Jack and Mort heaved the sacks of money out of the Mack and stood them against the side wall of the shuttered service station, where the slanting sleet began to crust on the canvas. Mort climbed back in the cab and wiped down all the surfaces they might have touched.

Jack stood by the bags, looking at the street beyond the end of the rig, where an occasional car crept past on the glistening pavement. None of the motorists would be interested in a truck parked at a long-abandoned service station. But if a police car cruised by on patrol . . .

At last Tommy pulled in from the side street and parked between the rows of pumps. Mort grabbed two sacks, hustled them toward the car, slipped, fell, got right up, made for the Rabbit again. Dragging the other pair of bags, Jack followed with greater care. By the time Jack reached the Rabbit, Mort was already in the back seat. Jack threw the last bags in with Mort, slammed the door, and got in front with Tommy.

He said, 'For God's sake, drive slow and careful.'

'You can count on it,' Tommy said.

The tyres spun on the sleet-skinned blacktop as they pulled out from between the pumps, and when they left the lot and moved into the street, they slid sideways before the tread gripped.

'Why does every job turn sour?' Mort asked mournfully.

'It hasn't turned sour,' Jack said.

The Rabbit hit a pothole, began to glide toward a parked car, but Tommy turned the wheel into the slide and got control. They continued at an even slower pace, found the expressway, and climbed a ramp under a sign that said NEW YORK CITY.

At the upper end of the ramp, as the tyres slithered one last time before gripping and carrying them onto the expressway, Mort said, 'Why'd it have to *sleet*?'

'They've got a lot of salt and cinders on these lanes,' Tommy said. 'It's going to be all right now, all the way into the city.'

'We'll see,' Mort said glumly. 'What a bad night. Jesus.'

'Bad?' Jack said. 'Bad? Mort, they would never in a thousand years let you in the Optimists Club. For God's sake, we're all of us millionaires. You're sitting back there on a fortune!'

Under his porkpie hat, which still dripped melting sleet, Mort blinked in surprise. 'Well, uh, I guess that does take some of the sting out of it.'

Tommy Sung laughed.

Jack laughed, and Mort too, and Jack said, 'The biggest score any of us ever made. And no taxes payable on it, either.'

Suddenly, everything seemed uproariously funny. They settled in a hundred yards behind a highway maintenance truck with flashing yellow beacons, cruising at a safe and leisurely speed, while they gleefully recalled the highlights of their escape from the warehouse.

Later, when the tension was somewhat relieved, when their giddy laughter had subsided to pleased smiles, Tommy said, 'Jack, I gotta tell you that was a first-rate piece of work. The way you used the computer to create paperwork for the crate . . . and that little electronic gizmo you used to open the safe so we didn't need to blow it . . . well, you are one hell of an organiser.'

'Better than that,' Mort said, 'in a crisis you're just about the best knockover artist I've ever seen. You think fast. I tell you, Jack, if you ever decided to put your talents to work in the straight world, for a good cause, there's no telling what you could do.'

'Good cause?' Jack said. 'Isn't getting rich a good cause?'

'You know what I mean,' Mort said.

'I'm no hero,' Jack said. 'I don't want any part of the straight world. They're all hypocrites out there. They talk about honesty, truth, justice, social conscience . . . but most of them are just looking out for number one. They won't admit it, and that's why I can't stand them. *I* admit it. I'm looking out for number one, and to hell with them.' He heard the tone of his own voice changing from amusement to sullen resentment,

91

but he could not help that. He scowled through the wet windshield, past the thumping wipers. 'Good cause, huh? If you spend your life fighting for good causes, the so-called good people will sure as hell break your heart in the end. Fuck 'em.'

'Didn't mean to touch a nerve,' Mort said, clearly surprised.

Jack said nothing. He was lost in bitter memories. Two or three miles later, he said quietly, 'I'm no damn hero.'

In days to come, when he recalled those words, he would have occasion to wonder how he could have been so wrong about himself.

It was 1:12 a.m., Wednesday, December 4.

3.

CHICAGO, ILLINOIS

By 8:20, Thursday morning, December 5, Father Stefan Wycazik had celebrated the early Mass, had eaten breakfast, and had retreated to his rectory office for a final cup of coffee. Turning away from his desk, he faced the big French window that presented a view of the bare, snow-crusted trees in the courtyard, and he tried not to think about any parish problems. This was *his* time, and he valued it highly.

But his thoughts drifted inexorably to Father Brendan Cronin. The rogue curate. The chalice-hurler. Brendan Cronin, the talk of the parish. The Berserk Priest of St. Bernadette's. Brendan Cronin of all people. It just did not make sense. No sense at all.

Father Stefan Wycazik had been a priest for thirty-two years, the rector of the Church of Saint Bernadette for nearly eighteen years, and throughout his life of service, he had never been tortured by doubt. The very concept baffled him.

Following ordination, he was assigned as a curate to St Thomas's, a small parish in the Illinois farm country, where seventy-year-old Father Dan Tuleen was shepherd. Father Tuleen was the sweetest-tempered, kindest, most sentimental, and most lovable man Stefan Wycazik had ever known.

Dan had also been troubled by arthritis and failing vision, too old for the job of running a parish. Any other priest would have been removed, gently forced into retirement. But Dan Tuleen had been permitted to remain at his post because he had been at St Thomas's for forty years and was an integral part of the life of his flock. The Cardinal, a great admirer of Father Tuleen, had looked around for a curate who could handle a good deal more responsibility than would usually be expected of a rookie, and he had finally settled on Stefan Wycazik. After only a day at St Thomas's, Stefan had realised what was expected of him and had not been intimidated. He'd shouldered virtually all the work of the parish. Few young priests would have been equal to such a task. Father Wycazik never doubted he could handle it.

Three years later, when Father Tuleen died quietly in his sleep, a new priest was assigned to St Thomas's, and the Cardinal sent Father Wycazik to another parish in suburban Chicago, where the rector, Father Orgill, was having troubles with alcohol. Father Orgill had not been a totally disgraced whisky priest. He had been a man with the power to salvage himself, and he had been well worth salvaging. Father Wycazik's job had been to give Father Orgill a shoulder to lean on and to guide him, subtly but firmly, toward the exit from his dilemma. Unhampered by doubt, he had provided what Francis Orgill had needed.

During the next three years, Stefan served at two more problem-plagued churches, and those who moved in the hierarchy of the archdiocese began to refer to him as 'His Eminence's troubleshooter.'

His most exotic assignment was to Our Lady of Mercy Orphanage and School in Saigon, Vietnam, where he was second in charge under Father Bill Nader for six nightmarish years. Our Lady of Mercy was funded by the Chicago Archdiocese and was one of the Cardinal's pet projects. Bill Nader had carried the scars of two bullet wounds, one in his left shoulder and one in his right calf, and had lost two Vietnamese priests and one previous American to Vietcong terrorists.

From the moment of Stefan's arrival, during his entire tour of duty in the war zone, he never doubted that he would survive or that his work in that hell-on-earth was worthwhile. When Saigon fell, Bill Nader, Stefan Wycazik, and thirteen nuns escaped the country with 126 children. Hundreds of thousands died in the subsequent bloodbath, but even in the face of mass slaughter, Stefan Wycazik never doubted that 126 lives were a *very* significant number, never allowed despair to grip him.

Back in the States, as a reward for his willingness to be the Cardinal's troubleshooter for a decade and a half, Stefan was offered a promotion to monsignor, which he modestly declined. Instead, he humbly requested – and was rewarded with – his own parish. At long last.

That was St Bernadette's. It had not been a prosperous parish when it was put into Stefan Wycazik's able hands. St Bernadette's was $125,000 in debt. The church was in desperate need of major repairs, including a new slate roof. The rectory was worse than decrepit; it threatened to come tumbling down in the next high wind. There was no parish school. Attendance at Sunday Masses had been on a steady decline for almost ten years. St Bette's, as some of the altar boys referred to it, was precisely the kind of challenge that excited Father Wycazik.

He never doubted that he could rescue St Bette's. In four years he raised the attendance at Mass by forty per cent, paid off the debt, and repaired the church. In five years he rebuilt the parish house. In seven years he doubled attendance and broke ground for a school. In recognition of Father Wycazik's unflagging service to Mother Church, the Cardinal, in his last week of life, had conferred the coveted honour of P.R. – permanent rector – on Stefan, guaranteeing him life tenure at the parish that he had single-handedly brought back from the edge of both spiritual and financial ruin.

The granite solidity of Father Wycazik's faith made it difficult for him to understand why, at the early Mass on the Sunday just past, Father Brendan Cronin's belief had dissolved so completely as to cause him to fling the sacred chalice across the chancel in despair and rage. In front of almost a hundred worshippers. Dear God. At least it had not happened at one of the three later Masses, which were better attended.

Initially, when Brendan Cronin had come to St Bette's more

than a year and a half ago, Father Wycazik had not wanted to like him.

For one thing, Cronin had been schooled at the North American College in Rome, reputedly the most splendid educational institution within the jurisdiction of the Church. But though it was an honour to be invited to attend that establishment, and though its graduates were considered the cream of the priesthood, they were often effete dainties, loath to get their hands dirty, with much too high an opinion of themselves. They felt that teaching catechism to children was beneath them, a waste of their complex minds. And visiting shut-ins was a task they found unspeakably distasteful after the glories that had been Rome.

In addition to the stigma of being trained in Rome, Father Cronin was fat. Well, not fat, really, but certainly plump, with a round soft face and liquid-green eyes that seemed, at first encounter, to betoken a lazy and perhaps easily corrupted soul. Father Wycazik, on the other hand, was a big-boned Pole whose family had not contained a single fat man. The Wycaziks were descended from Polish miners who had emigrated to the United States at the turn of the century, taking physically demanding jobs in steel mills, quarries, and the construction trades. They had produced big families that could be supported only through long hours of honest labour, so there wasn't time to get fat. Stefan had grown up with an instinctual sense that a *real* man was solid but lean, with a thick neck, big shoulders, and joints gnarled from hard work.

To Father Wycazik's surprise, Brendan Cronin had proved to be a hard worker. He had acquired no pretensions and no elitist opinions while in Rome. He was bright, good-natured, amusing, and he thrived on visiting shut-ins, teaching the children, and soliciting funds. He was the best curate Father Wycazik had been given in eighteen years.

That was why Brendan's outburst on Sunday – and the loss of faith that had inspired it – was so distressing to Stefan Wycazik. Of course, on another level, he looked forward to the challenge of bringing Brendan Cronin back into the fold. He had begun his career in the Church as a strong right arm for priests in trouble, and now he was being called upon to fill that role once more, which reminded of his youth and engendered in him a buoyant feeling of vital purpose.

Now, as he took another sip of coffee, a knock came at the office door. He turned his gaze to the mantel clock. It was of ormolu and inlaid mahogany with a fine Swiss movement, a gift from a parishioner. That timepiece was the only elegant object in a room boasting strictly utilitarian – and mismatched – furniture and a threadbare imitation-Persian carpet. According to the clock, the time was 8:30, precisely, and Stefan turned to the door, saying, 'Come in, Brendan.'

As he came through the door, Father Brendan Cronin looked no less distressed than he had on Sunday, Monday, Tuesday, and Wednesday, when they had met in this office to discuss his crisis of faith and to search for ways to re-establish his belief. He was so pale that his freckles burned like sparks on his skin, and by contrast his auburn hair looked more red than usual. The bounce had left his step.

'Sit down, Brendan. Coffee?'

'Thank you, no.' Brendan by-passed the tattered Chesterfield and the Morris chair, slumping in the sag-bottomed wingback.

Did you eat a good breakfast? Stefan wanted to ask, or did you just nibble at some toast and swill it down with coffee?

But he did not want to seem to be mothering his curate, who was thirty years old. So he said, 'You've done the reading I suggested?'

'Yes.'

Stefan had relieved Brendan of all parish duties and had given him books and essays that argued for the existence of God and against the folly of atheism from an intellectual point of view.

'And you've reflected on what you've read,' Father Wycazik said. 'So have you found anything so far that . . . helps you?'

Brendan sighed. Shook his head.

'You continue to pray for guidance?'

'Yes. I receive none.'

'You continue to search for the roots of this doubt?'

'There don't seem to be any.'

Stefan was increasingly frustrated by Father Cronin's taciturnity, which was utterly unlike the young priest. Usually.

Brendan was open, voluble. But since Sunday he had turned inward, and he had begun to speak slowly, softly, and never at length, as if words were money and he a miser who begrudged the paying out of every penny.

'There must be roots to your doubt,' Father Wycazik insisted. 'There must be something from which doubt's grown – a seed, a beginning.'

'It's just there,' Brendan muttered, barely audible. 'Doubt. It's just there as if it's always been there.'

'But it wasn't: you *did* believe. So when did doubt begin? Last August, you said. But what sparked it? There must've been a specific incident or incidents that led you to re-evaluate your philosophy.'

Softly exhaled: 'No.'

Father Wycazik wanted to shout at him, shake him, shock him out of his numbing gloom. But he patiently said, 'Countless good priests have suffered crises of faith. Even some saints wrestled angels. But they all had two things in common: their loss of faith was a gradual process that continued many years before reaching a crisis; and they could all point to specific incidents and observations from which doubt arose. The unjust death of a child, for instance. Or a saintly mother stricken with cancer. Murder. Rape. Why does God allow evil in the world? Why war? The sources of doubt are innumerable if familiar, and though Church doctrine answers them, cold doctrine is sometimes little comfort. Brendan, doubt *always* springs from specific contradictions between the concept of God's mercy and the reality of human sorrow and suffering.'

'Not in my case,' Brendan said.

Gently but insistently, Father Wycazik continued. 'And the only way to assuage that doubt is to focus on those contradictions that trouble you and discuss them with a spiritual guide.'

'In my case, my faith just . . . collapsed under me . . . suddenly . . . like a floor that seemed perfectly solid but was rotten all along.'

'You don't brood about unjust death, sickness, murder, war? Like a rotten floor, then? Just collapsed overnight?'

'That's right.'

'*Bullshit!*' Stefan said, launching himself up from his chair. The expletive and the sudden movement startled Father

Cronin. His head snapped up, and his eyes widened with surprise.

'Bullshit,' Father Wycazik repeated, matching the word with a scowl as he turned his back on his curate. In part he intended to shock the younger priest and force him out of his half-trance of self-pity, but in part he was also irritated by Cronin's uncommunicative funk and stubborn despair. Speaking to the curate but facing the window, where patterns of frost decorated the panes and where wind buffeted the glass, he said, 'You didn't fall from committed priest in August to atheist in December. *Could* not. Not when you claim to've had no shattering experiences that might be responsible. There must be reasons for your change of heart, Father, even if you're hiding them from yourself, and until you're willing to admit them, face them, you'll remain in this wretched state.'

A plumbless silence filled the room.

Then: the muffled ticking of the ormolu and mahogany clock.

At last, Brendan Cronin said, 'Father, please don't be angry with me. I have such respect . . . and I value our relationship so highly that your anger . . . on top of everything else . . . is too much for me right now.'

Pleased by even a thread-thin crack in Brendan's shell, delighted that his little stratagem had produced results, Father Wycazik turned from the window, moved quickly to the wingback chair, and put a hand on his curate's shoulder. 'I'm not angry with you, Brendan. Worried. Concerned. Frustrated that you won't let me help you. But not angry.'

The young priest looked up. 'Father, believe me, I want nothing more than your help in finding a way out of this. But in truth, my doubt doesn't spring from any of the things you mentioned. I really don't know where it comes from. It remains . . . well, mysterious.'

Stefan nodded, squeezed Brendan's shoulder, returned to his chair behind the desk, sat down, and closed his eyes for a moment, thinking.

'All right, Brendan, your inability to identify the cause of your collapsed faith indicates it's not an intellectual problem, so no amount of inspirational reading will help. If it's a psychological problem, the roots lie in your subconscious, awaiting revelation.'

When he opened his eyes, Stefan saw that his curate was intrigued by the suggestion that his own inner mind was simply malfunctioning. Which meant God hadn't failed Brendan, after all: *Brendan* had failed *God*. Personal responsibility was far easier to deal with than the thought that God was unreal or had turned His back.

Stefan said, 'As you may know, the Illinois Provincial of the Society of Jesus is Lee Kellog. But you may not know that he oversees two psychiatrists, both Jesuits themselves, who deal with the mental and emotional problems of priests within our order. I could arrange for you to begin analysis with one of those psychiatrists.'

'Would you?' Brendan asked, leaning forward in his chair.

'Yes. Eventually. But not right away. If you begin analysis, the Provincial will refer your name to the province's Prefect of Discipline, who will begin to pick through your actions of the past year to see if you've violated any of your vows.'

'But I never –'

'I *know* you never,' Stefan said reassuringly. 'But the Prefect of Discipline's job is to be suspicious. The worst thing is . . . even if your analysis leads to a cure, the Prefect will scrutinise you for years to come, to guard against a lapse into unpriestly conduct. Which would limit your prospects. And until your current problem, Father, you struck me as a priest who'd go far – monsignor, perhaps higher.'

'Oh, no. Certainly not. Not me,' Brendan said self-deprecatingly.

'Yes, you. And if you beat this problem, you could still go far. But once you're on the Prefect's danger list, you'll always be suspect. At best you'll wind up no better than me, a simple parish priest.'

A smile flickered at the corners of Brendan's mouth. 'It would be an honour – and a life well spent – to be, as you say, no better than you.'

'But you can go farther and be of great service to the Church. And I'm determined you'll have that chance. So I want you to give me until Christmas to help you find a way out of this hole. No more pep talks. No debates about the nature of good and evil. Instead, I'll apply some of my own theories about psychological disorders. You'll get amateur treatment from me, but

99

give it a chance. Just until Christmas. Then, if your distress is still as great, if we're no nearer an answer, I'll put you in the hands of a Jesuit psychiatrist. Deal?'

Brendan nodded. 'Deal.'

'Terrific!' Father Wycazik said, sitting up straight, rubbing his hands together briskly, as if about to chop wood or perform some other invigorating exercise. 'That gives us more than three weeks. For the first week, you'll put away your ecclesiastical suits, dress in ordinary clothes, and report to Dr James McMurtry at St Joseph's Hospital for Children. He'll see that you're assigned to the hospital staff.'

'As chaplain?'

'As an orderly – emptying bedpans, changing bedclothes, whatever is required. Only Dr McMurtry will know you're a priest.'

Brendan blinked. 'But what's the point of this?'

'You'll figure it out before the week is up,' Stefan said happily. 'And when you understand why I sent you to the hospital, you'll have one important key to help you unlock your psyche, a key that'll open doors and give you a look inside yourself, and maybe then you'll see the cause of your loss of faith – and overcome it.'

Brendan looked doubtful.

Father Wycazik said, 'You promised me three weeks.'

'All right.' Brendan unconsciously fingered his Roman collar and seemed disturbed by the thought of removing it, which was a good sign.

'You'll move out of the rectory until Christmas. I'll give you funds to pay for meals and an inexpensive hotel room. You'll work and live in the real world, beyond the shelter of the ecclesiastic life. Now, change clothes, pack your suitcases, and report back to me. Meanwhile, I'll call Dr McMurtry and make the necessary arrangements.'

Brendan sighed, got up, went to the door. 'There's one thing maybe supports the notion that my problem's psychological, not intellectual. I've been having these dreams . . . actually the same dream every time.'

'A recurring dream. That's very Freudian.'

'I've had it several times a month since August. But this week it's become a regular occurrence – three out of the last four nights. It's a bad one, too – a short dream that I have over and over again in one night. Short but . . . intense. It's about these black gloves.'

'Black gloves?'

Brendan grimaced. 'I'm in a strange place. Don't know where. I'm lying in bed, I think. I seem to be . . . restrained. My arms are held down. And my legs. I want to move, run, get out of there, but I can't. The light is dim. Can't see much. Then these hands . . .' He shuddered.

'Hands wearing black gloves?' Father Wycazik prompted.

'Yes. Shiny black gloves. Vinyl or rubber. Tightly fitted and shiny, not like ordinary gloves.' Brendan let go of the door-knob, took two steps toward the middle of the room, and stood with his hands raised before his face, as if the sight of them would help him recollect the details of the menacing hands in his dream. 'I can't see whose hands they are. Something wrong with my vision. I can see the hands . . . the gloves . . . but only up to the wrists. Beyond that, it's all . . . blurry.'

By the off-handed way that Brendan had mentioned the dream, almost as an after-thought, he obviously wanted to believe that it was of no consequence. However, his face was paler than before, and there was a vague but unmistakable flutter of fear in his voice.

A burst of winter wind rattled a loose window pane, and Stefan said, 'The man with black gloves – does he say anything to you?'

'He never speaks.' Another shudder. Brendan lowered his hands, thrust them in his pockets. 'He touches me. The gloves are cold, slick.' The curate looked as if he could feel those gloves even now.

Acutely interested, Father Wycazik leaned forward in his chair and said, '*Where* do these gloves touch you?'

The young priest's eyes glazed. 'They touch . . . my face. Forehead. Cheeks. Neck . . . chest. Cold. They touch me almost everywhere.'

'They don't hurt you?'

'No.'

'But you're afraid of these gloves, of the man wearing them?'

'Terrified. But I don't know why.'

101

'One can't help but see how Freudian a dream it is.'

'I suppose,' the curate said.

'Dreams are a way for the subconscious mind to send messages to the conscious, and in this case it's easy to see Freudian symbolic meanings in these black gloves. The hands of the devil, reaching out to pull you down from grace. Or the hands of your own doubt. Or they could be symbols of temptations, of sins seeking your indulgence.'

Brendan seemed grimly amused by the possibilities. 'Especially sins of the flesh. After all, the gloves *do* touch me all over.' The curate returned to the door and put his hand on the knob, but paused again. 'Listen, I'll tell you something odd. This dream . . . I'm half-sure it's not symbolic.' Brendan let his gaze slide away from Stefan's down to the worn rug. 'I think those gloved hands represent nothing more than gloved hands. I think . . . somewhere, someplace, at some time or other, they were real.'

'You mean you were once in a situation like the one in your dream?'

Still looking at the rug, the curate said, 'I don't know. Perhaps in my childhood. See, this might not have anything to do with my crisis of faith. The two things might be – probably are – unconnected.'

Stefan shook his head. 'Two unusual and serious afflictions – a loss of faith and a recurring nightmare – troubling you at the same time, and you want me to think they've no relation? Too coincidental. There must be some connection. But tell me, at what point in your childhood would you've been menaced by this unseen, gloved figure?'

'Well, I had a couple of serious illnesses as a boy. Maybe during a fever I was examined by a doctor who was a little rough or scary-looking. And maybe the experience was so traumatic that I repressed it, and now it's coming back to me in a dream.'

'When doctors wear gloves for an examination, they use throw-away white latex. Not black. And not heavy rubber or vinyl gloves.'

The curate took a deep breath, blew it out. 'Yeah, you're right. But I just can't shake the feeling that the dream's not symbolic. It's crazy, I suppose. But I'm sure those black gloves are real, as real as that Morris chair, as real as those books on the shelf.'

On the mantel, the clock struck the hour.

The soughing of the wind in the eaves became a howl.

'Creepy,' Stefan said, referring not to the wind or the hollow striking of the clock. He crossed the room and clapped the curate on the shoulder. 'But I assure you, you're wrong. The dream *is* symbolic, and it *is* related to your crisis of faith. The black hands of doubt. It's your subconscious warning you that you're in for a real battle. But it's a battle in which you're not alone. You've got me beside you.'

'Thank you, Father.'

'And God. He's beside you as well.'

Father Cronin nodded, but there was no conviction in his face or in the defeated hunching of his shoulders.

'Now go pack your suitcases,' Father Wycazik said.

'I'm leaving you short-handed when I go.'

'I've got Father Gerrano and the sisters at the school. Now, off with you.' When his curate had gone, Stefan returned to his desk.

Black gloves. It was only a dream, not particularly frightening in its essence, yet Father Cronin's voice had been so haunted when he spoke of it that Stefan was still affected by the image of shiny black rubber-clad fingers reaching out of a blur and prodding, poking. . . .

Black gloves.

Father Stefan Wycazik had a hunch that this was going to be one of the most difficult salvage jobs upon which he had ever embarked.

Outside, snow fell.

It was Thursday, December 5.

BOSTON, MASSACHUSETTS

On Friday, four days after the catastrophic fugue that followed the aortal graft on Viola Fletcher, Ginger Weiss was still a patient at Memorial Hospital, where she had been admitted after George Hannaby led her out of the snowy alleyway in which she had regained consciousness.

For three days, they had put her through exhaustive tests. An EEG study, cranial X-rays, sonograms, pneumoventriculography, a lumbar puncture, an angiogram, and more, repeating several procedures (though fortunately *not* the lumbar puncture) for cross-checked results. With the sophisticated tools and processes of modern medicine, they searched her brain tissue for neoplasms, cystic masses, abscesses, clots, aneurysms, and benign gummatuous lumps. For a while they concentrated on the possibility of malignancies of the perineural nerves. They checked for chronic intracranial pressure. They analysed the fluid from the spinal tap in search of abnormal protein, cerebral bleeding, a low sugar count that would indicate bacterial infection, or signs of a fungus infection. Because they were physicians who always gave their best to a patient, but especially because Ginger was one of their own colleagues, her doctors were diligent, determined, thoughtful, thorough, and firmly committed to pin-pointing the cause of her problem.

At two o'clock Friday afternoon, George Hannaby came to her room with the results of the final battery of tests and with the reports of consultants who had given one last round of opinions. The fact that he had come himself, rather than let the oncologist or the brain specialist (who were in charge of her case) bring the news, most likely meant that it was bad, and for once Ginger was sorry to see him.

She was sitting in bed, dressed in blue pyjamas that Rita Hannaby, George's wife, had been kind enough to fetch (along with a suitcase full of other necessities) from the Beacon Hill apartment. She was reading a paperback mystery, pretending to be confident that her seizures were the result of some easily corrected malady, but she was scared.

But what George had to tell her was so bad that she could no longer hold fast to her composure. In a way, it was wórse than anything for which she had prepared herself.

They had found nothing.

No disease. No injury. No congenital defect. Nothing.

As George solemnly outlined the final results and made it clear that her wild flights, performed in a fugue, were without a discernible pathological cause, she finally lost control of her emotions for the first time since she had broken into tears in the alleyway. She wept, not noisily, not copiously, but quietly and with enormous anguish.

A physical ailment might have been correctable. And once cured, it would not have prevented her from returning to a career as a surgeon.

But the test results and the opinions of the specialists all conveyed the same unbearable message: her problem was entirely in her mind, a psychological illness beyond the reach of surgery, antibiotics, or controlling drugs. When a patient suffered repeated incidents of fugue for which no physiological cause could be found, the only hope of ending the seizures was psychotherapy, though the finest psychiatrists could not boast of a high cure rate with patients thus afflicted. Indeed, a fugue was often an indication of incipient schizophrenia. Her chances of managing her condition and living a normal life were small; her chances of institutionalisation were dismayingly high.

Within reach of her lifelong dream, within months of beginning her own surgical practice, her life had been shattered as thoroughly as a crystal gobiet struck by a bullet. Even if her condition was not that extreme, even if psychotherapy gave her a chance to control her strange outbursts, she'd never be able to obtain a licence to practise medicine.

George plucked several Kleenex from the box on the nightstand and gave them to her. He poured a glass of water. He got a Valium and made her take it, though at first she resisted. He held her hand, which seemed like that of a very small girl when clasped in his large mitt. He spoke softly, reassuringly. Gradually he calmed her.

When she could speak, she said, 'But George, damn it, I

wasn't raised in a psychologically destructive atmosphere. Our home was happy, at peace. And I certainly got more than my share of love and affection. I wasn't physically, mentally, or emotionally abused.' She angrily snatched the box of tissues from the nightstand, tore Kleenex from it. 'Why me? How could *I*, coming from my background, develop a psychosis? *How*? With my fantastic mother, my special papa, my damned-if-it-wasn't-happy childhood, how could *I* wind up seriously mentally disturbed? It isn't fair. It isn't right. It isn't even *believable*.'

He sat on the edge of her bed, and he was so tall that he still loomed over her. 'First of all, Doctor, the consulting specialists tell me there's a whole school of thought that says many mental illnesses are the result of subtle chemical changes in the body, in the brain tissue, changes we're not yet advanced enough to detect or understand. So this doesn't have to mean that you're screwed up by your childhood. I don't think you've got to re-evaluate your whole life because of this. Second, I'm not – I repeat not – at all convinced that your condition is anything as serious as debilitating psychosis.'

'Oh, George, please don't coddle –'

'Coddle a patient? *Me*?' he said, as if no one had ever suggested anything half as astonishing to him. 'I'm not just trying to lift your spirits. I mean what I say. Sure, we didn't find a physical cause for this, but that doesn't mean there *isn't* a physical problem involved. You might have a condition that's not yet sufficiently advanced to be detectable. In a couple of weeks, or a month, or as soon as there's any worsening of the problem, any indication of deterioration, we'll run more tests; we'll take another look, and I'd bet everything I own that we'll eventually put our finger on the problem.'

She allowed herself to hope. Discarding a wadded mass of tissues, she fumbled for the Kleenex box. 'You really think it could be like that? A brain tumour or an abscess so small it doesn't show up yet?'

'Sure. I find that a hell of a lot easier to believe than that you're psychologically disturbed. You? You're one of the steadiest people I've ever known. And I can't accept that you could be psychotic or even psychoneurotic and not exhibit unusual behaviour *between* these fugues. I mean, serious mental illness isn't expressed in neatly contained little bursts. It slops over into the patient's entire life.'

She had not thought about that before. As she considered his point, she felt a little better, though not wildly hopeful and certainly not happy. On the one hand, it seemed weird to be *hoping* for a brain tumour, but a tumour could be excised, perhaps without gross damage to cerebral tissues. Madness, however, responded to no scalpel.

'The next few weeks or months are probably going to be the most difficult of your life,' he said. 'The waiting.'

'I suppose I'm restricted from hospital work for the duration.'

'Yes. But depending on how you come along, I don't see why you can't help me out at the office.'

'And what if I . . . threw one of these fits?'

'I'd be there to keep you from hurting yourself until it passed.'

'But what would your patients think? Wouldn't exactly help your practice any, would it? To have an assistant who suddenly turns into a *meshugene* and runs shrieking through the office?'

He smiled. 'Let me worry about what my patients think. Anyway, that's for the future. Right now, at least for a week or two, you've got to take it easy. No work at all. Relax. Rest. These last few days have been emotionally and physically exhausting.'

'I've been in bed. Exhausting? Don't knock a teapot.'

He blinked, confused, 'Don't what?'

'Oh,' she said, surprised to have heard those four words pop out of her, 'it's something my father used to say. It's a Yiddish expression. *Hok nit kayn tshaynik*: don't knock a teapot. It means, don't talk nonsense. But don't ask me *why* it means that. It's just something I used to hear all the time when I was a kid.'

'Well, I'm not knocking a teapot,' he said. 'You may have been in bed all week, but it's been an exhausting experience nonetheless, and you need to take it easy for a while. I want you to move in with Rita and me for the next few weeks.'

'What? Oh, I couldn't impose on you –'

'It's no imposition. We have a live-in maid, so you won't

107

even have to make you bed in the morning. From the guestroom window, you'll have a nice view of the bay. Living around water is calming. In fact, it's quite literally what the doctor ordered.'

'No. Really. Thank you, but I couldn't.'

He frowned. 'You don't understand. I'm not just your boss but your doctor, and I'm telling you this is what you're going to do.'

'I'll be perfectly fine at the apartment –'

'No,' he said firmly. 'Think about it. Suppose one of these seizures struck while you were making dinner. Suppose you knocked over a pot on the stove. It could start a fire, and you might not even be aware of it until you came out of the fugue, by which time the whole apartment could be ablaze and you could be trapped. That's only one way you might hurt yourself. I can think of a hundred. So I have to insist that . . . for a while you must not live alone. If you don't want to stay with me and Rita, do you have relatives who'd take you in for a while?'

'Not in Boston. In New York, I've got aunts, uncles . . .'

But Ginger could not stay with any of her relatives. They would be happy to have her, of course – especially Aunt Francine or Aunt Rachael. However, she did not want them to see her in her current condition, and the thought of pitching a fit in front of them was intolerable. She could almost see Francine and Rachael huddling over a kitchen table, speaking in low voices, clucking their tongues: 'Where did Jacob and Anna go wrong? Did they push her too hard? Anna always pushed her too hard. And after Anna died, Jacob relied on the girl too much. She had to take over the house at twelve. It was too much for her. Too much pressure too young.' Ginger would receive considerable compassion, understanding, and love from them, but at the risk of sullying the memory of her parents, a memory she was determined to honour, always.

To George, who still sat upon the edge of the bed and awaited her response with an obvious concern that touched her deeply, she said, 'I'll take the guestroom with the view of the bay.'

'Splendid!'

'Though I think it's a horrible imposition. And I warn you, if

I really like it there, you might never get rid of me. You'll know you're in a trouble if you come home some day, and I've hired people to repaint the walls and hang new drapes.'

He grinned. 'At the first mention of painters or draperies, we'll throw your butt out in the street.' He kissed her lightly on the cheek, got up from the edge of the bed, and walked to the door. 'I'm going to start the release procedures now, so you should be out of here in two hours. I'll call Rita and have her come pick you up. I'm sure you can beat this thing, Ginger, but you've got to keep thinking positive.'

When he left the room and his footsteps faded down the hall, she stopped struggling to maintain her smile, and it collapsed instantly. She leaned back against her pillows and stared morosely at the age-yellowed acoustic tile on the ceiling.

After a while she got out of bed and went into the adjoining bathroom, where she approached the sink with trepidation. After a brief hesitation, she turned on the water and watched it whirling around and around and into the drain. On Monday, at the surgical scrub sink, after successfully performing the aortal graft on Viola Fletcher, Ginger had been panicked by the sight of water swirling into a drain, but she could not imagine why.

Damn it, *why*? She desperately wanted to understand.

Papa, she thought, I wish you were alive, here to listen, to help.

Life's nasty surprises had been the subject of one of Papa's little sayings that Ginger had once found amusing. When anyone fretted about the future, Jacob would shake his head and wink and say, 'Why worry about tomorrow? Who knows what'll hit you *today*?'

How true. And how utterly *un*amusing now.

She felt like an invalid. She felt lost.

It was Friday, December 6.

LAGUNA BEACH, CALIFORNIA

When Dom went to the doctor's office on Monday morning, December 2, in the company of Parker Faine, Dr Cobletz did not recommend immediate diagnostic procedures, for he had only recently given Dom a thorough examination and had seen no signs of physical disorder. He assured them there were other treatments to be tried before jumping to the conclusion that it was a brain disorder that sent the writer scurrying upon errands of fortification and self-defence in his sleep.

After Dom's previous visit, on November 23, the physician had, he said, become curious about somnambulism and had done some reading on the subject. With most adults the affliction was short-lived; however, in a few cases, there was a danger of it becoming habitual, and in its most serious forms it resembled the inflexible routines and pattern-obsessed behaviour of worst-case neurotics. Once habitual, somnambulism was much harder to cure, and it could become the dominant factor in the patient's life, generating a fear of night and sleep, producing profound feelings of helplessness culminating in more serious emotional disorders.

Dom felt he was already in that danger zone. He thought of the barricade he had built across his bedroom door. The arsenal on the bed.

Cobletz, intrigued and concerned but not worried, had assured Dominick – and Parker – that in most instances of persistent somnambulism, the pattern of nocturnal rambling could be broken by the administration of a sedative before bed. Once a few untroubled nights had passed, the patient was usually cured. In chronic cases, the nightly sedative was augmented with a diazepam compound during the day when the patient was plagued by anxiety. Because the tasks that Dominick performed in his sleep were unnaturally strenuous for a somnambulist, Dr Cobletz had prescribed both Valium during the day and a 15-milligram tablet of Dalmane, just before slipping under the covers each night.

On the drive back to Laguna Beach from Dr Cobletz's offices

in Newport, with the sea on the right and hills on the left, Parker Faine argued that, until the sleepwalking stopped, it was not wise for Dom to continue living alone. Hunched over the steering wheel of his Volvo, the bearded and shaggy-haired artist drove fast, aggressively but not recklessly. He seldom glanced away from the Pacific Coast Highway, yet he gave the impression, through the sheer force of his personality, that his eyes and attention were fixed constantly and entirely upon Dom. 'There's plenty of room at my place. I can keep an eye on you. I won't hover, mind you. I won't be a mother hen. But at least I'll *be* there. And we would have plenty of opportunity to talk about this, really get into it, just you and me, and try to figure how this sleepwalking is related to the changes you went through the summer before last, when you threw away that job at Mountainview College. I'm definitely the guy to help you. I swear, if I hadn't become a goddamned painter, I'd have become a goddamned psychiatrist. I have a knack for getting people to talk about themselves. How about it? Come stay with me for a while, and let me play therapist.'

Dom had refused. He wanted to stay at his own house, alone, for to do otherwise seemed to be a retreat into the same rabbit hole in which he had hidden from life for so many years. The change he had undergone during his trip to Mountainview, Utah, the summer before last, had been dramatic, inexplicable, but for the better. At thirty-three, he had finally seized the reins of life, had mounted it with a flourish, and had ridden into new territory. He liked the man he had become, and he feared nothing more than slipping back into his dreary former existence.

Perhaps his somnambulism was mysteriously related to the previous changes of attitude that he had undergone, as Parker insisted, but Dom had his doubts that the relationship was either mysterious or complex. More likely, the connection between the two personality crises was simple: the sleepwalking was an excuse to retreat from the challenges, excitement, and stress of his new life. Which could not be allowed. Therefore, Dom would stay in his own house, alone, take the Valium and Dalmane as Dr Cobletz had prescribed them, and tough this thing out.

That was what he had decided in the Volvo, on Monday morning, and by Saturday, the seventh of December, it seemed that he had made the correct decision. Some days he needed a Valium and some days he did not. Every evening he took a Dalmane tablet with milk or hot chocolate. Somnambulism disturbed his nights less frequently. Before beginning drug therapy, he walked in his sleep every night, but in the past five nights he journeyed just twice, leaving his bed only in the pre-dawn hours of Wednesday and Friday mornings.

Furthermore, his activities in his sleep were far less bizarre and less disturbing than they had been. He no longer gathered up weapons, built barricades, or tried to nail the windows shut. On both occasions, he merely left his Beautyrest for a makeshift bed in the back of the closet, where he woke stiff and sore and frightened by some unknown and nameless threat that had pursued him in dreams he could not recall.

Thank God, the worst seemed past.

By Thursday he had begun to write again. He worked on the new novel, picking up where he left off weeks ago.

On Friday, Tabitha Wycombe, his editor in New York, called with good news. Two pre-publication reviews of *Twilight in Babylon* had just come in, and both were excellent. She read them to him, then revealed even better news: bookseller excitement, aroused by industry publicity and by several hundred advance reading copies, continued to grow, and the first printing, which had already been raised once, was now being raised again. They talked for almost half an hour, and when Dom hung up, he felt that his life was back on the rails.

But Saturday night brought a new development, which might have been either a turn for the better or the worse. Every night that he had gone walking in his sleep, he had been unable to recall even the smallest detail of the nightmares that drove him from his bed. Then, Saturday, he was plagued by an uncannily vivid, terrifying dream that sent him fleeing through the house in somnambulistic panic, but this time he remembered part of it when he woke, not most of it but at least the end.

In the last minute or two of the dream, he was standing in a half-glimpsed bathroom, everything blurred. An unseen man shoved him against a sink, and Dom bent over it, his face

112

thrust down into the porcelain bowl. Someone had an arm around him and was holding him on his feet, for he was too weak to stand on his own. He felt rag-limp, his knees were quivering, and his stomach was twisting and rolling. A second unseen person had two hands on his head, forcing his face into the sink. He could not speak. He could not draw breath. He knew he was dying. He had to get away from these people, out of this room, but he did not have the physical resources to take flight. Though his vision remained bleary, he could see the smooth porcelain and the chrome-plated rim of the drain in detail, for his face was only inches from the bottom of the sink. It was an old-fashioned drain without a mechanically operated stopper. The rubber plug had been removed and set aside, somewhere out of sight. The water was running, spewing out of a faucet, past his face, splattering against the bottom of the basin, whirling around and around, down into the drain, around and down. The two people forcing him into the sink were shouting, though he could not understand them. Around and down . . . around . . . Staring hypnotically into the miniature whirlpool, he grew terrified of the gaping drain, which was like a sucking orifice intent upon drawing him into its reeking depths. Suddenly he was sure they wanted to stuff him down into the drain, dispose of him. Might be a garbage disposal in there, something that would chop him to pieces and flush him away –

He woke, screaming. He was in his bathroom. He had walked in his sleep. He was at the sink, bent over, screaming into the drain. He leapt back from that gaping hole, stumbled, nearly fell over the edge of the bathtub. He grabbed a towel rack to steady himself.

Gasping for breath, shaking, he finally got up enough nerve to return to the sink and look into it. Glossy white porcelain. A brass drain rim and a dome-shaped brass stopper. Nothing else, nothing worse.

The room in his nightmare had not been this room.

Dominick washed his face and returned to the bedroom.

According to the clock on the nightstand, it was only 2:25 a.m.

Though it made no sense at all and seemed to have no symbolic or real connection with his life, the nightmare was profoundly disturbing. However, he had not nailed windows shut or gathered up weapons in his sleep, so it seemed that this was only a minor setback.

In fact, it might be a sign of improvement. If he remembered his dreams, not just pieces but all of them from beginning to end, he might discover the source of the anxiety that had made a night rambler of him. Then he would be better able to deal with it.

Nevertheless, he did not want to go back to bed and risk returning to that strange place in his dream. The bottle of Dalmane was in the top drawer of the nightstand. He was not supposed to take more than one tablet each evening, but surely one indulgence couldn't hurt.

He went out to the bar cabinet in the living room, poured Chivas Regal. With a shaky hand, he popped the pill in his mouth, drank the Chivas, and returned to bed.

He was improving. Soon, the sleep walking would stop. A week from now, he'd be back to normal. In a month, this would seem like a curious aberration, and he'd wonder how he'd allowed it to get the better of him.

Precariously prone upon the trembling wire of consciousness above the gulf of sleep, he began to lose his balance. It was a pleasant feeling, a soft slipping away. But as he floated down into sleep, he heard himself murmuring in the darkness of the bedroom, and what he heard himself saying was so strange it startled him and peaked his interest even as the Dalmane and whiskey inexorably had their way with him. 'The moon,' he whispered thickly. 'The moon, the moon.' He wondered what he could possibly mean by that, and he tried to push sleep away at least long enough to ponder his own words. The moon? 'The moon,' he whispered again, and then he was gone.

It was 3:11 a.m., Sunday, December 8.

6

NEW YORK, NEW YORK

Five days after stealing more than three million dollars from the *fratellanza*, Jack Twist went to see a dead woman who still breathed.

At one o'clock Sunday afternoon, in a respectable neighbourhood on the East Side, he parked his Camaro in the underground garage beneath the private sanitarium and took the elevator up to the lobby. He signed in with the receptionist and was given a visitor's pass.

One would not think the place was a hospital. The public area was tastefully decorated in Art Deco style suited to the building's period. There were two small Erté originals, sofas, one armchair, tables with neatly arranged magazines, and all the furniture had a 1920s look.

It was too damn luxurious. The Ertés were unnecessary. A hundred other economies were obvious. But the management felt that image was important in order to continue to attract upper-crust clientele and keep the annual profit around the hundred per cent mark. The patients were of all types – middle-aged catatonic schizophrenics, autistic children, the long-term comatose both young and old – but they had two things in common: their conditions were all chronic rather than acute, and they were from well-to-do families who could afford the best care.

Thinking about the situation, Jack invariably became angry that no place in the city provided fine custodial care for the catastrophically brain-injured or mentally ill at a reasonable price. In spite of huge expenditures of tax money, New York's institutions, like public institutions everywhere, were a grim joke that the average citizen had to accept for a lack of alternatives.

If he had not been a skilled and highly successful thief, he would not have been able to pay the sanitarium's exorbitant monthly charges. Fortunately, he had a talent for larceny.

Carrying his visitor's pass, he went to another elevator and rode up to the fourth of six floors. The hallways in the upper levels were more reminiscent of a hospital than the lobby had been. Fluorescent lights. White walls. The clean, crisp, minty smell of disinfectant.

At the far end of the fourth-floor hall, in the last room on the right, lived the dead woman who still breathed. Jack hesitated with his hand on the push-plate of the heavy swinging door, swallowed hard, took a deep breath, and finally went inside.

The room was not as sumptuous as the lobby, and it was not Art Deco, either, but it was very nice, resembling a medium-priced room at the Plaza: a high ceiling and white moulding; a fireplace with a white mantel; a deep hunter-green carpet; pale green drapes; a green leaf-patterned sofa and pair of chairs. The theory was that a patient would be happier in a room like this than in a clinical room. Although many patients were oblivious of their surroundings, the cosier atmosphere at least made visiting friends and relatives feel less bleak.

The hospital bed was the only concession to utilitarian design, a dramatic contrast to everything else. But even that was dressed up with green-patterned designer sheets.

Only the patient spoiled the lovely mood of the chamber.

Jack lowered the safety railing on the bed, leaned over, and kissed his wife's cheek. She did not stir. He took one of her hands and held it in both of his. Her hand did not grip him in return, did not flex, remained slack, limp, senseless, but at least it was warm.

'Jenny? It's me, Jenny. How are you feeling today? Hmmmmm? You look good. You look lovely. You always look lovely.'

In fact, for someone who had spent eight years in a coma, for someone who had not taken a single step and had not felt sunshine or fresh air upon her face in all that time, she looked quite good indeed. Perhaps only Jack could say that she was still lovely – and mean it. She was not the beauty she had once been, but she certainly did not look as if she had spent almost a decade in solemn flirtation with death.

Her hair was not glossy any more, though still thick and the same rich chestnut shade as when he had first seen her at her job, behind the men's cologne counter in Bloomingdale's, fourteen years ago. The attendants washed her hair twice a week here and brushed it every day.

116

He could have moved his hand under her hair, along the left side of her skull, to the unnatural depression, the sickening concavity. He could have touched it without disturbing her, for nothing disturbed her any more, but he did not. Because touching it would have disturbed *him*.

Her brow was uncreased, her face unlined even at the corners of her eyes, which were closed. She was gaunt though not shockingly so. Motionless upon those green designer sheets, she seemed ageless, as if she were an enchanted princess awaiting the kiss that would wake her from a century of slumber.

The only signs of life were the vague, rhythmic rise and fall of her breast as she breathed, and the soft movement of her throat as she occasionally swallowed saliva. The swallowing was an automatic, involuntary action and not a sign of awareness on any level whatsoever.

The brain damage was extensive and irreparable. The movements she made here and now were virtually the only movements she would ever make until, at last, she gave a dying shudder. There was no hope. He knew there was no hope, and he accepted the permanence of her condition.

She would have looked much worse if she had not received such conscientious care. A team of physical therapists came to her room every day and put her through passive exercise routines. Her muscle tone was not the best, but at least she *had* muscle tone.

Jack held her hand and stared down at her for a long time. For seven years, he had been coming to see her two nights a week and for five or six hours every Sunday afternoon, sometimes on other afternoons as well. But in spite of the frequency of his visits and in spite of her unchanging condition, he never tired of looking at her.

He pulled up a chair and sat next to the bed, still holding her hand, staring at her face, and for more than an hour he talked to her. He told her about a movie that he had seen since his previous visit, about two books he had read. He spoke of the weather, described the force and bite of the winter wind. He painted colourful word pictures of the prettiest Christmas displays he had seen in shop windows.

She did not reward him with even a sigh or a twitch. She lay as always, unmoving and unmoved.

Nevertheless, he talked to her, for he worried that a fragment of awareness might survive, a gleam of comprehension down in the black well of the coma. Maybe she *could* hear and understand, in which case the worst thing for her was being trapped in an unresponsive body, desperate even for one-way communication, but receiving none because they thought she could not hear. The doctors assured him that these worries were groundless; she heard nothing, saw nothing, knew nothing, they said, except what images and fantasies might sputter across short-circuiting synapses of her shattered brain. But if they were wrong – if there was only one chance in a million that they were wrong – he could not leave her in that perfect and terrible isolation. So he talked to her as the winter day beyond the window changed from one shade of grey to another.

At 5:15, he went into the adjoining bathroom and washed his face. He dried off and blinked at his reflection in the mirror. As on countless other occasions, he wondered what Jenny had ever seen in him.

Not one feature or aspect of his face could be called handsome. His forehead was too broad, ears too big. Although he had 20-20 vision, his left eye had a leftward cast, and most people could not talk to him without nervously shifting their attention from one eye to the other, wondering which was looking at them when, in fact, *both* were. When he smiled he looked clownish, and when he frowned he looked sufficiently threatening to send Jack the Ripper scurrying for home and hearth.

But Jenny had seen something in him. She had wanted, needed, and loved him. In spite of her own good looks, she had not cared about appearances. That was one of the reasons he had loved her so much. One of the reasons he missed her so much. One of a thousand reasons.

He looked away from the mirror. If it was possible to be lonelier than he was now, he hoped to God that he never slipped down that far.

He returned to the other room, said goodbye to his unheeding wife, kissed her, smelled her hair once more, and got out of there at 5:30.

In the street, behind the wheel of his Camaro, Jack looked at

118

passing pedestrians and other motorists with loathing. His fellow men. The good, kind, gentle, righteous people of the straight world would regard him with disdain and possibly even disgust if they knew he was a professional thief, though it was what they had done to him and to Jenny that had driven him to crime.

He knew anger and bitterness solved nothing, changed nothing, and hurt no one but himself. Bitterness was corrosive. He did not want to be bitter, but there were times when he could not help it.

*   *   *

Later, after dinner alone at a Chinese restaurant, he returned to his apartment. He had a spacious one-bedroom flat in a first-class building on Fifth Avenue, overlooking Central Park. Officially, it was owned by a Lichtenstein-based corporation, which had purchased it with a cheque written on a Swiss bank account, and each month the utilities and the association fees were paid by the Bank of America out of a trust account. Jack Twist lived there under the name 'Philippe Delon.' To the doormen and other building employees, to the few neighbours with whom he spoke, he was known as the odd and slightly disreputable scion of a wealthy French family who had sent him to America ostensibly to scout investments but actually just to get him out of their hair. He spoke French fluently and could speak English with a convincing French accent for hours without slipping up and revealing his deception. Of course, there was no French family, and both the corporation in Lichtenstein and the Swiss bank account were his, and the only wealth he had to invest was that which he had stolen from others. He was not an *ordinary* thief.

In his apartment, he went directly to the walk-in closet in the bedroom and removed the false partition at the rear of it. He pulled two bags from the secret, three-foot-deep storage space and took them into the dark living room, not bothering to turn on lights. He piled the bags beside his favourite armchair, which stood by a large window.

He got a bottle of Beck's from the refrigerator, opened it, and returned to the living room. He sat in the darkness for a while, by the window, looking down on the park, where lights reflected off the snow-covered ground and made strange shadows in the bare-limbed trees.

He was stalling, and he knew it. Finally he switched on the reading lamp beside the chair. He pulled the smallest of the two bags in front of him, opened it, and began to scoop out the contents.

Jewels. Diamond pendants, diamond necklaces, glittering diamond chokers. A diamond and emerald bracelet. Three diamond and sapphire bracelets. Rings, brooches, barrettes, stick pins, jewelled hat pins.

These were the proceeds of a heist that he had pulled off single-handedly six weeks ago. It should have been a two-man job, but with extensive and imaginative planning, he had found a way to handle it himself, and it had gone smoothly.

The only problem was that he had got no kick whatsoever from that heist. When a job had been successfully concluded, Jack was usually in a grand mood for days after. From his point of view, these were not simply crimes but also acts of retribution against the straight world, payment for what it had done to him and to Jenny. Until the age of twenty-nine, he had given much to society, to his country, but as a reward he had wound up in a Central American hellhole, in a dictator's prison, where he had been left to rot. And Jenny . . . He could not bear to think about the condition in which he had found her when, at last, he had escaped and come home. Now, he no longer gave to society but *took* from it, and with intense pleasure. His greatest satisfaction was breaking the rules, taking what he wanted, getting away with it – until the jewellery heist six weeks ago. At the end of that operation, he had felt no triumph, no sense of retribution. That lack of excitement scared him. It was, after all, what he lived for.

Sitting in the armchair by the window, he piled the jewellery in his lap, held selected pieces up to the light, and tried once more to gain a feeling of accomplishment and revenge.

He should have disposed of the jewellery in the days immediately following the burglary. But he was reluctant to part with it until he had squeezed at least a small measure of satisfaction from it.

Troubled by his continued lack of feeling, he put the jewels back into the sack from which he had taken them.

The other sack contained his share of the proceeds from the robbery at the *fratellanza* warehouse five days ago. They had been able to open only one of the two safes, but that had contained over $3,100,000, more than a million apiece, in untraceable twenties, fifties, and hundreds.

By now he should have begun to convert the cash into cashier's cheques and other negotiable instruments for deposit, by mail, in his Swiss accounts. However, he held onto it because, as with the jewellery, the possession of it had not yet given him a sense of triumph.

He removed thick stacks of tightly banded currency from the bag and held them, turned them over in his hands. He brought them to his face and smelled them. That singular scent of money was usually exciting in itself – but not this time. But he did not feel triumphant, clever, lawless, or in any way superior to the obedient mice who scurried through society's maze exactly as they were taught. He just felt empty.

If this change in him had occurred with the warehouse job, he would have attributed it to having stolen from other thieves, rather than from the straight world. But his reaction subsequent to the jewellery heist had been the same, and that victim had been a legitimate business. It was his ennui following the jewellery store action that caused him to move on to another job sooner than he should have. Usually he pulled off one job every three or four months, but only five weeks had elapsed between his most recent operations.

All right, so maybe the usual thrill eluded him on both these recent jobs because the money was no longer important to him. He had set aside enough to support himself in style for as long as he lived and to take care of Jenny even if she endured a normal lifespan in her coma, which was unlikely. Perhaps, all along, the most important thing about his work had not been the rebellion and defiance of it, as he had thought; perhaps, instead, he had done it all just for the money, and the rest of it had been merely cheap rationalisation and self-delusion.

But he could not believe that. He knew what he had felt, and he knew how much he missed those feelings now.

Something was happening to him, an inner shifting, a sea-change. He felt empty, adrift, without purpose. He dared not lose his love of larceny. It was the only reason he had for living.

He put the money back into the bag. He turned out the light and sat in the darkness, sipping Beck's and staring down at Central Park.

In addition to his recent inability to find joy in his work, he had been plagued by a recurring nightmare more intense than any dream he had ever known. It had begun six weeks ago, before the jewellery store job, and he'd had it eight or ten times since. In the dream, he was fleeing from a man in a motorcycle helmet with a darkly tinted visor. At least he thought it was a motorcycle helmet, although he could not see many details of it or anything else of the man who wore it. The faceless stranger pursued him on foot through unknown rooms and along amorphous corridors and, most vividly, along a deserted highway that cut through an empty moon-washed landscape. On every occasion, Jack's panic built like steam pressure in a boiler, until it exploded and blew him awake.

The obvious interpretation was that the dream was a warning, that the man in the helmet was a cop, that Jack was going to get caught. But that was not the way the nightmare *felt*. In the dream, he never had the impression that the guy in the helmet was a cop. Something else.

He hoped to God he would not have the dream tonight. The day had been bad enough without that mid-night terror.

He got another beer, returned to the chair by the window, and sat down in the darkness once more.

It was December 8, and Jack Twist – former officer in the elite United States Army Rangers, former POW in an undeclared war, a man who had helped save the lives of over a thousand Indians in Central America, a man who functioned under a burden of grief that might have broken some people, a daring thief whose reservoir of courage had always been bottomless – wondered if he had run out of the simple courage to go on living. If he could not regain the sense of purpose he had found in larceny, he needed to find a new purpose. Desperately.

122

7

ELKO COUNTY, NEVADA

Ernie Block broke all the speed limits on the drive back from Elko to the Tranquillity Motel.

The last time he had driven so fast and recklessly had been on a gloomy Monday morning during his hitch with Marine Intelligence in Vietnam. He had been behind the wheel of a Jeep, passing through what should have been friendly territory, and had unexpectedly come under enemy fire. The incoming shells had spewed up geysers of dirt and chunks of macadam only feet away from his front and rear bumpers. By the time he had broken out of the fire zone, he had escaped more than twenty near-misses, he had been hit by three small but painfully jagged pieces of mortar, had been rendered temporarily deaf from the thunderous explosions, and had found himself struggling to control a Jeep that was running on its wheel rims with four flat tyres. Having survived, he figured he had known fear as profound as it could ever be.

But coming back from Elko, his fear was building toward a new peak. Nightfall was approaching. He had driven to the Elko freight office in the Dodge van to take delivery of a shipment of lighting fixtures for the motel. He had set out shortly after noon, leaving Faye in charge of the front desk, giving himself plenty of time to make the round-trip before twilight. But he had a flat tyre and lost time changing it. Then, once he reached Elko, he wasted almost an hour having the tyre repaired because he had not wanted to start home without a spare. With one thing or another, he had left Elko almost two hours later than expected, and the sun had westered to the far edge of the Great Basin.

He kept the accelerator most of the way to the floor, whipping around other traffic on the superhighway. He did not think he would be able to finish the drive home if he had to do it in full darkness. In the morning they would find him behind the wheel of the van, still parked along the roadside, stark raving mad from having spent long hours in horrified contemplation of the perfectly black landscape.

In the two and a half weeks since Thanksgiving, he had continued to conceal his irrational fear of darkness from Faye. After she returned from her visit to Wisconsin, Ernie found it more difficult to sleep without a lamp burning, having indulged himself with a night light while she was gone. Every morning he used Murine to clear his bloodshot eyes. Fortunately, she had not suggested going into Elko at night for a movie, so Ernie had not been required to make excuses. A few times, after sunset, he'd had to go from the office to the Tranquillity Grille next door, and even though the walk was well-lighted by the motel's outdoor lamps and signs, he had been nearly overwhelmed by a sense of fragility, vulnerability. But he had kept his secret.

All his life, in the Marine Corps and out of it, to the best of his ability, Ernie Block had done what was required of him, all that could be expected. And now, by God, he was not going to fail his own wife.

Behind the wheel of the Dodge van, racing westwards toward the Tranquillity Motel under a smeary orange-purple sky, Ernie Block wondered if his problem was premature senility, `Alzheimer's disease. Even though he was only fifty-two, it almost had to be something like Alzheimer's. Although it frightened him, at least he could understand it.

Understand it, yes, but he could not accept it. Faye depended on him. He could not become a mental invalid, a burden to her. The men in the Block family never let their womenfolk down. Never. Unthinkable.

The highway rounded a small hillock, and a mile ahead, north of the Interstate, lay the motel, the only building in that vast panorama. Its blue and green neon sign was already switched on, shining fiercely bright against the twilight sky. He'd never seen a more welcome sight.

Complete darkness was still ten minutes away, and he decided it was foolish to risk being stopped by a cop when he was this close to sanctuary. He eased up on the accelerator, and the speedometer needle swiftly dropped: *ninety . . . eighty-five . . . seventy-five . . . sixty . . .*

He was three-quarters of a mile from home when a curious thing happened: he glanced southward, away from the road, and his breath caught. He did not know what startled him.

Something about the landscape. Something about the way the light and shadow played across those down-sloping fields. He was suddenly gripped by the odd idea that a particular piece of ground – a half-mile ahead, on the opposite side of the highway – was of supreme importance in understanding the bizarre changes that had been taking place in him during the past few months.

. . . fifty . . . forty-five . . . forty . . .

He could see nothing to make that piece of land different from the tens of thousands of acres around it. Besides, he had seen it countless times before and had been unimpressed by it. Nevertheless, in the slope of the terrain, in the gently folded contours of the earth, in the bisecting wound of an arroyo, in the configuration of sagebrush and grass, and in the scattered gnarled outcropping of rock, something seemed to cry out for investigation.

He felt as if the land itself were saying, 'Here, here, here is part of the answer to your problem, part of the explanation for your fear of the night. Here. Here . . .' But that was ridiculous.

To his surprise, he found himself pulling to the shoulder of the highway, stopping a quarter-mile from home, not far from the exit ramp to the county road that led past the motel. He squinted south across the highway, at the place that had mysteriously captured his attention.

He was gripped by the most amazing sense of impending epiphany, an overwhelming feeling that something of monumental importance was about to happen to him. The skin prickled along the back of his neck.

He got out of the van, leaving it behind him. In a state of tremulous expectation that he could not understand, he headed toward the far side of the interstate, where he could have a better look at the plot of ground that fascinated him. He traversed two lanes of blacktop, clambered into the twenty-foot-wide gulley that divided the halves of the interstate, and scrambled up the far slope. He waited for three huge trucks to roar past, then crossed the eastbound lanes in the windy wake of those rigs. His heart was pounding with an inexplicable excitement, and for the moment he had forgotten the advent of night.

He stopped on the far berm, at the crest of the highway's elevated bed, looking south and slightly west. He wore a bulky suede jacket with sheepskin lining, but his brush-cut grey hair provided little protection from the chilly wind, which scrubbed its cold knuckles across his skull.

He began to lose the feeling that something of immense importance was about to happen. Instead, he was seized by the even creepier notion that something had *already* happened to him on that patch of shadow-banded ground out there, something that accounted for his recent fear of the dark. Something he had assiduously banned from his memory.

But that made no sense. If important events had transpired here, they simply would not have slipped his mind. He was not forgetful. And he was not the kind of person who repressed unpleasant memories.

Still, the back of his neck continued to tingle. Out there, not far into those trackless Nevada plains, something had happened to him that he had forgotten but that now pricked him from his subconscious, where it was deeply embedded, much the way a needle, accidentally left in a quilt, might jab and startle a sleeper out of a dream.

With his legs spread wide and his feet planted firmly in the berm, with his blocky head hunched down on his blocky shoulders, Ernie seemed to be challenging the landscape to speak more clearly to him. He strained to resurrect the dead memory of this place – if, indeed, there was one – but the harder he tried to grasp the elusive revelation, the faster it receded from him. Then it was gone altogether.

The *deja vu* deserted him as completely as the sense of impending epiphany had evaporated before it. The tingle left his scalp and neck. His frantically pounding heart settled slowly into a more normal pace.

Bewildered and somewhat dizzy, he studied the fast-fading scene before him – the angled land, the spines and teeth of rock, the brush and grass, the weathered convexities and concavities of the ancient earth – and now he could not imagine why it had seemed special to him. It was just a portion of the high plains virtually indistinguishable from a thousand other spots from here to Elko or from here to Battle Mountain.

Disoriented by the suddenness of his plunge from the

brink of transcendent awareness, he looked back towards the van, which waited on the north side of the interstate. He felt conspicuous and foolish when he thought of the way he had dashed from there to here in the grip of a strange excitement. He hoped Faye had not seen him. If by chance she had been looking out a window in this direction, she could not have missed his performance, for the motel was only a quarter of a mile away, and the flashing emergency blinkers on the truck made it by far the most noticeable thing in the swiftly descending darkness.

Darkness.

Abruptly, the nearness of nightfall hit Ernie Block hard. For a while, the mysterious magnetism that had drawn him to this place had been stronger than his fear of the dark. But that changed in an instant when he realised that the eastern half of the sky was purple-black and that only minutes of vague light remained in the western realm.

With a cry of panic, he bolted across the eastbound lanes, in front of a motor home, oblivious of the danger. A horn blared at him. He did not care, did not pause, just ran pell-mell because he could feel the darkness clutching at him and pressing down on him. He reached the shallow gully that served as a lane divider, fell as he started down into it, rolled back onto his feet, terrified of the blackness that was welling up out of each depression in the land and from under every rock. He flung himself up the other side of the gully, fled into the westbound lanes. Fortunately there was no oncoming traffic, for he did not look to see if the way was clear. At the van, he fumbled with the door handle, acutely conscious of the perfect blackness *under* the truck. It was grappling at his feet. It wanted to pull him under the Dodge and devour him. He yanked the door open. Tore his feet loose of the hands of darkness. Clambered into the cab. Slammed the door. Locked it.

He felt better but far from safe, and if he had not been so close to home he would have frozen stiff. But he only had a quarter of a mile to go, and when he switched on his headlights, the gloom fell back, which encouraged him. He was shaking so violently that he did not trust himself to pull back into traffic, so he drove along the shoulder of the interstate until he came to the exit ramp. There were sodium-arc lamps along the ramp and at the base of it, and he was tempted to stop there at the bottom, in the yellow glare, but he gritted his teeth and turned onto the county road, out of the light. After driving only two hundred yards, Ernie reached the entrance to the Tranquillity Motel. He swung through the parking area, slid the van into a slot in front of the office, switched off the headlights, and cut the engine.

Beyond the big windows of the office, he could see Faye at the front desk. He hurried inside, closing the door behind himself with too much force. He smiled at Faye when she glanced up, and he hoped the smile looked more convincing than it felt.

'I was beginning to worry, dear,' she said, returning his smile.

'Had a flat tyre,' Ernie said, unzipping his jacket.

He felt somewhat relieved. Nightfall was easier to accept when he was not alone; Faye gave him strength, but he was still uneasy.

She said, 'I missed you.'

'I was only gone the afternoon.'

'I guess I'm hooked, then. Seemed longer. Guess I've got to have my Ernie fix every couple of hours or go through withdrawal symptoms.'

He leaned across the counter, and she leaned from her side, and they kissed. There was nothing half-hearted about their kiss. She put one hand to his head to hold him close. Most long-married couples, even if they remained in love, were perfunctory in their displays of affection, but that was not the case with Ernie and Faye Block. After thirty-one years of marriage, she could still make him feel young.

She said, 'Where are the new lighting fixtures? They did come in, didn't they? The freight office didn't make a mistake?'

That question jolted him back to an acute awareness of the night outside. He glanced at the windows, then quickly away. 'Uh, no. I'm tired. I don't really feel up to hauling them in here tonight.'

'Just four crates —'

'Really, I'd rather do it in the morning,' he said, striving to keep a tremor out of his voice. 'The stuff will be all right in the truck. Nobody'll touch it. Hey, you put up the Christmas decorations!'

128

'You mean you *just* noticed?'

A huge wreath of pinecones and nuts hung on the wall above the sofa. A life-size cardboard figure of Santa Claus stood in the corner beside the rack of postcards, and a small ceramic sleigh with ceramic reindeer was displayed at one end of the long counter. Red and gold Christmas-tree balls hung from the ceiling light fixture on lengths of transparent fishing line.

'You had to get up on a ladder for some of this,' he said.

'Just the stepladder.'

'But what if you'd fallen? You should've left this for me to do.'

Faye shook her head. 'Honey, I swear to God I'm not the fragile type. Now, hush up. You ex-Marines carry macho too far sometimes.'

'Is that so?'

The outer door opened, and a trucker came in, asking about a room.

Ernie held his breath until the door closed.

The trucker was a lanky man in a cowboy hat, denim jacket, cowboy shirt, and jeans. Faye complimented him on the hat, which had an elaborately sculpted leather band brightened with chips of turquoise. In that easy way of hers, she made the stranger feel like an old friend as she shepherded him through the check-in process.

Leaving her to it, trying to forget his curious experience on the interstate, trying not to dwell on the night that had come, Ernie moved behind the counter, hung his coat on the brass rack in the corner by the file cabinets, and went to the oak desk, where mail was stacked on the blotter. Bills, of course. Advertisements. A charity solicitation. The first Christmas cards of the year. His military pension cheque.

Finally, there was a white envelope without a return address, which contained only a Polaroid colour photograph that had been taken in front of the motel, beside the door to Room 9. It was of three people – man, woman, child. The man was in his late twenties, darkly tanned and good-looking. The woman was a couple of years younger, a pretty brunette. The little girl, five or six, was very cute. All three were smiling at the camera. Judging from their clothes – shorts and T-shirts –

and the quality of sunlight in the picture, Ernie assumed that the snapshot had been taken in the middle of summer.

Puzzled, he turned the photo over, looking for a scribbled note of explanation. The back was blank. He checked the envelope again, but it was empty: no letter, no card, not even a business card to identify the sender. The postmark was Elko, December 7, last Saturday.

He looked again at the people in the picture, and although he did not remember them, he felt his skin prickle, just as it had done when he had been drawn to that place along the highway. His pulse accelerated. He quickly put the picture aside and looked away from it.

Faye was still chatting with the cowboy-trucker as she took a room key off the pegboard and passed it across the counter.

Ernie kept his eyes on her. She was a calming influence. She had been a lovely farmgirl when he'd met her, and had grown into a lovelier woman. Her blonde hair might have begun to turn white, but it was hard to tell. Her blue eyes were clear and quick. Hers was an open, friendly Iowa face, slightly saucy but always wholesome, even beatific.

By the time the cowboy-trucker left, Ernie had stopped shaking. He took the Polaroid snapshot to Faye. 'What do you make of this?'

'That's our Room 9,' she said. 'They must've stayed with us.' She frowned at the young couple and little girl in the photograph. 'Can't say I remember them, though. Strangers to me.'

'So why would they send us a photo without a note?'

'Well, obviously, they thought we *would* remember them.'

'But the only reason they'd think that was if maybe they stayed for a few days and we got to know them. And I don't know them at all. I think I'd remember the tyke,' Ernie said. He liked children, and they usually liked him. 'She's cute enough to be in movies.'

'I'd think you'd remember the *mother*. She's gorgeous.'

'Postmarked Elko,' Ernie said. 'Why would anybody who lives in Elko come out here to stay?'

'Maybe they don't live in Elko. Maybe they were here last summer and always meant to send us a photo, and maybe they recently passed through and meant to stop and leave this

130

off but didn't have time. So they mailed it from Elko.'

'Without a note.'

'It is odd,' Faye agreed.

He took the picture from her. 'Besides, this is a Polaroid. Developed a minute after it was taken. If they wanted us to have it, why didn't they leave it with us when they stayed here?'

The door opened, and a curly-haired guy with a bushy moustache came into the office, shivering. 'Got any rooms left?' he asked.

While Faye dealt with the guest, Ernie took the Polaroid back to the oak desk. He meant to gather up the mail and go upstairs, but he stood by the desk, studying the faces of the people in the snapshot.

It was Tuesday evening, December 10.

8.

CHICAGO, ILLINOIS

When Brendan Cronin went to work as an orderly at St Joseph's Hospital for Children, only Dr Jim McMurtry knew that he was really a priest. Father Wycazik had obtained a guarantee of secrecy from the physician, as well as the solemn assurance that Brendan would be assigned as much work – and as much *unpleasant* work – as any orderly. Therefore, during his first day on the job, he emptied bedpans, changed urine-soaked bed linen, assisted a therapist with passive exercises for bed-ridden patients, spoon-fed an eight-year-old boy who was partially paralysed, pushed wheelchairs, encouraged despondent patients, cleaned up the vomit of two young cancer victims nauseous from chemotherapy. No one pampered him, and no one called him 'Father.' The nurses, doctors, orderlies, candy-stripers, and patients called him Brendan, and he felt uncomfortable, like an imposter engaged upon a masquerade.

That first day, overcome with pity and grief for St Joseph's children, he twice slipped away to the staff men's room and locked himself in a stall, where he sat and wept. The twisted legs and swollen joints of those who suffered from rheumatoid arthritis, that mangler of the innocent young, was a sight almost too terrible to be borne. The wasted flesh of the muscular dystrophy victims, the suppurating wounds of the burn victims, the battered bodies of those whose parents had abused them: he wept for all of them.

He could not imagine why Father Wycazik thought this duty would help him regain his lost faith. If anything, the existence of so many pain-racked children only reinforced his doubt. If the merciful God of Catholicism really existed, if there *was* a Jesus, why would He allow the innocent to endure such atrocities? Of course, Brendan knew all the standard theological arguments on that point. Mankind had brought all forms of evil upon itself by choice, the Church said, by turning away from the grace of God. But theological arguments were inadequate when he came face to face with these smallest victims of fate.

By the second day, the staff was still calling him Brendan, but the children were calling him Pudge, a long-unused nickname which he divulged to them in the course of telling a funny story. They liked his stories, jokes, rhymes, and silly puns, and he found he could nearly always get a laugh or at least a smile out of them. That day, he went to the men's room and wept only once.

By the third day, both the children and staff called him Pudge. If he had another metier besides the priesthood, he had found it at St Joseph's. In addition to performing the usual tasks expected of an orderly, he entertained the patients with comic patter, teased them, drew them out. Wherever he went, he was greeted with cries of '*Pudge*!' that were a better reward than money. And he did not cry until he was back in the hotel room that he had taken for the duration of Father Wycazik's unconventional therapy.

By Wednesday afternoon, the seventh day, he knew why Father Wycazik sent him to St Joseph's. Understanding came while he was brushing the hair of a ten-year-old girl who'd been crippled by a rare bone disease.

Her name was Emmeline, and she was rightfully proud of

her hair. It was thick, glossy, raven-black, and its healthy lustre seemed to be a defiant response to the sickness that had wasted her body. She liked to brush her hair a hundred strokes every day, but often her knuckles and wrist-joints were so inflamed that she could not hold the brush.

On Wednesday, Brendan put her in a wheelchair and took her to the X-ray department, where they were monitoring a new drug's effects on her bone marrow, and when he brought her back to her room an hour later, he brushed her hair for her. Emmeline sat in the wheelchair, looking out a window, while Brendan pulled the soft bristles through her silken tresses, and she became enchanted with the winterscape beyond the glass.

With a gnarled hand more suited to the body of an eighty-year-old woman, she pointed down to the roof of another, lower wing of the hospital. 'See that patch of snow, Pudge?' Rising heat within the building had caused most of the snow to loosen and slide off the pitched roof. But a large patch remained, outlined by dark slate shingles. 'It looks like a ship,' Emmy said. 'The shape. You see? A beautiful old ship with three white sails, gliding across a slate-coloured sea.'

For a while Brendan could not see what she saw. But she continued to describe the imaginary vessel, and the fourth time that he looked up from her hair, he suddenly was able to see that the patch of snow did, indeed, bear a remarkable and delightful resemblance to a sailing ship.

To Brendan, the long icicles that hung in front of Emmy's window were transparent bars, the hospital a prison from which she might never be released. But to Emmy, those frozen stalactites were wondrous Christmas decorations that, she said, put her in the holiday mood.

'God likes winter as much as He likes spring,' Emmy said. 'The gift of the seasons is one of His ways of keeping us from getting bored with the world. That's what Sister Katherine told us, and right away I could see it must be true. When the sun hits those icicles just right, they cast rainbows across my bed. Ever-so-pretty rainbows, Pudge. The ice and snow are like . . . like jewels . . . and ermine cloaks that God uses to dress up the world in winter to make us ooohh and ahhhh. That's why He never makes two snowflakes alike: it's a way

133

of reminding us that the world He made for us is a wonderful, wonderful world.'

As if on cue, snowflakes spiralled down from the grey December sky.

In spite of her nearly useless legs and twisted hands, in spite of the pain she had endured, Emmy believed in God's goodness, and in the inspiring *rightness* of the world that He had created.

Strong faith was, in fact, a trait of nearly all the children in St Joseph's Hospital. They remained convinced that a caring Father watched over them from His kingdom in the sky, and they were encouraged.

In his mind he could hear Father Wycazik saying: *If these innocents can suffer so much and not lose their faith, what sorry excuse do you have, Brendan? Perhaps, in their very innocence and naivety, they know something that you have forgotten while chasing your sophisticated education in Rome. Perhaps there is something to be learned from this, Brendan. Do you think so? Just maybe? Something to be learned?*

But the lesson was not powerful enough to restore Brendan's faith. He continued to be deeply moved, not by the possibility that a caring and compassionate God might actually exist, but by the children's amazing courage in the face of such adversity.

He gave Emmy's hair a hundred strokes, then ten more, which pleased her, and then he lifted her from the wheelchair and put her into bed. As he pulled the covers over her pathetic bent-stick legs, he felt a surge of that same rage that had filled him during Mass at St Bette's two Sundays ago, and if a sacred chalice had been close at hand, he would not have hesitated to hurl it at the wall once more.

Emmy gasped, and Brendan had the odd notion that she had read his blasphemous thoughts. But she said, 'Oh, Pudge, did you hurt yourself?'

He blinked at her. 'What do you mean?'

'Did you burn yourself? Your hands. When'd you hurt your hands?'

Bewildered by her question, he looked down at the backs of his hands, turned them over, and was surprised by the marks on his palms. In the centre of each palm was a red ring of

134

inflamed and swollen flesh. Each ring was two inches in diameter and sharply defined along all its edges. The circular band of irritated tissue which formed the ring was no more than half an inch wide, inscribing a perfect circle; the skin around and within the circle was quite normal. It almost looked as if the marks had been painted on his hands, but when he touched one of the rings with a fingertip, he could feel the bump it made in his palm.

'That's strange,' he said.

*   *   *

Dr Stan Heeton was the resident physician on duty in St Joseph's emergency room. Standing at the examining table on which Brendan sat, peering with interest at the odd rings in Brendan's hands, he said. 'Do they hurt?'

'No. Not at all.'

'Itching? A burning sensation?'

'No. Neither.'

'Do they at least tingle? No? You've never had these before?'

'Never.'

'Do you have any allergies that you're aware of? No? Hmmmm. At first glance, it looks like a mild burn, but you'd have remembered leaning against something hot enough to cause this. There'd be pain. So we can rule that out. Same for acid contact. Did you say you'd taken a little girl to radiology?'

'Yes, but I didn't stay in the room while the X-rays were taken.'

'Doesn't really look like a radiation burn. Maybe dermato-mycosis, a fungal infection, perhaps in the ringworm family, though the symptoms aren't sufficiently indicative of ringworm. No scaling, no itching. And the ring is much too clearly defined, not like the inflammation patterns you get with a Microsporum or Trichophyton infection.'

'So what does all this boil down to?'

Heeton hesitated, then said, 'I don't think it's anything serious. The best guess is a rash related to an unidentified allergy. If the problem persists, you'll have to take the standard patch tests and find the source of your problem.' He let go of Brendan's hands, went to a chair at a corner desk, and began to fill out a prescription form.

Puzzled, Brendan stared at his hands a moment longer, then folded them in his lap.

At the corner desk, still writing, Heeton said, 'I'll start with the simplest treatment, a cortisone lotion. If the rash doesn't disappear in a couple of days, come see me again.' He returned to the examining table, holding out the prescription form.

Brendan took the paper from him. 'Listen, is there any chance I might pass on an infection to the kids or anything like that?'

'Oh, no. If I thought there was the slightest chance, I'd have told you,' Heeton said. 'Now, let me have one last look.'

Brendan turned his hands palms-up for examination.

'What the devil?' Dr Heeton said, surprised.

The rings were gone.

*   *   *

That night, in his room at the Holiday Inn, Brendan again endured the by-now familiar nightmare about which he had spoken with Father Wycazik. It had disturbed his sleep twice before in the past week.

He dreamed he was lying in a strange place, with his arms and legs restrained by straps and braces. From out of a haze, a pair of hands reached for him. Hands encased in shiny black gloves.

He woke in knots of sweat-soaked sheets, sat up in bed, and leaned back against the headboard, letting the dream evaporate as sweat dried on his forehead. In the dark he brought his hands to his face to blot it – and went rigid when his palms touched his cheeks. He switched on the lamp. The swollen, inflamed rings had returned to his palms. But as he watched, they faded.

It was Thursday, December 12.

9

LAGUNA BEACH, CALIFORNIA

Dom Corvaisis thought he had slept Wednesday night straight through in peace. He woke in bed, in precisely the same position in which he had gone to sleep, as if he had not moved an inch during the night.

But when he went to work at his Displaywriter, he was dismayed to find proof of his somnambulistic wandering on the current work diskette. As on a few other occasions, he apparently had gone to the Displaywriter in his night-trance and had repeatedly typed two words. Previously, he had typed, 'I'm scared,' but this time there were two different words:

The moon. The moon. The moon. The moon.
The moon. The moon. The moon. The moon.

There were hundreds of repetitions of those seven letters, and he was at once reminded that he had heard himself murmuring the same words in a state of drowsy disorientation, just as he had fallen asleep last Sunday. Dominick stared at the screen for a long time, chilled, but he had no idea what special meaning 'the moon' held for him, if any.

The Valium and Dalmane therapy was working well. Until now, there had been no new episodes of sleepwalking and no dreams since last weekend, when he'd had that nasty nightmare about being forced face-down into a sink. He had seen Dr Cobletz again, and the physician had been pleased by his swift progress.

Cobletz had said, 'I'm going to extend your prescriptions, but be sure not to take the Valium more than once – or at most, twice – a day.'

'I never do,' Dom had lied.

'And only one Dalmane a night. I don't want you becoming drug-dependent. I'm sure we'll beat this thing by the first of the year.'

Dom believed Cobletz was correct, which was why he did not want to worry the doctor by confessing that there were days when he only made it through with the aid of Valium and nights when he took two or even three Dalmane tablets, washing some of them down with beer or Scotch. But in a couple of weeks he could stop taking them without fear that the somnambulism would get a new grip on him. The treatment was working. That was the important thing. The treatment was, thank God, working.

Until now.

The moon.

Frustrated and angry, he deleted the words from the diskette, a hundred lines of them, four repetitions to the line.

He stared at the screen a long time, growing increasingly nervous.

Finally he took a Valium.

*　　　*　　　*

That morning Dom got no work done, and at 11:30 he and Parker Faine picked up Denny Ulmes and Nyugen Kao Tran, the two boys assigned to them by the Orange County chapter of Big Brothers of America. They had planned a lazy afternoon at the beach, dinner at Hamburger Hamlet, and a movie, and Dominick had been looking forward to the outing.

He had become involved in the Big Brothers programme years earlier in Portland, Oregon. It had been his only community involvement, the only thing that had been able to bring him out of his rabbit hole.

He had spent his own childhood in a series of foster homes, lonely and increasingly withdrawn. Some day, when he finally got married, he hoped to adopt kids. In the meantime, when he spent time with these kids, he was not only helping them but was also comforting the lonely child within himself.

Nyugen Kao Tran preferred to be called 'Duke,' in imitation of John Wayne, whose movies he loved. Duke was thirteen, the youngest son of boat people who had fled the horrors of 'peacetime' Vietnam. He was bright, quick-witted, as startlingly agile as he was thin. His father – after surviving a brutal war, a concentration camp, and two weeks in a flimsy boat upon the open sea – had been killed three years ago in a hold-up while working at his second job as a night-shift clerk at a Seven-Eleven store in sunny southern California.

Denny Ulmes, the twelve-year-old who was Parker's little brother, lost his father to cancer. He was more reticent than

Duke, but the two got along famously, so Dom and Parker frequently combined their outings.

Parker became a Big Brother at Dom's insistence, with curmudgeonly reluctance. 'Me? *Me*? I'm not father material – or surrogate father material,' Parker had said. 'Never was and never will be. I drink too much, womanise too much. It'd be downright criminal for any kid to turn to me for advice. I'm a procrastinator, a dreamer, and a self-centred egomaniac. And I *like* me that way! What in God's name would I have to offer a kid? I don't even like dogs. Kids like dogs, but I hate 'em. Damn dirty flea-bitten things. Me, a Big Brother? Friend, you have lost your marbles for sure.'

But Thursday afternoon at the beach, when the water proved too cold for swimming, Parker organised a volleyball game and surfside races. He got Dom and the boys involved in a complicated game of his own devising, involving two frisbees, a beachball, and an empty soda can. Under his direction they also built a sandcastle complete with a menacing dragon.

Later, during an early dinner at Hamburger Hamlet in Costa Mesa, while the kids were in the bathroom, Parker said, 'Dom, good buddy, this Big Brother thing was sure one of the best ideas I've ever had.'

'*Your* idea?' Dominick said, shaking his head. 'I had to drag you into it kicking and screaming.'

'Nonsense,' Parker said. 'I've always had a way with kids. Every artist is a bit of a kid at heart. We have to stay young to create. I find kids invigorate me, keep my mind fresh.'

'Next, you'll be getting a dog,' Dom said.

Parker laughed. He finished his beer, leaned forward. 'You okay? At times today, you seemed . . . distracted. A little out of it.'

'Lot on my mind,' Dom said. 'But I'm fine. The sleep walking's pretty much stopped. And the dreams. Cobletz knows what he's doing.'

'Is the new book going well? Don't shit me, now.'

'It's going well,' Dom lied.

'At times you have that look,' Parker said, watching him intently. 'That . . . doped up. Following the prescribed dosage, I assume?'

The painter's perspicacity disconcerted Dom. 'I'd have to be

139

an idiot to snack on Valium as if it was candy. Of course I follow the prescribed dosage.'

Parker stared hard at him, then apparently decided not to push it.

* * *

The movie was good, but during the first thirty minutes Dom grew nervous without reason. When he felt the nervousness building towards an anxiety attack, he slipped out to the men's room. He'd brought another Valium for just such an emergency.

The important thing was that he was winning. He was getting well. The somnambulism was losing its grip on him. It really was.

Beneath a strong pine-scented disinfectant, there was an acrid strench from the urinals. Dom felt slightly nauseous. He swallowed the Valium without water.

* * *

That night, in spite of the pills, he had the dream again, and he remembered more of it than just the part where people were forcing his head into a sink.

In the nightmare, he was in a bed in an unknown room, where there seemed to be an oily saffron mist in the air. Or perhaps the amber fog was only in his eyes, for he could not see anything clearly. Furniture loomed beyond the bed, and at least two people were present. But those shapes rippled and writhed as if this were purely a realm of smoke and fluid, where nothing had a fixed appearance.

He almost felt as if he were under water, very deep beneath the surface of some mysterious cold sea. The atmosphere in the dream-place had more weight than mere air. He could barely draw breath. Each inhalation and exhalation was agony. He sensed that he was dying.

The two blurred figures came close. They seemed concerned about his condition. They spoke urgently to each other. Although he knew they were speaking English, he could not understand them. A cold hand touched him. He heard the clink of glass. Somewhere a door shut.

With the flash-cut suddenness of a scene transition in a film, the dream shifted to a bathroom or kitchen. Someone was forcing his face down into the sink. Breathing became even more difficult. The air was like mud: with each inhalation it clogged his nostrils. He choked and gasped and tried to blow out the mud-thick air, and the two people with him were shouting at him, and as before he could not understand what they were saying, and they pressed his face down into the sink—

Dom woke and was still in bed. Last weekend he had been flung free of the dream only to discover that he had walked in his sleep and had been acting out the nightmare at his own bathroom sink. This time, he was relieved to find himself beneath the sheets.

I *am* getting better, he thought.

Trembling, he sat up and switched on the light.

No barricades. No signs of somnambulistic panic.

He looked at the digital clock: 2:09 a.m. A half-empty can of warm beer stood on the nightstand. He washed down another Dalmane tablet.

I am getting better.

It was Friday the thirteenth.

10.

ELKO COUNTY, NEVADA

Friday night, three days after his weird experience on the I-80, Ernie Block couldn't sleep at all. As darkness embraced him, his nerves wound tighter, tighter, until he thought he would start screaming and be unable to stop.

Slipping out of bed as soundlessly as he could, pausing to make sure that Faye's slow and even breathing had not changed, he went into the bathroom, closed the door, turned on the light. Wonderful light. He revelled in the light. He put down the lid of the commode and sat for fifteen minutes in his underwear, just letting the brightness sear him, as mindlessly happy as a lizard on a sun-washed rock.

Finally he knew he must return to the bedroom. If Faye woke, and if he remained in here too long, she would begin to think something was wrong. He was determined to do nothing that would make her suspicious.

Although he had not used the toilet, he flushed it for cover, and went to the sink to wash his hands. He had just finished rinsing off the soap and had plucked the towel off the rack when his eyes were drawn to the only window of the room. It was above the bathtub, a rectangle about three feet wide and two feet high, which opened outwards on an overhead piano hinge. Although the glass was frosted and provided no view of the night beyond, a shiver passed through Ernie as he stared at the opaque pane. More disturbing than the shiver was the sudden rush of peculiar, urgent thoughts that came with it:

The window's big enough to get through, I could get away, escape, and the roof of the utility room is under the window, so there's not a long drop, and I could be off, into the arroyo behind the motel, up into the hills, make my way east, get to a ranch somewhere and get help. . . .

Blinking furiously as that swift train of thoughts flashed through his mind and faded away, Ernie discovered that he had stepped from the sink to the bathtub. He did not remember moving.

He was bewildered by the urge to escape. From whom? From what? Why? This was his own home. He had nothing to fear within these walls.

Yet he could not take his gaze from the milky window. A dreaminess had come over him. He was aware of it but unable to cast it off.

Got to get out, get away, there won't be another chance, not another chance like this, now, go now, go, go . . .

Unwittingly, he had stepped into the tub and was directly in front of the window, which was set in the wall at face-level. The porcelain coating of the tub was cold against his bare feet.

Slide back the latch, push up the window, stand on the rim of the tub, pull yourself up onto the sill, out and away, a three- or four-minute headstart before you're missed, not much but enough . . .

Panic rose in him without reason. There was a fluttering in his guts, a tightness in his chest.

Without knowing why he was doing it, yet unable to stop

142

himself, he slid the bolt from the latch on the bottom of the window. He pushed out. The window swung up.

He was not alone.

Something was at the other side of the window, out there on the roof, something with a dark, featureless, shiny face. Even as Ernie recoiled in surprise, he realised it was a man in a white helmet with a tinted visor that came all the way down over his face, so darkly tinted that it was virtually black.

A black-gloved hand reached through the window, as if to grab him, and Ernie cried out and took a step backwards and fell over the edge of the tub. Toppling out of the tub, he grabbed wildly at the shower curtain, tore it loose from several of its rings, but could not arrest his fall. He hit the bathroom floor with a crash. Pain flashed through his right hip.

'*Ernie!*' Faye cried, and a moment later she pushed open the door. 'Ernie, my God, what's wrong, what happened?'

'Stay back.' He got up painfully. 'Someone's out there.'

Cold night air poured through the open window, rustling the half-wrecked, bunched-up shower curtain.

Faye shivered, for she slept in only a pyjama-shirt and panties.

Ernie shivered, too, though partly for different reasons. The moment the pain had throbbed through his hip, the dreaminess had left him. In the sudden rush of clear-mindedness, he wondered if the helmeted figure had been imaginary, a hallucination.

'On the roof?' Faye said. 'At the window? Who?'

'I don't know,' Ernie said, rubbing his sore hip as he stepped back into the tub and peered out the window again. He saw no one this time.

'What'd he look like? Faye asked.

'I couldn't tell. He was in motorcycle gear. Helmet, gloves,' Ernie said, realising how outlandish it sounded.

He levered himself up on the windowsill far enough to lean out and look across the full length and breadth of the utility room's roof. Shadows were deep in places, but nowhere deep enough to hide a man. The intruder was gone – if he had ever existed.

Abruptly Ernie became aware of the vast darkness behind the motel. It stretched across the hills, off to the distant mountains, an immense blackness relieved only by the stars. Instantly, a crippling weakness and vulnerability overwhelmed him. Gasping, he dropped off the sill, back into the tub, and started to turn away from the window.

'Close it up,' Faye said.

Squeezing his eyes shut to guard against another glimpse of the night, he turned once more to the in-rushing cold air, fumbled blindly for the window and pulled it shut so hard that he almost broke the pane. With unsteady hands he struggled to secure the latch bolt.

When he stepped out of the tub, he saw concern in Faye's eyes, which he expected. He saw surprise, which he also expected. But he saw a penetrating awareness for which he was unprepared. For a long moment they looked at each other, neither of them speaking.

Then she said, 'Are you ready to tell me about it?'

'Like I said . . . I thought I saw a guy on the roof.'

'That's not what I'm talking about, Ernie. I mean, are you ready to tell me what's wrong, what's been eating at you?' Her eyes did not waver from his. 'For a couple of months now. Maybe longer.'

He was stunned. He thought he had concealed it so well.

She said, 'Honey, you've been worried. Worried like I've never seen you before. And scared.'

'No. Not scared exactly.'

'Yes. Scared,' Faye said, but there was no scorn in her, just an Iowan's forthrightness and a desire to help. 'I've only ever seen you scared once before, Ernie – back when Lucy was five and came down with that muscle fever, and they thought it might be muscular dystrophy.'

'God, yes, I was scared shitless then.'

'But not since.'

'Oh, I was scared in Nam sometimes,' he said, his admission echoing hollowly off the bathroom walls.

'But *I* never saw it.' She hugged herself. 'It's rare that I see you like this, Ernie, so when you're scared *I'm* scared. Can't help it. I'm even more scared because I don't know what's *wrong*. You understand? Being in the dark like I am . . . that's worse than any secret you're withholding from me.'

144

Tears came to her eyes, and Ernie said, 'Oh, hey, don't cry. It's going to be all right, Faye. Really it is.'

'*Tell me!*' she said.

'Okay.'

'Now. Everything.'

He had woefully underestimated her, and he felt thick-headed. She was a Corps wife, after all, and a good one. She had followed him from Quantico to Singapore to Pendleton in California, even to Alaska, almost everywhere but Nam and, later, Beirut. She had made a home for them wherever the Corps allowed dependents to follow, had weathered the bad times with admirable aplomb, had never complained, and had never failed him. She was tough. He could not imagine how he had forgotten that.

'Everything,' he agreed, relieved to be able to share the burden.

*   *   *

Faye made coffee, and they sat in their robes and slippers at the kitchen table while he told her everything. She could see that he was embarrassed. He was slow to reveal details, but she sipped her coffee, remained patient, and gave him a chance to tell it in his own way.

Ernie was about the best husband a woman could want, but now and then his Block-family stubbornness reared its head, and Faye wanted to shake some sense into him. Everyone in his family suffered from it, especially the men. Blocks did things *this* way, never *that* way, and you better never question why. Block men liked their undershirts ironed but never their underpants. Block women *always* wore a bra, even at home in the worst summer heat. Blocks, both men and women, always ate lunch at precisely twelve-thirty, always had dinner at six-thirty sharp, and God forbid if the food was put on the table two minutes late: the subsequent complaining would burst eardrums. Blocks drove only General Motors' vehicles. Not because GM products were notably better than others, but because Blocks had *always* driven only General Motors' vehicles.

Thank God, Ernie was not a tenth as bad as his father or brothers. He had been wise enough to get out of Pittsburgh, where the Block clan had lived for generations in the same neighbourhood. Out in the real world, away from the Kingdom of the Blocks, Ernie had loosened up. In the Marine Corps he could not expect every meal at precisely the time that Block tradition demanded. And soon after their marriage, Faye had made it clear that she would make a first-rate home for him but would not be bound by senseless traditions. Ernie adapted, though not always easily, and now he was a black sheep among his people, guilty of such sins as driving a variety of vehicles not made by General Motors.

Actually, the only area where the Block-family stubbornness still had a hold on Ernie was in some man-woman matters. He believed that a husband had to protect his wife from a variety of unpleasantness that she was just too fragile to handle. He believed that a husband should never allow his wife to see him in a moment of weakness. Although their marriage had never been conducted according to those rules, Ernie did not always seem to realise they had abandoned the Block traditions more than a quarter of a century ago.

For months, she had been aware something was seriously wrong. But Ernie continued to stonewall it, straining to prove he was a happy retired Marine blissfully launched on a second career in motels. She had watched an unknown fire consuming him from within, and her subtle and patient attempts to get him to open up had gone right over his head.

During the past few weeks, ever since returning from Wisconsin after Thanksgiving, she had been increasingly aware of his reluctance – even inability – to go out at night. He could not seem to make himself comfortable in a room where even one lamp was left unlit.

Now, as they sat in the kitchen with cups of steaming coffee, the blinds tightly closed and all the lights on, Faye listened intently to Ernie, interrupting only when he seemed to need a word of encouragement to keep him going, and nothing he told her was more than she could cope with. Indeed, her spirits rose, for she was increasingly certain that she knew what was wrong with him and how he might be helped.

He finished, his voice low and thin. 'So . . . is that the reward for all the years of hard work and careful financial planning? Premature senility? Now, when we can really start

146

enjoying what we've earned, am I going to wind up with my brains all scrambled, drooling, pissing my pants, useless to myself and a burden on you? Twenty years before my time? Christ, Faye, I've always realised that life isn't fair, but I never thought the deck was stacked against me *this* bad.'

'It won't be like that.' she reached across the table and took his hand. 'Sure, Alzheimer's can strike people even younger than you, but this isn't Alzheimer's. From what I've read, from the way it was with my father, I don't think the onset of senility – premature or otherwise – is ever like this. What it sounds like is a simple phobia. Phobia. Some people have an irrational fear of flying or heights. For some reason, you've developed a fear of the dark. It can be overcome.'

'But phobias just don't develop overnight, do they?'

Their right hands were still clasped. She squeezed his as she said, 'Do you remember Helen Dorfman? Almost twenty-four years ago. Our landlady when you were first assigned to Camp Pendleton.'

'Oh, yeah! The building on Vine Street, lived in number one, first floor front. We lived in number six.' He seemed to take heart from his ability to recall those details. 'She had a cat . . . Sable. Remember how the damn cat took a liking to us, left little gifts on our doorstep?'

'Dead mice.'

'Yeah. Right there beside the morning paper and the milk.' He laughed, blinked, and said, 'Hey, I see what you mean by bringing up Helen Dorfman! She was afraid to go out of her apartment. Couldn't even walk out on her own lawn.'

'The poor woman had agoraphobia,' Faye said. 'An irrational fear of open spaces. She was a prisoner in her own home. Outside, she was overwhelmed with fear. Doctors call it a "panic attack" I think.'

'Panic attack,' Ernie said softly. 'Yeah, that's it, all right.'

'And Helen didn't develop her agoraphobia till she was *thirty-five*, after her husband died. Phobias *can* spring up suddenly, later in life.'

'Well, whatever the hell a phobia *is*, wherever it comes from . . . I guess it's a lot better than senility. But good God, I don't want to spend the rest of my life being afraid of the dark.'

'You won't have to,' Faye said. 'Twenty-four years ago,

147

nobody understood phobias. There hadn't been much study done. No effective treatments. But it's not like that now. I'm sure it's not.'

He was silent for a moment. 'I'm not crazy, Faye.'

'I know that, you big jerk.'

He mulled over the word 'phobia,' and he plainly wanted to believe her answer. In his blue eyes, she saw a rebirth of hope.

He said, 'But the weird experience I had on the interstate on Tuesday . . . And the hallucination – I'm sure it must've been an hallucination – of the motorcyclist on the roof . . . How does stuff like that fit this explanation? How could that be a part of my phobia?'

'I don't know. But an expert in the field could explain it all and tie it together. I'm sure it's not as unusual as it seems, Ernie.'

He pondered for a moment, then nodded. 'Okay. But how do we begin? Where do we go for help? How do I *beat* this damn thing?'

'I already have it figured out,' she said. 'No doctor in Elko is going to know how to treat a case like this. We need a specialist, someone who deals with phobic patients every day. Probably isn't anyone like that in Reno, either. We'll have to go to a bigger city. Now, I suspect Milwaukee's big enough to have a doctor with experience in these things, and we could stay with Lucy and Frank –'

'And at the same time get to see a lot of Frank Jr. and Dorie,' Ernie said, smiling at the thought of his grandchildren.

'Right. We'll go there for Christmas a week sooner than planned, this Sunday instead of next. Which is tomorrow, in fact. It's already Saturday. When we get to Milwaukee, we'll look up a doctor. If, by New Year's it looks like we'll have to stay there a while, then I'll fly back here, find a full-time couple to manage the place, and rejoin you. We were planning to hire somebody this spring, anyway.'

'If we close the motel a week early, Sandy and Ned will lose out on some money over at the Grille.'

'Ned will still get truckers off the interstate. And if he doesn't do as well as usual, we'll make it up to him.'

Ernie shook his head and smiled. 'You've got it all worked out. You're something, Faye. You sure are. You're an absolute wonder.'

'Well, I will admit I can be dazzling sometimes.'

'I thank God every day that I found you,' he said.

'I don't have any regrets either, Ernie, and I know I never will.'

'You know, I feel a thousand per cent better than when we first sat down here. Why'd it take me so damn long to ask you for help?'

'Why? Because you're a Block,' she said.

He grinned and finished the old joke: 'Which is only one step removed from a blockhead.'

They laughed. He grabbed her hand again and kissed it. 'That's the first *real* laugh I've had in weeks. We're a terrific team, Faye. We can face anything together, can't we?'

'Anything,' she agreed.

It was Saturday, December 14, near dawn, and Faye Block was sure they would come out on top of their current problem, just as they had always come out on top before when they worked together, side by side.

She, like Ernie, had already forgotten the unidentified Polaroid photograph that they had received in a plain envelope last Tuesday.

11.

BOSTON, MASSACHUSETTS

On an intricately crocheted doily, on the highly polished maple dresser, lay black gloves and a stainless-steel ophthalmoscope.

Ginger Weiss stood at a window to the left of the dresser, looking out at the bay, where the grey water seemed to be a mirror image of the ashen mid-December sky. Farther shores were hidden by a lingering morning mist that shimmered with a pearly luminosity. At the end of the Hannaby property, at the bottom of a rocky slope, a private dock thrust out into the choppy bay. The dock was covered with snow, as was the long expanse of lawn leading back to the house.

149

It was a big house, built in the 1850s, with new rooms added in 1892, in 1905, and again in 1950. The brick driveway curved beneath an enormous front portico, and broad brick steps led up to massive doors. Pillars, pilasters, carved granite lintels above doors and windows, a multitude of gables and circular dormers, bay-facing second-storey balconies at the back, and a large widow's walk on the roof contributed to an impression of majesty.

Even for a surgeon as successful as George, the house might have been too expensive, but he had not needed to buy it. He had inherited the place from his father, and his father had inherited it from George's grandfather, and *his* father had bought it in 1884. The house even had a name – Baywatch – like ancestral homes in British novels, and more than anything else, that inspired awe in Ginger. Houses in Brooklyn, where she came from, did not have their own names.

At Memorial, Ginger never felt uncomfortable around George. There, he was a figure of authority and respect, but he seemed to have his roots in common stock like everyone else. At Baywatch, however, Ginger was aware of the patrician heritage and that made George different from her. He never never invoked a claim to privilege. That would not be like him. But the ghost of the New England patriciate haunted the rooms and corridors of Baywatch, often making her feel out of place.

The corner guest suite – bedroom, reading alcove, and bath – in which Ginger had been settled for the past ten days, was simpler than many chambers in Baywatch, and there she was almost as comfortable as in her own apartment. Most of the pegged-oak floor was covered by a figured Serapi carpet in shades of blue and peach. The walls were peach, the ceiling white. The maple furniture, which consisted of various kinds of chests used as nightstands and tables and dressers, had all come off 19th-century sailing ships owned by George's great-grandfather. There were two upholstered armchairs covered in peach-coloured silk from Brunschwig & Fils. On the night-stands, the bases of the lamps were actually Baccarat candlesticks, a reminder that the apparent simplicity of the room was built upon an elegant foundation.

Ginger went to the dresser and stared down at the black

gloves that lay upon the doily. As she had done countless times during the past ten days, she put the gloves on, flexed her hands, waiting for a rush of fear. But they were only ordinary gloves that she had bought the day she had been discharged from the hospital, and they did not have the power to bring her to the trembling edge of a fugue. She took them off.

A knock sounded at the door, and Rita Hannaby said, 'Ginger, dear, are you ready?'

'Coming,' she said, snatching her purse from the bed and taking one last quick glance at herself in the dresser mirror.

She was wearing a lime-green knit suit with a creamy-white blouse that had a simple lime-green bow at the throat. Her ensemble included a pair of green pumps that matched the suit, an eel-skin purse that matched the pumps, a gold and malachite bracelet. The outfit perfectly complemented her complexion and golden hair. She thought she looked chic. Well, perhaps not chic, but at least reasonably stylish.

However, when she stepped into the hall and got a look at Rita Hannaby, Ginger felt at a disadvantage, a mere pretender to class.

Rita was as slim as Ginger, but at five-eight she was six inches taller, and everything about her was queenly. Her chestnut-brown hair swept back from her face in a perfectly feathered cut. If her facial bones had been more exquisitely chiselled, she would have looked severe. However, beauty and warmth were assured by her luminous grey eyes, translucent skin, and generous mouth. Rita was wearing a grey St John's suit, pearls, pearl earrings, and a broad-brimmed black hat.

To Ginger, the amazing thing was that Rita's fashionable appearance did not seem planned. One had no sense that she had spent hours getting ready. Instead, she seemed to have been *born* with impeccable grooming and a fashionably tailored wardrobe; elegance was her natural condition.

'You look smashing!' Rita said.

'Next to you, I feel like a frump in bluejeans and a sweatshirt.'

'Nonsense. Even if I were twenty years younger, I'd be no match for you, dear. Wait and see who the waiters pamper the most at lunch.'

Ginger had no false modesty. She knew she was attractive. But her beauty was more that of a pixie, while Rita had the

151

blueblood looks of one who could sit upon a throne and convince the world she belonged.

Rita did nothing to cause Ginger's newfound inferiority complex. The woman treated her not like a daughter but like a sister and an equal. Ginger's feelings of inadequacy were, she knew, a direct result of her pathetic condition. Until two weeks ago, she had not been dependent on anyone in ages. Now she was dependent again, not entirely able to look after herself, and her self-respect slipped a bit further every day. Rita Hannaby's good humour, carefully planned outings, woman-to-woman *shmoosing*, and unflagging encouragement were not enough to distract Ginger from the cruel fact that fate once more had cast her, at thirty, in the frustrating role of a child.

Together, they descended to the marble-floored foyer, where they got their coats from the closet, then went out the door and down the steps under the portico to the black Mercedes 500 SEL in the driveway. Herbert, who was sort of a cross between a butler and a man-Friday, had brought the car around five minutes ago and had left the engine running, so the interior was a toasty-warm haven from the frigid winter day.

Rita drove with her usual confidence, away from the old estates, out of quiet streets lined with bare-limbed elms and maples, through ever-busier thoroughfares, heading to Dr Immanuel Gudhausen's office on bustling State Street. Ginger had an eleven-thirty appointment with Gudhausen, whom she had seen twice last week. She was scheduled to visit him every Monday, Wednesday, and Friday until they got to the bottom of her attacks of fugue. In her bleaker moments, Ginger was sure she'd still be lying on Gudhausen's couch thirty years from now.

Rita intended to do a bit of shopping while Ginger was with the doctor. Then they would go to lunch at some exquisite restaurant in which, no doubt, the decor would seem to have been planned to flatter Rita Hannaby and in which Ginger would feel like a schoolgirl foolishly trying to pass for a grown-up.

'Have you given some thought to what I suggested last Friday?' Rita asked as she drove. 'The Women's Auxiliary at the hospital?'

'I don't really think I'm up to it. I'd feel so . . . awkward.'

'It's important work,' Rita said, expertly slipping the Mercedes out from behind a *Globe* newspaper truck, into a gap in traffic.

'I know. I've seen how much money you've raised for the hospital, the new equipment you've bought . . . but I think I've got to stay away from Memorial right now. It'd be too frustrating to be around the place, too constant a reminder that I can't do the work I've been trained for.'

'I understand, dear. Don't give it another thought. But there's still the Symphony Committee, the Women's League for the Aged, and the Children's Advocacy Committee. We could use your help at any of those.'

Rita was an indefatigable charity worker, ably chairing committees or serving on them, not only organising beneficent societies but getting her hands dirty in the operation of them. 'What about it?' she pressed. 'I'm sure you'd find working with children especially rewarding.'

'Rita, what if I had one of my attacks while I was with the children? It would frighten them, and I –'

'Oh, pish-posh,' Rita said. 'Every time I've got you out of the house these last two weeks, you've used that same excuse to try to resist leaving your room. "Oh, Rita," you say, "I'll have one of my awful fits and embarrass you." But you haven't, and you won't. Even if you *did*, it wouldn't embarrass me. I don't embarrass easily, dear.'

'I never thought for a moment you were a shrinking violet. But you haven't seen me in this fugue state. You don't know what I'm like or –'

'Oh, for goodness sake, you make it sound as if you're a regular Dr Jekyll and Mr Hyde – or *Ms*. Hyde – which I'm sure you're not. You haven't beaten anyone to death with a cane yet, have you, Ms Hyde?'

Ginger laughed and shook her head. 'You're something else, Rita.'

'Excellent. You'll bring so much to the organisation.'

Although Rita probably did not think of Ginger as another charity case, she had approached this recuperation and rehabilitation as a new cause. She rolled up her sleeves and *committed* herself to seeing Ginger through the current crisis, and nothing on earth was going to stop her. Ginger was touched

153

by Rita's concern – and depressed by the need for it.

They stopped at a traffic light, third car from the intersection, with cars, trucks, buses, taxis, and delivery vans crowding them on all sides. In the Mercedes, the cacophony of the city was muffled but not silenced altogether, and when Ginger looked out the window at her side to search for the source of a particularly annoying engine roar, she saw a large motorcycle. The rider turned his head towards her at that moment, but she could not see his face. He was wearing a helmet with a tinted visor that came all the way down to his chin.

For the first time in ten days, the amnesic mist descended over Ginger. It happened much faster this time than it had with the black gloves, opthalmoscope, or sink drain. She looked into the blank and shiny visor, and her heart stuttered, and her breath was pinched off, and she was instantly swept away by a massive wave of terror, gone.

*   *   *

First, Ginger became aware of horns. Car horns, bus horns, the air-horns of trucks. Some like the high squeals of animals, some low and ominous. Wailing, whooping, barking, shrieking, honking, bleating.

She opened her eyes. Her vision swam into focus. She was still in the car. The intersection was still in front of them, though evidently a couple of minutes had passed and the traffic ahead had moved. With the engine running but the gearshift in park, the Mercedes was ten feet closer the crosswalk and angled slightly into the next lane, which was what was causing the horn blowing as other vehicles tried to get around.

Ginger heard herself whimpering.

Rita Hannaby was leaning across the console that separated the driver's and passenger's seats, very close, gripping both of Ginger's hands, holding them down and holding them very tightly. 'Ginger? Are you there? Are you all right? Ginger?'

Blood. After the jarring blasts of the horns, after Rita's voice, Ginger became aware of the blood. Red spots marked her lime-green skirt. A dark smear stained the sleeve of her suit jacket. Her hands were gloved in blood, as were Rita's hands.

'Oh, my God,' Ginger said.

'Ginger, are you with me? Are you back? Ginger?' One of Rita's manicured nails was torn off, with only a splintered stub sticking up jaggedly from the cuticle, and both her hands appeared to have been *gouged*. Scratches on the woman's fingers, on the backs of her hands, and on her palms were bleeding freely, and as far as Ginger could tell, all of the blood was Rita's, none of it her own. The cuffs of the grey St John's suit were wet with blood. 'Ginger, talk to me.'

Horns continued to blare.

Ginger looked up and saw that Rita's perfectly coiffured hair was now in disarray. A two-inch-long scratch furrowed her left cheek, and blood tinted with make-up was trickling along her jaw to her chin.

'You're back,' Rita said with obvious relief, letting go of Ginger's hands.

'What've I done?'

'Only scratches,' Rita said. 'It's all right. You had an attack, panicked, tried to leave the car. I couldn't let you go. You might've been hit in traffic.'

A passing driver, manoeuvering around the Mercedes, angrily shouted something unintelligible at them.

'I've hurt you,' Ginger said. Sickness throbbed through her at the thought of the violence she had done.

Other drivers sounded their horns with increasing impatience, but Rita ignored them. She took Ginger's hands again, not to restrain her this time but to offer comfort and reassurance. 'It's all right, dear. It's passed now, and a little iodine will patch me up just fine.'

The motorcyclist. The dark visor.

Ginger looked out the side window; the cyclist was gone. He had, after all, been no threat to her, just a stranger passing in the street.

Black gloves, an ophthalmoscope, a sink drain, and now the dark visor of a motorcyclist's helmet. Why had those particular things set her off? What did they have in common, if anything?

As tears spilled down her face, Ginger said, 'I'm so sorry.'

'No need to be. Now, I better get us out of the way,' Rita said. She pulled handfuls of Kleenex from the box on the console and used them to grip the wheel and gearshift, to avoid spreading bloodstains.

Her own hands wet with Rita's blood, Ginger sagged back against her seat and closed her eyes and tried to stop the tears but could not.

Four psychotic episodes in five weeks.

She could no longer glide placidly through the grey winter days, defenceless, docile in the face of this vicious turn of fate, merely waiting for another attack or for a shrink to explain what was wrong.

It was Monday, December 16, and Ginger was suddenly determined to *do* something before she suffered a fifth fugue. She could not imagine what she possibly could do, but she was sure she'd think of something if she put her mind to it and stopped feeling sorry for herself. She had reached bottom now. Her humiliation, fear, and despair could not bring her to any greater depths. There was nowhere to go but up. She would claw her way back to the surface, damned if she wouldn't, up toward the light, out of the dark into which she had fallen.

THREE

Christmas Eve – Christmas Day

1.

LAGUNA BEACH, CALIFORNIA

At 8:00 a.m. Tuesday, December 24, when Dom Corvaisis got out of bed, he went through his morning ablutions in a haze resulting from the lingering effects of yesterday's indulgence in Valium and Dalmane.

For the eleventh night in a row, he had been troubled by neither somnambulism nor the bad dream that involved the sink. The drug therapy was working, and he was willing to tolerate a period of pharmaceutically induced detachment to put an end to his unnerving midnight journeys.

He did not believe he was in danger of becoming physically addicted to – or even psychologically dependent on – Valium or Dalmane. He *had* been exceeding the prescribed dosage, but he was still not worried. He had almost run out of pills, and in order to get another prescription from Dr Cobletz, he had fabricated a story about a break-in at his house, claiming that the drugs had been taken along with his stereo and TV set. Dom had *lied* to his doctor in order to obtain drugs, and sometimes he saw his action in exactly that harsh and un-favourable light; but most of the time, in the soft haze that accompanied continuous tranquillisation, he was able to dress the shabby truth in self-delusion.

He dared not think about what would happen to him if the episodes of somnambulism returned in January, after the drugs were discontinued.

At ten o'clock, unable to concentrate enough to work, he put

157

on a light corduroy jacket and left the house. The late-December morning was cool. Except for a few unseasonably warm days now and then, the beaches would not be busy again until April.

As Dom descended the hills in his Firebird, heading for the centre of town, he noticed that Laguna looked dull under a sombre grey sky. He wondered how much of the leaden gloom was real and how much resulted from the dulling effect of the drugs, but he quickly abandoned that disturbing line of thought. In acknowledgement of his somewhat fuzzy perceptions and impaired responsiveness, he drove with exaggerated care.

Dom received most mail at the post office. Because he subscribed to so many publications, he rented a large drawer rather than just a box, and that day before Christmas, the drawer was more than half full. He didn't look at the return addresses but carried everything back to the car with the intention of reading his mail at breakfast.

The Cottage, a popular restaurant for decades, was on the east side of Pacific Coast Highway, on the slope above the road. At that hour, the breakfast rush had passed, and the lunch crowd had not yet arrived. Dom was given a table by the window with the best view. He ordered two eggs, bacon, cottage fries, toast, and grapefruit juice.

As he ate, he went through the mail. In addition to magazines and bills, there was a letter from Lennart Sane, the wonderful Swedish agent who handled translation rights in Scandinavia and Holland, and a padded envelope from Random House. As soon as he saw the publisher's address on the label, he knew what he had. Finally, his mind began to clear, the fuzziness partially dispelled by excitement. He put down the toast he had been eating and tore open the large envelope, and an advance copy of his first novel slid out. No man can know what a woman feels when taking her newborn child in her arms for the first time, but a novelist who holds the first copy of his first book must experience a joy similar to that of the mother who looks upon the face of her baby for the first time and feels its warmth through the swaddling clothes.

Dom kept the book beside his plate and could barely look

away from it. He had finished his meal and had ordered coffee by the time he was able to tear his attention from *Twilight* and examine what mail remained. Among other things, there was a plain white envelope with no return address, which contained a single page of white paper on which had been type-written two sentences that rocked him:

> The sleepwalker would be well-advised to search the past for the source of his problem. That is where the secret is buried.

He read the message again, astonished. The sheet of paper rattled as a tremor passed through him. The back of his neck went cold.

2.
BOSTON, MASSACHUSETTS

When Ginger got out of the cab, she was in front of a six-storey, brick, Victorian Gothic building. A blustery wind slapped her, and the bare-limbed trees along Newbury Street rasped, clattered, and clicked: the sound of rattling bones. Huddling against the bitter wind, she scurried past a low iron fence and entered 127 Newbury, the former Hotel Agassiz, one of the city's finest historic landmarks, now converted into condominiums. She had come to see Pablo Jackson, about whom she knew only what she had read in yesterday's *Boston Globe*.

She had left Baywatch after George departed for the hospital and after Rita went off to do some last-minute Christmas shopping, for she had been afraid they would try to stop her. In fact, the maid, Lavinia, had pleaded with her not to go out alone. Ginger had left a note, explaining her whereabouts, and she hoped they would not be too upset.

When Pablo Jackson opened his door, Ginger was surprised. That he was a black man, that he was in his eighties – those things were not surprising, for she had learned as much about him from the article in the *Globe*. However, she was not prepared for such a vital and vigorous octogenarian. He was about five-eight, slight, but age had not bowed his legs, bent his back, or rounded his shoulders. He stood militarily erect, in white shirt and sharply creased black trousers, and there was a sprightliness and youthfulness in his smile and in the way he waved her into the apartment. His thick kinky hair had not receded, but it had gone so white that it seemed to glow with a spectral light, giving him a curiously mystical aura. He escorted Ginger into the living room, moving with the stride of a man forty or fifty years his junior.

The living room was a surprise, too, not what she expected either of a sedate old monument like the Hotel Agassiz or of Pablo Jackson, an elderly bachelor. The walls were cream-coloured, and the contemporary sofas and chairs were uphol-stered in a matching fabric. An Edward Fields carpet of the same creamy shade provided relief from the dominant scheme by means of a deeply sculpted wave pattern. Colour was provided by pastel accent pillows – yellow, peach, green, and blue – on the sofas, and from two large oil paintings, one a Picasso. The result was an airy, bright, warm, and modern decor.

Ginger settled into one of two armchairs that faced each other across a small table near a long, bay window. She declined coffee and said, 'Mr Jackson, I'm afraid I'm here under false pretences.'

'What an interesting beginning,' he said, smiling, crossing his legs, resting his long-fingered black hands on the arms of his chair.

'No, really, I'm not a reporter.'

'Not from *People*?' He studied her speculatively. 'Well, that's all right. I knew you weren't a reporter when I let you in. These days, reporters have an oily smoothness about them, and they're an arrogant lot. Soon as I saw you standing at the door, I said to myself, "Pablo, this bitty girl is no reporter. She's a *real* person."'

'I need some help that only you can provide.'

'A damsel in distress?' he said, amused. He seemed not at all angry or uneasy, which she had expected he would be.

She said, 'I was afraid you wouldn't see me if I told you my real reasons for wanting to meet you. You see, I'm a doctor, a

160

surgical resident at Memorial, and when I read the article about you in the *Globe*, I thought you might be able to help.'

'I'd be delighted to see you even if you were selling magazines. An eighty-one-year-old man can't afford to turn anyone away . . . unless he prefers to spend his days talking to the walls.'

Ginger appreciated his efforts to put her at ease, though she suspected that his social life was more interesting than her own.

He said, 'Besides, not even a burnt-out old fossil like me would turn away such a lovely girl as you. But now tell me what this help is that only I can give you.'

Ginger leaned forward in her chair. 'First, I've got to know if the article in the newspaper was accurate.'

He shrugged. 'As accurate as newspaper articles ever are. My mother and father were expatriate Americans living in France, just as the newspaper said. She was a popular chanteuse, a cafe singer in Paris, before and after World War I. My father was a musician, as the *Globe* said. And it's true that my parents knew Picasso and recognised his genius early on. I was named after him. They bought two score of Picasso's pieces when his work was cheap, and he gave them several paintings as gifts. They had *bon gout*. They didn't own a hundred works, as the paper said, but fifty. Still, that collection was an embarrassment of riches. Sold gradually over the years, it cushioned their retirement and gave me something to fall back on as well.'

'You *were* an accomplished stage magician?'

'For over fifty years,' he said, raising both hands in a graceful and elegant expression of amazement at his own longevity. That gesture was marked by the rhythm and fluidity of prestidigitation, and Ginger half-expected him to pluck living white doves from thin air. 'And I was famous, too. *Sans pareil*, even if I say so myself. Not famous over here so much, you understand, but all over Europe and in England.'

'And your act involved hypnotising a few members of the audience?'

He nodded. 'That was the centrepiece. It always wowed them.'

'And now you're helping the police by hypnotising

161

witnesses to crimes, so they can recall details they've forgotten.'

'Well, it's not a full-time job,' he said, waving one slender hand as if to dismiss any such thoughts she might have had. The gesture seemed likely to end with the magical appearance of a bouquet of flowers or deck of cards. 'In fact, they've only come to me four times in the past two years. I'm usually their last resort.'

'But what you've done has worked for them?'

'Oh, yes. Just as the newspaper said. For instance, a by-stander might see a murder take place and get a glimpse of the car in which the killer escaped, but not be able to recall the licence number. Now, if he glanced at the licence even for a split second, that number is buried in his subconscious mind, 'cause we never really forget anything we see. Never. So if a hypnotist puts the witness in a trance, regresses him in time – that is, takes him back in his memories to the shooting – and tells him to look at the car, then the licence number can be obtained.'

'Always?'

'Not always. But we win more than we lose.'

'Why turn to you? Aren't the police department's psychia-trists capable of using hypnosis?'

'Certainly. But they're psychiatrists not hypnotists. Hypno-sis is not what they *specialised* in. I've made it a lifelong study, developed my own techniques that often succeed where standard methods fail.'

'So when it comes to hypnotism, you're a maven.'

'An expert? Yes, that's true. Even a *maven's maven*. But why does any of this interest you, Doctor?'

Ginger had been sitting with her purse in her lap and her hands at rest upon it. But as she told Pablo Jackson about her attacks, she clutched the purse tighter, tighter, until her knuckles were white.

Jackson's relaxed demeanour changed to shocked interest and concern. 'You poor child. You poor, poor little thing. *De mal en pis – en pis*! From bad to worse – to worse! How horrible. You wait there. Don't you move.' He popped up from the chair and hurried from the room.

When he returned, he was carrying two glasses of brandy. She tried to refuse hers. 'No thank you, Mr Jackson. I don't

162

drink much, and certainly not at this hour of the morning.'

'Call me Pablo. How much sleep did you get last night? Not much? You were up most of the night, woke up hours ago, so for *you* this isn't morning, it's the middle of the afternoon. And there's no reason a person can't have a drink in the afternoon, is there?'

He settled into his chair again, and for a moment they were silent as they sipped their brandies.

Then she said, 'Pablo, I want you to hypnotise me, regress me back to the morning of November 12, to Bernstein's Delicatessen. I want you to hold me at that point in time and question me relentlessly until I can explain *why* the sight of those black gloves terrified me.'

'Impossible!' He shook his head. 'No, no.'

'I can pay whatever —'

'Money is not the issue. I don't need money.' He frowned. 'I'm a magician, not a physician.'

'I'm already seeing a psychiatrist, and I've broached the subject with him, but he won't do it.'

'He must have his reasons.'

'He says it's too soon for hypnotic regression therapy. He admits the technique might help me discover the cause of my attacks, but he says that might be a mistake because I might not yet be ready to face up to the truth. He says premature confrontation with the source of my anxieties might contribute to . . . a breakdown.'

'You see? He knows best. I would be meddling.'

'He does *not* know best,' Ginger insisted, angered by the vivid recollection of her recent conversation with the psychiatrist, in which he had been infuriatingly condescending. 'Maybe he knows what's best for most patients, but he doesn't know what's best for *me*. I can't go on like this. By the time Gudhausen's willing to resort to hypnosis, maybe in a year, I'll no longer be sane enough to benefit. I've got to get a grip on this problem, take control, *do* something.'

'But surely you see that I can't be responsible —'

'Wait,' she interrupted, putting her brandy aside. 'I anticipated your reluctance.' She opened her purse, withdrew a folded sheet of typing paper, and held it out to him. 'Here. Please take this.'

163

He took the paper. Though Pablo was half a century older than she, his hands were far steadier than hers. 'What is it?'

'A signed release making it clear that I came here in desperation, exonerating you in advance for anything that goes wrong.'

He did not bother to read it. 'You don't understand, dear lady. I'm not concerned about being sued. Considering my age and the snail's pace of the courts, I wouldn't live to see a judgment placed against me. But the mind is a delicate mechanism, and if something went wrong, if I led you into a breakdown, I would surely roast in Hell.'

'If you don't help me, if I've got to spend long months in therapy, uncertain of the future, I'll have a breakdown anyway.' Desperate, Ginger raised her voice, venting her frustration and anger. 'If you send me away, leave me to the well-meaning mercy of friends, abandon me to Gudhausen, I'm finished. I swear, that'll be the end of end of me. *I can't go on like this!* If you refuse to help me, you'll still be responsible for my breakdown because you could've prevented it.'

'I'm sorry,' he said.

'*Please.*'

'I can't.'

'You cold, black bastard,' Ginger said, startled by the epithet even as she spoke it. The hurt expression on his benign and gnomish face stung and shamed her. Now it was her turn to say, 'I'm sorry. So sorry.' She brought her hands to her face, bent forward in her chair, and wept.

Her came to her, stooped down in front of her. 'Dr Weiss, please don't cry. Don't depair. It'll be all right.'

'No. It never will,' she said. 'Not ever like it was.'

He gently pried her hands away from her face. He put one of his hands under her chin, lifted her head until she was looking at him. He smiled, winked, and held a hand before her eyes to show her that it was empty. Then, to her surprise, he plucked a quarter from her right ear.

'Hush now,' Pablo Jackson said, patting her shoulder. 'You've made your point. And I certainly don't have an *ame de boue*, a soul of mud, an ungenerous spirit. A woman's tears can move the world. Against my better judgment, I'll do what I can.'

164

Instead of putting an end to her crying, his offer of help renewed her weeping, though these were tears of gratitude.

* * *

'. . . and now you are in a deep sleep, deep, very deep, utterly relaxed, and you will answer all my questions. Is that understood?'

'Yes.'

'You cannot refuse to answer. Cannot refuse. Cannot.'

Pablo had drawn the drapes over the three-bay window and had turned out all the lights except the lamp beside Ginger Weiss's chair. The amber beams fell over her, giving her hair the appearance of real gold filaments and emphasising the unnatural paleness of her skin.

He stood before her, looking down at her face. She had a fragile beauty, an exquisite femininity, yet in her face there was also a great strength almost masculine in quality. *Juste milieu*: perfect balance, the golden mean, was nowhere better defined than in her countenance, where character and beauty were given equal weight.

Her eyes were closed, and they moved very little beneath her lids, an indication that she was in a deep trance.

Pablo returned to his chair, which stood in shadow, beyond the amber light from the single lamp. He sat, crossed his legs. 'Ginger, why were you frightened by the black gloves?'

'I don't know,' she said softly.

'You cannot lie to me. Do you understand? You can withhold nothing from me. Why were you afraid of the black gloves?'

'I don't know.'

'Why were you afraid of the ophthalmoscope?'

'I don't know.'

'Why were you afraid of the sink drain?'

'I don't know.'

'Did you know the man on the motorcycle on State Street?'

'No.'

'Then why were you frightened of him?'

'I don't know.'

Pablo sighed. 'Very well. Ginger, we'll now do something amazing, something that might seem impossible but which I assure you is possible. In fact, it's easy. We're going to make time run backward, Ginger. Nothing to it. We're going to send you slowly but surely back in time. You are going to get younger. It's already happening. You can't resist it . . . time like a river . . . flowing backwards . . . ever back . . . and now it's no longer December twenty-fourth. It's December twenty-third, Monday, and still the clock runs backwards . . . a little faster . . . now it is the twenty-second . . . now the twentieth . . . the eighteenth. . . .' He continued in that manner until he had regressed Ginger to the twelfth of November. 'You are in Bernstein's Delicatessen, waiting for your order to be filled. Can you smell the hot baked goods, the spices?' She nodded, and he said, 'Tell me what you smell.'

She drew a deep breath, and a pleased look overtook her face. Her voice became more animated: 'Pastrami, garlic . . . honey cookies . . . cloves and cinnamon . . .' She remained in her chair, with her eyes closed, but she lifted her head and turned left and right, as if surveying the deli. 'Chocolate. Just *smell* that cocoa pound cake!'

'It's wonderful,' Pablo said. 'Now, you pay for your order, turn from the counter . . . head towards the door, preoccupied with your purse.'

'I can't get my wallet in,' she said, scowling.

'You have the bag of groceries in one arm.'

'Got to clean out this purse.'

'*Bang*! You bump into the man in the Russian hat.'

Ginger gasped and twitched in surprise.

'He grabs your grocery bag to keep it from falling,' Pablo said.

'Oh!' she said.

'He tells you he's sorry.'

'My fault,' Ginger said. Pablo knew she was not talking to him but to the doughy-faced man in the Russian hat, who was now as real to her as he had been that Tuesday in the deli. Apologetically, she said, 'I wasn't looking where I was going.'

'He holds out your bag of groceries, which you take from him.' The aged magician watched her closely. 'And you notice . . . his gloves.'

Her transformation was instantaneous and electrifying. She sat straight up; her eyes popped open. 'The gloves! Oh, God, the gloves!'

'Tell me about the gloves, Ginger.'

'Black,' she said in a small, quavering voice. 'Shiny.'

'What else?'

'*No!*' she cried, starting to get up from the chair.

'Sit down please,' Pablo said.

She froze, half out of her seat.

'Ginger, I am ordering you to sit down and relax.'

She sat rigidly, her small hands fisted. Her radiant blue eyes were open wide, focused not on Pablo but on the gloves in her memory. She looked as if she would bolt again at the slightest provocation.

'You will relax now, Ginger. You will be calm . . . calm . . . very calm. Do you understand?'

'Yes. All right,' she said. Her breath came less rapidly than it had done, and her shoulders slumped a bit, but she was still tense.

Ordinarily, when he put someone into a trance, he maintained total and instantaneous control of the subject. He was surprised and made uneasy by this woman's continued distress in spite of his admonitions to relax, but he could not calm her further. Finally he said, 'Tell me about the gloves, Ginger.'

'Oh, my god.' Her face twisted in fear.

'Relax and tell me about the gloves. Why are you afraid of them?'

She shook. 'D-Don't let them t-t-touch me.'

'Why are you afraid of them?' he persisted.

She hugged herself and shrank back into her chair.

'Listen to me, Ginger. That moment in time is frozen. The clock is moving neither forward nor back. The gloves cannot touch you. I will never let them touch you. Time is suspended. I have the power to suspend time, and I have stopped it. You are safe. Do you hear me?'

'Yes,' she said, but as she cringed against the back of her armchair, there was doubt and barely suppressed terror in her voice.

'You are perfectly safe.' Pablo was distressed to see this sweet girl so oppressed by fear. 'Time has been stopped, so you can study those black gloves without being afraid they'll get hold of you. You will study them and tell me why they frighten you.'

167

She was silent, shaking.

'You must answer me, Ginger. Why are you afraid of the gloves?' She only whimpered, so he thought a moment, then said, 'Is it really *this* pair of gloves that frighten you?'

'N-No. Not exactly.'

'The gloves on this man in the deli . . . they remind you of a pair of other gloves, perhaps from some incident long ago? Is that it?'

'Oh, yes. Yes.'

'When did this other incident take place? Ginger, what other gloves do these remind you of?'

'I don't know.'

'Yes, you do.' Pablo rose from his chair, moved to the draped windows, and observed her from those shadows. 'All right . . . the hands of the clock are moving again. Time is moving backwards again . . . back . . . back . . . all the way back to the time when you were *first* frightened by a pair of black gloves. You are drifting back . . . back . . . and now you are *there*. You are at the very time, at the very place, at the precise moment and spot where you were first frightened by black gloves.'

Ginger's eyes were fixed on a horror in a different time, not in this room or in Bernstein's Delicatessen, but in some other place.

Pablo watched her anxiously. 'Where are you, Ginger?' When she remained silent, he said, 'You must tell me where you are.'

'The face,' she said in a haunted voice that made Pablo shiver. 'The face. The blank face.'

'Explain yourself, Ginger. What face? Tell me what you see.'

'The black gloves . . . the dark glass face.'

'Do you mean . . . like the motorcyclist?'

'The gloves . . . the visor.' A spasm of fear throbbed through her.

'Be calm, relax, You're safe. Safe. Now, wherever you are, do you see a man wearing a helmet and visor? And black gloves?'

She began a monotonous chant of stark terror: 'Uh, uh, uh, uh . . .'

'Ginger, you must be calm. Be calm, relaxed, and at ease.

Nothing can harm you. You're safe.' Afraid that he was losing control of her and would have to bring her out of the trance soon, Pablo moved quickly to her chair, knelt at her side, put one hand on her arm, and stroked gently as he spoke to her. 'Where are you, Ginger? How far back in time have you gone, Ginger? Where are you? *When* are you?'

'Uh, uh, *uhhhhhhhh.*' A pathetic cry escaped her, an echo out of time, the tortured response to a long-suppressed terror and despair.

He became very stern, switching from a soft to a hard voice. 'I am in command of you. You are deeply asleep and completely in my control, Ginger. I demand that you answer me, Ginger.'

A shudder, worse than any previous spasm, passed through her.

'I demand that you answer. Where are you, Ginger?'

'Nowhere.'

'Where are you?'

'No place.' Abruptly, she stopped shaking. She sagged in the chair. The fear melted out of her face, and her features went soft, slack. In a thin and emotionless voice, she said, 'Dead.'

'What do you mean? You're not dead.'

'Dead,' she insisted.

'Ginger, you must tell me where you are and how far back in time you've gone, and you must tell me about the black gloves, that *first* pair of black gloves, the ones you were reminded of when you saw the gloves on that man in the delicatessen. You absolutely must tell me.'

'*Dead.*'

Suddenly, because he was kneeling beside her chair and was close to her, Pablo realised her breathing was extremely shallow. He took her hand and was startled by how cold it was. He pressed two fingers to her wrist, feeling for her pulse. Weak. *Very* weak. Frantic, he put his fingertips to her throat and located a slow and weak heartbeat.

To avoid answering his questions, she seemed to be withdrawing into a sleep far deeper than her hypnotic trance, perhaps into a coma, into an oblivion where she could not hear his demanding voice. He had never encountered a reaction like this before, had never even read of such a thing. Was it possible for Ginger to *will* herself dead merely to escape his questions? Memory blocks erected around traumatic experiences were not uncommon; his reading in psychology journals sometimes turned up accounts of these psychological barricades to recollection, but they were barriers that could be dismantled without killing the subject. Surely no experience could be so horrendous that a person would rather die than remember it. Yet even as Pablo pressed his fingers to her throat, the throbbing of her pulse grew fainter and more irregular.

'Ginger, listen,' he said urgently. 'You don't have to answer me. No more questions. You can come back. I won't insist on answers.'

She seemed suspended on a terrible brink, teetering.

'Ginger, listen to me! No more questions. I'm finished asking questions. I swear it.' After a long and frightening hesitation, he detected a slight improvement in her pulse rate. 'I'm no longer interested in the black gloves or anything else, Ginger. I just want to bring you back to the present and out of your trance. Do you hear me? Please hear me. *Please*. I'm finished questioning you.'

Her pulse stuttered shockingly, but then it throbbed more steadily. Respiration improved, too. As he talked to her in that reassuring manner, she quickly got better. Colour returned to her lovely face.

In less than a minute, he returned her to December 24 and woke her.

She blinked. 'It didn't work, huh? You couldn't put me under.'

'You were under,' he said shakily. 'Too far under.'

She said, 'Pablo, you're trembling. Why're you trembling? What's wrong? What happened?'

This time, she went to the kitchen and poured the brandy.

*　　　*　　　*

Later, at the door of Pablo's apartment, as Ginger was leaving to meet the taxi that Pablo had summoned for her, she said, 'I still can't think what it could be. Nothing so terrible has ever happened to me, certainly nothing so bad I'd rather die than reveal it.'

170

'There's something very traumatic in your past,' Pablo said. 'An incident involving a man wearing black gloves, a man with what you said was a "dark glass face." Perhaps a motorcyclist like the one that panicked you on State Street. It's an incident you've buried very deep . . . and which you seem determined to keep buried at any cost. I really think you should tell Dr Gudhausen what happened here today and let him proceed from there.'

'Gudhausen is too traditional, too slow. I want *your* help.'

'I won't risk putting you in a trance and questioning you again.'

'Unless your research turns up a similar case.'

'Not much chance of that. I've done a lot of reading in psychology and hypnosis for fifty years, and I've never heard of anything like it.'

'But you're going to research it, aren't you? You promised.'

'I'll see what I can find,' he said.

'And if you discover that someone developed a workable technique for getting through a memory block like this, you'll use it on me.'

Ginger was mystified, but she was also considerably less distraught than she had been when she first arrived at Pablo Jackson's apartment. At least they had got somewhere, even if they did not yet know where. They had found the problem, some mysterious traumatic experience in the past, and though they had not learned a single detail of it, they knew it was back there, a dark shape waiting to be explored. In time they would find a way to throw a light on it, and when it was revealed, she would know the cause of her fugues.

'Tell Dr Gudhausen,' Pablo said again.

'I'm pinning all my hopes on you.'

'You're damn stubborn,' the old magician said, shaking his head.

'No. Just persistent.'

'Wilful.'

'Just determined.'

'*Acharnement*!'

'When I get back to Baywatch I'll look up that word, and if it's an insult, you'll be sorry when I come back on Thursday,' she teased.

171

'Not Thursday,' he said. 'The research is going to take time. I'm not going to hypnotise you again unless I can find a record of a similar case and can follow someone else's procedures, knowing they succeeded.'

'Okay, but if you don't call by Friday or Saturday, I'll probably come back and bust my way in. Remember, you're my best hope.'

'I am your best hope . . . only for want of anything better.'

'You underrate yourself, Pablo Jackson.' She kissed him on the cheek. 'I'll be waiting for your call.'

'*Au revoir.*'

'*Shalom.*'

Outside, as she got into the cab, she remembered one of her father's favourite aphorisms, and like a lead weight, it counteracted her new buoyancy: *It's always brightest just before the dark.*

3.

CHICAGO, ILLINOIS

Winton Tolk – the tall, black, jovial patrolman riding shotgun – got out of the police cruiser to buy three hamburgers and Cokes at a corner sandwich shop, leaving his partner, Paul Armes, behind the wheel, and Father Brendan Cronin in the back seat. Brendan glanced at the shop, but he could not see inside, for the big front windows were painted with festive holiday images: Santa, reindeer, wreaths, angels. A light snow had just began to fall, and the weather forecast called for eight inches by midnight, which meant tomorrow would be a white Christmas.

As Winton got out of the car, Brendan leaned forward and said to Paul Armes, 'Yeah, well, nobody's knocking *Going My Way*, but what about *It's a Wonderful Life*? Now there was a terrific picture!'

'Jimmy Stewart and Donna Reed,' Paul said.

'What a cast.' They had been talking about great Christmas

films, and now Brendan was sure he had hit upon the best of the best. 'Lionel Barrymore played the skinflint. Gloria Grahame was in that, too.'

'Thomas Mitchell,' Paul Armes said as, outside, Winton reached the door of the sandwich shop. 'Ward Bond. *God, what a cast!*' Winton had gone into the sandwich shop. 'But you're forgetting another great one. *Miracle on 34th Street.*'

'That was terrific, sure, but I still think Capra's better –'

It seemed that the gunshots and the startling cascade of shattering glass came at the same instant, with not a fraction of a second between. Even with the car doors shut, the heater fan making noise, and the policeband radio crackling and chirruping, the shots were loud enough to halt Brendan in mid-sentence. As the explosions blew away the Christmas peace of the Uptown street, the sandwich shop's painted window tableau dissolved, erupted in a glittering spray. New shots overlaid the echo of old reports, and the blasts were accompanied by a brittle and atonal music of glass smashing on the roof, hood, and trunk of the cruiser.

'Oh, shit!' Paul Armes tore the dash-mounted riot gun free of its clasps, throwing open his door even as the glass was still raining. 'Stay down,' he shouted back at Brendan, and then he was out, crouching, moving around the car and using it as a shield.

Stunned, Brendan looked through the window at his side, back towards the sandwich-shop entrance. Abruptly, that door was flung wide, and two young men appeared, one black, one white. The black man wore a knitted cap and a long navy peacoat – and carried a semi-automatic, sawed-off shotgun. The white man, in a plaid hunting jacket, was armed with a revolver. They came out fast, half-crouched, and the black man swung the shotgun toward the patrol car. Brendan was looking directly into the muzzle. There was a flash, and he was sure he had been shot, but the rear passenger-side window in front of his face remained intact. Instead, the front window exploded inward, fragments of glass and lead pellets showering across the seat, rattling off the dashboard. The near-miss shocked Brendan out of his daze, and he rolled off his seat, to the floor, his heart hammering almost as loud as the gunfire.

Winton Tolk had had the bad luck to walk unsuspecting into

the middle of an armed robbery. He was probably dead.

As Brendan pressed himself to the floor of the squad car, he heard Paul Armes shouting outside: '*Drop it!*'

Two shots cracked. Not a shotgun. Revolver fire. But who pulled the trigger? Paul Armes or the guy in the plaid hunting jacket?

Another shot. Someone screamed.

But who had been hit? Armes or one of the robbers?

Brendan wanted to look, but he did not dare show himself.

Thanks to an arrangement Father Wycazik had made with the local precinct captain, Brendan had been riding as an observer with Winton and Paul for five days. In an ordinary suit, tie and topcoat, he was supposed to be a lay consultant employed by the Church to study the need for Catholic charity out-reach programmes, a cover story which everyone seemed to accept. Winton's and Paul's beat was Uptown, an area bordered by Foster Avenue on the North, Lake Shore Drive highrises on the east, Irving Park Road on the south, and North Ashland Avenue on the west. It was Chicago's poorest and most crime-ridden neighbourhood, home to blacks, Indians, but mostly Appalachians and Hispanics. After five days with Winton and Paul, Brendan developed a strong liking for both men and a deep sympathy for all the honest souls who lived and worked in those decaying buildings and filthy streets – and who were prey to the packs of human jackals among them. He had learned to expect anything riding with these guys, but the sandwich-shop shootout was the worst incident yet.

Another shotgun blast slammed into the car, rocking it.

Brendan curled fetally on the floor and tried to pray, but no words came. God was still lost to him, and he cowered in terrible solitude.

Outside, Paul Armes shouted, 'Give it up!'

The gunman said, 'Fuck you!'

When he'd reported to Father Wycazik after a week at St Joseph's, Brendan had been sent to another hospital, where he'd been given work on the terminal ward, a dreadful place with no children at all. There, as at St Joseph's, Brendan quickly discovered the lesson that Stefan Wycazik expected him to learn. To most who were at the end of life, death was not to be feared but welcomed, a blessing for which they thanked God rather than cursing Him. And in dying, many who had never been believers became believers at last, and those who had fallen away from faith came back. There was frequently something noble and deeply moving in the suffering that accompanied a person's exit from this world, as if each shared, for a while, the mystical burden of the cross.

Yet, that lesson learned, Brendan remained unable to believe. Now, the fierce beating of his heart hammered the words of the prayer to dust before he could speak them, and his mouth was as dry as powder.

Outside, there was shouting, but he could not make sense of the words any more, maybe because the people shouting were incoherent and maybe because he was partially deaf from the gunfire.

He did not yet fully understand the lesson that Father Wycazik had hoped he would learn from this Uptown portion of his unconventional therapy. And now as he listened to the chaos outside, he knew that the lesson, regardless of its nature, would be insufficient to convince him that God was as real as bullets. Death was a bloody, stinking, foul reality, and in the face of it, the promise of a reward in the afterlife was not the least persuasive.

The shotgun discharged again, followed by the roar of the riot gun, then by shouting and the *slap-slap-slap* of running feet. It sounded like a war out there. Another blast from the riot gun. More shattering glass. Another scream, more horrible than the one that had rent the air before it. Yet another shot. Silence. Silence perfect and profound.

The driver's door was jerked open.

Brendan cried out in surprise and terror.

'Stay down!' Paul Armes said from the front seat, keeping a low profile himself. 'Two dead, but there might be other shitheads inside.'

'Where's Winton?' Brendan asked.

Paul did not answer. Instead, he grabbed the radio microphone up front and called Central. 'Officer down. Officer down!' Armes gave his position, the address of the sandwich shop, and requested back-up.

Lying on his side on the floor of the squad car, Brendan

closed his eyes and saw, with heart-breaking clarity, the pictures that Winton Tolk carried in his wallet and that he proudly displayed when queried about his family – pictures of his wife, Raynella, and his three children.

'Those rotten fucking bastards,' Paul Armes said, his voice shaking.

Brendan heard soft clicking and scraping sounds that puzzled him until he realised Armes was reloading. He said, 'Winton's been shot?'

'Bet on it,' Armes said.

'He might need help.'

'It's on the way.'

'But he may need help *now*,' Brendan said.

'Can't go in there. Might be another one. Two more. Who knows? We gotta wait for back-up.'

'Winton might need a tourniquet . . . other first-aid. He might be dead by the time help gets here.'

'Don't you think I *know* that?' Paul Armes said bitterly, furiously. He finished reloading and slid out of the car to take up a position from which he could watch the shop.

The more Brendan thought about Winton Tolk sprawled on the floor in there, the angrier he became. If he had still believed in God, he might have quenched his anger in prayer. But now it fed on itself and grew into a hot rage. His heart pounded even harder than when the shotgun blasts were crashing into the car inches from him. The injustice of Winton's fate – the unfairness, the *wrongness* – was like an acid eating at Brendan.

He got out of the car and started across the sidewalk, through the falling snow, towards the entrance to the sandwich shop.

'Brendan!' Paul Armes shouted from the far side of the police cruiser. 'Stop! For God's sake, don't!'

Brendan kept going, driven by his rage and by the thought that Winton Tolk might need immediate first-aid to survive.

A dead man in a plaid hunting jacket was lying on his back on the sidewalk. A round from Armes's revolver had taken him in the chest, a second round in the throat. There was a stink of loosed bowels. In the snow beside the corpse lay a handgun, perhaps the very one with which Winton Tolk had been shot.

'Cronin!' Paul Armes yelled. 'Get your ass back here, you idiot!'

Moving past the broken windows, Brendan could see into the shop, which was surprisingly dark. The lights had been shot out or a switch thrown, and the grey daylight penetrated only a couple of feet inside. He could not see anyone, but that did not mean it was safe to enter.

'Cronin!' Paul Armes shouted.

Brendan went to the entrance, where he found the black man in the peacoat. This one had been hit by a shotgun blast that also demolished the glass door; he was crumpled in a thousand bright fragments.

Stepping over the body, Brendan entered the sandwich shop. He did not have his Roman collar, which might have been something of a shield if he had been wearing it. On the other hand, degenerates like these would probably kill a priest as reflexively and as happily as they blew away police officers. In his suit and tie and topcoat, he was as ordinary and vulnerable as any man, but he did not care. He was *that* furious. Furious that God did not exist or, existing, did not care.

At the back of the small shop was a service counter. Behind the counter was a grille, other equipment. On this side were five very small tables and ten chairs, most of which had been toppled. On the floor were a couple of napkin dispensers, ketchup and mustard bottles, scattered one- and five-dollar bills, a lot of blood, and Winton Tolk.

Not bothering to study the overturned tables to see if a gunman was sheltering behind them, Brendan went to the officer, knelt beside him. Winton had been hit twice in the chest. Not with the shotgun. Probably the other thug's revolver. The wounds were sickening, far too traumatic to respond dramatically to a mere tourniquet or first-aid procedures. His breast was mantled with blood, and blood trickled from his mouth. The pool of blood in which he lay was so deep that he appeared to be floating in it. He was still, eyes closed, either unconscious or dead.

'Winton?' Brendan said.

The cop did not respond. His eyelids did not even flutter. Filled with a rage akin to that which had caused him to heave the holy chalice against the wall during Mass, Brendan Cronin gently put both hands to Winton Tolk's neck, one on each side, feeling for the throbbing carotid arteries. He detected no life, and in his mind he saw the photographs of Raynella and the Tolk children again, and now he was *seething* with resentment at the indifference of the universe. 'He can't die,' Brendan said angrily. 'He can't.' Suddenly he thought he felt a thready pulse, so faint it was virtually non-existent. He moved his hands, seeking confirmation that Tolk lived. He found it: a less feeble beat than that first phantom drumming, though no less irregular.

'Is he dead?'

Brendan looked up and saw a man coming around the side of the service counter, an Hispanic in a white apron, the owner or an employee. A woman, also in a white apron, had risen from behind the counter.

Outside, distant sirens were growing nearer.

Under Brendan's hands, the throbbing in Winton Tolk's neck seemed to be getting stronger and more regular, which was surely not the case. Winton had lost too much blood to stage even a limited spontaneous recovery. Until the paramedics arrived with life-support machines, his vital signs would deteriorate unavoidably, and even expert medical care might not stabilise his condition.

The sirens were no more than two blocks away.

Puffs of snow blew in through the shattered windows.

The sandwich-shop employees edged closer.

Numb with shock, in a haze of anger at fate's capricious brutality, Brendan trailed his hands from Winton's neck to the wounds in the chest. When he saw the blood oozing up between his fingers, his rage gave way to overwhelming helplessness and uselessness, and he began to cry.

Winton Tolk choked. Coughed. Opened his eyes. Breath rattled thinly and wetly in his throat, and a soft groan escaped him.

Amazed, Brendan felt for a pulse in the man's throat again. It was weak but definitely not as weak as before, and hardly irregular at all.

Raising his voice over the shrieking sirens, which were now so near that the air trembled, Brendan said, 'Winton? Winton, do you hear me?'

The cop did not seem to recognise Brendan – or even to know where he was. He coughed again and choked more violently than before.

Brendan quickly lifted Tolk's head a few inches and turned it to one side, to let the blood and mucous drain more freely from his mouth. Immediately the wounded man's respiration improved, though it remained noisy, each inhalation hard-won. He was still in critical condition, in desperate need of medical attention, but he was alive.

Alive.

Incredible. All this blood, and he was still alive, hanging on.

Outside, three sirens died one after the other. Brendan shouted for Paul Armes. Excited by the hope that Winton could be saved, but also panicked by the possibility that medical attention would arrive seconds too late, he glanced at the sandwich-shop employees and shouted 'Go! Get them in here. Let them know it's safe. Paramedics, damn it!'

The man in the apron hesitated, then moved towards the door.

Winton Tolk expelled bloody mucous and finally drew an unobstructed breath. Brendan carefully lowered Winton's head to the floor again. The cop continued to breathe shallowly, with difficulty, but steadily.

Outside there were shouts and doors slamming and running feet coming toward the sandwich shop.

Brendan's hands were wet with Winton Tolk's blood. Unthinking, he blotted them on his coat – and it was then that he realised the rings had reappeared on his hands for the first time in nearly two weeks. One on each palm. Twin bands of raised and inflamed tissue.

Cops and paramedics burst through the front door, stepping over the dead man in the navy peacoat, and Brendan quickly moved out of their way. He backed up until he bumped against the service counter, where he leaned in sudden exhaustion, staring at his hands.

For a few days following the first appearance of the rings, he had used the cortisone prescribed by Dr Heeton at St Joseph's, but when the rings had not reappeared, he had soon stopped applying the lotion. He had almost forgotten about the marks. They had been a curiosity, baffling, but of little concern. Now, as he looked at the strange marks, he heard the voices of those around him, fuzzy and strange:

'Jesus, the blood!'

'Can't be alive . . . twice in the chest.'

'Get the fuck out of my way!'

'Plasma!'

'Type his blood. No! Wait . . . do it in the ambulance.'

Brendan finally looked at the crowd around Winton Tolk. He watched the paramedics as they worked to keep the wounded man alive, get him on a stretcher, and move him out of the sandwich shop.

He saw a cursing policeman dragging the dead man out of the doorway to make it easier for the paramedics to exit with Tolk.

He saw Paul Armes moving along beside the stretcher.

He saw that the blood in which Tolk had been lying was not merely a pool but a *lake*.

He looked at his hands again. The rings were gone.

4.

LAS VEGAS, NEVADA

The Texan in the yellow Day-Glo polyester pants would not have tried to get Jorja Monatella into bed if he had known she was in the mood to castrate someone.

Although it was the afternoon of December 24, Jorja was not yet in the Christmas spirit. Usually even-tempered and easygoing, she was in an exceedingly sour state of mind as she strode back and forth through the casino, from the bar to the blackjack tables and back to the bar again, delivering drinks to the gamblers.

For one thing, she hated her job. Being a cocktail waitress was bad enough in a regular bar or lounge, but in a hotel casino bigger than a football field, it was a killer. At the end of a shift, her feet ached, and often her ankles were swollen. The hours were irregular, too. How were you supposed to provide a stable home for a seven-year-old daughter when you did not have a job with normal hours?

She also hated the costume: a little red nothing, cut high in the crotch and hips, very low at the bustline, smaller than a bathing suit. An elastic corset was built in to minimise the waistline and emphasise the breasts. If you were already small-waisted, with generous breasts – as Jorja was – the get-up made you look almost freakishly erotic.

And she hated the way the pit bosses and casino floormen were always hitting on her. Maybe they figured any girl who would strut her stuff in an outfit like that was an easy lay.

She was sure that her name had something to do with their attitude as well: Jorja. It was cute. Too cute. Her mother must have been drunk when she got creative with the spelling of Georgia. It was all right when people heard it because they had no way of knowing she spelled it cute, but she had to wear a name tag on her costume – JORJA – and at least a dozen people a day commented on it. It was a frivolous name, mis-spelled like that, so it gave them the idea she was a frivolous person. She had considered going to court to have the proper spelling made legal, but that would hurt her mother. However, if guys at work kept hitting on her, she might even have it changed to Mother Teresa, which ought to cool off some of the horny bastards.

And fending off the bosses was not the worst of it. Every week, some high-roller – a bigshot from Detroit or LA or Dallas, dropping a bundle at the tables – would take a shine to Jorja and ask the pit boss to fix him up with her. A few cocktail waitresses *were* available, not many but a few. But when the pit bosses approached Jorja, her answer was always the same: 'To hell with him. I'm a waitress, not a hooker.'

Her routine, cold refusal did not stop them from pressuring her to relent, which they had done an hour ago. A wart-faced, bug-eyed oilman from Houston – in phosphorescent yellow pants, a blue shirt, and a red string tie – one of the hotel's favoured clients, had got the hots for her and had made

181

inquiries. His breath stank of the burritos he had eaten for lunch.

Now the bosses were angry with her for refusing a highly valued customer, for being 'too stuffy.' Rainy Tarnell, the blackjack pit boss on the day-shift, had the gall to put it just like that – 'Honey, don't be so stuffy!' – as if falling on her back and spreading her legs for a stranger from Houston was merely the equivalent of a fashion gaucherie like wearing white shoes either before Memorial Day or after Labour Day.

Though she hated being a casino cocktail waitress, she could not afford to quit. No other job would pay her as well. She was a divorced mother raising a daughter without benefit of child-support payments, and in order to protect her credit rating, she was still paying off bills that Alan had run up in her name before walking out on her, so she was acutely aware of the value of a dollar. Her wages were low, but the tips were exceedingly good, especially on those occasions when one of her customers started winning big at cards or dice.

On this day before Christmas, the casino was two-thirds empty, and tips were bad. Vegas was always slow Thanksgiving to Christmas, and the crowds did not return until December 26. The whizzing-rattling-ringing of slot machines was muted. Many of the blackjack dealers stood idle and bored in front of empty tables.

No wonder I'm in a sour mood, Jorja thought. Sore feet, back pain, a horny creep who figures I ought to be as available as the drinks I serve, an argument with Rainy Tarnell, and no tips to show for it.

When her shift ended at four o'clock, she hurried to the changing room downstairs, punched the time-clock, slipped out of her costume and into street clothes, and was out of the door into the employee parking lot with a speed that would have drawn praise from an Olympic runner.

The unpredictable desert weather did nothing to instill the Christmas spirit in her. A Las Vegas winter day could be cold, with bone-numbing wind, or it could be warm enough for shorts and halters. This year, the holiday was warm.

Her dusty, battered Chevette started on only the third try, which should have improved her mood. But listening to the

182

starter grind and the engine cough, she was reminded of the shiny new Buick that Alan had taken with him fifteen months ago, when he had abandoned her and Marcie.

Alan Rykoff. More than her job, more than any of the other things that irritated her, Alan was the cause of Jorja's foul mood. She had shed his name when the marriage had been dissolved, reverting to her maiden name, Monatella, but she could not as easily shed the memories of the pain he had inflicted on her and Marcie.

As she drove out of the parking lot into the street behind the hotel, Jorja tried to banish Alan from her thoughts, but he remained at centre stage. The bastard. With his current bedmate, an airhead blonde bearing the unlikely name 'Pepper,' he had flown off to Acapulco for a week, not even bothering to leave a Christmas gift for Marcie. What did you tell a seven-year-old girl when she asked why her daddy didn't buy her anything for Christmas – or even come to see her?

Although Alan left Jorja saddled with bills, she had willingly forgone alimony because, by then, she loathed him so much that she had not wanted to be dependent on him. However, she had gone after child-support and had been shocked when he countered by insisting Marcie was not his child and, there-fore, not his responsibility. Damn him. Jorja had married him when she was nineteen and he was twenty-four, and she'd never been unfaithful. Alan knew she hadn't cheated, but protecting his jazzy lifestyle – he needed every dollar for clothes, fast cars, and women – was more important to him than his wife's reputation or his daughter's happiness. To spare little Marsha humiliation and pain, Jorja had released Alan from responsibility before he could voice his sleazy accusations in the courtroom.

So she was finished with him. She could put him out of her mind.

But as she drove past the mall at the intersection of Mary-land Parkway and Desert Inn Road, Jorja thought about how young she had been when she tied herself to Alan, too young for marriage and too naive to see through his facade. When she was nineteen, she thought he was *tres* sophisticated, charming. For more than a year, their union had seemed blissful, but gradually she began to see him for what he was: shallow, vain, lazy; a shockingly promiscuous womaniser.

The summer before last, when their relationship had been rocky, she had tried to salvage the marriage by coercing Alan into a carefully planned three-week vacation. She believed that part of their problem was that they spent too little time together. He was a baccarat dealer in one hotel, and she was employed in another, and they frequently worked different shifts, slept on different schedules. Just the two of them – and Marcie – embarked upon an adventurous three-week car trip, seemed a good way to repair their damaged relationship.

Unfortunately but predictably, her scheme had not worked. After the vacation, upon their return to Vegas, Alan had been more promiscuous than before. He seemed determined – *driven* – to take a poke at anything in skirts. In fact, it was almost as if the car trip had somehow pushed him over the edge, for the number and intensity of his one-night stands developed a manic quality, a frightening desperation. Three months later, in October of that year, he walked out on her and Marcie.

The only good thing about the car trip had been the brief encounter with that young woman doctor who had been driving cross-country from Stanford to Boston on, she'd said, her first vacation ever. Jorja still remembered the woman's name: Ginger Weiss. Although they had met only once, and then for little more than an hour, Ginger Weiss had quite unwittingly changed Jorja's life. The doctor had been so very young – so slender, pretty, feminine – it had been difficult to accept that she was really a doctor, yet she'd been uncommonly self-assured and competent. Deeply impressed by Ginger Weiss during that encounter, Jorja was later motivated by the doctor's example. She'd always thought of herself as a born cocktail waitress, incapable of anything more challenging, but when Alan walked out, she had remembered Dr Weiss and decided to make more of herself than she had previously thought possible.

During the past eleven months, Jorja had taken business management courses at UNLV, squeezing them into an already hectic schedule. When she finished paying the bills that Alan had left her, she would build a nest egg with which

184

to eventually open her own business, a dress shop. She had worked out a very detailed plan, revising and honing it until it was realistic, and she knew she would stick with it.

It was a shame that she would never have a chance to thank Ginger Weiss. Of course, it was not any favour that Dr Weiss had performed that so deeply affected Jorja; it was not so much what the doctor had done as what she *was*. Anyway, at twenty-seven, Jorja's prospects were more exciting than they had been previously.

Now, she turned off Desert Inn Road onto Pawnee Drive, a street of comfortable homes behind the Boulevard Mall. She stopped in front of Kara Persaghian's house and got out of the car. The front door opened before she reached it, and Marcie rushed out, into her arms, shouting happily. 'Mommy! Mommy!' And Jorja was at last able to forget about her job, the Texan, the argument with the pit boss, and the dilapidated condition of the Chevette. She squatted down and hugged her daughter. When all else failed to cheer her, she could count on Marcie for a lift.

'Mommy,' the girl said, 'did you have a great day?'

'Yes, honey, I did. You smell like peanut butter.'

'Cookies! Aunt Kara made peanut-butter cookies! I had a great day, too. Mommy, do you know why elephants came . . . ummm, why they came all the way from Africa to live in this country?' Marcie giggled. ''Cause we got orchestras here, and elephants just *love* to dance!' She giggled again. 'Isn't that *silly*.'

Even allowing for maternal prejudice, Jorja knew that Marcie was an adorable child. The girl had her mother's hair, so dark brown that it was virtually black, and her mother's dusky complexion. Her eyes were a striking contrast to the rest of her, not brown like Jorja's but blue like her father's. She had an immensely appealing gamine quality.

Marcie's huge blue eyes opened wide. 'Hey, know what day it is?'

'I sure do. Almost Christmas Eve.'

'Will be soon as it's dark. Aunt Kara's giving us cookies to take home. You know, Santa's already left the North Pole, and he's started going down chimneys already, but in other parts of the world, of course, where it's dark, not chimneys here.

185

Aunt Kara says I been so bad all year I'll only get a necklace made out of coal, but she's just teasing. Isn't she just teasing, Mommy?'

'Just teasing,' Jorja confirmed.

'Oh, no, I'm not!' Kara Persaghian said. She came through the doorway, onto the front walk, a grandmotherly woman in a housedress and apron. 'A coal necklace . . . and *maybe* a set of matching coal earrings.'

Marcie giggled again.

Kara was not Marcie's aunt, merely her after-school baby-sitter. Marcie called her 'Aunt Kara' from the second week she knew her, and the sitter was obviously delighted by that affectionately bestowed, honorary title. Kara was carrying Marcie's jacket, a big colouring-book picture of Santa that they had been working on for a few days, and a plate of cookies. Jorja gave the picture and jacket to Marcie, accepted the cookies with expressions of gratitude and with some chatter about diets, and then Kara said, 'Jorja, could I speak with you a moment – just the two of us?'

'Sure.' Jorja sent Marcie to the car with the cookies and turned inquisitively to Kara. 'It's about . . . Marcie. What's she done?'

'Oh, nothing bad. She's an angel, that one. Couldn't misbe-have if she tried. But today . . . well, she was talking about how the thing she wants most for Christmas is that Little Ms Doctor play kit –'

'It's the first time she's ever really *nagged* me about a toy,' Jorja said. 'I don't know why she's obsessed with it.'

'She talks about it every day. You are getting it for her?'

Jorja glanced at the Chevette, confirming that Marcie was out of earshot, then smiled. 'Yes, Santa definitely has it in his bag.'

'Good. She'd be heartbroken if you didn't. But the oddest thing happened today, and it made me wonder if she'd ever been seriously ill.'

'Serious illness? No. She's an exceptionally healthy kid.'

'Never been in the hospital?'

'No. Why?'

Kara frowned. 'Well, today she started talking about the Little Ms Doctor kit, and she told me she wanted to be a doctor when she grew up because then she could treat herself when she got sick. She said she never wanted a doctor to touch her again because she was once hurt real bad by doctors. I asked her what she meant, and she got quiet for a while, and I thought she wasn't going to answer me. Then finally, in this *very* sombre voice, she said some doctors had once strapped her down in a hospital bed, so she couldn't get out, and then they stuck her full of needles and flashed lights in her face and did all sorts of horrible things to her. She said they hurt her real bad, so she was going to become her own doctor and treat herself from now on.'

'Really? Well, it's not true,' Jorja said. 'I don't know why she'd made up such a story. That *is* odd.'

'Oh, that's not the odd part. When she told me all this, I was concerned. I was surprised you'd never told me. I mean, if she'd been seriously ill, I ought to've been told in case there was a possibility of a recurrence. So I questioned her about it – just casually, the way you coax things out of a child – and suddenly the poor little thing just *burst* into tears. We were in the kitchen, making cookies, and she started to cry . . . and shake. Just shaking like a leaf. I tried to calm her, but that only made her cry harder. Then she pulled away from me and ran. I found her in the living room, in the corner behind the big green Lay-Z-Boy, huddled down as if she was hiding from someone.'

'Good heavens,' Jorja said.

Kara said, 'Took me at least five minutes to get her to stop crying and another ten to coax her out of her hidey-hole behind that chair. She made me promise, if those doctors ever came for her again, that I'd let her hide behind the chair and not tell them where she was. I mean, Jorja, she was in a real *state*.'

*　　*　　*

On the way home, Jorja said, 'That was some story you told Kara.'

'What story?' Marcie asked, looking straight ahead, barely able to see over the dashboard.

'That story about the doctors.'

'Oh.'

187

'Being strapped in bed. Why'd you make up a thing like that?'

'It's true,' Marcie said.

'But it isn't.'

'Yes, it is.' The girl's voice was little more than a whisper.

'The only hospital you were ever in was the one where you were born, and I'm *sure* you don't remember that.' Jorja sighed. 'A few months ago we had a little talk about fibbing. Remember what happened to Danny Duck when he fibbed?'

'The Truth Fairy wouldn't let him go to the woodchuck's party.'

'That's right.'

'Fibbing's bad,' Marcie said softly. 'Nobody likes fibbers – 'specially not woodchucks and squirrels.'

Disarmed, Jorja had to bite back a laugh and struggle to keep a stern tone in her voice. '*Nobody* likes fibbers.'

They stopped at a red traffic light, but Marcie still looked straight ahead, refusing to meet Jorja's eyes. The girl said, 'It's 'specially bad to fib to your mommy or your daddy.'

'Or to *anyone* who cares about you. And making up stories to scare Kara – that's the same as fibbing.'

'Wasn't tryin' to scare her,' Marcie said.

'Trying to get sympathy, then. You were never in a hospital.'

'Was.'

'Oh, yeah?' Marcie nodded vigorously, and Jorja said, 'When?'

'Don't 'member when.'

'You don't remember, huh?'

'Almost.'

'Almost isn't good enough. Where was this hospital?'

'I'm not sure. Sometimes . . . I 'member it better than other times. Sometimes I can hardly 'member it at all, and sometimes I 'member it real good, and then I . . . I get scared.'

'Right now you don't remember too well, huh?'

'Nope. But today I 'membered real good . . . and scared myself.'

The traffic light changed, and Jorja drove in silence, wondering how best to handle the situation. She had no notion what to make of it. It was foolish ever to believe that you

188

understood your child. Marcie had always been able to surprise Jorja with actions, statements, big ideas, musings, and
questions that seemed not to have come from within herself
but which it seemed she had carefully selected from some
secret book of startling behaviour that was known to all kids
but not to adults, some cosmic volume perhaps titled *Keeping
Mom and Dad Off-Balance*.

As if she had just dipped into that book again, Marcie said,
'Why were all Santa Claus's kids deformed?'

'*What*?'

'Well, see, Santa and Mrs Claus hade a whole bunch of kids,
but all of them was *elves*.'

'The elves aren't their children. They work for Santa.'

'Really? How much does he pay 'em?'

'He doesn't pay them anything, honey.'

'How do they buy food then?'

'They don't have to buy anything. Santa gives them all they
need.' This was certainly the last Christmas that Marcie would
believe in Santa. Recently, she had been asking these probing
questions. Jorja would be sorry to see the fantasy disproved,
the magic lost. 'The elves are part of his family, honey, and
they work with him simply for the love of it.'

'You mean the elves are adopted? So Santa doesn't have real
kids of his own? That's sad.'

'No, 'cause he's got all the elves to love.'

God, I love this kid, Jorja thought. Thank you, God. Thank
you for this kid, even if I did have to get tied up with Alan
Rykoff to get her. Dark clouds and silver linings.

She turned into the two-lane driveway that encircled Las
Huevos Apartments and parked the Chevette in the fourth
carport. Las Huevos. The Eggs. After five years in the place,
she still couldn't understand why anyone would name an
apartment complex The Eggs.

The instant the car stopped, Marcie was out of it with the
poster from the colouring book and the plate of cookies,
dashing up the walkway to their entrance. The girl had deftly
changed the subject just long enough to finish the ride and
escape from the confines of the car.

Jorja wondered if she should press the issue further. It was
Christmas Eve, and she had no desire to spoil the holiday.

189

Marcie was a good kid, better than most, and this business about being hurt by doctors was an extremely rare instance of fabrication. Jorja had made the point that fibbing was not acceptable, and Marcie had understood (even if she had persisted a bit with her medical fantasy), and her sudden change of subject had probably been an admission of wrong-doing. So it was an aberration. Nothing would be gained by harping on it, especially not at the risk of ruining Christmas.

Jorja was confident she would hear no more about it.

5.

LAGUNA BEACH, CALIFORNIA

During the afternoon, Dominick Corvaisis must have read the unsigned typewritten note a hundred times:

The sleepwalker would be well-advised to search the past for the source of his problem. That is where the secret is buried.

In addition to the letter's lack of signature and return address, the postmark on the plain white envelope was double-struck and badly smeared, so he could not determine whether it had been mailed in Laguna Beach or from another city.

After he paid for his breakfast and left the Cottage, he sat in his car, the copy of *Twilight in Babylon* forgotten on the seat beside him, and read the note half a dozen times. It made him so nervous that he withdrew a pair of Valium from his jacket pocket and almost took one without water. But as he put the capsule to his lips, he hesitated. To explore all the ramifications of the note, he would need a clear mind. For the first time in weeks, he denied himself chemical escape from his anxieties; he returned the Valium to his pocket.

He drove to South Coast Plaza, a huge shopping mall in Costa Mesa, to buy some last-minute Christmas gifts. In each store he visited, while he waited for the clerks to gift-wrap his purchases, he took the curious message from his pocket and read it again and again.

For a while Dom had wondered if the note had come from Parker, if perhaps the artist had sent it to jolt him and intrigue him and propel him out of his drug-induced haze. Parker might be capable of such highly theatrical, amateur psychotherapy. But finally Dom dismissed that idea. Machiavellian manoeuvres were simply not aspects of the painter's personality. He was, in fact, almost excessively forthright.

Parker was not the author of the note, but he was certain to have some original speculations about who might be behind it. Together, they might be able to decide just how the arrival of this letter changed things and how they ought to proceed.

Later, back in Laguna, when Dom was within a block of Parker's house, he was suddenly shaken by a previously unconsidered, profoundly troubling possibility. This new idea was so disconcerting that he pulled the Firebird to the kerb and stopped. He got the note from his pocket, read it again, fingered the paper. He felt cold inside. He looked into the reflection of his own eyes in the rearview mirror, and he did not like what he saw.

Could he have written the note himself?

He could have composed it on the Displaywriter while asleep. But it was outlandish to suppose he'd dressed, gone to a mailbox, deposited the note, returned home, and changed into pyjamas again without waking up. Impossible. Wasn't it? If he had done such a thing, his mental imbalance was worse than he had thought.

His hands were clammy. He blotted them on his trousers.

Only three people in the world were aware of his sleepwalking: himself, Parker Faine, and Dr Cobletz. He had already eliminated Parker. Dr Cobletz had certainly not sent the note. So if Dom himself had not sent it – who had?

When he pulled away from the kerb at last, he did not continue to Parker's house but headed home instead.

Ten minutes later, in his study, he took the by-now rumpled note from his pocket. He typed those two sentences, which appeared on the Displaywriter's dark screen in glowing green letters. Then he switched on the printer and instructed the computer to produce a hard copy of the document. He watched as it hammered out those twenty-three words.

The Displaywriter came with two printwheels in two type faces. He had bought two more to provide options for different tasks. Now, Dom used the three additional printwheels to produce a total of four copies of the note, and with a pencil he labelled each according to the style of type used for it: PRESTIGE ELITE, ARTISAN 10, COURIER 10, LETTER GOTHIC.

He smoothed out the original rumpled note and placed each of the copies beside it for comparison. He hoped to eliminate all four type styles that he possessed, disproving the theory that he had sent the note to himself. But the Courier 10 appeared to be a perfect match.

That did not conclusively prove he'd written the note. In offices and homes all over the country, there must be millions of printwheels and printer elements in the Courier face.

He compared the paper of the original note to that of the copy he had made. They were both twenty-pound, 8½" × 11", standard products sold under a dozen labels in thousands of stores in all fifty states. Neither sheet was of sufficient quality to contain fibres. Dom held them up to the light and saw that neither page featured a mill seal or brand-name watermark, which might have proven that the original note had not been typed on paper from his own stock.

He thought: Parker, Dr Cobletz, and me. Who else could know?

And what was the note trying to tell him, exactly? What secret was buried in his past? What suppressed trauma or forgotten event lay at the root of his somnambulism?

Sitting at his desk, staring at the night beyond the big window, straining blindly toward understanding, he grew tense. Again, he felt a need for Valium, almost a craving, but he resisted.

The note engaged his curiosity, logic, and reason. He was able to focus his intellect on the search for a solution and concentrate with an intensity of which he had not been capable recently, and thus he found the will power to forsake the solace of tranquillisation.

He was beginning to feel good about himself for the first time in weeks. In spite of the helplessness in which he had been wallowing, he now realised that, after all, he still had the power to shape and direct the course of his own life. All he had needed was something like the note, something tangible on which he could focus.

He paced around the house, carrying the note, thinking.

Eventually he came to a front window from which he could see his kerbside mailbox – a brick column with a metal receptacle mortared into it – standing in the bluish fall of light from a mercury-vapour streetlamp.

Because he kept the post office drawer in town, the only mail he got at home was that addressed to 'Occupant' and occasional cards or letters from friends who had both his mailing and street addresses but who sometimes forgot that all correspondence was to go to the former. Standing at the window, staring at the kerbside receptacle, Dom realised that he had not picked up today's delivery.

He went outside, down the front walk to the street, and used a key to unlock the receptacle. Except for the breeze that rustled the trees, the night was quiet. The wind carried the scent of the sea, and the air was chilly. The overhead mercury-vapour lamp was sufficiently bright for Dom to identify the mail as he withdrew it from the box: six advertising flyers and catalogues, two Christmas cards . . . and a plain white business-size envelope with no return address.

Excited, fearful, he hurried back into the house, to his study, tearing open the white envelope and extracting a single sheet of paper as he went. At his desk, he unfolded the letter.

The moon.

No other words could have shocked him as badly as those. He felt as if he had fallen into the White Rabbit's hole and was tumbling down into a fantastic realm where logic and reason no longer applied.

The moon. This was *impossible*. No one knew he had awakened from bad dreams with those words on his lips, repeating them in panic: 'The moon, moon. . . .' And no one knew that, while sleepwalking, he had typed those words on the Displaywriter. He'd told neither Parker nor Cobletz, because those incidents had transpired after he'd begun drug therapy and after the drugs seemed to be working, and he had not wanted to appear to be slipping backwards. Besides, although those two words filled him with dread, he did not understand their significance. He did not know *why* they had the power to raise gooseflesh, and he instinctively felt that it was unwise to mention this development to anyone until he had got a better handle on it. He had been afraid Cobletz would conclude that the drugs were not helping him and would discontinue them in favour of psychotherapy – and Dom had *needed* the drugs.

The moon.

No one knew, damn it. No one but . . . Dom himself.

In the streetlamp's dim glow, he had not checked for a postmark. Now, he saw that its point of origin was not a mystery, as was the case with the letter that had come this morning. It was clearly stamped NEW YORK, NEW YORK, and dated December 18. Wednesday of last week.

He almost laughed out loud. He was not insane, after all. He was not sending these cryptic messages to himself – could not *possibly* be sending them – because he had been in Laguna last week. Three thousand miles separated him from the mailbox in which this – and undoubtedly the other – strange message had first been deposited.

But who had sent him the notes – and why? Who in New York could know that he was sleepwalking . . . or that he had repeatedly typed 'the moon' on his word processor? A thousand questions crowded Dom Corvaisis' mind, and he had no answers to any of them. Worse, at the moment, he could see no way even to *seek* answers. The situation was so bizarre that there was no logical direction for his inquiries to take.

For two months, he had thought that his sleepwalking was the strangest and most frightening thing that had ever happened – or ever would happen – to him. But whatever lay behind the somnambulism must be even stranger and more frightening than the night-walking itself.

He recalled the first message he had left for himself on the word processor: *I'm afraid*. What *had* he been hiding from in closets? When he had started to nail the windows shut while sound asleep, what had he hoped to keep out of his house?

Dom saw now that his sleepwalking had not been caused by stress. He was not suffering anxiety attacks because he feared the success or failure of his first novel. It was nothing as mundane as that.

Something else. Something very strange and terrible.

What did he know in his sleep that he did not know when awake?

6.

NEW HAVEN COUNTY, CONNECTICUT

The sky had cleared before darkfall, but the moon had not yet risen. The stars shed little light upon the cold earth.

With his back against a boulder, Jack Twist sat in the snow atop a knoll, at the edge of a copse of pines, waiting for the Guardmaster armoured truck to appear. Only three weeks after personally netting more than a million dollars from the Mafia warehouse job, he was already setting up another heist. He was wearing boots, gloves, and a white ski suit, with the hood over his head and tied securely under his chin. Three hundred yards behind him and to the southwest, beyond the small woods, the darkness was relieved by the lights of a housing development; however, Jack waited in utter blackness, his breath steaming.

In front of him, two miles of night-clad fields lay northeast, barren but for a few widely spaced trees and some winter-stripped brush. In the distance beyond the emptiness, there were electronics plants, then shopping centres, then residential neighbourhoods, none of which was visible from Jack's position, though their existence was indicated by the glow of electric lights on the horizon.

At the far edge of the fields, headlights appeared over a low rise. Raising a pair of night binoculars, Jack focused on the approaching vehicle, which was following the two-lane county road with bisected the fields. In spite of the leftward cast of his left eye, Jack had superb vision, and with the help of the night binoculars, he ascertained that the vehicle was not the Guardmaster truck, therefore of no consequence to him. He lowered the glasses.

In his solitude upon the snowy knoll, he thought back to another time and a warmer place, to a humid night in a Central American jungle, when he had studied a nocturnal landscape with binoculars just like these. Then, he had been searching anxiously for hostile troops that had been stalking and encircling him and his buddies. . . .

*　　　*　　　*

His platoon – twenty highly trained Rangers under the leadership of Lieutenant Rafe Eikhorn, with Jack as second in command – had crossed the border illegally and gone fifteen miles inside the enemy state without being detected. Their presence could have been construed as an act of war; therefore, they wore camouflage suits stripped of rank and service markings, and they carried no identification.

Their target was a nasty little 're-education' camp, cynically named the Institute of Brotherhood, where a thousand Miskito Indians were imprisoned by the People's Army. Two weeks earlier, courageous Catholic priests had led another fifteen hundred Indians through the jungles and out of the country before they could be imprisoned, too. Those clergymen had brought word that the Indians at the Institute would be murdered and buried in mass graves if not rescued within a month.

The Miskitos were a fiercely proud breed with a rich culture that they refused to forsake for the anti-ethnic, collectivist philosophy of the country's latest leaders. The Indians' continued loyalty to their own traditions would ensure their extermination, for the ruling council did not hesitate to call up the firing squads to solidify its power.

Nevertheless, twenty Rangers in mufti would not have been committed to such a dangerous raid merely to save Miskitos. Both left- and right-wing dictatorial regimes routinely slaughtered their citizenry in every corner of the world, and the United States did not – could not – prevent those state-sanctioned murders. But in addition to the Indians at the Institute, there were eleven others whose rescue, along with the Indians, made the risky operation worthwhile.

Those eleven were former revolutionaries who had fought the just war against the now-deposed right-wing dictator, but who had refused to remain silent when their revolution had been betrayed by totalitarians of the left. Undoubtedly, those eleven possessed valuable information. The opportunity to debrief them was more important than saving the lives of a thousand Indians – at least as far as Washington was concerned.

Undetected, Jack's platoon reached the Institute of Brotherhood in a farming district at the edge of the jungle. It

196

was a concentration camp in all but name, a place of barbed-wire fences and guard towers. Two buildings stood outside the fenced perimeter of the camp: a two-storey concrete-block structure from which the government administered the district, and a dilapidated wooden barracks housing sixty troops.

Shortly after midnight, the platoon of Rangers stealthily took up positions and launched a rocket attack on the barracks and the concrete building. The initial artillery barrages were followed by hand-to-hand combat. Half an hour after the last shot was fired, the Indians and other prisoners – as jubilant a group as Jack had ever seen – were formed into a column and moved out towards the border, fifteen miles away.

Two Rangers had been killed. Three were wounded.

As first in command of the platoon, Rafe Eikhorn led the exodus and oversaw security along the column's flanks, while Jack stayed behind with three men to be sure the last of the prisoners got out of the camp in orderly fashion. It was also his responsibility to gather up files relating to the interrogation, torture, and murder of Indians and district peasants. By the time he and his four men left the Institute of Brotherhood, they were two miles behind the last of the Miskitos.

Though Jack and his men made good time, they never caught up with their platoon and were still miles from the Honduran border when, at dawn, hostile army helicopters, like giant black wasps, came in low over the trees and began off-loading enemy troops wherever a clearing could be found. The other Rangers and all the Indians reached freedom, but Jack and his three men were captured and transported to a facility similar to the Institute of Brotherhood. However, the place was so much worse than the concentration camp that it had no official existence. The ruling council did not admit that such a hellhole existed in the new workers' paradise – or that monstrous inquisitions were conducted within its walls. In true Orwellian tradition, because the four-storey complex of cells and torture chambers had no name, it did not exist.

Within those nameless walls, in cells without numbers, Jack Twist and the three other Rangers were subjected to psychological and physical torture, relentless humiliation and degradation, controlled starvation, and constant threats of death.

197

One of the four died. One went mad. Only Jack and his closest friend, Oscar Weston, held on to both life and sanity during the eleven and a half months of their incarceration. . . .

*   *   *

Now, eight years later, leaning against a boulder atop a knoll in Connecticut, waiting for the Guardmaster truck, Jack heard sounds and detected odours which were not of this wind-swept winter night. The hard footfalls of jackboots on concrete corridors. The stench from the overflowing slops bucket, which was the cell's only toilet. The pathetic cry of some poor bastard being taken from his cell to another session with interrogators.

Jack took deep breaths of the clean, cold Connecticut air. He was seldom troubled by bad memories of that time and name-less place. He was more often haunted by what had happened to him *after* his escape – and by what had happened to his Jenny in his absence. It was not his suffering in Central America that turned him against society; rather, subsequent events were what had soured him.

He saw other headlights out on the black fields, and raised his night binoculars. It was the Guardmaster armoured transport.

He looked at his watch. 9:38. It was right on schedule, as it had been every night for a week. Even with the holiday tomor-row, the truck kept to its route. Guardmaster Security was nothing if not reliable.

On the ground beside Jack was an attache case. He lifted the lid. The blue numerals of a digital scanner were locked on the Guardmaster's open radio link to the company dispatcher. Even with his state-of-the-art equipment, he had needed three nights to discover the truck's frequency. He turned the volume dial on his own receiver. Static crackled, hissed. Then he was rewarded by a routine exchange between the driver and the distant dispatcher.

'Three-oh-one,' the dispatcher said.

'Reindeer,' the driver said.

'Rudolph,' the dispatcher said.

'Rooftop,' the driver said.

The hiss and crackle of static settled in once more.

The dispatcher had opened the exchange with the truck's number, and the rest of it had been the day's code which served as confirmation that 301 was on schedule and in no trouble of any kind.

Jack switched off his receiver. The lighted dials went dark.

The armoured transport passed less than two hundred feet from his position on the knoll, and he turned to watch its dwindling tail-lights.

He was confident of Guardmaster 301's schedule now, and he would not be returning to these fields until the night of the stick-up, which was tentatively scheduled for Saturday, January 11. Meanwhile, there was a great deal more planning to be done.

Ordinarily, planning a job was nearly as exciting and satisfying as the actual commission of the crime. But as he left the knoll and headed towards the houses to the southwest, where he had parked his car on a quiet street, he felt no elation, no thrill. He was losing the ability to take delight in even the *contemplation* of a crime.

He was changing. And he did not know why.

As he drew near the first houses to the southwest of the knoll, he became aware that the night had grown brighter. He looked up. The moon swelled fat on the horizon, so huge it seemed to be crashing to earth, an illusion of enormousness created by the odd perspective of the early stages of the satellite's ascension. He stopped abruptly and stood with his head tilted back, staring up at the luminous lunar surface. A chill seized him, an inner iciness unrelated to the winter cold.

'The moon,' he said softly.

Hearing himself speak those words aloud, Jack shuddered violently. Inexplicable fear welled in him. He was gripped by an irrational urge to run and hide from the moon, as if it's luminescence were corrosive and would, like an acid, dissolve him as he stood bathed in it.

The compulsion to flee passed in a minute. He could not understand why the moon had so suddenly terrified him. It was only the ancient and familiar moon of love songs and romantic poetry. Strange.

He headed towards the car again. The looming lunar face

still made him uneasy, and several times he glanced up at it, perplexed.

However, by the time he got in the car, drove into New Haven, and picked up Interstate 95, that curious incident had faded from his mind. He was once more preoccupied with thoughts of Jenny, his comatose wife, whose condition haunted him worse than usual at Christmastime.

Later, in his apartment, as he stood by a big window, staring out at the great city, a bottle of Beck's in one hand, he was sure that from 261st Street to Park Row, from Bensonhurst to Little Neck, there could be no one in the Metropolis whose Christmas Eve was lonelier than his.

7.

CHRISTMAS DAY

Elko County, Nevada.

Sandy Sarver woke soon after dawn came to the high plains. The early sun glimmered vaguely at the bedroom windows of the house trailer. The world was so still that it seemed time must have stopped.

She could turn over and go back to sleep if she so desired, for she had eight more days of vacation ahead of her. Ernie and Faye Block had closed the Tranquillity Motel and had gone to visit their grandchildren in Milwaukee. The adjacent Tranquillity Grille, which Sandy operated with her husband Ned, was also closed over the holidays.

But Sandy knew she could not get back to sleep, for she was wide awake – and horny. She stretched like a cat beneath the blankets. She wanted to wake Ned, smother him with kisses, and pull him atop her.

Ned was merely a shadowy form in the dark bedroom, breathing deeply, sound asleep. Although she wanted him badly, she did not wake him. There would be plenty of time for love-making later in the day.

She slipped quietly out of bed, into the bathroom, and

200

showered. She made the end of it a *cold* shower.

For years she had been uninterested in sex, frigid. Not long ago the sight of her own nude body had embarrassed her and filled her with shame. Although she did not know the reason for the new feelings that had risen in her lately, she definitely had changed. It had started the summer before last, when sex had suddenly seemed . . . well, appealing. That sounded silly now. *Of course* sex was appealing. But prior to that summer, love-making had always been a chore to be endured. Her late erotic blossoming was a delightful surprise and an inexplicable mystery.

Nude, she returned to the shadowy bedroom. She took a sweater and a pair of jeans from the closet, and dressed.

In the small kitchen, she started to pour orange juice but stopped when stricken by the urge to go for a drive. She left a note for Ned, put on a sheepskin-lined jacket, and went outside to the Ford pick-up.

Sex and driving were the two new passions in her life, and the latter was almost as important to her as the former. That was another funny thing: until the summer before last, she hated going anywhere in the pick-up except to work and back, and she seldom drove. She'd not only disliked highway travel but had dreaded it the way some people were afraid of aeroplanes. But now, other than sex, there was nothing she liked better than to get behind the wheel of the truck and take off, journeying on a whim, without a destination, speeding.

She had always understood why sex repelled her; that had been no mystery. She could blame her father, Horton Purney, for her frigidity. Though she had never known her mother, who had died giving birth, Sandy had known her father far too well. They had lived in a ramshackle house on the outskirts of Barstow, on the edge of the lonely California desert, just the two of them, and Sandy's earliest memories were of sexual abuse. Horton Purney had been a moody, brooding, mean, and dangerous man. Until Sandy escaped from home at fourteen, her father had used her as if she had been an erotic toy.

Only recently had she realised that her strong dislike for highway travel was also related to something else that her father had done to her. Horton Purney had run a motorcycle repair shop out of a sagging, sun-burnt, unpainted barn on the same property as his house, but he had never made much money from it. Therefore, twice a year, he put Sandy in the car and made the two-and-a-half-hour drive across the desert to Las Vegas, where he knew an enterprising pimp, Samson Cherrik. Cherrik had a list of perverts with a special interest in children, and he was always happy to see Sandy. After a few weeks in Vegas, Sandy's father packed, put Sandy in the car, and drove back to Barstow, his pockets bulging with cash. For Sandy, the long drive to Vegas was a nightmare journey, for she knew what awaited her at their destination. The trip back to Barstow was worse, for it was not an escape from Vegas but a return to the grim life in that ramshackle house and the dark, urgent, insatiable lust of Horton Purney. In either direction, the road had led to hell, and she had learned to loathe the rumble of the car's engine, the hum of tyres on the pavement, and the unspooling highway ahead.

Therefore, the pleasure she now took from driving and sex seemed miraculous. She could not understand where she'd found the strength and will to overcome her horrible past. Since the summer before last, she simply . . . *changed*, was still changing. And, oh, it was glorious to feel the chains of self-loathing and the bonds of fear breaking apart, to feel self-respect for the first time in her life, to feel *free*.

Now, she got into the Ford pick-up and started the engine. Their house trailer was set on an unlandscaped half-acre lot at the southern edge of the tiny – almost non-existent – town of Beowawe, along Route 21, a two-lane blacktop. As Sandy drove away from the trailer, there seemed to be nothing but empty plains, rolling hills, scattered buttes, rocky outcroppings, grass, brush, and waterless arroyos for a thousand miles in every direction. The intensely blue morning sky was immense, and as she got the Ford up to speed, Sandy felt as if she might take flight.

If she headed north on 21, she would pass through Beowawe and soon come to Interstate 80, which led east towards Elko or West towards Battle Mountain. Instead, she went south, into a beautifully barren landscape. With skill and ease, she guided the four-wheel-drive pick-up over the badly weathered county road at seventy miles an hour.

In fifteen minutes, Route 21 petered out into a gravel

roadbed that led south through another eighty-three miles of uninhabited and desolate territory. She did not follow it, choosing instead to turn east on a one-lane dirt track flanked by wild grass and scrub.

Some snow lay on the ground this Christmas morning, though not much. In the distance, the mountains were white, but down here, the annual precipitation was less than fifteen inches a year, little of it in the form of snow. Here was an inch-deep skin of snow, there a small hillock against which a shallow drift had formed, and here a sparkling bush on which wind-driven snow had hardened into a lacy garment of ice, but by far the largest portion of the land was bare and dry and brown.

Sandy drove fast on the dirt, too, and behind her a cloud of dust plumed up. In time she left the track, headed overland – north, then west, coming at last to a familiar place, though she had not set out with this destination in mind. For reasons she did not understand, her subconscious often guided her to this spot during her solitary drives, seldom in a direct line but by wandering routes, so her arrival was usually a surprise to her. She stopped, set the brake. With the engine idling, she stared for a while through the dusty windshield.

She came here because it made her feel better, though she did not know why. The slopes, the spines and teeth of rock, the grass and brush, formed a pleasing picture, though the scene was no prettier and no different from thousands of other places nearby. Yet here she felt a sublime peacefulness that could not be attained anywhere else.

She switched off the engine and got out of the pick-up, and for a while she strolled back and forth, hands jammed into the pockets of her sheepskin-lined jacket, oblivious of the stingingly cold air. Her drive through the wildlands had brought her back towards civilisation, and Interstate 80 lay only a couple of hundred yards to the north. The occasional roar of a passing truck echoed like a distant dragon's growl, but the holiday traffic was light. Beyond the highway, on the uplands to the northwest, lay the Tranquillity Motel and Grille, but Sandy glanced just once in that direction. She was more interested in the immediate terrain, which exerted a mysterious and powerful attraction for her, and which seemed to radiate peace the way a rock, in evening, radiated the heat of the sun that it had absorbed during the day.

She wasn't trying to analyse her affinity for this patch of ground. Evidently, there was some subtle harmony in the contours of the land, an interplay of line, form, and shadow that defied definition. Any attempt to decode its attraction would be as foolish as trying to analyse the beauty of a sunset or the appeal of a favourite flower.

That Christmas morning, Sandy did not yet know that Ernie Block had been drawn, as if possessed, to the same patch of ground on December 10, when he had been on his way home from the freight office in Elko. She did not know that it aroused, in Ernie, an electrifying sense of pending epiphany and more than a little fear – emotions quite unlike those that it stirred in her. Weeks would pass before she learned that her special retreat had a strong attraction for others besides herself – both friends and strangers.

*　　　*　　　*

Chicago, Illinois.

For Father Stefan Wycazik – that stocky Polish dynamo, rector of St Bernadette's, rescuer of troubled priests – it was the busiest Christmas morning he had ever known. And as the day wore on, it swiftly became the most meaningful Christmas of his life.

He celebrated the second Mass at St. Bernadette's, spent an hour greeting parishioners who stopped by the rectory with fruit baskets and boxes of homemade cookies and other gifts, then drove to University Hospital to pay a visit to Winton Tolk, the policeman who had been shot in an uptown sandwich shop yesterday afternoon. Following emergency surgery, Tolk had been in the Intensive Care Unit yesterday afternoon and all through the night. Christmas morning he had been moved to a semi-private room adjacent to the ICU, for although he was no longer in critical condition, he still needed to be monitored constantly.

When Father Wycazik arrived, Raynella Tolk, Winton's wife, was at her husband's bedside. She was quite attractive, with chocolate-brown skin and stylish close-cropped hair. 'Mrs Tolk? I'm Stefan Wycazik.'

'But –'

He smiled. 'Relax. I'm not here to give anyone the last rites.'

'Good,' Winton said, ''cause I'm sure not planning on dying.'

The wounded policeman was not only fully conscious but alert and apparently suffering no pain. His bed was raised to a sitting position. Although his broad chest was heavily bandaged, and although a cardiac telemetry device hung around his neck, and in spite of the IV line that was dripping glucose and antibiotics into the median basilic vein in his left arm, he looked remarkably well considering his recent misadventure.

Father Wycazik stood at the foot of the bed, his tension betrayed only by the way he kept turning his black fedora around and around in his strong hands. When he realised what he was doing, he quickly put the hat on a chair.

He said, 'Mr Tolk, if you feel up to it, I've come to ask you a few questions about what happened yesterday.'

Both Tolk and his wife looked puzzled by Stefan's curiosity.

The priest gave a partial explanation for his interest – through only partial. 'The fellow who cruised the Uptown district with you for the past week, Brendan Cronin, was in my employ,' he said, maintaining Brendan's cover as a lay worker for the Church.

'Oh, I'd like to meet *him*,' Raynella said, her face brightening.

'He saved my life,' Tolk said. 'He did a *crazy*-brave thing, which he shouldn't have done in a million years, but I'm sure glad he did it.'

Raynella said, 'Mr Cronin walked into that sandwich shop not knowing if all the gunmen were dead, not knowing if he might be shot.'

'It's strictly against police procedure to walk into a situation like that,' Winton said. 'I'd have handled it by the book myself if I'd been one of those outside. I can't exactly applaud what Brendan did, Father, but I owe him my life for doing it.'

'Amazing,' Father Wycazik said, as if this were the first time he had heard of Brendan's bravery. In fact, yesterday he had spoken at length with Winton Tolk's precinct captain, an old friend, and had heard Brendan praised for courage and damned for foolishness. 'I've always known Brendan's a dependable fellow. Did he also provide first-aid?'

'He might have,' Winton said. 'Don't really know. I remember regaining consciousness . . . and there he was . . . sort of looming over me . . . calling my name . . . but I was still in a haze, you see.'

'It's a miracle Win survived,' Raynella said in a tremulous voice.

'Now, now, honey,' Winton said softly. 'I *did* make it, and that's all that counts.' When he was sure his wife would be all right, he looked at Stefan and said, 'Everyone's amazed that I could lose so much blood and pull through. From what I hear, I must've lost buckets.'

'Did Brendan apply a tourniquet?'

Tolk frowned. 'Don't know. Like I said, I was in a haze, a daze.'

Father Wycazik hesitated, wondering how to find out what he needed to know without revealing the extraordinary possibility that motivated this visit. 'I know you're not very clear about what happened but . . . did you notice anything peculiar about . . . Brendan's hands?'

'Peculiar? What do you mean?'

'He touched you, didn't he?'

'Sure. I guess he felt for a pulse . . . then checked around to see where the bleeding was coming from.'

'Well, did you feel anything . . . anything unusual when he touched you . . . anything odd,' Stefan asked carefully, frustrated by the need to be vague.

'I don't seem to be following your line of thought, Father.'

Stefan Wycazik shook his head. 'Never mind. The important thing is that you're well.' He glanced at his watch and, feigning surprise, said, 'Good heavens, I'm late for an appointment.' Before they could respond, he snatched his hat from the chair, wished them Godspeed, and hurried out, no doubt leaving them astonished by his behaviour.

When people saw Father Wycazik walking towards them, they were usually reminded of drill sergeants or football coaches. His solid body and the self-confident, aggressive way he used it were not what one expected of a priest. And when he was in a hurry, he was not so much like a drill sergeant or a football coach as he was like a *tank*.

From Tolk's room, Father Wycazik blitzed down the hall, shoved through a pair of heavy swinging doors, then through another pair, into the Intensive Care Unit, where the wounded policeman had been until just an hour ago. He asked to speak with the physician on duty, Dr Royce Albright. With the hope that God would forgive a few little white lies told in a good cause, Stefan identified himself as the Tolk family's priest and implied that Mrs Tolk hade sent him to get the full story of her husband's condition, about which she was not yet entirely clear.

Dr Albright looked like Jerry Lewis and had a deep rumbling voice like Henry Kissinger, which was disconcerting, but he was willing to answer whatever questions Father Wycazik wished to pose. He was not Winton Tolk's personal physician, but he was interested in the case. 'You can assure Mrs Tolk that there's almost no danger of a setback. He's coming along marvellously. Shot twice in the chest, pointblank with a .38. Until yesterday, no one here would've believed that anyone could take two shots in the chest from a large-calibre handgun *and be out of intensive care in twenty-four hours*! Mr Tolk is incredibly lucky.'

'The bullets missed the heart, then . . . and all vital organs?'

'Not only that,' Albright said, 'but neither round did major damage to any veins or arteries. A .38-calibre slug has lots of punch, Father. Ordinarily, it chews up the victim. In Tolk's case, one major artery and vein were nicked, but neither was severed. Very fortunate, indeed.'

'Then I suppose the bullets were stopped by bone at some point.'

'Deflected, yes, but not stopped. Both slugs were found in soft tissue. And that's another amazing thing – no shattered bones, not even a small fracture. A *very* lucky man.'

Father Wycazik nodded. 'When the two slugs were removed from his body, was there any indication they were underweight for .38-calibre ammunition? I mean, maybe the cartridges were faulty, with too little lead in the bullets. That would explain why, even though it was a .38 revolver, the shots did less damage than a pair of .22s.'

Albright frowned. 'Don't know. Could be. You'd have to

ask the police . . . or Dr Sonneford, the surgeon who took the slugs out of Tolk.'

'I understand Officer Tolk lost a great deal of blood.'

Grimacing, Albright said, 'Must be a mistake about that on his chart. I haven't had a chance to talk to Dr Sonneford today, it being Christmas, but according to the chart, Tolk received over four litres of whole blood in the operating room. Of course, that can't be correct.'

'Why not?'

'Father, if Tolk actually lost four litres of blood before they got him to the hospital, there wouldn't have been enough in him to maintain even minimal circulation. He'd have been dead. Stone cold dead.'

*   *   *

Las Vegas, Nevada.

Mary and Pete Monatella, Jorja's parents, arrived at her apartment at 6:00 Christmas morning, bleary-eyed and grumpy from too little sleep, but determined to take up their rightful posts by the brightly trimmed tree before Marcie awoke. Mary, as tall as Jorja, had once been almost as shapely as her daughter too; now she was heavy, girdled. Pete was shorter than his wife, barrel-chested, a bantam rooster who seemed to strut when he walked but was one of the most self-effacing men Jorja had ever known. They came burdened with presents for their only grandchild.

They had a present for Jorja – plus the usual gifts they brought every time they visited: well-meant but annoying criticism, unwanted advice, guilt. Mary was hardly through the door before she announced that Jorja should clean the ventilation hood above the range, and she rummaged under the sink until she found a spray bottle of Windex and a rag, with which she performed the chore herself. She also observed that the tree looked underdecorated –' It needs more lights, Jorja!' – and when she saw how Marcie's presents were wrapped, she professed despair. 'My God, Jorja, the wrapping papers aren't bright enough. The ribbons aren't big enough. Little girls like bright papers with Santa Claus on them and lots of ribbons.'

For his part, her father was content to focus all of his discontent upon the huge tray of cookies on the kitchen counter. 'These are all store-bought, Jorja. Didn't you make any homemade cookies this year?'

'Well, Dad, I've been working a little overtime lately, and then there're the classes I'm taking at UNLV, and –'

'I know it's hard being a single mother, baby,' he said, 'but we're talking fundamentals here. Homemade cookies are one of the best parts of Christmas. It's an absolute fundamental.'

'Fundamental,' Jorja's mother agreed.

The Christmas spirit had been late in coming to Jorja this year, and even now she had a tenuous grip on it. Subject to her parents' well-intentioned but infuriating non-stop commentary on her shortcomings, she might have lost the holiday mood altogether if Marcie had not put in a timely appearance at 6:30, just after Jorja had slipped a fourteen-pound turkey into the oven for the big meal later in the day. The girl shuffled into the living room in her pyjamas, as cute as any idealised child in a Norman Rockwell painting.

'Did Santa bring my Little Ms Doctor kit?'

Pete said, 'He brought you more than that, pumpkin. Look here! Just *look* at all Santa brought.'

Marcie turned and saw the tree – which 'Santa' had put up during the night – and the mountain of gifts. She gasped. 'Wow!'

The child's excitement was transmitted to Jorja's parents, and for the time being they forgot about such things as dusty ventilation hoods and store-bought cookies. For a while the apartment was filled with joyous, busy sounds.

But by the time Marcie had opened half her gifts, the celebratory mood began to change, and in crept a little of the darkness that would reappear in a far more frightening form later in the day. In a whiny voice that was out of character, the girl grumped that Santa had not remembered the Little Ms. Doctor kit. She discarded a much-wanted doll without even taking it out of its box, moving to the next package in the hope that it contained Little Ms Doctor, clawing at the wrappings. Something in the child's demeanour, a queerness in her eyes, disquieted Jorja. Soon Mary and Pete noticed it as well. They began urging Marcie to take more time with each present, to get more pleasure out of each before rushing on to the next, but their entreaties were not successful.

Jorja had not put the doctor play-kit under the tree; it was hidden in a closet as a final surprise. But with only three boxes left, Marcie was pale and trembling in anticipation of Little Ms Doctor.

In God's name, what was so important about it? Many of the toys already unwrapped were more expensive and more interesting than the play-doctor's bag. Why was her attention so intently and unnaturally focused on that single item? Why was she so obsessed with it?

When the last of the gifts beneath the tree and the last of those from Mary and Pete were opened, Marcie let out a sob of purest misery. 'Santa didn't bring it! He forgot! He forgot!'

Considering all the wondrous presents strewn across the room, the girl's despondency was shocking. Jorja was disconcerted and displeased by Marcie's rudeness, and she saw that her own parents were startled, dismayed, and impatient with this unexpected and unjustified tantrum.

Suddenly afraid that Christmas was collapsing into ruins around her, Jorja ran to the bedroom closet, plucked the crucial gift from behind the shoe boxes, and returned to the living room with it.

With frenzied desperation, Marcie snatched the box from her mother.

'What's got into the child?' Mary asked.

'Yeah,' Pete said, 'what's so important about this Little Doctor?'

Marcie tore frantically at the wrappings until she saw that the package contained the item she most desired. Immediately, she grew calm, stopped trembling. 'Little Ms Doctor. Santa didn't forget!'

'Honey, maybe it's not from Santa,' Jorja said. She was relieved to see the child she loved emerging from that strange and unpleasant mood. 'Not all your gifts came from Santa. Better look at the tag.'

Marcie dutifully searched for the tag, read the few words on it, and looked up with an uncertain smile. 'It's from . . . Daddy.'

Jorja felt her parents staring at her, but she did not meet their eyes. They knew that Alan had gone off to Acapulco with his latest bimbo, the airhead blonde named Pepper, and that he had not bothered to leave so much as a card for Marcie, and they no doubt disapproved of Jorja letting him off the hook like this.

Later, when Jorja was in the kitchen, squatting in front of the oven, checking on the turkey, her mother stooped down beside her and said softly, 'Why'd you do it, Jorja? Why'd you put that louse's name on the gift she wanted most of all?'

Jorja slid the rack part way out of the oven, bringing the turkey into the light. With a ladle, she scooped the drippings from the pan and basted the roasting bird. Finally she said, 'Marcie shouldn't have her Christmas ruined just because her father's a jackass.'

'You shouldn't protect her from the truth,' Mary said quietly.

'The truth's too ugly for a seven-year-old.'

'The sooner she knows what a louse her father is, the better. You know what your dad heard about this woman Alan's living with?'

'I sure hope this bird's going to be done by noon.'

Mary would not drop the subject. 'She's on the call list of two casinos, Jorja. That's what Pete heard. You know what I mean? She's a call girl. Alan's living with a call girl. What's *wrong* with him?'

Jorja closed her eyes and took a deep breath.

Mary said, 'Well, if he wants nothing to do with Marcie, that's fine. God knows what diseases he's picked up living with *that* woman.'

Jorja pushed the turkey back into the oven, closed the door, and stood up. 'Could we not talk about this any more?'

'I thought you'd want to know what the woman is.'

'So now I know.'

Their voices dropped lower, became more intense: 'What if he comes around some day and says, "Pepper and I want Marcie to go to Acapulco with us," or Disneyland or maybe just stay at their place for a while?'

Exasperated, Jorja said, 'Mother, he doesn't want anything to do with Marcie because she reminds him of his responsibilities.'

'But what if –'

'*Mother, damn it!*'

Although Jorja had not raised her voice, there was such anger in those three words that the effect on her mother was immediate. A hurt look crossed Mary's face. Stung, she turned away from Jorja. She went quickly to the refrigerator, opened it, and looked over the contents of the overloaded shelves. 'Oh, you made gnocchi.'

'Not store-bought,' Jorja said shakily. 'Homemade.' She meant to be conciliatory, but she realised that her comment might be misconstrued as a snide reference to her father's dismay over store-brought cookies. She bit her lip, and fought back scalding tears.

Still looking into the refrigerator, a tremor still in her voice, Mary said, 'You're going to have potatoes, too? And what's this – oh, you've already grated the cabbage for coleslaw. I thought you'd need help, but I guess you've thought of everything.' She closed the refrigerator door and looked for something she could do to occupy her and get them through this awkward moment. Tears were visible in her eyes.

Jorja virtually flung herself away from the counter and threw her arms around her mother. Mary returned the hug, and for a while they clung to each other, finding speech both unnecessary and impossible.

Holding fast, Mary said, 'I don't know why I'm like this. My mother was the same with me. I swore I'd never be like this with you.'

'I love you just the way you are.'

'Maybe it's because you're my only. If I'd been able to have a couple others, I wouldn't be so tough on you.'

'It's partly my fault, Mom. I've been so touchy lately.'

'And why shouldn't you be?' her mother said, holding her tight. 'That louse walks out on you, you're supporting yourself and Marcie, going to school. . . . You got every *right* to be touchy. We're so proud of you, Jorja. It takes such courage to do what you're doing.'

In the living room, Marcie began shrieking.

What now? Jorja wondered.

When she got to the living room archway, she saw her father trying to persuade Marcie to play with a doll. 'Look here,' Pete said, 'dolly cries when you tilt her this way, giggles when you tilt her that way!'

'I don't want to play with the dumb doll,' Marcie pouted. She was holding the make-believe, plastic and rubber hypodermic syringe from the Little Ms Doctor kit, and that unsettling intensity and urgency had taken possession of her again. 'I want to give you another *shot*.'

'But honey,' Pete said, 'you've already given me twenty shots.'

'I've got to practise,' Marcie said. 'I'll never grow up to be my own doctor if I don't start practising *now*.'

Pete looked at Jorja with exasperation.

Mary said, 'What *is* it with this Little Ms Doctor thing?'

'I wish I knew,' Jorja said.

Marcie grimaced as she pushed the plunger of the fake hypodermic. Perspiration glistened on her brow.

'I wish I knew,' Jorja repeated uneasily.

*　　　*　　　*

Boston, Massachusetts.

It was the worst Christmas of Ginger Weiss's life.

Although Jewish, her beloved father had always celebrated Christmas in a secular spirit, because he liked the harmony and goodwill that the holiday promoted, and after his death, Ginger had continued to regard December 25th as a special day, a time of joy. Until today, Christmas had never depressed her.

George and Rita did all they could to make Ginger feel a part of their celebration, but she was acutely aware that she was an outsider. The Hannabys' three sons had brought their families to Baywatch for several days, and the huge house was filled with the silvery laughter of children. Everyone made an effort to include Ginger in all the Hannaby traditions from popcorn-stringing to neighbourhood carolling.

Christmas morning, she was there to watch the children attack the mountain of gifts, and following the example of the other adults, she crawled around on the floor with the kids, helping them assemble and play with their new toys. For a couple of hours, her despair abated, and she was assimilated by the Hannaby family in spite of herself.

However, at lunch – rich with holiday delicacies yet essentially a light meal, just a hint of the extravagant dinner feast to come that evening – Ginger felt out of place again. Much conversation involved reminiscences of previous holidays of which she'd not been a part.

After lunch, she pleaded a headache and escaped to her room. The splendid view of the bay calmed her but couldn't arrest her spiral into depression. She desperately hoped Pablo Jackson would call tomorrow and say that he had studied the problem of memory-blocks and was ready to hypnotise her again.

Ginger's visit to Pablo had distressed George and Rita less than she had expected. They were upset that she had gone out alone, risking an amnesic seizure with no friend to help her, and they made her promise she would allow either Rita or one of the servants to drive her to and from Pablo's apartment in the future, but they did not attempt to argue against the unconventional treatment she had sought from the magician.

The bay view's capacity to calm Ginger was limited. She turned from the window, got up, and went to the bed, where she was surprised to find two books on the nightstand. One was a fantasy by Tim Powers, an author she had read before, the other a copy of something called *Twilight in Babylon*, and she had no idea where they had come from.

There were half a dozen other books in the room, borrowed from the library downstairs, for during the past few weeks she had had little to do but read. But this was the first time she'd seen Powers' book and *Twilight in Babylon*. The former, a tale of time-travelling trolls fighting their own secret war against British goblins during the American revolution, looked delightful, the type of exotic story that her father had enjoyed. A slip of paper laid loosely in the front identified it as an advance review copy. Rita had a friend who was a reviewer for the *Globe*, and who sometimes passed along intriguing books before they were available in the stores. Evidently, these had come within the last day or two and Rita, aware of Ginger's tastes in fiction, had put them in her room.

She set the Powers book aside for later delectation, and she took a closer look at *Twilight in Babylon*. She had never heard of the author, Dominick Corvaisis, but the brief summary of the story was intriguing, and when she had read the first page, she was hooked. However, before continuing, she moved

214

from the bed to one of the comfortable chairs and, only then, glanced at the author's photograph on the back of the jacket.

Her breath caught in her throat. Fear filled her.

For a moment she thought the photograph was going to be the kicker that knocked her into another fugue. She tried to fling the book aside but could not, tried to stand up but could not. She drew deep breaths, closed her eyes, and waited for her pulse rate to sink towards normal.

When she opened her eyes and looked at the author's photograph again, it still disturbed her, though not as badly as it had at first. She knew that she had seen this man before, had met him somewhere, and not in the best of circumstances, though she could not remember where or when. His brief biography on the jacket flap informed her that he had lived in Portland, Oregon, and now resided in Laguna Beach, California. As she had never been in either of those places, she could not imagine when their paths might have crossed. Dominick Corvaisis, about thirty-five, was a striking man who reminded Ginger of Anthony Perkins when that actor had been younger. His looks were compelling enough that she could not imagine having forgotten where she had met him.

Her instant reaction to the photo was strange, and some might have dismissed it as a meaningless fillip of an overwrought mind. But during the past two months she had learned to respect strange developments and to look for meaning in them, no matter how meaningless they seemed.

She stared at Corvaisis' photograph, hoping to nudge her memory. Finally, with an almost clairvoyant sense that *Twilight in Babylon* would somehow change her life, she opened it and began to read.

*   *   *

Chicago, Illinois.

From University Hospital, Father Stefan Wycazik drove across town to the laboratory operated by the Scientific Investigation Division of the Chicago Police Department. Though it was Christmas Day, municipal workers were still cleaning last night's snowfall from the streets.

Only a couple of men were on duty at the police lab, which was located in an ageing government building, and the old rooms had the deserted feeling of an elaborate Egyptian tomb buried far beneath desert sands. Footsteps echoed resoundingly back and forth between the tile floors and the high ceilings.

Ordinarily, the lab did not share its information with anyone from outside the police and judicial systems. But half the police officers in Chicago were Catholics, which meant that Father Wycazik had more than a few friends on the force. Stefan had importuned some of those friends to make petitions in his name and to pave the way for him at the SID.

He was greeted by Dr Murphy Aimes, a paunchy man with a perfectly bald head and walrus moustache. They'd spoken on the telephone earlier, before Stefan left the rectory for University Hospital, and now Murphy Aimes was ready for him. They settled on two stools at a laboratory bench. A tall opaque window loomed in front of them, decorated with dark streaks of pigeon dung. On the marble top of the bench, Aimes had laid out a file folder and several other items.

'I must say, Father, I'd never compromise case information like this if there were any possibility of a trial arising from the shootout at that sandwich shop. But I suppose, as both perpetrators are dead, there's no one to be put on trial.'

'I appreciate that, Dr Aimes. I really do. And I'm grateful for the time and energy you've expended on my behalf.'

Curiosity ruled Murphy Aimes's face. He said, 'I don't really understand the reason for your interest in the case.'

'I'm not entirely sure of it myself,' Stefan said cryptically.

He had not revealed his purpose to the higher authorities who had made him welcome at the lab, and he did not intend to enlighten Aimes, either. For one thing, if he told them what was on his mind, they would think he was dotty and would be less inclined to cooperate with him.

'Well,' Aimes said, miffed at not being taken into Stefan's confidence, 'you asked about the bullets.' He opened a manila envelope of the type that ties shut with a string, and emptied its contents into his palm: two grey lumps of lead. 'The surgeon removed these from Winton Tolk. You said you were particularly interested in them.'

'I certainly am,' Stefan said, taking them in his own hand when Aimes offered them. 'You've weighed these, I suppose.

216

I understand that's standard procedure. And they weigh what .38 slugs should?'

'If you mean, did they fragment on impact – they did not. They're so misshapen they must've impacted bone, so it's surprising they didn't fragment a little – or a lot – but in fact they're both intact.'

'Actually,' Father Wycazik said, staring at the slugs in his hand, 'I meant were they underweight for .38s? Malformed ammunition, factory mistakes? Or were they the right size?'

'Oh, the right size. No doubt of that.'

'Big enough to do plenty of damage, terrible damage,' Father Wycazik said thoughtfully. 'The gun?'

From a larger envelope, Aimes produced the revolver with which Winton Tolk was shot. 'A snubnose Smith & Wesson .38 Chief's Special.'

'You've examined it, test-fired it?'

'Yes. Standard procedure.'

'No indication that anything's wrong with it? Specifically, is the bore poorly machined or is there some other anomaly that'd result in the bullet leaving the muzzle at a much slower velocity than it should?'

'That's a peculiar question, Father. The answer is no. It's a fine Chief's Special, up to the usual high standards of Smith & Wesson.'

Putting the two expended bullets back into the small envelope from which he had seen Aimes take them, Father Wycazik said, 'What about the cartridges these bullets came from? Is there any chance they were filled with too little powder, that they carried an inadequate charge?'

The SID man blinked. 'I gather one thing you're trying to find out is why two .38s in the chest didn't do more damage.'

Stefan Wycazik nodded but offered no elaboration. 'Were there any unexpended cartridges in the revolver?'

'A couple. Plus spare ammunition in one of the gunman's jacket pockets – another dozen.'

'Did you cut open any of the unexpended shells to see if maybe they carried an inadequate charge?'

'No reason to,' Murphy Aimes said.

'Would it be possible for you to check one of them now?'

'Possible. But why? Father, what in the world is this all about?'

Stefan sighed. 'I know this is an imposition, Dr Aimes, and it behooves me to repay your kindness with an explanation. But I can't. Not yet. Priests, like physicians and attorneys, must sometimes respect confidences, keep secrets. But if I'm ever at liberty to reveal what lies behind my curiosity, you'll be the first to know.'

Aimes stared and Stefan met his eyes forthrightly. Finally the SID man opened another envelope. This contained the unexpended cartridges from the dead gunman's .38 Chief's Special. 'Wait here.'

In twenty minutes, Aimes returned with a white enamel lab tray in which were two dissected .38 Special cartridges. Using a pencil as a pointer, he commented on the disassembled elements. 'This is the case head in which the primer assembly is seated. The firing pin strikes here. This opening on the other side of the case head is the flashhole that leads from the primer packet to the powder compartment. There's no problem with this, no manufacturing errors. At the other end of the cartridge, you've got a lead semiwadcutter bullet with a copper gascheck crimped onto its base to retard bore leading. The tiny cannelures around the bullet are packed with grease to ease its passage through the barrel. Nothing out of order here, either. And in between the case head and the bullet is the powder compartment – or it's sometimes called the combustion chamber – out of which I've taken this small pile of grey, flaky material. This is nitrocellulose, a highly combustible material; it's ignited by the spark that comes through the flashhole from the primer; it explodes, ejecting the bullet from the cartridge. As you can see, there's enough nitrocellulose to fill the powder chamber. Just to be sure, I opened another round.' Aimes pointed the pencil at the second disassembled cartridge. 'There was nothing wrong with this, either. The gunman was using well-made, reliable, Remington ammunition. Officer Tolk was just a lucky man, Father, a very lucky man.'

*   *   *

New York, New York.

Jack Twist spent Christmas in the sanitarium room with Jenny, his wife of thirteen years. Being with her on holidays was especially grim. But being anywhere else, leaving her alone, would have been grimmer.

218

Although Jenny had spent almost two-thirds of their marriage in a coma, the years of lost communion had not diminished Jack's love for her. More than eight years had passed since she had smiled at him or spoken his name or been able to return his kisses, but in his heart, at least, time was stopped, and she was still the beautiful Jenny Mae Alexander, a fresh-faced young bride.

Incarcerated in that Central American prison, he had been sustained by the knowledge that Jenny waited at home for him, missed him, worried about him, and prayed each night for his safe return. Throughout his ordeal of torture and periodic starvation, he had clung to the hope that he would one day feel Jenny's arms around him and hear her marvellous laugh. That hope had kept him alive and sane.

Of the four captured Rangers, only Jack and his buddy Oscar Weston survived and came home, though their escape was a near thing. They had waited almost a year to be rescued, confident that their country would not leave them to rot. Sometimes they debated whether they would be freed by commandos or through diplomatic channels. After eleven months, they still believed their countrymen would bail them out, but they no longer dared wait. They had lost weight and were dangerously thin, undernourished. They had also suffered unknown tropical fevers without treatment, which had further debilitated them.

Their only opportunity for escape was during one of their regular visits to the People's Center for Justice. Every four weeks, Jack and Oscar had been taken from their cells and driven to the People's Center – a clean, well-lighted, unwalled, unbarred institution in the heart of the capital – a model prison meant to impress foreign journalists with the current regime's humanitarianism. There, they were given showers, deloused, put in clean clothes, handcuffed to prevent gesturing, and seated before videotape cameras to be politely questioned. Usually, they answered questions with obscenities or wisecracks. Their answers did not matter because the tape was edited, and answers they had never made were dubbed in by linguists who could speak unaccented English.

Once the propaganda film had been made, they were interviewed over closed-circuit television by foreign reporters gathered in another room. The cameras never provided close-ups of them, and their answers were not heard by those who asked the questions; instead, once again, unseen intelligence men, stationed at another microphone outside the camera's range, answered for them.

At the start of their eleventh month in captivity, Jack and Oscar began making plans to escape the next time they were transported to that far less secure, less heavily guarded propaganda facility.

The once-formidable strength of their young bodies had been leached away, and their only weapons were shivs and needles made of rat bones, which they had painstakingly shaped and sharpened by rubbing them against the stone walls of the cells. Wickedly sharp, those instruments nevertheless made pathetic weapons; yet Jack and Oscar hoped to triumph over gun-toting guards.

Surprisingly, they *did* triumph. Once inside the People's Center, they were remanded into the custody of a single guard who escorted them to the showers on the second floor. The guard kept his gun holstered, probably because the facility was a detention centre inside the larger detention centre of the capital city itself. The guard was certain Jack and Oscar were demoralised, weak, and unarmed, so he was surprised when they suddenly turned on him and, with shocking savagery, stabbed him with the bone shivs they had concealed in their clothes. Pierced twice in the throat, his right eye skewered, he succumbed without producing a scream that might have drawn other police or soldiers.

Before their break was discovered, Jack and Oscar confiscated the dead guard's handgun and ammunition, then made bold use of the hallways, risking notice, alarm, and capture. But it was, after all, a minimum security 're-education' centre, and they were able to make their way to a stairwell and down to a dimly lighted basement, where they progressed swiftly and stealthily through a series of musty storage rooms. At the end of the building, they found the loading docks and a way out.

Seven or eight large boxes had just been off-loaded from a delivery truck, which was backed up to the nearest of the two big bays, and the driver was engaged in an argument with another man, both of whom were shaking clipboards at each other. Those two were the only men in sight, and as they turned and headed towards a glass-enclosed office, Jack and Oscar raced silently to the recently unloaded boxes and from there into the back of the delivery truck, where they made a nest for themselves behind other, as yet undelivered packages. In a few minutes the driver returned, cursing, slammed the truck's cargo-bay door, and drove away into the city before the alarm sounded.

Ten minutes and many blocks from the People's Center, the truck stopped. The driver unbolted the rear doors, took out a single package without realising Jack and Oscar were inches from him behind a wall of boxes, and went into the building before which he'd parked. Extricating themselves from their burrow, Jack and Oscar fled.

Within a few blocks they found themselves in a district of muddy streets and dilapidated shanties, where the poverty-stricken residents were no fonder of the new tyrants than they had been of the old and were willing to hide two Yankees on the lam. After nightfall, supplied with what little food the slum-dwellers could spare, they departed for the outskirts. When they came to open farmland, they broke into a barn and stole a sharp sickle, several withered apples, a leather blacksmith's apron and some burlap bags which could be used to fashion makeshift shoes when their shabby prison-issue eventually fell apart – and a horse. Before dawn, they had reached the edge of the true jungle, where they abandoned the horse and set out on foot once more.

Weak, poorly provisioned, armed only with the sickle – and the gun they had taken off the guard – without a compass and therefore required to plot a course by the sun and the stars, they headed north through the tropical forests toward the border, eighty miles away. Throughout that nightmare journey, Jack had one vital aid to survival: Jenny. He thought of her, dreamed of her, longed for her, and seven days later, when he and Oscar reached friendly territory, Jack knew that he had made it as much because of Jenny as because of his Ranger training.

At that point he thought the worst was behind him. He was wrong.

Now, sitting beside his wife's bed, with Christmas music on the tape deck, Jack Twist was suddenly overcome with grief. Christmas was a bad time because he could not help but remember how dreams of her had sustained him through his Christmas in prison – when in fact she had already been in a coma and lost to him.

Happy holidays.

*　　　*　　　*

Chicago, Illinois.

As Father Stefan Wycazik moved through the halls and wards of St Joseph's Hospital for Children, his spirits soared. That was no small thing, for he was already in a buoyant and elevated state.

The hospital was crowded with visitors, and Christmas music issued from the public address system. Mothers, fathers, brothers, sisters, grandparents, other relatives, and friends of the young patients were on hand with gifts, goodies, and good wishes, and there was more laughter in that usually grim place than one might ordinarily hear echoing through its chambers in an entire month. Even most of the seriously afflicted patients were smiling broadly and talking animatedly, their suffering forgotten for the time being.

Nowhere in the hospital was there more hope or laughter than among those people gathered around the bed of ten-year-old Emmeline Halbourg. When Father Wycazik introduced himself, he was greeted warmly by Emmy Halbourg's parents, two sisters, grandparents, one aunt, and one uncle, who assumed he was one of the hospital's chaplains.

Because of what he'd learned from Brendan Cronin yesterday, Stefan expected to find a happily mending little girl; but he was unprepared for Emmy's condition. She was positively *glowing*. Only two weeks ago, according to Brendan, she had been crippled and dying. But now her dark eyes were clear, and her former pallor was gone, replaced by a wholesome flush. Her knuckles and wrists were not swollen, and she seemed to be completely free of pain. She looked not like a sick child valiantly fighting her way back to health; rather, she seemed *already* cured.

Most startling of all, Emmy was not lying in bed but stand-

222

ing with the aid of crutches, moving among her delighted and admiring relatives. Her wheelchair was gone.

'Well,' Stefan said, after a brief visit, 'I must be going, Emmy. I only stopped by to wish you a merry Christmas from a friend of yours. Brendan Cronin.'

'Pudge!' she said happily. 'He's wonderful, isn't he? It was awful when he stopped working here. We miss him a lot.'

Emmy's mother said, 'I never met this Pudge, but from the way the kids talked about him, he must've been good medicine for them.'

'He only worked here one week,' Emmy said. 'But he comes back – did you know? Every few days he comes back to visit. I was hoping he'd come today, so I could give him a big Christmas kiss.'

'He wanted to stop by, but he's spending Christmas with his folks.'

'Oh, that's good! That's what Christmas is for – isn't it, Father? Being together with your folks, having fun and loving each other.'

'Yes, Emmy,' Stefan Wycazik said, thinking that no theologian or philosopher could have put it better. 'That's what Christmas is for.'

If Stefan had been alone with the girl, he would have asked her about the afternoon of December 11. That was the day Brendan had been brushing her hair while she sat in her wheelchair before this very window. Stefan wanted to know about the rings on Brendan's hands, which had appeared for the first time that day, and which Emmeline had noticed before Brendan himself spotted them. He wanted to ask Emmy if she had felt anything unusual when Brendan had touched her. But there were too many adults around, and they would surely ask awkward questions. Stefan was not yet prepared to reveal the reasons for his curiosity.

*　　　*　　　*

Las Vegas, Nevada.

After getting off to a rocky start, Christmas at the Monatella apartment improved dramatically. Mary and Pete stopped hammering Jorja with their well-meant but unwanted advice and criticism. They loosened up and involved themselves in

223

Marcie's play the way grandparents should, and Jorja was reminded of just why she loved them so much. The holiday dinner was on the table at 12:50, only twenty minutes late, and it was delicious. By the time Marcie sat down to eat, she had worked off her all-consuming interest in Little Ms Doctor, and she did not rush through her meal. It was a leisurely dinner with much chit-chat and laughter, the Christmas tree twinkling in the background. Those were golden hours until, during dessert, the trouble started with surprising suddenness. With frightening speed, it escalated to total disaster.

Teasing Marcie, Pete said, 'Where does a little bitty thing like you put so much food? You've eaten more than the rest of us combined!'

'Oh, Grandpa.'

'It's true! You've been really shovelling it in. One more bite of that pumpkin pie, and you're going to *explode*.'

Marcie lifted another forkful, held it up for all to see, and with great theatricality, she moved it towards her mouth.

'No, don't!' Pete said, putting his hands in front of his face as if to protect himself from the blast.

Marcie popped the morsel into her mouth, chewed, and swallowed. 'See? I didn't explode.'

'You will with the *next* bite,' Pete said. 'I was just one bite too soon. You'll explode . . . or else we'll have to rush you to the hospital.'

Marcie frowned. 'No hospital.'

'Oh, yes,' Pete said. 'You'll be all swollen up, ready to burst, and we'll have to rush you to the hospital and have them deflate you.'

'No hospital,' Marcie repeated adamantly.

Jorja realised that her daughter's voice had changed, that the girl was no longer participating in the game but was, instead, genuinely if inexplicably frightened. She was not scared of exploding, of course, but evidently the mere *thought* of a hospital had caused her to go pale.

'No hospital,' Marcie repeated, a haunted look in her eyes.

'Oh, yes,' Pete said, not yet aware of the change in the child.

Jorja tried to deflect him: 'Dad, I think we –'

But Pete said, 'Of course, they won't take you in an ambulance 'cause you'll be too big. We'll have to rent a truck to haul you.'

The girl shook her head violently. 'I won't go to a h-h-hospital in a million years. I won't ever let those doctors touch me.'

'Honey,' Jorja said, 'grandpa's only *teasing*. He doesn't really –'

Unplacated, the girl said, 'Those hospital people will h-hurt me like they hurt me before. I won't let them hurt me again.'

Mary looked at Jorja, baffled. 'When was she in the hospital?'

'She wasn't,' Jorja said. 'I don't know why she –'

'I was, I was, I was! They t-tied me down in bed, stuck me full of n-needles, and I was scared, and I won't ever let them touch me again.'

Remembering the strange tantrum that Kara Persaghian had reported yesterday, Jorja moved swiftly to forestall a similar scene. She put one hand on Marcie's shoulder and said, 'Honey, you were never –'

'I *was*!' The girl's anger and fear burgeoned into rage and terror. She threw her fork, and Pete ducked to avoid being hit by it.

'Marcie!' Jorja cried.

The girl slipped off her chair and backed away from the table, white-faced. 'I'm going to grow up and be my own doctor, so nobody else'll stick n-needles in me.' Words gave way to a pitiful moaning.

Jorja went after Marcie, reaching for her. 'Honey, don't.'

Marcie held her hands out in front of her, as if warding off an attack, although it was not her mother that she feared. She was looking *through* Jorja, perhaps seeing some imaginary threat, though her terror was real. She was not merely pale but translucent, as if the very substance of her was evaporating in the tremendous heat of her terror.

'Marcie, what is it?'

The girl stumbled backwards into a corner, shuddering.

Jorja gripped her daughter's defensively raised hands. 'Marcie, talk to me.' But even as Jorja spoke, a sudden stench of urine filled the air, and she saw a dark stain spreading from

225

the crotch down both legs of Marcie's jeans. 'Marcie!'

The girl was trying to scream, but could not.

'What's happening?' Mary asked. 'What's wrong?'

'I don't know,' Jorja said. 'God help me, I don't know.'

With her eyes still focused on some figure or object that remained visible only to her, Marcie began a wordless keening.

*   *   *

New York, New York.

The tape deck still played Christmas music, and Jenny Twist lay immobile and insensate, but Jack no longer engaged in the frustrating one-way communication with which he had filled the first few hours of his visit. Now he sat in silence, and inevitably his thoughts drifted back through the years to his homecoming from Central America. . . .

Upon returning to the States, he had discovered that the rescue of the prisoners at the Institute of Brotherhood had been misrepresented, in some quarters, as a terrorist act, a mass kidnapping, a provocation meant to spark a war. He and every Ranger involved were painted as criminals in uniform, and those taken prisoner were for some reason the special focus of the opposition's anger.

In a political panic, Congress had banned *all* covert activities in Central America, including a pending plan to rescue the four Rangers. Their release was to be arranged strictly through diplomatic channels.

That was why they had waited in vain for rescue. Their country had abandoned them. At first Jack had trouble believing it. When at last he believed, it was the second-worst shock of his life.

Having won his freedom, home again, Jack was relentlessly pursued by hostile journalists and subpoenaed to appear before a Congressional committee to testify about his involvement in the raid. He expected to have a chance to set the record straight, but he quickly discovered that they weren't interested in his viewpoint, and that the televised hearing was merely an opportunity for politicians to do some grandstanding in the infamous tradition of Joe McCarthy.

In a few months, most people had forgotten him, and when

226

he regained the pounds he had lost in prison, they ceased to recognise him as the alleged war criminal they had seen on television. But the pain and the sense of betrayal continued to burn fiercely in him.

If being abandoned by his country was the second-worst shock of his life, the worst was what had happened to Jenny while he had been stuck in that Central American prison. A thug had accosted her in the hallway of her own apartment building as she was coming home from work. He put a gun to her head, hustled her into her apartment, sodomised and raped her, clubbed her brutally with his pistol, and left her for dead.

When Jack came home at last, he found Jenny in a state institution, comatose. The level of care she had been getting was abominable.

Norman Hazzurt, the rapist who attacked Jenny, had been tracked down through fingerprints and witnesses, but a clever defence attorney had managed to delay the trial. Undertaking an investigation of his own, Jack satisfied himself that Hazzurt, with a history of violent sex offences, was the guilty man. He also became convinced that Hazzurt would be acquitted on a technicality.

Throughout his ordeal with the press and politicians, Jack made plans for the future. There were two primary tasks ahead of him: first, he would kill Norman Hazzurt in such a way as to avoid any suspicion falling upon himself; second, he would get enough money to move Jenny to a private sanitarium, though the only way to obtain so much cash in a hurry was to steal it. As an elite Ranger, he was trained in most weapons, explosives, martial arts, and survival techniques. His society had failed him, but it had also provided him with the knowledge and the means by which he could extract his revenge, and it had taught him how to break whatever laws stood in his way without punishment.

Norman Hazzurt died in an 'accidental' gas explosion two months after Jack returned to the States. And two weeks later, Jenny's transference to a private sanitarium was financed by the proceeds from an ingenious bank robbery executed with military precision.

The murder of Hazzurt did not satisfy Jack. In fact, it

depressed him. Killing in a war was different from killing in civilian life. He did not have the detachment to kill except in self-defence.

Robbery, however, was enormously appealing. After the successful bank job, he'd been excited, exalted, exhilarated. Daring robbery had a medicinal quality. Crime gave him a reason to live. Until recently.

Now, sitting at Jenny's bedside, Jack Twist wondered what would keep him going, day after day, if not grand larceny. The only other thing he had was Jenny. However, he no longer needed to provide for her; he had already piled up more than enough money for that. So his only reason for living was to come here several times a week, look upon her serene face, hold her hand – and pray for a miracle.

It was ironic that a man like him – a hard-headed, self-reliant individualist – should have no hope but mysticism.

As he brooded on that, he heard Jenny make a soft gurgling sound. She took two quick, deep breaths and produced a long, rattling sigh. For one crazy moment as he rose from his chair, Jack half-expected to find her eyes open, filled with awareness for the first time in more than eight years, the miracle having come to pass even as he had been day-dreaming of it. But her eyes were closed, and her face was slack. He put a hand against her face, then moved it to her throat. He felt for her pulse. What had happened was not, in fact, miraculous but *anti*-miraculous, mundane, and inevitable: Jenny Twist had died.

*   *   *

Chicago, Illinois.

Few physicians were on duty at St Joseph's that Christmas, but a resident named Jarvil and an intern named Klinet were eager to talk to Father Wycazik about Emmeline Halbourg's amazing recovery.

Klinet, an intense wiry-haired young man, escorted Stefan to a consultation room to review Emmy's file and X-rays. 'Five weeks ago, she was started on namiloxiprine – a new drug, just approved by the FDA.'

Dr Jarvil, the resident, was soft-spoken, with heavy-lidded eyes, but when he joined them in the consultation room, he too was visibly excited by Emmeline Halbourg's dramatic turn for the better.

'Namiloxiprine has several effects in bone diseases like Emmy's,' Jarvil said. 'In many instances it puts a stop to the destruction of the periosteum, promotes the growth of healthy osteocytes, and somewhat induces the accumulation of intercellular calcium. And in a case like Emmy's, where the bone marrow is the primary target of the disease, namiloxiprine creates an unusual chemical environment in the marrow cavity and in the Haversian canals, an environment that's extremely hostile to micro-organisms but actually *encourages* the growth of marrow cells, the production of blood cells, and haemoglobin formation.'

'But it's not supposed to work *this* fast,' Klinet said.

'And it's basically a stop-loss drug,' Jarvil said. 'It can arrest the progress of a disease, put a stop to bone deterioration. But it doesn't make regeneration possible. Sure, it's supposed to promote *some* reconstruction, but not the kind of rebuilding we're seeing in Emmy.'

'*Fast* rebuilding,' Klinet said, smacking his forehead with the heel of his hand, as if to knock this amazing fact into his unwilling brain.

They showed Stefan a series of X-rays taken over the past six weeks, in which the changes in Emmy's bones and joints were obvious.

Klinet said, 'She'd been on namiloxiprine for three weeks without noticeable effect, and then suddenly, two weeks ago, her body not only went into a state of remission but began rebuilding damaged tissues.'

The timing of the girl's turnaround coincided perfectly with the first appearance of the strange rings on Brendan Cronin's hands. However, Stefan Wycazik made no mention of that coincidence.

Jarvil produced more X-rays and tests that showed a remarkable improvement in the child's haversian canals, the elaborate network that carried small blood vessels and lymphatics throughout the bone for the purpose of maintenance and repair. Many of these had been clogged with a plaque-like substance that pinched off the vessels passing through them. In the past two weeks, however, the plaque had almost disappeared, allowing the full circulation required for healing and regeneration.

'No one even knew that namiloxiprine could clean out the canals this way,' Jarvil said. 'No record of it. Oh, yes, minor unclogging, but only as a consequence of getting the disease itself under control. Nothing like this. Amazing.'

'If regeneration continues at this rate,' Klinet said, 'Emmy could be a normal, healthy girl in three months. Really phenomenal.'

Jarvil said, 'She could be well again.'

They grinned at Father Wyczazik, and he did not have the heart to suggest that neither their hard work nor the wonder drug was responsible for Emmeline Halbourg's cure. They were euphoric, so Stefan kept to himself the possibility that Emmy's cure had been effected by some power far more mysterious than modern medicine.

* * *

Milwaukee, Wisconsin.

Christmas Day with Lucy, Frank, and the grandchildren was fun and therapeutic for Ernie and Faye Block. By the time they went out for a walk (just the two of them) towards the end of the afternoon, they were feeling better than they had in months.

The weather was perfect for walking: cold, crisp, but without wind. The most recent snowfall was four days old, so the sidewalks were clear. As twilight approached, the air shimmered with a purple radiance.

Bundled in heavy coats and scarves, Faye and Ernie strolled arm-in-arm, talking animatedly about the day's events, enjoying the Christmas displays that Lucy's and Frank's neighbours had erected on their front lawns. The years slipped away, and Faye felt as if she and Ernie were still newlyweds, young and full of dreams.

From the moment they had arrived in Milwaukee on December 15, ten days ago, Faye had reason to hope that everything was going to work out all right. Ernie had seemed better – a new bounciness in his step, more genuine good humour in his smile. Evidently, just basking in the love of his daughter, son-in-law, and grandchildren was sufficient to burn away some of the crippling fear that had become the central fact of his life.

The therapy sessions with Dr Fontelaine, six so far, had also been remarkably beneficial. Ernie was still afraid of the dark but far less terrified than when they left Nevada. Phobias, according to the doctor, were easy to treat compared to many other psychiatric disorders. In recent years therapists had discovered that, in most cases, the symptoms *were* the disease rather than merely shadows cast by unresolved conflicts in the patient's subconscious. It was no longer considered necessary – or even possible or desirable – to seek the psychological causes of the condition in order to treat it. Long courses of therapy had been abandoned in favour of teaching the patient desensitisation techniques that could eradicate the symptoms in months or even weeks.

Approximately a third of all phobics could not be helped by these methods and, instead, required long-term treatment and even panic-blocking drugs like alprazolam. But Ernie had improved at a pace that even Dr Fontelaine, an optimist by nature, found astonishing.

Faye had been reading extensively about phobias and had discovered she could help Ernie by digging up amusing, curious facts that allowed him to view his condition from a different – less fearsome – perspective. He was especially fond of hearing about bizarre phobias that made his terror of the dark seem reasonable by comparison. For example, knowing there were pteronophobics out there, people who lived in constant and unreasonable fear of feathers, made his abhorrence of nightfall seem not only bearable but almost ordinary and logical, as well. Ichthyophobes were horrified by the prospect of encountering a fish, and pediophobes ran screaming at the sight of a doll. And Ernie's nyctophobia was certainly preferable to coitophobia (the fear of sexual inter-course), and not a fraction as debilitating as autophobia (the fear of oneself).

Now, walking through the twilight, Faye tried to keep Ernie's mind off the descending darkness by telling him about the late author, John Cheever, winner of the National Book Award, who'd been gephyrophobic. Cheever had suffered from a crippling fear of crossing high bridges.

Ernie listened in fascination, but he was no less aware of the onset of nightfall. As the shadows lengthened across the snow, his hand steadily tightened on her arm until it would have been painful if she had not been wearing a thick sweater and heavy coat.

By the time they had gone seven blocks, they were too far from the house to have any hope of returning to it before full darkness settled on the land. Two-thirds of the sky was black already, and the other third was deep purple. The shadows had spread like spilt ink.

The streetlamps had come on. Faye halted Ernie in a cone of light, giving him a brief reprieve. His eyes had a wild look, and his steaming exhalations rushed from him at a rate that indicated incipient panic.

'Remember to control your breathing,' Faye said.

He nodded and began at once to take deeper, slower breaths.

When all the light in the sky had been extinguished, she said, 'Ready to go back?'

'Ready,' he said hollowly.

They stepped out of the glow of the streetlamp, into darkness, heading back toward the house, and Ernie hissed between clenched teeth.

What they were engaged upon, for the third time, was a dramatic therapeutic technique called 'flooding,' in which the phobic was encouraged to confront the thing he feared and to endure it long enough to break its hold on him. Flooding is based on the fact that panic attacks are self-limiting. The human body cannot sustain a very high level of panic indefinitely, cannot produce endless adrenalin so the mind must adapt to, and make peace – or at least a truce – with what it fears. Unmodified flooding can be a cruel, barbaric method of cracking a phobia, for it puts the patient at risk of a breakdown. Dr Fontelaine preferred a modified version of the technique involving three stages of confrontation with the source of fear.

The first stage, in Ernie's case, was to put himself in darkness for fifteen minutes, but with Faye at his side for support and with lighted areas easily accessible. Now, each time they arrived at the lighted sidewalk beneath a streetlamp, they paused to let him gather his courage, then went on into the next patch of darkness.

The second stage, which they would try in another week or two, after more sessions with the doctor, would involve driving to a place where there were no streetlamps, no easily reached lighted areas. There, they would walk together arm in arm across an unrelieved vista of darkness until Ernie could tolerate no more, at which time Faye would switch on a flashlight and give him a moment's respite.

In the third stage of treatment, Ernie would go for a stroll alone in a completely dark area. After a few outings like that, he would almost certainly be cured.

But he was not cured yet, and by the time they covered six blocks of the seven-block return journey to the house, Ernie was breathing like a well-run racehorse, and he bolted for the safety of the light inside. Not bad, though – six blocks. Better than before. At this rate, he would be cured in no time.

As Faye followed him into the house, where Lucy was already helping him out of his coat, she tried to feel good about his progress to date. If this pace held, he would complete the third and final stage weeks – maybe even a couple of months – ahead of schedule. That was what worried Faye. His rapid improvement was amazing; it seemed too rapid and too amazing to be real. She wanted to believe the nightmare would be put behind them quickly, but the pace of his recuperation made her wonder if it was lasting. Striving always to think positive, Faye Block was nevertheless plagued by the instinctive and unnerving feeling that something was wrong. Very wrong.

*   *   *

Boston, Massachusetts.

Inevitably, given his exotic background as a godson of Picasso and a once-famous European stage performer, Pablo Jackson was a star in Boston social circles. Furthermore, during World War II, he had been a liaison between British Intelligence and the French resistance forces, and his recent work as a hypnotist with police agencies had only added to his mystique. He never lacked invitations.

On the evening of Christmas Day, Pablo attended a black-tie

233

dinner party for twenty-two at the home of Mr and Mrs Ira Hergensheimer in Brookline. The house was a splendid brick Georgian Colonial, as elegant and warmly welcoming as the Hergensheimers themselves, who had made their money in real estate during the 1950s. A bartender was on duty in the library, and white-jacketed waiters circulated through the enormous drawing room with champagne and canapés, and in the foyer a string quartet played just loudly enough to provide pleasant background music.

Among that engaging company, the man of most interest to Pablo was Alexander Christophson, former Ambassador to the Court of St James, one-term United States Senator from Massachusetts, later Director of the Central Intelligence Agency, now retired almost a decade, whom Pablo had known half a century. Seventy-six, Christophson was the second-eldest guest, but old age had been nearly as kind to him as to Pablo. He was tall, distinguished, with remarkably few lines in his classic Bostonian face. His mind was as sharp as ever. The true length of his journey on the earth was betrayed only by a mild trace of Parkinson's Disease which, in spite of medication, left him with a tremor in his right hand.

Half an hour before dinner, Pablo eased Alex away from the other guests and led him to Ira Hergensheimer's oak-panelled study, adjacent to the library, for a private conversation. The old magician closed the door behind them, and they carried their glasses of champagne to a pair of leather wingback chairs by the window. 'Alex, I need your advice.'

'Well, as you know,' Alex said, 'men our age find it especially satisfying to give advice. It compensates for no longer being able to set a bad example ourselves. But I can't imagine what advice I could give on any problem that you wouldn't already have thought of yourself.'

'Yesterday,' Pablo said, 'a young woman came to see me. She's an exceedingly lovely, charming, and intelligent woman who's accustomed to solving her own problems, but now she's bumped up against something very strange. She desperately needs help.'

Alex raised his eyebrows. 'Beautiful young women still come to you for help at eighty-one? I am impressed, humbled, and envious, Pablo.'

234

'This is not a *coup de foudre*, you filthy-minded old lizard. Passion isn't involved.' Without mentioning Ginger Weiss's name or occupation, Pablo discussed her problem – the bizarre and inexplicable fugues – and recounted the session of hypnotic regression that had ended with her frightening withdrawal. 'She actually seemed about to retreat into a deep self-induced coma, perhaps even into death, to avoid my questions. Naturally, I refused to put her in a trance again and risk another withdrawal of that severity. But I promised to do some research to see if any similar case was on record. I found myself poring through books most of last evening and this morning, searching for references to memory blocks with self-destruction built into them. At last I found it . . . in one of your books. Of course, you were writing about an *imposed* psychological condition as a result of brainwashing, and this woman's block is of her own creation; but the similarity is there.'

Drawing on his experiences in the intelligence services during World War II and the subsequent cold war, Alex Christophson had written several books, including two that dealt with brainwashing. In one, Alex had described a technique he called the Azrael Block (naming it for one of the angels of death) that seemed uncannily like the barrier which surrounded Ginger Weiss's memory of some traumatic event in her past.

As distant string music came to them muffled by the closed study door, Alex put down his champagne glass because his hands trembled too violently. He said, 'I don't suppose you'd drop this matter and forget all about it? Because I'm telling you that's the wisest course.'

'Well,' Pablo said, a bit surprised by the ominous tone of his friend's voice, 'I've promised her I'll try to help.'

'I've been retired eight years, and my instincts aren't what they once were. But I have a very bad feeling about this. Drop it, Pablo. Don't see her again. Don't try to help her any more.'

'But, Alex, I've promised her.'

'I was afraid that'd be your position.' Alex folded his tremulous hands. 'Okay. The Azrael Block . . . It's not something that Western intelligence services use often, but the Soviets find it invaluable. For example, let's imagine a top-notch Russian agent named Ivan, an operative with thirty years service to the KGB. In Ivan's memory there'll be an incredible amount of highly sensitive information that, were it to fall into Western hands, would devastate Russian espionage networks. Ivan's superiors constantly worry that, on some foreign assignment, he'll be identified and interrogated.'

'As I understand it, with current drugs and hypnotic techniques, no one can withhold information from a determined interrogator.'

'Exactly. No matter how tough he is, Ivan will spill all he knows without being tortured. For that reason, his superiors would prefer to send younger agents who, if caught, would have less valuable information to reveal. But many situations require a seasoned man like Ivan, so the possibility of all his knowledge falling into enemy hands is a nightmare with which his superiors must live, whether they like it or not.'

'The risk of doing business.'

'Exactly. However, let's imagine that, among all the sensitive knowledge in his head, Ivan knows two or three things that're *especially* sensitive, so explosive that their revelation could destroy his country. These particular memories, less than one per cent of his knowledge about KGB operations, could be suppressed without affecting his performance in the field. We're talking here about the suppression of a very tiny portion of his memories. Then, if he fell into enemy hands, he'd still give up a great deal of valuable stuff during interrogation – but at least he would not be able to reveal those few most crucial memories.'

'And this is where the Azreal Block comes in,' Pablo said. 'Ivan's own people use drugs and hypnosis to seal off certain parts of his past before sending him overseas on his next assignment.'

Alex nodded. 'For example . . . say that years ago Ivan was one of the agents involved in the attempted assassination of Pope John Paul II. With a memory block in place, his awareness of that involvement could be locked in his subconscious, beyond the reach of potential interrogators, without affecting his work on new assignments. But not just any block will do. If Ivan's interrogators discover a standard memory block, they'll work diligently to unlock it, because they'll know that what lies behind it is of enormous importance. So the barrier must be one that cannot be tampered with. The Azreal Block is perfect. When the subject is questioned about the forbidden topic, he's programmed to retreat into a deep coma where he cannot hear the inquisitor's voice – and even into death. In fact, it should more accurately be called the Azrael Trigger, because if the interrogator probes into the blocked memories, he pulls that trigger, shooting Ivan into a coma, and if he continues to pull the trigger he may eventually kill the subject.'

Fascinated, Pablo said, 'But isn't the survival instinct strong enough to overcome the block? When it comes to the point that Ivan must either remember and reveal what he has forgotten . . . or die . . . well, surely the repressed memory would surface.'

'No.' Even in the warm amber light of the floorlamp beside his chair, Alex's face appeared to have gone grey. 'Not with the drugs and hypnotic techniques we have these days. Mind control is a frighteningly advanced science. The survival instinct is the strongest we've got, but even that can be over-ridden. Ivan can be programmed to self-destruct.'

Pablo found his champagne glass empty. 'My young lady-friend seems to have invented a sort of Azrael Block of her own to hide from herself some extraordinarily distressing event in her past.'

'No,' Alex said, 'she didn't form the block herself.'

'She must have. She's in a bad state, Alex. She just . . . slips away when I try to question her. So, as you know this field, I thought you might have a few ideas about how I can deal with it.'

'You still don't understand why I warned you to drop this whole thing,' Alex said. He pushed up from his chair, moved to the nearby window, shoved his trembling hands in his pockets, and stared out at the snow-covered lawn. 'A self-imposed, naturally generated Azrael Block? Such a thing isn't possible. The human mind will not, of its own volition, put itself at risk of death merely to conceal something from itself. An Azrael Block is *always* an externally applied control. If you've encountered such a barrier, then someone planted it in her mind.'

'You're saying she's been brainwashed? Ridiculous. She's no spy.'

'I'm sure she's not.'

'She's no Russian. So why would she've been brainwashed? Ordinary citizens don't become targets for that sort of thing.'

Alex turned from the window and faced Pablo. 'This is just an educated guess . . . but perhaps she accidentally saw something she was not supposed to see. Something extremely important, secret. Subsequently, she was subjected to a sophisticated process of memory repression, to make sure she never told anyone about it.'

Pablo stared at him, astonished. 'But what could she possibly have seen to've made such extreme measures necessary?'

Alex shrugged.

'And who could've tampered with her mind?'

Alex said, 'The Russians, the CIA, the Israeli Mossad, Britain's MI6 – any organisation with the knowledge of how such things are done.'

'I don't think she's travelled outside the US, which leaves the CIA.'

'Not necessarily. All the others operate in this country for their own purposes. Besides, intelligence organisations are not the only groups who're familiar with mind-control techniques. So are some crackpot religious cults, fanatical political fringe groups . . . others. Knowledge spreads fast, and evil knowledge spreads faster. If people like that want her to forget something, you sure don't want to help her remember. It wouldn't be healthy for either you or her, Pablo.'

'I can't believe –'

'Believe,' Alex said sombrely.

'But these fugues, these sudden fears of black gloves and helmets . . . these would seem to indicate that her memory block is cracking. Yet the people you've mentioned wouldn't have done a half-baked job, would they? If they'd implanted a block, it would be perfect.'

Alex returned to his chair, sat, leaned forward, fixing Pablo with an intense gaze, obviously striving to impress him with the gravity of the situation. 'That's what worries me most, old friend. Ordinarily, such a firmly implanted mental barrier would never weaken on its own. The people capable of doing this to your lady-friend are absolutely expert at it. They wouldn't screw up. So her recent problems, her deteriorating psychological condition, can mean only one thing.'

'Yes?'

'The forbidden memories, the secrets buried behind this Azrael Block, are apparently so explosive, so frightening, so traumatic, that not even an expertly engineered barrier can contain them. Buried in this woman is a shocking memory of immense power, and it's straining to break out of its prison in her subconscious, into her conscious mind. These objects that trigger her blackouts – the gloves, the sink drain – are very likely elements of those repressed memories. When she fixates on one of these things, she's close to a breakthrough, trembling on the edge of remembrance. Then her programme kicks in, and she blacks out.'

Pablo's heart quickened with excitement. 'Then, after all, it might be possible to use hypnotic regression to probe at this Azrael Block, widen the cracks already in it, without driving her into a coma. One would have to be extremely cautious, of course, but with –'

'You're not listening to me!' Alex said, bolting up again. He stood between their chairs, looming over Pablo, pointing one trembling finger at him. 'This is incredibly dangerous. You've stumbled into something much too big for you to handle. If you help her to remember, you're going to make powerful enemies somewhere.'

'She's a sweet girl, and her life is in ruins because of this.'

'You can't help her. You're too old, and you're just one man.'

'Listen, maybe you don't understand enough of the situation. I haven't told you her name or profession, but I'll tell you now that –'

'I don't want to know who she is!' Alex said, his eyes widening.

'She's a physician,' Pablo persisted. 'Or almost. She's spent the past fourteen years training herself for medical practice, and now she's losing everything. It's tragic.'

'Think about this, damn it: she's almost certain to discover that knowing the truth is even worse than not knowing. If the repressed memories are breaking through like this, then they must be so traumatic that they could destroy her psychologically.'

'Maybe,' Pablo acknowledged. 'But shouldn't *she* be the one to decide whether or not to keep digging for the truth?'

Alex was adamant. 'If the memory itself doesn't destroy her, then she'll probably be killed by whoever implanted the block. I'm surprised they didn't kill her straightaway. If it *is* an intelligence agency behind this, ours or theirs, then you've got to remember that to them civilians are entirely expendable. She got a rare and amazing reprieve when they used brainwashing instead of a bullet. A bullet's quicker and cheaper. They won't give her a second reprieve. If they discover that the Azrael Block has crumbled, if they learn that she's uncovered the secret they've hidden from her, they'll blow her brains out.'

'You can't be sure,' Pablo said. 'Besides, she's a real go-getter, Alex, an achiever, a mover and shaker. So from her point of view, her current situation is almost as bad as having her brains blown out.'

Making no effort to conceal his frustration with the old magician, Alex said, 'You help her, and they'll blow your brains out as well. Doesn't that give you pause?'

'At eighty-one,' Pablo said, 'not much of interest happens. You can't afford to turn your back on that rare bit of excitement when it comes along. *Vogue la galère* – I must chance it.'

'You're making a mistake.'

'Maybe I am, my friend. Maybe. But . . . then why do I feel so good?'

*　　　*　　　*

Chicago, Illinois.

Dr Bennet Sonneford, who had operated on Winton Tolk yesterday subsequent to the shooting at the sandwich shop, ushered Father Wycazik into a spacious den, where the walls were covered with mounted fish: marlin, an immense albacore, bass, trout. More than thirty glass eyes stared sightlessly down upon the two men. A trophy case was filled with silver and gold cups, bowls, medallions. The doctor sat at a pine desk in the shadow of a forever-swimming, open-mouthed marlin of startling proportions, and Stefan sat beside the desk in a comfortable chair.

Although the hospital had provided only Dr Sonneford's

240

office number, Father Wyczazik had been able to track down the surgeon's home address with the aid of friends at the telephone company and police department. He had arrived at Sonneford's doorstep at 7:30 Christmas night, effusively apologetic about interrupting holiday celebrations.

Now, Stefan said, 'Brendan works with me at St Bernadette's, and I think very highly of him, so I don't want to see him in trouble.'

Sonneford, who looked a bit like a fish – pale, slightly protuberant eyes, a naturally puckered mouth – said, 'Trouble?' He opened a kit of small tools, choosing a miniature screwdriver, and turned his attention to a fly-casting reel that lay on the blotter. 'What trouble?'

'Interfering with officers in the performance of their duties.'

'Ridiculous.' Sonneford carefully removed tiny screws from the reel housing. 'If he hadn't tended to Tolk, the man would be dead now. We gave him four and a half litres.'

'Really? That isn't a mistake on the patient's chart.'

'No mistake.' Sonneford removed the metal case from the automatic reel, peered intently into its mechanical guts. 'An adult has seventy millilitres of blood per kilogram of body weight. Tolk is a big man – one hundred kilos. He'd normally contain seven litres. So when I first ordered blood in the ER, he'd lost over sixty percent of his own.' He put down the screwdriver and picked up an equally small wrench. 'And they gave him another litre in the ambulance before I saw him.'

'You mean he'd actually lost over seventy-five percent of his blood by the time they got him out of that sandwich shop? But . . . can a man lose so much blood and survive?'

'No,' Sonneford said quietly.

A pleasant shiver passed through Stefan. 'And both bullets lodged in soft tissue but damaged no organs. Deflected by ribs, other bones?'

Sonneford was still squinting at the reel but had stopped tinkering with it. 'If those .38s had hit bone, the impact would've resulted in chipping, splintering. I found nothing like that. On the other hand, if they were *not* deflected by bone, they should've passed through him, leaving massive exit wounds. But I found them lodged in muscle tissue.'

Stefan stared at the surgeon's bent head. 'Why do I have the feeling there's something more you want to tell me, but that it's something you're afraid to talk about?'

At last Sonneford glanced up. 'And why do I get the feeling that you've not told the truth about your reasons for coming here, Father?'

'Touché,' Stefan said.

Sonneford sighed and put the tools away in the kit. 'All right. The entry wounds make it clear that one bullet hit Tolk in the chest, impacted with the lower portion of the sternum, which should've snapped off or fractured; splinters like shrapnel should've pierced organs, vital blood vessels. Apparently, none of that happened.'

'Why do you say "apparently?" Either it happened, or it didn't.'

'From the entry wound in the flesh, I *know* that bullet hit the sternum, Father, and I found it lodged harmlessly in tissue on the other side of the sternum, therefore . . . somehow . . . it passed *through* that bone without damaging it. Impossible, of course. Yet I found just an entry wound over the sternum, the undamaged bone directly under the wound – and then the bullet lodged inside behind the sternum, with no indication how it had got from one place to the other. Furthermore, the entry wound of the second slug was over the base of the fourth rib, right side, but that rib was undamaged as well. The bullet should have shattered it.'

'Maybe you're wrong,' Stefan said, playing the Devil's Advocate. 'Maybe the bullet entered just slightly off the rib, between ribs.'

'No.' Sonneford raised his head but did not look at Stefan. The physician's uneasiness still seemed peculiar and was not explained by what he had said thus far. 'I don't make diagnostic errors. Besides, inside the patient, those bullets were lodged where you'd expect them to be if they *had* hit bone, had punched through, and had had the last of their energy absorbed by the muscle. But there were no damaged tissues *between* the point of entry and the expended slugs. Which is impossible. Bullets can't pass through a man's chest and leave no trail at all!'

'Almost seems as if we have a minor miracle.'

'More than minor. Seems like a pretty damn *major* miracle to me.'

'If only one artery and vein were injured, and if both were only nicked, how did Tolk lose so much blood? Were those nicks big enough to account for it?'

'No. He couldn't have haemorrhaged so massively from those trauma.'

The surgeon said nothing more. He seemed gripped in the talons of some dark fear that Stefan could not understand. What had he to fear? If he believed that he had witnessed a miracle, should he not be joyous?

'Doctor, I know it's difficult for a man of science and medicine to admit he's seen something that his education can't explain, something that in fact is in opposition to everything he had believed to be true. But I beg you to tell me everything you saw. What are you holding back? How did Winton Tolk lose so much blood if his injuries were so small?'

Sonneford slumped back in his chair. 'In surgery, after beginning transfusions, I located the bullets on the X-rays and made the necessary incisions to remove them. In the process, I found a tiny hole in the superior mesenteric artery and another small tear in one of the superior intercostal veins. I was certain there must be other severed vessels, but I couldn't locate them immediately, so I clamped off both the superior mesenteric and the intercostal for repair, figuring to search further when those were attended to. It only took a few minutes, an easy task. I sewed the artery first, of course, because the bleeding was in spurts and was more serious. Then . . .'

'Then?' Father Wycazik urged gently.

'Then, when I had quickly finished stitching the artery, I turned to the torn intercostal vein . . . and the tear was gone.'

'Gone,' Stefan said. A quiver of awe passed through him, for this was the thing he had expected – yet it was also a revelation of such astounding importance that it seemed too much to have hoped for.

'Gone,' Sonneford repeated, and at last he met Stefan's gaze. In the surgeon's watery grey eyes, a shadow moved like the half-perceived passage of a leviathan through the depths of a murky sea, the shadow of fear, and Stefan confirmed that for some inexplicable reason the miracle occasioned dread in the doctor. 'The torn vein healed itself, Father. I *know* the tear had been there. Clamped it off myself. My technician saw it. My nurse saw it. But when I was ready to sew it up, the rent was gone. Healed. I removed the clamps, and blood flowed again through the vein, and there was no leakage. And later . . . when I excised the bullets, the muscle tissue appeared to . . . knit up before my eyes.'

'Appeared to?'

'No, that's an evasion,' Sonneford admitted. 'It *did* knit before my eyes. Incredible, but I saw it. Can't prove it, Father, but I know those two slugs *did* smash Tolk's sternum and shatter his rib. They *did* send bone fragments through him like shrapnel. Major, mortal damage *was* done, had to've been. But by the time he was on the table in surgery, his body had almost entirely healed itself. The shattered bones had . . . reformed. The superior mesenteric artery and the intercostal vein were severed to begin with, which is why he lost blood so fast, but by the time I opened him, both vessels had knitted up except for a small tear in each. Sounds crazy, but if I hadn't moved to repair the artery, I'm sure it would've finished closing on its own . . . just as the vein did.'

'What did your nurse and other assistants think of this?'

'Funny thing is . . . we didn't talk much about it. I can't account for how little we discussed it. Maybe we didn't talk about it because . . . we're living in a rational age when the miraculous is unacceptable.'

'How sad if true,' Stefan said.

With the shadow of dread still shimmering anemone-like in the depths of his eyes, Sonneford said, 'Father, if there is a God – and I'm not admitting there is – why would He save this particular cop?'

'He's a good man,' Father Wycazik said.

'So? I've seen hundreds of good men die. Why should this one be saved and none of the others?'

Father Wycazik pulled a chair around from the side of the desk in order to be able to sit near the surgeon. 'You've been frank with me, Doctor, so I'll be upfront with you. I sense a force behind these events that's more than human. A Presence. And that Presence isn't primarily concerned with Winton Tolk but with Brendan, the man . . . the *priest* who first reached Officer Tolk in that sandwich shop.'

Bennet Sonneford blinked in surprise. 'Oh. But you wouldn't have got such a notion unless . . .'

'Unless Brendan was linked to at least one other miraculous event,' Stefan said. Without using Emmy Halbourg's name, he told Sonneford about the girl's mending limbs that had once been crippled by disease.

Instead of taking hope from what Stefan told him, Bennet Sonneford shrivelled farther in the heat of his strange despair.

Frustrated by the physician's relentless gloominess, Father Wyczak said, 'Doctor, maybe I'm missing something, but it seems to me you've got every reason to be joyous. You were privileged to witness what – I personally believe – was the hand of God at work.' He held one hand out to Sonneford and was not surprised when the doctor gripped it tightly. 'Bennet, why're you so despondent?'

Sonneford cleared his throat and said, 'I was born and raised a Lutheran, but for twenty-five years I've been an atheist. And now . . .'

'Ah,' Stefan said, 'I see. . . .'

Happily, Stefan began angling for Bennet Sonneford's soul in the fish-lined den. He had no suspicion that, before the day was done, his current euphoria would be dispelled and that he would experience a bitter disappointment.

*   *   *

Reno, Nevada.

Zeb Lomack had never imagined that his life would end in bloody suicide at Christmas, but by that night he had sunk so low that he longed to end his existence. He loaded his shotgun, put it on the filthy kitchen table, and promised himself that he would use it if he was unable to get rid of all the goddamned moon stuff before midnight.

His bizarre fascination with the moon had begun the summer before last, though at first it had seemed innocent enough. Toward the end of August that year, he had taken to going out on the back porch of his cosy little house and watching the moon and stars while sipping Coors. In mid-September, he purchased a Tasco 10VR refracting telescope and bought a couple of books on amateur astronomy.

Zebediah was surprised by his own sudden interest in stargazing. For most of his fifty years, Zeb Lomack, a professional gambler, had shown little interest in anything but cards. He worked Reno, Lake Tahoe, Vegas, occasionally one of the smaller gambling towns like Elko or Bullhead City, playing poker with the tourists and local would-be poker champs. He was not only good at card games: he *loved* cards more than he loved women, booze, food. Even the money was not important to Zeb; it was just a handy by-product of playing cards. The important thing was staying in the game.

Until he got the telescope and went crazy.

For a couple of months he used the scope on a casual basis, and he bought a few more books on astronomy, and it was just a hobby. But by last Christmas he began to focus his attention less on the stars than on the moon, and thereafter something strange happened to him. The new hobby soon became as interesting as card games, and he found himself cancelling planned excursions to the casinos in order to study the lunar surface. By February, he was glued to the eyepiece of the Tasco every night that the moon was visible. By April he built a collection of books about the moon that numbered more than one hundred, and he went out to play cards only two or three nights a week. By the end of June, his book collection had grown to five hundred titles, and he had begun to paper the bedroom walls and ceiling with pictures of the moon clipped from old magazines and newspapers. He no longer played cards, but began living off his savings, and thereafter his interest in things lunar ceased to bear any resemblance to a hobby and became a mad obsession.

By September, his book collection had grown to more than fifteen hundred volumes stacked throughout his small house. During the day, he read about the moon or, more often, sat for hours staring intently at photographs of it, unable either to understand or to resist its allure, until its craters and ridges and plains became as familiar to him as the five rooms of his own house. On those nights when the moon was visible, he studied it through the telescope until he could no longer stay awake, until his eyes were bloodshot and sore.

Before this obsession took control of him, Zeb Lomack had

been a ruggedly hewn and relatively fit man. But as his pre-occupation with things lunar tightened its grip, he stopped exercising and began eating junk food – cake, ice cream, TV dinners, bologna sandwiches – because he no longer had time to prepare good meals. Furthermore, the moon not only fascinated him but also made him uneasy, not only filled him with wonder but with dread, so he was always nervous; and he tranquillised himself with food. He became softer, flabbier, though he was only minimally aware of the physical changes he was undergoing.

By early October, he thought about the moon every hour of every day, dreamed of it, and could go nowhere in his house without seeing hundreds of images of the lunar face. He had not stopped re-papering the walls when he had finished his bedroom in June, but had carried that project throughout. The full-colour and black-and-white moon pic-tures came from astronomy journals, magazines, books, and newspapers. On one of his infrequent ventures out of the house, he had seen a three-by-five-foot poster of the moon, a colour photograph taken by astronauts, and he had bought fifty copies, enough to paper the ceiling and every wall in the living room; he had even taped the poster over the windows, so every square inch of the room was decorated with that repeating image, except for doorways. He moved the furniture out, transforming the empty cham-ber into a planetarium where the show never changed. Sometimes he'd lie on his back on the floor and stare up and around at those fifty moons, transported by an exhilarating sense of wonder and an inexplicable terror, neither of which he could understand.

Christmas night, as Zeb was sprawled on the floor with half a hundred bloated moons hanging over him, bearing down on him, he suddenly noticed writing on one of them, a single word scrawled across the lunar image with a felt-tip pen, where there had never been a word before. The picture had been defaced with a name: *Dominick*. He recognised his own handwriting, but he could not remember having scrawl-ed that name across the moon. Then his eye was caught by another name written on another poster: *Ginger*. And then a third name on a third poster: *Faye*. And a fourth: *Ernie*.

Suddenly anxious, Zeb stumbled around the room, checking the other posters, but he found no more names.

In addition to being unable to recall writing those words, he could not think of anyone he knew named Dominick, Ginger, or Faye. He knew a couple of Ernies, though neither was a close friend, and the appearance of that name on one of the moons was no less mysterious than the three others. Staring at the names, he grew increasingly uneasy, for he had the odd feeling that he *did* know them, that they had played a terribly important role in his life, and that his very sanity and survival depended on remembering who they were.

Some long-forgotten memory swelled in him like a steadily inflating balloon, and intuitively he knew that when the balloon popped he would recollect everything, not only the identities of these four people, but also the origins of his fevered fascination with – and underlying fear of – the moon. But as the memory-balloon swelled within him, his fear grew as well, and he began to sweat and then to shake uncontrollably.

He turned from the posters, suddenly terrified of remembering, and lurched out to the kitchen, driven by that gnawing hunger that was always occasioned by thoughts that made him nervous. He wrenched open the refrigerator door and was startled to discover that the shelves were bare. They held dirty bowls and empty plastic containers in which food had been kept, two empty milk cartons, an egg carton with one broken and dried egg. He looked in the freezer, found only frost.

Zeb tried to remember when he had last been to the supermarket. It might have been days or weeks since his most recent shopping expedition. He could not remember because, in his moon-filled world, time no longer had any meaning. And how much time had passed since his last meal? He vaguely remembered having some canned pudding, but he was not clear whether that had been earlier today or yesterday or even two days ago.

Zebediah Lomack was so shocked by this development that his mind cleared for the first time in weeks, and when he looked around the kitchen, he made a strangled sound of disgust and fear. For the first time he saw – *really* saw – the mess in which he'd been living, a situation previously masked by his all-encompassing fascination with the moon. Garbage covered the floor: discarded cans sticky with fruit juices, slimy with traces of rancid gravy; empty cereal boxes and a score of drained milk cartons; dozens of wadded-up and discarded potato-chip bags and candy wrappers. And roaches. They squirmed, scuttled, and jigged through the garbage, raced across the floor, climbed walls, crouched on counters, and lurked in the sink.

'My God,' Zeb said in a voice that was hardly more than a croak, 'what's happened to me? What've I been doing? What's *wrong* with me?'

He put one hand to his face and twitched with surprise when he felt a beard. He had always been clean-shaven, and he had thought he shaved just this morning. The wiry hair on his face sent him in a panic to the bathroom, where he could look in the mirror. He saw a stranger: filthy, matted hair hanging in tangled clumps; pale, soft, sickly looking skin; a two-week beard crusted with food and dirt; wild eyes. He became aware of his body odour: his stink was so rank that he gagged on his own aroma. Apparently, he had not bathed in days, weeks.

He needed help. He was sick. Confused and sick. He could not understand what had happened to him, but he knew that he must go to the telephone and call for help.

But he did not go immediately to the phone because he was afraid they'd say he was hopelessly insane and would lock him away forever. Like they had locked away his father. When Zebediah was eight, his father had a terrible fit, ranting and raving about lizard-things that were crawling out of the walls, and the doctors took him to the hospital to dry him out. But that time, unlike before, the DTs had not gone away, and Zeb's dad had been institutionalised for the rest of his life. Ever after, Zeb had been afraid his own mind might be flawed, too. Staring at his pale face in the mirror, he knew he could not call for help until he made himself presentable and straightened up the house; otherwise, they would lock him up and throw away the key.

He could not bear to look at his reflection long enough to shave, so he decided to deal with the house first. Keeping his

249

head down to avoid seeing the moons, which exerted a tidal force on him as real as the true moon's effect on the seas, he scurried into the bedroom, opened the closet, shoved the clothes aside, located his Remington .12-gauge and a box of shells. Head bowed, fighting the urge to look up, he made his way to the kitchen, where he loaded the shotgun and put it on the garbage-strewn table. Speaking aloud, he made a bargain with himself:

'You get rid of the moon books, tear down the pictures so this place don't look so crazy, clean the kitchen, shave, bathe. Then maybe you'll get your head clear enough to figure what the hell's wrong with you. Then you can get help – just not while things are like this.'

The shotgun was the unspoken part of the bargain. He had been fortunate to rise briefly out of the moon-dream in which he had been living, shocked to his senses by the lack of food in the refrigerator, but if he drifted back into that nightmare, he could not count on being jolted awake again. Therefore, if he could not resist the siren song of the moons on the walls, he would quickly return to the kitchen, pick up the shotgun, put it in his mouth, and pull the trigger.

Death was better than this.

And death was better than being locked up forever like his father.

Now, in the living room once more, keeping his eyes on the floor, he began to gather up the books. Some had once boasted jackets with photos of the moon, but he had clipped those pictures. He hefted an armload of them and went outside to the snow-covered back yard, where there was a barbecue pit lined with concrete blocks. Shivering in the crisp winter air, he dumped the books into the pit and headed back to the house for more, not daring to look at the night sky for fear of the great luminous body suspended in it.

As he worked, the urge to return to the study of the moon was as intense and demanding as the hideous need that forced a heroin addict to return again and again to the needle, but Zeb fought it.

Likewise, as he made trip after trip to the barbecue pit, he felt that memory of some long-forgotten event continuing to swell within him: *Dominick, Ginger, Faye, Ernie.* . . .

250

Instinctively, he knew that he would understand the cause of his fascination with the moon if only he could recall who those four people were. He concentrated on the names, trying to use them to block out the alluring summons of the moon, and it seemed to work because soon he had disposed of two or three hundred volumes in the barbecue pit and was ready to set them ablaze.

But when he struck a match and leaned down to light the pages of a book, he discovered the pit was empty. He stared in shock and horror. Dropping the matches, he raced back to the house, threw open the kitchen door, stumbled inside, and saw what he had been most afraid of seeing. The books were piled there, damp with snow, smeared with wet ashes from the pit. He had indeed disposed of them, but then the lunacy had taken him again; under its spell and without knowing what he was doing, he had carried every volume back into the house.

He began to cry, but he was still determined he would not wind up in a padded room. He picked up a score of books and headed back toward the barbecue pit, feeling as if he were in hell and condemned, for eternity, to the performance of this frantic ritual.

When he figured he had filled the pit again, he suddenly realised he was not carrying books *to* the place of burning but away from it. Again, he had drifted off into his moon-dream and, instead of destroying the objects of his obsession, he was re-collecting them.

As he headed back towards the house, he noticed how the crust of snow glimmered with a scintillant, reflected light. Against his will, his head came up. He looked into the deep and cloudless sky.

He said, 'The moon.'

He knew then that he was a dead man.

*   *   *

Laguna Beach, California.

For Dominick Corvaisis, Christmas was usually not much different from other days. He had no wife or children to make it special. Raised in foster homes, he had no relatives with whom he could share a turkey and mincemeat pie. A couple of friends, including Parker Faine, always invited him to join in their festivities, but he declined, for he knew he would feel like the proverbial fifth wheel. However, Christmas was not sad or lonely. He was never bored by his own company, and his home overflowed with good books that could fill the day with delight.

But this Christmas Dom could not concentrate to read, for he was preoccupied by the mysterious mail he had received the previous day and by the need to resist the urge to pop a Valium. Though he had been afraid that he would dream and walk in his sleep, he had taken no Valium yesterday and no Dalmane last night. He was determined to avoid any further reliance on chemicals, though he continued to crave them.

In fact, the craving became so bad that he emptied the pills into the toilet and flushed them away, because he did not trust himself. As the day wore on, his anxiety rose to the level he had experienced before he had begun drug therapy.

At seven o'clock Christmas night, Dom arrived at Parker's rambling hillside contemporary and accepted a glass of homemade eggnog with a cinnamon stick in it. The burly painter's beard, usually bushy and untamed, was neatly trimmed, and his mane of hair was newly cut and combed in honour of the holiday. Though he was more conservatively groomed and more subdued in dress than was his habit, he was every bit as ebullient as one expected him to be. 'What a Christmas! Peace and love reigned in this house today, I tell you! My cherished brother made only forty or fifty nasty and envious remarks about my success, which is not half as many as he lets loose with on a less blessed occasion. My sainted half-sister Carla only *once* called her sister-in-law Doreen a bitch, and even that might be considered justified in light of the fact that Doreen started it by calling Carla a 'brainless New Age crackpot full of psychobabble.' Ah, truly a day of fellowship and caring! Not one punch thrown this year, if you can believe it. And Carla's husband, though he got plastered as usual, did not throw up or fall down a flight of stairs, as in past years, though he did insist on doing his Bette Midler imitation at least a dozen times.'

As they moved toward a grouping of chairs by the window-wall overlooking the sea, Dom said, 'I'm going on a trip, a long drive. I'll fly to Portland and rent a car up there. Then I'll retrace the journey I took the summer before last, from Portland down to Reno, across Nevada and half of Utah on Interstate 80, then to Mountainview.'

Dom sat down as he spoke, but Parker remained on his feet, very still. The announcement pleasantly electrified him. 'What's happened? That's no vacation. That's not a route you'd take for pleasure. Are you sleepwalking again? Must be. And something's happened to convince you this is related to the changes you underwent that summer.'

'I haven't begun sleepwalking again, but I'm sure I will, probably tonight, because I've thrown the damn drugs away. They weren't curing me. I lied. I was getting hooked, Parker. I didn't care because it seemed that being hooked was better than enduring the things I did while sleepwalking. But now all that's changed because of these.' He held up the two notes from his unknown correspondent. The problem's not just within me, not just psychological. There's something stranger at work here.' He gave the first note to Parker. His fearful state of mind was betrayed by the sheet of paper, which shook in his hand.

When the painter read it, he looked baffled.

Dom said, 'It came in the mail yesterday at the post office. No return address. There was another note delivered to the house.' He explained about having typed the words 'the moon' on his word processor hundreds of times in his sleep and about waking from a dream with those same words on his lips, then passed the second note to Parker.

'But if I'm the first one you've told about this moon thing, how could anyone have known enough to send such a note?'

'Whoever he is,' Dom said, 'he knows about my sleepwalking, maybe because I've gone to a doctor about it –'

'You're saying you're being watched?'

'Apparently, to a degree. Periodically monitored if not constantly watched. But while the monitor knows about my sleepwalking, he probably doesn't know about my typing those words on the Displaywriter, or that I woke up repeating them in the night. Not unless he was standing beside my bed, which he wasn't. However, he indisputably *does* know that I'll react to "the moon", that those words'll frighten me. So he must know what lies behind this whole crazy mess.'

253

At last Parker sat down on the edge of a chair. 'Find him, and you'll know what's going on.'

'New York is a big place,' Dom said. 'I have no starting point there. But when I got this first note – this business about the answer to my sleepwalking lying in the past – I realised you must be right about *this* personality crisis being tied to the previous one. The dramatic change I went through on the trip from Portland to Mountainview is somehow connected. If I make that trip again, stop at the same motels, eat in the same roadside restaurants, try to recreate it as exactly as I can . . . something might turn up. My memory might be jogged.'

'But how could you have forgotten something so major?'

'Maybe I didn't forget it. Maybe the memory was *taken* from me.'

Leaving that possibility for later exploration, Parker said, 'Whoever the hell this guy is – what reasons would he have for sending these notes? I mean, you've imagined a situation where it's you against Them, some unknown *Them*, and so this guy is on their side, not yours.'

'Maybe he doesn't agree with everything that's been done to me – whatever it is that I've forgotten was done to me.'

'Done to you? What're we talking about here?'

Dom nervously turned his glass of eggnog around and around in his hands. 'I don't know. But this correspondent . . . he obviously wants me to know my problem's not psychological, that there's something more behind it. I think maybe he wants to help me find the truth.'

'So why doesn't he just call you up and tell you the truth?'

'The only thing I can figure is that he doesn't dare *risk* telling me. He must be part of some conspiracy, God knows what, but part of some group that doesn't want the truth to come out. If he approaches me directly, the others will know, and he'll be in deep shit.'

As if it helped him think, Parker ran one hand through his hair several times, mussing it badly. 'You make this sound like some all-knowing secret society is on your ass – like the Illuminatus Society, Rosicrucians, CIA, and the Fraternal Order of Masons all rolled into one! You actually think you've been brainwashed?'

'If you want to call it that. Whatever traumatic episode I've forgotten, I didn't forget it without assistance. Whatever I saw or experienced was apparently so shocking, so traumatic, that it's still festering in my subconscious, trying to reach me through sleepwalking and through the messages I leave on the Displaywriter. It was so damned big that even brainwashing hasn't been able to wipe it out, so big that one of the conspirators is risking his own neck to send me hints.'

After reading them one more time, Parker returned the two notes to Dom, chugged down his own eggnog. 'Shit. I think you've got to be right, which upsets me. I don't want to believe it. It sounds too much as if you've let your novelistic imagination run wild, as if you're trying out the plot of a new book on me, something a bit more colourful than you should write. But crazy as the whole thing sounds, I can't think of any other answer.'

Dom realised he was squeezing the eggnog glass so tightly that he was in danger of shattering it. He put it on a small table and blotted his hands on his slacks. 'Me neither. There's nothing else that explains both the crazy damn sleepwalking, *and* my personality change between Portland and Mountainview, *and* those two notes.'

His face lined with worry, Parker said, 'What could it have been, Dom? What did you stumble into when you were out there on the road?'

'I don't have the foggiest.'

'Have you considered that it might be something so bad . . . so damn dangerous that you'd be better off not knowing?'

Dom nodded. 'But if I don't learn the truth, I won't be able to stop the sleepwalking for good. In my sleep I'm running from the memory of whatever happened to me out there on the road, the summer before last, and to stop running I've got to find out what it was, face up to it. 'Cause if I don't stop the sleepwalking, it'll eventually drive me mad. That might sound a bit melodramatic, too, but it's true. If I don't learn the truth, then the thing I fear in my dreams is going to start haunting the waking hours as well, and I'm not going to have a moment's peace, waking or sleeping, and eventually the only solution will be to put a gun to my mouth and pull the trigger.'

'Jesus.'

'I mean it.'

'I know you do. God help you, my friend, I know you do.'

* * *

Reno, Nevada.

A cloud saved Zeb Lomack. It drifted across the moon before the grip of the lunar obsession had completely reclaimed him. With the empyreal lantern briefly dimmed, Zebediah abruptly became aware that he was standing coatless in the freezing December night, gaping up at the sky, mesmerised by moonbeams. If the cloud had not broken the trance, he might have stood there until the object of his grim fascination had descended past the horizon. Then, having sunk back into his lunacy, he might have returned to one of the rooms papered with the ancient god-face that the Greeks called Cynthia, that the Romans called Diana, there to lie in a stupor until, days hence, he had starved to death.

Reprieved, he let out a wretched cry and ran to the house. He slipped and fell in the snow, fell again on the porch steps, but immediately scrambled up, desperately seeking the safety of the indoors, where the face of the moon could not work its charms on him. But of course there was no safety inside, either. Though he closed his eyes and began at once to tear blindly at the moon pictures, ripping them from the kitchen walls and casting them on the garbage-covered floor, he began to succumb to his obsession yet again. Eyes tightly shut, he could not see the cratered images, but he could *feel* them. He could feel the pale light of a hundred moons upon his face, and he could feel the roundness of the moons in his hands as he tore them off the wall, which was crazy because they were only pictures that could not produce light or warmth and could not convey by touch the roundness of the lunar globe, yet he nevertheless felt those things strongly. He opened his eyes and was instantly captured by the familiar celestial body.

Just like my dad. Asylum-bound.

Like a distant crackle of lightning, that thought flickered through Zeb Lomack's rapidly dimming mind. It jolted him and allowed him to recover just long enough to turn away from the living room door and fling himself towards the kitchen table, where the loaded shotgun waited.

*　　*　　*

Chicago, Illinois.

Father Stefan Wycazik, descendant of strong-willed Poles, rescuer of troubled priests, was not accustomed to failure, and he did not handle it well. 'But after everything I've told you, how can you still not believe?' he demanded.

Brendan Cronin said, 'Father Stefan, I'm sorry. But I simply don't feel any stronger about the existence of God than I did yesterday.'

They were in a bedroom on the second floor of Brendan's parents' gingersnap brick house in the Irish neighbourhood called Bridgeport, where the young priest was spending the holiday according to Father Wycazik's orders, issued yesterday after the Uptown shootout. Brendan, dressed in grey slacks and a white shirt, was sitting on the edge of a double bed that was covered by a worn, yellow chenille spread. Stefan, choosing to feel needled by his curate's stubbornness, moved constantly around the room from dresser to highboy to window to bed to dresser again, as if trying to avoid the prickling pain of his failure.

'Tonight,' Father Wycazik said, 'I met an atheist who was half-converted by Tolk's incredible recovery. But you're unimpressed.'

'I'm happy for Dr Sonneford,' Brendan said mildly, 'but his renewed belief doesn't rekindle my own.'

The curate's refusal to be properly impressed by recent miraculous events was not the only thing that irritated Father Wycazik. The young priest's pacific demeanour was also bothersome. If he could not find the will to believe in God again, then it seemed he should at least be disheartened and downcast by his continued lack of faith. Instead, Brendan appeared untroubled by his miserable spiritual condition, which was quite different from his attitude when Father Wycazik had seen him last. He had changed dramatically; for reasons that were not at all clear, a great peace seemed to have settled over Brendan.

Still determinedly pressing his argument, Stefan said, 'It

257

was *you*, Brendan, who cured Emmy Halbourg and healed Winton Tolk. It was you, through the power of those stigmata on your hands. Stigmata that God visited upon you as a sign.'

Brendan looked at his palms, now unmarked. 'I believe . . . somehow I did heal Emmy and Winton. But it wasn't God acting through me.'

'Who else but God could've granted you such curing power?'

'I don't know,' Brendan said. 'Wish I did. But it wasn't God. I felt no divine presence, Father.'

'Good grief, how much more strongly do you expect Him to make His presence felt? Do you expect Him to thump you on the head with His great Staff of Justice, tip His diadem to you, and introduce Himself? You've got to meet Him halfway, Brendan.'

The curate smiled and shrugged. 'Father, I know these amazing events seem to have no explanation other than a religious one. But I feel very strongly that something other than God lies behind it.'

'Like what?' Stefan challenged.

'I don't know. Something tremendously important, something really wonderful and magnificent . . . but not God. Look, you've said that the rings were stigmata. But if that's what they were, why wouldn't they have been in a form that had some Christian significance? Why rings – which seem to have no relation to the message of Christ?'

When Brendan began Stefan's unconventional course of psychological therapy at St Joseph's Hospital for Children three weeks ago, the young priest had been so troubled by his loss of faith that he'd been growing rapidly thinner. Now he had stopped losing weight. He was still thirty pounds lighter than usual, but he was no longer as wan and haggard as he had been following his shocking outburst during Mass on the first of December. In spite of his spiritual fall, there was a glow to his skin and a light in his eyes that was almost . . . beatific.

'You feel splendid, don't you?' Stefan asked.

'Yes, though I'm not sure why.'

'Your soul's no longer troubled.'

'No.'

'Even though you've still not found your way back to God.'

'Even though,' Brendan agreed. 'Maybe it has something to do with the dream I had last night.'

'The black gloves again?'

'No. Haven't had that one in a while,' Brendan said. 'Last night I dreamed that I was walking in a place of pure golden light, beautiful light, so bright I could see nothing around me, and yet it didn't hurt my eyes.' A peculiar note, perhaps of reverence, entered the curate's voice. 'In the dream, I keep walking and walking, not knowing where I am or where I'm going, but with the sense that I'm approaching a thing or a place of monumental importance and unbearable beauty. Not just approaching but . . . being called to it. Not an audible call but a summons that just . . . reverberates in me. My heart is pounding, and I'm a little afraid. But it isn't a bad fear, Father, what I feel in that bright place, not bad at all. So I just keep walking through the light, toward something magnificent that I can't see but that I *know* is there.'

Drawn by Brendan's hushed voice as if by a magnet, Father Wycazik moved to the bed and sat upon the corner of it. 'But surely this is a spiritual dream, the call of God coming to you in sleep. He's calling you back to your faith, back to the duties of your office.'

Brendan shook his head. 'No. There was no religious quality to the dream, no sense of a divine presence. It was a different kind of awe that filled me, a joy unlike the joy I knew in Christ. I woke up four times during the night, and each time I woke, the rings were on my hands. And each time that I fell back to sleep, I dropped into the same dream again. Something very strange and important is happening, Father, and I'm a part of it; but whatever it is, it's not anything that my education, experiences, or previous beliefs have prepared me for.'

Father Wycazik wondered if the call that had come to Brendan in the dream had been from Satan instead of God. Perhaps the devil, aware that a priest's soul was in jeopardy, had dressed his hateful form in this deceptively attractive golden light, the better to lead the curate from the righteous path.

Still firmly determined to bring his curate back into the fold, but temporarily out of winning strategies, Stefan Wycazik decided to call a truce. He said, 'So . . . what now? You aren't ready to put on your Roman collar and resume your duties, as I

259

thought you'd be by now. Do you want me to contact Lee Kellog, the Illinois Provincial, and ask him to authorise psychiatric counselling?'

Brendan smiled. 'No. That doesn't appeal to me any more. I don't believe it'd do any good. What I'd like to do – if it's all right with you, Father – is move back into my room in the rectory and wait this out, see what happens. Of course, as I remain a fallen-away priest, I can't hear confessions or say Mass. But while I'm waiting to see what happens, I could do some cooking, help you catch up on the filing.'

Father Wycazik was relieved. He had expected Brendan to express the intention of returning to a secular life. 'You're welcome, of course. There's much you can do. I'll keep you busy; no need to worry about that. But tell me, Brendan . . . you *do* think there's a possibility that you'll find your way back?'

The curate nodded. 'I don't feel *alienated* from God any more. Just empty of Him. As this situation develops, perhaps it'll lead me back to the Church, as you're convinced it will. I just don't know.'

Still frustrated and disappointed by Brendan's refusal to see the miraculous presence of God in the healing of Emmy and Winton, Father Wycazik was nonetheless glad that he would have the curate close and be provided with the opportunity to continue guiding him back to salvation.

Brendan went downstairs with Father Wycazik, and at the front door the two men embraced in such a way that a stranger, without any knowledge of their occupation, would have thought them father and son.

Accompanying Father Wycazik as far as the front stoop, where a blustery wind gave a howl more suited to Halloween than to Christmas, Brendan said, 'I don't know why or how, Father Stefan, but I feel we're about to embark upon an amazing adventure.'

'The discovery – or rediscovery – of faith is always an amazing adventure, Brendan,' Father Wycazik said. Then, having got in the last clean jab, as a good fighter for souls should always do, he left.

* * *

Reno, Nevada.

Whimpering, gasping for breath, struggling valiantly against the narcotising effect of his lunar obsession, Zeb Lomack clambered through the garbage and squirming roaches that carpeted the kitchen, grabbed the shotgun that lay upon the table, jammed the barrel between his teeth – and suddenly realised that his arms were not long enough to reach the trigger. The urge to look up at the bewitching moons on the walls was so overpowering that he felt as if someone had hold of him by the hair and was pulling his head back to force his gaze up from the floor. And when he closed his eyes defensively, it seemed as if some invisible adversary began to pry insistently at his eyelids. In his horror of being committed to a madhouse like his father, he found the strength to resist the mesmeric moon-call. Eyes still closed, he collapsed into a chair, kicked off one shoe, stripped away the sock, braced the shotgun with both hands, put the barrel in his mouth, raised his unshod foot, and touched one bare toe to the cold trigger. Imagined moonlight on his skin and imagined lunar tides in his blood (no less forceful for being imaginary) demanded his attention with such sudden power that he opened his eyes, saw the many moons on the walls, and cried 'No!' into the barrel of the gun. Even as the spellbinding moon-call pulled him back towards a trance, even as he pressed his foot down upon the trigger, the swelling memory-balloon at last burst in his mind, and he remembered everything that had been taken away from him: *the summer before last, Dominick, Ginger, Faye, Ernie, the young priest, the others, Interstate 80, the Tranquillity Motel, oh God the motel, and oh God the moon!*

Perhaps Zebediah Lomack was unable to check the downward motion of his bare foot or perhaps, instead, the suddenly revealed memory was so terrible that it encouraged suicide. Whichever the case, the .12-gauge went off with a roar, and the back of his head blew out, and for him (though for no one else) the terror ended.

*   *   *

Boston, Massachusetts.

All Christmas afternoon, Ginger Weiss read *Twilight in Baby-lon*, and at seven o'clock that evening, when it was time to go

261

downstairs for drinks and dinner with the Hannaby family, she resented the interruption and did not want to put the book aside. She was a willing captive of the engrossing story, but she was more captivated by the photo of the author. Dominick Corvaisis' commanding eyes and dark good looks continued to arouse in her an uneasiness bordering on fear, and she could not overcome the peculiar feeling that she knew him.

Dinner with her hosts, their children and grandchildren, might have been pleasurable if Dominick Corvaisis had not exerted a mysteriously powerful claim on her attention. At 10:00, when she could at last gracefully withdraw without offending anyone, she cast out and gathered in a final series of Christmas wishes for happiness and good health, then returned to her room.

She began reading where she had left off, and with a minimum of interruptions to scrutinise the author's photograph, she finished the book at 3:45 a.m. In the deep post-midnight silence that had settled over Baywatch, Ginger sat with the book in her lap, the jacket photo turned up, her eyes fixed on Dominick Corvaisis' hauntingly familiar face. Minute by minute, as she sat in her strange, silent, one-sided communion with the writer's image, Ginger became increasingly convinced that she had met the man somewhere and that he was, in some unimaginable fashion, part of her recent troubles. Although her steadily growing conviction was tempered by the realisation that this intuition might be part of the same mental disturbance that generated her fugues, and might therefore be unreliable, her agitation and excitement increased until, shaky and distraught, she was finally driven to action.

Leaving her room with exaggerated stealth, she went downstairs through the dark and untenanted rooms of the great slumbering house, into the kitchen. She switched on the light and used the wall phone to call information in Laguna Beach. It was one o'clock in the morning in California, too rude an hour to wake Corvaisis. But if she could get a number for him, she would sleep better, knowing that she could get in touch with him in the morning. To her dismay though not to her surprise, his number was unlisted.

Switching off the kitchen light and creeping quietly back to her room, Ginger made up her mind to write Corvaisis in the morning, care of his publisher. She would dispatch the message by express mail, with an urgent plea to the publisher to forward the letter immediately.

Perhaps attempting to contact him was precipitate and irrational. Perhaps she had never met him, and perhaps he had nothing to do with her bizarre affliction. Perhaps he'd think she was a crackpot. But if this million-to-one shot proved a good bet, the pay-off might be her very salvation, which was sufficient reward to risk making a fool of herself.

*   *   *

Laguna Beach, California.

As yet unaware that an advance review copy of his book had made a vital link between himself and a deeply troubled woman in Boston, Dom remained at Parker Faine's house until midnight, discussing the possible nature of the conspiracy that he had theorised. Neither he nor Parker had enough information to put together a detailed or even slightly useful picture of the conspirators, but the very process of sharing and exploring the mystery with a friend made it less frightening.

They agreed that Dom should not fly to Portland and begin his odyssey until he saw how bad his sleepwalking became now that he had thrown away the Valium and Dalmane. Maybe somnambulism would not recur, as he expected it would, in which case he could travel without fear of losing control of himself in a distant place. But if he resumed his night rambling, he would need a couple of weeks to decide on the best way of restraining himself during sleep, before heading to Portland.

Besides, by waiting a while, he might receive additional letters from his unknown correspondent. Those clues might make the trek from Portland to Mountainview unnecessary or might target a specific area along that route as the place where Dom would encounter some sight or experience that would free his imprisoned memories.

By midnight, when Dom rose to leave Parker's hillside house, the artist had become so intrigued by the situation that he looked as if he would be up for hours yet, his mind spinning. 'You're sure it's wise to be alone tonight?' he asked at the front door.

263

Dom stepped outside onto a walkway patterned with spiky geometric forms of darkness and wedge-shaped slices of yellow light, which were formed by the beams of a decorative iron lantern half obscured by shadow-casting palm fronds. Looking back at his friend, he said, 'We've been through this before. It might not be wise, but it's the only way.'

'You'll call if you need help?'

'I'll call,' Dom said.

'And take those precautions we talked about.'

Dom attended to those precautions a short while later at home. He removed the pistol from his nightstand, locked it in a drawer of his office desk, and buried the desk key under a package of ice cream in the freezer. Better to be unprepared for a burglar than to risk firing the gun while sound asleep. Next, from a coil of rope in the garage, he cut a ten-foot length. After brushing his teeth and undressing, he knotted one end of the line securely around his right wrist in such a way that he could escape only by untying four difficult knots. He secured the other end of the rope to one post of the headboard, taking care to fasten it tightly. With one foot of the line's length used for the knots, he was left with nine feet of play, enough to assure his comfort while keeping him tethered within a safe distance of the bed.

In previous somnambulistic episodes, he had performed complex tasks that had required some concentration, though nothing quite so tedious as the unravelling of well-made knots, which were often a challenge to him when he was *awake*. In his sleep, he would surely lack the coordination and mental focus to free himself, and the effort to do so would be frustrating enough to wake him.

Being thus hampered involved some danger. If a fire broke out in the night or if the house were damaged in an earthquake, he might be so delayed by the need to untie himself that he would perish in the smoke or beneath a collapsing wall. He had to risk it.

When he turned out the bedside light and slipped under the blanket, trailing the rope from one arm, the glowing red numerals of the digital clock read 12:58. Staring at the dark ceiling, wondering what in the name of God he had become involved in out there on the road the summer before last, he waited for sleep to creep upon him.

On the nightstand, the telephone was silent. If his number had not been unlisted, he might have received, at that moment, a long-distance call from a lonely and frightened young woman in Boston, a call that would have radically changed the course of the next few weeks and might have saved lives.

*　　　*　　　*

Milwaukee, Wisconsin.

In the guest room of her only daughter's house, where a nightlight burned in consideration of Ernie's phobia, Faye Block listened to her husband as, asleep and dreaming, he mumbled into his pillow. A few minutes ago, she had been awakened when he had let out a soft cry and had thrashed for a moment in the sheets. Now she raised herself on one elbow, cocked her head, and listened intently, trying to decipher his muffled speech. He was saying the same thing again and again into the pillow. The almost panicky urgency in his voice made Faye nervous. She leaned closer to him, straining to understand.

Suddenly he shifted his head just enough to turn his mouth from the pillow, and his words became clear though no less mysterious than when they had been muffled: 'The moon, the moon, the moon, the moon . . .'

*　　　*　　　*

Las Vegas, Nevada.

Jorja took Marcie into her own bed that night, because it did not seem like a good idea to let the girl alone after the disturbing events of the day. She did not get much rest because all night Marcie seemed to phase in and out of nightmares, frequently kicking at the sheets, squirming vigorously as if to free herself from restraining hands, and talking in her sleep about doctors and needles. Jorja wondered how long this had been going on. Their bedrooms were separated by back-to-back closets insulated by hanging clothes, and the child's sleep-talk was very soft, so it was possible that she had passed a lot of nights in unconscious terror without Jorja being aware of it. Her voice raised gooseflesh on Jorja's arms.

In the morning, she would take Marcie to the doctor. Given her unexplained dread of all physicians, the girl might cause a hell of a scene. But as much as Marcie feared going to a doctor, Jorja feared *not* going. If it had not been so hard to locate the right physician on Christmas Day, Jorja would have gone for help already. She was scared.

Following Marcie's outburst, when her grandfather's teasing about taking her to a hospital had driven her away from the table in a mad panic, the day had gone downhill. The girl was so overcome by fear that she peed her pants, and for ten or fifteen hideously embarrassing and terrifying minutes, she resisted all Jorja's efforts to get her cleaned up. She screamed, scratched, and kicked. The tantrum passed at last, and she submitted to a bath. But she was like a little zombie, slack-faced and empty-eyed, as if the terror, in passing out of her, had taken with it all her strength and her mind as well.

That quasi-catatonic state lasted almost an hour while Jorja made a dozen telephone calls in an attempt to track down Dr Besancourt, the pediatrician who treated Marcie on those rare occasions when she was sick. As Mary and Pete tried unsuccessfully to get a smile or at least a word of response from the stricken girl, and as Marcie continued to act as if she were deaf and mute, Jorja's mind was increasingly filled with half-remembered magazine articles about autistic children. She couldn't recall whether autism was a condition that began in infancy or whether it was possible for a perfectly normal little girl of seven to suddenly withdraw into a private place and close out the rest of the world forever. Not being able to remember made her a little crazy.

Gradually, however, Marcie came out of her daze. She began to answer Mary and Pete, though in one-word replies delivered in a flat, emotionless voice nearly as unsettling as her screams had been earlier. Sucking on her thumb as she had not done in at least two years, she went into the living room to play with her new toys. Most of the afternoon, she played without any visible pleasure, a faint scowl·having taken unchallenged possession of her small face. Jorja was no less worried because of this change, but she was relieved to see that Marcie showed no further interest in the Little Ms Doctor kit.

266

By four-thirty, the girl's scowl had faded, and she had become sociable once more. In a good mood again, she was such a natural charmer that she almost made it seem as if her outburst at the table had been no worse than any child's temper tantrum.

In fact, on the outside stairs of the apartment complex, beyond Marcie's hearing, Jorja's mother paused on the way down to the car and said, 'She's just trying to let us know that she's hurt and confused. She doesn't understand why her father left, and right now she needs a lot of special attention, Jorja, a lot of love. That's all.'

Jorja knew the problem was worse than that. She had no doubt that Marcie was still disturbed by her father's behaviour, deeply hurt by his abandonment, and full of unresolved conflicts. But something else was eating the girl, something that seemed disturbingly irrational, and Jorja was scared of it.

Not long after Pete and Mary left, the girl began playing Little Ms Doctor with the same unnerving intensity she had exhibited earlier, and when bedtime came she wanted to take the kit with her. Now, some of the Little Ms Doctor things lay on the floor at Marcie's side of the bed, some on the nightstand. And in the dark bedroom the child dreamed and whimpered about doctors, nurses, needles.

Jorja would have been unable to sleep even if Marcie had been perfectly still and quiet. Worry induced insomnia even more effectively than a dozen cups of coffee. Since she was awake anyway, she listened attentively to her daughter's every dreamy utterance, hoping that she would hear something that would help her understand or that would assist the doctor in arriving at his diagnosis. It was after two o'clock in the morning when Marcie mumbled something different from what she had mumbled before, something that had nothing to do with doctors and nurses and big sharp needles. With a flurry of violent kicks, the girl flopped from her stomach onto her back, gasped, and went rigid, perfectly still, 'The moon, moon, the moon,' she said in a voice that was filled with both amazement and fear, 'the moon,' a voice of such chilling whispery urgency that Jorja knew it was not just meaningless sleeptalk. 'The moon, moon, *moooooooonnn . . .*'

*　　　*　　　*

Chicago, Illinois.

Brendan Cronin, priest on probation, slept warmly under a blanket and patchwork quilt, smiling at something in a dream. The winter wind sighed through the giant pine tree outside, fluted and soughed in the eaves, and moaned at his window, exerting itself in evenly spaced gusts as if nature were ventilating the night with a huge mechanical bellows that faithfully produced eight exhalations to the minute. Even lost in his dream, Brendan must have been aware of the wind's slow pulse, for when he began to talk in his sleep, the words issued from him in a sympathetic rhythm: 'The moon . . . the moon . . . the moon . . . the moon. . . .'

* * *

Laguna Beach, California.

'The moon! The moon!'

Dominick Corvaisis was awakened by his own fearful shouting and by a burning pain in his right wrist. He was on his hands and knees in the darkness beside his bed, wrenching frantically at something that had a grip on his arm. He continued to struggle for a few seconds until the mists of sleep cleared, whereupon he realised that he was being held by nothing more sinister than the rope with which he had tethered himself.

Breathing raggedly, heart pounding, he fumbled for the lamp switch and winced as the sudden light stung his eyes. A quick look at the restraining rope showed that in his sleep (and in the dark) he had completely untied one of the four tightly drawn knots and partially unravelled a second before losing patience for the task. Then, in the panic that always accompanied his sleepwalking, he evidently had begun to pull and tug and twist against the belaying line as if he were a dumb animal protesting at a leash, painfully abrading his right wrist.

Dom got off the floor, pushed aside the tangled blankets, and sat on the edge of the bed.

He knew he had been dreaming, though he could not recall anything about the dream. However, he was pretty sure that it was not the nightmare he had endured on other occasions during the past month, for that one had had nothing to do with the moon. This was another dream, equally terrifying but in a different way.

His shouts, which had been partly responsible for waking him, had been so importunate, so haunted, so fright-filled that he could even now summon them in memory as clearly as he had first heard them: *'The moon! The moon!'* He shuddered and raised his hands to his throbbing head.

The moon. What did it mean?

* * *

Boston, Massachusetts.

Ginger sat straight up in bed with a shrill cry.

Lavinia, the Hannaby's housekeeper, said, 'Oh, I'm sorry, Dr Weiss. Didn't mean to scare you. You were having a nightmare.'

'Nightmare?' Ginger had no recollection of a dream.

'Oh, yes,' Lavinia said, 'and a really bad one from the sound of it. I was passing in the hall when I heard you crying out. I almost came in right away, until I realised you must be dreaming. I hesitated then, but you went on and on, shouting it over and over again, until I thought I'd better wake you.'

Blinking, Ginger said, 'Shouting? What was I shouting?'

'Over and over again,' the housekeeper said. 'The moon, the moon, the moon.' You sounded so frightened.'

'I don't remember.'

'"The moon,"' Lavinia assured her, '"the moon," over and over again, in such a voice that I half-thought someone was killing you.'

PART TWO

Days of Discovery

Courage is resistance to fear, mastery of fear – not absence of fear.

– Mark Twain

Is there some meaning to this life?
What purpose lies behind the strife?
Whence do we come, where are we bound?
These cold questions echo and resound
Through each day, each lonely night.
We long to find the splendid light
That will cast a revelatory beam
Upon the meaning of the human dream.

– The Book of Counted Sorrows

A friend may well be reckoned the masterpiece of Nature.

– Ralph Waldo Emerson

FOUR

December 26 – January 11

1.

BOSTON, MASSACHUSETTS

Between December 27 and January 5, Dr Ginger Weiss went to Pablo Jackson's Back Bay apartment seven times. On six of those visits he used hypnotic therapy to probe cautiously and patiently at the Azrael Block that sealed off a portion of her memory.

To the old magician, she grew more beautiful each time she arrived at his door – more intelligent, charming, and appealingly tough-minded, too. Pablo saw in her the kind of woman he would have wanted as a daughter. Ginger had stirred in him protective fatherly feelings that he had never known before.

He told her nearly everything he had learned from Alexander Christophson at the Hergensheimers' Christmas party. She resisted the idea that her memory block had not developed naturally but had been implanted by persons unknown. 'Too bizarre. Things like that don't happen to ordinary people like me. I'm just a *farmishteh* from Brooklyn, not someone who gets involved in international intrigue.'

The only thing about his conversation with Alex Christophson that he did not tell her was that the retired espionage officer had warned against becoming involved with her. If Ginger knew Alex had been deeply disturbed, she might decide that the situation was too dangerous to justify Pablo's involvement. Out of concern for her and out of a selfish desire to be part of her life, he withheld that information.

At their first meeting on December 27, prior to the session of hypnosis, he prepared a lunch of quiche and salad. As they ate, Ginger said, 'But, I've never been around a sensitive military installation, never been involved in any defence research, never associated with anyone who could conceivably be part of a spy ring. It's ludicrous!'

'If you stumbled on some dangerous bit of knowledge, it wasn't in a high security area. It was someplace you had every right to be . . . except you just happened to be there at the wrong time.'

'But listen, Pablo, if they brainwashed me, that would've taken time. They'd have had to hold me in custody somewhere. Right?'

'I imagine it would take a few days.'

'So you can't be right,' she said. 'Of course, I realise that while they were forcing me to forget the things I'd accidentally seen, they'd also repress the memory of the place where they held me for the brainwashing. But there'd be a blank spot in my past somewhere, an empty time when I couldn't remember where I'd been or what I'd done.'

'Not at all. They'd implant a set of false recollections to cover the missing days, and you'd never know the difference.'

'*Good God*! Really? They could do that?'

'One thing I hope to do is locate those false memories,' Pablo explained as he finished his quiche. 'It'll take a long time, slowly regressing you back through your life week by week, but when I find the phony memories, I'll recognise them *tout de suite* because they won't have the detail, the substance, of genuine memories. Mere stage sets, you see. If we find two or three days of tissue-thin memories, we'll have pinpointed the origin of your problem because those will be the dates when you were in the hands of these people . . . whoever they may be.'

'Yes, yes, I see,' she said, suddenly excited. 'The first day of the mushy memories will be the day that I saw something I shouldn't have seen. And the last day will be the day they finished brainwashing me. It's terribly difficult to believe. . . . But if someone really did *implant* this memory block, and if all my symptoms – the fugues – are a result of those repressed memories struggling to the surface, then my problem isn't really psychological. There's a chance I could practise medicine again. All I've got to do is dig out the memories, bring them into the light, and then the pressure will be relieved.'

Pablo took her hand and gave it a squeeze. 'Yes, I believe there's real hope. But it's not going to be easy. Every time I probe at the block, I risk plunging you into a coma . . . or worse. I intend to be oh-so-careful, but the risk remains.'

*   *   *

The first two sessions of deep hypnosis were conducted in armchairs by the huge bay window, one on December 27, one on Sunday the twenty-ninth, each lasting four hours. Pablo regressed her day by day through the previous nine months but found no obviously artificial memories.

Also on Sunday, Ginger suggested he question her about Dominick Corvaisis, the novelist whose picture affected her in such a peculiar manner. When Pablo hypnotised her and established that he was speaking to the inner Ginger, to her deep subconscious self, he asked if she had ever met Corvaisis, and after a brief hesitation she said, 'Yes.' Pablo pursued the point cautiously and diligently, but he could get almost nothing more out of her. At last a thin vapour of memory escaped her: 'He threw salt in my face.'

'Corvaisis threw salt on you?' Puzzled, Pablo asked, 'Why?'

'Can't . . . quite . . . remember.'

'Where did this happen?'

Her frown deepened, and when he continued to pursue the subject, she withdrew, sinking into that frightening comatose state. He quickly retreated before she had spiralled down as deep as she had done before. He assured her that he would ask no further questions about Corvaisis if only she would return, and gradually she responded to that promise.

Clearly, Ginger had at one time met Corvaisis. And her encounter with him was associated with the memories of which she had been robbed.

*   *   *

In the next two sessions – Monday the thirtieth, and Wednesday, first day of the new year – Pablo regressed Ginger another eight months, to the end of July, two summers ago,

275

without discovering any tissue-thin memories that would indicate the work of mind-control specialists.

Then on Thursday, January 2, Ginger asked him to question her about her previous night's unremembered dream. For the fourth time since Christmas, she had cried out in her sleep – 'The moon!' with such insistence that she woke others in Baywatch. 'I think the dream's about the place and time that's been stolen from me. Put me in a trance, and maybe we'll learn something.'

But when hypnotised and returned to last night's dream, she refused to answer questions and drifted into a deeper sleep than a mere hypnotic trance. He had pulled the Azrael Trigger once more, which was proof positive that her dreams involved those forbidden memories.

*   *   *

On Friday they did not meet. Pablo needed the day to read further about memory blocks of all kinds and to think about how best to proceed.

In addition, he had recorded all five post-Christmas sessions, so he sat at the reproduction Sheraton desk in his book-lined study and listened to portions of those tapes for hours. He was searching for a single word or a change in Ginger's voice that might make a particular answer seem more important on rehearing than it had seemed at the time.

He found nothing startling, though he noticed that, during hypnotic regression, a subtle note of anxiety had entered her voice when their backward journey through time had reached August 31 of the year before last. It was nothing dramatic that would have caught his attention at the time the recordings were made. But by telescoping all the sessions into one afternoon, using the fast-forward control to skip from day to day, he saw the pattern of steadily building anxiety, and he suspected they were getting close to the event now hidden behind the Azrael Block.

Therefore, during their sixth post-Christmas session on Saturday, January 4, Pablo was not surprised when the breakthrough came. As usual, Ginger was sitting in one of the armchairs by the bay window, beyond which a fine snow was falling. Her silver-blonde hair glowed with spectral light. As he regressed her back through July of the previous year, her brows knitted, and her voice became whispery and tense, and Pablo knew she was drawing closer to the moment of her forgotten ordeal.

Since they were going backwards in time, he had already taken her through her busy months as a surgical resident at Memorial Hospital, back to the moment when she first reported to George Hannaby for duty on Monday, July 30, more than seventeen months ago. Her memories remained sharp and richly detailed as Pablo conveyed her into Sunday, July 29, when she still had been settling into her new apartment. July 28, 27, 26, 25, 24 . . . through those days she had been unpacking and shopping for furniture . . . all the way back to July 21, 20, 19. . . . On July 18, the moving van arrived with her household goods, which she had shipped from Palo Alto, California, where she had lived the previous two years while taking an advanced course of study in vascular surgery. Further back . . . On July 17, she arrived in Boston by car and booked a room overnight at the Holiday Inn Government Center, as close to Beacon Hill as possible, not yet able to stay at her new apartment because she had no bed there.

'By car? You drove cross-country from Stanford?'

'It was the first vacation I ever really had. I like to drive, and it was a chance to see a little of the country,' Ginger said, but in such an ominous voice that she might have been talking about a journey through hell rather than a trans-continental holiday.

So Pablo began to regress her through the days of her journey, back across the Midwestern heartland, around the northernmost horn of the Rocky Mountains, through Utah, into Nevada, until they came to Tuesday morning, July 10. She had stayed the previous night at a motel, and when he asked for the name of it, a shudder passed through her.

'T-Tranquillity.'

'Tranquillity Motel? Where is this place? Describe it, too.'

On the arms of her chair, her hands curled into fists. 'Thirty miles west of Elko, on Interstate 80.' Haltingly, reluctantly, she described the twenty-unit Tranquillity Motel and Grille. Something about the place terrified her. Every muscle in her body went rigid.

Pablo said, 'So you stayed the night of July ninth at the motel. That was a Monday. All right, so now it's Monday, July ninth. You're just arriving at the motel. You haven't stayed there yet; you're just driving up to it. . . . What time of the day is it?'

She did not answer, and her tremors grew more pronounced, and when he asked again, she said, 'I didn't arrive on Monday. F-Friday.'

Startled, Pablo said, 'The previous Friday? You stayed at the Tranquillity Motel from Friday, July sixth, through Monday, July ninth? Four nights at this small motel in the middle of nowhere?' He leaned forward in his chair, sensing that they had found the time when her mind had been tampered with. 'Why would you want to stay so long?'

In a slightly wooden voice, she said, 'Because it was peaceful. I was on vacation, after all,' she said, her strangely stilted voice becoming more flat and devoid of nuance with each word she spoke. 'I needed to relax, you see, and this was a perfect place to relax.'

The old magician looked away from her, watched the faintly luminous snow slanting down through the dreary grey afternoon beyond the window, and carefully considered his next question. 'You said this motel has no swimming pool. And the rooms you've described aren't luxurious. Not resort-style rooms for long-term visits. What on earth did you do for four days out there in the middle of nowhere, Ginger?'

'Like I said, I relaxed. Just relaxed. Napped. Read a couple of books. Watched some TV. They have good TV even way out there on the plains because they've got their own little satellite receiver dish on the roof.' Her manner of speech was now entirely altered, and she sounded as if she were reading from a script. 'After two intense years at Stanford, I needed a few days of doing absolutely nothing.'

'What books did you read while at the motel?'

'I . . . I don't remember.' Her hands were still fisted, and she was still rigid. Fine pearly beads of sweat popped out along her hairline.

'Ginger, you're there now, in the motel room, reading. Understand? You are reading whatever you were reading then. Now look at the title of the book and tell me what it is.'

'I . . . no . . . no title.'

'Every book has a title.'

'No title.'

'Because there really is no book – is there?' he said.

'Yes. I just relaxed. Napped. Read a couple of books. Watched some TV,' she said in a soft, dead, emotionless voice. 'They have good TV even way out there on the plains because they've got their own little satellite receiver dish on the roof.'

'What TV shows did you watch?' Pablo asked.

'News. Movies.'

'What movies?'

She flinched. 'I . . . don't remember.'

Pablo was quite sure that the reason she did not remember these things was precisely because she had never done them. She had been at that motel, all right, because she could describe it in minute detail, but she could not recall the books and the TV programmes because she had never passed any of that time in those pursuits. Through clever post-hypnotic suggestions, she had been instructed to say that she had done those things, and she had actually been made to remember vaguely having done them, but they were merely artificial memories designed to cover what had really transpired at that motel. A specialist in brainwashing could insert false memories in a subject's mind, but even if he worked very hard at it and built an intricate web of interlocking details, he could not make phoney memories as convincing as real ones.

Pablo said, 'Where did you eat dinner each night?'

'The Tranquillity Grille. It's a small place, and it doesn't have much of a menu, but the food is reasonably good.' That response was, once again, delivered in a flat and hollow voice.

Pablo said, 'What did you eat at the Tranquillity Grille?'

She hesitated. 'I . . . I don't remember.'

'But you told me the food was good. How could you make that judgment if you don't remember what you ate?'

'Uhhh . . . it's a small place, and it doesn't have much of a menu.'

The more insistently he pressed for details, the more tense she became. Her voice remained emotionless as she spewed out her programmed responses, but her face twisted and hardened with anxiety.

Pablo could have told her that her apparent memories of

those four days at the Tranquillity Motel were false. He could have ordered her to blow them out of her mind the way one might blow dust from an old book, and she would have done it. Then he could have told her that her true memories were locked behind an Azrael Block, and that she must hammer it into more dust. But if he had done so, she would have plunged, as programmed, into a coma – or worse. He would have to spend many days, possibly weeks, looking for tiny cracks to exploit cautiously.

For today, he contented himself with identifying the precise number of hours of her life that had been stolen from her. He took her back to Friday, July sixth of the summer before last, and asked exactly when she signed the register at the Tranquillity Motel.

'A little after eight o'clock.' She no longer spoke in a wooden voice because these were real memories. 'It was still an hour before sunset, but I was exhausted. All I wanted was dinner, a shower, and bed.' She described the man and woman behind the check-in counter in detail. She even recalled their names: Faye and Ernie.

Pablo said, 'Once you had checked in, you ate at the Tranquillity Grille next to the motel. So describe the place.'

She did so, and in convincing detail. But when he jumped her ahead to the moment at which she left the grille, her recollections were phony again, thin and without colour. Clearly, her memories had been altered from some point after she had gone into the Tranquillity Grille on that Friday evening until she had left the motel and had headed towards Utah the following Tuesday morning.

Pablo backtracked, returning Ginger to the small restaurant once more, searching for the exact moment at which the genuine memories ended and the false began. 'Tell me about your dinner from the moment you went into Tranquillity Grille that Friday evening. Minute by minute.'

Ginger sat up straight in her chair. Her eyes were still closed, but under the shuttered lids, they moved visibly, as if she were looking left and right upon entering the Tranquillity Grille. She unfisted her hands and got up, much to Pablo's surprise. She walked away from her chair, towards the centre of the room. He walked beside her to prevent her from

280

bumping into furniture. She did not know she was in his apartment but imagined herself to be making her way between the tables in the restaurant. As she moved, the tension and fear left her, for now she was wholly in that time, prior to all her trouble, when she had had nothing about which to be tense or afraid.

In a quiet, anxiety-free voice she said, 'Took me awhile to freshen up and get over here, so it's almost twilight. Outside, the plains are orange in the late sunlight, and the inside of the diner is full of that glow. I think I'll take that booth over in the corner by the window.'

Pablo went with her, guiding her past the Picasso painting toward one of the sofas that was decorated with colourful pastel accent pillows.

She said, 'Mmmm. Smells good. Onions . . . spices . . . French fries . . .'

'How many people in the diner, Ginger?'

She paused and turned her head, surveying the room with closed eyes. 'The cook behind the counter and a waitress. Three men . . . truck drivers, I guess . . . on stools at the counter. And . . . three at that table . . . and the chubby priest . . . another guy over at that booth . . .' Ginger continued pointing and counting. 'Oh, eleven in all, plus me.'

'All right,' Pablo said, 'let's go to that booth by the windows.'

She began walking again, smiled vaguely at someone, side-stepped an obstacle that only she could see, then suddenly twitched in surprise, jerked one hand to her face. 'Oh!' She stopped in her tracks.

'What is it?' Pablo asked. 'What's happened?'

She blinked furiously for a moment, smiled, and spoke to someone in the Tranquillity Grille back there on July sixth of last year. 'No, no, I'm all right. It's nothing. I've already brushed it off.' She wiped her face with one hand. 'See?' She had been looking down, as if the other person was seated, and now she raised her eyes as he got up.

Pablo waited for her to continue the conversation.

She said, 'Well, when you spill salt you'd *better* throw some over your shoulder, or God knows what'll happen. My father used to throw it three times, so if you'd been him, you'd have buried me in the stuff.'

281

She started walking again, and Pablo said, 'Stop. Wait, Ginger. The man who threw salt over his shoulder – tell me what he looks like.'

'Young,' she said. 'Thirty-two or thirty-three. About five-ten. Lean. Dark hair. Dark eyes. Sort of handsome. Seems shy, sweet.'

Dominick Corvaisis. No doubt about it.

She began to move again. Pablo stayed at her side until, realising she was about to sit in the restaurant booth, he guided her gently to the sofa. She sat back on it and looked out a window, smiling at her private panorama of Nevada plains washed in the light of a dying sun.

Pablo watched and listened while Ginger exchanged pleasantries with the waitress and ordered a bottle of Coors. The beer was served, and Ginger pantomimed sipping it while she watched the sun fade. Seconds ticked past, but Pablo didn't speed her through the scene because he knew they were approaching the crucial moment when her real memories gave way to phoney ones. The event – the thing that she saw and should not have seen – had transpired around this time, and Pablo wanted to learn everything he could about the minutes leading up to it.

Twilight arrived back there in the past.

When the waitress returned, Ginger ordered a bowl of the homemade vegetable soup and a cheeseburger with all the trimmings.

Night fell out there in Nevada.

Abruptly, before her food had been served, Ginger frowned and said, 'What's that?' She looked out the imagined window, scowling.

'What do you see?' Pablo asked, chained to his inconvenient vantage point in present-day Boston.

A worried look came over her face, and she stood up. 'What the devil *is* that noise?' She looked towards other people in the restaurant with a puzzled expression, and she spoke to them: 'I don't know. I don't know what it is.' She suddenly tottered sideways and nearly fell. '*Gevalt!*' She reached out as if supporting herself against the side of a booth or table. 'Shaking. Why's everything shaking?' She jumped in surprise. 'It's knocked over my beer glass. Is it an earthquake? What's happening? What *is* that sound?' She stumbled again. Now she was frightened. 'The door!' She started to run across the living room, though in her mind she was heading toward the exit from the restaurant that, in reality, she had long ago departed. 'The door,' she cried again, but then she stopped abruptly, swaying, gasping, shuddering.

When Pablo caught up with her, she dropped to her knees and hung her head. 'What's happening, Ginger?'

'Nothing.' She had changed in an instant.

'What's that noise?'

'What noise?' The robot voice again.

'Ginger, damn it, what's happening in the Tranquillity Grille?'

Horror was on her face, but she merely said, 'I'm having dinner.'

'That's a false memory.'

'Having dinner.'

He tried to make her continue with the crucial memory of the frightening thing that had been about to happen. But at last he had to accept that the Azrael Block, behind which her memories were repressed, took form when she had been running for the restaurant door, and it did not end until the following Tuesday morning, when she drove east towards Salt Lake City. In time, he might be able to chip it down to smaller dimensions, but enough had been accomplished for one day.

At last they were making real headway. They knew that on the night of Friday, July sixth, the year before last, Ginger had seen something she had not been meant to see. Having seen it, she had almost certainly been detained in a room at the Tranquillity Motel, where someone had used sophisticated brainwashing techniques to conceal the memory of that event from her and thereby prevent her from carrying word of it to the world. They had worked on her for three days – Saturday, Sunday, and Monday – releasing her, with sanitised recollections, on Tuesday.

But in God's name who were these omnipotent strangers? And what had she seen?

2.

PORTLAND, OREGON

Sunday, January 5, Dominick Corvaisis flew to Portland and took a hotel room near the apartment house in which he had once lived. Rain was falling hard, and the air was cold.

Except for dinner in the hotel restaurant, he spent the remaining hours of Sunday afternoon and evening at a table by the window of his room, alternately staring out at the rain-lashed city and studying the roadmaps. Again and again, he mentally reviewed the trip he had taken the summer before last (and would take again starting tomorrow).

As he had told Parker Faine at Christmas, he was convinced that he had stumbled into a dangerous situation out there on the road, and that (paranoid as it sounded) the memory of it had been wiped from his mind. The mail from his unknown correspondent pointed to no other conclusion.

Two days ago, he had received a third envelope without a return address, postmarked New York. Now, when Dom tired of looking at the maps and staring thoughtfully out at the Oregon rain, he picked up that envelope, shook out the contents, and studied them. This time there had been no note, just two Polaroid photographs.

The first picture had the least effect on him, although it made him tense – unaccountably tense, considering that it was a photograph of someone who, as far as he knew, was a stranger to him. A young, pudgy priest with unruly auburn hair, freckles, and green eyes. He was facing the camera, sitting in a chair near a small writing desk, a suitcase at his side. He was very erect, head up and shoulders squared off, hands limp in his lap, knees together. The picture disturbed Dom because the expression on the priest's face was only one step removed from the lifeless, sightless stare of a corpse. The man was alive; that much was evident from his rigid posture, yet his eyes were chillingly empty.

The second photograph hit Dom much harder than the first, and its powerful effect did not diminish with familiarity. A young woman was the subject of the snapshot, and she was no

284

stranger. Although Dom could not recall where they had met, he knew they were acquainted. The sight of her made his heart quicken with a fear similar to that which filled him when he woke from one of his episodes of sleepwalking. She was in her late twenties. Blue eyes. Silver-blonde hair. Exquisitely proportioned face. She would have been exceptionally beautiful if her expression had not been precisely that of the priest: slack, dead, empty-eyed. She had been photographed from the waist up, lying in a narrow bed, sheets pulled up chastely to her neck. Restraining straps held her down. One arm was partially bared to allow clearance for an IV needle in her wrist vein. She looked small, helpless, oppressed.

The photograph instantly brought to mind his own nightmare in which unseen men were shouting at him and forcing his face into a sink. A couple of times, that bad dream had not begun at the sink itself but in a bed in a strange room, where his vision was blurred by a saffron mist. Looking at the young woman, Dom was convinced that somewhere there was a Polaroid shot of him in similar circumstances: strapped to a bed, an IV needle in his arm, his face without expression.

When he had shown the two photographs to Parker Faine on Friday, the day they came in the mail, the artist jumped to similar conclusions. 'If I'm wrong, roast me in hell and make sandwiches for the devil, but I swear this is a snapshot of a woman in a trance or drug-induced stupor, undergoing the brainwashing that you evidently underwent. Christ, this situation gets more bizarre and fascinating day by day! It's something you ought to be able to go to the cops about – but you can't because who's to say which side *they'd* be on? It may have been a branch of our own government you ran afoul of out there on the road. Anyway, you weren't the only one who got in trouble, good buddy. This priest and this woman also stumbled into it. Whoever went to this much trouble is hiding something damned big, a lot bigger than I thought before.'

Now, sitting at the table by his hotel-room window, Dom held one picture in each hand, side by side, and let his gaze travel back and forth from the priest to the woman. 'Who are you?' he asked aloud. 'What're your names? What happened to us out there?'

Outside, lightning cracked whiplike in the night over Portland, as if a cosmic coachman were urging the rain to fall faster. Like the drumming hooves of a thousand harried horses, fat hard-driven raindrops hammered against the wall of the hotel and galloped down the window.

*　　*　　*

Later, Dom fastened himself to the bed with a tether that he had improved considerably since Christmas. First he wrapped a length of surgical gauze around his right wrist and secured it with adhesive tape, a barrier between rope and flesh to prevent abrasion. He was no longer using an ordinary all-purpose line but a hawser-laid nylon rope, only a quarter-inch in diameter but with a breaking strength of twenty-six hundred pounds. It was expressly made for rock- and mountain-climbing.

He had switched to the sturdier rope because, on the night of December 28, he had slipped his previous tether by chewing all the way through it while asleep. The mountaineering rope was fray-resistant and nearly as impervious to teeth as copper cable would have been.

That night in Portland, he woke three times, wrestling furiously with the tether, perspiring, panting, his racing heart's accelerator floored beneath a heavy weight of fear. 'The moon! The moon!'

3.

LAS VEGAS, NEVADA

The day after Christmas, Jorja Monatella took Marcie to Dr Louis Besancourt, and the examination turned into an ordeal that frustrated the physician, frightened Jorja, and embarrassed them both. From the moment Jorja took her into the doctor's waiting room, the girl screamed, screeched, wailed, and wept. 'No doctors! They'll hurt me!'

On those rare occasions when Marcie misbehaved (and they were rare, indeed), one hard slap on the bottom was usually all

286

that was required to restore her senses and induce contrition. But when Jorja tried that now, it had the opposite effect of what she intended. Marcie screamed louder, wailed more shrilly, and wept more copiously than before.

The assistance of an understanding nurse was required to convey the shrieking child from the waiting area into an examination room, by which time Jorja was not only mortified but worried sick by Marcie's complete irrationality. Dr Besancourt's good humour and bedside manner were not enough to quiet the girl, and in fact she had become more frightened and violent the moment he appeared. Marcie pulled away from him when he tried to touch her, screamed, struck him, kicked him, until it became necessary for Jorja and a nurse to hold her down. When the doctor used an ophthalmoscope to examine her eyes, her terror reached a crescendo indicated by a sudden loosening of her bladder that was dismayingly reminiscent of the fiasco on Christmas Day.

Her uncontrolled urination marked an abrupt change in her demeanour. She became sullen, silent, just she had for a while at Christmas. She was shockingly pale, and she shivered constantly. She had that eerie detachment that made Jorja think of autism.

Lou Besancourt had no simple diagnosis with which to comfort Jorja. He spoke of neurological and brain disorders, and psychological illness. He wanted Marcie to check into Sunrise Hospital for a few days of tests.

The ugly scene at Besancourt's office was just a warm-up for a series of fits Marcie threw at the hospital. The mere sight of doctors and nurses catapulted her into panic, and invariably the panic became outright hysteria that escalated until, exhausted, the child fell into that semi-catatonic trance from which she needed hours to recover.

Jorja took a week of sick-leave from the casino and virtually lived at Sunrise for four days, sleeping on a roll-away bed in Marcie's room. She didn't get much rest. Even in a drugged sleep, Marcie twitched, kicked, whimpered, and cried out in her dreams: 'The moon, the moon . . .' By the fourth night, Sunday December 29, worried and weary, Jorja almost needed medical attention for herself.

Miraculously, on Monday morning, Marcie's irrational

terror simply went away. She still did not like being hospitalised, and she pleaded aggressively to go home. But she no longer appeared to feel that the walls were going to close in and crush her. She remained uneasy in the company of doctors and nurses, but she did not shrink from them in horror or strike them when they touched her. She was still pale, nervous, and watchful. But for the first time in days, her appetite was normal, and she ate everything on her breakfast tray.

Later in the day, after the final testing had been completed, while Marcie was sitting in bed eating lunch, Dr Besancourt spoke with Jorja in the hall. He was a hound-faced man with a bulbous nose and moist, kind eyes. 'Negative, Jorja. Every test, negative. No brain tumours, no cerebral lesions, no neurological dysfunction.'

Jorja almost burst into tears. 'Thank God.'

'I'm going to refer Marcie to another doctor,'Besancourt said. 'Ted Coverly. He's a child psychologist, and a good one. I'm sure he'll ferret out the cause of this. Funny thing is . . . I have a hunch we *may* have cured Marcie without realising we were doing it.'

Jorja blinked. 'Cured her? What do you mean?'

'In retrospect I can see that her behaviour had all the earmarks of a phobia. Irrational fear, panic attacks . . . I suspect she'd begun to develop a severe phobic aversion to all things medical. And there's a treatment called 'flooding,' wherein the phobic patient is purposefully, even ruthlessly exposed to the thing he fears for such a long time – hours and hours – that the power of the phobia is shattered. Which is what we might've inadvertently done to Marcie when we forced her into the hospital.'

'Why would she have developed such a phobia?' Jorja asked. 'Where would it've come from? She never had a bad experience with doctors or hospitals. She's never been seriously ill.'

Besancourt shrugged, sidled out of the way of some nurses pushing a patient on a trolley. 'We don't know what causes phobias. You don't have to've nearly crashed in an plane in order to be afraid of flying. Phobias just . . . spring up. Even if we accidentally cured her, there'll be a residual apprehension that Ted Coverly can identify. He'll root out any remaining traces of phobic anxiety. Don't worry, Jorja.'

That afternoon, Monday December 30, Marcie was released from the hospital. In the car on the way home, she was almost her old self, happily pointing out animal-shapes in the clouds. At home, she dashed into the living room and settled down immediately among the piles of new Christmas toys which she had not yet had much opportunity to enjoy. She played with the Little Ms Doctor kit, though not exclusively or with that disturbing intensity that she had exhibited on Christmas Day.

Jorja's parents raced over to the apartment. Jorja had kept them away from the hospital by arguing that they might disturb Marcie's delicate condition. Marcie remained in a splendid mood at dinner, sweet and amusing, leaving Jorja's parents disarmed.

For the next three nights, Marcie slept in Jorja's bed in case she suffered an anxiety attack, but none materialised. The nightmares came with less frequency and less power than before, and Marcie's sleeptalk awakened Jorja only twice in three nights. 'The moon, moon, the moon!' But now it was a soft and almost forlorn call rather than a shout.

In the morning, at breakfast, she asked Marcie about the dream, but the girl could not remember it. 'The moon?' she said, frowning into her bowl of Trix. 'Didn't dream about the moon. Dreamed about horses. Can I have a horse someday?'

'Maybe, when we don't live in an apartment any more.'

Marcie giggled. 'I *know* that. You can't keep a horse in an apartment. The neighbours would complain.'

*　　　*　　　*

Thursday, Marcie saw Dr Coverly for the first time. She liked him. If she still had an abnormal fear of doctors, she hid it well.

That night Marcie slept in her own bed, with only the company of a teddy bear named Murphy. Jorja got up three times between midnight and dawn to look in on her daughter. Once she heard the now-familiar chant – 'moon, moon, moon' – in a whisper that, because it was an eerie blend of fear and delight, made the hair prickle on her scalp.

And on Friday, with three days of school vacation still ahead for Marcie, Jorja put her in Kara Persagian's care once more and returned to work. It was almost a relief to get back to the noise and smoke of the casino. Cigarettes, stale beer, and the occasional blast of halitosis were infinitely more pleasing than the antiseptic stink of the hospital.

She picked up Marcie at Kara's place, and on the way home the girl excitedly showed her the product of a day spent drawing on butcher's paper: scores of pictures of the moon in every imaginable hue.

* * *

On Sunday morning, January fifth, when Jorja got out of bed and went to brew coffee, she found Marcie at the dining-room table, engaged upon a curious task. The girl, still in her pyjamas, was taking all the photographs out of their picture album and making neat stacks of them.

'I'm putting the pictures in a shoebox, because I need the . . . ablum,' the girl said, frowning over the hard word. 'I need it for my moon collection.'

'Why? Baby, why're you so interested in the moon?'

'It's pretty,' Marcie said. She put the picture on a blank page of the photo album and stared at it. In her fixed gaze, in the intensity of her fascination with the photograph, there was an echo of the single-mindedness with which she had played Little Ms Doctor.

With a quiver of apprehension, Jorja thought: This is how the damn doctor phobia started. Quietly. Innocently. Has Marcie merely traded one phobia for another?

She had the urge to run to the telephone and somehow get hold of Dr Coverly, even if it was Sunday and his day off.

But as she stood by the table, studying her daughter, Jorja decided she was over-reacting. Marcie certainly had not traded one phobia for another. After all, the girl wasn't *afraid* of the moon. Just . . . well, strangely fascinated by it. A temporary enthusiasm. Any parent of a bright seven-year-old was accustomed to these short-lived but fiercely burning fascinations and infatuations.

Nevertheless, Jorja decided she would tell Dr Coverly about it when she took Marcie to his office for a second session on Tuesday.

* * *

At 12:20 a.m. Monday, before she turned in for the night, Jorja looked in on Marcie to see if she was sleeping soundly. The girl was·not in bed. In her dark room, she had drawn a chair up to the window and was sitting there, staring out.

'Honey? What's wrong?'

'Nothing's wrong. Come see,' Marcie said softly, dreamily.

Heading toward the girl, Jorja said, 'What is it, Peanut?'

'The moon,' Marcie said, her eyes fixed on the silvery crescent high in the black vault of the sky. 'The moon.'

4.

BOSTON, MASSACHUSETTS

On Monday, January 6, the wind from the Atlantic was bitterly cold and unrelenting, and all of Boston was humbled by it. On the blustery streets, heavily bundled and bescarfed people hurried towards sanctuary with their shoulders drawn up and heads tucked down. In the hard grey winter light, the modern glass office towers appeared to be constructed of ice, while the older buildings of historic Boston huddled together, presenting a drab and miserable face utterly unlike their charm and stateliness in better weather. Last night, sleet had fallen. The barren trees were jacketed in glittering ice, bare black branches poking through the white crust like the marrow-core revealed beneath the outer layers of shattered bones.

Herbert, the efficient major domo who kept the Hannaby household functioning smoothly, drove Ginger Weiss to her seventh post-Christmas meeting with Pablo Jackson. The wind and the previous night's ice-storm had brought down power lines and disrupted the traffic lights at more than half the intersections. They finally reached Newbury Street at 11:05 a.m., just five minutes past Ginger's eleven o'clock appointment.

After the breakthrough during Saturday's session, Ginger had wanted to contact the people at the Tranquillity Motel in Nevada and broach the subject of the unremembered event that had transpired there on the night of July 6, the summer before last. Either the owners of that motel were accomplices of those who had tampered with Ginger's memory, or they were victims like her. If they had been subjected to brainwashing, perhaps they also were experiencing anxiety attacks of one sort or another.

Pablo was firmly opposed to immediate confrontation. He felt the risks were too great. If the owners of the motel were not victims but associates of the victimisers, Ginger might be putting herself in grave danger. 'You've got to be patient. Before approaching them, you must have as much information as you can possibly obtain.'

She had suggested they go to the police, seeking protection and an investigation, but Pablo had convinced her that the police would not be interested. She had no proof that she had been the victim of a mental mugging. Besides, the local constabulary could not unravel a crime across state lines. She'd have to go to the federal authorities or local Nevada police, and in either case she might be unwittingly seeking help from the very people responsible for what had been done to her.

Frustrated but unable to find a hole in Pablo's arguments, Ginger had agreed to continue following his programme of treatment. He had wanted Sunday to himself, so he could review the crucial tape of Saturday's session, and he had said he was not available Monday morning because he intended to see a friend in the hospital. 'But you come back at, say, one o'clock Monday afternoon, and we'll begin chipping away at the edges of that memory block – en pantoufles, "in slippers" as they say, in a relaxed manner.'

This morning he had called her from the hospital to say that his friend was being discharged sooner than expected, and that he, Pablo, would be home by eleven o'clock if she would like to come earlier than planned. 'You can help me make lunch.'

Now, disembarking from the elevator and stepping quickly along the short hall to Pablo's apartment, Ginger decided that she would make every effort to control her natural impatience and to settle for making progress en pantoufles, as the magician was determined they would.

The front door was ajar. Assuming he had left it open for

her, she stepped into the foyer. Closing the door, she said, 'Pablo?'

In another room, someone grunted. Something clattered softly. Something thudded to the floor.

'Pablo?' He did not answer. Moving into the living room, she called out louder than before. 'Pablo?'

Silence.

One of the library's double doors was open, and a light was on. Ginger entered – and saw Pablo face-down on the floor near the Sheraton desk. He had evidently just returned from his visit to his hospitalised friend, for he was still wearing galoshes and an overcoat.

As she rushed to him and knelt at his side, grim possibilities occurred to her – cerebral haemorrhage, thrombosis, or embolism; massive heart attack – but she was not prepared for what she found when she eased him onto his back. Pablo had been shot high in the chest, and bright red arterial blood welled from the bullet hole.

His eyes fluttered open, and although they looked unfocused, he seemed to know who she was. Blood bubbled over his lower lip. He got out a single word in an urgent whisper: 'Run.'

Her instinctive reaction upon seeing him prone before the desk had been that of a friend and physician: anguished, she had gone immediately to his aid. But until Pablo said, 'Run,' Ginger did not understand that her own life might be in jeopardy. Suddenly she realised that she had heard no gunfire, which meant a silencer-equipped pistol. The assailant was no ordinary burglar. Someone infinitely more dangerous. All those considerations flashed through her mind in an instant.

Heart pounding, she rose and turned toward the door. The gunman – tall and broad-shouldered, wearing a leather topcoat belted tightly at the waist – came out from behind the door, holding the silencer-equipped pistol. He was big, but surprisingly less threatening in appearance than she had expected. He was her age, clean-cut, with innocent blue eyes and a face unsuited for menace.

When he spoke, the disparity between his unremarkable appearance and his murderous actions was even greater, for his first words were a tremulous apology of sorts. 'Shouldn't have happened. Didn't have to happen, for Christ sake. I just . . . I was duping those tapes on a high-speed recorder. That's all I wanted – dupes of the tapes.'

He was pointing to the desk, and for the first time Ginger noticed an open attaché case in which was nestled a compact piece of electronic equipment. Tape cassettes were scattered across the top of the desk, and she knew at once what tapes they were.

'Let's call an ambulance,' she said. She edged toward the phone, but he stopped her by gesturing pointedly and angrily with the gun.

'High-speed duplication,' he said, torn between rage and tears. 'I could've made copies of all six of your sessions and been out of here. He wasn't supposed to be home for another fucking hour at least!'

Ginger grabbed a chair cushion and used it to prop up Pablo's head, so he would not choke on the blood and phlegm in his throat.

Obviously stunned by what had happened, the gunman said, 'He just comes in so quiet, gliding in here like a goddamned ghost.'

Ginger remembered how gracefully and elegantly the magician carried himself, as if each movement was prelude to an act of prestidigitation.

Pablo coughed, closed his eyes. Ginger wanted to do more for him, but the only remedy was heroic surgery. At the moment, she could only keep a hand on his shoulder in a feeble attempt to reassure him.

She looked up entreatingly, but the gunman said, 'And what the hell's he doing packing a gun? A fucking eighty-year-old man, a gun in his fist, as if he knows how to handle something like this.'

Until now, Ginger had not noticed the pistol on the carpet, a few feet from Pablo's out-flung hand. When she saw it, a cripplingly sharp pang of horror went through her, and she nearly passed out, for in that instant she knew Pablo had been aware all along that it was dangerous to help her. She had not suspected that the mere attempt to probe at the memory block would quickly draw the unwanted attentions of men like this one in the leather topcoat. Because this meant she was being watched. Maybe not hour by hour or even every day. But *They* were keeping tabs on her. The moment she first called Pablo, she unwittingly endangered his life. And somehow he had known, for he had been packing a gun. Now, Ginger felt the weight of guilt.

'If he hadn't pulled that stupid .22,' the gunman said miserably, 'and if he hadn't insisted on calling the cops, I'd have walked away without laying a hand on him. I didn't want to hurt him. Shit.'

'For God's sake,' Ginger said beseechingly, 'let me call an ambulance. If you didn't mean to hurt him, then let's get help.'

The gunman shook his head, and his gaze moved to the crumpled magician. 'Too late anyway. He's dead.'

Those last two words, like a pair of hard punches, knocked the breath out of her and drew the shadowy curtain of unconsciousness to the edges of her vision. One glance at the old man's glassy eyes was enough to confirm what the gunman had said, yet she resisted the truth. She lifted his left hand and put her fingertips to his thin black wrist, feeling for a pulse. Finding none, she searched along the carotid artery in his throat, but in spite of the remaining warmth of the flesh, there was only an awful stillness where once had been the throb of life. 'No,' she said. 'Oh, no.' She touched Pablo's dark brow, not with the diagnostic intent of a physician but tenderly, lovingly. Her heart was so painfully constricted with grief that it was difficult to believe she had known the magician only two weeks. Like her father, she was quick to give her heart, and because Pablo was the man he was, the gift of affection and love was even more easily bestowed than usual.

'I'm sorry,' the killer said shakily. 'I'm really sorry. If he hadn't tried to stop me, I'd have walked right out of here. Now, I've killed someone, haven't I? And . . . you've seen my face.'

Blinking back her tears, suddenly aware that she could not afford to grieve right now, Ginger rose slowly to her feet and faced him.

As if thinking aloud, the gunman said, 'You've got to be dealt with now, too. I'll have to ransack the place, empty out drawers, take a few things of value, and make it look like you two walked in on a burglar.' He chewed worriedly on his lower lip. 'Yeah, it'll work. Instead of copying the tapes, I'll just take them, so they won't be here to raise suspicions.' He looked at Ginger and winced. 'I'm sorry. Jesus, I really am, but that's the way it'll have to be. I wish it didn't. It's partly my fault. Should've heard the old bastard coming in. Shouldn't have let him surprise me.' He moved towards her. 'Should I maybe rape you, too? I mean, would a burglar just shoot a good looking girl like you? Wouldn't he rape you first? Wouldn't that make this look more real?' He came closer, and she began to back away. 'God, I don't know if I can do it. I mean, how can I get a hardon and do it to you when I know I've got to kill you afterwards?' He kept coming, and she backed up against the bookshelves. 'I don't like this. Believe me, I don't. This shouldn't have to happen. I really *hate* this.'

His apparently genuine pity, repeated apologies, and sorrowful self-recriminations gave Ginger the creeps. He would have been less frightening if he had been pitiless and bloodthirsty. The fact that he had scruples but could set them aside long enough to commit one rape and two murders . . . that made him more of a monster.

He stopped six feet from her and said, 'Please take off your coat.'

It was useless to beg, but she hoped to make him overconfident. 'I won't give a good description of you. I swear. Please let me go.'

'Wish I could.' His face defined remorse. 'Take off your coat.'

Buying time while she arrived at a course of action, Ginger slowly unbuttoned the coat. Her hands were shaking, but she exaggerated those genuine tremors and fumbled with the buttons. At last she shrugged out of the coat and let it drop to the floor.

He stepped closer. The pistol was only inches from her chest. He was more relaxed, holding the gun less rigidly than before, thrusting it forward less aggressively, though he was by no means lax with it.

'Please don't hurt me.' She continued to beg because, if he thought she was nearly paralysed with abject fear, he might slip up and give her an opportunity for escape.

'I don't *want* to hurt you,' he said, as if deeply offended by the implication that he had any choice in the matter. 'Didn't want to hurt him, either. That old fool was responsible for this. Not me. Listen, I'll make it as painless as I can. I promise you that.'

Still holding the gun in his right hand, he used his left hand to touch her breasts through her sweater. She endured his fondling because he might become careless as he grew aroused. In spite of his claims that his empathy would render him impotent, Ginger was certain he'd have no difficulty raping her. Beneath his regret and sympathy, beneath the sensitivity he wished to project more for his own benefit than for hers, he was taking an unconscious savage pleasure in what he had done and would do. In spite of his gentle voice, violence burned in every word he spoke; he stank of violence.

He said, 'Very pretty. Petite yet so nicely built.' He slipped his hand under her sweater, gripped her bra, gave it a hard yank that broke it. As elastic snapped, the bra straps dug painfully into her shoulders; the metal clasp at her back bit the skin. He grimaced as if her pain was transmitted to him. 'I'm sorry. Did I hurt you? I didn't meant it. I'll be more careful.' He pushed aside the ruined brassiere and put his cool, clammy hand on her bare breasts.

Filled equally with terror and revulsion, Ginger pressed back even harder against the bookshelves, which jabbed painfully into her back. The gunman was less than an arm's length away from her now, but he kept the pistol between them. The muzzle was pressed coldly against her bare midriff, leaving her no room to manoeuvre. If she tried to twist free of him, she would be gut-shot for her temerity.

Fondling her, he continued to speak softly and to express great sadness at the necessity of raping and killing her, as though she simply must understand, as though it would be unthinkably cruel of her not to bestow upon him full absolution for the sin of taking her life.

With nowhere to run, with his monotonous self-justifications washing over her in numbing waves of words, subjected to his groping hand, Ginger was gripped by a claustrophobia so intense she felt the urge to claw at him and force him to pull the trigger, just to end it. His Certs-scented breath had a cloying minty aroma that, by its pervasiveness, gave her the feeling she was closed up in a bell-jar with him. She whimpered, pleaded with wordless sounds, turned her head from side to side as if trying to deny the reality of the assault. The picture of demoralisation and terror that she presented could not have been more convincing if she'd had days to practise, but there was unfortunately little calculation in it.

Further inflamed by her distress, he pawed at her more roughly than before. 'I think I can do it, baby. I think I can do it to you. Feel me, baby. Just feel me.' He pressed his body to hers and ground his pelvis against her. Incredibly, he seemed to think that, under such stressful and tragic circumstances, his rampant tumescence was a tribute to her erotic appeal and that somehow she ought to be flattered.

Her reaction could only have been a disappointment for him.

When he pressed and rubbed himself against her, he was obliged to stop jamming the gun into her belly. Swept away by his own excitement, convinced that Ginger was weak and helpless, he did not even keep the weapon pointed at her but held it to one side with the muzzle aimed at the floor. Ginger's terror was exceeded by her loathing and anger, and the moment the pistol swung away from her, she translated those pent-up emotions into action. Turning her head to the side, she slumped against him as if about to faint in fear or in a swoon of reluctant passion, an action that brought her mouth to his throat. In swift succession, she bit him hard in the adam's apple, slammed one knee into his crotch, and clawed at his gun hand to keep the pistol away from her.

He partially blocked the knee, limiting the damage to his privates, but he was unprepared for the bite. Shocked, horrified, and reeling from the devastating pain in his throat, the gunman pushed away from her and stumbled backwards two steps.

She had bitten deep, and now she gagged on the taste of his blood, though she did not permit her revulsion to delay her counter-attack. She grabbed his gun hand, brought it to her mouth, and bit his wrist.

A sharp cry of pain and astonishment burst from him. Because she was delicate, waiflike, he had not taken her seriously.

As she bit him again, he dropped the gun, but simultaneously he made a fist of his other hand and with tremendous force slammed it into her back. She was driven to her knees and thought for a moment that he had broken her spine. Pain as bright and scintillant as an electric current shot up her back into her neck, flashed through her skull.

Stunned, her vision briefly blurred, Ginger almost did not see him bending to retrieve the gun. Just as his fingers touched the butt, she frantically threw herself at his legs. Seeing her coming and hoping to jump out of her reach, he whipped upright as if he were a lashed-down sapling suddenly cut loose. When she hit him a fraction of a second later, he windmilled his arms in a brief attempt to keep his balance. Falling backwards, he crashed into one of the library's chairs, knocked over a small table and a lamp, and rolled onto Pablo Jackson's corpse.

Equally breathless, staring warily at each other, they were both petrified for a moment. They were on their sides on the floor, curled fetally in reaction to their pains, gasping for breath.

To Ginger, the gunman's eyes seemed as wide and round as clock faces, proof that he was filled with fevered thoughts of his own mortality ticking close. The bite would not kill him. She had not bitten through the jugular vein or the carotid artery, had merely pierced the thyroid cartilage, mangling tissue, severing a few small vessels. However, it was easy to understand why he might be convinced it was a mortal wound; the pain must be excruciating. He put his unbitten hand to his damaged throat, then pulled it away and stared aghast at his own gore dripping off his fingers. The killer thought he was dying, and that might make him either less or more dangerous.

Simultaneously, they saw that his pistol had been kicked halfway across the library during their tussle. It was closer to him than to Ginger. Bleeding from throat and wrist, making a strange wheezing-gurgling noise, he scrambled across the floor toward the weapon, and Ginger had no option but to get up and run.

She fled from the library into the living room, hobbling more than running, slowed by the pain in her back, which pulsed through her in diminishing but still debilitating waves. She intended to leave the apartment by the front door, but then she realised there was no escape in that direction because the only exits from the public corridor were the elevator and the stairs. She could not wait for the elevator, and in the stairwell she could easily be trapped.

Instead, hunched because of her aching back, she scurried crablike across the living room, down a long hall, into the kitchen, where the swinging door softly swished shut behind her. She went directly to the utensils rack on the wall by the stove and took down a butcher's knife.

She became aware that a shrill, eerie keening was issuing from her. She held her breath, cut off the sound, and got a grip on herself.

The gunman did not immediately burst into the kitchen, as Ginger expected. After a few seconds she realised that she was lucky he had not yet appeared, because the butcher's knife was of no use against a pistol at a distance of ten feet. Silently cursing herself for almost having made a fatal error, she quickly and light-footedly returned to the door and took up a position to one side of it. Her back still ached, but the sharpest pain was gone. Now she was able to stand straight and flat against the wall. Her heart was pounding so loud that it seemed as if the wall against which she leaned was a drumhead, responding to her heartbeat, amplifying it until the hollow booming of atrium and ventricle must be echoing throughout the entire apartment.

She held the knife low, ready to swing it up and into him in a deadly arc. However, that desperate scenario depended on his slamming through the kitchen door in a fit of hysteria and rage, reckless, crazed by the conviction that he was dying from his throat wound, bent on blind revenge. If instead he came slowly, cautiously, nudging the swinging door open inch by inch with the barrel of the gun, Ginger would be in trouble. But every second that passed without his appearance made it less likely that he would play the drama out in the way she hoped.

Unless the throat wound was far worse than she had realised. In that case, he might be still in the library, bleeding to death on the Chinese carpet. She prayed that was what had happened to him.

But she knew better. He was alive. And he was coming.

She could scream and perhaps alert a neighbour who would call the police, but the gunman would not be driven off in time. He would not run until he killed her. Screaming was a waste of energy.

She pressed harder against the wall, as if trying to melt into it. The swinging door, just inches from her face, riveted her as a blacksnake might command the full attention of a field-mouse. She was tense, poised to react to the first sign of movement, but the door remained still, maddeningly still.

Where the hell was he?

Five seconds passed. Ten. Twenty.

What was he doing?

The taste of blood in her mouth became more rather than less acrid as the seconds ticked past, and nausea worked its greasy fingers in her. As she had more time to consider what she'd done to him in the library, she grew acutely aware of the bestiality of her actions, and she was shaken by her own potential for savagery. She had time, as well, to think about what she still intended to do to him. She had a mental image of the wide blade of the butcher's knife spearing deep into his body, and a shudder of revulsion shook her. She was not a killer. She was a healer, not merely by education but by nature as well. She tried to stop thinking about stabbing him. It was dangerous to think too much about it, dangerous and confusing and enervating.

Where *was* he?

She could not wait any longer. Afraid that her inaction was damping the animal cunning and savage ferocity that she needed if she were to survive, uneasily certain that each passing second was somehow giving him a greater advantage, she eased to the doorway and put one hand on the edge of the door. But as she was about to pull it open a crack and peer out at the hallway and into the living room, she was chilled by the sudden feeling that he was there, inches away, on the other side of the portal, waiting for her to make the first move.

Ginger hesitated, held her breath, listened.

Silence.

She brought her ear to the door, still could not hear anything.

The handle of the knife had grown slippery in her sweaty hand.

At last, she took hold of the edge of the door and cautiously pulled it inward, until a half-inch gap opened. No shots rang out, so she put one eye to the crack. The gunman was not right in front of her, as she had feared, but at the far end of the hall where it met the foyer; he was just re-entering the apartment from the public corridor, pistol in hand. Evidently, he had first looked for her at the elevator and on the stairs. Not finding her, he had returned. Now, by the way he closed the door, locked it, and engaged the chain to delay her exit, it was clear that he had decided she was still in the apartment.

He held his bitten hand to his bitten throat. Even at a distance she could hear his wheezy breathing. However, he was clearly no longer panicked. Having survived this long, he was gaining confidence by the second. He had begun to realise that he would live.

Moving to the edge of the foyer, he looked left towards the living room and right toward the bedrooms. Then he looked straight backdown the long shadowy hall, and Ginger's heart stumbled through a flurry of irregular beats as, for a moment, he seemed to be staring directly at her. But he was too far away to see that the door was being held half an inch ajar. Instead of coming straight towards her, he went into the bedroom. He moved with a quiet purposefulness that was disheartening.

She let the kitchen door go shut, unhappily aware that her plan would no longer work. He was a professional, accustomed to violence, and although he was initially thrown off balance by the unexpected ferocity of her attack, he was rapidly regaining his equilibrium. By the time he searched the bedrooms and the closets in there, he would be completely cool and calculating once more. He would not come charging into the kitchen and make an easy target of himself.

She had to get out of the apartment. Fast.

She had no hope of reaching the front door. He might already be finished in the bedrooms and on his way back into the hall.

Ginger put the knife down. She reached under her sweater, pulled off her ruined bra, and dropped it on the floor. She stepped silently around the kitchen table, pulled the curtains away from the window, and looked out at the fire-escape landing in front of her. Quietly, she twisted the latch. She slid up the lower sash, which unfortunately was *not* quiet. The wooden frame, swollen by the winter dampness, moved with a squeak and squeal and scrape. When it abruptly loosened and slid all the way up with a solid thump and a rattle of glass, she knew she had alerted the gunman. She heard him coming at a run along the hallway.

She climbed hastily out of the window, onto the iron fire escape, and started down. The bitter wind lashed her, and the piercing sub-zero cold penetrated to her bones. The metal steps were encrusted with ice from last night's storm, and icicles hung from the handrails. In spite of the treacherous condition of those switchback stairs, she had to descend quickly or risk a bullet in the back of her head. Repeatedly, her feet almost slipped out from under her. She could not get a secure grip on the icy railing with her ungloved hands, but it was even worse when she took hold of the bare metal, for she stuck to the frigid iron, pulling loose only by sacrificing the top layer of skin.

When she was still four steps from the next landing, she heard someone curse above her, and she glanced back. Pablo Jackson's killer was coming out of the kitchen window in frantic pursuit of her.

Ginger took the next step too fast, and the ice did its work. Her feet flew out from under her, and she fell over the final three steps onto the landing, crashing down on her side, re-igniting the pain in her back. Her fall shattered the ice that coated the metal grid, and chunks fell through lower levels of the fire escape, making brittle music, disintegrating as they struck the steps below.

In the wind's maniacal howling, the whisper of the silenced pistol was lost altogether, but Ginger saw sparks leap off the iron inches from her face, and she knew a shot had narrowly missed her. She looked up in time to see the gunman taking aim – and to see him slip and stumble down several treads. He pitched forward, and she thought he was going to fall on top of her. He grabbed at the railing three times before he was able to halt his uncontrolled descent.

He was sprawled on his back across several risers, clutching a step with one hand, one leg shot out into space between two of the narrow iron balusters. His other arm was hooked around a baluster, which was how he had arrested his fall; that was the hand holding the pistol, which was why he could not immediately take another shot at her.

Ginger scrambled to her feet, intent upon making as rapid a descent as possible. But when she cast one last quick look at the gunman, she was arrested by the sight of the buttons on his topcoat, which were the only colourful objects in that wintry gloom. Bright brass buttons, each decorated with the raised image of a lion passant, the familiar cadence mark from English heraldry. She had seen nothing special about the buttons before, they were similar to those on many sports jackets, sweaters, coats. But now her eyes fixed on them, and everything else faded away, as if only the buttons were real. Even the gabbling-hooting wind, which filled the day and blustered coldly in every corner of it, could not keep a grip on her awareness. The buttons. Only the buttons held her attention, and they generated in her a terror far more powerful than her fear of the gunman.

'No,' she said, uselessly denying what was happening to her. *The buttons*. 'Oh, no.' *The buttons*. This was the worst possible time and place to lose control of herself. *The buttons*.

She could not forestall the attack. For the first time in three weeks, Ginger was overwhelmed by a crushing, irrational terror. It made her feel small, doomed. It plunged her into a strange and lightless interior landscape through which she was compelled to run blindly.

Turning from the buttons, she fled down the fire escape, and as total blackness claimed her, she knew that her reckless flight would terminate in a broken leg or fractured spine. Then, while she lay paralysed, the killer would come to her, put the gun to her head, and blow her brains out.

Darkness.

*   *   *

Cold.

When the world returned to Ginger – or she to the world – she was huddled in dead leaves and snow and shadows at the foot of a set of exterior cellar steps behind a townhouse, an unguessable distance along Newbury Street from Pablo's building. A dull pain throbbed the length of her back. Her entire right side ached. The badly abraded palm of her left hand burned. But the severe cold was the worst discomfort. A chill lanced up through her from the snow and ice in which she sat. A frost passed into her by osmosis from the concrete retaining wall against which she leaned. The raw wind rushed down the single flight of ten steep steps, snuffling and growling like a living creature.

She did not know how long she had been cowering there, but she ought to get moving or risk pneumonia. However, the gunman might be nearby, searching for her, and if she revealed herself, the chase would be on again, so she decided to wait a minute or two.

She was astonished that she had clambered all the way down the ice-sheathed fire escape and had fled, by whatever roundabout route, to this hiding place without breaking her neck. Evidently, in her fugue, reduced to the miserable condition of a frightened and mindless animal, there was at least the compensation of an animal-like fleetness and sure-footedness.

Like a pair of industrious morticians, the wind and cold continued to drain the warmth from her. The narrow, grey concrete stairwell increasingly resembled an unlidded sarcophagus. Ginger decided it was time to go. She rose slowly. The small backyard was deserted, as were the yards of houses on both sides. Ice-crusted snow. A few bare trees. Nothing threatening. Shivering, sniffing, blinking away tears, Ginger climbed the stairs and followed a brick walkway that linked the rear of the house to the gate at the end of the small property.

She intended to find her way back to Newbury Street, locate a telephone, and call the police, but as she reached the gate, that plan was abruptly forgotten. On each of the two gate-posts was a wrought-iron carriage lamp with amber panes of glass. Either they'd been left burning by accident or were activated by a solenoid that had mistaken the dreary winter morning for twilight. They were electric lamps but had those flickering bulbs that imitated gas flames, so the lantern-glass was alive with shimmering, dancing amber light. That throbbing, yellowish luminosity made Ginger's breath catch,

305

and she was once more pitched into a state of unreasoning panic.

No! Not again.

But yes. Yes. The mist. Nothingness. Gone.

*   *   *

Colder.

Her feet and hands were going numb.

She was apparently on Newbury Street again. She had crawled under a parked truck. Lying in the gloom under the oil pan, she peered out from beneath her sanctuary, getting a wheel-level view of the vehicles parked on the other side of the street.

Hiding. Every time she recovered from a fugue, she was hiding from something unspeakably terrifying. Today, of course, she was hiding from Pablo's killer. But what about other days? What had she been hiding from then? Even now, she was hiding not only from the gunman but from something else that hovered tantalisingly at the edge of remembrance. Something she had seen out in Nevada. Something.

'Miss? Hey, Miss?'

Ginger blinked and turned stiffly toward the voice, which came from the back of the truck. She saw a man on his hands and knees, looking under the tailgate. For a moment she thought it was the gunman.

'Miss? What's wrong?'

Not the gunman. Evidently, he had given up when he couldn't find her quickly and had fled. This was someone she had never seen before, and this was one occasion when a stranger's face was welcome.

He said, 'What the hell are you doing under there?'

Ginger was filled with self-pity. She realised how she had looked, running crazily through the neighbourhood like some demented freak. All dignity had been stolen from her.

She squirmed toward the man who had spoken to her, grasped the gloved hand he offered, and allowed him to help her slide out from beneath the truck, which proved to be a Mayflower Moving Company van. The rear doors were open. She glanced inside and saw boxes, furniture. The guy who had pulled her out was young, brawny, and dressed in quilted

306

thermal coveralls with the Mayflower logo stitched across the chest.

'What's going on?' he asked. 'Who're you hiding from, lady?'

As the Mayflower man spoke, Ginger noticed a policeman standing in the middle of the intersection half a block away, directing traffic, where a signal light had failed. She ran towards him.

The Mayflower man called after her.

She was surprised she could run at all. She felt as if she were a creature constructed of nothing but aches and pains and chills. Yet she ran with a dreamy effortlessness into the shrieking wind. The gutters were full of icy slush, but the street itself was relatively dry and calcimine-streaked with de-icing compounds. Dodging out of the way of a couple of oncoming cars, she even found the strength to call out to the cop as she drew near him. 'There's been a man killed! Murder! You've got to come! Murder!' Then, when he started toward her with a look of concern on his broad Irish face, she saw the shiny brass buttons on his heavy, winter-weight uniform coat, and all was lost again. They were not exactly like the buttons on the leather topcoat the killer had been wearing; they were not decorated with a lion passant, but with some other raised figure. But one glimpse sent her thoughts flashing towards remembrance of buttons she had seen *then*, during the mysterious events at the Tranquillity Motel. Some forbidden recollection began to surface, and that pulled the Azrael Trigger.

As she lost control and ran off into her private darkness, the last thing she heard was her own pathetic cry of despair.

*   *   *

Coldest.

That morning, at least for Ginger Weiss, Boston was the coldest place on earth. Bitter, polar, piercing, marrow-freezing, the January day induced a glaciation of the spirit as well as the flesh. When the fugue receded, she was sitting on the ground in ice and snow. Her hands and feet were numb, stiff. Her lips were chapped and cracked.

This time she had taken refuge in the narrow space between a row of well-manicured bushes and a brick building, in a shadowy corner where the angled wall of a bay-windowed tower met a flat portion of the main facade. The former Hotel Agassiz. Where Pablo had his apartment. Where he had been killed. She had come nearly full circle.

She heard someone approaching. Between the hoary branches of the snow-dressed and ice-laced shrubs, she saw someone climbing over the low wrought-iron fence that separated the front lawn from the sidewalk. She did not see the person himself, merely his booted feet, legs clad in blue trousers, and the flaps of a long, heavy, navy-blue coat. But as he came across the narrow strip of lawn towards the shrubbery, she knew who he was: the traffic cop from whom she had turned and run.

Fearing yet another seizure at the sight of his coat buttons, Ginger closed her eyes.

Perhaps irreversible psychological damage was a side-effect of the brainwashing she had undergone, an inevitable result of the tremendous and constant stress generated by the artificially repressed memories struggling mightily to make themselves known. Even if she could find another hypnotist to do for her what Pablo had done, perhaps there was no way the block could be broken or the pressure relieved, in which case she was destined to deteriorate further. If she was stricken by three fugues in one morning, what was to prevent three more in the next hour?

The policeman's boots crunched noisily through the sleet-skinned snow. He stopped in front of her. She heard him pressing against the low bushes and parting them to look into her hiding place. 'Miss? Hey, what's wrong? What were you shouting about murder? Miss?'

Maybe she would fall into a fugue and *remain* there forever.

'Oh, now, what're you crying about?' the cop said sympathetically. 'Darlin', I can't help if you won't tell me what's wrong.'

She would not be the daughter of Jacob Weiss if she failed to respond warmly and eagerly to the slightest sign of kindness in others, and the policeman's concern finally affected her. She opened her eyes and looked up at the topmost brass button on his coat. The sight of it did not bring the hateful darkness upon her. But that meant nothing, for the ophthalmoscope, black gloves, and other triggering items had not affected her later, when she had forced herself to confront them again.

In a crackle of ice, the cop pushed between the bushes.

She said, 'They've killed Pablo. They murdered Pablo.'

And as she spoke those words, her distress over her condition was made worse by a rush of guilt. The sixth of January would forever be a black day in her life. Pablo was dead. Because he tried to help her.

Such a very cold day.

5.

ON THE ROAD

Monday morning, the sixth of January, Dom Corvaisis cruised his old Portland neighbourhood in a rented Chevrolet, trying to recapture the mood he had been in when he had left Oregon for Mountainview, Utah, more than eighteen months ago. The rain, as heavy as any he had ever seen, had stopped near dawn. Now the sky, though still cloudy from horizon to horizon, was a particularly powdery, dry-looking shade of grey, like a burnt field, as if there had been a fire behind the clouds that had forced out all that precipitation. He drove through the university campus, stopping repeatedly to let the familiar scenes stir feelings and attitudes of times past. He parked across the street from the apartment where he'd lived, and as he stared up at the windows, he tried to recall the man he had been then.

He was surprised at how difficult it was to recollect the timidity with which that other Dom Corvaisis had viewed life. Though he could bring to mind the way he had been, there was no intimacy or poignancy to those memories. He could see those old days again, but he could not *feel* them, which seemed to indicate that he could never be that old Dom again, regardless of how much he feared the possibility.

He was convinced that he had seen something terrible on

the road the summer before last, and that something monstrous had been done to him. But that conviction generated both a mystery and a contradiction. The mystery was that the event had wrought in him an undeniably positive change. How could an experience fraught with pain and terror effect a beneficial change in his outlook? The contradiction was that, in spite of the beneficial effect on his personality, the event filled his dreams with horror. How could his ordeal have been both terrifying and uplifting at the same time?

The answer, if it could be found, was not here in Portland but out on the highway. He started the engine, put the Chevy in gear, pulled away from his old apartment building, and went looking for trouble.

*   *   *

The most direct route from Portland to Mountainview began with Interstate 80-North. But as he had done nineteen months ago, Dom took a more roundabout trail, heading south on Interstate 5. That special summer, he had scheduled a lay-over in Reno for a few days to do some research for a series of short stories about gambling, so the less direct route had been necessary.

Now in his rented Chevy, he followed the familiar highway, keeping his speed down to fifty, even as low as forty on the steeper hills, for he had been pulling a U-Haul trailer that last day in June, and he had not made good time. And, as before, he stopped for lunch in Eugene.

Hoping to spot something that would goose his memory and provide a link with the mysterious events of the previous trip, Dom looked over the small towns that he passed. However, he saw nothing that made him uneasy, and nothing bad happened all the way to Grant's Pass, where he arrived shortly before six o'clock that evening, right on schedule.

He stayed in the motel where he had been a guest eighteen months ago. He remembered the number of the room – ten – because it was near the soft drink and ice machines, which had been the source of irritating noises half the night. It was unoccupied, and he took it, vaguely explaining to the clerk that it had sentimental associations for him.

He ate in the same restaurant, across the road from the motel.

He was seeking satori, which was a Zen word meaning 'sudden enlightenment,' a profound revelation. But enlightenment eluded him.

All day he had used the rearview mirror, hoping to spot a tail. During dinner, he surreptitiously watched the other customers. But if he was being followed, his tail was masterful, invisible.

At nine o'clock, rather than use the telephone in his room, he walked to a nearby service station pay phone. With his credit card, he placed a call to the number of another pay phone in Laguna Beach. By pre-arrangement, Parker Faine was waiting there with a report on the mail that he had collected for Dom earlier in the day. There was little chance that either of their phones was tapped; however, after receiving those two disturbing Polaroid snapshots, Dom had decided (and Parker had agreed) that in this case prudence and paranoia were synonymous.

'Bills,' Parker said, 'advertisements. No more strange messages, and no more Polaroids. How's it going at your end?'

'Nothing so far,' Dom said, leaning wearily against the Plexiglas and aluminium wall of the phone booth. 'Didn't sleep well last night.'

'But you didn't go for a walk?'

'Didn't even get one knot untied. Had a nightmare, though. The moon again. Anybody follow you to that pay phone?'

'Not unless he was as thin as a dime and a master of camouflage,' Parker said. 'So you can call me here again tomorrow night and not have to worry that they've tapped the line.'

'We sound like two madmen,' Dom said.

'I'm kind of having fun,' Parker said. 'Cops and robbers, hide and seek, spies – I was always good at games like that when I was a kid. You just hang in there, my friend. And if you need help, I'll come fast.'

'I know,' Dom said.

He walked back to the motel through a cold damp wind. As in the hotel in Portland, he woke three times before

311

dawn, always surfacing from an unremembered nightmare, always shouting about the moon.

*   *   *

Tuesday, January 7, Dom rose early and drove to Sacramento, then took Interstate 80 east toward Reno. Rain fell, silvery and cold, for most of the drive, and by the time he reached the foothills of the Sierras, it was snowing. He stopped at an Arco station, bought tyre chains, and put them on before heading into the mountains.

The summer before last, he had taken more than ten hours to get from Grant's Pass to Reno, and this time the drive took even longer. When he finally checked in at Harrah's Hotel where he had stayed before, called Parker Faine from a pay phone, and had a bite of dinner in the coffee shop, he was too tired to do anything but pick up a copy of the Reno newspaper and return to his room. So at eight-thirty that evening, sitting in bed in his underwear, he saw the story about Zebediah Lomack.

MOON MAN'S ESTATE
WORTH HALF A MILLION DOLLARS

RENO – Zebediah Harold Lomack, 50, whose suicide on Christmas Day led to the discovery of his bizarre obsession with the moon, left an estate valued at more than $500,000. According to documents filed with the probate court by Eleanor Wolsey, sister of the deceased and executrix of Lomack's will, most of the funds are in accounts at various savings & loan associations and in treasury bills. The modest house in which Lomack lived at 1420 Wass Valley Road has an appraised value of only $35,000.

Lomack, a professional gambler, is said to have amassed his wealth primarily from the game of poker. 'He was one of the best players I ever knew,' said Sidney 'Sierra Sid' Garfork of Reno, another professional gambler and winner of last year's World Championship of Poker at Binion's Horseshoe Casino in Las Vegas. 'He took to cards when he was just a kid the way some others might have a natural knack for baseball or math or physics.' According to Garfork and other friends of Lomack, the gambler's estate

312

would have been even larger if he had not had a weakness for dice games. 'He lost back more than half his winnings at the craps tables, and the IRS took a big chunk, of course,' Garfork said.

On Christmas night, responding to a neighbour's report of shotgun fire, Reno police officers found Lomack's body in the garbage-strewn kitchen of his home. Upon further investigation, they found thousands of photographs of the moon decorating walls, ceilings, and furniture.

There was more to the story, which had apparently been a local sensation for the past two weeks. Dom read with growing fascination and uneasiness. Most likely, Zebediah Lomack's mad obsession with the moon had nothing to do with Dom's own problems. Coincidence. Yet . . . he felt a stirring of precisely that fear – part terror, horror, and awe – that filled him when he woke from his nightmares, that also overwhelmed him when he went sleepwalking and tried to nail windows shut.

He pored over the article several times, and at 9:15, in spite of his weariness, he decided that he had to get a look in the Lomack house. He dressed, retrieved his rented car from the hotel's valet parking, and got directions to Wass Valley Road from the attendant. Reno was below the snowline, so the night was dry and the roads clean. Dom stopped at an all-night Sav-On drugstore to buy a flashlight. He arrived at 1420 Wass Valley Road shortly after ten o'clock and parked across the street.

The house was actually a bungalow with large porches, every bit as modest as the news account had indicated. It sat on a half-acre lot. From previous storms, snow lay in patches on the roof, covered the lawn, weighted the branches of several large pines. The windows were dark.

According to the article in the Reno newspaper, Eleanor Wolsey, Zebediah Lomack's sister, had flown in from Florida three days after his death, on December 28. She arranged the funeral services, which had been conducted on the thirtieth, and was staying over until the estate was settled. However, she was at a hotel rather than in her brother's house, because the bungalow was too depressing.

Dom was a law-abiding citizen; the prospect of breaking into the house gave him no thrill. But it had to be done because there was no way he could see it except by forced entry. He saw no point in trying to persuade Eleanor Wolsey to allow a visit tomorrow, for she had been quoted in the newspaper as saying that she was sick and tired of gawkers and that she was repelled by the perverse curiosity of strangers.

Five minutes later, on the back porch of the Lomack bungalow, Dom discovered that the door was equipped with a deadbolt in addition to its regular lock. He tried the windows that faced onto the porch. The one above the kitchen sink was unlatched. He slid it open and clambered inside.

Hooding the flashlight with one hand to avoid drawing the notice of anyone outside, he swept the narrowed beam around the kitchen, which was no longer in the disgusting condition in which Reno policemen had found it at Christmas. According to the newspaper, just two days ago Lomack's sister began cleaning the house and preparing it for sale. Evidently she had started here. The garbage had gone. The counters were clean, and the floor was spotless. The air was filled with the stink of new paint and Spectracide. A single startled roach scurried along the baseboard and disappeared behind the refrigerator, but there was no longer a gross infestation. And there were no pictures of the moon.

Dom was suddenly worried that Eleanor Wolsey and her helpers might have made too much progress. Perhaps all traces of Zebediah Lomack's obsession had been stripped down, scrubbed out, and thrown away.

But that concern was quickly put to rest when Dom followed the pale probing beam of the flashlight into the living room, where the walls and ceiling and windows were still papered with big posters of the moon. It seemed as if he were hanging in deep space, in some crowded realm where half a hundred cratered worlds orbited impossibly close to one another. The effect was disorientating. He felt dizzy, and his mouth went dry.

He moved slowly out of the living room into a hallway, where hundreds of pictures of the moon – some colour and some black-and-white, some large and some small, some overlapping others – had been fixed to every inch of the walls with glue, Scotch tape, masking tape, and staples. The same decorations had been applied in both bedrooms as well, so the omnipresent moons seemed almost like a fungus that had spored and spread throughout the house, creeping into every corner.

The newspaper report had said that no one but Lomack had been in the house for more than a year prior to his suicide. Dom believed it, for if visitors had seen the work of this lunatic, cut-and-paste Michelangelo, they would have contacted the mental health authorities at once. The neighbours told of the gambler's rapid metamorphosis from a hail-fellow to a recluse. Apparently his fascination with the moon had begun the summer before last.

The summer before last . . . The timing uncannily paralleled the changes in Dom's own life.

Second by second, Dom grew more uneasy. He could not understand the insane behaviour that had created this eerie display, could not put himself inside the fevered mind of Lomack, but he *could* empathise with the gambler's terror. Just moving through the moon-crowded house, shining his flashlight on the lunar faces, Dom felt a tingling along the back of his neck. The moons did not mesmerise him as they had evidently mesmerised Lomack, but as he stared at them he sensed instinctively that the impulse which had driven Lomack to paper his house with moon-images was the same impulse that drove Dom himself to dream of them.

He and Lomack had shared some experience in which the moon had figured or of which it was an apt and powerful symbol. The summer before last they had been in the same place at the same time. The wrong place at the wrong time.

Lomack had been driven mad by the stress of repressed memories.

Will I be driven mad, too? Dom wondered as he stood in the master bedroom, turning slowly in a circle.

A new and grim thought struck him. Suppose Lomack had not killed himself out of despair over his unshakable obsession but had, instead, been compelled to shove the shotgun barrel into his mouth *because he had finally remembered what had happened to him the summer before last.* Maybe the memory was far worse than the mystery. Maybe, if the truth were revealed, sleepwalking and nightmares would seem less terrifying than what had happened during that drive from Portland to Mountainview.

The oppressiveness of those pendulant forms drastically increased. The claustrophobic mural made breathing difficult. The moons seemed to portend some unreadable but manifestly evil fate that awaited him, and he stumbled out of the room, suddenly eager to flee from them.

Among a herd of leaping and prancing shadows whipped up by the bobbling beam of the flashlight, he ran down the short hall, into the living room, tripped over a stack of books, and fell with a jarring crash. For a moment he lay stunned. But his senses swiftly cleared, and he was jolted to find himself staring at the word 'Dominick,' which was scrawled in felt-tip pen across the luminous moon-face in one of the dozens of identical big posters. He had not noticed it when he had come through from the kitchen earlier, but now he had fallen so that the flash in his right hand was aimed just right.

A chill rippled through Dom. He had read nothing about this in the newspaper, but the handwriting surely belonged to Lomack. To the best of his knowledge, he had not known the gambler. Yet to pretend that this was *another* Dominick would be to embrace an outrageous coincidence.

He got up from the floor and took a couple of steps toward the poster that bore his name, stopping six feet from it. In the penumbra of the flashlight beam, he saw writing on an adjacent poster. His own name was only one of four that Lomack had scribbled across four lunar images: DOMINICK, GINGER, FAYE, ERNIE. If his name was here because he had shared a forgotten nightmarish experience with Lomack, then the other three must have been fellow sufferers as well, though Dom could remember nothing whatsoever about them.

He thought of the priest in the Polaroid snapshot. Was that Ernie?

And the blonde strapped to the bed. Was she Ginger? Or Faye?

As he moved the light from one name to the other and back again, some dark and awesome memory did indeed stir in him. But it remained far down in his subconscious, an amor-

316

phous blur like a giant ocean-creature swimming past below the mottled surface of a murky sea, its existence revealed only by the rippled wake of its passage and by the flicker of shadow and light in the water. He tried to reach out for the memory and seize it, but it dived deep and vanished.

From the moment he had come into the Lomack place, Dom had been in the hands of fear, but now frustration took an even tighter grip on him. He shouted in the empty house, and his voice echoed coldly off the moon-papered walls. 'Why can't I remember?' He knew why, of course: someone had mucked with his mind, scrubbing out certain memories. But still he shouted – fearful, furious. 'Why can't I remember? I've got to *remember*!' He held his left hand toward the poster that featured his name, as if to wrench from its substance the memory that had been in Lomack's mind when he had scrawled 'Dominick.' His heart thumped. He roared with hot anger: 'Goddamn it, goddamn you whoever you are, I will remember. I will remember you sons of bitches. You bastards! *I will*.'

Suddenly, impossibly, even though he was not touching it, though his hand was still a few feet from it, the poster bearing his name tore loose from the wall. It was fixed in place with four strips of masking tape angled across its corners, but the tape peeled up with the sound of zippers opening, and the poster *leapt* off the wall as if a wind had blown straight through the lathe and plaster behind it. With a rattle and rustle of paper wings, it swooped at him, and he staggered back across the living room in surprise, nearly falling over the books again.

In his unsteady hand, his flashlight revealed that the poster had stopped a few feet from him. It hung at eye-level, unsupported in thin air, undulating slightly from top to bottom, first bulging out at him and then bending away when the direction of undulation reversed itself. As the pocked surface of that moon rippled, his own handwritten name fluttered and writhed as if it were the legend on a wind-stirred banner.

Hallucination, he thought desperately.

But he knew it was really happening.

He could not breathe, as if the cold air were so syrup-thick with miraculous power that it could not be inhaled.

The poster floated closer.

His hand shook. The flashlight jiggled. Sharp glints of light lanced off the undulant surface of the glossy paper.

After a timeless moment in which the only sound was the crackle of the animated poster, other noise abruptly arose from every part of the room: the zipper-sound of masking tape being pulled loose. On the ceiling, walls, and windows, the other posters simultaneously disengaged themselves. With a brittle clatter-rattle-whoosh, half a hundred moon images exploded towards Dom from every direction, and he cried out in surprise and fear.

The loosed cry was like a blockage expelled from his windpipe, for he was suddenly able to breathe.

The last of the tape pulled loose. Fifty posters hung unmoving in mid-air, not even rippling, as if pasted firmly to nothing whatsoever. The silence in the dead gambler's house was as profound as in a temple devoid of worshippers, a cold and penetrating silence that seemed to pierce to the core of Dom, seeking to replace even the soft liquid susurration of his blood's movement through his arteries and veins.

Then as if they were fifty parts of a single mechanism brought to life with the flick of a switch, the three-by-five-foot lunar images shivered, rustled, flapped. Although there was not the slightest breeze to propel them, they began to whirl around the room in the orderly manner of horses on a carousel. Dom stood in the middle of that eerie merry-go-round, and the moons circled him; they capered and twirled, curled and uncurled, flexed and flapped, here seen as half moons and here as crescents and here full-face, and they waxed and waned, ascended and descended, faster, faster, faster still. In the flashlight glow, it seemed like a procession set in motion by the sorcerer's apprentice who, in the old story, had magically imparted life to a bunch of broomsticks.

Dom's fear receded, making room for wonder. At the moment there seemed no threat in the phenomenon. In fact a wild delight burgeoned in him. He could think of no explanation for what he was witnessing, but stood in dumb astonishment, puzzled and amazed. Usually nothing was so terrifying as the unknown, but perhaps he sensed a benign power at work. Wonderstruck, he turned slowly in a circle, watching the moons parade around him, and at last a tremulous laugh escaped him.

In an instant, the mood changed dramatically. In a cacophony of imitation wings, the posters flew at Dom as if they were fifty enormous and furious bats. They swooped and darted over his head, slapped his face, beat against his back. Though they were not alive, he attributed malevolent intent to their assault. He put one arm across his face and flailed at the moons with the hand that held the flashlight, but they did not fall back. The noise grew louder and more frantic as the paper wings beat on the chilly air and on one another.

His previous delight forgotten, Dom stumbled across the room in a panic, searching for the way out. But he could see nothing but zooming, soaring, spinning moons. No doors. No windows. He staggered one way, then another, disoriented.

The noise grew still worse as, in the hallways and other rooms of the bungalow, a thousand moons began to tear free of their petrified orbits upon the walls. Tape pulled loose, and staples popped out of plaster, and glue suddenly lost its adhesiveness. A thousand cratered moonforms – and then a thousand more – detached themselves and rose into suspension with ten thousand rustles, spun and swooped towards the living room with a hundred thousand clicks and crackles and hisses, swinging into orbit around Dom with a steadily swelling roar that sounded as if he were immersed in raging flames. The glossy full-colour pictures torn from magazines and books now flashed and sparkled and shimmered as they darted through the flashing beam, contributing to the scintillant illusion of fire, and the black-and-white pictures cascaded down and spiralled up like bits of ash caught in thermal currents.

Gasping for breath, he sucked in slick-paper and newsprint moons and had to spit them out. Thousands of small paper worlds seethed around him in layer upon layer, and when he hysterically parted one curtain composed of false planetoids, there was only another behind it.

Intuitively, he perceived that this impossible display was meant to help him break through to a full recollection of his unremembered nightmares. He had no idea who or what lay behind the phenomenon, but he sensed the purpose. If he immersed himself in the storm of moons and let them sweep him away, he'd understand his dreams, understand the frightening cause of them, and know what had happened to

319

him on the road eighteen months ago. But he was too scared to let go and be drawn into a trance by the mesmerising weave and-wobble of the pale spheres. He longed for that revelation but was terrified of it. He said, 'No. No.' He pressed his hand over his ears and squeezed his eyes shut. 'Stop it! Stop it!' His heart hammered two beats to each exclamation. 'Stop it!' His throat cracked as his cries broke loose: '*Stop it!*'

He was astonished when the tumult was cut off with the suddenness of a symphony orchestra terminating a thunder ous crescendo on one last bone-shaking note. He did not expect his shouted commands to be obeyed, and he still did not think his words had done the trick.

He took his hands away from his ears. He opened his eyes.

A galaxy full of moons hung around him.

With a trembling hand, he plucked one of the pictures from its unsupported perch upon the air. Wonderingly, he turned it over in his hand. Tested its substance between two fingers. There was nothing special about the picture, yet it had been suspended magically before him, just as thousands more were still suspended, motionless.

'How?' he said shakily, as if the moons, being able to levitate, ought also to be able to speak. 'How? Why?'

The moons fell as one. As by the breaking of some spell, the thousands of pieces of paper dropped straight to the floor where they lay in uneven heaps, in a drift over Dom's winter boots, with no lingering trace of the mysterious life-force that had possessed them.

Bewildered and half in shock, Dom shuffled toward the doorway that led to the hall. The moons crunched and rustled like dry autumn leaves. At the door he stopped and played his flashlight beam slowly over the short corridor, where not a single lunar image remained moored by staples, tape, or glue. The walls had been stripped bare.

Turning, he took a couple of steps into the centre of the living room once more, then knelt among the debris. He put down the glowing flashlight and sifted paper moons through his trembling hands, trying to understand what he had seen.

Within him, fear fought delighted amazement and terror battled awe. But in truth he could not decide how he ought to feel, because there was no precedent for what he had experi

•nced. One moment a giddy laugh began to build, but then joy vas frozen by a breath of cold horror. Now he felt he'd been n the presence of something unspeakably evil, but *now* he was ust as convinced it had been something good and pure. Evil. food. Perhaps both . . . or neither. Just . . . well *something*. iome mysterious thing beyond the descriptive, definitive)ower of words.

He knew one thing only: whatever had happened to him the iummer before last was far stranger then he had realised leretofore.

Still sifting paper moons through his fingers, he noticed omething unusual on his hands. He brought them palms-up nto the direct beam of the flashlight. Rings. On each palm)lazed a ring of swollen, red skin, each as perfect as if the nflamed tissues had conformed to a pattern drawn with a lraftsman's compass.

Even as he watched, the stigmata faded, vanished.

It was Tuesday, January 7.

6.

CHICAGO, ILLINOIS

n his bedroom on the second floor of St Bernadette's rectory, 'ather Stefan Wycazik woke to the thump of a drum. The beat lad the deep boom of a base drum and the hollow reverber-ation of a timpani. It sounded like the pounding of an enor-nous heart, although it embellished the simple two-stroke hythm of the heart with an extra beat: *LUB-DUB-dub* . . . *LUB-DUB-dub* . . . *LUB-DUB-dub*. . . .

Bewildered and still half asleep, Stefan switched on the amp, squinted in the blaze of light, and looked at his alarm lock. It was 2:07, Thursday morning, certainly not a reason-ble hour for a parade.

LUB-DUB-dub . . . *LUB-DUB-dub* . . .

After each triad of thumps, there was a three-second pause, hen a set of beats identical to all the others, then another

321

three-second pause. The precise timing and unfaltering repetition of the noise began to seem less like the work of a drummer and more like the laborious piston-stroke of an enormous machine.

Father Wycazik threw back the covers and padded barefoot to the window that looked out on the courtyard between the rectory and the church. He saw only snow and bare-limbed trees in the backwash of the carriage lamp above the sacristy door.

The beats grew louder, and the pause between the groups shortened to about two seconds. He took his robe from the back of a chair and slipped it on over his pyjamas. The sonorous pounding was so loud now that it was no longer merely an annoyance and puzzlement. It had begun to frighten Stefan. Each burst of sound rattled the windowpanes and shook the door in its frame.

He hurried into the upstairs hall. He fumbled in the dark for the wall switch and finally turned on the overhead light.

Farther along the short hall, on the right, another door opened, and Father Michael Gerrano, Stefan's other curate, dashed out of his room, struggling into his own robe. 'What is that?'

'Don't know,' Stefan said.

The next triple-thud was twice as loud as the group preceding it, and the entire house reverberated as if it had been struck by three gigantic hammers. It was not a hard sharp sound, but muffled in spite of its loudness – as if the hammers were thinly padded yet swung with tremendous force. The lights flickered. Now the thumps were separated by no more than a second of silence, not long enough for the echo of the previous fulminations to fade away. And with each powerful hammering, the lights flickered again and the floor under Stefan trembled.

In the same instant, Father Wycazik and Father Gerrano perceived the locus of the noise: Brendan Cronin's room. They moved swiftly to that door, which was directly across the hall from Father Gerrano.

Incredibly, Brendan was fast asleep. In spite of the thunderous explosions that made Father Wycazik flash back to the mortar fire of Vietnam, Brendan dreamed on, untroubled. In fact, in the pulsing light, there seemed to be a vague smile tugging at the young priest's lips.

The windows rattled. Drapery hooks clicked against the rods to which they were attached. On the dresser, a hairbrush bounced up and down, and several coins clinked together, and Brendan's breviary slid first to the left and then to the right. On the wall above the bed, a crucifix jiggled wildly under the picture hook from which it was hung.

Father Gerrano shouted, but Stefan could not hear what the curate said, for now there were no pauses between muffled detonations. With each tripartite beat, Father Wycazik retreated further from his initial mental image of a huge drum and became increasingly convinced that what he was hearing was the throbbing of some enormous and immeasurably powerful machine. But it seemed as if the sound came from all sides, as if the machinery was hidden within the walls of the house itself, labouring at some mysterious and unknowable task.

As the breviary finally slid off the dresser and the coins began to spill to the floor, Father Gerrano backed to the doorway and stood there wide-eyed, as if he might flee.

But Stefan went to the bed, bent over the dozing priest, and shouted his name. When that had no effect, he grabbed Brendan by the shoulders and shook him.

The auburn-haired curate blinked and opened his eyes.

The hammering stopped abruptly.

The sudden cessation of thunderous noise jolted Father Wycazik as badly as the first boom that had shattered his sleep. He let go of Brendan and looked around the room, disbelieving.

'I was so close,' Brendan said dreamily. 'I wish you hadn't wakened me. I was so close.'

Stefan pulled aside the covers, took hold of the curate's hands, and turned them palms-up. There was an angry red ring in each palm. Stefan stared at them in fascination, for this was the first time that he had seen the stigmata.

What in God's name is this all about? he wondered.

Breathing hard, Father Gerrano approached the bed. Staring at the rings, he said, 'What're those from?'

Ignoring the question, Father Wycazik spoke to Brendan: 'What was that sound? Where did it come from?'

'Calling,' Brendan said in a voice still thick with sleep – and with a soft, excited pleasure. 'Calling me back.'

'What was calling you?' Stefan demanded.

Brendan blinked, sat up and leaned against the headboard. His eyes had been out of focus. Now his gaze cleared, and he really looked at Father Wycazik for the first time. 'What happened? You heard it, too?'

'Somehow, yes,' Stefan said. 'It shook the whole house. Amazing. What was it, Brendan?'

'A call. It was calling me, and I was following the call.'

'But what was calling you?'

'I . . . I don't know. Something. Calling me back . . .'

'Back where?'

Brendan frowned. 'Back into the light. The golden light of the dream I told you about.'

'What's this all about?' Father Gerrano persisted. His voice was shaky, for he was not as accustomed to the miraculous as were his rector and his fellow curate. 'Will somebody clue me in?'

The other priests continued to ignore him.

To Brendan, Stefan said, 'This golden light . . . what is it? Could it have been God calling you back to His fold?'

'No,' Brendan said. 'Just . . . something. Calling me back. Next time, maybe I'll get a better look at it.'

Father Wycazik sat on the edge of the bed. 'You think this will happen again? You think it'll keep calling to you?'

'Yes,' Brendan said. 'Oh, yes.'

It was Thursday, January 9..

7.

LAS VEGAS, NEVADA

Friday afternoon, Jorja Monatella was at the casino, working, when she learned that her ex-husband, Alan Rykoff, had killed himself.

The news came by way of an emergency telephone call from

Pepper Carrafield, the hooker with whom Alan had been living. Jorja took the call on one of the phones in the blackjack pit, cupping a hand over one ear to block out the roar of voices, the click and snap of cards being dealt and shuffled, the ringing of slot machines. When she heard that Alan was dead, she was shocked and sickened, but she felt no grief. By his own selfish and cruel behaviour, Alan had ensured she would have no reason to grieve for him. Pity was the best emotion she could summon.

'He shot himself this morning, two hours ago,' Pepper elaborated. 'The police are here now. You've got to come.'

'The police want to see me?' Jorja said. 'But why?'

'No, no. The police don't want to see you. You got to come and clean his stuff out. I want his stuff out of here as soon as possible.'

'But I don't want his things,' Jorja said.

'It's still your job, whether you want them or not.'

'Miss Carrafield, it was a bitter divorce. I neither want nor –'

'He had a will drawn up last week. He named you executor, so you got to come. I want his stuff out of here *now*. It's your job.'

*   *   *

Alan had lived with Pepper Carrafield in a highrise condominium, a ritzy place called The Pinnacle, on Flamingo Road, where the call-girl owned an apartment. It was a fifteen-storey white concrete monolith with bronze windows. Surrounded by undeveloped desert land, it appeared to be even taller than it was. And because it stood alone, it looked oddly like a monument, the world's largest, swankiest tombstone. The grounds were lushly planted with sprinkler-tended lawns and flowerbeds, but a few dry tumbleweeds had blown in from the bordering plots of sand and scrub. The chill and desolate wind which stirred the tumbleweeds also fluted hollowly under the condominium's portico.

Two police cars and a morgue wagon stood in front of the building, but no cops were in the lobby; just a young woman on a mauve sofa near the elevators, forty feet away; and at a desk near the entrance, a man in grey slacks and blue blazer, who was security guard and doorman. The travertine marble

325

floor, crystal chandeliers, oriental carpet, Henredon sofas and chairs, and brass elevator doors contributed to a decor that strained too hard to convey class – but conveyed it nonetheless.

As Jorja asked the doorman to announce her, the young woman on the sofa rose and said, 'Mrs Rykoff, I'm Pepper Carrafield. Er . . . I think you use your maiden name now.'

'Monatella,' Jorja said.

Like the building in which she lived, Pepper strained for Fifth Avenue class, but her efforts were less successful than those of the interior designers who had worked on The Pinnacle. Her blonde hair had been cut in an excessively shaggy carefree style that hookers preferred, perhaps because when you spent your work-day in a series of beds, shaggy hair required less grooming. She wore a purple silk blouse that might have been a Halston, but she'd left too many buttons open, revealing a daring amount of cleavage. Her grey slacks were well tailored but too tight. She wore a Cartier watch encrusted with diamonds, but the elegant effect of the watch was spoiled by her indulgence in flashy diamond rings: she wore four of them.

'I couldn't bear to stay upstairs in the apartment,' Pepper said, motioning for Jorja to join her on the sofa. 'I'm not going back up there until they've taken the body away.' She shivered. 'We can talk right here, just so we keep our voices low.' She nodded toward the doorman at the desk. 'But if there's going to be a scene, I'll just get up and walk away. You understand? People here don't know what I do for a living. I intend to keep it that way. I never do business out of my home. I'm strictly out-call.' Her grey-green eyes were flat.

Jorja stared coldly at her. 'If you think I'm a scorned, suffering wife, you can relax, Miss Carrafield. Anything I ever felt for Alan is gone now. Even knowing he's dead, I feel nothing. Nothing much. I'm not proud of it. I was in love with him once, and we created a lovely child together. I should feel *something*, and I'm ashamed that I don't. But I'm definitely not going to cause a scene.'

'Great,' Pepper said, genuinely pleased, so involved with herself and her own concerns that she was oblivious of the domestic tragedy Jorja had just described. 'There're a lot of high-class people live here, you know. When they hear my boyfriend killed himself, they're going to be stand-offish for a long time. These kind of people don't like messy scenes. And if they found out what I do for a living . . . well, there'd be no way I'd ever fit in here again. You know? I'd have to move, and I sure don't want to. No way, honey. I like it here a lot.'

Jorja looked at Pepper's ostentatiously diamond-encumbered hands, looked at her plunging neckline, looked into her avaricious eyes, and said, 'What do you suppose they think you are – an heiress?'

Astonishingly, missing the sarcasm, Pepper said, 'Yeah. How'd you know? I paid for the condo with hundred-dollar bills, so no credit check was necessary, and I've let them all think my family has money.'

Jorja did not bother to explain that heiresses did not pay for condominiums with bundles of hundred-dollar bills. She simply said, 'Could we talk about Alan? What happened? What went wrong? I would never have thought Alan was the type to . . . to kill himself.'

Glancing at the doorman to make sure he had not left his post and drifted nearer, Pepper said, 'Me neither, honey. I'd never have pegged him as the type. He was so . . . macho. That's why I wanted him to move in and take care of me, manage me. He was strong, tough. Of course, a few months ago he started acting a little weird, and lately he was downright creepy. Weird and creepy enough that I was thinking about maybe finding someone else to look after me. But I didn't expect he'd screw things up for me by killing himself. Christ, you just never know, do you?'

'Some people have no consideration,' Jorja said. She saw Pepper's eyes narrow, but before the hooker could say anything, Jorja said, 'Am I to understand that Alan was pimping for you?'

Pepper scowled. 'Listen, I don't need a pimp. Whores need pimps. I'm no whore. Whores give fifty-dollar blow-jobs, screw eight or ten johns a day for whatever they can get, spend half their lives with the clap, and wind up broke. That's not *me*, sister. I'm an escort for gentlemen of means. I'm on the approved escort lists of the finest hotels, and last year I made two hundred thousand bucks. What do you think of that? I got

327

investments'. Whores don't have investments, honey. Alan wasn't my pimp. He was my *manager*. In fact, he managed a couple of my girlfriends, too. I fixed him up with them because, at first, before he started getting strange, he was the best.'

Dazzled by the woman's self-delusion, Jorja said, 'And Alan took a managerial fee for handling your career – and theirs?'

Her scowl fading, somewhat placated by Jorja's willingness to use euphemisms, Pepper said, 'No. That was one of the best things about our arrangement with him. He was still a blackjack dealer, see; that's where he made his money. He had all the contacts needed to manage us, but all he wanted for his trouble was free trade. I never knew a man who needed so much pussy. He couldn't get enough. In fact, the last couple of months, he seemed obsessed with pussy. Was he like that with you, honey?' Repelled by this sudden intimacy, Jorja tried to stop the woman, but Pepper would not be quiet. 'In fact, the last few weeks he was so horny all the time that I started to think maybe I should dump him. I mean, there was something a little crazy about it. He'd do it and do it and do it until he just couldn't get his pecker up to do it any more, and then he'd want to watch X-rated videotapes.'

Jorja was suddenly angry that Alan had made her executor, forcing her to witness the moral squalor in which he had passed the last year of his life. And she was angry because she would have to find a way to explain his death to Marcie, who was already treading a psychological tightrope. But she was not really angry with Pepper Carrafield; not angry but appalled, yes, because even Alan deserved a little mourning and respect from his live-in lover, more than this shark could ever give him. But there was no point in blaming the shark for *being* a shark.

One of the elevators opened, disgorging uniformed policemen, morgue employees, and a trolley bearing a corpse in an opaque plastic body bag.

Jorja and Pepper rose from the sofa.

Even as the stretcher was being rolled out of the first elevator, the doors of the second opened, and four more cops appeared, two in uniform plus a team of plainclothes detectives. A detective came to Pepper Carrafield and asked a few final questions.

No one asked any questions of Jorja. She stood rigid and

suddenly numb, staring at the body bag that contained her ex-husband.

They rolled the trolley across the travertine. The wheels squeaked.

Jorja watched it moving away.

Two cops held the lobby doors while the morgue attendants pushed the trolley outside. It moved past the lobby windows. Jorja turned to observe its progress. She still felt no grief, but she was swept by a powerful wave of melancholy, a profound sadness at what might have been.

From the nearest of the elevators, where she was holding a door open, Pepper said, 'Let's go up to my place.'

Outside, they closed the doors of the coroner's van.

*   *   *

In the elevator on the way up, and in a discreet whisper in the fourteenth-floor hallway, then continuing in a normal tone of voice as they entered her big livingroom, Pepper insisted on describing Alan's peculiar sexual hunger. He had always had the carnal appetite of a gourmand, but apparently sex had become a sick obsession with him as his life had wound down through its last couple of months.

Jorja did not want to hear about it, but stopping the hooker seemed more difficult than simply enduring her chatter.

In recent weeks, Alan's days had been devoted to erotic pursuits, though it all sounded feverish and desperate rather than pleasurable. He had used sick leave and vacation time to spend long – often frantic – hours in bed with Pepper or others whose 'careers' he managed, and there was no variation or perversion that he failed to explore to excess. The hooker chattered on: Alan had developed a fascination with lascivious substances, devices, appliances, and clothing – dildos, penis rings, spike-heeled shoes, vibrators, cocaine ointment, handcuffs. . . .

Jorja, already weak-kneed and dizzy since seeing the body bag, grew queasy. 'Please stop. What's the point? He's dead, for God's sake.'

Pepper shrugged. 'I thought you'd want to know. He threw away a lot of his money on this . . . this sex binge.

329

Since you're the executor of the estate, I thought you'd want to know.'

*   *   *

The last will and testament of Alan Arthur Rykoff, which he had left with Pepper for safe-keeping, was a simple pre-printed one-page form of the type obtainable at any business supply store.

Jorja sat on a cobalt-blue Ultrasuede chair beside a lacquered black Tavola table, quickly scanning the will in the light from a high-tech, burnished-steel, cone-shaped lamp. The most surprising thing was not that Alan had named Jorja as executor, but that he had left what he owned to Marcie, whose fatherhood he had been prepared to deny.

Pepper sat on a black lacquered chair with white upholstery, near a wall of windows. 'I don't figure it's much of an estate. He spent money pretty freely. But there's his car, some jewellery.'

Jorja noticed that Alan's will had been notarised just four days ago, and she shivered. 'He must've been considering suicide when he had this notarised; otherwise, he wouldn't have felt the need for it.'

Pepper shrugged. 'I guess.'

'But didn't you see the danger? Didn't you see he was troubled?'

'Like I told you, honey, he'd been weird for a couple of months.'

'Yes, but there must've been a noticeable change in him during the last few days, something different from that other strangeness. When he told you he'd made out a will and asked you to put it in that lockbox of yours, didn't you wonder? Wasn't there anything about him – his manner, his look, his state of mind – that worried you?'

Pepper stood up impatiently. 'I'm no psychologist, honey. His stuff's in the bedroom. If you want to give his clothes to Goodwill, I'll call them. But his other stuff – jewellery, personal things – you can get them out of here right now. I'll show you where everything is.'

Jorja was sickened by the moral squalor into which Alan had sunk, but she also felt a measure of guilt for his death. Could

330

she have done something to save him? By leaving his few possessions to Marcie and by naming Jorja executor of his will, he seemed to have reached out to them in his last days, and although that gesture was pathetic and inadequate, it touched Jorja. She tried to remember how he had sounded on the telephone before Christmas, when she had last spoken with him. She remembered his coldness, arrogance, and selfishness, but perhaps there had been other more subtle things that she should have heard beneath the surface cruelty and bravado: distress, confusion, loneliness, fear.

Brooding on that, she followed Pepper towards the bedroom. She loathed this task, pawing through Alan's things, but it had to be done.

Halfway down a long hall, Pepper stopped at a door, pushed it inwards. 'Oh, shit. I can't believe the damned cops left it like this.'

Jorja looked in the open door before she realised that this was the bathroom in which Alan had killed himself. Blood was all over the beige tile floor. More blood was spattered over the glass door of the shower stall, sink, towels, wastecan, and toilet. The wall behind the toilet was stained with dried blood in a macabre pattern resembling a Rorschach blot, as if Alan's psychological condition and the meaning of his death were there to be read by anyone with sufficient insight.

'Shot himself twice,' Pepper said, supplying details Jorja did not want to hear. 'First in the crotch. Is that queer or what? Then he put the gun in his mouth and pulled the trigger.'

Jorja could smell the vague coppery scent of blood.

'The damned cops should've cleaned up the worst of it,' Pepper said, as if she thought policemen ought to be armed not only with guns but with scrub brushes and soap. 'My housekeeper doesn't come until Monday. And she's not going to want to deal with this disgusting mess.'

Jorja broke the bloody bathroom's hypnotic hold on her and stumbled blindly a few steps along the hall.

'Hey,' Pepper Carrafield said, 'you okay?'

Jorja gagged, clenched her teeth, moved quickly along the hall, and leaned against the jamb of another doorway.

'Hey, honey, you *were* still carrying a torch for him, weren't you?'

'No,' Jorja said softly.

Pepper moved closer, too close, putting an unwanted consoling hand upon her shoulder. 'Sure, you were. Jesus, I'm sorry.' Pepper oozed unctuous sympathy, and Jorja wondered if the woman was capable of any genuine emotion that did not have its roots in self-interest. 'You said you were burnt out on him, but I should've seen.'

Jorja wanted to shout: *You stupid bitch, I'm not carrying a torch for him, but he was still a human being, for Christ's sake. How can you be so callous? What's wrong with you? Is something missing in you?*

But she only said, 'I'm all right. I'm all right. Where are his things? I want to sort through them and get out of here.'

Pepper ushered Jorja through the doorway in which she had been leaning, into a bedroom. 'He had the bottom drawers of the highboy, plus the left side of the dresser, and that half of the closet. I'll help.' She pulled out the lowest drawer of the highboy.

For Jorja, the room suddenly was as eerie and unreal as a place in a dream. Her heart began to pound, and she moved around the bed toward the first of three things that had filled her with fear. Books. Half a dozen books were stacked on the nightstand. She had seen the word 'moon' on the spines of two of them. With trembling hands, she sorted through them and found that all six dealt with the same subject.

'Something wrong?' Pepper asked.

Jorja moved to the dresser, on which stood a globe the size of a basketball. A cord trailed from it. She clicked a switch on the cord and found the globe was opaque with a light inside. It was not a globe of the earth but of the moon, with geological features – craters, ridges, plains – clearly named. She gave the glowing sphere a spin.

The third thing that frightened her was a telescope on a tripod beside the dresser, in front of a window. Nothing about the instrument was different from other amateur telescopes, but to Jorja it seemed ominous, even dangerous, with dark and unknowable associations.

'Those're Alan's things,' Pepper said.

'He was interested in astronomy? Since when?'

'For the past couple months,' Pepper said.

The similarities between Alan's and Marcie's conditions

troubled Jorja. Marcie's irrational fear of doctors. Alan's compulsive sex drive. Those were different psychological problems – obsessive fear in one case, obsessive attraction in the other – but they shared the element of obsession. Apparently, Marcie had been cured of her phobia. Alan was not as fortunate. He'd had no one to help him, and he had snapped, shooting off the genitals that had come to control him, putting a bullet in his brain. Jorja shuddered. It was too coincidental that father and daughter had been stricken by psychological problems simultaneously, but what made it more than coincidence was the *other* strangeness they shared: their interest in the moon. Alan had not seen Marcie in six months, and their most recent phone conversation had been in September, weeks before either had become fascinated by the moon. There had been no contact by which either could have transmitted that fascination to the other; it appeared to have sprung up spontaneously in each of them.

Remembering Marcie's moon-troubled sleep, Jorja said, 'Do you know if he was having unusual dreams? About the moon?'

'Yeah. How'd you figure that? He was having them, but he could never remember any details when he woke up. They started . . . back in late October, I think it was. Why? What's it matter?'

'These dreams – were they nightmares?'

Pepper shook her head. 'Not exactly. I'd hear him talking in his sleep. Sometimes he sounded afraid, but lots of times he'd smile, too.'

Jorja felt as if ice had formed in her marrow.

She turned to look at the lighted globe of the moon.

What in the hell is going on? she wondered. A shared dream? Is that possible? How? Why?

Behind her, Pepper said, 'Are you okay?'

Something had driven Alan to suicide.

What might happen to Marcie?

8

SATURDAY, JANUARY 11

Boston, Massachusetts.

The memorial service for Pablo Jackson was held at 11:00 Saturday morning, January 11, in a nondenominational chapel in the grounds of the cemetery where he was to be buried. The coroner and police pathologists had not been finished with the body until Thursday, so five days had passed between Pablo's murder and his funeral.

When the last eulogy was delivered, the mourners adjourned to the grave, where the casket waited. Snow had been cleared around Pablo's plot, but the space was insufficient. Scores of people stood outside the prepared area, some in snow deeper than their boots. Others remained on the sidewalks that criss-crossed the memorial park, watching from a distance. Three hundred had come to pay their last respects to the old magician. The chilly air steamed with the breath of the rich and the poor, the famous and the unknown, Boston socialites, magicians.

Ginger Weiss and Rita Hannaby stood in the first circle around the gravesite. Since Monday, Ginger had not had much of an appetite and had got little sleep. She was pale, nervous, and very tired.

Both Rita and George had argued against Ginger's attendance at the services. They were concerned that such a wrenchingly emotional experience would trigger a fugue. But the police had encouraged her, hoping she might see Pablo's killer at the services. In self-defence she'd hidden the truth from the cops, leading them to believe that the killer was an ordinary burglar, and sometimes burglars were driven by such sick compulsions. But she knew that he was no mere burglar and that he would not risk arrest by coming to the cemetery.

Ginger wept during the eulogies, and by the time she walked from the chapel to the grave, her grief was a vice squeezing her heart. But she did not lose control. She was determined not to make a circus of this solemn occasion, determined to pay her respects with dignity.

Besides, she had come with a second purpose that could not be fulfilled if she spiralled down into a fugue or suffered an emotional collapse. She was sure that Alexander Christophson – former ambassador to Great Britain, former United States Senator, and former Director of the CIA – would be at the funeral of his old friend, and she wanted very much to speak with him. It was to Christophson, on Christmas Day, that Pablo had turned for advice about Ginger's problems. And it was Alex Christophson who had told him about the Azrael Block. She had an important question to ask Christophson, though she dreaded the answer.

She had seen him in the chapel, recognised him from his days in public life when he had been on television and in newspapers. He was a striking figure, tall, thin, white-haired, unmistakable. Now, they stood on opposite sides of the grave, the draped casket between them. He had glanced at her a couple times, though without recognition.

The minister said a brief final prayer. After a moment, some of the mourners greeted one another, formed small groups to talk. Others, including Christophson, moved away through a forest of headstones, past snow-laden pines and winter-stripped maples, toward the parking lot.

'I've got to talk to that man,' Ginger told Rita. 'Be right back.'

Startled, Rita called after her, but Ginger did not pause or offer further explanation. She caught up with Christophson in the jagged shadows cast by the skeletal branches of an immense oak that was all black bark and crusted snow. She called his name, and he turned. He had piercing grey eyes, which widened when she told him who she was.

'I can't help you,' he said, and began to turn away from her.

'Please,' she said, putting a hand on his arm. 'If you blame me for what happened to Pablo –'

'Why should you care what I think, Doctor?'

She held fast to his arm. 'Wait. Please, for God's sake.'

Christophson surveyed the slowly dispersing crowd in the cemetery, and Ginger knew that he was afraid the wrong people – dangerous people – might see him with her and assume he was helping her as Pablo had done. His head twitched slightly, and Ginger thought it was an indication of his nervousness, but then she realised it was the faint tremor

335

of Parkinson's disease. He said, 'Dr Weiss, if you're seeking some form of absolution, then by all means let me provide it. Pablo knew the risks, and he accepted them. He was the captain of his own fate.'

'*Did* he understand the risks? That's what I've got to know.'

Christophson seemed surprised. 'I warned him myself.'

'Warned him about who? About what?'

'I don't know who or what. But considering the enormous effort expended to tamper with your memories, you must've seen something of tremendous importance. I warned Pablo that whoever had brainwashed you was no amateur and that if they realised the two of you were trying to break through the Azrael Block, they might come after not just you but him as well.' Christophson's grey eyes searched her eyes for a moment, and then he sighed. 'He *did* tell you about his conversation with me?'

'He told me everything – except about your warning.' Her eyes filled with tears again. 'He didn't breathe a word of that.'

He withdrew one elegant but palsied hand from his pocket and gripped her arm reassuringly. 'Doctor, now that you've told me this, I can't possibly lay any of the blame at your doorstep.'

'But *I* blame me,' Ginger said in a voice thin with misery.

'No. You can't blame yourself for any of it.' Looking around again to make sure they were not under surveillance, Christophson opened the top two buttons of his overcoat, reached inside, plucked the display handkerchief from the breast pocket of his suit jacket, and gave it to Ginger. 'Please stop punishing yourself. Our friend lived a full and fortunate life, Doctor. His death might've been violent, but it was relatively quick, which can be a blessing.'

Drying her eyes on the swatch of pale blue silk that he had given her, Ginger said, 'He was a dear man.'

'He was,' Christophson agreed. 'And I'm beginning to understand why he took the risks he did for you. He said *you* were a very dear woman, and I see his judgment was as accurate and reliable as usual.'

She finished blotting her eyes. Her heart still felt pinched in a vice, but she began to believe there was a chance that guilt and grief would eventually give way to grief alone. 'Thank you.' As much to herself as to him, Ginger said, 'What now? Where do I go from here?'

'I'm in no position to help you,' he said at once. 'I've been out of the intelligence business for almost a decade, and I've no contacts any more. I've no idea who might be behind your memory block or why.'

'I wouldn't ask you to help me. I'm not risking any more innocent lives. I just thought you might have some idea how I can help myself.'

'Go to the police. It's their *job* to help.'

Ginger shook her head. 'No. The police are slow, too slow. Most of them are overworked, and the rest are just bureaucrats in uniforms. My problem's too urgent to wait for them to solve it. Besides, I don't trust them. Suddenly I don't trust authorities of any kind. The tapes Pablo made of our sessions were gone when I took the police back to his apartment, so I didn't mention them. I spooked. I didn't tell the cops about my fugues or about how Pablo had been helping me. I just said we'd been friends, that I'd stopped by to have lunch and walked in on the killer. I let them think it was an ordinary burglary. Sheer paranoia. Didn't trust them. Still don't. So the cops are out.'

'Then find another hypnotist to regress you –'

'No. I'm not risking any more innocent lives,' she repeated.

'I understand. But those are the only suggestions I have.' He shoved both hands into the deep pockets of his overcoat. 'I'm sorry.'

'No need to be,' she said.

He started to turn away, hesitated, sighed. 'Doctor, I want you to understand me. I served in the war, the big war, with some distinction. Later, I was a good ambassador. As head of the CIA and as a Senator, I made many difficult decisions, some that put me in personal danger. I never backed away from risk. But I'm an old man now. Seventy-six, and I feel older. Parkinson's. A bad heart. High blood pressure. I have a wife I love very much, and if anything happens to me, she'll be alone. I don't know how well she'd deal with being alone, Dr Weiss.'

'Please, there's no need to justify yourself,' Ginger said. She realised how completely and quickly their roles had reversed.

In the beginning, he had been the one full of reassurances and absolution; now she was returning the favour. Jacob, her father, had often said that the capacity for mercy was humankind's greatest virtue, and that the giving and receiving of mercy formed a bond unbreakable. Ginger remembered Jacob's words now because, in allowing Alex Christophson to allay her guilt and in trying to allay his, she felt that bond.

Apparently, he felt it, too, for although he did not stop trying to explain himself, his explanations became more intimate and were offered now in a tone of voice that was less defensive and more conspiratorial. 'Quite frankly, Doctor, my reluctance to get involved is not so much because I find life infinitely precious but because I am increasingly afraid of death.' As he spoke, he reached into an inside pocket and withdrew a notepad and pen. 'In my life I've done some things of which I'm not proud.' Holding the pen in his palsied right hand, he began to print. 'True, most of those sins were committed in the line of duty. Government and espionage are both necessary, but neither is a clean business. In those days, I didn't believe in God or an afterlife. Now I wonder. . . . And wondering, I'm sometimes afraid.' He tore the top page from the pad. 'Afraid of what might await me after death, you see. That's why I want to hold on to life as long as I can, Doctor. That's why, God help me, I've become a coward in my old age.'

As Christophson folded and passed to her the slip of paper on which he had been printing, Ginger realised that he had managed to put his back to all of the remaining mourners before he had removed the notepad and pen from his coat. No one could have seen what he had done.

He said, 'I've just given you the phone number of an antique store in Greenwich, Connecticut. My younger brother, Philip, owns the place. You can't call me direct because the wrong people may have seen us talking; my telephone might be tapped. I won't risk associating with you, Dr Weiss, and I won't pursue any investigation of your problem. However, I have many years of broad experience in these matters, and there may be times when that experience will be of help to you. You may encounter something you don't understand, a situation you don't now how to deal with, and I may be able to offer advice. Just call Philip and leave your number with him. He'll immediately call me at home and use a prearranged codeword. Then I'll go out to a pay phone, return his call, get the number you left with him, and contact you as quickly as possible. Experience, my peculiar kind of malevolent experience, is all I'm willing to offer you, Dr Weiss.'

'It's more than enough. You're not obligated to help me at all.'

'Good luck.' He turned abruptly and walked away, his boots crunching in the frozen snow.

Ginger returned to the grave, where Rita, the mortician, and two labourers were the only people remaining. The velvet curtain around the grave had been collapsed and removed. A plastic tarpaulin had been pulled off a waiting mound of earth.

'What was that all about?' Rita asked.

'Tell you later,' Ginger said, bending down to pick up a rose from the pile of flowers beside Pablo Jackson's final resting place. She leaned forward and tossed the bloom into the hole, on top of the casket. '*Alav ha-sholem*. May this sleep be only a little dream between this world and something better. *Baruch ha-Shem*.'

As she and Rita walked away, Ginger heard the labourers begin to shovel dirt onto the casket.

* * *

Elko County, Nevada.

On Thursday, Dr Fontelaine was satisfied that Ernie Block was cured of his disabling nyctophobia. 'Fastest cure I've ever seen,' he said. 'I guess you Marines are tougher than ordinary mortals.'

On Saturday, January 11, after only four weeks in Milwaukee, Ernie and Faye went home. They flew into Reno on United, then caught a ten-seat commuter flight to Elko, arriving at 11:27 in the morning.

Sandy Sarver met them at the airport in Elko, though Ernie did not immediately recognise her. She was standing by the small terminal, in the crystalline winter sunshine, waving as Ernie and Faye disembarked. Gone was the pale-faced mouse, the familiar slump-shouldered frump. For the first time since Ernie had known her, Sandy was wearing a little make-up, eye shadow, and lipstick. Her nails were no longer bitten. Her hair, always limp and dull and neglected in the past, was now full, glossy. She had gained ten pounds. She had always looked older than she was. Now she looked years younger.

She blushed when Ernie and Faye raved about her make-over. She pretended the changes were of little consequence, but she was clearly pleased by their praise, approval, and delight.

She had changed in other ways, as well. For one thing, she was usually reticent and shy, but as they walked to the parking lot and put the baggage in the back of her red pick-up, she asked lots of questions about Lucy, Frank, and the grandchildren. She did not ask about Ernie's phobia because she knew nothing of it; they had kept his condition secret and had explained the extension of their Wisconsin visit by saying they wanted to spend more time with the grandchildren. In the truck, as Sandy drove through Elko and onto the interstate, she was downright garrulous as she spoke of the Christmas just past and of business at the Tranquillity Grille.

As much as anything, Sandy's driving surprised Ernie. He knew she had an aversion to four-wheel travel. But now she drove fast, with an ease and skill Ernie had never seen in her before.

Faye, sitting between Ernie and Sandy, was aware of this change, too, for she gave Ernie meaningful looks when Sandy manoeuvred the pick-up with special fluidity and audacity.

Then a bad thing happened.

Less than a mile from the motel, Ernie's interest in Sandy's metamorphosis was suddenly displaced by the queer feeling that had first seized him on December 10, when he'd been coming home from Elko with the new lighting fixtures: the feeling that a particular piece of ground, half a mile ahead, south of the highway, was *calling* him. The feeling that something strange had happened to him out there. As before, it was simultaneously an absurd and gripping feeling, characterised by the eerie attraction of a talismanic place in a dream.

This was an unsettling development because Ernie had supposed that the peculiar magnetism of that place had been, somehow, a part of the same mental disturbance that resulted in his crippling dread of the dark. His nyctophobia cured, he had assumed that all other symptoms of his temporary psychological imbalance would disappear along with his fear of the night. So this seemed like a bad sign. He did not want to consider what it might indicate about the permanency of his cure.

Faye was telling Sandy about Christmas morning with the grandkids, and Sandy was laughing, but to Ernie the laughter and conversation faded. As they drew nearer the plot of ground that exerted a mesmeric attraction on him, Ernie squinted through the sun-streaked windshield, possessed by a sense of impending epiphany. Something of monumental importance seemed about to happen, and he was filled with fear and awe.

Then, as they were passing that beguiling place, Ernie became aware that their speed had dropped. Sandy had slowed to under forty miles an hour, half the speed she had maintained since Elko. Even as Ernie realised the truck had slowed, it accelerated again. He looked at Sandy too late to be certain that she also had been temporarily spellbound by that same portion of the landscape, for now she was listening to Faye and watching the road ahead and bringing the pick-up back to speed. But it seemed to him there was a strange look on her face, and he stared at her in bewilderment, wondering how she could share his mysterious and irrational fascination with that piece of quite ordinary land.

'It's good to be home,' Faye said as Sandy switched on the right-turn signal and steered the truck toward the exit lane.

Ernie watched Sandy for an indication that she had slowed the truck in answer to the same eerie call that he felt, but he saw none of the fear that the call engendered in him. She was smiling. He must have been wrong. She had slowed the truck for some other reason.

A chill had taken residence in his bones, and now as they drove up the sloped county road and turned into the motel lot, he felt a cold damp dew of sweat on his palms, on his scalp.

He looked at his watch. Not because he needed to know the time. But because he wanted to know how long until sundown. About five hours.

What if it wasn't darkness in general that he feared? What if it was a *specific* darkness? Perhaps he had quickly overcome his phobia in Milwaukee because he was only mildly frightened by the night out there. Perhaps his real fear, his deep fear, was of the darkness of the Nevada plains. Could a phobia be that narrowly focused, that localised?

Surely not. Yet he looked at his watch.

Sandy parked in front of the motel office, and when they got out of the truck and went around to the tailgate to get the luggage, she hugged both Faye and Ernie. 'I'm glad you're back. I missed you both. Now I'd better get over to the diner and help Ned. Lunch hour's started.'

Ernie and Faye watched Sandy as she hurried away, and Faye said, 'What on earth do you suppose happened to her?'

'Damned if I know,' Ernie said.

Her breath steaming in the cold air, Faye said, 'At first, I thought she must've learned she's pregnant. But now I don't think so. If she was pregnant and overjoyed about it, she'd have told us. She'd have been *bursting* with the news. I think it's something . . . else.'

Ernie pulled two of the four suitcases out of the back of the truck and stood them on the ground, surreptitiously glancing at his watch as he put the bags down. Sundown was five minutes closer.

Faye sighed. 'Well, whatever the cause, I'm sure happy for her.'

'Me, too,' Ernie said, lifting the other two bags out of the truck.

'"Me, too,"' Faye said, affectionately mimicking him as she picked up the two lightest suitcases. 'Don't play cool with me, you big softy. I know you've worried about her almost like you used to worry about our own Lucy. When you first saw the change in Sandy back at the airport, I was watching you, and I thought your heart was going to melt.'

He followed her with the two heavier bags. 'Do they have a medical term for a calamity like that, for a melting heart?'

'Sure. Cardio-liquefaction.'

He laughed in spite of the tension that knotted his stomach. Faye was always able to make him laugh – usually when he needed it most. When they got inside, he would put his arms around her, kiss her, and convey her straight upstairs and into bed. Nothing else would be as certain to chase away the fear that had popped up in him like a jack-in-the-box. Time spent with Faye was always the best medicine.

She put her two bags down by the office door and fished her keys out of her purse.

When it had become clear, early on, that Ernie was likely to have an exceptionally swift recovery and that they would not need to stay in Milwaukee for months, Faye had decided against flying home to search for a motel manager. They simply kept the place closed. Now they needed to unlock, turn up the thermostat, clean away the accumulated dust.

A lot of work to be done . . . but still enough time for a little horizontal dancing first, Ernie thought with a grin.

He was standing behind Faye as she put the key in the office door, so fortunately she did not see him twitch and jump in surprise when the bright day was suddenly claimed by shadows. They were not actually plunged into darkness; a large cloud merely moved across the sun; the level of light dropped by no more than twenty percent. Yet even that was sufficient to startle and unnerve him.

He looked at his watch.

He looked toward the east, from whence the night would come.

I'll be all right, he thought. I'm cured.

*   *   *

On the road: Reno to Elko County.

Following the paranormal experience in Lomack's house on Tuesday, when countless paper moons took orbit around him, Dominick Corvaisis spent a few days in Reno. On his previous journey from Portland to Mountainview, he had laid-over to research a series of short stories about gambling. Recreating that trip, he passed Wednesday, Thursday, and Friday in 'The Biggest Little City in the World.'

Dom wandered from casino to casino, watching gamblers. There were young couples, retirees, pretty young women, middle-aged women in stretch pants and cardigans, leather-faced cowboys fresh from the range and soft-faced rich men on junkets from far cities, secretaries, truckers, executives, doctors, ex-cons and off-duty cops, hustlers and dreamers, escapees from every social background, drawn together by the

343

hope and thrill of organised games of chance, surely the most democratising industry on earth.

As during his previous visit, Dom gambled only enough to be part of the scene, for his primary purpose was to observe. After the storm of paper moons, he had reason to believe that Reno was the place where his life had been changed forever and where he would find the key to unlock his imprisoned memories. Those around him laughed, chattered, grumbled about the unkindness of cards, shouted to encourage the rolling dice, but Dom remained cool and alert, among them yet distanced from them, the better to spot any clue to the unremembered events in his past.

No clue was revealed.

Each night he contacted Parker Faine in Laguna Beach, hoping that the unknown correspondent had sent an additional message.

No message was received.

Each night before sleep came, he tried to understand the impossible dance of paper moons. And he sought an explanation of the circular, swollen, red rings in his hands, which he had watched fade as he knelt in a drift of moons in Lomack's living room. No understanding came.

Day by day, his craving for Valium and Dalmane diminished, but his unremembered nightmares – *The moon* – grew worse. Each night, he fought fiercely against the tether with which he moored himself to his bed.

By Saturday, Dom still suspected that the answer to his night fear and somnambulism lay in Reno. But he decided that he must not change his plans, must go on to Mountainview. If he concluded the journey without achieving satori, he could return to Reno at that time.

The summer before last, he departed Harrah's at 10:30 a.m. Friday, July 6, after an early lunch. On Saturday, January 11, he therefore followed that timetable, driving onto I-80 at 10:40, heading northeast across the Nevada wasteland toward distant Winnemucca, where Butch Cassidy and the Sundance Kid had robbed a bank in another age.

The immense unpopulated expanses of land were little different from the way they had been a thousand years ago. The highway and power lines, often the only signs of civilsation, followed the route that had been called the Humboldt Trail in the days of wagon trains. Dom drove over barren plains and hills bearded with scrub, through an uninviting yet starkly beautiful primeval world of sagebrush, sand, alkaline flats, dry lakes, solidified lava beds with columnar crystallisations, distant mountains. Sheered bluffs and veined monoliths showed traces of borax, sulphur, alum, and salt. Isolated rocky buttes were splendidly painted in ochre, amber, umber, and grey. North of the trackless Humboldt Sink, where the Humboldt River simply vanished into the thirsty earth, were more streams, as well as the Humboldt itself, and here the forbidding land featured some contrastingly fertile valleys with lush grasses and trees – cottonwoods, willows, though not in profusion. Adequate water meant communities and agriculture, but even in the hospitable valleys, the settlements were small, the grip of civilisation tenuous.

As always, Dom was humbled by the vastness of the West. But the landscape also aroused new feelings this time: a sense of mystery and an unsettling awareness of limitless – and eerie – possibilities. Hurtling through this lonely realm, it was easy to believe something frightening had happened to him here.

At 2:45 he stopped for gasoline and a sandwich in Winnemucca, a town of only five thousand souls yet by far the largest in a county of sixteen thousand square miles. Then I-80 turned eastwards. The land rose gradually toward the rim of the Great Basin. More mountains peaked on every horizon, with snow far down their slopes, and more bunch-grass appeared midst the sagebrush, and there were genuine meadows in some places, though the desert was by no means left entirely behind.

At sunset, Dom pulled off the interstate at the Tranquillity Motel, parked near the office, got out of the car, and was surprised by a cold wind. Having driven so long through deserts, he was psychologically prepared for heat, though he knew it was winter on the high plains. He reached into the car, grabbed a fleece-lined suede jacket, and put it on. He started toward the motel . . . then stopped, suddenly apprehensive.

This was the place.

He did not know *how* he knew. But he knew.

Here, something strange had happened.

He had stopped here on Friday evening, July 6, the summer before last. He had found the curious isolation of the place and the majesty of the land enormously appealing and inspiring. Indeed, he had become convinced that this territory was good material for fiction, and he had decided to stay a couple of days to familiarise himself with it and to brood about story ideas suitable to the background. He had not left for Mountainview, Utah, until Tuesday morning, the tenth of July.

Now, he turned slowly, studying the scene in the fast-fading light, hoping to prick his memory. As he turned, he became convinced that what had happened to him here was more important than anything that would ever happen to him, anywhere, as long as he lived.

The diner, with its big windows and blue neon sign, was at the western end of the complex, detached from the motel, surrounded by a large parking lot to accommodate long-haul trucks, of which three were in attendance. The entire length of the single-storey white motel was served by a breezeway sheltered under an aluminium awning that glistened darkly with a well-kept coat of forest-green enamel. The west wing had ten rooms with glossy green doors. It was separated from the east wing by a two-storey section that housed the office on the first floor and, no doubt, the owner's quarters on the second. Unlike the west wing, the east wing was L-shaped, with six rooms in the first section, four in the shorter arm. Dom kept turning and saw the dark sky in the east, the interstate dwindling into that gloom, then the immense and uninhabited panorama of shadowed land to the south. More plains and mountains lay in the west, where the sky above was streaked crimson by the sunset.

Moment by moment, Dom's apprehension grew, until he had turned in a complete circle and was looking once more at the Tranquillity Grille. As if in a dream, he moved toward the diner. By the time he reached the door, his heart was hammering. He had the urge to flee.

Steeling himself, he opened the door and went inside.

It was a clean well-lighted place, cosy and warm. Delicious odours filled the air: french fries, onions, fresh hamburger sizzling on the griddle, frying ham.

In dreamlike fear, he crossed to an empty table. A ketchup

346

bottle, a squeeze-bottle of mustard, a sugar bowl, salt and pepper shakers, and an ashtray were clustered in the centre. He picked up the salt shaker.

For a moment he did not know why he had picked it up, but then he remembered sitting at this very table the summer before last, his first night at the Tranquillity Motel. He had spilled a bit of salt and had reflexively cast a pinch of it over his shoulder, inadvertently throwing it in the face of a young woman approaching behind him.

He sensed that the incident was important, but he did not know why. Because of the woman? Who had she been? A stranger. What had she looked like? He tried to recall her face but could not.

His heart raced without apparent reason. He felt as if he were on the brink of some devastating revelation.

He strove to recall additional details, but they eluded him.

He put the salt shaker down. Still moving dreamily, shivering with unfocused anxiety, he crossed to the corner booth by the front windows. It was unoccupied, but Dom was sure that the young woman, having blinked the salt out of her eyelashes, had come here that *other* night.

'Can I help you?'

Dom was aware that a waitress in a yellow sweater was standing beside him and had spoken to him, but he remained spellbound by the tantalising ascension of some terrible memory. It had not swum into view yet, but it was rising, rising. The woman out of his past, whose face remained a blank to him, had sat in this booth, radiantly beautiful in the orange light of the sunset.

'Mister? Is something wrong?'

The young woman had ordered dinner, and Dom had gone on with his meal, and the sunset had faded, and night had fallen, and. . . . *No*!

The memory swam out of the deeps, almost broke through the murky surface into light, into his consciousness, but at the last moment he recoiled from it in panic, as if he had seen the horrible face of some monstrously evil leviathan streaking toward him. Abruptly not wanting to remember, refusing, Dom loosed a wordless cry, stumbled back, turned away from the startled waitress, and ran. He was aware of people staring,

347

aware that he was making a scene, but he did not give a damn. All he cared about was getting out. He hit the door, flung it open, and rushed out under a post-sunset, black, purple, and scarlet sky.

He was afraid. Afraid of the past. Afraid of the future. But afraid mostly because he did not know *why* he was afraid.

*   *   *

Chicago, Illinois.

Brendan Cronin was saving his announcement for after dinner, when Father Wycazik, with a full belly and a glass of brandy in hand, would be in his best mood of the day. Meanwhile, in the company of Fathers Wycazik and Gerrano, he ate a hearty dinner: double portions of potatoes and beans and ham, disposing of a third of a loaf of homemade bread.

Though he had regained his appetite, he had not regained his faith. When his belief in God had collapsed, it had left in him a terrible dark emptiness and despair, but now the despair was gone, and the emptiness, though not entirely filled, was shrinking. He was beginning to perceive that one day he might lead a meaningful life *that had nothing to do with the Church.* For Brendan – for whom no temporal pleasures had been as enticing as the spiritual joy of the Mass – the mere contemplation of a secular life was a revolutionary development.

Perhaps his despair had lifted because, since Christmas, he had at least journeyed from atheism to a qualified agnosticism. Recent events had conspired to make him consider the existence of a Power that, though not necessarily God, was nevertheless above nature.

After dinner, Father Gerrano went upstairs to spend a few hours with the latest novel by James Blaylock, the fantasist whom Brendan, too, found interesting, but whose colourful tales of bizarre fantasy creatures and even more bizarre human beings were too imaginative for a hard-nosed realist like Father Wycazik. Adjourning to the study with Brendan, the rector said, 'He writes well, but when I'm finished with one of his stories, I get the peculiar feeling that nothing's what it seems to be, and I don't like that feeling.'

'Maybe nothing *is* what it seems to be,' Brendan said.

The rector shook his head, and his grey hair caught the

light in such a way that it looked like steel wire. 'No, when I read for entertainment, I prefer it in big, solid, heavy blocks that let you grapple with the *reality* of life '

Grinning broadly, Brendan said, 'If there's a heaven, Father, and if I somehow manage to get there with you, I hope I'll have a chance to arrange a meeting between you and Walt Disney. I'd love to see you convince him that he should've spent his time animating the collected works of Dostoevsky instead of the adventures of Mickey Mouse.'

Laughing at himself, the rector poured their drinks, and they settled into armchairs, the fallen priest with a glass of schnapps, his superior with a small brandy.

Deciding there would be no better time for his news, Brendan said, 'If it's all right with you, I'll be going away for a while, Father. I'd like to leave on Monday, if I can. I need to go to Nevada.'

'*Nevada*?' Father Wycazik made it sound as if his curate had just said Bangkok or Timbuktu. 'Why Nevada?'

With the taste of peppermint schnapps on his tongue and the scent burning his sinuses, Brendan said, 'That's where I'm being called. Last night, in the dream, though I still saw nothing but a brilliant light, I suddenly knew where I was. Elko County, Nevada. And I knew I must go back there in order to find an explanation for Emmy's cure and Winton's resurrection.'

'*Back* there? You've been there before?'

'The summer before last. Just before I came to St Bernadette's.'

Upon leaving his post with Monsignor Orbella in Rome, Brendan had flown directly to San Francisco to carry out a final assignment from his Vatican mentor. He stayed two weeks with Bishop John Santefiore, an old friend of Orbella. The bishop was writing a book on the history of papal selection, and Brendan came laden with research material provided by the monsignor in Rome. It was his job to answer any questions about those documents. John Santefiore was a charming man with a sly dry wit, and the days flashed past.

His task concluded, Brendan was left with two weeks to himself before he was required to report to his superiors in Chicago, his hometown, where he would be assigned as

349

curate to some parish in that archdiocese. He spent a few days in Carmel, on the Monterey Peninsula. Then, making up his mind to see some of the country that he had never seen before, Brendan set out on a long drive eastwards in a rental car.

Now, Father Wycazik leaned forward, brandy snifter clasped in both hands. 'I remembered about Bishop Santefiore, but I'd forgotten you drove from there to here. And you passed through Elko County, Nevada?'

'Stayed there, at a motel in the middle of nowhere. Tranquillity Motel. I stopped for the night, but it was so peaceful, the countryside so beautiful, that I stayed a few days. Now I've got to go back.'

'Why? What happened to you out there?'

Brendan shrugged. 'Nothing. I just relaxed. Napped. Read a couple books. Watched TV. They have good TV reception even way out there because they've got their own little receiver dish on the roof.'

Father Wycazik cocked his head. 'What's wrong? There for a moment you sounded . . . odd. Wooden . . . as if repeating something you'd memorised.'

'I was just telling you what it was like.'

'So if nothing happened to you there, why is the place so special? What will happen when you go back there?'

'I'm not sure. But it's going to be something . . . incredible.'

Finally revealing his frustration with his curate's obtuseness, Father Wycazik put the question bluntly: 'Is it *God* calling you?'

'I don't think so. But maybe. A slim maybe. Father, I want your permission to go. But if I can't have your blessing, I'll go anyway.'

Father Wycazik took a larger swallow of brandy than was his habit. 'I think you should go, but I don't think you should go alone.'

Brendan was surprised. 'You want to come with me?'

'Not me. I've got St Bette's to run. But you should be in the company of a qualified witness. A priest familiar with these things, one who can verify any miracle or miraculous visitation –'

'You mean some cleric who has the Cardinal's imprimatur to investigate every hysterical report of weeping statues of the Holy Mother, bleeding crucifixes, and divine manifestations of all kinds?'

Father Wycazik nodded. 'That's right. Someone who knows the process of authentication. I had in mind Monsignor Janney of the archdiocese's office of publications. He's had a lot of practice.'

Reluctant to disappoint his rector but determined to proceed in his own fashion, Brendan interrupted: 'There's no visitation involved here, so there's no need for Monsignor Janney. None of this has an obvious Christian significance or source.'

'And who ever said God isn't permitted to be subtle?' Father Wycazik asked. His grin made it clear he expected to win this argument.

'These things could all be merely psychic phenomena.'

'Bah! Claptrap. Psychic phenomena are just the non-believer's pathetic explanation for glimpses of the divine hand at work. Examine these events closely, Brendan; open your heart to the meaning of them, and you'll see the truth. God's calling you back to His bosom. And I believe a divine visitation is what this may be building towards.'

'But if this is building to a divine manifestation, why couldn't it happen right here? Why's it necessary to go all the way to Nevada?'

'Perhaps it's a test of your obedience to the will of God, a test of your underlying desire to believe again. If your desire's strong enough, you'll discomfit yourself by taking this long journey, and as reward you'll be shown something to make you believe again.'

'But why Nevada? Why not Florida or Texas – or Istanbul?'

'Only God knows.'

'And why would God go to all this trouble to recapture the heart of one fallen priest?'

'To Him who made the earth and stars, this is no trouble at all. And one heart is as important to Him as a million hearts.'

'Then why did He let me lose my faith in the first place?'

'Perhaps losing and regaining it is a tempering process. You may have been put through it because God needs you to be stronger.'

Brendan smiled and shook his head in admiration. 'You're never caught without an answer, are you, Father?'

Looking self-satisfied, Stefan Wycazik settled back in his chair. 'God blessed me with a quick tongue.'

Brendan was aware of Father Wycazik's reputation as a saviour of troubled priests, and he knew the rector would not give up easily – or at all. But Brendan was determined not to go to Nevada with Monsignor Janney in tow.

From the other armchair, over the rim of his brandy snifter, Father Wycazik watched Brendan with evident affection and iron determination, waiting eagerly for another argument that he could swiftly refute, for another thrust that he could parry with his unfailing Jesuitical aplomb.

Brendan sighed. It was going to be a long evening.

*   *   *

Elko County, Nevada.

After hurrying out of the Tranquillity Grille in fear and confusion, into the last fading scarlet and purple light of dusk, Dom Corvaisis went directly to the motel office. There, he walked into the middle of a scene that initially appeared to be a domestic quarrel, though he quickly saw that it was something stranger than that.

A squarely built man in tan slacks and a brown sweater stood in the centre of the room, this side of the counter. He was only two inches taller than Dom, but in other dimensions he was considerably larger. He seemed to have been hewn from massive slabs of oak. The grey of his brush-cut hair, the weathered lines of his face, indicated he was in his fifties, although his bull-strong body had a younger presence and power.

The big man was shaking, as if enraged. A woman stood beside him, staring up at him with an odd and urgent expression. She was a blonde with vivid blue eyes, younger than him, though it was difficult to judge her age. The man's pale face was shiny with sweat. As Dom stepped across the threshold, he realised that his flash impression was wrong: this guy was not enraged but terrified.

'Relax,' the woman said. 'Try to control your breathing.'

The big man was gasping. He stood with his thick neck bent, head lowered, shoulders hunched, staring at the floor, inhalation following exhalation in an arhythmic pattern that betrayed a growing panic.

'Take deep slow breaths,' the woman said. 'Remember what

352

Dr Fontelaine taught you. When you're calm, we'll go outside for a walk.'

'No!' the big man said, shaking his head violently.

'Yes, we will,' the woman said, putting a reassuring hand on his arm. 'We'll go outside for a walk, Ernie, and you'll see that this darkness is no different from the darkness in Milwaukee.'

Ernie. The name chilled Dom and immediately brought to mind those four posters of the moon on which names had been scrawled in Zebediah Lomack's living room, in Reno.

The woman glanced at Dom, and he said, 'I need a room.'

'We're full,' she said.

'The vacancy sign is lit.'

'Okay,' she said. 'Okay, but not now. Please. Not now. Go over to the diner or something. Come back in half an hour. *Please.*'

Until that exchange, Ernie had seemed unaware of Dom's intrusion. Now, he looked up from the floor, and a moan of fear and despair escaped him. 'The door. Close it before the darkness comes in!'

'No, no, no,' the woman told him, her voice firm yet full of compassion. 'It's not coming in. Darkness can't hurt you, Ernie.'

'It's coming in,' he insisted miserably.

Dom realised that the room was unnaturally bright. Table lamps, a floor lamp, a desk lamp, and the ceiling fixtures blazed.

The woman turned to Dom again. 'For God's sake, close the door.'

He stepped in, rather than out, and shut the door behind him.

'I meant, close it as you leave,' the woman said pointedly.

The expression on Ernie's face was part terror, part embarrassment. His eyes shifted from Dom to the window. 'It's right there at the glass. All the darkness . . . pressing, pressing.' He looked sheepishly at Dom, then lowered his head again, shut his eyes tight.

Dom stood transfixed. Ernie's irrational fear was horribly like the terror which drove Dom to walk in his sleep and to hide in closets.

353

Using anger to repress her tears, the woman turned to Dom. 'Why won't you go? He's nyctophobic. He's afraid of the dark sometimes, and when he has one of these attacks, we have to work it out together.'

Dom remembered the other names scrawled on the posters in Lomack's house – Ginger, Faye – and he chose one by instinct. 'It's all right, Faye. I think I understand a little of what you're going through.'

She blinked in surprise when he used her name. 'Do I know you?'

'Do you? I'm Dominick Corvaisis.'

'Means nothing to me,' she said, staying with the big man as he turned and, eyes still closed, shuffled toward the back of the office.

Ernie moved blindly toward the gate in the counter. 'Got to get upstairs, where I can pull the drapes, keep the dark out.'

Faye said, 'No, Ernie, wait. Don't run from it.'

Stepping in front of Ernie, putting a hand on the man's chest to halt him, Dom said, 'You have nightmares. When you wake up, you can't remember what they were, except they had something to do with the moon.'

Faye gasped.

Ernie opened his eyes in surprise. 'How'd you know that?'

'I've had nightmares for over a month,' Dom said. 'Every night. And I know a man who suffered from them so bad he killed himself.'

They stared at him in astonishment.

'In October,' Dom said, 'I started walking in my sleep. I'd creep out of bed, hide in closets, or gather weapons to protect myself. Once, I tried to nail the windows shut to keep something out. Don't you see, Ernie, I'm afraid of something in the dark. I'll bet that's what you're afraid of, too. Not just the dark itself but something else, something specific that happened to you' – he gestured toward the windows – 'out there in the darkness on that same weekend, the summer before last.'

Still baffled by this turn of events, Ernie glanced at the night beyond the windows, then immediately looked away. 'I don't understand.'

'Let's go upstairs, where you can draw the drapes,' Dom said. 'I'll tell you what I know. The important thing is you

354

aren't alone in this. You're not alone any more. And, thank God, neither am I.'

*   *   *

New Haven County, Connecticut.

Clockwork. Jack Twist's heists always ticked along like clockwork mechanisms. The armoured-car job was no exception.

The night was solidly roofed with clouds. No stars, no moon. No snow was falling, but a cold moist wind swept up from the southwest.

The Guardmaster truck rumbled past empty fields, coming from the northeast toward the knoll from which Jack had watched it Christmas Eve. Its headlights bored through thin ragged sheets of patchy winter fog. In the snow-wrapped fields, the county lane resembled a strip of black satin ribbon.

Dressed in a white ski suit with hood, Jack lay half buried in snow, south of the roadway, across from the knoll. On the other side of the road, at the foot of the knoll, the second member of the team, Chad Zepp, also in white camouflage, sprawled in another drift.

The third member of the team, Branch Pollard, was halfway down the knoll with a Heckler and Koch HK91 heavy assault rifle.

The truck was two hundred yards away. Refracting the headlights, fog formations drifted across the road, into the lightless fields.

Suddenly the muzzle of the HK91 flashed up on the hillside. A shot cracked above the sound of the grinding engine.

The HK91, perhaps the finest combat rifle made, could fire hundreds of rounds without jamming. Extremely accurate, effective at a thousand yards, the HK91 could put a 7.62 NATO round through a tree or concrete wall, with sufficient punch left to kill someone on the other side.

Tonight, however, they did not intend to kill anyone. Aided by an infra-red telescopic sight, Pollard put the first shot where he wanted it, blowing out the right front tyre of the Guardmaster transport.

The truck swerved wildly. Encountering ice, it began to slide.

355

Even while the armoured transport was sliding, its fate unsettled, Jack was up and running. He leaped a ditch and dashed onto the road in front of the vehicle, which loomed like a tank. At the last moment, when it seemed bound inexorably for the ditch, the driver regained control and brought the truck to a jerky halt thirty feet from Jack.

He saw one of the Guardmaster crewmen talking excitedly into a radio handset. That call for help was futile. The moment Pollard had fired from the knoll, Chad Zepp, still concealed in the snow north of the road, had switched on a battery-powered transmitter, jamming the transport's radio frequency with shrill electronic static.

As the rising wind harried fog-ghosts past Jack, he stood in the middle of the road, feeling naked in the blazing headlights, taking time to aim the tear-gas rifle at the truck's grille. The gun was of British manufacture, designed for anti-terrorist squads. Other tear-gas weapons fired grenades that spewed disabling fumes on impact, requiring the marksman to aim at windows. But upon seizing an embassy, terrorists usually boarded up the windows. The new British gun, which Jack had acquired from a blackmarket arms dealer in Miami, had a two-inch bore and fired a high-velocity, steel-jacketed tear-gas *shell* that could penetrate most wooden doors or punch through a boarded window. When Jack fired, the shell smashed through the truck's grille into the engine compartment. A noxious yellow vapour began roiling into the cab by way of its ventilation system.

The guards had been trained to remain in their secure roost in a crisis, for the cab had steel doors and bullet-proof glass. But when they switched off the heater and closed the vents too late, they found themselves choking in the gas-filled cabin. They opened their locked doors, spilled out into the cold winter night, wheezing, coughing.

In spite of the blinding, suffocating gas, the driver had drawn his revolver. Dropping to his knees, gagging, he squinted his copiously watering eyes in search of a target.

But Jack kicked the gun out of his hand, grabbed him by the coat, and dragged him to the front of the truck, where he handcuffed him to a support strut on the bumper.

After firing the shot that disabled the truck, Branch Pollard had sprinted down the knoll. Now, at the other end of the front bumper, he handcuffed the other protesting guard to another strut.

Both guards were blinking furiously, trying to clear their gas-blurred vision to get a look at their attackers' faces, but that was wasted effort because Jack, Pollard, and Zepp were wearing ski masks.

Leaving the securely shackled men, Jack and Pollard ran to the back of the truck, moving fast, though not because they feared being seen by other traffic on that lonely road. No traffic would pass until they were gone. The moment the Guardmaster unit had entered the flats, the last two members of the robbery team, Hart and Dodd, had sealed off both ends of the road with stolen vans that had been repainted and equipped with Department of Highway signs. Against an impressive backdrop of emergency beacons flashing on the roofs of their vans and on sawhorses they had set out on the pavement, Dodd and Hart would turn back everyone who wanted through, spinning a tale of a tanker-truck accident.

Clockwork.

When Jack and Pollard got to the rear of the truck, Chad Zepp was already there. In the glow of a battery-powered light that he had fixed to the truck with a magnet, Zepp was unscrewing the faceplate that covered the lock mechanism on the doors to the cargo hold.

They had brought explosives, but when trying to peel a truck as well-constructed as the Guardmaster, there was a risk that explosives would fuse the lock pins, sealing the honeypot even tighter. They had to try going in through the lock, leaving explosives as a last resort.

Some older armoured cars had locks that operated with a key or pair of keys, and some had combination dials, but this was a new vehicle with state-of-the-art equipment. This lock was engaged and disengaged by pressing a sequence of code numbers on a ten-digit keyboard that was the size and appearance of the 'dial' on a touch-tone telephone. To activate the lock, the guard closed the doors and simply punched in the middle number of the three-number code. To deactivate it, he pressed all three numbers in the correct order. The code was changed every morning, and of the two men crewing the truck, only the driver knew it.

There were a thousand possible three-number sequences in ten digits. Because it would take between four and five seconds to key in each sequence and wait for it to be accepted or rejected, they would have to delay at least an hour and a quarter to try every combination. That was far too risky.

Chad Zepp removed the faceplate from the lock. The ten numbered buttons remained, but now it was possible to see a bit of the mechanism between and behind them.

Hung on a strap from Zepp's shoulder was a battery-powered, attaché-size computer, which could assess and control the circuitry of electronic locks and alarms. It was SLICKS, an acronym for Security Lock Intervention and Circumvention Knowledge System. Intended solely for military or intelligence-agency personnel with security clearance, SLICKS was unavailable to the public. Unauthorised possession was a criminal violation of the Defence Security Act. To obtain a SLICKS, Jack had gone to Mexico City and had paid $25,000 to a blackmarket arms dealer who had a contact inside the firm that manufactured the device.

Zepp unslung the computer and held it so he and Jack and Pollard could see the four-inch-square video display, which was dark. Three retractable probes were slotted in the SLICKS, and Jack withdrew the first of these from its niche: it looked like a copper-tipped steel thermometer on a two-foot wire umbilical. Jack looked closely at the partially exposed guts of the electronic lock and carefully inserted the slender probe between the first two buttons, touching it to the contact point at the base of the button marked '1.' The display screen remained dark. He moved the probe to button number 2, then 3. Nothing. But when he touched number 4, a pale green word – CURRENT – appeared on the screen, plus numbers that measured trace-electricity in the contact.

This meant that the middle number of the three-digit lock-code was 4. After loading sacks of money and cheques into the cargo-hold at the last stop on the route, the driver had pushed 4 to activate the lock. The contact point of that button would remain closed until the entire code was punched in, thereby unlocking the door.

With three unknown numbers, the possible combinations had been one thousand. But now that they needed to find only the first and last numbers, the search was reduced to one hundred combinations.

Ignoring the howling wind, Jack withdrew another instrument from the SLICKS. This was also on a two-foot cord but resembled a watercolour brush though with a single bristle. The bristle glowed with light and was thicker than a sixty-pound fishing line, stiff yet flexible. Jack inserted it into a crack at the base of the 1 button on the lock keyboard, glanced at the computer video display, but was not rewarded. He moved the bristle-probe from number to number. The display screen blinked, then showed a partial diagram of a circuit board.

The bristle that he had thrust inside the mechanism was actually the end filament of an optical laser, a more sophisticated cousin of the similar device which, in supermarket cash registers, read the bar codes on grocery items. The SLICKS was not programmed to read bar codes but to recognise circuitry patterns and render models of them on the display screen. The screen would register nothing whatsoever until the bristle-probe was aimed directly at a circuit or portion thereof, but then it would faithfully reproduce the hidden pattern that it saw.

Jack had to move the probe three times, insert it into the lock mechanism at three different points, before the computer was able to piece together a picture of the entire circuitry from partial views. The diagram glowed in bright green lines and symbols on the miniature video display. After three seconds of consideration, the computer drew boxes around two small portions of the diagram to indicate those points at which a tap could easily be applied to the circuitry. Then it superimposed an image of the ten-digit keyboard over the diagram, to show where those two weak points were in relation to that portion of the lock mechanism that was visible to Jack.

'There's a good tap-in spot below the number 4 button,' Jack said.

'You need me to drill?' Pollard asked.

'I don't think so.'

Jack returned the optical probe to its slot and withdrew a third slender instrument with a spongy mesh tip of some material he could not identify, which the designer of SLICKS had labelled the 'tap-wand.' He inserted it through the tiny gap in the lock mechanism at the base of the 4 button, slowly moved it up and down, left and right, until the computer beeped and flashed INTERVENTION on the miniature video display.

While Jack held the tap-wand in place and Chad Zepp held the SLICKS upright, Pollard used the computer's small programming board to quickly type instructions. INTERVENTION disappeared, and onto the screen came other words: SYSTEM CONTROL ESTABLISHED. The computer could now feed commands directly to the microchip that processed the lock codes and that directed the sliding steel bolts to either close or open.

Pollard hit two more keys, and the SLICKS began to send sequences of three numbers to the microchip, one combination every six-hundredths of a second, all of which used the already-known 4 as the middle digit of the code. SLICKS hit the right code – 545 – in only nine seconds.

With four simultaneous thumps, the lock bolts retracted as one.

Jack returned the tap-wand to its niche, switched off the computer. Only four minutes had passed since the rifle-shot that had blown out the truck's right front tyre.

Clockwork.

As Zepp slung the SLICKS over his shoulder again, Pollard opened the rear doors of the armoured car. The money was theirs for the taking.

Zepp laughed with delight. With a gleeful whoop, Pollard clambered into the truck and began to push out bulging canvas bags.

But Jack still felt empty and cold inside.

A few snow flurries suddenly appeared in the wind.

The unexplained change in Jack, which had begun weeks ago, had now reached completion. He no longer cared about getting even with society. He felt purposeless, as adrift as the wind-borne flakes of snow.

*   *   *

Elko County, Nevada.

Faye Block had turned on the NO VACANCY notice to ensure that they would not be disturbed.

360

Sitting around the table in the cheery kitchen of their apartment above the motel office, with the blinds shut against the night, the Blocks sipped coffee and listened spellbound as Dom told his story.

The only point at which they registered disbelief was when he told them of the impossible dance of paper moons in Zebediah Lomack's house in Reno. But he was able to describe that startling event in such sharp detail that he felt gooseflesh pimpling his arms, and he saw that his own awe and fear were being transmitted to Faye and Ernie

They appeared most impressed by the two Polaroid photographs that had arrived in the mail from the unknown correspondent two days before Dom had flown to Portland. They studied the picture in which the zombie-faced priest was sitting at a writing desk, and they were certain it had been taken in one of their motel rooms. The photo of the blonde in bed with an IV line in her arm was a close-up that showed nothing of the room, but they recognised the floral-patterned bedspread visible in one corner of the shot; it was the kind that had been in use in some units until ten months ago.

To Dom's surprise, they had been sent a similar photograph. Ernie remembered receiving it in a plain envelope on December 10, five days before they had flown to Milwaukee. Faye got it from the centre drawer of the desk in the downstairs office, and they hunched conspiratorially over the kitchen table, studying the print. It was a shot of three people – man, woman, child – standing in sunshine by the door to Room 9. All three were dressed in shorts, T-shirts, and sandals.

'Do you recognise them?' Dom asked.

'No,' Faye said.

'But I feel like I *ought* to remember them,' Ernie said.

Dom said, 'Sunshine . . . summer clothes . . . so we can almost certainly conclude it was taken the summer before last, *that* weekend, between Friday the sixth of July and the following Tuesday. These three people were part of whatever happened. Maybe innocent victims like us. And our unknown correspondent wants us to think about them, remember them.'

Ernie said, 'Whoever sent the pictures would've been one of

the people who erased our memories. So why would he want to stir us up like this after so much trouble was taken to make us forget?'

Dom shrugged. 'Maybe he never believed it was right – what was done to us. Maybe he only went along with it because he had to, and maybe it's been on his conscience ever since. Whoever he is, he's afraid to come right out with what he knows. He's got to do it indirectly.'

Abruptly, Faye pushed her chair back from the table. 'Five weeks of mail piled up while we were away. Might be something more in it.'

As the sound of Faye's descending footsteps echoed up from the stairs, Ernie said, 'Sandy – that's our waitress at the grille – sorted through the mail and paid the bills as they arrived. But the rest of the mail she just dropped in a paper sack. Since we came back this morning, we've been so busy getting the place open, we didn't bother looking to see what the postman brought.'

Faye returned with two plain white envelopes. In a state of high excitement, they opened the first. It contained a Polaroid of a man lying on his back in bed, an intravenous needle in his arm. He was in his fifties. Dark hair, balding. In ordinary circumstances, he probably had a jovial look, for he resembled W. C. Fields. But he was staring blankly toward the camera, face bleak, zombie eyes.

'My God, it's Calvin!' Faye said.

'Yeah,' Ernie said, 'Cal Sharkle. He's a long-haul trucker movin' freight between Chicago and San Francisco.'

'He stops at the grille most every trip,' Faye said. 'Sometimes when he's beat, he stays overnight. Calvin's such a nice man.'

'What company's he drive for?' Dom asked.

'He's independent,' Ernie said. 'Owns his own rig.'

'Would you know how to get in touch with him?'

'Well,' Ernie said, 'he signs the registry every time he checks in, so we'll have his address . . . around Chicago somewhere, I think.'

'We'll check later. First, let's look in that other envelope.'

Faye opened it and produced another Polaroid. Again, it was a shot of a man lying in one of the Tranquillity Motel's beds, an IV line in one arm. Like all the others, he had no expression whatsoever, and soulless eyes that reminded Dom of horror movies about the living dead.

But this time, they all recognised the man in the bed. It was Dom.

*   *   *

Las Vegas, Nevada.

When Marcie's bedtime came, she was sitting at the little desk in the corner of her room, occupied with her collection of moons.

Jorja stood in the doorway, watching. The girl was so thoroughly engaged by the task that she remained unaware she was being observed.

A box of crayons lay beside the album full of moons. Marcie was hunched over the work surface, carefully colouring one of the lunar faces. This was a new development, and Jorja wondered what it meant.

In the week since Marcie had begun her collection with magazine clippings, she had filled the album. She had few sources for photos, so she drew hundreds of pictures to add to the monotonous gallery. Using templets as varied as coins, jar lids, vases, drinking glasses, cans, and thimbles, she traced lunar forms of all sizes on tablet paper, construction paper, paper bags, envelopes, and wrapping paper. She did not spend most of her time with the album, but each day she devoted a bit more time to it than she had the day before.

Dr Ted Coverly, the psychologist treating Marcie, believed the anxiety that had generated the girl's irrational fear of doctors had not been relieved. Now, the child was expressing that anxiety through her lunar preoccupation. When Jorja noted that Marcie did not seem to be particularly frightened of the moon, Coverly said, 'Well, her anxiety doesn't have to seek expression in another *phobia*. It can show itself in other ways . . . such as an obsession.' Jorja could not understand where her daughter's extraordinary anxiety came from. Coverly said, 'That's why the therapy – to seek understanding. Don't worry, Miss Monatella.'

But Jorja *was* worried.

She was worried because Alan had killed himself only yesterday. Jorja had not yet told Marcie of her father's death. On leaving Pepper Carrafield's apartment, she had called Coverly to ask his advice. He was astonished that Alan, too, had been dreaming of the moon and had independently developed an intense lunar fascination of his own. *That* one would take time to ponder. Meanwhile, Coverly thought it wise to withhold the bad news from Marcie until Monday. 'Come with her to the appointment. We'll tell her together.' Jorja was afraid that, in spite of Alan's inattention, Marcie would be devastated by his death.

As she stood in the bedroom doorway, watching Marcie diligently applying a crayon to one of the moons, Jorja was stricken by an acute awareness of the girl's fragility. Although she was seven years old and in second grade, the three-quarter-scale chair was still too big for her, and only the toes of her sneakers touched the floor. Even for a macho man armoured with muscles, life was tenuous, and every additional day of existence was against the odds. But for a child as petite as Marcie, continued life seemed downright miraculous. Jorja realised how easily her precious daughter could be taken from her, and her heart swelled and ached with love.

When at last Jorja said, 'Honey, better put your pyjamas on and brush your teeth,' she could not keep a tremor out of her voice.

The girl looked bewildered, as if she were not quite sure where she was or who Jorja was. Then her eyes cleared, and she gave her mother a smile that could melt butter. 'Hi, Mommy. I been colouring moons.'

'Well, now it's time to get ready for bed,' Jorja said.

'In a little while, okay?' The girl appeared to be relaxed, yet she was gripping a crayon so tightly that her knuckles were white. 'I want to colour some more moons.'

Jorja wanted to destroy the hateful album. But Dr Coverly had warned that arguing with the child about the moons and forbidding her to collect them would only strengthen her obsession. Jorja was not sure he was right, but she stifled the urge to destroy the album.

'Tomorrow, you'll have lots of time to colour, Peanut.'

Reluctantly, Marcie closed the album, put away her

crayons, and went to the bathroom to brush her teeth.

Alone beside the child's desk, Jorja was overcome by weariness. In addition to working a full shift, she'd arranged a mortician for Alan's body, ordered flowers, and settled details with the cemetery for Monday's funeral. She had also called Alan's estranged father in Miami to break the bad news. She was drained. Wearily, she opened the album.

Red. The girl was colouring all the moons red, both those she had drawn and those clipped from newspapers and magazines. She had already painted more than fifty lunar images. The obsessive quality of the girl's work was evident in the great care she had taken to keep the crayon from slipping past the outline of each moon. The crayon had been applied more heavily picture by picture, until some moons were coated with so much scarlet wax that they had a glisteningly wet look.

The use of red – and red alone – profoundly disturbed Jorja. It almost seemed as if Marcie had glimpsed an augury of some onrushing terror, a premonition of blood.

*   *   *

Elko County, Nevada.

Faye Block had gone downstairs to the file cabinets, from which she had extracted the motel registry that had been in use the summer before last. Upon her return, she put the book on the kitchen table, in front of Dom, open to the guest lists of Friday and Saturday, July 6 and 7.

'There, just like Ernie and I remembered. That Friday was the night they closed the interstate because of a toxic spill. A truckload of dangerous chemicals headed out to Shenkfield. That's a military installation about eighteen miles southwest of here. We had to close the motel until Tuesday, until they got the situation under control.'

Ernie said, 'Shenkfield's an isolated testing ground for chemical and biological weapons, so the crap in that truck was damned nasty.'

Faye continued, a new wooden note in her voice, as if reciting carefully memorised lines. 'They erected roadblocks and ordered us to evacuate the danger zone. Our guests left in their own cars.' Her face remained expressionless. 'Ned

365

and Sandy Sarver were allowed to go up to their trailer near Beowawe because it was outside the quarantine area.'

Astonished and confused, Dom said, 'Impossible. I don't remember any evacuation. I was *here*. I remember reading, researching the geography for a series of short stories . . . but those memories are so thin I suspect they aren't real. No substance to them. Still, I was here and nowhere else, and something weird was done to me.' He indicated the Polaroid snapshot of himself. 'There's the proof.'

When Faye spoke, she sounded stiffer than before, and Dom saw a strangeness in her eyes, a slightly glazed look. 'Until the all-clear was given, Ernie and I stayed with friends who have a small ranch in the mountains ten miles northeast of here – Elroy and Nancy Jamison. It was a difficult spill to clean up. The Army needed more than three days to do the job. They wouldn't let us back here until Tuesday morning.'

'What's wrong with you, Faye?' Dom asked.

She blinked. 'Huh? What do you mean?'

'You sound as if you'd been . . . programmed with that little speech.'

She seemed genuinely baffled. 'What're you talking about?'

Frowning, Ernie said, 'Faye, your voice went . . . flat.'

'Well, I was only explaining what happened.' She leaned over and put one finger on Friday's page of the registry. 'See, we'd rented out eleven rooms by the time they closed the interstate that night. But nobody paid for the rooms because nobody stayed. They were evacuated.'

'There's your name, seventh on the list,' Ernie said.

Dom stared at his signature and at the Mountainview, Utah, address to which he had been moving at the time. He could remember checking in, but he sure as hell could not remember climbing back into his car and driving out the same night in response to an evacuation order. He said, 'Did you actually see the accident, the tanker truck?'

Ernie shook his head. 'No, the truck overturned a couple miles from here.' He spoke in that by-rote tone that had marked Faye's speech. 'The Army experts from Shenkfield were concerned the chemicals would be dispersed by the wind, so the quarantine zone was very large.'

Chilled by the unconscious artificiality in Ernie's voice, Dom looked at Faye and saw that she too had noticed her husband's unnatural tone. He said, 'That's what *you* sounded like a moment ago, Faye.' He looked at Ernie. 'You two have been programmed with the same script.'

Faye frowned. 'Are you saying the spill never happened?'

'It happened, all right,' Ernie told Dom. 'For a while we saved a bunch of newspaper clippings about it from the *Elko Sentinel*. But I think we eventually threw them out. Anyway, people around these parts still wonder what might've happened if we'd got big winds and been contaminated with that top-secret stuff before the evacuation order was even given. No, it's not just some delusion of Faye's and mine.'

'You can ask Elroy and Nancy Jamison,' Faye said. 'They were here that night, visiting. When we had to evacuate, they offered to take us back to their place and put us up for the duration.'

Dom smiled sourly. 'I wouldn't put much credence in their recall of events. If they were here, then they saw what the rest of us saw, and it was scrubbed from their minds. They remember taking you back to their place because that's what they were *told* to remember. In fact they were probably right here, being brainwashed with the rest of us.'

'My head's swimming,' Faye said. 'This is positively Byzantine.'

'But, damn it, the toxic spill and evacuation happened,' Ernie said. 'It was in the newspapers.'

Dom thought of a disturbing explanation that made his scalp crawl. 'What if everyone here at the motel that night *was* contaminated with some chemical or biological weapon headed for Shenkfield? And what if the Army and the government covered it up to avoid bad press, millions of dollars in law suits, and the disclosure of top-secret information? Maybe they closed the highway and announced that everyone was safely evacuated, when in fact we had *not* been got out in time. Then they used the motel as a clinic, decontaminated us as much as they could, scrubbed the memory of the incident out of our minds, and reprogrammed us with false memories, so we'd never know what had happened to us.'

They stared at one another in shocked silence for a moment.

Not because the scenario sounded entirely right, which it did not. But because it was the first scenario they'd come up with that made sense of the psychological problems they had been having and explained the drugged people in those Polaroid snapshots.

Then Ernie and Faye began to think of objections. Ernie voiced the first: 'In that case, the logical thing for them to've done was to make our false memories tie in closely with their cover story about the toxic spill and evacuation. That's exactly what they did with Faye and me, with the Jamisons, Ned and Sandy Sarver. So why didn't they do the same with you? Why'd they programme you with different memories that didn't have anything to do with the evacuation? That was irrational and risky. I mean, the radical differences between our memories is virtually proof that you or we – or all of us – were brainwashed.'

'Don't know,' Dom said. 'That's just one more mystery to unravel.'

'And here's another flaw in that theory,' Ernie said. 'If we'd been contaminated by a biological weapon, they wouldn't have let us go in just three days. They'd have been afraid of contagion, epidemic.'

Dom said, 'All right. So it was a *chemical* agent, not a virus or bacterium. Something they could wash off or flush out of our systems.'

'That doesn't make sense, either,' Faye said. 'Because the things they test as Shenkfield are meant to be deadly. Poison gas. Nerve gas. Hideous damn stuff. If we'd got caught in a cloud like that, we'd have been dead on the spot or brain-damaged or crippled.'

'Maybe it was a slow-acting agent,' Dom said. 'Something that generates tumours, leukemia, or other conditions that only begin to show up two or three or five years from the date of contamination.'

That thought also shocked them into silence. They listened to the ticking of the kitchen clock, to the mournful fluting of the wind at the windows, wondering if malignancies were even now sprouting within them.

Finally, Ernie said, 'Maybe we were contaminated, and maybe we're all slowly rotting inside, but I don't think so.

After all, they test potential *weapons* at Shenkfield. And what use would a weapon be that didn't kill the enemy for years and years?'

'Virtually no use at all,' Dom acknowledged.

'And,' Ernie said, 'how could chemical contamination explain that bizarre experience you had in Lomack's house in Reno?'

'I've an idea,' Dom said. 'But now that we know they cordoned off this whole area using the excuse of a toxic spill – whether it was a real spill or not – my theory that we were brainwashed is a lot more credible. Because, see, before this I wasn't able to explain how someone could've rounded us up at will and held us long enough to make us forget the thing we saw. But the quarantine gave them the time they needed, and it also kept away prying eyes. So . . . at least now we have a good idea who we're up against. The United States Army, maybe acting in collusion with the government, maybe acting alone, has been trying to hide something that happened here, something it did but shouldn't have done. I don't know about you, but the thought of being up against an enemy that big and that potentially ruthless scares the hell out of me.'

'An old Leatherneck like me is bound to be scornful of the Army,' Ernie said. 'But they're not devils, you know. We can't leap to the conclusion we're victims of a wicked right-wing conspiracy. That crackpot stuff makes millions for paranoid novelists and for Hollywood, but in the real world, evil is more subtle, less identifiable. If Army and government officials are behind what happened to us, they don't necessarily have immoral motives. They probably think they did the only wise thing they could've done in the circumstances.'

'But whether or not it's wise,' Faye said, 'we've got to dig into this situation. If we don't, Ernie's nyctophobia will surely get worse. And your sleepwalking will also get worse, Dom. And what then?'

They all knew 'what then.' 'What then' was a shotgun barrel jammed in the mouth, the route to peace that Zebediah Lomack had taken.

Dom looked down at the motel registry on the table before him. Four spaces above his own name, he saw another entry that electrified him. Dr Ginger Weiss. Her address was in Boston.

'Ginger,' he said. 'The fourth name on those moon posters.'

Furthermore, Cal Sharkle, the Blocks' trucker-friend from Chicago, the zombie-eyed subject of one of the Polaroid snapshots, had checked into the motel just before Dr Weiss. The first guests to sign in that day were Mr and Mrs Alan Rykoff and daughter, of Las Vegas. Dom was willing to bet that they were the young family photographed in front of the door to Room 9. Zebediah Lomack's name was not in the registry, so he had probably just been unlucky enough to stop at the Grille for dinner that night, on his way between Reno and Elko. One of the other names might have been that of the young priest in the other Polaroid, but if so, he had signed without appending his title.

'We'll have to talk to all these people,' Dom said excitedly. 'We can start calling them first thing tomorrow and see what *they* remember about those days in July.'

*　　　*　　　*

Chicago, Illinois.

By allowing no slightest hairline crack to appear in his resolve, by showing no equivocation whatsoever, Brendan managed to obtain Father Wycazik's permission to go to Nevada alone on Monday, without Monsignor Janney trailing him in expectation of miracles.

By 10:10, he was in bed with the lights out, lying on his side in blackness, staring at the window, where the palest light glistered softly in the frost that skinned the pane. The window looked out upon the courtyard, where no lights burned at this hour, so Brendan knew that he was seeing indirect moonglow refracted by the thin layer of ice that had welded itself to the glass. It had to be indirect light because the moon was traversing the sky on a course that had made it visible from the study windows earlier in the evening, and the study was on the other side of the rectory; the moon could not now be over the courtyard unless it had made a sudden ninety-degree turn in the path it had previously been following, which was not possible. As he patiently lay waiting for sleep, he became increasingly intrigued by the subtle patterns made by the second-hand moonbeams that had been trapped in the frost; light splintered at every point where one ice-crystal interfaced with another, each beam shattering into a hundred beams, a hundred more.

'The moon,' he whispered, surprised by his voice. 'The moon.'

Gradually, Brendan realised that something uncanny was happening.

At first he was merely fascinated by the harmonious interaction of frost and moonlight, but soon fascination evolved into a more intense attraction. He could not look away from the pearly window. It offered an indefinable promise, and he was drawn as a sailor by a siren's song. Before he knew what he intended, he had slipped one arm out from beneath the blankets and was reaching towards the window, though it was ten feet away and could not be touched from where he lay. The black silhouette of his spread-fingered hand was clearly defined against the niveous pane of glass that glowed softly beyond, and his futile straining was the essence of yearning. Brendan longed to be within the light, not the light that lived in the frost but that *other* golden light of his dreams.

'The moon,' he whispered, again surprised that he had spoken.

His heartbeat accelerated. He began to tremble.

Suddenly, upon the glass, the sugary-looking frost underwent an inexplicable change. As Brendan watched, the thin rime melted away from the edges of the pane, towards the centre. In a few seconds, when the melting stopped, there remained only a perfect circle of ice, about ten inches in diameter, glowing eerily in the middle of an otherwise clear, dry, dark rectangle of glass.

The moon.

Brendan knew it was a sign, though he did not know from whom or what or where it came, nor did he understand it.

On Christmas night, when he had stayed at his parents' house in Bridgeport, Brendan had apparently had a dream featuring the moon, for he had awakened his mother and father with his loud and panicky cries. But he could remember nothing of the dream. Since then, as far as he knew, none of his dreams had involved the moon, but were concerned exclusively with that mysterious place full of dazzling golden light, where he felt himself called towards some incredible revelation.

Now, as he still reached with one hand toward the glimmering frost on the window, the vaguely phosphorescent rime grew brighter, as if some peculiar chemical reaction was at work within the ice-crystals. The moon-image changed from a milky hue to the crisper white of sun-dappled snow, then grew even brighter, until it was a scintillant circle of silver blazing on the glass.

Heart pounding furiously, certain he was teetering on the edge of some astounding epiphany, Brendan continued to hold his hand towards the window, and he gasped in shock as a shaft of light leapt out from the frost-moon and fell across the bed. It was like the beam of a spotlight and every bit as brilliant. As he squinted into the glare, trying to see how such fierce incandescence could possibly originate from ordinary hoarfrost and glass, the light changed to pale red, to darker red, to crimson, to scarlet. Around him, the rumpled blankets shone like molten steel, and his outstretched hand appeared to be wet with blood.

He was gripped by *deja vu*, absolutely convinced that he had once really stood under a scarlet moon, bathed in its bloody glow.

Although he wanted to understand how this strange red light related to the wondrous golden light of his dreams, although he still felt himself being called by something unknown that waited in that radiance, he was suddenly afraid. As the scarlet beams intensified, as his room became a cauldron of heatless red fire and red shadows, his fear grew into terror of such power that it made him shake and sweat.

He pulled his hand back, and the scarlet light rapidly faded to silver, and the silver dimmed as well, until the circle of frost on the window shone with only a natural reflection of the January moon.

As darkness laid claim to his room once more, Brendan sat up and hastily switched on the lamp. Damp with sweat, as full of the nightshakes as any child frightened by fantasies of carnivorous goblins, he went to the window. The icy circle was still there, a moon-image in the centre of the otherwise unfrosted pane of glass.

He had wondered if the light had been but a dream or hallucination. In a way, he almost wished it had been only that. But the frost-moon was still there, proof that what he had seen was real, not a delusion.

Hesitantly he touched the glass. He felt nothing unusual. Just the bitter cold of winter pressing against the other side of the pane.

With a start, he realised that he felt the swollen rings in his palms. He turned his hands over and watched as the stigmata faded.

He returned to bed. For a long while he sat with his back against the headboard, with his eyes open and the light on, waiting for the courage to lie down in darkness.

*   *   *

Elko County, Nevada.

Ernie stood by the tub in the bathroom, trying to recall precisely what he had thought and felt in the early hours of Saturday, December 14, when he had been driven by some strange impulse to open the window and had suffered that frightening hallucination. The writer, Dominick Corvaisis, stood by the sink, and Faye watched from the doorway.

Reflections of the ceiling light and the light above the mirror imparted a warmth to the ceramic-tile floor, glimmered in the chrome faucets and shower rod, gave a bright flat sheen to the plastic shower curtain, and gradually illuminated the memories that Ernie sought.

'Light. I came in here for the light. My fear of the dark was at a peak then, and I was trying to hide it from Faye. Couldn't sleep, so I slipped out of bed, came here, closed the door, and just . . . just sort of *revelled* in the light.' He told how his gaze was drawn to the window above the tub and how he was overcome by an irrational and urgent need to escape. 'It's hard to explain. But suddenly crazy thoughts . . . *whirled* into my head. For some reason, I panicked. I thought "This is my one chance to escape, so I'd better take it, go through that window, head up into the hills . . . get to a ranch, get help."'

'Help for what?' Corvaisis asked. 'Why did you need help? Why did you feel you needed to escape from your own home?'

Ernie frowned. 'Don't have the foggiest notion.' He remembered the way he had felt that night – the eerieness, urgency strangely mixed with dreaminess. He pointed to the window. 'I actually slid back the bolt. Opened it. Might've crawled out,' too, except I saw someone outside. On the roof of the utility room.'

'Who?' Corvaisis asked.

'Sounds silly. It was a guy in motorcycle gear. White crash helmet. Dark visor over his face. Black gloves. In fact, he reached one hand through the window, as if making a grab for me, and I stepped backwards, fell over the edge of the tub.'

'That's when I came running,' Faye said.

'I got off the floor,' Ernie said, 'went back to the window, looked out on the roof. No one there. It'd been just . . . hallucination.'

Faye said, 'In extreme cases of phobia, when the sufferer is in almost constant anxiety, hallucinations sometimes occur.'

The writer stared at the opaque window above the tub, as if hoping to find some vital secret revealed in the uneven milky texture of the glass. At last he said, 'It wasn't exactly a hallucination. I have a hunch that what you saw, Ernie, was a . . . well, call it a memory-flash. From the summer before last. From the lost days. For a moment, back on December 14, your repressed memories surged towards the surface. You had a flashback to a time when you really *were* a prisoner in your own home, when you really did try to escape.'

'And I was stopped by that guy on the roof of the utility room? But what was he doing there in a motorcycle helmet? Strange, isn't it?'

Dom said, 'A man in a decontamination suit, sent to deal with a spill of chemicals of biological toxins, would wear an airtight helmet.'

'Decontamination,' Ernie said. 'But if they were actually here in suits like that, then there must've really been a spill.'

'Maybe,' Dom said. 'We still don't know enough to decide.'

Faye said, 'But listen, if we all went through this experience, like you think we did, then how come only you and Ernie and that Mr Lomack are suffering repercussions? How come *I'm* not having bad dreams and psychological problems?'

The writer's gaze drifted back to the window. 'I don't know. But those are some of the questions we've got to answer if we've any hope of relieving the subconscious anxiety that this experience left in us, if we've any hope of getting on with normal lives.'

*　　　*　　　*

Connecticut to New York City.

After the money had been removed from the armoured car, Jack and his men drove only nine miles and parked the two phoney Department of Highway vans in a four-stall rented garage leased with fake ID, where they had left their cars. The garage was one of a long row that faced both sides of a litter-strewn alley in a shabby neighbourhood, where relaxed zoning laws permitted intermingling of commercial and industrial facilities with residences. The area was characterised by peeling paint, grime, broken streetlamps, empty storefronts, and mean-looking mongrel dogs on the loose.

They emptied the contents of the canvas bags on the oily concrete floor of the garage and did a hasty count of the cash. They split it quickly into five shares of approximately $350,000 each, all in used bills that could never be traced.

Jack felt no triumph, no thrill. Nothing.

In five minutes, the gang had dispersed like dandelion fluff on a brisk wind. Clockwork.

As Jack headed home to Manhattan, spits of snow fell in brief squalls, though not enough to dust the highway or interfere with travel.

During the drive from Connecticut, in a strange mood, he underwent a change he could not have anticipated. Minute by minute and mile by mile, the greyness in him began at last to be coloured by emotion; his ennui gave way to feelings that surprised him. He would not have been surprised by a new welling-up of grief or loneliness, for Jenny had been dead only seventeen days. But the emotion that steadily tightened its grip on him was *guilt*. The stolen $350,000 in the trunk of the car began to weigh on his conscience as heavily as if it were the first ill-gotten money ever to fall into his hands.

Through eight busy years of meticulously planned and triumphantly executed larcenies, several on an even grander scale than the armoured car, he had never experienced the mildest quiver of guilt. Until now. He had seen himself as a just avenger. Until now.

Cruising to Manhattan through the blustery winter night, he had begun to see himself as little more than a common thief. Guilt wrapped him like fly-paper. He tried repeatedly to shake it off. It clung.

Sudden as it seemed, the guilt had actually been building for a long time; that was where his growing dissatisfaction had been leading for months. Disillusionment had set in noticeably with the jewellery-store job last October, and he'd thought the changes had begun then. But now, forced into self-analysis, he realised he had stopped getting a full measure of pleasure from his work long ago. As he scrolled backwards in his memory, seeking the most recent job that had left him fulfilled, he was startled to discover it was the McAllister burglary in Marin County, north of San Francisco, the summer before last.

Ordinarily, he worked only in the East near Jenny, but Branch Pollard – with whom he had pulled off the just-completed Guardmaster heist – had settled in California for a while, and during that Pacific sojourn he had spotted Avril McAllister, a sheep waiting to be sheared. McAllister, an industrialist worth two hundred million, lived on an eight-acre estate in Marin County, protected by stone walls, a complex electronic security system, and guard dogs. With information developed from a half-dozen sources, Branch had determined that McAllister was a collector of rare stamps and coins, two eminently fenceable commodities. Besides, the industrialist was a gambler who went to Vegas three times a year, usually dropping a quarter of a million each visit, but sometimes winning big; he always took his winnings in cash to avoid the taxman, and some of that cash was surely in the mansion. Branch needed Jack's sense of strategy and expertise in electronics, and Jack needed a change of scenery, so they pulled it off with the help of a third man.

After considerable planning, getting onto the estate and into the house went smoothly. They were prepared with an electronic listening device that could detect the soft tick of a safe's tumblers and amplify them, which made deducing the combinations mere child's play, but as insurance they also took a full set of safe-cracking tools *and* a plastic explosive. The problem was that Avril McAllister had no mere safe. He had a damn *vault*. The industrialist was so certain of the vault door's inviolability that he'd made no effort to conceal it with a sliding partition or tapestry; it was in one wall of the immense gameroom, a massive stainless-steel portal as big as anything in a first-class bank. The listening device Jack had brought was not sensitive enough to detect the movement of tumblers through twenty inches of stainless-steel. The plastic explosive would have peeled any safe, but the vault was blast-proof. The set of safe-cracker's tools was a joke.

They left the estate with no stamps or coins, but with sterling silver, a complete collection of Raymond Chandler and Dashiell Hammett first editions, a few jewels that Mrs McAllister carelessly left out of the vault, and a handful of other items, which they fenced for only sixty thousand dollars, split three ways. The take was by no means a pittance, but it was far less than anticipated, insufficient to cover their expenses and to make their time, planning and risks worthwhile.

In spite of this debacle, Jack had got a kick out of the job. Once they had safely fled the McAllister estate, he and Branch had seen the humour in the catastrophe and had been able to laugh about it. They spent two days relaxing in the California sun; then, on a whim, Jack took his twenty thousand to Reno to see if he could do better at craps and blackjack than he had done at burglary. Twenty-four hours after checking into Harrah's, he checked out, the twenty thousand having grown to an amazing $107,455. The exquisite symmetry of bad-luck money bringing good luck was enormously appealing. Deciding to extend his vacation, he rented a car and drove back to New York, all the way across the country, in a splendid mood, eager to see Jenny.

Now, more than eighteen months later, as he entered Manhattan on his return trip from Connecticut, Jack realised that, curiously, the fiasco at the McAllister estate had been the last enterprise to provide untainted satisfaction. At that point he had begun a long journey from dead-end amorality all the way across the moral spectrum until he had become, once more, capable of guilt.

But *why*? What had initiated the change in him? What conti
nued to power it? He had no answers.

All he knew was that he was no longer able to think o
himself as a melancholy and romantic bandit with a jus
mission to redress the wrongs done to him and to his beloved
wife. He was merely a thief. For eight years he had beer
deluding himself. Now he saw himself for what he really was
and the sudden insight was devastating.

He had not merely become a man without purpose. Worse
without realising it, he had been lacking a worthwhile purpose
for eight years.

He drove aimlessly through the streets of Manhattan, going
nowhere in particular, unwilling to return straightaway to the
apartment.

He soon found himself on Fifth Avenue, approaching S
Patrick's, and on impulse he pulled to the kerb, parked ille
gally before the main doors of the immense cathedral. He go
out of the car, went around to the trunk, opened it, and pulled
half a dozen banded stacks of twenty-dollar bills from the
plastic garbage bag.

It was foolhardy to leave the car illegally parked in so promi
nent a location when it's trunk contained more than a third of a
million dollars in stolen money, an illegally obtained device
like SLICKS, and guns. If a cop stopped to give him a ticke
and became suspicious and demanded to search the car, Jack
would be finished. But he had ceased to care. In some ways, he
was a dead man who still walked, just as Jenny had been
dead woman who still breathed.

Though not a Catholic, he pulled open one of the sculpted
bronze doors of St Patrick's, went inside, into the nave, where
a handful of people knelt in the front pews, praying or saying
the rosary, and where an old man was lighting a votive candle
even at this hour. Jack stood for a moment looking up at the
elegant baldachin above the main altar. Then he located the
poor-boxes, removed the bundles of twenty-dollar bills from
inside his winter jacket, broke the paper bands that bound
them, and stuffed the money into the containers as if he were
jamming garbage into trash receptacles.

Outside again, as he was descending the granite steps, he
stopped abruptly and blinked at the night-draped cityscape

for something was different about Fifth Avenue. As a few huge snowflakes spiralled lazily through the glow of street-lamps and through the lights of cars moving along the thoroughfare, Jack gradually realised that the city had re-acquired a fraction of the glitter, glamour, and mystery it always had for him before he'd gone to Central America but which it had not possessed in ages. It seemed *cleaner* now than it had been in a long time, and the air was crisper, less polluted.

Staring around in amazement, he slowly understood that the city had not undergone a metamorphosis during the past few minutes. It was the same city that it had been an hour ago – and yesterday. But when he had come back from Central America, he had been a different man from the one who had gone away, and on returning he had been unable to see anything good in the metropolis or in any other works of the society he hated. Much of the Big Apple's dreariness and degeneration had been merely a reflection of his own blasted, burnt-out, corrupted inner landscape.

Jack returned to the Camaro, went west to the Avenue of the Americas, north to Central Park, made a right turn, then another right onto Fifth Avenue again, heading south, not sure where he was going until he reached the Fifth Avenue Presbyterian Church. Once more, he parked ille-gally, took cash from the trunk, and went into the church.

There was no poor-box as in St Patrick's, but Jack found a young assistant minister in the process of closing the place for the night. From various pockets, Jack produced bundles of ten- and twenty-dollar bills wrapped with rubber bands, and handed them to the startled cleric, claiming to have won a fortune in the casinos of Atlantic City.

In two stops, he had given away thirty thousand dollars. But that was not even one-tenth of what he had brought back from Connecticut, and these dispensations did not allay his guilt. In fact, his newfound shame was growing stronger by the minute. The bag of money in the trunk was, to him, like the tell-tale heart buried under the floor-boards in the story by Poe, a throbbing annunciator of his guilt, and he was as anxious to be rid of it as Poe's narrator had been anxious to silence the incriminating heartbeat of his dismembered victim.

$330,000 remained. For some New Yorkers, Christmas was about to come two and a half weeks late.

*   *   *

Elko County, Nevada.

The summer before last, Dom had stayed in Room 20. He remembered it well because it was the last unit in the motel's L-shaped east wing.

Ernie Block's curiosity was more compelling than his nyctophobia so he decided to accompany Faye and Dom to Room 20, where it was hoped that Dom's memories would be stirred by the sight of the familiar walls and furnishings. Ernie walked between Faye and Dom, who held his arms. During the trip along the breezeway, the frigid night wind made Dom glad of his fleece-lined jacket. More concerned about the black night than the chill, Ernie kept his eyes shut for the entire journey.

Faye went in first, snapping on the lights, closing drapes. Dom followed with Ernie, who opened his eyes only when Faye shut the door.

Upon entering the room, Dom was filled with apprehension. He walked to the queen-size bed, stared down at it. He tried to remember lying here, drugged and helpless.

Faye said, 'The bedspread's not the same, of course.'

The Polaroid had shown the corner of a floral-patterned spread. The current model was brown- and blue-striped.

'The bed itself is the same, and all the furniture,' Ernie said.

The padded headboard was upholstered with a coarse brown fabric, slightly snagged and worn. The nightstands with plain two-drawer chests with laminated walnut veneer. The bases of the lamps resembled large hurricane lanterns, black metal with two panes of smokey amber glass in each side; the cloth shades were the same amber hue as the glass in the base. Each lamp had two bulbs: the main one, under the shade, provided most of the light; the second bulb, inside the base, was shaped like a candle flame and gave off a dim flickering glow that imitated a real flame and was used only for its decorative effect, to enhance the illusion of hurricane lanterns.

380

Dom remembered every detail of the place now that he was standing in it, and he had the impression that a multitude of ghosts flitted teasingly through the room, staying just at the periphery of his vision. The ghosts were actually bad memories rather than spirits, and they haunted not the room but the shadowy corners of his own mind.

'Remember anything?' Ernie asked. 'Is it coming back to you?'

'I want to have a look at the john,' Dom said.

It was small and strictly functional, with a shower stall but no bathtub, a speckled tile floor, and durable Formica counter tops.

Dom was interested in the sink, for it was surely the one in his recurring nightmare. But when he looked into the bowl, he was surprised to see a mechanical stopper. And an inch below the rim of the bowl, the overflow drain consisted of three round holes, a more modern design than the six slanted lozenge-shaped outlets in the sink of his dreams.

'This isn't the same,' he said. 'The sink was old, with a rubber stopper attached to a bead-chain and hung from the cold-water faucet.'

'We're always upgrading the place,' Ernie said from the doorway.

'We took that out eight or nine months ago,' Faye said. 'We replaced the Formica then, too, although it's the same colour as before.'

Dom was disappointed because he had been convinced that at least some memories from those lost days would begin to return to him when he touched the sink. After all, judging from the stark terror of the nightmare, something particularly frightening had happened to him at that very spot; therefore, it seemed likely that the sink might act as a lightning rod upon the supercharged memories that drifted in the darkness of his subconscious, drawing them back in a sudden crackling blaze of recollection. He put his hands on the new sink, but he felt only cold porcelain.

'Anything?' Ernie asked again.

'No,' Dom said. 'No memories . . . but bad vibrations. If I give it time, I think the room might break down the

381

barriers. I'll sleep here tonight, give it a chance to work on me . . . if that's all right.'

'No problem,' Faye said. 'The room's yours.'

Dom said, 'I have a hunch the nightmare will be worse here than it's ever been before.'

*   *   *

Laguna Beach, California.

Although Parker Faine was one of the most respected of living American artists, although his canvasses were assiduously collected by major museums, although he had been commissioned to create works for the President of the United States and other luminaries, he was not too old and certainly not too dignified to get a thrill from the intrigue upon which he was engaged on Dominick Corvaisis' behalf. To be a successful artist, one needed maturity, an adult's perception and sensitivity and dedication to craftsmanship, but one also had to hold on to a child's curiosity, wonder, innocence, and sense of fun. Parker held tighter to those things than most artists did; therefore, he fulfilled his role in Dom's plans with a spirit of adventure.

Each day, when he picked up Dom's mail, Parker pretended to go about his business without the slightest suspicion that he might be under surveillance, but in fact he searched surreptitiously, diligently for the watchers – spies, cops, or whoever they might be. He never saw anyone observing him, and he never detected a tail.

And each night, when he left his house and went to a different pay phone to await Dom's pre-arranged call, he drove miles out of his way, turned back on his own route, made sudden turns calculated to throw off a tail, until he was sure that he was not being followed.

A few minutes before nine o'clock, Saturday night, he arrived by his usual devious means at a telephone booth beside a Union 76 station. A hard rain fell, sluicing down the Plexiglas walls, distorting the world beyond and screening Parker from prying eyes.

He was wearing a trenchcoat and a rain-proof khaki hat with the rim turned down all the way around to let the rain run off. He felt as if he belonged in a John Le Carré tale. He loved it.

382

Promptly at nine o'clock, the phone rang. It was Dom. 'I'm on schedule, at the Tranquillity Motel. This is the place, Parker.'

Dom had a lot to tell: a disturbing experience in the Tranquillity Grille; Ernie Block's nyctophobia. . . . And by indirection, he managed to convey that the Blocks had received strange Polaroid snapshots, too.

Discretion was essential; if the Tranquillity Motel was, indeed, the centre of the unremembered events of the summer before last, the Blocks' phones might be tapped. If the listeners heard about the photographs, they would know they had a traitor in their midst, and they would surely find him, and there would be no more notes or photos forthcoming.

'I've got news, too,' Parker said. 'Ms Wycombe, your editor, left a message on your answering machine. *Twilight in Babylon* had another printing, and there're now a hundred thousand copies in the stores.'

'Good God, I'd forgotten the book! Since Lomack's house four days ago, I haven't thought about anything but this crazy situation.'

'Ms Wycombe has more good news she wants to share, so you're to call her as soon as you get a chance.'

'I'll do that. Meanwhile . . . seen any interesting pictures?' Dom asked, indirectly inquiring if any more Polaroids had been received.

'Nope. No amusing notes, either.' When the headlights of passing cars swept across the booth, the thin skin of flowing water on the transparent walls flared briefly with a rippling-shimmering brilliance. Parker said, 'But something came in the mail that'll knock your socks off, buddy. You've identified three of the names on those moon posters at Lomack's. So how'd you like to hear who the fourth one is?'

'Ginger? I forgot to tell you. I think her name's on the motel registry. Dr Ginger Weiss of Boston. I intend to call her tomorrow.'

'You've stolen some of my thunder. But you'll be surprised to hear you got a letter today from Dr Weiss. She sent it to Random House on December 26, but it got caught in their bureaucracy. Anyway, she's at the end of her rope, see, and then she gets hold of a copy of your book, gloms your photo, and she gets this feeling she's met you before, and that *you* are a part of what's been happening to her.'

'Do you have the letter with you?' Dom asked excitedly.

Parker had it in his hand, waiting. He read it, glancing now and then at the night beyond the booth.

'I've got to call her right away,' Dom said when Parker finished the letter. 'Can't wait till morning now. I'll talk to you again tomorrow night. Nine o'clock.'

'If you'll be calling from the motel, where the phones are likely to be tapped, there's no point in my running out to a phone booth.'

'You're right. I'll call you at home. Take care,' Dom said.

'You too.' With mixed feelings, Parker put the receiver on the hook, relieved that these inconvenient nightly journeys to a pay phone were at an end, but also certain that he would miss the intrigue.

He stepped out of the phone booth, into the rain, and he was almost disappointed when no one took a shot at him.

* * *

Boston, Massachusetts.

Pablo Jackson had been buried that morning, but he was with Ginger Weiss throughout the afternoon and evening. Like a ghost, his memory haunted her, a smiling revenant in the chambers of her mind.

Keeping to herself in the guestroom at Baywatch, she tried to read, could not concentrate. When not preoccupied with memories of the old magician, she was eaten up by worry, wondering what would become of her.

She got into bed at a quarter past midnight and was reaching for the switch to turn off the lamp when Rita Hannaby came to tell her that Dominick Corvaisis was on the phone and that she could take the call in George's study, down the hall, adjacent to the master bedroom. Excited and trepidatious, Ginger put on a robe over her pyjamas.

The study was warm and shadowy with dark oak panelling. The Chinese carpet was beige and forest-green, and the stained-glass lamp on the desk was either a genuine Tiffany or a superb reproduction.

George's puffy eyes made it clear that the call woke him. He

384

began surgery early most mornings and was usually in bed by nine-thirty.

'I'm sorry,' Ginger told him.

'No need,' George said. 'Isn't this what we've been hoping for?'

'Maybe,' she said, unwilling to raise her hopes.

Rita said, 'We'll give you privacy.'

'No,' Ginger said. 'Stay. Please.' She went to the desk, sat down, picked up the uncradled handset. 'Hello? Mr Corvaisis?'

'Dr Weiss?' His voice was strong yet melodic. 'Writing to me was the best thing you could've done. I don't think you're nuts. Because you're not alone, Doctor. There are more of us with strange problems.'

Ginger tried to respond, but her voice cracked. She cleared her throat. 'I . . . I'm sorry . . . I'm not . . . I don't . . . don't usually cry.'

Corvaisis said, 'Don't try to talk until you're ready. I'll tell you about *my* problem: sleepwalking. And my dreams . . . about the moon.'

A thrill, half cold fear and half exultation, throbbed through her. 'The moon,' she agreed. 'I never remember the dreams, but they must involve the moon because that's what I wake up screaming about.'

He told her about a man named Lomack in Reno, dead by his own hand, driven to suicide by an obsession with the moon.

Ginger sensed some vast gulf beneath her, a fearful unknown.

'We've been brainwashed,' she blurted. 'All these problems we're having are the result of repressed memories trying to surface.'

For a moment there was a stunned silence on the line. Then the writer said, 'That's been my theory, but you sound sure of it.'

'I am. I underwent hypnotic regression therapy after I wrote to you, and we turned up evidence of systematic memory repression.'

'Something happened to us the summer before last,' he said.

'Yes! The summer before last. The Tranquillity Motel in Nevada.'

'That's where I'm calling from.'

Startled, she said, 'You're there *now*?'

'Yes. And if possible, you ought to come. A lot has happened that I can't risk talking about on the phone.'

'Who *are* they?' she asked in frustration. 'What are they hiding?'

'We'll have a better chance finding out if we all work together.'

'I'll come. Tomorrow, if I can book a flight that quickly.'

Rita started to protest that Ginger was in no condition to travel. In the many-coloured light of the Tiffany lamp, George's scowl deepened.

To Corvaisis, Ginger said, 'I'll call you later to let you know how and when I'll arrive.' When Ginger hung up, George said, 'You can't possibly go all that way in your condition.'

Rita said, 'What if you blackout on the aeroplane, become violent?'

'I'll be all right.'

'Dear, you had *three* seizures last Monday, one after the other.'

Ginger sighed and slumped back in the green leather chair, 'Rita, George, you've been wonderful to me, and I can never adequately repay you. I love you, I really do. But I've been living with you for five weeks, five helpless weeks during which I've been more like a dependent child than an adult, and I'm just not capable of going on that way. I've got to go to Nevada. I've no other option. I've got to.'

* * *

New York, New York.

A couple of blocks farther down Fifth Avenue from the Presbyterian Church, Jack stopped again, in front of St Thomas's Episcopal Church. In the nave, he stared in fascination at the huge reredos of Dunville stone behind the altar. He met the strangely portentous gazes of the statues in the shadowy niches along the walls – Saints, Apostles, the Blessed Virgin, Christ – and he realised that the primary purpose of religion was the expiation of guilt, to provide people with

386

forgiveness for being less than they were meant to be. The human species seemed incapable of living up to its potential, and some would be driven mad by guilt if they did not believe that a god – be it Jesus, Yahweh, Mohammed, Marx, or some other – looked on them with favour in spite of themselves. But Jack found no comfort in St Thomas's, no expiation of his sins, not even when he left twenty thousand dollars in the charity box.

In the Camaro again, he set out to dispose of the rest of the cash from the Guardmaster heist, not because giving it away would salve his guilt; it would not, for redistribution of the funds was not the moral equivalent of repayment. He had too much to atone for to expect to shrive himself of all his transgressions in one night. But he did not need or want the money any more, could not simply throw it in the trash, so giving the damn stuff away was his only possible course of action.

He stopped at more churches and temples. Some were open, some locked. Where he could gain entrance, he left money.

He drove down to the Bowery and left forty thousand dollars with the startled night attendant at the Salvation Army Mission.

On Bayard Street in nearby Chinatown, Jack saw a sign in a second-floor window that proclaimed, in both Chinese characters and in English: THE ALLIANCE AGAINST OPPRESSION OF CHINESE MINORITIES. The place was above a quaint apothecary that specialised in the herbs and powdered roots of traditional Chinese medicines. The apothecary was closed, but a light shone in a window of The Alliance offices. Jack rang the bell at the street-level door, rang it and rang it until an elderly and wizened Chinese man came down the stairs and spoke to him through a small grille. When Jack ascertained that The Alliance's current major project was the rescue of brutalised Chinese families from Vietnam (and resettlement in the States), he passed twenty thousand in cash through the grille. The Chinese gentleman reverted to his native language in surprise and came out into the cold winter wind, insistent upon shaking hands. 'Friend,' the elderly mandarin said. 'You can't know what suffering this gift will relieve.' Jack echoed the old man, 'Friend.' In that single word, and in the warm grasp of the venerable oriental's calloused hand, Jack found something he thought he had lost forever: a sense of belonging, a feeling of community, fellowship.

In his car again, he drove up Bayard to Mott Street, turned right, and had to pull to the kerb. A flood of tears blurred his vision.

He could not remember ever having been more confused than he was now. He wept in part because the stain of guilt, for the moment at least, seemed an ineradicable mark upon his soul. Yet some of the tears were tears of joy, for he was abruptly brimming over with brotherhood. For the better part of a decade, he had been outside society, distanced in mind and spirit if not in body. But now, for the first time since Central America, Jack Twist had the need, desire, *and* ability to reach out to the society around him, to make friends.

Bitterness was a dead-end. Hatred hurt no one more than he who harboured it. The wine of alienation was loneliness.

During the past eight years, he had often wept for Jenny, and he had sometimes wept in fits of self-pity. But *these* tears were different from all others he had let previously, for they were cleansing tears, purging tears, washing all the rage and resentment out of him.

He still did not understand the cause of these radical and rapid changes taking place in him. However, he sensed that his evolution – from outcast and criminal to law-abiding citizen – was not finished and would generate several more surprises before it reached a conclusion. He wondered where he was bound and by what route he would arrive there.

That night in Chinatown, hope swept back into his world like a summer breeze stirring music from a cluster of windchimes.

*   *   *

Elko County, Nevada.

Ned and Sandy Sarver were able to run the diner by themselves because they were hard workers by nature, but also because their menu was simple and because Ned had learned efficient food service as a cook in the US Army. A hundred tricks were employed to make the Tranquillity Grille function smoothly with as little effort as possible.

Nevertheless, at the end of work, Ned was always glad that Ernie and Faye provided the motel's guests with a free continental breakfast in their rooms, so it was not necessary to open the diner before noon.

Saturday evening, while he grilled hamburgers and made french fries and served chili-dogs, Ned Sarver glanced frequently at Sandy as she worked. He still could not get used to the change in her, the sudden flowering. She had added ten pounds, and her figure had acquired an appealing female roundness it never possessed before. And she no longer shuffled slump-shouldered through the diner, but moved with a fluid grace and a jaunty good humour that Ned found enormously appealing.

He was not the only man who had eyes for the new Sandy. Some of the truckers watched the roll of her hips and the flex of her buttocks as she crossed the room with plates of food or bottles of cold beer.

Until recently, although Sandy had been unfailingly polite to the customers, she had not been chatty. That changed, too. She was still somewhat shy, but she responded to the truckers' teasing and even teased them in return, and came up with some damn good quips.

For the first time in eight years of marriage, Ned Sarver feared losing Sandy. He knew she loved him, and he told himself that these changes in her appearance and personality would not also change the nature of their relationship. But that was precisely what he feared.

This morning, when Sandy went to Elko to meet Ernie and Faye at the airport, Ned had worried that she would not come back. Maybe she would just keep going until she found a place she liked better than Nevada, until she met a man who was handsomer, richer, and smarter than Ned. He knew that he was being unfair to Sandy by harbouring such suspicions, that she was incapable of infidelity or cruelty. Maybe his fear lay in the fact that he'd always thought Sandy deserved better than him.

At nine-thirty, when the dinner crowd thinned to seven customers, Faye and Ernie came into the Grille with that dark, good-looking guy who had caused a scene earlier in the evening when he had wandered through the door as if in a

389

dream and then had turned and run out as though hell hounds were at his heels. Ned wondered who the guy was, how he knew Faye and Ernie, and whether *they* knew their friend was a little weird.

Ernie looked pale and shaky, and to Ned it seemed as if his boss was taking considerable care to keep his back to the windows. When he raised a hand in greeting to Ned, there was a visible tremor in it.

Faye and the stranger sat facing each other across the table, and from the looks they gave Ernie, you could see they were concerned about him. They didn't look so good themselves.

Something peculiar was going on. Intrigued by Ernie's condition, Ned was briefly distracted from thoughts of Sandy leaving him.

But when Sandy stopped at their table, she was so long taking their order that Ned's concern rose again. From his post behind the counter, with a hamburger and a pair of eggs sizzling noisily on the griddle, he could not hear what they were saying over there, but he had the crazy notion that the stranger was taking undue interest in Sandy and that she was responding to his slick patter. Jealous nonsense, of course. Yet the guy was handsome, and he was younger than Ned, closer Sandy's age, and apparently successful, just the kind of guy she *ought* to run off with because he would be better for her than Ned could ever be.

In his own view, Ned Sarver was not much to brag about. He was not ugly, but certainly not handsome. His brown hair had receded from his forehead in a deep widow's peak; unless you were Jack Nicholson, such a hairline was not sexy. He had pale-grey eyes that perhaps had been startling and magnetic when he was a young man, but with the passing years, they merely made him appear tired and washed-out. He was neither rich nor destined to be rich. And at forty-two, ten years older than Sandy, Ned Sarver was not likely to be gripped suddenly by the driving need to make something of himself.

All of this dismaying self-criticism roiled through his mind as he watched Sandy finally leave the stranger's table and come to the counter. With an odd and troubled expression, she handed the order-slip to him and said, 'What time we closing? Ten or ten-thirty?'

'Ten.' Indicating the few customers, Ned added: 'No profit hanging around tonight.'

She nodded and went back to Faye, Ernie – and the stranger.

Her brusqueness and her speedy return to the stranger aggravated Ned's worries. As far as he could see, he had only three qualities that gave Sandy any reason to stay with him. First, he could always make a decent living as a short-order cook because he was good. Second, he had a talent for fixing things, both inanimate objects and living creatures. If a toaster, blender, or radio went on the blink, Ned set to work with a tool kit and soon had the appliance back in operation. Likewise, if he found a panicky bird with a broken wing he stroked it until it grew calm, took it home, nursed it back to health, then sent it on its way. Having the talent to fix things seemed important, and Ned was proud of it. Third, he loved Sandy with all his body, mind, and heart.

Preparing the order for Faye, Ernie, and the stranger, Ned glanced repeatedly at Sandy, and he was surprised when she and Faye started moving around the room, lowering the Levolor blinds over the windows.

Something unusual was going on. Returning to Ernie's table, Sandy leaned forward in earnest conversation with the good-looking stranger.

It was ironic that he was worried about losing Sandy, for it had been his talent for fixing things that contributed to her transformation from duckling to swan. When Ned first met her at a diner in Tucson, where they worked, Sandy was not just bashful and self-conscious but painfully shy, fearful. She was a hard worker, always willing to lend a hand to other waitresses when they got behind in their orders, but she was incapable of interacting with anyone on a personal level. A pale, scuttling girl (twenty-three but still more girl than woman), she was reluctant to open the door on friendship, for fear she would put her trust in someone who might hurt her. She had been drab, mousy, meek, beaten by life – and the instant Ned had seen her, he had felt the need to *fix* things for her. With enormous patience, he began work on her, so subtly that, at first, she was not aware that he was interested in her.

They were married nine months later, although his repair-work on her was far from finished. She was more badly broken than any creature he'd encountered before, and there were times when, in frustration, he felt that, even with his talent, he would be unable to fix her and would spend the rest of his life tinkering endlessly without much effect.

During their first six years of marriage, however, he *had* witnessed a slow healing in her, maddeningly gradual. Sandy had an indisputably bright mind, but she was retarded emotionally; she learned to take and give affection only with tremendous effort, much as a dim-witted child struggles mightily to learn to count to ten.

The first indication Ned had had that *major* changes were taking place in Sandy was the sudden marked improvement in her sexual appetite. The turn-around had come in late August, two summers ago.

She'd never been a hesitant lover. She exhibited extensive carnal knowledge, but she made love more like a machine than a woman, with a joyless expertise. He had never known a woman as silent in bed as Sandy had been. He suspected something in her childhood had stunted her, the same thing that had broken her spirit. He tried to get her to talk about it, but she was adamant about letting the past stay buried, and his persistence was the one thing that might have caused her to leave him; so he asked about it no more, though it was difficult to fix something when you could not get at the part of it that was broken.

Then, in August of the summer before last, she came to the conjugal bed with a noticeably different attitude. Nothing dramatic at first. No sudden release of long-imprisoned passions. Initially, the change involved only a subtle new relaxation during the act of love. Sometimes she smiled or murmured his name as he made love to her.

Slowly, slowly, she blossomed. By that Christmas, four months after the change began, she no longer lay upon the bed as if she were made of metal. She strove to find and match his rhythm, searching for the fulfilment that still eluded her.

Slowly, slowly, she freed the erotic power chained within her. Finally, on April 7, last year, a night Ned would never forget, Sandy had an orgasm for the first time. It was a climax of such power that for a moment it frightened Ned. Afterwards, she wept with happiness and clung to him with such gratitude, love, and trust that he wept as well.

He thought her orgasmic breakthrough would finally enable her to speak of the source of her long-hidden pain. But when he cautiously inquired, she rebuffed him: 'The past is past, Ned. Won't help to dwell on it. If I talk about it . . . that might just give it a new hold on me.'

Through last spring, summer, and early autumn, Sandy gradually achieved satisfaction more often until, by September, their love-making nearly always brought her fulfilment. And by Christmas Day, less than three weeks ago, it was clear that her sexual maturation was not the only change in her but was accompanied by a new pride and self-respect.

Concomitant with her sexual development, Sandy learned to enjoy driving, an activity she had once found even less pleasurable than sex. Initially, she expressed the modest intention of driving to work from their trailer out near Beowawe. Before long she was lighting out in the truck on solo spins. Sometimes Ned stood at a window and watched his uncaged bird soar off, and he viewed each flight with delight but also with an uneasiness he could not explain.

By New Year's Day, just past, the uneasiness became dread and was with him twenty-four hours a day, and by then he understood it. He was afraid Sandy would fly away from him.

Maybe with the stranger who'd come in with Ernie and Faye.

I'm probably over-reacting, Ned thought as he put three hamburger patties on the griddle. Fact is, I know damn well I'm over-reacting.

But he worried.

By the time Ned prepared cheeseburgers with all the fixings for the Blocks and their friend, the other customers were gone. As Sandy served the loaded plates, Faye locked the door and switched on the CLOSED sign that was visible from I-80, though it was shy of ten o'clock.

Ned joined them for a closer look at the stranger, and to insinuate himself between the guy and Sandy. When he got to their table, he was surprised to see that Sandy had a bottle of beer and had opened one for him, too. He did not drink much; Sandy drank less.

'You'll need it when you hear what they have to tell us,' Sandy said. 'In fact, you might even need a couple more bottles.'

The guy's name was Dominick Corvaisis, and he had an amazing tale that drove all worries of infidelity from Ned's mind. When Corvaisis was finished, Ernie and Faye had an incredible story of their own, and that was when Ned first learned about the ex-Marine's fear of the dark.

'But I remember we were evacuated,' Ned said, 'We couldn't have been here at the motel those three days, 'cause I remember we had a sort of mini-vacation at home – watching TV, reading Louis L'Amour.'

'I believe that's what you were *told* to remember,' Corvaisis said. 'Did anyone visit you at the trailer during that time? Any neighbours drop by. Anyone who could confirm that you were actually there?'

'We're outside Beowawe, where we don't really have neighbours. Far as I remember, we didn't see anybody who could swear we was there.'

Sandy said, 'Ned, they wondered if anything strange has been happening to either of us.'

Ned met his wife's eyes. Without words, he let her know it was up to her whether she told them about the changes she had been undergoing.

Corvaisis said, 'The two of you were here the night it happened. Whatever it was, it started while I was having dinner. So you must have been a part of it. But the memory was stolen from you.'

The thought of strangers messing with his mind gave Ned the creeps. Uneasy, he studied the five Polaroid snapshots that Faye had fanned out on the table, especially the picture of Corvaisis staring empty-eyed.

To Sandy, Faye said, 'Honey, Ernie and I would have to've been blind not to've noticed the changes in you recently. I don't mean to embarrass you, and I don't want to pry, but if those changes might be related to whatever happened to us, then we ought to know about it.'

Sandy reached for Ned's hand, held it. Her love for him was so evident that he was ashamed of himself for the ridiculous thoughts of betrayal that had preoccupied him earlier.

Staring intently at her beer, she said, 'Most all my life, I've had the lowest opinion of myself. I'll tell you why, because you've got to know how bad it was for me when I was a kid if you want to understand how miraculous it is that I ever found any self-respect. It was Ned who first lifted me up, believed in me, gave me a chance to be somebody.' Her hand tightened on his. 'Almost nine years ago, he started courting me, and he was the first person ever treated me like a lady. He married me knowing that inside I was tied up in tangled knots, and he's spent eight years doing his best to untie and untangle them. He thinks I don't know how hard he's tried to help me, but I know all right.'

Her voice cracked with emotion. She paused for a swallow of beer.

Ned was unable to speak.

Sandy said, 'The thing is . . . I want everyone to know that maybe what happened the summer before last, the thing none of us remembers . . . maybe it *did* have a powerful effect on me. But if Ned hadn't taken me under his wing all those years ago, I never would've had a chance.'

Love enwrapped Ned as if it were bands of iron, closing his throat, constricting his chest, applying a pleasant pressure to his heart.

She glanced at him, returned her gaze to the bottle of beer, and recounted a childhood in hell. She did not describe her father's violations of her in explicit detail, and she spoke demurely – almost primly – of her periodic exploitation as a child prostitute under the management of a Vegas pimp. Her account of this monstrous abuse was all the more shocking and moving because she related it without drama. Everyone at the table listened in a silence resulting not merely from shock but from respect for her suffering and from a certain reverence for her ultimate triumph.

When Sandy finished, Ned embraced her, held her close. He was amazed by her strength. He had always known she was special, and the things she told them tonight only strengthened his love and admiration.

Though he was deeply saddened by what had been done to Sandy, he was delighted that she was at last able to talk about it. Surely this meant that the past had lost its hold on her.

Faye and Ernie commiserated with her in the awkward manner of friends who want to help but who know they can offer only words.

Everyone needed another beer. Ned got five bottles of Dos Equis out of the cooler and brought them to the table.

Corvaisis, who no longer seemed like the enemy to Ned, shook his head and blinked as if Sandy's story had left him in a daze of horror. 'This turns things upside down. I mean, if our unremembered experience had one basic effect on the rest of us, it was *terror*. Oh, I benefited because I was brought out of my shell; I share that with Sandy. But Ernie, Dr Weiss, Lomack, and me . . . we were for the most part left with a residue of fear. Now Sandy tells us the effect on her was strictly beneficial, not frightening in the least. How could it affect us so differently? You really have no fear, Sandy?'

'None,' Sandy said.

Ever since Ernie pulled a chair up to the table, he'd been sitting with his shoulders hunched and his head lowered, as if protecting his neck from attack. Now, with one hand clamped around a bottle of Dos Equis, he leaned back and relaxed, though not much. 'Yeah, fear's the core of it. But you remember that place along the interstate I told you about, little more than a quarter-mile from here? I'm sure something weird happened there, something that relates to the brainwashing. But when I'm standing at that place, I feel more than just fear. My heart starts to race . . . and I get excited . . . but it's not entirely a *bad* excitement. Fear's a part of it, yeah, maybe the biggest part of it, but there's a stew of other emotions, as well.'

Sandy said, 'I think the place Ernie's talking about is where I often wind up when I take the truck out for a ride. I'm . . . *drawn* there.'

Ernie leaned forward, excited. 'I knew it! Coming back from the airport this morning, as we were passing that place, you let the truck slow way down. And I said to myself, "Sandy feels it, too."'

Faye said, 'Sandy, what exactly do *you* feel when you're drawn to that piece of ground?'

With a smile so warm that Ned could almost feel the heat of it, Sandy said, 'Peace. I feel at peace there. It's hard to explain . . . but it's as if the rocks, dirt, and trees all radiate harmony, tranquillity.'

'I don't feel peaceful there,' Ernie said. 'Fear, yes. A queer excitement. An eerie sense that something . . . shattering will happen. Something that I'm eager for, even though it scares the hell out of me.'

'And I feel none of what you feel,' Sandy said.

'We ought to go there,' Ned suggested. 'See if the place affects the rest of us.'

'In the morning,' Corvaisis said. 'When it's light.'

Faye said, 'I can see this might've had a different effect on each of us. But why has it changed Dom's and Sandy's and Ernie's lives – and the lives of that Mr Lomack in Reno and Dr Weiss in Boston – yet done nothing to Ned and me. Why aren't we having problems, too?'

Dom said, 'Maybe the brainwashers did a better job on you and Ned.'

That thought gave Ned the heebie-jeebies again.

For a while they discussed their situation, and then Ned suggested that Corvaisis try to recreate his actions on that Friday night, July 6, up to the point where his memories were erased. 'You recollect the early part of the evening better than we do. And when you came in the first time tonight, you were close to remembering something important.'

'Close,' Corvaisis agreed, 'but at the last moment, when I felt the memory within grasp, it scared the crap out of me . . . and the next thing I knew, I was running for the door. Made quite a spectacle of myself. I was totally freaked out. It was such a visceral thing, instinctual, so utterly uncontrollable, that I think it would probably happen again if I made a second attempt to force the memories.'

'Still, it's worth a try,' Ned said.

'And you've got us for moral support this time,' Faye said.

Corvaisis needed coaxing, which Ned interpreted as meaning that the experience earlier this evening had been considerably more unnerving than words could express. But at last the writer got up and, carrying his glass of beer, went to the front door of the diner. He stood with his back to the exit, chugged a long swallow of Dos Equis. He looked around the room, trying hard to see the people of that other time.

He said, 'There were three or four men sitting at the counter. Maybe a dozen customers altogether. I can't remember their faces.' Moving away from the door, he walked past

Ned and the others, to the next table, where he pulled out a chair and sat with his back turned partly toward them. 'This is where I sat. Sandy waited on me. I took a bottle of Coors while I looked at the menu. Ordered the ham-and-egg sandwich. French fries, coleslaw. As I was salting the fries, the shaker slipped out of my hand. Salt spilled on the table. I threw a pinch over my shoulder. Silly gesture. Threw it too hard. Dr Weiss! Ginger Weiss was the woman I threw the salt on. I didn't remember that before, but I can see her clearly now. The blonde in the photo.'

Faye tapped the Polaroid snapshot of Dr Weiss that was on the table in front of Ned.

Still sitting alone at the other table, Corvaisis said, 'Quite a beautiful woman. Pixie-cute yet also sophisticated-looking, a really interesting mix. Could hardly take my eyes off her.'

Ned looked more closely at the photo of Ginger Weiss. He supposed she might, indeed, be unusually attractive when her face was not so pale and slack, when her eyes were not so cold, empty, dead.

In a voice that had grown odd, as if he were actually speaking to them from out of the past, Corvaisis said, 'She sits in the corner booth by the window, facing this way. Sunset is near. The sun's out there on the horizon, balanced like a big red ball, and the diner's filled with orange light slanting in through the windows. Almost like firelight. Ginger Weiss looks especially lovely in that light. I can hardly keep from staring openly at her. . . . Twilight now. I've got a second beer.' He sipped some Dos Equis. When he continued, his voice was softer: 'The plains are all purple . . . then black . . . night. . . .'

Like Ernie and Faye and Sandy, Ned was spellbound by the writer's struggle to remember, for it stirred in him, at last, faint and shapeless – but compelling – memories of his own. He began to recall that particular evening out of the many he'd spent in the Tranquillity Grille. The young priest had been here, the one in the Polaroid snapshot now lying on the table. And the young couple with their little girl.

'Not long after nightfall . . . nursing my second beer mainly so I can stare at Ginger Weiss a little longer.' Corvaisis looked left, right, raised his right hand to his ear. 'An unusual sound of some kind. I remember that much. A distant rumble . . . getting louder.' He was silent for a while. 'Can't remember what happened next. Something . . . something . . . but it just won't come.'

As the writer spoke of the rumbling, Ned Sarver experienced the vaguest possible memory of that frightening, swelling sound, but he could not clearly call it to mind. He felt as if Corvaisis had brought him to the edge of a dark chasm into which he was desperately afraid to look but into which he *must* look, and now they were turning away without shining a light down in those black depths. Heart racing, he said, 'Concentrate on remembering the sound, the *exact* sound, and maybe that'll bring the rest of it back to you.'

Corvaisis pushed his chair back from the table, got up. 'Rumbling . . . like thunder, very distant thunder . . . but growing closer.' He stood beside the table, seeking the direction from which the sound had come, looking left, right, up, down at the floor.

Suddenly Ned heard the noise, not in memory but in reality, not back there in the past but *now*. The hollow roll of far-away thunder. But it came in one endless peal, not a series of rising and falling crashes, and it was growing louder, louder. . . .

Ned looked at the others. They heard it too.

Louder. Louder. Now he could feel the vibrations in his bones.

He could not remember what had happened that night, but he knew the astonishing events they had endured had started with this sound.

He pushed back his chair and got up. He was awash in a rising tide of fear, and he had to fight against the urge to run.

Sandy stood, and there was fear in her face, as well. Though the unknown events seemed to have had an entirely positive effect on her, she was frightened now. She put one hand on Ned's arm for reassurance.

Ernie and Faye were frowning, looking around for the source of the noise, but they did not yet appear frightened. Their memory of the sound was apparently more thoroughly scrubbed away, so they could not as easily connect it with the events of that Friday night in July.

Another sound arose, underlying the thunderlike rumble: a

queer, ululating whistle. That, too, was unpleasantly familiar to Ned.

It was happening again. Whatever had taken place that night more than eighteen months ago was somehow being repeated, Jesus, happening all over again, and Ned heard himself saying, 'No, no. *No!*'

Corvaisis backed a couple of steps away from his table, cast a glance at Ned and the others. He was white-faced.

The growing roar began to resonate in the window glass, behind the closed blinds. A loose pane, unseen, started rattling in its frame.

The Levalor blinds were vibrating now, adding a jangly chorus.

Sandy's hold on Ned became a panicky clutch.

Ernie and Faye were on their feet, and they were no longer merely bewildered but as afraid as everyone else.

The ululant whistle had grown in volume with the thunder. Now it became piercingly shrill, an oscillating electronic shriek.

'What *is* it?' Sandy cried, and the continuous fulminations attained such volume and power that the walls of the Tranquillity Grille shook.

On the table at which Corvaisis had been sitting, the beer glass fell on its side, cracking, spilling what Dos Equis remained in it.

Ned looked at the table beside him and saw the objects on it – ketchup bottle, mustard dispenser, salt and pepper shakers, ashtray, glasses, plates, and silverware – bouncing, clinking against one another, moving back and forth across the surface. A beer glass toppled, and another, and the ketchup bottle.

Wide-eyed, Ned and the others turned this way and that, as if in anticipation of the imminent materialisation of a demonic entity.

Throughout the room, objects fell off tables. The clock with the Coors logo leapt from the hook on which it hung, crashed to the floor.

This very thing had happened that night in July. Ned remembered as much. But he could not remember what had come next.

'Stop it!' Ernie shouted with the conviction and authority of a Marine officer accustomed to obedience – but without effect.

Earthquake? Ned wondered. A quake did not explain the electronic shriek that accompanied the thunder.

The chairs jittered across the floor, bumping against one another. One of them slid into Corvaisis, and the writer jumped in surprise.

Ned could feel the floor shaking.

The thunderlike rumble and the accompanying oscillatory shriek rose to an ear-splitting peak, and with the hard flat crash of a bomb blast, the big front windows imploded. Faye screamed and threw her arms up in front of her face, and Ernie stumbled backwards and nearly fell over a chair. Sandy buried her face against Ned's chest.

They might have been badly cut by flying glass if the closed blinds had not imposed a barrier between them and the shattering panes. Even so, the force of the implosion flung the blinds up as a strong wind might blow curtains at an open window, and some glittering shards fell onto the booths, rained over Ned, and smashed on the floor around him.

Silence. The implosion of the windows was followed by a profound silence disturbed only by a few last, loose, little pieces of glass falling out of window frames, one at a time.

On that Friday night in July, the summer before last, much more than this had happened, though Ned could not remember what. Tonight, however, the mysterious drama apparently was not going to progress as far as it had gone then. For now, it was over.

Dom Corvaisis was bleeding lightly from a nick in his cheek, hardly worse than a shaving cut. Ernie's forehead and the back of his right hand had been slightly scratched by splinters of glass.

When he had determined that Sandy was unhurt, Ned reluctantly left her and rushed to the front door. He went out into the night in search of the cause of the weird noise and destruction, but he found only the deep, dark, solemn silence of the plains. No smoke or blackened rubble marked the source of an explosion. At the bottom of the hill on which the Tranquillity Motel and Grille stood, widely separated cars and trucks moved on the interstate. Over at the motel, drawn by the commotion, a few guests had come outside in their nightclothes. The sky above was full of stars. The air was numbingly cold, but there was no wind, only a soft breeze, like the frigid sigh of Death. Nothing in sight could have caused the thunder, shaking, or implosion of the windows.

Dom Corvaisis came out of the Grille, bewildered. 'What the hell?'

'I was hoping *you'd* know,' Ned responded.

'It's what happened the summer before last.'

'I know.'

'But just the start of it. Damn it, I can't remember what happened that night *after* the windows blew in.'

'Me neither,' Ned replied.

Corvaisis turned his hands palms-up, held them out for inspection. In the blue neon light from the sign on the diner's roof, Ned saw rings of swollen flesh in the writer's palms. Because the light was blue, he could not ascertain the true colour of the marks. But from what Corvaisis had told them earlier, Ned knew the rings were an angry red.

'What the hell?' Corvaisis said again.

Sandy was standing in the open door of the diner, backlit by the fluorescent glow from inside, and Ned went to her, embraced her. He felt one shudder after another passing through her. But he did not realise how badly *he* was trembling until she said, 'You're shaking like a leaf.'

Ned Sarver was scared sick. With an almost clairvoyant vividness, he sensed that they were involved in something of monumental importance, something unimaginably danger- ous, and that it was likely to end in death for some or all of them. He was a natural-born fixer of both inanimate objects and people, a damned good repairman. But this time he was up against a force with which he did not know how to tinker. What if Sandy were killed? He took pride in his talents, but even the best fixer in the whole damned world could not undo the wreckage wrought by Death.

For the first time since meeting her in Tucson, Ned felt powerless to protect his wife.

At the horizon, the moon had begun to rise.

402

FIVE
January 12 – January 14

1.

SUNDAY, JANUARY 12

Air as dense as molten iron.

In the nightmare, Dom could not draw breath. A tremendous pressure bore down on him. He was choking violently. He was dying.

He could not see much; his vision was clouded. Then two men came close, both wearing white vinyl decontamination suits with dark-visored helmets similar to those of astronauts. One man was at Dom's right, frantically disconnecting the IV line, withdrawing the intravenous spike from his arm. The other man, on the left, was cursing the cardiological data on the video read-out of the ECG machine. One of them unbuckled the straps and tore off the electrodes connecting Dom to the ECG, and the other lifted him into a sitting position. They pressed a glass to his lips, but he could not drink, so they tipped his head back and forced his mouth open and poured some noxious stuff down his throat.

The men communicated with each other via radios built into their helmets, but they were leaning so close to Dom that he could hear their voices clearly even through the muffling Plexiglas of their dark visors. One of them said, 'How many detainees were poisoned?' And the other said, 'Nobody's sure yet. Looks like at least a dozen.' The first said, 'But who'd want to poison them?' And the second said, 'One guess.' The first said, 'Colonel Falkirk. Colonel fucking Falkirk.' The second man said, 'But we'll never prove it, never nail the bastard.'

Flash-cut. The motel bathroom. The men were holding Dom on his feet, forcing his face down into the sink. This time, he understood what they were saying to him. With growing urgency, they were insisting that he vomit. Colonel fucking Falkirk had somehow had him poisoned, and these guys had made him drink a foul-tasting emetic, and now he was supposed to purge himself of the poison that was killing him. But even as sick as he was, he still could not puke. He gagged, retched; his stomach roiled; sweat poured off him like melting fat off a broiling chicken; but he could not rid himself of the poison. The first man said, 'We need a stomach pump.' And the second said, 'We don't *have* a stomach pump.' They pressed Dom's face deeper into the porcelain bowl. The crushing pressure grew worse, and Dom could hardly breathe at all now, and hot greasy waves of nausea washed through him, and sweat *gushed* from him, but he could not puke, could not, could not. And then he did.

Flash-cut. In bed again. Weak, kitten-weak. But able to breathe, thank God. The men in the decontamination suits had cleaned him up and strapped him to the mattress once more. The one on the right prepared a hypodermic and administered an injection of something apparently meant to counteract the remaining effects of the poison. The one on the left reconnected him to the intravenous drip from which he was receiving drugs, not nourishment. Dom was woozy, holding onto consciousness only with considerable effort. They hooked him to the ECG again, and as they worked, they talked. 'Falkirk's an idiot. We can keep a lid on this, given half a chance.' 'He's afraid the memory block will wear off. He's afraid that some of them will eventually remember what they saw.' 'Well, he may be right. But if the asshole kills them all, how's he going to explain the bodies? *That's* going to draw reporters like raw meat draws jackals, and then there'll be no way to keep the lid on. A nice memory wipe – that's the only sensible answer.' 'You don't have to convince me. Go burn Falkirk's ear about it.'

The dream-figures faded away, as did their voices, and Dom passed into a different nightmare country. He no longer felt weak, no longer sick, but his fear exploded into stark terror, and he begun to run with that maddening slow-motion panic indigenous to nightmares. He did not know what he was running from, but he was certain that something was pursuing him, something threatening and inhuman, he could sense it right behind him, closer, reaching for him, closer, and finally he knew he could not outrun it, knew he must face it, so he stopped and turned and looked up and cried out in surprise: 'The moon!'

Dom was awakened by his own cry. He was in Room 20, on the floor beside the bed, kicking, flailing. He got up and sat on the bed.

He looked at his travel clock. 3:07 a.m.

Shivering, he blotted his damp palms on the sheets.

Room 20 was having precisely the effect on him that he had thought it would. The bad vibrations of the place stimulated his memory, made his nightmares more vivid and more detailed than ever.

These dreams were radically different from all others he had ever known, for they were not fantasies but glimpses of a past reality seen through a distorting lens. They were not dreams as much as they were memories, forbidden recollections that had been weighted and dropped into the black sea of his subconscious, like dead bodies encumbered with cement shoes and thrown from a bridge into the deeps. Finally, the memories had slipped out of the cement and were surging to the surface.

He really *had* been imprisoned here, drugged, brainwashed. And during that ordeal, someone named Colonel Falkirk had actually poisoned him to prevent him from talking about whatever he had seen.

Falkirk was right, Dom thought. Eventually, we'll overcome the brainwashing and remember the truth. He *should* have killed us all.

*   *   *

Sunday morning, Ernie purchased panels of plyboard from a friend in Elko who owned a building supply. With his portable tablesaw, he cut the panels to fit the busted-out diner windows. Ned and Dom helped nail the plyboard in place, and by noon they had completed the job.

Ernie did not want to call a glazier and have the windows

405

replaced because last night's phenomena might recur. Until they knew what had caused the thunderous noise and shaking, installing new glass seemed foolhardy. In the interim, the Tranquillity Grille would not be open.

The Tranquillity Motel also would be closed. Ernie did not want business to distract him from helping Dom and the others probe into the mystery of the 'toxic spill.' When the last of yesterday's check-ins departed later today, the motel would house only Ernie, Faye, Dom, and any other victims who, when contacted, might decide to journey to Elko County to participate in the investigation. He did not know how many rooms he might need for those fellow-sufferers, so he decided to reserve all twenty. For the time being, the Tranquillity was less a motel than a barracks, where the troops would be quartered until this war with an unknown enemy was finally brought to a conclusion.

* * *

When the diner was boarded up, they all got into the motel's Dodge van, and Faye drove them down to the interstate and just over a quarter of a mile east, where she parked on the shoulder of the highway near the place that had a special attraction for Ernie and Sandy. The five of them stood along the guardrail, staring south, seeking a communion with the landscape that might illuminate the past. The winter solstice was three weeks behind them, so the sunlight was almost as hard and flat and cold as fluorescent light. In the grip of January, the scrub- and grass-covered plains, rugged hills, arroyos and gnarled rock formations were basically trichromatic, rendered in browns and greys and deep reds, with only an occasional patch of white sand, snow, or vein of borax. The scene was stark and dreary under a sky that grew more clouded and grey by the hour, but it also possessed an undeniable austere grandeur.

Faye wanted very much to feel something special about this place, for if she felt nothing, that would mean the people who brainwashed her had totally controlled her, totally *violated* her. She allowed no room in her self-image for the concept of absolute submission. She was a proud, capable woman. But she felt nothing other than the winter wind.

Ned and Dom appeared to be no more moved than Faye was, but she could see that Ernie and Sandy were receiving some cryptic message from the vista before them. Sandy was smiling beatifically. But Ernie had that look he got when night fell: pale, drawn, with haunted eyes.

'Let's go closer,' Sandy said. 'Let's go right down there.'

All five climbed over the guardrail and plunged down the steep embankment of the elevated road. They moved across the plain – fifty yards, a hundred – carefully avoiding the cold-weather prickly pear which grew in profusion near the foot of the interstate but soon disappeared in favour of sagebrush and bunch-grass, which in turn gave way to another kind of grass which was also brown but thicker, silkier. Portions of the plain were rocky and sandy and in the grip of worthless bristly scrub, while other portions were almost like small lush meadows, for this was a land in transition from the semi-desert of the south to the rich mountain pastures of the north. More than two hundred yards from the interstate, they stopped on a patch of ground not appreciably different from surrounding territory.

'Here,' Ernie said with a shudder, jamming his hands in his pockets and pulling his neck down into the rolled sheepskin collar of his coat.

Sandy smiled and said, 'Yes. Here.'

They spread out and moved back and forth across the ground. Here and there, in one shadowed niche or another, meagre patches of snow lay hidden from the evaporating effect of the dry wind and from the cold winter sun. Those traces of winter, plus the lack of green grass and scattered late-blooming wildflowers, were the only things that made the landscape different from the way it had looked two summers ago. After a minute or two, Ned announced that he did, indeed, feel an inexplicable connection with the place, though it did not bring him peace as it did his wife. His fear became so acute that, expressing surprise and embarrassment at his reaction, he turned and walked away. As Sandy hurried after Ned, Dom Corvaisis admitted that he was strangely affected by the place, too. However, he was not merely frightened, like Ned; Dom's fear, like Ernie's, was spiced by an unexplained awe and a sense of impending epiphany. Only Faye remained unaffected, unmoved.

Standing in the middle of the area in question, Dom turned slowly in a circle. 'What was it? What the hell happened here?'

The sky had turned to grey slate.

The blunt wind became sharp. Faye shivered.

She remained unable to feel what Ernie and the others felt, and that inability increased her sense of violation. She hoped she would one day meet the people who had messed with her mind. She wanted to look in their eyes and ask them how they could have so little respect for the personal integrity of another human being. Now that she knew she had been manipulated, she would never again feel entirely secure.

Stirred by the wind, the dry sagebrush made a scraping-rustling noise. Ice-crusted twigs clicked against one another with a sound that, fancifully, made Faye think of small, scurrying skeletons of little animals long-dead but somehow reanimated.

*　　　*　　　*

Back at the motel, in the Blocks' apartment, Ernie and Sandy and Ned sat at the kitchen table, while Faye made coffee and hot chocolate.

Dom perched on a stool by the wall phone. On the counter in front of him lay the Tranquillity Motel's registration book that had been in use the year before last. Referring to the page for Friday, July 6, he began to call those who must have shared the unremembered but important experiences of that far-away summer night.

In addition to his own name and that of Ginger Weiss, there were eight on the list. One of them, Gerald Salcoe of Monterey, California, had rented two rooms for himself, his wife, and two daughters. He had entered an address but no telephone. When Dom tried to get it from the Area Code 408 Information Operator, he was told the number was unlisted.

Disappointed, he moved on to Cal Sharkle, the long-haul trucker, a repeat customer known to Faye and Ernie. Sharkle lived in Evanston, Illinois, a suburb of Chicago. He had included his telephone number in the motel registry. Dom dialled it but discovered that the telephone had been disconnected and that no new number was listed.

'We can check his more recent entries on the current registry,' Ernie said. 'Maybe he's moved to another town. Maybe we have his new address somewhere.'

Faye put a cup of coffee on the counter where Dom could reach it, then joined the others at the table.

Dom had better luck on his third attempt, when he dialled Alan Rykoff in Las Vegas. A woman answered, and he said, 'Mrs Rykoff?'

She hesitated. 'I was Mrs Rykoff. My name's Monatella now, since the divorce.'

'Oh. I see. Well, my name's Dominick Corvaisis. I'm calling from the Tranquillity Motel up here in Elko County. You, your former husband, and your daughter stayed here for a few days in July, two summers ago?'

'Uh . . . yes, we did.'

'Miss Monatella, are either you or your daughter or your ex-husband having . . . difficulties, frightening and extraordinary problems?'

This time her hesitation was pregnant with meaning. 'Is this some sick joke? Obviously, you know what happened to Alan.'

'Please, Miss Monatella, believe me: I don't know what happened to your ex-husband. But I do know there's a good chance that you or him or your daughter – or all of you – are suffering from inexplicable psychological problems, that you're having frightening and repetitive nightmares you can't remember, and that some of these nightmares involve the moon.'

She gasped twice in surprise as Dom was speaking, and when she tried to respond she had difficulty talking.

When he realised she was on the verge of tears, he interrupted 'Miss Monatella, I don't know what's happened to you and your family, but the worst is past. The worst is past. Because whatever might still be to come . . . at least you're not alone any more.'

*　　　*　　　*

Over twenty-four hundred miles east of Elko County, in Manhattan, Jack Twist spent Sunday afternoon giving away more money.

On returning from the Guardmaster heist in Connecticut the previous night, he had driven through the city, looking for those who were both in need and deserving, and he had not rid himself of all the cash until five o'clock in the morning. On the edge of physical and emotional collapse, he'd returned to his Fifth Avenue apartment, gone immediately to bed and instantly to sleep.

He dreamed again of the deserted highway in an empty moon-washed landscape, and of the stranger in the dark-visored helmet who pursued him on foot. As the moonlight suddenly turned blood-red, he woke from the dream in panic at one o'clock Sunday afternoon, flailing at his pillow. A blood-red moon? He wondered what that meant, if anything.

He showered, shaved, dressed, and took time for only a quick breakfast consisting of an orange and a half-scale croissant.

In the large walk-in closet that served the master bedroom, he removed the cleverly concealed false panel and inventoried the contents of the three-foot-deep secret storage space. The jewellery from the job in October was finally gone, success-fully fenced, and most of the money from the *fratellanza* ware-house in early December had been converted to scores of cashiers' cheques and mailed to Jack's accounts at three Swiss banks. Only $125,000 remained, his emergency get-away fund.

He transferred most of the cash to a briefcase: nine banded packets of hundred-dollar bills, a hundred bills in each, and five packets of twenty-dollar bills, a hundred in each. That left $25,000 still in his cache, which seemed more than enough now that he was no longer involved in criminal activity and would not be putting himself in situations that might necessi-tate a swift exit from the state or country.

Although Jack intended to dispose of a considerable portion of his ill-gotten wealth, he certainly did not plan to give away all of it and leave himself penniless. That might be good for his soul, but it would be bad for his future and undeniably foolish. However, he had eleven safe-deposit boxes in eleven of the city's banks – additional emergency caches in case he needed to escape but could not reach the money behind the false partition in his bedroom closet – and those caches contained more than another quarter of a million. His Swiss accounts were worth in excess of four million. It was far more than he needed. He was looking forward to shedding half of that fortune during the next couple of weeks, at which point he would pause to decide what he wanted to do with his future. Eventually, he might give away even more.

At three-thirty Sunday afternoon, he carried his money-filled briefcase out into the city. All the strangers' faces, which for eight years had seemed fiercely hostile, every one, now seemed like animated portraits of promise and dazzling possibilities, every one.

*   *   *

The Block kitchen smelled of coffee and hot chocolate, then of cinnamon and pastry dough when Faye took a package of breakfast rolls from the freezer and popped them in the oven.

While the others sat at the table, listening, Dom continued to call the people who had registered at the motel on that special Friday night.

He reached Jim Gestron, who turned out to be a photographer from L.A. Gestron had driven throughout the West that summer, shooting on assignment for *Sunset* and other magazines. Initially, he was friendly, but as he heard more of Dom's story, he cooled off. If Gestron had been brainwashed, the mind-control experts had been as successful with him as with Faye Block. The photographer was having no dreams, no problems. Dom's tale of brainwashing, somnambulism, nyctophobia, obsessions with the moon, suicides, and paranormal experiences struck Gestron as the babbling of a seriously disturbed person. He said as much and hung up in the middle of the conversation.

Next, Dom called Harriet Bellot in Sacramento, who was no more troubled than Gestron. She was, she said, a fifty-year-old unmarried schoolteacher who had developed an interest in the Old West when, as a young WAC, she was stationed in Arizona. Every summer, she travelled old wagontrain routes and visited the sites of the forts and Indian settlements of another age, usually sleeping in her little camper but sometimes splurging on a motel room. She sounded like one of those likeable, dedicated, but stern teachers who brooked no nonsense from her pupils, and she brooked none from Dom. When he started talking about fanciful stuff like poltergeist phenomena, she hung up, too.

'Does that make you feel better, Faye?' Ernie asked. 'You're not the only one whose memories were so thoroughly scrubbed away.'

'Doesn't make me feel one damn bit better,' Faye said. I'd rather be suffering problems like you or Dom than feel nothing. I feel as if a piece of me was cut out and thrown away.'

Perhaps she's right, Dom thought. Perhaps nightmares, phobias, and terrors of one kind or another *are* better than having a little pocket of absolute emptiness inside, cold and dark, which would be like carrying a fragment of death around within her for the rest of her life.

*   *   *

When Dominick Corvaisis telephoned St Bernadette's rectory at 4:26 Sunday afternoon, seeking Brendan Cronin, Father Wycazik was in the study with officers of the Knights of Columbus, concluding the first of many planning sessions for the annual St Bernadette's Spring Carnival.

At four-thirty, Father Michael Gerrano interrupted with the news that the call he had just taken on the kitchen phone was from Father Wycazik's 'cousin' in Elko, Nevada. Only a few hours ago, one day ahead of schedule, Brendan Cronin had boarded a United flight to Reno, taking advantage of cancellations that had opened up some seats, and intending to use a small commuter airline from Reno to Elko on Monday. At the moment, Brendan was still in the air with United, not yet even as far as Reno and in no position to be calling anyone, so Michael's message intrigued Father Wycazik and instantly pried him loose of the planning session without alerting the visitors that something extraordinary was happening in the lives of their parish clergy.

Leaving the young priest to conclude matters with the Knights, the rector hurried to the kitchen phone and took the call meant for Brendan. Dominick Corvaisis, with a writer's appreciation for the fantastic, and Stefan, with a priest's appreciation for mystery and mysticism, became increasingly excited and voluble as they spoke to each other. Stefan swapped his knowledge of Brendan's problems and adventures –

412

lost faith, miraculous cures, strange dreams – for Corvaisis' stories of poltergeist phenomena, somnambulism, nyctophobia, lunar obsessions, and suicides.

Finally, Stefan could not resist asking, 'Mr Corvaisis, do you see any reason for an old unregenerate religious like me to hold out the hope that what is happening to Brendan is somehow divine in nature?'

'Quite frankly, Father, in spite of the miraculous cures of that police officer and the little girl you mentioned, I don't see the hand of God in this. There are too many indications of human connivery in this to support the interpretation you'd like to put on it.'

Stefan sighed. 'I suppose that's true. But I'll still cling to the hope that what Brendan's being called to witness there in Nevada is something meant to bring him back into the hands of Christ. I won't give up on the possibility.'

The writer laughed softly. 'Father, just from what I've learned of you during this conversation, I suspect you'd *never* give up on the possibility of redeeming any soul, anywhere, any time. I'd guess you don't save souls quite the way other priests do – by finesse, by gentle and genteel encouragement. You strike me more as . . . well, as a blacksmith of the soul, hammering out the salvation of others by the sweat of your brow and the application of plenty of muscle. Please understand: I mean this as a compliment.'

Stefan laughed, too. 'How else could I possibly take it? I firmly believe that nothing easy is worth doing. A blacksmith bent over a glowing forge? Yes, I do rather like the image.'

'I'll look forward to Father Cronin's arrival here tomorrow. If he's anything like you, Father, we'll be glad to have him on our side.'

'I'm on your side as well,' Father Wycazik said, 'and if there's anything I can do to help with your investigation, please call on me. If there's the slightest chance these strange events involve the manifest presence of God, then I do not intend to sit on the sidelines and miss all the action.'

*   *   *

The next entry on the guest list was for Bruce and Janet Cable of Philadelphia. Neither of them were having trouble of the

413

sort that plagued Dom, Ernie, and the others. However, they were more willing to hear Dom out than Jim Gerston and Harriet Bellot had been, but in the end they were no more swayed by his story.

The final name on the list was Thornton Wainwright, who had given a New York City address and telephone number. When Dom dialled it, he reached a Mrs Neil Karpoly, who said the number had been hers for more than fourteen years and that she had never heard of Wainwright. When Dom read the Lexington Avenue address from the registry and inquired if that was where Mrs Karpoly lived, she asked him to repeat it, then laughed. 'No, sir, that's not where I live. And your Mr Wainwright's not a trustworthy sort if he told you that's *his* address. Nobody lives there, although I'm sure there are thousands who might enjoy it. That's the address of Bloomingdale's.'

Sandy was astonished when Dom reported this news: 'Phoney name and address? What's that mean? Was he really a guest that night? Or did someone add the name to the registry just to confuse us? Or . . . what?'

* * *

Jack Twist possessed complete sets of sophisticated false ID — driver's licences, birth certificates, Social Security cards, credit cards, passports, even library cards — in eight names, including 'Thornton Bains Wainwright,' and he always employed an alias when planning and executing a heist. But he worked anonymously that Sunday afternoon, portioning out another hundred thousand dollars to startled recipients all over Manhattan. The largest gift was fifteen thousand to a young sailor and his bride of one day, whose battered old Plymouth had broken down on Central Park South, near the statue of Simon Bolivar. 'Get a new car,' Jack told them as he stuffed money into their hands and playfully stuck a wad of bills under the sailor's hat. 'And if you're wise, you won't tell anyone about this, especially not the newspapers. That'll just bring the IRS down on you. No, you don't need to know my name, and there's no need to thank me. Just be kind to each other, all right? Always be kind to each other, because we never know how much time we have on this world.'

In less than an hour, Jack gave away the entire hundred thousand that he had taken from the secret compartment in the back of his bedroom closet. With plenty of time on his hands, he bought a bouquet of coral-red roses and drove out to Westchester County, an hour from the city, to the memorial park in which Jenny had been buried over two weeks ago.

Jack had not wanted to put her to rest in one of the city's crowded and grim cemeteries. Although he knew he was being sentimental, he felt that the only suitable resting place for his Jenny was in open country, where there would be expansive green grassy slopes and shade trees in the summer and peaceful vistas of snow in the winter.

He arrived at the memorial park shortly before twilight. Although the uniform headstones were set flush with the earth, with no features to distinguish one from another, and although most of them were covered with snow, Jack went directly to Jenny's plot, the location of which was branded on his heart.

While the dreary day faded into a drearier dusk, in a world colourless except for the blazing roses, Jack sat in the snow, oblivious of the dampness and cold, and spoke to Jenny as he had spoken to her during her years in a coma. He told her about the Guardmaster heist yesterday, about giving away all the money. As the curtain of twilight pulled down the heavier drape of night, the memorial park's security guard began driving slowly around the grounds, warning the few late visitors that the gates would soon close. Finally Jack stood and took one last look at Jenny's name cast in bronze letters on the headstone plaque, now illuminated by the vaguely bluish light of one of the streetlamps that lined the park's main drive. 'I'm changing, Jenny, and I'm still not sure why. It feels good, right . . . but also sort of strange.' What he said next surprised him: 'Something big is going to happen, Jenny. I don't know what, but something big is going to happen to me.' He suddenly sensed that his newfound guilt and subsequent peace with society were only the beginning steps of a great journey that would take him places he could not yet imagine. 'Something big is going to happen,' he repeated, 'and I sure wish you were here with me, Jenny.'

*   *   *

415

The blue Nevada sky had been armouring itself with dark storm clouds ever since Ernie, Ned, and Dom had begun boarding up the diner's broken windows. Hours later, when Dom drove his rental car to the Elko airport to pick up Ginger Weiss, the world turned under a gloomy light, girdled in battlefield grey. He was too restless to wait inside the small terminal. He stood on the windswept tarmac, huddled in his heavy winter jacket, so he heard the twin engines of the ten-seat commuter craft even before he saw it descend through the low clouds. The roar of the engines contributed to the mood of impending warfare, and Dom realised uneasily that, in a sense, they were assembling their army; war against their unknown enemy loomed nearer day by day.

The plane taxied within eighty feet of the terminal, and Dr Weiss was the fourth passenger to disembark. Even in a bulky, thoroughly unattractive car-coat, she looked petite and beautiful. The wind made a streaming banner of her silky silver-blonde hair.

Dom hurried towards her; she stopped and put down her bags. They hesitated, staring at each other in silence, with a peculiar mixture of amazement, excitement, pleasure and apprehension. Then with an impulsiveness that obviously surprised her as much as it did him, they virtually threw themselves at each other, embracing as if they were old and dear friends too long apart. Dom held her close, and she held him tightly, and he felt her heart pounding as hard and fast as his.

What the hell is happening here? he wondered.

But he was in too much turmoil to analyse the situation. For the moment, he could *feel* but not think.

Neither of them wanted to let go, and when they finally separated, neither could speak. She tried to say something, but her voice cracked with emotion, and Dom was incoherent. So she picked up one of her bags, and he picked up the other, and they went out to the parking lot.

In the car, with the engine running and the heater blowing warm air in their faces, Ginger said, 'What was *that* all about?'

Still shaken, but curiously not embarrassed by the bold greeting he had given her, Dom cleared his throat. 'Don't really know. But I think maybe, together, you and I went

416

through something so shattering that the experience created a special bond between us, a powerful bond we weren't entirely aware of until we saw each other in the flesh.'

'When I first came across your picture on the book jacket, it had a very odd effect on me, but nothing like this. Stepping off the plane, seeing you there . . . it was as if we'd known each other all of our lives. No, not exactly that. More precisely . . . it was as if we'd known each other far better, more completely, than we'd ever known anyone else, as if we shared some tremendous secret that all the world might want to know but that only we possessed. Does that sound crazy?'

He shook his head. 'No. Not at all. You've put into words what I was feeling . . . as nearly as words can explain it.'

'You've met some of the others,' Ginger said. 'Was it like this when you first encountered them?'

'No. I instantly felt . . . a certain warmth towards them, a strong sense of community, but nothing a fraction as powerful as what I felt when you got off that plane. All of us went through something unusual that linked our lives, our futures, but evidently you and I shared an experience even stranger and more affecting than anything we shared with tham. Damn. It's as layered as an onion, one strangeness on another.'

For half an hour they sat in the car, in the airport parking lot, talking. Outside, cars and pick-ups came and went around them, and the January wind buffeted the Chevy and moaned at the windows; however, they were seldom aware of anything but each other.

She told him about her fugues, the hypnotic regression sessions with Pablo Jackson, and the mind-control technique know as the Azrael Block. She told him about Pablo's murder and her own narrow escape.

Although, clearly, Ginger sought neither sympathy for her suffering nor praise for the way she had handled herself in trying cirumstances, Dom's respect and admiration for her grew by the minute. She was only five-two, a hundred pounds, but somehow she had a physical presence more imposing than many men twice her size.

Dom recounted the events of the past twenty-four hours, and when Ginger heard about his dream of the previous night and about the new memories that surfaced in it, she appeared immensely relieved. In Dom's dream, there was proof of Pablo Jackson's theory: her fugues were not caused by mental aberration; they were, instead, always triggered by objects associated with her imprisonment at the motel two summers ago. The black gloves and dark-visored helmet had terrified her because they made a direct connection with the repressed memories of the people in decontamination suits who tended her while she underwent brainwashing. The drain in the hospital scrub-sink threw the panic switch because she probably had been one of those 'detainees' poisoned by Colonel Falkirk (whoever the hell he was), then forced to vomit up the deadly substance, just as Dom had been. While strapped in the motel bed, she must have undergone many eye examinations to determine the depth of her drug-induced trance, which was why an ophthalmoscope had sent her reeling away in a dark terror that night in George Hannaby's office. Dom saw a relaxation of the tension at this irrefutable evidence that her blackouts were not a sign of madness and were, in fact, a desperate but entirely rational method of avoiding the repressed memories that the mind-control experts had forbidden her to recall.

She said, 'But what about the brass buttons on the coat of the man who killed Pablo? And on the policeman's uniform? Why did they terrify me and throw me into a fugue?'

'We know the military is involved in this cover-up,' Dom said, turning up the heater to counteract the cold air pouring off the car's wind-buffeted windows, 'and officers' uniforms have brass buttons like that, though not a lion passant. Most likely . . . raised images of eagles. The buttons on the killer's and cop's coats were probably similar to the buttons on the uniforms of those who imprisoned us in the motel.'

'Okay, but you said they wore decontamination suits, not uniforms.'

'Maybe they didn't wear the decon suits for the entire three and a half days. At some point they decided it was safe to take them off.'

She nodded. 'I'm sure that's right. Which leaves only one thing. That carriage lamp behind the house on Newbury Street, the day Pablo was murdered. I told you about it: black

418

iron with pebbled amber panes of glass. It had those bulbs
that flickered like a gas flame. A perfectly innocent lamp.
But it kicked me into another blackout.'

'The bases of the lamps in the rooms at the Tranquillity
Motel are designed like hurricane lamps, with little windows of amber glass.'

'I'll be damned. So every blackout was triggered by an
object that reminded me of something from those days
when I was being brainwashed.'

Dom hesitated, then reached inside his sweater and withdrew the Polaroid photograph from his shirt pocket and
handed it to her.

She paled and shuddered when she saw herself staring
up with vacant eyes at the camera. '*Gevalt*!' She looked away
from the picture.

Dom gave her time to recover from the shock of the
snapshot.

Outside, in the fading dirty-grey light, a score of vehicles
waited silently like dark, dumb, brooding beasts. The wind
harried collections of litter, dead leaves, and miscellaneous
debris across the macadam.

'It's *meshugge*,' she said, lowering her troubled gaze to the
photo again. 'It's crazy. What could possibly have happened
to us that would justify this elaborate, risky conspiracy?
What could we have seen that was so dreadfully goddamned important?'

'We'll find out,' he promised.

'Will we? Will they let us? They killed Pablo. Won't they
do whatever's necessary to keep us from uncovering the
truth?'

Adjusting the heater again, Dom said, 'Well, I figure
there're two factions among the conspirators. There are the
hardasses represented by Colonel Falkirk and his people,
and the better guys – can't call them *good* guys exactly –
represented by the fella who sent us these snapshots and by
the two men in decontamination suits in my dream last
night. The hardasses wanted to kill all of us right at the
start, so there'd never be any doubt that the cover-up would
be permanent. But the better guys wanted to scrub our
memories, use mind-control techniques instead of violence,

so we could go on living, and the better guys must be the stronger of the two factions because they got their way.'

'The gunman who killed Pablo was most likely one of the hardasses.'

'Yeah. Working for Falkirk. The colonel's evidently *still* willing to kill anyone who jeopardises the cover-up, which means none of us is safe. But there's the other faction that doesn't believe in Falkirk's ultimate solution, and they're still trying to protect us, I think. So we have a chance. Anyway, we can't walk away. We can't go home and try to get on with our lives just because the enemy looks formidable.'

'No,' Ginger agreed, 'we can't. Because until we find out what happened, we don't really *have* lives to get on with.' The wind blew withered leaves against the windshield, over the roof. Ginger swept the parking lot with her gaze. 'They must know we're gathering at the motel, that things are falling apart. Do you think they're watching us now?'

'Very likely they've got the motel under surveillance,' Dom said. 'But no one followed me to the airport. I watched for a tail.'

'They wouldn't need to tail you here,' she said grimly. 'They knew where you were going. They knew who you were picking up.'

'Are we labouring under a delusion of free will? Are we only bugs on a giant's palm, and can the giant crush us whenever he wants?'

'Maybe,' Ginger Weiss said. 'But by God, we can at least give him a couple of nasty bites before he smashes us.'

She spoke with a fierce determination that was convincing but also amusing in the context of a metaphor as basically comic as a giant and a bunch of bugs. Though he was pleased by her fierce resolution in the face of such overwhelmingly poor odds, Dom could not help laughing.

Blinking at him in surprise, she laughed too. 'Hey, am I spunky, or what? Might be smashed by a giant, but I feel triumphant 'cause I'll be able to bite him just before he reduces me to a bloody smear.'

'Spunky should be your middle name,' Dom agreed, laughing harder.

As he watched Ginger laughing at her own expense, Dom

was again stricken by her beauty. His response to her, on seeing her disembark from the plane, had been instant and powerful because of unremembered experiences they shared. But even if they had been complete strangers whose lives had never crossed, he would have felt something more at the sight of her than he felt when he saw other beautiful women. Under any circumstances, she would have turned his head. She was special.

He drew a deep breath. 'Shall I take you to meet the others?'

'Oh, yes,' she said, dabbing her slender fingers at the corners of her eyes to wipe away tears that her graveyard laughter had occasioned. 'Yes, I'm eager to meet them. The other bugs on the giant's hand.'

* * *

Less than half an hour before nightfall, the shadows on the high plains were long, and the muddy grey light of the overcast dusk lent an air of mystery even to such ordinary objects as clumps of sagebrush, rock formations, and twisted mounds of dead brown bunch-grass.

Before taking her to the motel, Dom Corvaisis had brought Ginger to what he called 'the special place,' more than two hundred yards south of Interstate 80. The wind rustled half-seen vegetation. The ice on the grass and sagebrush, when glimpsed at all, looked black, shiny black.

The writer stood away from her, hands jammed in his jacket pockets, silent. He had told her that he did not want to influence her reaction to the place or colour her first feelings with a description of his own.

Ginger wandered slowly back and forth, feeling slightly foolish, as if taking part in a half-baked experiment in psychic perception, seeking clairvoyant vibrations. But she quickly stopped feeling foolish when the vibrations actually began to shake her. A queer uneasiness arose, and she found herself staying away from the deeper pockets of shadows, as if something hostile lurked in them. Her heart pounded. Uneasiness became fear, and she heard the tempo of her breathing change.

'It's inside me. It's inside me.'

She whirled toward that voice. It was Dom's voice, but it

had not come from him. The words had been spoken behind her. But no one was there: only dry sagebrush, and a thin patch of snow glowing softly, luminously within a nest of shadows.

'What's the matter?' Dom asked, moving toward her.

She was wrong. Dom's other voice, the ghostly-sounding voice, had not come from behind her. It had come from within her. She heard that other Dom again, and she realised she was hearing a fragment of memory, an echo from the past, something he had said to her that Friday night, July 6, perhaps when they had both stood in this same place. The scrap of memory came with no visual or olfactory element because it was part of the events locked behind the Azrael Block. There were just those three urgent words repeated twice: '*It's inside me. It's inside me.*'

Abruptly, her simmering fear flashed bright. The landscape around her seemed to embody a nameless but monstrous threat. She started back toward the highway, walking fast, and Dom asked what was wrong, and she walked even faster, unable to answer because fear was like a paste in her mouth and throat. He called her name, and she began to run. Every object in sight seemed to have been wounded on its eastern flank, for black blood-shadows spilled in that direction.

She was not able to speak until they were back in the Chevy, with the doors locked, the engine running, and the heater blowing warm air on her chilled face. Shakily, she told him about the nameless threat she had felt on that ordinary-looking piece of ground, and about the memory of his urgent voice and the three-word sentence.

'''It's inside me,''' he said thoughtfully. 'You're sure it's really something I said to you that night?'

'Yes.' She shivered.

'It's inside me. What in the world did I mean by that?'

'I don't know,' Ginger said. 'But it gives me the creeps.'

He was silent a moment. Then he said, 'Yeah. Me too.'

* * *

That evening, at the motel, Ginger Weiss felt almost as if she was with her family on a holiday gathering like Thanksgiving. In spite of the difficulties in which they found themselves, their spirits were high; for in the manner of a real family, they drew strength from one another. The six of them crowded into the kitchen and prepared dinner together, and through that domestic labour, Ginger got to know the others better and felt a strengthening of the ties that bound her to them.

Ned Sarver, being a professional cook, prepared the main dish – chicken breasts baked in a spicy green tomatillo sauce with sour cream. Initially, Ginger mistakenly thought Ned was a brooding, unfriendly sort, but she soon changed her opinion. Taciturnity sometimes could be a sign of a healthy ego that did not require constant gratification, which was the case with Ned. Besides, Ginger could not help but like a man who loved his wife as deeply as Ned loved Sandy, a love apparent in every word he spoke to her, in every glance he cast her way.

Sandy, the only one of them to be affected *only* positively by their mysterious ordeal, was so sweet-tempered, so delighted with the recent changes in herself, that she was especially good company. Together, she and Ginger prepared the dinner salad and vegetables, and as they worked, an almost sisterly affection developed between them.

Faye Block made the dessert, a refrigerator pie with a chocolate crust and banana-cream filling. Ginger liked Faye, who reminded her of Rita Hannaby. That cultured society woman was different from Faye in many ways, but in fundamental respects they were alike: efficient take-charge types, tough of mind, tender of spirit.

Ernie Block and Dom Corvaisis put the extra leaf in the table and arranged six place settings. Ernie had seemed gruff and intimidating at first, but now she saw he was a sweetheart. He inspired much affection because of his fear of darkness, which made him seem boyish in spite of his size and age.

Of the five people among whom Ginger found herself, only Dominick Corvaisis stirred emotions that she could not understand. For him, she felt the same friendship that she felt for the others, and she was aware of a special bond between them related to an unremembered experience just the two of them had shared. But she was also sexually attracted to him. That surprised her because she never felt desire for a man until she knew him for several weeks, at least, and knew him well.

Wary of her romantic yearnings, Ginger kept a tight rein on her emotions, and she tried hard to convince herself that Dom did not feel a similar attraction for her, which he so patently did.

Through dinner, the six of them continued to discuss their strange predicament and search for clues that might have been overlooked.

Like Dom, Ginger had no recollection of the toxic spill two years ago, though the Blocks and Sarvers recalled it clearly. I-80 had really been closed, and an environmental emergency had been declared; there was no doubt about that much. Last night, however, Dom convinced the Blocks that their memories of evacuating to Elroy and Nancy Jamison's mountain ranch were phoney and that both they *and* the Jamisons had almost surely been kept at the motel. (According to Faye and Ernie, the Jamisons had not mentioned having any nightmares or odd problems lately, so their brainwashing must have been effective, thought it would be necessary to talk to them soon.) Likewise, Ned and Sandy had reluctantly concluded that their own recollections of sitting out the crisis at their trailer were too shallow to be real and that they had been strapped into motel beds, drugged, and brainwashed like everyone else in those Polaroids.

'But,' Faye wondered, 'why wouldn't they give us all approximately the same false memories?'

Ginger said, 'Maybe all you locals have had the toxic spill and the highway closure woven into your false memories. That'd be necessary because, later, people would be asking you where you went during the emergency, and you'd have to know what they were talking about. But Dom and I are from distant places, unlikely ever to return, unlikely to run into anyone who would know that we'd been within the quarantine zone, so they didn't bother including that bit of reality in the set of fake memories they gave us.'

Sandy paused with a morsel of chicken on her fork. 'But wouldn't it be safer and easier to make your memories fit the toxic spill, too?'

'Ever since Pablo Jackson helped me discover that my mind had been tampered with,' Ginger said, 'I've been reading about brainwashing, and I think maybe it's a lot less difficult to implant recollections that are *entirely* false than it is to weave in threads of reality such as the environmental emergency and the road closure. It probably takes a lot longer to construct fake memories that have some reality to them, and maybe they simply didn't have time to do that with all of us. So they gave the super-deluxe brainwashing job only to you locals.'

'That feels like the truth,' Ernie said, and everyone agreed.

Faye said, 'But did the toxic spill really happen, or was it just a cover story that gave them an excuse to close I-80 and bottle us up, a way of preventing us from talking about what we'd seen Friday night?'

'I suspect there *was* contamination of some sort,' Ginger said. 'In Dom's nightmare, which we know is really more memory than dream, those men were wearing decontamination suits. Now, when they came into the quarantine zone, maybe they'd wear costumes like that for the benefit of newsmen or other onlookers. But once here, where only we could see them, they wouldn't keep the suits on unless they absolutely had to.'

Glancing uneasily at the blind-covered window nearest the table, as if he thought he had seen a trickle of darkness dribbling in from the night beyond, Ernie cleared his throat and said, 'Yeah, uh . . . well, which was it, do you think? You're the doctor? Does it sound like chemical or biological contamination? The story they gave the media was that it involved chemicals being delivered to Shenkfield's testing facilities.'

Ginger had been thinking about this question for some time, long before Ernie asked it. Chemical or biological contamination? She had arrived at an answer that deeply disturbed her. 'Generally speaking, the suits required for a chemical spill don't have to be air-tight. They just have to cover the worker from head to toe in order to prevent any caustic or toxic substance from coming into contact with his skin, and they have to include a respirator, rather like a scuba diver's tank and mask, so he won't breathe deadly fumes. They're usually made of lightweight non-porous cloth, and the headgear consists of a simple cloth hood with a plastic visor. But Dom described heavy-looking suits with an outer level of thick vinyl, with gloves that were of one piece with the sleeves, and

425

a hard helmet that locked into an airtight seal at the collar. That is unquestionably gear that's been designed to prevent exposure to a dangerous *biological* agent, microbes.'

For a while no one said a word, pondering this disquieting news.

Then Ned took a long swallow of his Heineken for fortification and said, 'So we must've been infected with something.'

Faye said, 'Some virus they developed for biological warfare.'

'If it was headed for Shenkfield, that's the only kind of bug it could've been,' Ernie said. 'Something mean.'

'Yet we lived,' Sandy said.

'Because they were immediately able to quarantine us and treat us,' Ginger said. 'Surely they wouldn't be intending to test a genetically engineered virus, some new and deadly organism that could be used as a weapon, unless they had simultaneously developed an effective cure for it. So they had a supply of a new antibiotic or serum to guard against just such an accident. If they contaminated us, they also cured us.'

Ernie said, 'It sounds right, doesn't it? Maybe it's all starting to fall together, piece by piece.'

Dom disagreed. 'It still doesn't explain what happened on that Friday night, what we saw that they didn't want us to see. It doesn't explain what made the whole damned diner shake or what blew out the windows – either on that first night or again last night.'

'And it doesn't explain the other weird stuff,' Faye said. 'Like all those paper moons whirling around Dom in Lomack's house. Or Father Wycazik's claim that this young priest's been performing miracle cures.'

They looked at one another, waiting in silence for someone to put forth an explanation that would tie biological contamination with those paranormal events, but no one had an answer.

*   *   *

Less than three hundred miles west of the Tranquillity Motel, in another motel in Reno, Brendan Cronin had gone to bed and turned out the lights. Although it was only a few minutes after nine o'clock, he was still functioning on Chicago time, so for him it was after eleven.

However, sleep eluded him. After checking into the motel and having dinner at a nearby Bob's Big Boy, he had telephoned St Bette's rectory and had spoken with Father Wycazik, who had told him of the call from Dominick Corvaisis. Brendan was electrified by the news that he was not the only one caught up in this mystery. He considered calling the Tranquillity, but they already knew he was on his way, and whatever they could say on the phone could be said better in person, tomorrow. Thoughts of tomorrow and speculations about what might happen were what kept sleep at bay.

He had lain awake less than an hour and his thoughts had drifted to the eerie luminescence that had filled his rectory bedroom two nights ago, when suddenly that phenomenon appeared once more. This time, there was no visible source of light, not even one so unlikely as the frost-moon upon the window from which the uncanny radiance had sprung last Friday night. Now, the glow appeared above him and on all sides, as if the very molecules of the air had acquired the ability to produce light. It was a lunar-pale, milky shimmer at first, growing brighter by the second, until it seemed as if he must be lying in an open field, under the looming countenance of a full moon.

This was different from the peaceful golden light that was featured in his recurring dream, and as it had done two nights ago, it filled him with conflicting emotions – horror and rapture, fear and wild excitement.

As in his rectory bedroom, the lactescent light changed colour, darkening to scarlet. He seemed suspended in a radiant bubble of blood.

It's inside me, he thought, wondering what that meant. *Inside me*. The thought reverberated in his mind. Suddenly he was cold with fear.

His thundering heart seemed about to explode. He lay rigid. In his hands, the rings appeared. Throbbing.

MONDAY, JANUARY 13

When they gathered in Ernie and Faye's kitchen for breakfast the next morning, Dom was excited to learn that the previous night had been an ordeal for most of them. 'It's unravelling the way I hoped it might,' he said. 'By gathering together here, by recreating the group that was gathered here *that* night, and by working together to get at the truth, we're putting constant pressure on the memory blocks that've been implanted in us. And now, that barrier is crumbling a bit faster.'

Last night, Dom, Ginger, Ernie, and Ned experienced exceptionally vivid nightmares of such similarity that they were surely fragments of forbidden memories. In every case they had involved being strapped to motel beds and tended by men in decontamination suits. Sandy had a pleasant dream, although it lacked the clarity and detail of the others' nightmares. Faye was the only one who did not dream at all.

Ned had been so disturbed by his nightmare that on Monday morning, when he and Sandy arrived from Beowawe for breakfast, he announced they were moving into a room at the motel for the duration. 'During the night, after the dream woke me, I couldn't get back to sleep. And while I was laying there, I got to thinking how lonely it is at our trailer, empty plains all around. . . . Maybe this Colonel Falkirk will decide to kill us like he wanted to do in the first place. And if he comes for us, I don't want me and Sandy to be alone out there at the trailer.'

Dom sympathised with Ned because these dark and vivid dreams were new to the cook. Over recent weeks, Dom, Ginger, and Ernie had learned a little about coping with the frighteningly powerful nightmares, but Ned had developed no armour, so he was badly shaken.

And, of course, Ned was well advised to fear Falkirk. The closer they came to exposing the conspiracy and learning the truth, the more likely they were to become targets for a pre-emptive strike. Dom did not think Falkirk would make a move until Brendan Cronin, Jorja Monatella, and perhaps other victims had gathered at the Tranquillity. But once they were in one place, they would need to be prepared for trouble.

Now, in the Blocks' kitchen, Ned Sarver picked at his breakfast without appetite as he spoke of the images that had disturbed his sleep. At first he had dreamed of being held prisoner by men in decontamination suits, but later they had worn either lab coats or military uniforms, an indication that the biological danger had passed. One of the uniformed men had been Colonel Falkirk, and Ned described that officer in detail: about fifty years old; black hair greying at the temples; grey eyes like circles of polished steel; a beakish nose; thin lips.

Ernie was able to confirm the word-portrait that Ned painted, for Falkirk had also been in his nightmare. The amazing coincidence of the same man appearing in both Ned's and Ernie's dreams made it clear that his face was not merely a figment of imagination but a memory of a real face that both Ernie and Ned had seen two summers ago.

'And in my nightmare,' Ernie said, 'another Army officer referred to Falkirk by his first name. Leland. Colonel Leland Falkirk.'

'He's probably stationed at Shenkfield,' Ginger said.

'We'll try to find out later,' Dom said.

The barriers to memory were definitely crumbling. That prospect boosted Dom's spirits higher than they had been in months.

In Ginger's nightmare, which she recounted for them, she had not been the only person being brainwashed in Room 5, the room she had occupied that summer and which she now occupied again. 'There was a rollaway bed in one corner, and the redhead in it was someone I'd never seen before. She was about forty years old. They had her connected to her own IV drip and ECG machine. She had that . . . vacant stare.'

Just as Ernie and Ned had shared a new development – the appearance by Colonel Falkirk – in their nightmares, Dom and Ginger had shared this other discovery. In Dom's dream, there had been a rollaway bed, flanked by an IV stand and an ECG monitor, and in the bed had been a young man in his twenties with a pale face, bushy moustache, and zombie eyes.

'What does it mean?' Faye Block asked. 'Did they have so many subjects for brainwashing that they more than filled all twenty rooms.'

'But,' Sandy said, 'the registry showed only eleven rooms rented.'

Ginger said, 'There must've been people on the interstate, in transit, who saw what we saw. The Army managed to stop them and bring them here. None of their names would appear on the registry.'

'How many?' Faye wondered.

'We'll probably never know for sure,' Dom said. 'We never actually met them; we only shared rooms with them while we were drugged. We might eventually remember the faces of those we saw, but we can't possibly remember names and addresses we never knew in the first place.'

But at least those programmed memories, those tissues of lies, were dissolving, allowing the truth to show through. Dom was grateful for that much. In time, they would uncover the entire story – if Colonel Falkirk did not first come after them with heavy artillery.

*　　　*　　　*

Monday morning, while the group at the Tranquillity ate breakfast, Jack Twist was being escorted to a safe-deposit box in a vault of the Fifth Avenue branch of Citibank, in New York. The attending bank employee, an attractive young woman, kept calling him 'Mr Farnham,' for that was the false identity under which he had acquired the box.

After they used their separate keys to remove the box from the wall of the vault, when he was alone with it in a cubicle, he opened the lid and stared in shock at the contents. The rectangular metal container held something that he had not put there, which was an impossibility since only he knew about the box and possessed the only master key.

It should have contained five white envelopes, each filled with five thousand dollars in hundred-dollar and twenty-dollar bills, and indeed that money appeared to be untouched. This was one of eleven emergency caches he kept in safe-deposit boxes all over the city. He had set out this morning to remove fifteen thousand dollars from each, a total of $165,000, which he intended to give away. He opened each of the five envelopes and counted the contents with trembling hands. Not a single bill was missing.

Jack was not even slightly relieved. Though his money was still there, the presence of the other object proved that his false identity had been penetrated, his privacy violated, and his freedom jeopardised. Someone knew who 'Gregory Farnham' really was, and the item that had been left in the box was a bold notification that his elaborately constructed cover had been penetrated.

It was a postcard. There was no writing on the back, no message; the presence of the card itself was message enough. On the front was a photograph of the Tranquillity Motel.

The summer before last, after he and Branch Pollard and a third man had burglarised the Avril McAllister estate in Marin County, north of San Francisco, and after Jack paid a profitable visit to Reno, he rented a car and drove east, stopping the first night at the Tranquillity Motel along Interstate 80. He had not thought about the place since, but he recognised it the instant he saw the photograph.

Who could possibly know he had stayed at that motel? Not Branch Pollard. He'd never told Branch about Reno or about his decision to drive back to New York. And not the third man on the McAllister job, a guy named Sal Finrow from Los Angeles; Jack had never seen him again after they had split the take from that sour job.

Then Jack realised that at least *three* of his phoney IDs had been penetrated. He rented this safe-deposit box as 'Farnham,' but he stayed at the Tranquillity Motel as 'Thornton Wainwright.' Both *noms de guerre* were now blown, and the only way anyone could have linked them was by connecting Jack with his 'Philippe Delon' identity, under which he resided at his Fifth Avenue apartment, so that name was blown as well.

Jesus.

He sat in the bank cubicle, stunned but thinking furiously, trying to decide who his enemy might be. It could not be the police or the FBI or any other legitimate authority, for they would simply have arrested him once they had accumulated this much evidence; they would not play games. Nor could it

431

be any of the men with whom he ever worked on a heist, for he took great care to keep his acquaintances in the criminal underworld well out of his life on Fifth Avenue. None of them knew where he really lived; in the event they scouted a job requiring his planning skills and special knowledge, they could reach him only through a series of mail drops or through a chain of pseudonymously listed phone numbers backed up by answering services and answering machines. He was confident of the effectiveness of those precautions. Besides, if some hoodlum had got into this box, he would not have left the twenty-five thousand bucks untouched; he would have taken every dollar of it.

So who's on to me? Jack wondered.

He focused on the *fratellanza* warehouse robbery that he and Mort and Tommy Sung had pulled off December 3. Was the mafia after him? When they wanted to find someone, those boys had more contacts, sources, determination, and sheer perseverance than the FBI. And the *fratellanza* would most likely not have taken the twenty-five thousand, leaving it as an ominous notice that they wanted more than the money he had stolen from them. It was also in character for the *fratellanza* to leave a teaser like the postcard, because those guys enjoyed making a target sweat a lot before they finally pulled the trigger.

On the other hand, even if the mob tracked him down, then somehow searched back through his criminal career to see who else he had hit, they would not have gone to the trouble of acquiring cards from the Tranquillity Motel just to put the fear of God in him. If they had wanted to leave an upsetting teaser in the safe-deposit box, they would have left a photo of the warehouse that he had robbed in New Jersey.

So it was not the mafia. Then who? Damn it, who?

The tiny cubicle began to seem even smaller than it was. Jack felt claustrophobic and vulnerable. As long as he was in the bank, there was nowhere to run, nowhere to hide. He stuffed the twenty-five thousand into his overcoat pockets, no longer intending to give away any of it; suddenly, it had become his escape money. He put the postcard in his wallet, closed the empty box, and rang the buzzer for the attendant.

Two minutes later, he was outside, drawing deep breaths of

the freezing January air, studying the people on Fifth Avenue for one who might be tailing him. He saw no one suspicious.

For a moment he stood rocklike in the river of people that flowed around him. He wanted to get out of the city and the state as quickly as possible, flee to an unlikely destination, where they would not look for him. Whoever *they* were. Yet he was not entirely sure that flight was necessary. In Ranger training, he had been taught never to act until he understood why he was acting and until he knew what he hoped to achieve by his actions. Besides, fear of his faceless enemy was outweighed by curiosity; he needed to know who he was up against, how they had broken his various covers, and what they wanted from him.

Outside the Citibank Building, Jack hailed a cab and went to the corner of Wall Street and William Street, in the heart of the financial district, where he had six safe-deposit boxes in six banks. He went to four of them, from each of which he collected twenty-five thousand dollars and a postcard of the Tranquillity Motel.

He decided to stop after the third, because his coat pockets were already bulging with $125,000, a sufficiently dangerous sum to be carrying, and because, by now, he knew beyond a doubt that his other six phoney identities and clandestine safe-deposit boxes had been found out as well. He had enough money with which to travel, and he was not particularly worried about leaving the remaining $150,000 in the other six boxes. For one thing, Jack had four million in his Swiss accounts; and for another thing, the distributor of the postcards would already have taken the available money if that had been his intention.

By now, he'd had time to think about that motel out in Nevada, and he had begun to realise something was strange about the time that he had spent at the place. He had remained there for three days, relaxing, enjoying the quiet and the scenery. But now, for the first time, it seemed to him that he would have done no such thing. Not with so much cash in the trunk of his rental car. Not when he had already been away from New York (and Jenny) for two weeks. He would have driven straight home from Reno.

433

Now that he was forced to contemplate it, the three-day stay at the Tranquillity Motel did not make much sense.

Another taxi conveyed him to his Fifth Avenue apartment building, where he arrived shortly before eleven. He promptly telephoned Elite Flights, a company that chartered small jets, with whom he had dealt previously, and he was relieved to discover that, fortuitously, they had an unbooked Lear available for departure at his convenience.

He took the twenty-five thousand from the secret compartment in the back of his bedroom closet. With the funds he had removed from the safe-deposit boxes, he now had $150,000 in immediate operating capital, enough to deal with virtually any contingency that might arise.

He hurriedly packed three suitcases, distributing a few clothes in each, but leaving most of the space for other items. He stowed away two handguns: a Smith & Wesson Model 19 Combat Magnum, chambered for the .357 Magnum cartridge but also capable of firing .38 Special cartridges with considerably less kick; and a .32 Beretta Model 70, its stubby barrel grooved to accept a screw-on, pipe-type silencer, of which Jack included two. He also took an Uzi submachine gun, which he'd illegally modified for full automatic fire, plus plenty of ammunition.

Jack's newly acquired guilt had substantially transformed him during the past forty-eight hours, but it had not overwhelmed him to such an extent that he was incapable of dealing violently with those who might deal violently with him. His determination to be an honest and upstanding citizen did not interfere with his instinct for self-preservation. And considering his background, no one was better prepared to preserve himself than Jack Twist.

Besides, after eight years of alienation and loneliness, he had begun to rejoin society, had begun to hope for a normal life. He would not let anyone destroy what might be his last chance for happiness.

He also packed the portable SLICKS computer, which he had used to get through the armoured transport's sophisticated electronic lock the night before last in Connecticut. In addition, he decided he might need a Police Lock Release Gun, a tool that could instantly open any type of pin-tumbler lock –

434

mushroom, spool, or regular – without damaging the mechanism, and which was sold only to law-enforcement agencies.
And a Star Tron MK 202A, a compact, hand-held 'night vision'
device which could also be rifle-mounted. And a few other
things.

Although he distributed the heaviest weapons and equipment equally among the three large suitcases, none of the bags
was light when he finally closed and locked them. Anyone
who helped him with his luggage might wonder about the
contents, but no one would ask embarrassing questions or
raise an alarm. That was the advantage of leasing a Lear jet for
the journey: he would not be required to pass through airport
security, and no one would inspect his baggage.

From his apartment, he taxied to La Guardia.

The waiting Lear would take him to Salt Lake City, Utah, the
nearest major airport to Elko, a shade closer than Reno International, and a lot closer if you considered the necessity of
over-flying to Reno and then doubling back in a conventional-
engine commuter plane to Elko. Elite Flights had told him that
Reno was anticipating a major snowstorm that might close
them down later in the day, and the same was true of the two
smaller fields in southern Idaho that were capable of handling
Lear-size jets. But the weather forecast for Salt Lake City was
good throughout the day. At Jack's request, Elite was already
arranging the lease of a conventional-engine plane from a
Utah company to carry him from Salt Lake to the little county
airport in Elko. Although it was in the eastern-most fourth of
Nevada, Elko was still within the Pacific time zone, so he
would benefit from a gain of three hours, though he did not
think he would arrive in Elko much before nightfall.

That was all right. He'd need darkness for what he was
planning.

To Jack, the taunting postcards, retrieved from his safe-
deposit boxes, implied there were people in Nevada who had
learned everything worth knowing about his criminal life. The
cards seemed to be saying that he could reach those people
through the Tranquillity Motel or perhaps find them in
residence there. The postcard was an invitation. Or a
summons. Either way, he could ignore it only at his peril.

He did not know if he was being followed to La Guardia; he

435

did not bother looking for a tail. If his apartment phone was tapped, they knew he was coming the moment he called Elite Flights. He wanted them to see him approaching openly, for then they might be off-guard when, on arrival in Elko, he suddenly shook loose of them and went underground.

*   *   *

Monday morning, after breakfast, Dom and Ginger went into Elko, to the offices of the *Sentinel*, the county's only newspaper. The biggest town in the county, Elko boasted a population of less than ten thousand, so its newspaper's offices were not housed in a gleaming glass highrise but in a humble one-storey concrete-block building on a quiet street.

Like most papers, the *Sentinel* provided access to its back-issue files to anyone with legitimate research needs, though permission for the use of the files was granted judiciously.

In spite of the financial success of his first novel, Dom still had difficulty identifying himself as a writer. To his own ears, he sounded pretentious and phoney, though he realised his uneasiness was a holdover from his days as an excessively self-effacing milquetoast.

The receptionist, Brenda Hennerling, did not recognise his name, but when he mentioned the title of his novel that Random House had just shipped to the stores, she said, 'It's the book-club selection this month! You wrote it? Really?' She had ordered it a month ago from the Literary Guild, and it had just arrived in the mail. She was (she said) an avid reader, two books a week, and it was truly a thrill to meet a genuine novelist. Her enthusiasm only added to Dom's embarrassment. He was of a mind with Robert Louis Stevenson, who had said, 'The important thing is the tale, the well-told tale, not he who tells it.'

The *Sentinel's* back-issue files were kept in a narrow, windowless chamber. There were two desks with typewriters, a microfilm reader, a file of microfilm spools, and six tall filing cabinets with oversize drawers containing those editions of the newspaper that had not yet been transferred to film. The exposed concrete-block walls were painted pale grey, and the acoustic-tile ceiling was grey, and the fluorescent lights shed a cold glare. Dom had the odd sensation that they were in a submarine, far beneath the surface of the sea.

After Brenda Hennerling explained the filing system to them and left them alone to do their work, Ginger said, 'I'm so caught up in our problems that I keep forgetting you're a famous author.'

'So do I,' Dom said, reading the labels on the filing cabinets that held issues of past *Sentinels*. 'But of course, I'm not famous.'

'Soon will be. It's a shame: with all that's happening to us, you're getting no chance to savour the publication of your first novel.'

He shrugged. 'This isn't a picnic for any of us. You've had to put an entire medical career on hold.'

'Yes, but now I know I'll be able to go back to medicine once we've dug to the bottom of this,' Ginger said, as if there was no doubt they would triumph over their enemies. By now, Dom knew that conviction and determination were as much a part of her as the blueness of her eyes. 'But this is your *first* book.'

Dom had not yet recovered from his embarrassment at being treated like a celebrity by the receptionist. Now Ginger's kind comments kept a blush on his cheeks. However, this was not the mark of embarrassment; it was an indication of the intense pleasure he took in being the object of her concern. No woman had ever affected him as this one did.

Together, they went through the file drawers and removed the pertinent back issues of the *Sentinel*. They would not need to use the microfilm reader, for the newspaper was running two years behind in the transferral to film. They withdrew a full week's editions, beginning with Saturday, July 7, of the summer before last, and took them to one of the desks, where they both pulled up chairs.

Although the unremembered event that they had witnessed, and the possible contamination, and the closure of I-80 had happened on Friday night, July 6, the Saturday paper carried no report of the toxic spill. The *Sentinel* was primarily a source of local and state news and, though it included some national and international material, was not interested in fast-breaking stories. Its halls would never ring with that dramatic cry, 'Stop press!' There would be no last-minute recomposition of the front page. The pace of life in Elko County was rural, relaxed, sensible, and no one felt a burning need to be breathlessly up-to-the-minute on anything. The *Sentinel* was put to bed late in the evening, for distribution in the morning; therefore, since no Sunday edition was published, the story of the toxic spill and the closure of I-80 did not appear until the edition of Monday, July 9.

But Monday's and Tuesday's editions were emblazoned with urgent headlines: TOXIC SPILL CLOSES I-80, and ARMY ESTABLISHES QUARANTINE ZONE, and NERVE GAS LEAKING FROM DAMAGED TRUCK?, and ARMY SAYS EVERYONE EVACUATED FROM DANGER ZONE, and WHERE ARE EVACUEES?, and SHENKFIELD ARMY TESTING GROUNDS: WHAT REALLY GOES ON THERE?, and I-80 CLOSURE ENTERS FOURTH DAY, and CLEAN-UP ALMOST FINISHED; HIGHWAY OPEN BY NOON.

For both Dom and Ginger, it was eerie to read about these events that had transpired during days when they remembered nothing more than relaxing quietly at the Tranquillity Motel. As Dom read about the crisis, he became convinced Ginger's theory was correct; it seemed obvious that the mind-control technicians would have needed an extra week or two in order to have incorporated this elaborate toxic-spill cover-story into the phoney memories of both Elko County locals *and* passers-through, and there was no way they could have kept the highway closed and the area sealed tight for that long.

The edition of Wednesday, July 11, continued the saga: I-80 OPENS!, and QUARANTINE REMOVED: NO LONG-TERM CONTAMINATION, and FIRST EVACUEES LOCATED: THEY SAW NOTHING.

Editions of the *Sentinel*, distinctly a small-town paper, averaged between sixteen and thirty-two pages. During those days in July, most of its news space was given to reports of the toxic crisis, for this event had drawn reporters from all over the country, and the low-key *Sentinel* found itself at the centre of a big story. Poring over that wealth of material, Dom and Ginger discovered a lot that was pertinent to their quest and that would help them plan their next move.

For one thing, the degree of security imposed by the United States Army was soberly instructive of the lengths to which they would go to keep the lid on the truth. Although it was not strictly within their authority to do so, Army units attached to

Shenkfield had established roadblocks and closed a ten-mile stretch of I-80 immediately after the accident; they had not even informed the Elko County Sheriff or the Nevada State Police of the crisis until they had secured the quarantine zone. That was a startling breach of standard procedure. Throughout the emergency, the sheriff and state police complained with increasing vehemence that the Army was freezing them out of every aspect of crisis management and usurping civilian authority; state and local police were neither included in the maintenance of the quarantine line nor consulted on essential contingency planning for the possibility that increased winds or other factors might spread the nerve gas beyond the initial area of danger. Clearly, the military trusted only its own people to keep the secret of what was actually happening in the quarantine zone.

Following two days of frustration, Foster Hanks, the Elko County Sheriff, had complained to a *Sentinel* reporter that: 'This here's *my* bailiwick, by God, and the people elected *me* to keep peace. This is no military dictatorship. If I don't get some cooperation from the Army, I'll see a judge first thing tomorrow and get a court order to make them respect the legal jurisdictions in this matter.' The Tuesday *Sentinel* reported that Hanks had, indeed, gone before a judge, but before a determination could be made, the crisis was drawing to an end and the argument about jurisdiction was moot.

Huddling over the newspaper with Dom, Ginger said, 'So we don't have to worry that *all* authorities are aligned against us in this. The state and local police weren't part of it. Our only adversary is . . .'

'The United States Army,' Dom finished, laughing at the unconscious element of graveyard humour in her assessment of the enemy.

She also laughed sourly. 'Us against the Army. Even with state and local police out of the battle, it's hardly a fair match, is it?'

According to the *Sentinel*, the Army kept sole and iron control of the roadblocks on I-80, the only east-west artery through forbidden territory, and also closed eight miles of the north-south county road. Civilian air traffic was restricted from passing over the contaminated area, necessitating the rerouting of flights, while the Army maintained continuous helicopter patrols of the perimeter of the proscribed land. Obviously, substantial manpower was required to secure eighty square miles, but regardless of expense and difficulty, they were determined to stop anyone entering the danger zone on foot, on horseback, or in four-wheel-drive vehicles. The choppers flew in daylight and after dark, as well, sweeping the night with searchlights. Rumours circulated that teams of soldiers, equipped with infra-red surveillance gear, were also patrolling the perimeter at night, looking for interlopers who might have slipped past the big choppers' searchlights.

'Nerve gases rate among the deadliest substances known to man,' Ginger said as Dom turned a page of the newspaper they were currently perusing. 'But even so, this much security seems excessive. Besides, though I'm no expert on chemical warfare, I can't believe *any* nerve gas would pose a threat at such a distance from a single point of release. I mean, according to the Army, it was only one cylinder of gas, not an enormous quantity, not a whole tanker truck as Ernie and Faye remembered it. And it's the nature of gas to disperse, to expand upon release. So by the time the stuff spread a couple of miles, it would've been diluted to such a degree that surely the air would've contained no more of it than a few parts per billion. In three miles . . . not even one part per billion. Not enough to endanger anyone.'

'This supports your idea that it was biological contamination.'

'Possibly,' Ginger said. 'It's too early to say. But it was certainly more serious than the nerve-gas story they put out.'

By Saturday, July 7, less than one day after the interstate was closed, an alert wire-service reporter had noted that the uniforms of many of soldiers in the quarantine operation bore – in addition to rank and standard insignia – an unusual company patch: a black circle with an emerald-green star in the centre. This was different from the markings on the uniforms of the men from Shenkfield Testing Grounds. Among those wearing the green star, the ratio of officers to enlisted men was high. When questioned, the Army identified the green-star soldiers as a little-known, super-elite company of Special Forces troops. 'We call them DERO, which stands for Domestic

Emergency Response Organisation,' an Army spokesman was quoted by the *Sentinel*. 'The men of DERO are superbly trained, and they've all had extensive field experience in combat situations, *and* all of them carry top-security clearances, as well, which is essential because they may find themselves operating in highly classified areas, witness to sensitive sights.'

Dom translated that to mean DERO men were chosen, in part, for their ability and willingness to keep their goddamn mouths shut.

The *Sentinel* quoted the Army spokesman further: 'They're the cream of our young career soldiers, so naturally many have attained the rank of at least sergeant by the time they qualify for DERO. Our intention is to create a superbly trained force to deal with extraordinary crises, such as terrorist attacks on domestic military installations, nuclear emergencies on bases housing atomic weapons, and other unusual problems. Not that there's any aspect of terrorism involved in this case. And there's no nuclear emergency here, either. But several DERO companies are stationed around the country, and since one was near when this nerve-gas situation arose, it seemed prudent to bring in the best we had to ensure public safety.' He refused to tell reporters where this DERO company had been stationed, how far they had been flown, or how many were involved. 'That's classified information.' Not one of the DERO men would speak with any member of the press.

Ginger grimaced and said, '*Shmontses*!'

Dom blinked. 'Huh?'

'Their whole story,' she said, leaning back in her chair and rolling her head from side to side to work out a cramp in her lovely neck. 'It's all just *shmontses*.'

'But what's *shmontses*?'

'Oh. Sorry. Yiddish word, adapted from German, I guess. One of my father's favourites. It means something of no value, something foolish, absurd, nonsense, worthy of contempt or scorn. This stuff the Army put out is just *shmontses*.' She stopped rolling her head, leaned forward in her chair, and stabbed one finger at the newspaper. 'So this DERO team just happened to be hanging around here in the middle of nowhere precisely when this crisis arose, huh? Too damned neat.'

Dom frowned. 'But, Ginger, according to these stories,

441

although the roadblocks on I-80 were set up by men from Shenkfield, the DERO team took over little more than an hour later. So if they didn't just happen to be nearby, the only way they could've gotten here so quickly was if they were airborne and on their way *before the accident ever happened.*'

'Exactly.'

'You're saying they knew in advance there'd be a toxic spill?'

She sighed. 'At most, I'm willing to accept that a DERO team might've been at one of the nearest military bases . . . in western Utah or maybe up in southern Idaho. But even that's not near enough to make the Army's scenario work. Even if they dropped everything and flew in here the moment they heard about the spill, they couldn't have been manning those roadblocks within an hour. No way. So, yeah, it sure looks to me as if they had a little advance warning that something was going to happen out at the western end of Elko County. Not much warning, mind you. Not days. But maybe a one- or two-hour advance notice.'

'Which means the toxic spill couldn't have been an accident. In fact, probably wasn't a spill at all, neither chemical nor biological. So why in hell were they wearing decontamination suits when they were treating us?' Dom was frustrated by the elaborate maze of this mystery, which twisted and turned inwards but not towards a solution, towards nothing but twistier and more complex pathways that led into ever deeper puzzlement. He had the irrational urge to tear the newspapers to shreds, as if, by ripping them to pieces, he would also be ripping apart the Army's lies and would somehow find the truth revealed, at last, in the resultant confetti.

With a note of frustration that matched his own, Ginger said, 'The only reason the Army called in a DERO company to enforce the quarantine was because the men patrolling the zone would have a view of something highly classified, something absolutely top-secret. The Army felt they couldn't trust ordinary soldiers who didn't have the very highest security clearance. That's the sole reason the DERO team was used.'

'Because they could be trusted to keep their mouths shut.'

'Yes. And if it'd been nothing more than a toxic spill out there on I-80, the DERO men wouldn't have been required for the job. I mean, if it was just a spill, what would there've been

442

to see except maybe an overturned truck and a damaged, leaking canister of gas or liquid?'

Turning their attention once more to the newspapers spread before them, they soon found additional evidence indicating the Army had had at least some warning that unusual and spectacular trouble would erupt in western Elko County that hot July night. Both Dom and Ginger distinctly remembered that the Tranquillity Grille had been filled with a strange sound and shaken by earthquake-like tremors about half an hour after full darkness had settled on the land; and because sunset came later during the summer (even at 40° North Latitude), the trouble must have started approximately at 8:10. Their memory blocks began at the same time, which further pinpointed The Event. Yet Dom spotted a line in one of the *Sentinel's* stories stating that the roadblocks on I-80 had been erected almost at eight o'clock on the dot.

Ginger said, 'You mean the Army had the highway closed off five or ten minutes before the 'accidental' toxic spill even happened?'

'Yeah. Unless we're wrong about the time of the sunset.'

They checked the weather column in the July 6 edition of the *Sentinel*. It painted a more than adequate portrait of that fateful day. The high temperature had been expected to hit ninety degrees, with an overnight low of sixty-four. Humidity between twenty and twenty-five per cent. Clear skies. Light to variable winds. And sunset at 7:31.

'Twilight's short out here,' Dom said. 'Fifteen minutes, tops. Figure full darkness at 7:45. Now, even if we're wrong to think it was half an hour after nightfall that trouble hit, even if it came just fifteen minutes after dark, the Army *still* had its roadblocks up first.'

'So they knew what was coming,' Ginger said.

'But they couldn't stop it from happening.'

'Which means it must've been some process, some series of events, that they initiated and then were unable to control.'

'Maybe,' Dom said. 'But maybe not. Maybe they weren't really at fault. Until we know more, we're just speculating. No point to it.'

Ginger turned the page of the *Sentinel's* edition for Wednesday, July 11, which they were currently examining, and her gasp of surprise directed Dom's attention to a head-and-shoulders photograph of a man in an Army officer's uniform and cap. Although Colonel Leland Falkirk had appeared in neither Dom's nor Ginger's dreams last night, they both recognised him at once because of the description that Ernie and Ned had supplied from their nightmares: dark hair greying at the temples, eyes with an eerie translucency, a beakish nose, thin lips, a face of flat hard planes and sharp angles.

Dom read the caption under the picture: *Colonel Leland Falkirk, commanding officer of the company of DERO troops manning the quarantine line, has been an elusive target for reporters. This first photograph was obtained by* Sentinel *photographer, Greg Lunde. Caught by surprise, Falkirk was angry about being photographed. His answers to the few questions asked him were even shorter than the standard 'no comment.'*

Dom might have smiled at the quiet humour in the last sentence of the caption, but Falkirk's stony visage chilled him. He instantly recognised the face not only because of Ernie's and Ned's description, but because he had seen it before, the summer before last. Furthermore, there was a ferocity in that hawklike countenance and in those predatory eyes that was dismaying; this man routinely got what he wanted. To be at his mercy was a frightening prospect.

Staring at the photograph of Falkirk, Ginger softly said, *'Kayn ayn hore.'* Aware of Dom's puzzlement, she said, 'That's Yiddish, too. *Kayn ayn hore.* It's an expression that's used to . . . to ward off the evil eye. Somehow, it seemed appropriate.'

Dom studied the photograph, half mesmerised by it.

After a moment, he said, 'Yes. Quite appropriate.'

Colonel Falkirk's sharply chiselled face and cold pale eyes were so striking that it seemed as if he were alive within this photograph, as if he were returning their scrutiny.

*   *   *

While Dom and Ginger were examining the back-issue files at the *Elko Sentinel*, Ernie and Faye Block were working in the office of the Tranquillity Motel, trying to contact the people whose names were on the guest list for July 6, two summers ago, but who had thus far been unreachable. They were

444

behind the check-in counter, sitting opposite each other at the oak desk, which had kneeholes on both sides. A pot of coffee stood within reach on an electric warming-plate.

Ernie composed a telegram to Gerald Salcoe, the man who had rented two rooms for his family on July 6, the summer before last, and who was unreachable by phone because his number in Monterey, California, was unlisted. Meanwhile, Faye went back through last year's guest book, day by day, looking for the most recent entry for Cal Sharkle, the trucker who had stayed with them on that July 6. Yesterday, Dom had tried the telephone number Cal had printed in the guest registry that night, but it had been disconnected. The hope was that a more recent entry would provide his new address and phone number.

As they performed their separate tasks, Ernie was reminded of countless other times throughout their thirty-one years of marriage when they had sat facing each other at a desk or, more often, at a kitchen table. In one apartment or another, in one house or another, at one end of the world or another, from Quantico to Pendleton to Singapore, nearly everywhere the Marines sent him, the two of them had spent long evenings at a kitchen table, working or dreaming or worrying or happily planning together, often late into the night. Ernie was suddenly filled with poignant echoes of those thousands of huddled conferences and shared labours. How very fortunate he had been to find and marry Faye. Their lives were so inextricably linked that they might as well have been a single creature. If Colonel Falkirk or others resorted to murder to terminate this investigation, if anything happened to Faye, then Ernie hoped he would die, too, simultaneously.

He finished composing the telegram to Gerald Salcoe, called it in to Western Union, and requested immediate delivery – all the while warmed by a love that was strong enough to make their dangerous situation seem less threatening than it really was.

Faye found five occasions during the past year when Cal Sharkle had stayed overnight, and in every case he had listed the same Evanston, Illinois, address and phone number that he had entered in the registry for July 6 of the previous year. Apparently, he had not moved, after all. Yet, when they dialled his number, they obtained the recording that Dom had got yesterday, informing them that the telephone had been disconnected and that no new Evanston listing existed.

On the chance that Cal had moved out of Evanston into the 'Windy City' itself, Faye dialled Area Code 312 Information and asked if there was a number for Calvin Sharkle in Chicago. There was not. Using a map of Illinois, she and Ernie placed calls to Information in the Chicago suburbs: Whiting, Hammond, Calumet City, Markham, Downer's Grove, Oak Park, Oakbrook, Elmhurst, Des Plaines, Rolling Meadows, Arlington Heights, Skokie, Wilmette, Glencoe. . . . No luck. Either Cal Sharkle had moved out of the Chicago area, or had dropped off the face of the earth.

*   *   *

While Faye and Ernie worked in the first-floor office, Ned and Sandy Sarver were already preparing dinner in the kitchen upstairs. This evening, after Brendan Cronin arrived from Chicago, after Jorja Monatella and her little girl flew in from Vegas, there would be nine for dinner, and Ned did not want to leave preparations until the last minute. Yesterday, when all six of them joined forces to prepare and serve the evening meal, Ginger Weiss had observed that the occasion was almost like a family holiday gathering; and indeed, they felt an extraordinary closeness though they hardly knew one another. With the idea that reinforcement of their special affection and camaraderie might give them strength to face whatever lay ahead of them, Ned and Sandy had decided that tonight's meal ought to be like a Thanksgiving feast. Therefore, they were preparing a sixteen-pound turkey, pecan stuffing, scalloped potatoes, baked corn, carrots with tarragon, pepper slaw, pumpkin pie, and made-from-scratch crescent rolls.

As they chopped celery, diced onions, cubed bread, and grated cabbage, Ned occasionally wondered if what they were cooking was not only a family feast but also the last hearty meal of the condemned. Each time that morbid thought rose, he chased it away by pausing to watch Sandy as she worked. She smiled almost constantly, and sometimes softly hummed a song. Surely, an event that had induced this

446

radical and wonderful change in Sandy could not ultimately culminate in their deaths. Surely, they had nothing to worry about. Surely.

*   *   *

After three hours at the *Elko Sentinel*, Ginger and Dom ate a light lunch – chef's salads – at a restaurant on Idaho Street, then returned to the Tranquillity Motel at two-thirty. Faye and Ernie were still in the office, which was filled with appetising aromas drifting down from the apartment upstairs: pumpkin, cinnamon, nutmeg, onions fried lightly in butter, the yeasty odour of baking bread dough.

'And you can't smell the turkey yet,' Faye said. 'Ned just put that in the oven half an hour ago.'

'He says dinner's at eight,' Ernie told them, 'but I suspect the odours'll drive us mad and force us to storm the kitchen before then.'

Faye said, 'Learn anything at the *Sentinel*?'

Before Ginger could tell them what she and Dom had uncovered, the front door of the motel office opened, and a slightly pudgy man entered in a burst of cold whirling wind. He had hurried from his car without bothering to put on a topcoat; although he wore grey slacks, a dark blue blazer, a light blue sweater, and an ordinary white shirt, rather than a black suit and Roman collar, his identity was not for a moment in doubt. He was the auburn-haired, green-eyed, round-faced young priest in the Polaroid snapshot that the unknown correspondent had sent to Dom.

'Father Cronin,' Ginger said.

She was as immediately and powerfully drawn to him as she'd been to Dominick Corvaisis. With the priest as with Dom, Ginger sensed a shared experience even more shattering than the one which she had shared with the Blocks and Sarvers. Within The Event that they had all witnessed that Friday in July, there had been a Second Event experienced by only some of them. Although it was a frightfully improper way to greet a man who was a virtual stranger *and* a priest, Ginger rushed to Father Cronin and threw her arms around him.

But apologies were not required, for Father Cronin evidently sensed the same thing she did. Without hesitation, he

447

returned her hug, and for a moment they clung to each other, not as if they were strangers but brother and sister greeting each other after a long separation.

Then Ginger stepped back as Dom said, 'Father Cronin,' and came forward to embrace the priest.

'There's no need to call me "Father." At the moment I neither want nor deserve to be considered a priest. Please just call me Brendan.'

Ernie shouted upstairs to Ned and Sandy, then followed Faye out from behind the check-in counter. Brendan shook Ernie's hand and embraced Faye, obviously feeling great affection for them, though not a closeness as powerful and inexplicable as the tremendous emotional magnetism that pulled him towards Dom and Ginger. When Ned and Sandy came downstairs, he greeted them the same as he had Ernie and Faye.

Just as Ginger had done last night, Brendan said, 'I have a truly wonderful sense of . . . being among family. You all feel it, don't you? As if we've shared the most important moments of our lives . . . went through something that'll always make us different from everyone else.'

In spite of his insistence that he did not deserve the deference accorded a priest, Brendan Cronin had a profoundly spiritual air about him. His somewhat pudgy face, sparkling eyes, and broad warm smile conveyed joy; and he moved among them, touched them, and spoke with an ebullience that was infectious and that somehow lifted Ginger's soul.

Brendan said, 'What I feel in this room only reassures me that I've made the right decision in coming. I'm *meant* to be with you. Something will happen here that'll transform us, that's already begun to transform us. Do you feel it? Do you *feel* it?'

The priest's soft voice sent a pleasant shiver up Ginger's spine, filled her with an indescribable sense of wonder reminiscent of what she'd felt the first time that, as a medical student, she had stood in an operating room and had seen a patient's thorax held open by surgical retractors to reveal the pulsing, mysterious complexity of the human heart in all its crimson grandeur.

'Called,' Brendan repeated. The softly spoken word echoed

448

eerily around the room. 'All of us. Called back to this place.'

'*Look*,' Dom said, packing a paragraph of amazement into that one syllable, raising his arms and holding his hands out to show them the red rings of swollen flesh that had appeared in his palms.

Surprised, Brendan raised his hands, which were also branded by the strange stigmata. As the men faced each other, the air thickened with unknown power. Yesterday, on the telephone, Father Wycazik had told Dom that Brendan was relatively certain no religious element was involved in the miraculous cures and other events that had recently transformed the young priest's life. Yet the motel office seemed, to Ginger, to be filled with a force that, if not supernatural, was certainly beyond the ken of any man or woman.

'Called,' Brendan said again.

Ginger was gripped by breathless expectancy. She looked at Ernie, who stood behind Faye with his hands on her shoulders, and both their faces were full of tremulous suspense. Ned and Sandy, who were by the rack of postcards, holding hands, were wide-eyed.

Ginger felt the flesh prickling on the back of her neck. She thought, *Something's going to happen*, and even as the thought took form, something did.

Every lamp in the motel office was aglow in deference to Ernie's uneasiness in the presence of deep shadows, but abruptly the place was even brighter than it had been. A milky-white light filled the room, springing magically from molecules of air. It shimmered on all sides but rained mostly from overhead, a silvery mist of luminosity. She realised this was the same light that featured in her unremembered lunar dreams. She turned in a circle, looking around and up through spangled curtains of brilliant yet soft radiance, not in search of the source but with the hope of remembering her dreams and, ultimately, the events of that long-lost summer night that had inspired the dreams.

Ginger saw Sandy reach into the glowing air with one hand, as if to grasp a fistful of the miraculous light. A tentative smile pulled at Ned's mouth. Faye smiled, too, and Ernie's expression of childlike wonder was almost laughably out of place on his ruggedly hewn face.

'The moon,' Ernie said.

'The moon,' Dom echoed, the stigmata still blazing on his hands.

For one thrilling moment, Ginger Weiss was poised on the brink of complete understanding. The black, blank membrane of her memory block trembled; revelation pressed strenuously against the far side, and that membrane seemed certain to split and spill forth everything that had been dammed beyond it.

Then the light changed from moon-white to blood-red, and with it the mood changed from wonder and growing delight to fear. She no longer sought revelation but dreaded it, no longer welcomed understanding but withdrew from it in terror and revulsion.

Ginger stumbled back through the bloody glow, bumped against the front door. Across the room, beyond Dom and Brendan, Sandy Sarver had ceased reaching up to seize a handful of light; she was holding tightly to Ned, whose smile had become a rictus of repulsion. Faye and Ernie were pressing back against the check-in counter.

As scarlet incandescence welled like fluid into the room and filled it from corner to corner, the stunning visual phenomena were augmented by sound. Ginger jumped in surprise as a loud three-part crash shook the sanguineous air, jumped once more as it repeated, then flinched but did not jump when it came again. It had a cardiac quality, like the thunderous beating of a great heart, though it featured one more stroke than a usual heartbeat: *LUB-DUB-dub, LUB-DUB-dub, LUB-DUB-dub.* . . . She knew at once that it was the apparitional noise of which Father Wycazik had spoken in his telephone conversation with Dom, the noise that had arisen in Brendan Cronin's bedroom and had shaken St Bernadette's.

But she also knew that she had heard this very thing before. This entire display – the moonlike light, the blood-red radiance, the noise – were part of something that had happened the summer before last.

LUB-DUB-dub . . . *LUB-DUB-dub* . . .

The window frames rattled. The walls shook. The bloody light and the lamplight began to pulse in time with the pounding.

LUB-DUB-dub . . . *LUB-DUB-dub* . . .

Again, Ginger was approaching a shocking recollection. With each crash of sound and throb of light, long-buried memories surged nearer.

However, her inhibiting fear grew; a towering black wave of terror bore down on her. The Azrael Block was doing what it was designed to do; rather than let remembrance have its way with her, she would plunge into a fugue state, as she had not done since the day Pablo Jackson had been killed, one week ago. The familiar signs of oncoming blackout were present: she was having difficulty breathing; she trembled with a sense of mortal danger so strong it was palpable; the world around her began to fade; an oily darkness seeped in at the edges of her vision.

Run or die.

Ginger turned her back on the phenomenal events transpiring in the office. With both hands, she gripped the frame of the front door, as if to anchor herself to consciousness and thwart the black wave that sought to sweep her away. In desperation, she looked through the glass at the vast Nevada landscape, at the sombre winter sky, trying to block out the stimuli – the impossible light and sound – that pushed her towards a dark fugue. Terror and mindless panic grew so unbearable that escape into a hateful fugue seemed almost preferable, yet she somehow held fast to the doorframe, held tight, held on, shaking and gasping, held on, terrified not so much by the strange events occurring behind her but by the unremembered events of *that* summer of which these phenomena were only dim echoes, and still she held on, held on . . . until the three-stroke thunder faded, until the red light paled, until the room was silent, and until the only light was that coming through the windows or from ordinary lighting fixtures.

She was all right now. She was not going to black out.

For the first time, she had successfully resisted a seizure. Maybe her ordeal of the past few months had toughened her. Maybe just *being* here, within reach of all the answers to the mystery, had given her the heart to resist. Or maybe she had drawn strength from her new 'family.' Whatever the reason, she was confident that, having once fended off a fugue, she would find it easier to deal with future attacks. Her memory blocks were crumbling. And her fear of facing up to what had happened that July 6 was now far outweighed by the fear of never knowing.

Shaky, Ginger turned toward the others again.

Brendan Cronin tottered to the sofa and sat, trembling visibly. The rings were no longer visible in either his hands or Dom's.

To the priest, Ernie said, 'Did I understand you? That same light sometimes fills your room at night?'

'Yes,' Brendan acknowledged. 'Twice before.'

'But you told us it was a *lovely* sight,' Faye said.

'Yeah,' Ned agreed. 'You made it sound . . . wonderful.'

'It is,' Brendan said. 'Partly, it is. But when it turns red . . . well, then it scares the hell out of me. But when it first starts . . . oh, it uplifts me and fills me with the strangest joy.'

The ominous scarlet light and the frightening three-part hammering had generated such terror in Ginger that she had temporarily forgotten the exhilarating moon-white glow that had preceded it and that had filled her with wonder.

Wiping his palms on his shirt, as if the vanished rings had left an unwanted residue upon his hands, Dom said, 'There was both a good and evil aspect to the events of that night. We long to relive a part of what happened to us, yet at the same time it scares us . . . scares us . . .'

'Scares us shitless,' Ernie said.

Ginger noticed that even Sandy Sarver, who heretofore had perceived only a benign shape to the mystery, was frowning.

*　　　*　　　*

When Jorja Monatella buried her ex-husband, Alan Rykoff, at eleven o'clock Monday morning, the Las Vegas sun beamed down between scattered iron-grey clouds. A hundred shafts of golden sunshine, some half a mile across, some only a few yards wide, like cosmic spotlights, left many buildings in winter shadows while highlighting others. Several shafts of sunshine moved across the cemetery, harried by the rushing clouds, sweeping eastwards across the barren floor of the desert. As the portly funeral director concluded a nondenominational prayer, as the casket was lowered into the waiting grave, a particularly bright beam illuminated the scene, the colour *burst* from the flowers.

In addition to Jorja and Paul Rykoff – Alan's father, who had flown in from Florida – only five people had shown up. Even Jorja's parents had not come. By his selfishness, Alan had assured an exit from life accom panied by a minimum of grieving. Paul Rykoff, too like his son in some respects, blamed Jorja for everything. He had been barely civil since his arrival yesterday. Now that his only child was in the ground, he turned from Jorja, stone-faced, and she knew she would meet him again only if his stubbornness and anger eventually were outweighed by a desire to see his grandchild. ·

She drove only a mile before she pulled to the side of the road, stopped, and finally wept. She wept neither for Alan's suffering nor for the loss of him, but for the final destruction of all the hope with which their relationship had begun, the burnt-out hopes for love, family friendship, mutual goals, and shared lives. She had not wished Alan dead. But now that he *was* dead, she knew it would be easier to make the new beginning toward which she had been planning and working, and that realisation made her feel neither guilty nor cruel; it was just sad.

Last night, Jorja told Marcie her father was dead, though not that he'd committed suicide. Initially, Jorja had not intended to tell her until this afternoon, in the presence of Dr Coverly, the psychologist. But the appointment with Coverly had to be cancelled because, later today, Jorja and Marcie were flying to Elko to join Dominick Corvaisis, Ginger Weiss, and the others. Marcie took the news of Alan's death surprisingly well. She cried, but not hard or long. At seven, she was old enough to understand death, but still too young to grasp the cruel finality of it. Besides, by his abandonment of Marcie, Alan unwittingly had done the girl a favour; in a sense, for her, he had died more than a year ago, and her mourning had already been done.

One other thing had helped Marcie overcome her grief: her obsession with the collection of moon pictures. Only an hour after she learned of her father's death, the child was sitting at the dining room table, eyes dry, small pink tongue poked between her teeth in total concentration, a crayon stub in one hand. She'd begun the moon-colouring project on Friday evening and pursued it through the weekend. By breakfast this morning, every one of the photographs and all but fifty of

453

the hundreds of hand-drawn moons had been transformed into fiery globes.

Marcie's obsession would have disturbed Jorja even if she had not known others shared it and that two had killed themselves. The moon was not yet the focus of the girl's every waking hour. However, Jorja required little imagination to see that, if the obsession progressed, Marcie might travel irretrievably into the land of madness.

Her anxiety about Marcie was so acute that she quickly overcame the tears that had forced her to pull to the side of the road. She put the Chevette in gear and drove to her parents' house, where Marcie waited.

The girl was at the kitchen table with the ubiquitous album of moons, applying a scarlet crayon. She glanced up when Jorja arrived, smiled weakly, and returned at once to the task before her.

Pete, Jorja's father, was also at the table, frowning at Marcie. Occasionally, he thought of a stratagem to interest her in some activity less bizarre and more wholesome than the endless colouring of moons, but all his attempts to lure her away from the album failed.

In her parents' bedroom, Jorja changed from her dress into jeans and a sweater for the trip north, while Mary Monatella badgered her. 'When will you take that book away from Marcie? Or let *me* take it away?'

'Mother, I told you before: Dr Coverly believes taking the book from her right now would only reinforce her obsession.'

'That doesn't make any sense to me,' Jorja's mother said.

'Dr Coverly says if we make an issue of the moon collection at this early stage, we'll be emphasising its importance and –'

'Nonsense. Does this Coverly have kids of his own?'

'I don't know, Mom.'

'I'll bet he doesn't have kids of his own. If he did, he wouldn't be giving you such dumb advice.'

Having put her dress on a hanger, having stripped down to bra and panties, Jorja felt naked and vulnerable, for this situation reminded her of when her mother used to watch her dress for dates with boys who did not meet approval. No boy ever met Mary's approval. In fact, Jorja married Alan in part because Mary disapproved of him. Matrimony as rebellion.

Stupid, but she had done it and paid dearly. Mary had driven her to it – Mary's suffocating and authoritarian brand of love. Now, Jorja grabbed the jeans that were laid out on the bed and slipped into them, dressing fast.

Mary said, 'She won't even say why she's collecting those things.'

'Because she doesn't know why. It's a compulsion. An irrational obsession, and if there's a reason for it, the reason is buried down in her subconscious, where even she can't get a look at it.'

Mary said, 'That book should be taken away from her.'

'Eventually,' Jorja said. 'One step at a time, Mom.'

'If it was up to me, I'd do it right now.'

Jorja had packed two big suitcases and had left them here earlier. Now, when it was time to go to the airport, Pete drove, and Mary went along for the opportunity to engage in more nagging.

Jorja and Marcie shared the back seat. On the way to the airport, the girl paged continuously, silently back and forth through her album.

Between Jorja and Mary, the subject of conversation had changed from the best way to deal with Marcie's obsession to the imminent trip to Elko. Mary had doubts about this expedition and did not hesitate to express them. Was the plane just a twelve-seater? Wasn't it dangerous to go up in a bucket of bolts owned by a small-time outfit that was probably short of cash and skimped on maintenance? What was the purpose of going, anyway? Even if some people in Elko were having problems like Marcie's, how could it possibly have anything to do with the fact that they'd all stayed at the same motel?

'This Corvaisis guy bothers me,' Pete said as he braked for a red traffic light. 'I don't like you getting involved with his kind.'

'What do you mean? You don't even know him.'

'I know enough,' Pete said. 'He's a writer, and you know what they're like. I read once where that Norman Mailer hung his wife out a high window by her heels. And isn't it Hemingway who's always getting in fist-fights?'

Jorja said, 'Daddy, Hemingway's dead.'

'*See*? Always getting in fights, drunk, using drugs. Writers are a flaky bunch. I don't like you being involved with writers.'

'This trip is a big mistake,' Mary said flatly.

It never ended.

At the airport, when she kissed them goodbye, they told her they loved her, and she told them the same, and the strange thing was that they were all telling the truth. Though they continuously sniped at her and though she had been deeply wounded by their sniping, they loved one another. Without love, they would have stopped speaking long ago. The parent-child relationship was sometimes even more perplexing than the mystery of what had happened at the Tranquillity Motel two summers ago.

The feeder line's bucket of bolts was more comfortable than Mary would have believed, with six-well padded seats on each side of a narrow aisle, free headphones providing bland but mellowing Muzak tapes, and a pilot who handled his craft as gently as a new mother carried her baby.

Thirty minutes out of Las Vegas, Marcie closed the album and, in spite of the daylight streaming through the portholes, she drifted off to sleep, lulled by the loud but hypnotic droning of the engines.

During the flight, Jorja thought about her future: the business degree towards which she was working, her hope of owning a dress shop, the hard work ahead – and loneliness, which was already a problem for her. She wanted a man. Not sexually. Although *that* would be welcome too! She had dated a few times since the divorce but had been to bed with no one. She was no female eunuch. Sex was important to her, and she missed it. But sex was not the main reason she wanted a man, one special man, a mate. She needed someone to share her dreams, triumphs, and failures. She had Marcie, but that was not the same. The human species seemed genetically compelled to make life's journey two-by-two, and the need was particularly strong in Jorja.

As the plane droned north-northeast, Jorja listened to Mantovani on the headphones and indulged in a bit of uncharacteristic, girlish fantasising. At the Tranquillity Motel, perhaps she would meet a special man with whom she could share this new beginning. She recalled Dominick Corvaisis's gentle but confident voice, and included him in her fantasy. If Corvaisis

456

was the one for her, imagine what her father would say when he learned she was marrying one of those flaky, drunken writers who held their wives by the heels and dangled them out high windows!

She scrapped that particular fantasy soon after the plane landed, for she quickly perceived that Corvaisis's heart was already claimed.

At four-thirty in Elko, half an hour before sunset, the sky was plated with dark clouds, and the Ruby Mountains were purple-black on the horizon. A penetratingly cold wind, sweeping in from the west, was ample proof that they had come four hundred miles north from Las Vegas.

Corvaisis and Dr Ginger Weiss were waiting on the tarmac beside the small terminal, and the moment that Jorja saw them, she had the odd but reassuring feeling that she was among family. That sensation was something of which Corvaisis had spoken on the phone, but Jorja had not understood what he meant until she experienced it.

Even Marcie – bundled in coat and scarf, her eyes still puffy from the nap on the plane, the album clutched to her chest – was stirred from her moody trancelike state by the sight of the writer and the physician. She smiled and answered their questions with more enthusiasm than had marked her speech in days. She offered to show them her album, and she submitted with a giggle when Corvaisis scooped her up in his arms to carry her to the parking lot.

We were right to come, Jorja thought. Thank God we did.

Carrying Marcie, Corvaisis led the way to the car, while Jorja and Ginger followed with the suitcases. As they walked, Jorja said, 'Maybe you don't remember, but you provided emergency treatment for Marcie that Friday evening in July, even before we checked into the Tranquillity.'

The physician blinked. 'In fact, I hadn't remembered. Was that you and your late husband? Was that Marcie? But of course it was!'

'We had parked along I-80, five miles west of the motel,' Jorja recalled. 'The view to the south was so spectacular, such a wonderful panorama, that we wanted to use it as a backdrop for some snapshots.'

Ginger nodded. 'And I was driving east in your wake. I saw

457

you up ahead, parked along the shoulder. You were focusing the camera. Your husband and Marcie had stepped over the guardrail and were standing a few feet farther out, posing at the edge of the highway embankment.'

'I didn't want them standing so close to the brink. But Alan insisted it was the best position for the best picture, and when Alan insisted on something, there was no use arguing with him.'

However, before Jorja had been able to click the shutter, Marcie had slipped and fallen backwards, over the edge, tumbling down the thirty- or forty-foot embankment. Jorja screamed – 'Marcie!' – flung the camera aside, vaulted the guardrail, and started down towards her daughter. Fast as she was, however, Jorja had just reached Marcie when she heard someone shouting: 'Don't move her! I'm a doctor!' That had been Ginger Weiss, and she had descended the slope so rapidly that she had arrived at Marcie's side simultaneously with Alan, who had started down before her. Marcie was still and silent but not unconscious, only stunned, and Ginger quickly determined that the girl had not sustained a head injury. Marcie began to cry, and because her left leg was tucked under her at a somewhat odd angle, Jorja was certain it was broken. Ginger was able to allay that fear, too. In the end, because the slope was rock-free and cushioned by bunch-grass, Marcie came through with only minor injuries – a few scrapes and bruises.

'I was so impressed by you,' Jorja said.

'Me?' Ginger looked surprised. She waited for an in-coming single-engine plane to pass overhead. Then: 'I did nothing special, you know. I only examined Marcie. She didn't need heroic care, just Bandaids.'

As they put the suitcases in the trunk of Dom's car, Jorja said, 'Well, I was impressed. You were young, pretty, feminine, yet you were a doctor – efficient, quick-thinking. I'd always thought of myself as a born cocktail waitress, nothing more, but that encounter with you started a fire in me. Later, when Alan walked out on us, I didn't fall apart. I remembered you, and I decided to make more of myself than I'd ever thought I could. In a way, you changed my life.'

Closing the trunk lid, locking it, handing the keys to Dom

(who had already put Marcie in the car), Ginger said, 'Jorja, I'm flattered. But you're giving me much too much credit. You changed your own life.'

'It wasn't what you did that day,' Jorja said. 'It's what you *were*. You were exactly the role model I needed.'

Embarrassed, the physician said, 'Good God! No one's ever called me a role model before! Oh, honey, you're definitely unbalanced!'

'Ignore her,' Dom told Jorja. 'She's the best role model I've ever seen. Her humble mutterings are pure *shmontses*.'

Ginger Weiss whirled on him, laughing. '*Shmontses*?'

Dom grinned. 'I'm a writer, so it's my job to listen and absorb. I hear a good expression, I use it. Can't fault me for doing my job.'

'*Shmontses*, huh?' Ginger Weiss said, pretending anger.

Still grinning, the writer said, 'If the Yiddish fits, wear it.'

That was the moment when Jorja knew Dominick Corvaisis's heart was already claimed and that she would have to exclude him from any romantic fantasies she might cook up in the future. The spark of desire and glimmer of deep affection shone brightly in his eyes when he looked at Ginger Weiss. The same heat warmed the physician's gaze. The funny thing was, neither Dom nor Ginger appeared quite to realise the true power of their feelings for each other. Not quite yet, but soon.

They drove out of Elko, toward the Tranquillity, thirty miles to the west. As twilight faded towards night in the east, Dom and Ginger told Jorja what had happened prior to her and Marcie's arrival. Jorja found it increasingly difficult to hold the good mood she'd been in since stepping off the plane. As they sped through the gloom-mantled barrens, with craggy and threatening black mountains thrusting up at the horizon under a blood-dark sky, Jorja wondered if this place was, as she had thought, the threshold of a new beginning . . . or a doorway to the grave.

*   *   *

After the Lear landed in Salt Lake City, Utah, Jack Twist quickly transferred to a chartered Cessna Turbo Skylane RG piloted by a polite but tight-lipped man with a huge handlebar moustache. They arrived in Elko, Nevada, at 4:53, in the last light of day.

459

The airport was too small to have Hertz and Avis counters, but a local entrepreneur operated a modest little taxi company. Jack had the cab take him – and his three big suitcases – to a local Jeep dealership, where they were getting ready to close, and where he startled the salesman by paying cash for a four-wheel-drive Cherokee wagon.

To this point, Jack took no evasive action to shake off a tail or even to determine if he had one. His adversaries clearly possessed great power and resources, and regardless of how frantically he tried to elude them, they would have sufficient manpower to keep tabs on a lone target trying to escape on foot or by taxi in a town as small as Elko.

Once the Cherokee was his, Jack drove away from the dealership, and for the first time he looked for a tail. He glanced repeatedly at the rearview and side mirrors, but he spotted no suspicious vehicles.

He went directly to an Arco Mini-Mart that he had noticed during the taxi ride from the airport. He parked at the dark end of the lot, beyond the reach of the arc lamps, got out of the wagon, and surveyed the shadowy street behind for an indication of a pursuer.

He saw no one.

That didn't mean they weren't out there.

In the Mini-Mart, the blindingly excessive fluorescent lighting and chrome display fixtures made him long for the good old days of quaint corner groceries operated by immigrant couples who spoke with appealing accents, where the air would have been redolent of Mama's homemade baked goods and Papa's made-to-order deli sandwiches. Here, the only aromas were a vague trace of disinfectant and the thin odour of ozone coming off the motors of refrigerated display cases. Squinting in the glare, Jack bought a map of the county, a flashlight, a quart of milk, two packages of dried beef, a little box of small chocolate doughnuts – and, on a morbid impulse, something called a 'Hamwich,' which was 'a guaranteed delicious one-piece sandwich of pulverised, blended, remolded ham-paste, bread, and spices,' and which was claimed to be especially 'convenient for hikers, campers, and sportsmen.' Ham paste? At the bottom of the airtight plastic package was this legend: 'REAL MEAT.'

Jack laughed. They had to tell you it was 'real meat' because, even though it was wrapped in clear plastic, you couldn't tell what the hell it was by looking at it. Yes sir, oh yes, ham paste and real meat: *that* was why he had gone to Central America to fight for his country.

He wished Jenny were alive and here with him. Real meat. As opposed to fake, polyester meat. She'd have got a kick out of that.

When he walked out of the Mini-Mart, he paused to study the street again, but again he saw no one suspicious.

He returned to the Cherokee at the dark end of the lot and put up the tailgate. He opened one of his suitcases, withdrew an empty nylon rucksack, the Beretta, a loaded clip, a box of .32 ammunition, and one of the pipe-type silencers. As his breath steamed from him in the cold air, he transferred the groceries from the paper bag to the rucksack. He screwed the silencer onto the gun, slammed the loaded clip into the butt. When he had distributed all the loose ammunition among the many pockets of his heavily insulated leather jacket, he closed the tailgate.

Behind the wheel of the Cherokee once more, Jack put the Beretta on the seat beside him and set the rucksack on top of it for concealment. Using the new flashlight, he passed a few minutes studying the map of Elko County. When he switched the flashlight off and put the map away, he was ready to engage the enemy.

For the next five minutes, he drove through Elko, using every trick he knew to reveal a tail, staying on quiet residential streets where traffic was light and where a surveillance team would be as obvious as a festering cold sore, no matter how good they were. Nothing.

He parked at the end of a cul-de-sac and got an anti-surveillance broadband receiver from one of the suitcases. This device, the size of two packs of cigarettes, with a short antenna that telescoped out of the top, received all possible radio bands from 30 to 120, including FM from 88 to 108. If a transmitter had been fixed to the Jeep while he was in the market, enabling a tail to follow at a distance, his broadband receiver would pick up the signals; a feedback loop would cause the receiver to emit an ear-piercing squeal. He pointed

461

the antenna at the Jeep and slowly circled the vehicle.

The Cherokee had not been bugged.

He put the broadband receiver away and got behind the wheel of the wagon again, where he sat for a minute in thought. He was under neither visual nor electronic surveillance. Did that make sense? When his adversaries put those Tranquillity Motel postcards in his safe-deposit boxes, they must have known he would come to Nevada at once. Surely they also knew that he was a potentially dangerous man, and surely they would not allow him to plot against them on their own turf unobserved. Yet that seemed to be precisely what they were doing.

Frowning, Jack twisted the key in the ignition. The engine roared.

On the Lear from New York, he had pondered the situation at length and had arrived at several theories (most of them half-baked) as to the identity and intentions of his adversaries. Now he decided that nothing he dreamed up was half as strange as whatever was actually happening.

No one was watching. That spooked him.

The inexplicable *always* spooked him.

When you couldn't understand a situation, that usually meant you were missing something important. If you were missing something important, that meant you had a blind side. If you had a blind side, you could get your ass shot off when you were least expecting it.

Alert, cautious, Jack Twist drove north from Elko on State Route 51. After a while, he turned west, following a series of gravel and dirt tracks, sneaking behind the Tranquillity Motel instead of making an open approach on I-80. Eventually he was reduced to travelling overland on sometimes dangerous terrain, from an elevation as high as four thousand feet, down across sloping foothills toward the plains. When the clouds parted, revealing a three-quarter moon, he switched off the headlights and continued, guided only by the glow of the lunar lamp, and his eyes soon adjusted to the night.

Jack topped a rise and saw the Tranquillity Motel, a lonely group of lights in a vast dark emptiness, a mile and a half below and southwest of him, this side of I-80. There were not as many lights as there ought to have been; either the place had little business or it was not open. He did not want to advertise his arrival, so he would proceed on foot.

He left the Beretta in the Jeep and took the Uzi submachine gun. Actually, he did not expect trouble. Not yet. His adversaries, whoever the hell they were, had not teased him into coming all this way merely to kill him. They could have killed him in New York if that was all they wanted. Nevertheless, he was prepared for violence.

In addition to the Uzi – and a spare magazine – he took the rucksack of groceries, a battery-powered directional microphone, and the Star Tron night-vision device. He pulled on gloves and a toboggan cap.

Jack found the hike invigorating. The night was cold, and when the wind gusted, it stung but not unpleasantly.

Because he'd expected to go to ground immediately upon arrival in Nevada, he had dressed suitably when he left New York. He wore high-topped hiking shoes with hard rubber soles and heavy tread, longjohns and jeans, a sweater, and a leather jacket with a thick quilted lining. The crew of the chartered Lear was surprised by his appearance, but they treated him as if he were in tuxedo and top hat; even an ugly man with one cast eye, dressed like an ordinary labourer, elicited respect when he could afford to lease a private jet rather than fly commercial airlines.

Now Jack walked. Ragged tears in the clouds disrobed the moon, and the few widely scattered patches of snow shone brightly, as if they were shards of bone glimpsed in the darker carcass of the hump-backed hills; the bare earth, rock formations, sagebrush, and plentiful dry grass accepted the caress of moonlight and were lined in a vague milky-blond hue. But when the moon slipped behind the clouds, deep rich darkness flooded forth.

At last he reached a suitable observation point on the southern slope of a hill, only a quarter of a mile behind the Tranquillity Motel. He sat down, putting the Uzi and his rucksack aside.

The Star Tron night-vision device took available light – starlight, moonlight, the natural phosphorescence of snow and of certain plants, meagre electric light if any – and amplified it eighty-five thousand times. With the gadget's single lens, Jack could transform all but the very blackest nights into grey daylight or better.

He propped his elbows on his knees, held the Star Tron in both hands, and focused on the Tranquillity. The rear of the structure popped into view with sufficient clarity for him to determine that no lookouts were posted in any shadowed niches. None of the motel units had windows along the back-wall, so no guards could be watching from those rooms. The centre third of the motel had a second floor, probably the owner's apartment, and light shone at most of those windows. However, he could not see into the apartment because the drapes and blinds were drawn.

He put the Star Tron in the rucksack and picked up the battery-powered, hand-held, directional microphone, which resembled a futuristic gun. Only a few years ago, 'rifle mikes' were effective to a distance of only two hundred yards. But these days, a good power-amplified unit could suck in a conversation up to a quarter of a mile, much farther if conditions were ideal. The device included a pair of compact earphones, which he put on. He aimed the mike at a window shielded by drapes, and at once heard animated voices. However, he got only scraps of their conversation because he was trying to pull their voices out of a closed room *and* through a quarter-mile of blustery wind.

With great caution, he grabbed the Uzi and other gear, and moved closer, choosing a second observation point less than a hundred yards from the building. When he aimed the mike at the window again, he picked up every word spoken beyond the glass, in spite of the muffling draperies. He heard six voices, maybe more. They were eating dinner and complimenting the cook (someone named Ned) and his helper (Sandy) on the turkey, the pecan stuffing, and other dishes.

They're not just eating dinner, Jack thought enviously, they're having a damned banquet in there.

He'd eaten a light lunch on the Lear but had taken nothing since. He was still on Eastern Standard Time, so for him it was almost eleven o'clock. He would probably be eavesdropping for hours, piecing together these people's identities, gradually determining if they were his adversaries. He was too hungry to wait that long for his own dinner, such as it was. With a few

464

rocks, he made a brace for the microphone to keep it angled towards the window. He unwrapped the Hamwich and bit into that 'pulverised, blended, and remolded' treat. It tasted like sawdust soaked in rancid bacon fat. He spat out the gummy mouthful, and settled down to a meagre meal of dried beef and doughnuts, which would have been more satisfying if he had not had to listen to those strangers indulging in a modern version of a harvest feast.

Soon, Jack had heard enough of the conversation in the apartment to know these people were not his enemies. Strangely, one way or another, they had been drawn or summoned here, as he'd been. Monitoring them, he began to think their voices were curiously familiar, and he was overcome with the feeling that he belonged among them as a brother among family.

A woman named Ginger and a man – either Don or Dom – began to tell the others about research they'd done earlier in the offices of the *Elko Sentinel*. Listening to talk of toxic spills, roadblocks, and highly trained DERO troops, Jack felt his appetite fading. DERO! Shit, he'd heard about the DERO companies, though they'd been formed after he'd left the service. They were gung-ho types who'd happily accept an order to go into a pit against a grizzly bear, armed only with a meat grinder; and they were tough enough to make sausages out of the bear. Forced to choose between a quick, painless suicide and hand-to-hand combat with a DERO, the ordinary man would be well-advised to blow his own brains out and save himself pain. Jack realised he was involved in something far bigger and more dangerous than *fratellanza* revenge or any of the other things he had hypothesised during his flight from New York.

Although the picture he got from eavesdropping was full of holes, he began to grasp that these people had come together to discover what had happened to them the summer before last, the same weekend Jack had stayed here. They'd made considerable headway in their investigation, and Jack winced as they openly discussed their progress. They were so naive that they thought closed doors and covered windows ensured privacy. He wanted to shout: *Hey, for God's sake, shut up already! If I can hear you, they can hear you.*

DERO. That bit of news made him even sicker than the Hamwich.

In the motel they continued to chatter, revealing their strategy to the enemy even as they worked it out, and at last Jack tore off the earphones, frantically grabbed his guns and equipment, and hurried down through the darkness towards the Tranquillity Motel.

* * *

The apartment had no dining room, just the alcove in the kitchen, but that area was too small to seat nine. In the living room, they moved the furniture against the walls, brought in the kitchen table, and used both extra leaves to extend it, accommodating everyone. To Dom, the impromptu arrangements contributed to the feeling of a family gathering and to the mood of cautious festivity.

Rather than have to repeat themselves, Dom and Ginger had waited until dinner, when the group was gathered, to report on their research at the newspaper in Elko. Now, over the clinking of silverware, they revealed that the Army had blockaded I-80 minutes *before* the toxic spill that Friday night. Which meant that choppers full of soldiers had been dispatched from distant Shenkfield at least half an hour earlier, and that the Army knew in advance the 'accident' was going to happen.

Tearing a crescent roll, Dom said, 'If Falkirk and a DERO company flew in and took over security on the quarantine line so soon after the crisis hit . . . well, it means the Army must've had advance warning.'

'But then why didn't they stop it from happening?' Jorja Monatella asked as she cut her daughter's serving of turkey into bite-size pieces.

'Apparently, they *couldn't* stop it,' Dom said.

'Maybe there was a terrorist attack on the truck, and maybe Army Intelligence only got wind of it just before it went down,' Ernie said.

'Maybe,' Dom said doubtfully. 'But they would've gone public with that kind of story if it happened. So it must've been something else. Something involving top-secret data of such importance that only DERO troops could be trusted to keep quiet about it.'

Brendan Cronin had a heartier appetite than anyone at the table, but his temporal appetite did not diminish the spiritual air that had surrounded him. He swallowed some baked corn and said, 'This explains why there weren't hundreds of people on those ten miles of interstate when the thing happened, as there should've been at that hour. If the Army sealed off ahead of the event, they had time to get most traffic out of the danger zone before anything actually happened.'

Dom said, 'Some didn't get out, saw too much, and were held and brainwashed with the rest of us who were already here at the motel.'

For a while everyone joined in the discussion and arrived at all the same theories and unanswerable questions that had occurred to Dom and Ginger at the newspaper offices earlier in the day.

Finally, Dom told them about the important discovery he and Ginger had made when, as an afterthought, they had looked through issues of the *Sentinel* published during the weeks *following* the toxic spill. When they had finishing poring through editions for the week of the crisis, Ginger had suggested that clues to the secret of what really happened on the closed highway that night might be hidden in other news, in unusual stories that appeared to have nothing to do with the crisis but were, in fact, related to it. They pulled more issues from the files, and by studying every story from a paranoid perspective, they soon found what they hoped for. One place in particular figured in the news in such a way that it seemed linked to the closure of I-80.

'Thunder Hill,' Dom said. 'We believe that's where our trouble came from. Shenkfield was just a ruse, a clever misdirection to focus attention away from the *real* source of the crisis. Thunder Hill.'

Faye and Ernie looked up from their plates in surprise, and Faye said, 'Thunder Hill's ten or twelve miles north-northeast of here, in the mountains. The Army has an installation up there, too – the Thunder Hill Depository. There're natural limestone caves in those hills, where they store copies of service records and a lot of other important files, so they won't lose all copies if military bases in other parts of the country are wiped out in a disaster . . . nuclear war, like that.'

467

Ernie said, 'The Depository was here before Faye and me. Twenty years or more. Rumours have it that files and records aren't the only things in storage there. Some believe there's also huge supplies of food, medicines, weapons, ammunition. Which makes sense. In case a big war breaks out, the Army wouldn't want all its weapons and supplies on ordinary military bases because those would be the first nuked. They've surely got fallback caches, and I guess Thunder Hill is one of those.'

'Then *anything* might be up there,' Jorja Monatella said uneasily.

'Anything,' Ned Sarver said.

'Is it possible that place isn't just a storage dump?' Sandy asked. 'Could they also maybe be doing some kind of experiments up there?'

'What kind of experiments?' Brendan asked, leaning over to look past Ned, beside whom he was seated.

Sandy shrugged. 'Any kind.'

'It's possible,' Dom said. The same thought had occurred to him.

'But if there wasn't a toxic spill on I-80, if it was something at Thunder Hill that went wrong,' Ginger said, 'how could it have affected us, more than ten miles to the south?'

No one could think of an answer.

Marcie, who had been preoccupied with her moon collection for most of the evening and who had said nothing during dinner, put down her fork and piped up with a question of her own: 'Why's it called Thunder Hill?'

'Sweetie,' Faye said, 'that's one I *can* answer. Thunder Hill's really one of four huge, connecting mountain meadows, a long sloping piece of high pastureland. It's surrounded by a great many high peaks, and during a storm, the place acts like a sort of . . . well, a sort of funnel for sound. The Indians named it Thunder Hill hundreds of years ago because thunder echoes between those peaks and rolls down the mountainsides, and it all pours in on that one particular meadow in a most peculiar way, so that it seems as if the roar isn't coming out of the sky, but as if it's coming right up out of the ground around you.'

'Wow,' Marcie said softly. 'I'd probably pee my pants.'

'Marcie!' Jorja said as everyone broke into laughter.

'Well, gee, I probably would,' the child replied. 'You 'member when Grandma and Grandpa came over to dinner at our place, and there was a big storm, really big, and some lightning struck the tree in our yard, and there was this *boom!* and I peed my pants?' Looking around the table at her new extended family, she said, 'I was *soooo* embarrassed.'

Everyone laughed again, and Jorja said, 'That was more than two years ago. You're a bigger girl now.'

To Dom, Ernie said, 'You haven't told us yet why Thunder Hill is the place, rather than Shenkfield. What'd you find in the newspaper?'

In the *Sentinel* for Friday, July 13, exactly one week after the closure of I-80 and three days after its re-opening, there was a report of two county ranchers – Norvil Brust and Jake Dirkson – who were having trouble with the Federal Bureau of Land Management. A disagreement between ranchers and the BLM was not unusual. The government owned half of Nevada, not merely deserts but a lot of the best grazing land, some of which it leased to cattlemen for their herds. Ranchers were always complaining that the BLM kept too much good land out of use, that the government ought to sell off part of its holdings to private interests, and that leases were too expensive. But Brust and Dirkson had a new complaint. For years they leased BLM land surrounding a three-hundred-acre Army installation, the Thunder Hill Depository. Brust held eight hundred acres to the west and south, and Dirkson was using over seven hundred acres on the east side of Thunder Hill. Suddenly, on Saturday morning, July 7, though four years remained on Brust's and Dirkson's leases, the BLM took five hundred acres from Brust, three hundred from Dirkson; and at the request of the Army, those eight hundred acres were incorporated into the boundaries of the Thunder Hill Depository.

'Which just happens to be the very morning after the toxic spill and the closure of I-80,' Faye observed.

'Brust and Dirkson showed up Saturday morning to inspect their herds, per their usual routine,' Dom said, 'and both discovered that their livestock had been driven off most of the leased pasture. A temporary barbed-wire fence was being thrown into place along the new perimeter of the Thunder Hill Depository.'

Having finished dinner, Ginger pushed her plate aside and said, 'The BLM simply told Brust and Dirkson it was unilaterally abrogating their leases, without compensation. But they didn't receive an official written notice till the following Wednesday, which is extremely unusual. Ordinarily, a notice of termination comes sixty days in advance.'

'Was that kind of treatment legal?' Brendan Cronin asked.

'Right there's the problem of doing business with the government,' Ernie told the priest. 'You're dealing with the very people who decide what's legal and what isn't. It's like playing poker with God.'

Faye said, 'The BLM's despised around these parts. No bunch of bureaucrats is more high-handed.'

'That's what we gathered from reading the *Sentinel*,' Dom said. 'Now, Ginger and I might've figured the Thunder Hill business was just coincidental, that the BLM just happened to go after that land the same time as the crisis on I-80. But the way the government dealt with Brust and Dirkson *after* the land was seized was so extraordinary it made us suspicious. When the ranchers hired attorneys, when stories about the cancellation of their leases began appearing in the *Sentinel*, the BLM did a sudden about-face and offered compensation, after all.'

'That's not a bit like the BLM!' Ernie said. 'They'll always make you drag them into court, hoping litigation will wear you down.'

'How much were they willing to pay Brust and Dirkson?' Faye asked.

'The figure wasn't revealed,' Ginger said. 'But it was evidently darned good, because Brust and Dirkson accepted it overnight.'

'So the BLM bought their silence,' Jorja said.

'I think it was the Army working secretly through the BLM,' Dom said. 'They realised the longer the story was in the news, the more chance there was of someone wondering about a link between the crisis on I-80 that Friday night and the unorthodox seizure of land the very next morning, even if the two events were ten or twelve miles apart.'

470

'Surprises me somebody *didn't* make the connection,' Jorja said. 'If you and Ginger could spot it this long after the fact, why didn't anyone think of it then?'

'For one thing,' Ginger said, 'Dom and I had the enormous benefit of hindsight. We know there was a lot more going on during the days of the crisis than anyone suspected at the time. So we were specifically *looking* for connections. But that July, all the hoopla about a toxic spill diverted attention from Thunder Hill. Furthermore, there was nothing extraordinary about ranchers fighting the BLM, so nothing in the situation linked it in anyone's mind with the I-80 quarantine. In fact, when the BLM made that totally out-of-character offer to Brust and Dirkson, a *Sentinel* editorial praised the repentant attitude of the government and prophesied a new age of reason.'

'But from what you've told us,' Dom said to Faye and Ernie, 'and from what else we've read, that was the first and last time the Bureau of Land Management dealt reasonably with ranchers. So it wasn't a new policy – just a one-time response to a crisis. And it's too coincidental to believe that the crisis evolving at Thunder Hill was unrelated to the crisis simultaneously underway here along the interstate.'

'Besides,' Ginger said, 'once our suspicion was aroused, we got to thinking that if the trouble that night *had* been related to Shenkfield, there'd have been no need for the Army to use DERO troops for security. Because the soldiers stationed at Shenkfield would already have full security clearance in all matters related to that base, and there would've been nothing about a Shenkfield crisis too sensitive for them to see. The only reason DERO would've been called in is if the crisis was utterly unrelated to Shenkfield, involving something the soldiers at that base were not cleared for.'

'So if there're answers to our problems,' Brendan said, 'we'll most likely find them at the Thunder Hill Depository.'

'We already suspected the story about a spill was less than half true,' Dom said. 'Maybe there was no truth to it at all. Maybe the crisis had nothing to do with Shenkfield. If the real source was Thunder Hill, the rest was just smoke they blew in the public's eyes.'

'It sure feels right,' Ernie said. He had finished dinner, too. His silverware was neatly arranged on the plate, which was

471

almost as clean as before dinner, evidence that his military discipline and order had not departed him. 'You know, part of my service career was in Marine Intelligence, so I'm speaking with some experience when I say this Shenkfield stuff truly does smack of an elaborate cover-story.'

Ned's frown exaggerated his pronounced widow's peak. 'There're a couple of things I don't understand. The quarantine didn't extend from Thunder Hill all the way down here. There were miles of territory in between that weren't sealed off. So how did the effects of an accident on Thunder Hill leap-frog over all that distance and come down on *our* heads, without causing trouble between there and here?'

'You're not dull-witted,' Dom said. 'I can't explain it, either.'

Still frowning, Ned said, 'Another thing: the Depository doesn't need a lot of land, does it? From what I've heard, it's underground. They've got a couple of big blast doors in the side of the hill, a road leading up to the doors, maybe a guard post, and that's it. The three hundred acres you mentioned – the area around the entrance – is plenty big enough for a security zone. So why the land-grab?'

Dom shrugged. 'Beats me. But whatever the hell happened up there on July sixth, it prompted two emergency actions on the part of the Army: first, a temporary quarantine down here, ten or twelve miles away, until we witnesses could be dealt with; second, an immediate enlargement of the security zone around the Depository, up there in the mountains, a secondary quarantine that's still in effect. I have a hunch . . . if we're ever going to find out what happened to us – what's *still* happening – we're going to have to dig into the activities up on Thunder Hill.'

They were all silent. Though everyone was finished with dinner, no one was ready for dessert. Marcie was using her spoon to draw circles in the greasy residue of turkey gravy on her plate, creating fluid and temporary moon-forms. No one moved to clear away the dirty dishes, for at this point in the discussion, no one wanted to miss a word. They were at the crux of their dilemma: how were they to move against enemies as mighty as the US Government and Army? How were they to penetrate an iron wall of secrecy that had been forged in the name of national security, with the full power of the state and the law behind it?

'We've put together enough to go public,' Jorja Monatella said. 'The deaths of Zebediah Lomack and Alan, the murder of Pablo Jackson. The similar nightmares that many of you have shared. The Polaroids. It's the kind of sensational stuff the media thrives on. If we let the world know what we think happened to us, we'll have the power of the press and public opinion on our side. We won't be alone.'

'No good,' Ernie said. 'That kind of pressure'll just make the military stonewall like hell. They'll construct an even more confusing and impenetrable cover-up. They don't crack under pressure the way politicians do. On the other hand, as long as they see us stumbling around on our own, fumbling for explanations, they'll be confident – which might give us time to probe for their weak spots.'

'And don't forget,' Ginger warned, 'apparently Colonel Falkirk advocated killing us instead of just blocking our memories, and we've no reason to believe he's mellowed since then. He was obviously overruled, but if we tried to go public, he might be able to persuade his superiors that a final solution is required, after all.'

'But even if it's dangerous, maybe we've got to go public,' Sandy said. 'Maybe Jorja's right. I mean, there's no way we can get inside the Thunder Hill Depository to see what's going on. They've got lots of security and a pair of blast-doors built to take a nuclear hit.'

Dom said, 'Well, it's like Ernie told us . . . we'll have to just stay loose and search for their weaknesses until we find a way.'

'But it looks like they don't *have* any weaknesses,' Sandy said.

'Their cover-up has been falling apart ever since they brainwashed us and let us go,' Ginger said. 'Each time one of us remembers another detail, that's another gaping hole in their cover-up.'

'Yeah,' Ned said, 'but seems to me they're in a better position to keep patching the holes than we are to keep poking new ones.'

'Let's can the goddamn negative thinking,' Ernie said gruffly.

473

Smiling beatifically, Brendan Cronin said, 'He's right. We must not be negative. We *need* not be negative because we're meant to win.' His voice was again infused with the eerie serenity and certitude which arose from his brief that the revelation of their special fate was inevitable. At moments like this, however, the priest's tone and manner did not comfort Dom, as they were meant to but, for some odd reason, stirred up a sediment of fear and muddied his emotions with anxiety.

'How many men are stationed at Thunder Hill?' Jorja asked.

Before Dom or Ginger could respond with information they'd gleaned from the *Sentinel*, a stranger appeared in the doorway at the head of the stairs that led up from the motel office. He was in his late-thirties, lean and tough-looking, dark-haired, dark-complexioned, with a crooked left eye that was not coordinated with his right. Though the downstairs door was locked, and although the linoleum on the stairs did nothing to quiet ascending footsteps, the intruder appeared with magical silence, as if he were not a real man but an ectoplasmic visitation.

'For God's sake, shut up,' he said, sounding every bit as real as anyone else in the room. 'If you think you can plot in privacy here, you're badly mistaken.'

*　　　*　　　*

Eighteen miles southwest of the Tranqullity Motel, at Shenk-field Army Testing Grounds, all the buildings – laboratories, administration offices, security command centre, cafeteria, recreation lounge, and living quarters – were underground. In the blazing summers on the edge of the high desert and in the occasionally bitter winters, it was easier and more economical to maintain a comfortable temperature and humidity-level in underground rooms than in structures erected on the less-than-hospitable Nevada barrens. But a more important consideration was the frequent open-air testing of chemical – and occasionally even biological – weapons. The tests were conducted to study the effects of sunlight, wind, and other natural forces on the distribution patterns and potency of those deadly gases, powders, and super-diffusible mists. If the buildings were above ground, any unexpected shift in the wind would contaminate them, making unwilling guinea pigs of base personnel.

474

No matter how involved they became in work or leisure, the staff of Shenkfield never forgot they were beneath the earth, for they had two constant reminders of their condition: the lack of windows; plus the susurration of the piped-in air coming through the wall vents, and the echoing hum of the motors that fanned the air along the pipes.

Sitting alone at a metal desk in the office to which he had been temporarily assigned, waiting impatiently and worriedly for the phone to ring, Colonel Leland Falkirk thought: *God, I hate this place!*

The never-ending whine and hiss of the air-supply system gave him a headache. Since his arrival on Saturday, Falkirk had been eating aspirin as though they were candy. Now he tipped two more out of a small bottle. He poured a glass of ice-water from the metal carafe that stood on the desk, but he did not use it to wash down the pills. Instead, he popped the dry aspirin into his mouth and chewed them.

The taste was bitter, disgusting, and he almost gagged.

But he did not reach for the water.

He did not spit out the aspirin, either.

He persevered.

A lonely, miserable childhood filled with uncertainty and pain, followed by an even worse adolescence, had taught Leland Falkirk that life was hard, cruel, and utterly unjust, that only fools believed in hope or salvation, and that only the tough survived. From an early age, he had forced himself to do things that were emotionally, mentally, and physically painful, for he had decided that self-inflicted pain would toughen him and make him less vulnerable. He tempered the steel of his will with challenges that ranged from chewing dry aspirin to major tests like the outings that he called 'desperation survival treks.' Those expeditions lasted two weeks or longer, and they put him face-to-face with death. He parachuted into a forest or jungle wilderness, far from the nearest outpost, without supplies, with only the clothes on his back. He carried no compass or matches. His only weapons were his bare hands and what he could fashion with them. The goal: reach civilisation alive. He spent many vacations in that self-imposed suffering, which he judged worthwhile because he came back a harder and more self-reliant man than he'd been at the start of each adventure.

Now he crunched dry aspirin. The tablets were reduced to powder, and the powder turned his saliva to an acidic paste.

'Ring, damn you,' he said to the telephone on the desk. He was hoping for news that would get him out of this hole in the ground.

In DERO, the Domestic Emergency Response Organisation, a colonel was less a desk jockey and more a field officer than in any other branch of the Army. Falkirk's home base was in Grand Junction, Colorado, not Shenkfield, but even in Colorado, he spent little time in his office. He thrived on the physical demands of the job, so the low-ceilinged, windowless rooms of Shenkfield felt like a many-chambered coffin.

If he had been engaged upon any mission but this one, he might have established temporary unit headquarters up at Thunder Hill Depository. That place was also underground but its caves were huge, high-ceilinged, not like these tomb-size rooms.

But there were two reasons he had to keep his men away from Thunder Hill. First, he dared not draw attention to the place because of the secret it harboured. Several ranchers lived in the highlands along the road leading to the gated Thunder Hill turn-off. If they spotted a fully equipped DERO company moving into the Depository, they'd speculate about it. Locals must not start wondering about Thunder Hill. Two summers ago, he'd used Shenkfield as a red herring to divert attention from the Depository. Now, with another crisis building, he would stay here at Shenkfield again, so he would be in position to spread the same kind of disinformation to the press and public that he'd spread before. The second reason he set up HQ at Shenkfield was because he had certain dark suspicions about everyone in the Depository: he trusted none of them, would not feel safe among them. They might be . . . changed.

The residue of crushed aspirin had been in his mouth so long that he had adjusted to the bitter taste. He was no longer sickened, no longer had to struggle against the gag reflex, so it was all right to drink the water now. He drained the glass in four swallows.

Leland Falkirk suddenly wondered if he had crossed the line that separated the constructive use of pain from the enjoyment of it. Even as he asked the question, he knew the answer: yes, to some degree, he had become a masochist. Years ago. He was a very well-disciplined masochist, one who benefited from the pain he inflicted on himself, one who controlled the pain instead of letting it control him, but a masochist nonetheless. At first he subjected himself to pain strictly to make himself tough. But along the way, he began to enjoy it, too. That insight left him blinking in surprise at the empty waterglass.

An outrageous image formed in his mind: himself more than a decade from now, a sixty-year-old pervert sticking bamboo shoots under his fingernails every morning for the thrill and to get his heart running. That grotesque picture was grim. It was also funny, and he laughed.

As recently as a year ago, Leland would not have been capable of self-critical insights of this nature. He had never been much of a laughter, either. Until recently. Lately, he was not merely noticing – and being amused by – traits in himself that he had never noticed before, but he was also becoming aware that he could and should change some of his attitudes and habits. He saw that he could become a better and more satisfied person, without losing the toughness he prized. This was a strange state of mind for him, but he knew the cause of it. After what had happened to him two summers ago, after all the things that he had seen, and considering what was happening right now up at Thunder Hill, he could not possibly go on with his life exactly as before.

The telephone rang. He grabbed it, hoping it was news about the situation in Chicago. But it was Henderson from Monterey, California, reporting that the operation at the Salcoe house was going smoothly.

The summer before last, Gerald Salcoe, with his wife and two daughters, rented a pair of rooms at the Tranquillity Motel. On the wrong night. Recently, all of the Salcoes had experienced marked deterioration of their memory blocks.

The CIA's experts in brainwashing, who were usually used only in covert foreign operations, had been borrowed for the Tranquillity job that July and had promised to repress witnesses' memories without fail; now they were embarrassed by the number of subjects whose conditioning was breaking down. The experience these people had undergone was too profound and shattering to be easily repressed; the forbidden memories possessed mythopoeic power and exerted relentless pressure on the memory blocks. The mind-control experts now claimed that *another* three-day session with the subjects would guarantee their eternal silence.

In fact, the FBI and CIA, working in conjunction, were illegally holding the Salcoe family incommunicado in Monterey at this very moment, putting·them through another intricate programme of memory repression and alteration. Although Cory Henderson, the FBI agent on the phone, claimed it was going well, Leland decided it was a lost cause. This was one secret that could not be kept.

Besides, too many agencies were involved: FBI, CIA, one entire DERO company, others. Which made too many chiefs and not enough Indians.

But Leland was a good soldier. In charge of the military side of the operation, he'd carry out his assignment even if it was hopeless.

In Monterey, Henderson said, 'When are you moving in on the other witnesses at the motel?'

That was the word they used for everyone who had been brainwashed that July – witnesses..Leland thought it was apt, for in addition to its obvious meaning, it also embodied mystical and religious overtones. He remembered, as a child, being taken to tent revivals at which scores of Holy Rollers writhed upon the floor while the raving minister screamed at them to 'be a witness to the miraculous, be a heartfelt witness for the Lord!' Well, what the witnesses at the Tranquillity Motel had seen was every bit as paralysing, amazing, humbling, and terrifying as the face of God that those spasming Pentecostals had longed to see.

To Henderson, Leland said, 'We're standing by, ready to seal off the motel with half an hour's notice. But I'm not giving the go-ahead until someone straightens out the mess in Chicago with Calvin Sharkle. Not until I know for sure what's going on out in Illinois.'

'What a screw-up! Why was the situation with Sharkle allowed to deteriorate so far? He should've been grabbed, put into a new memory-repression programme days ago, like we've done with the Salcoes here.'

'Wasn't my screw-up,' Leland said. 'Your Bureau is in charge of monitoring the witnesses. I only come in and mop up after you.'

Henderson sighed. 'I wasn't trying to shift the blame to your men, Colonel. And hell, you can't blame us, either. The trouble is, even though we're only doing visual surveillance of each witness four days a month and listening to only about half the tapes of their phone calls, we need twenty-five agents. But we only have twenty. Besides, the damn case is so highly classified that only three of the twenty know why the witnesses have to be watched. A good agent doesn't like being kept in the dark like that. Makes him feel he's not trusted. Makes him sloppy. So you get a situation like this Sharkle: the witness starts breaking through his memory block, and nobody notices until it's at crisis stage. Why'd we ever think we could maintain such an elaborate deception for an unlimited length of time? Nuts. I'll tell you what our problem was: we believed the CIA's brain-scrubbers. We believed those mother-fuckers could do what they said they could do. That was our mistake, Colonel.'

'I always said there was a simpler solution,' Leland reminded him.

'Kill them all? Kill thirty-one of our own citizens just because they were in the wrong place at the wrong time?'

'I wasn't proposing it seriously. My point was that short of barbarism, we couldn't contain the secret and shouldn't have tried.'

Henderson's silence made it clear he did not believe Leland's disclaimer. 'You *will* move on the motel tonight?'

'If the Chicago situation clears up, if I can figure what's going on there, we'll move tonight. But there're questions need answered. These strange . . . psychic phenomena. What's it mean? We both have ideas, don't we? And we're scared puke-sick. No, sir, I'm not moving against the motel and jeopardise my men until I understand the situation.'

Leland hung up.

Thunder Hill. He wanted to believe that what was happening up in the mountains would lead to a better future than mankind deserved. But in his heart he was afraid it was, instead, the end of the world.

*   *   *

479

When Jack stepped into the living room – which they had converted to a dining room – and spoke to the group, some gasped in surprise and started to rise, bumping the table in their eagerness to turn around, sending up a clatter of dishes and flatware. Others flinched in their chairs as if they thought he had been sent to kill them. He'd left the Uzi downstairs to avoid causing just such a panic, but his unexpected arrival still scared them. Good. They needed a nasty shock to make them more cautious. Only the little girl, playing in her gravy-smeared plate with a spoon, did not react to his arrival.

'All right, okay, be calm. Sit down, sit,' Jack said, gesturing impatiently. 'I'm one of you. That night, I registered at the motel as Thornton Wainwright. Which is how you've probably been looking for me. But that's not my real name. We'll get into that later. For now –'

Suddenly, everyone was excitedly pitching questions at him.

'Where did you –'

'– scared the bejesus –'

'How did you –'

' – tell us if –'

Raising his voice enough to silence them, Jack said, 'This isn't the place to discuss these things. You can be heard here, for God's sake. I've been eavesdropping for nearly an hour. And if I can listen in on everything you say, then so can the people you're pitted against.'

They stared dumbly at him, startled by his assertion that their privacy was an illusion. Then a big blocky man with grey brush-cut hair said, 'Are you telling us these rooms are bugged? 'Cause I find that hard to believe. I mean, I've searched, you know; I've checked, found nothing. And I've had some experience in these matters.'

'You must be Ernie,' Jack said, speaking in a sharp cold tone of voice meant to keep them on edge and get his message through to them. They had to understand, right away, that their conversations must be far better guarded, and the lesson had to be driven into them so hard and deep that they would not forget it. 'I heard you mention your years in Marine Intelligence, Ernie. Christ, how long ago was that? Better part of a decade, I'll bet. Things have changed since then, man.

480

Haven't you heard about the high-tech revolution? Shit, they don't need to come in here and physically plant listening devices. Rifle mikes are a hell of a lot better than they used to be. Or they can just hook up an infinity transmitter to their phone and dial your number.' Jack pushed rudely past Ernie and stepped to the living room extension, which stood on a table by the sofa. He put his hand on the phone. 'You know what an infinity transmitter is, Ernie? When they dial your number here, an electric tone oscillator deactivates the bell while it simultaneously opens the microphone in your telephone handset. There's no ringing for you to hear; you've no way of knowing you've been called, that your line's wide open. But they can monitor you in any room where you've got an extension.' He plucked up the handset and held it toward them with a calculated look of scorn. 'Here's your bug. You had it installed yourself.' He slammed the handset back into the cradle. 'You can bet your ass they've been tuning in on you a lot lately. Probably listened all through dinner. You people keep this up, you might as well just cut your own throats and save everybody a lot of trouble.'

Jack's caustic performance had been effective. They were stunned. He said, 'Now, is there a room without windows, big enough to hold a war council? Doesn't matter if there's a phone; we'll just unplug it.'

An attractive middle-aged woman, apparently Ernie's wife, whom Jack vaguely remembered from checking into the motel two summers ago, thought for a moment and said, 'There's the restaurant, the diner, next door.'

'Your restaurant doesn't have any windows?' Jack asked.

'They were . . . broken,' Ernie said. 'Right now they're boarded up.'

'Then let's go,' Jack said. 'Let's work out our strategy in privacy, then come back here for some of that pumpkin pie I heard you talking about. I had a *lousy* dinner while you people were in here eating yourselves into a stupor.'

Jack went quickly down the stairs, confident they would follow.

* * *

Ernie loathed the crooked-eyed bastard for five minutes. But slowly, the hatred turned to grudging respect.

481

For one thing, Ernie admired the caution and stealth with which the guy had answered his own call to the Tranquillity Motel. He had not just walked in like the others. He'd even brought a submachine gun.

But as he watched 'Thornton Wainwright' slip the carrying-strap of the Uzi over one shoulder and head out of the front door of the motel office, Ernie was still stung by the criticism he had endured. In fact, his rage was so great he did not pause to grab a coat, as most of the others did, but plunged after the stranger, through the door and across the macadam towards the diner, keeping pace with him in order to chew him out. 'Listen, what the hell's the point of being a wiseass? You could've made your point without being so goddamn snide.'

The stranger said, 'Yeah, but I couldn't have made it as fast.'

Ernie was about to reply when he abruptly realised he was outside, vulnerable, at night, in the *dark*. Halfway between the office and the diner. His lungs seemed to collapse; he could not draw the slightest wisp of breath. He made a disgustingly pitiful mewling sound.

To Ernie's surprise, the newcomer immediately grasped his arm, providing support, with no trace of the scorn he'd shown before. 'Come on, Ernie. You're halfway there. Lean on me, and you'll make it.'

Furious with himself for letting this bastard see him disabled and weak with childish fear, furious with the guy, too, for playing the Samaritan, humiliated, Ernie jerked his arm away from the helping hand.

'Listen,' the newcomer said, 'while I was eavesdropping, I heard about your problem, Ernie. I don't pity you, and I don't find your condition amusing. Okay? If your fear of the dark has something to do with this situation we all find ourselves in, it's not your fault. It's those bastards who messed with us. We need one another if we're going to get through this thing. Lean on me. Let me help you over to the diner, where we can turn on some lights. Lean on me.'

When the newcomer began to talk, Ernie was unable to breathe, but by the time the guy finished his spiel, Ernie had the opposite problem; he was hyperventilating. As though pulled by a magnetic force, he turned from the diner and looked southeast, out into the terrifyingly immense darkness of the barrens. And suddenly he *knew* the darkness itself was not what he feared, but something that had been out there on the night of July 6, that bad summer. He was looking towards that special place along the highway, where they had gone yesterday to commune with the land in search of clues. That strange place.

Faye had arrived, and Ernie had not shaken loose of her when she had taken hold of him. But now the crooked-eyed man tried to take his arm again, and he was still angry enough to reject *that* assistance.

'Okay, okay,' the guy said. 'You're a bull-headed old Leatherneck bastard, and it's going to take your hurt pride a while to heal. If you want to be a thick-skulled mule, go ahead, stay pissed at me. It was only your blind anger that got you this far into the dark, wasn't it? Sure as hell wasn't Marine backbone. Just dumb blind anger. So if you stay pissed at me, maybe you'll be able to get to the diner.'

Ernie knew the crooked-eye man was cleverly taunting him into completing the trip to the Tranquillity Grille, that he was not really being cruel. *Hate me enough*, the guy was saying, *and you'll fear the darkness less. Focus on me, Ernie, and take one step at a time*. This was not much different from taking the guy's arm and leaning on it, and if Ernie had not been scared half to death by the surging night on all sides of him, he would have been amused at being conned this way. But he held fast to his anger, fanned the flames of it, and used it to light his way to the diner. He stepped through the door after the newcomer, and sighed with relief when the lights came on.

'It's freezing in here,' Faye said. She went directly to the thermostat to switch on the oil furnace.

Sitting in a chair in the centre of the room, his back to the door, Ernie recuperated from his ordeal as the others entered behind him. He watched the crooked-eyed newcomer moving from window to window, checking the plyboard slabs that had been nailed up to replace the shattered glass. And that was when, to Ernie's surprise, he realised he no longer loathed the guy, merely harboured an extreme dislike for him.

The newcomer examined the payphone near the door.

Being a coin-operated unit, it did not unplug, so he lifted the receiver, tore the cord free of the wall-mounted box, and threw the useless handset aside.

'There's a private phone back of the counter,' Ned said.

The newcomer told him to unplug it, and Ned obliged.

Then he told Brendan and Ginger to push three tables together and pull up chairs to accommodate everyone, and they did as they were told.

Ernie watched the crooked-eyed man with keen interest.

The newcomer was concerned about the diner's front door, which had not shattered during the weird phenomena on Saturday night because it was made of much thicker glass than the windows had been. It was not boarded up, so it offered a weak point to anyone trying to monitor them with a directional microphone. He wanted to know if any plywood was left from the window job, and Dom told him there was, and he sent Ned and Dom to bring back a suitable piece from the stack in the maintenance room behind the motel. They soon returned with a section of wood that was slightly larger than the door, and the newcomer stood it in front of the glass portal, bracing it in place with a table. 'Not perfect,' he said, 'but good enough to defeat a rifle mike, I think.' Then he headed towards the back of the restaurant to 'have a look in the storeroom,' and on his way he told Sandy to plug in the jukebox, switch it to free-play, and punch in some songs. 'Some background noise makes eavesdropping more difficult.' Even before he explained why he wanted music, Sandy jumped up and headed for the jukebox, quick to obey him.

Abruptly, Ernie realised why the crooked-eyed man fascinated him. The guy's quick thinking, precision movements, and ability to command indicated that he was – or had once been – a career soldier, an officer, a damn good one. He could tune an intimidatingly hard edge into his voice one moment, and the next moment tune it out in favour of cajolery.

Hell, Ernie thought, he's fascinating because he reminds me of me!

That was also why the newcomer had been able to needle Ernie so effectively back in the apartment. The guy knew just where to stick the sharp points because he and Ernie were, in some ways, two of a kind.

Ernie laughted softly. Sometimes, he thought, I can be such a perfect jackass.

The crooked-eyed man returned from the storeroom and smiled with satisfaction when he saw everyone seated at the long table which he had told Brendan and Ginger to put together from three smaller ones. He came to Ernie and said, 'No hard feelings?'

'Hell, no,' Ernie said. 'And thanks . . . thanks a lot.'

The newcomer went to the head of the table, where a chair had been left for him. With Kenny Rogers crooning on the jukebox, the guy said, 'My name's Jack Twist, and I don't know any more than you what in hell's happening, probably less than you know. The whole thing gives me the heebie-jeebies, but I also have to tell you this is the first time in eight years that I've really and truly felt like I'm on the right side of an issue, the first time I've felt like one of the good guys – and dear God in Heaven, you can't know how much I've needed to feel *that*!'

*   *   *

Lieutenant Tom Horner, Colonel Falkirk's aide-de-camp, had enormous hands. The small tape recorder was totally concealed in his right hand when he carried it into the windowless office. His fingers were so large that he seemed certain to have trouble using the little control buttons. But he was remarkably dextrous. He produced the recorder, placed it on the desk, switched it on, and set it in the playback mode.

The tape had been duplicated from the reel-to-reel machine on which all phone-monitored conversations were recorded. It was a portion of an exchange that had taken place between several people at the Tranquillity only minutes ago. The first part of the tape concerned the witnesses' discovery that the source of their trouble was not Shenkfield but Thunder Hill. Leland listened with dismay. He had not anticipated that their quest would take the right trail so soon. Their cleverness worried and angered him.

On the tape: '*For God's sake, shut up. If you think you can plot in privacy here, you're badly mistaken.*'

'That's Twist,' Lieutenant Horner said. He had a big voice, too, which was as well controlled as his enormous hands: a

485

soft rumble. He stopped the tape. 'We knew he was coming here. And we know he's dangerous. We figured he'd be more cautious than the others, sure, but we didn't expect him to act as if he was at war from the get-go.'

As far as they knew, Jack Twist's memory block had not seriously deteriorated. He was not suffering fugues, sleepwalking, phobias, or obsessions. Therefore, only one thing might have motivated him to suddenly lease a plane and fly to Elko County: mail from the same traitor who had sent Polaroids to Corvaisis and to the Blocks.

Leland Falkirk was furious that someone involved in the cover-up, probably someone at Thunder Hill, was sabotaging the entire operation. He had made this discovery only last Saturday night, when Dominick Corvaisis and the Blocks had sat at the kitchen table and discussed the strange snapshots they'd been sent. Leland had ordered an immediate investigation and intense screening of everyone at the Depository, but that was going a lot slower than he had anticipated.

'There's worse,' Horner said. He switched on the tape again.

Leland listened to Twist tell the others about rifle microphones and infinity transmitters. Shocked, they adjourned to the diner, where they could discuss their strategy without being overheard.

'They're in the diner now,' Horner said, shutting off the recorder. 'Ripped out the phones. I've spoken by radio with the observers we have stationed south of I-80. They watched the witnesses move to the Grille, but they haven't had any luck tuning in with a rifle mike.'

'And won't,' Leland said sourly. 'Twist knows what he's doing.'

'Now that they're aware of Thunder Hill, we've got to move on them as soon as possible.'

'I'm waiting to hear from Chicago.'

'Sharkle's still barricaded in his house?'

'Last I heard, yes,' Leland said. 'I've got to know if his memory block has completely crumbled. If it has, and if he gets a chance to tell anyone what he saw that summer, then the operation's blown, anyway, and it'd be a mistake to

486

move against the witnesses at the motel. We'll have to fall back to another plan.'

*   *   *

Under the diner's wagonwheel lights, safe in her mother's lap, Marcie dozed off even as Jack Twist introduced himself. In spite of the nap the girl had taken on the plane, sooty rings of weariness encircled her eyes, and a tracery of blue veins marked her porcelain-pale skin.

Jorja was tired, too, but Twist's dramatic arrival was an effective antidote to the narcotising effects of the dinner. She was wide awake and eager to hear what he had to tell them of his own tribulations.

He began by briefly mentioning his imprisonment in Central America, with which his military career had ended. He made the experience sound more boring and frustrating than frightening, but Jorja sensed that he had endured gruelling hardship. From his matter-of-fact tone, she had the impression that he was a man so secure in his self-image, so certain of his emotional and physical and intellectual strengths, that he never needed to boast or to hear the praise of others.

When he spoke of Jenny, his late wife, he was less able to maintain an air of detachment. Jorja heard the cadences of lingering grief in this part of his story; a river of love and longing flowed beneath his feigned placidity. The intimacy of mind and spirit between Jack Twist and Jenny, prior to her coma, had surely been extraordinary, for only a special and magical relationship would have ensured his unflagging devotion through the woman's long deathlike sleep. Jorja tried to imagine what a marriage of that sort might be like, then realised that, regardless of how magical their marriage had been, Jack would not have committed himself so totally to his afflicted wife if he'd been any less than the man he was. Their relationship had been special, yes, but even more special was this man himself. That realisation increased Jorja's already strong interest in Twist and his story.

He was vague in describing the enterprises by which he had financed Jenny's long stay at a sanitarium. He made it clear only that what he had done was illegal, that he was not proud of it, and that his lawless days were over. 'At least I never

487

killed any innocent by-standers, thank God. Otherwise, I think it's best if you don't know any details that might somehow make you accessories-after-the-fact.'

Their mutual unremembered ordeal had affected Jack Twist. But as with Sandy, the mysterious events of that July night had wrought only beneficial changes in him.

Ernie Block said, 'I think what you've indirectly told us is that you were a professional thief.' When Jack Twist said nothing, Ernie continued: 'It occurs to me that you were almost certainly forced to reveal your criminal life to the people who brainwashed us. In fact, from what little you've said, I figure those safe-deposit boxes in which the postcards turned up were kept under the identities you also used when committing robberies; therefore, since that July, the Army and government must've known about your illegal activities.'

Jack's silence was confirmation that he had, indeed, been a thief.

Ernie said, 'Yet, once they'd blocked your memories of what really happened here that summer, they turned you loose and let you continue with what you'd been doing. Why in the hell would they do that? I can understand the Army and government bending – even breaking – the law to hide whatever happened at Thunder Hill if it involves national security. But otherwise, you'd expect them to uphold the law, wouldn't you? So why wouldn't they at least anonymously inform the New York police or arrange for you to be caught in the middle of a crime?'

Jorja said, 'Because from the start they've not been certain that our memory blocks would hold up. They've been monitoring us, at least checking in on us once in a while, to be sure we don't need a refresher course in forgetfulness. What happened to Ginger and Pablo Jackson seems to prove they're watching, all right. And if they decided it was necessary to grab Jack – or any of us – and put him through another session with the mind-control doctors, they'd want him where they could reach him without too much trouble. It'd be a lot easier to snatch Jack out of his apartment or from his car than to spirit him out of prison.'

Good grief,' Jack said, smiling at her, 'I think you've hit on it. Absolutely.' Although Jorja had been slightly chilled by his

488

smile the first time she'd seen it, she perceived it differently now; it was a warmer smile than it had seemed initially.

Marcie murmured wordlessly in her sleep. Suddenly and curiously shy about meeting Jack Twist's eyes, Jorja used her daughter's dreamy mutterings as an excuse to look away from him.

Jack said, 'Whatever secret they're protecting is so important they had to let me carry on with whatever crimes I chose to commit.'

Ginger Weiss shook her head. 'Maybe not. Maybe they engineered this guilt. Maybe they planted the seed, so you'd change.'

'No,' Jack said. 'If they didn't have time to weave the story of the toxic spill into everyone's false memories, they sure wouldn't have had time to finesse me toward the straight-and-narrow path. Besides . . . this is difficult to explain . . . but, since coming here tonight, I feel in my heart that I re-learned guilt and found my way back into society because something so important happened to us two summers ago that it put my own suffering in perspective and made me see that none of my bad experiences was *so* bad as to justify the warping of my entire life.'

'Yes!' Sandy said. 'I feel that, too. All the hell I went through as a child . . . none of it matters after what happened that July.'

They were silent, trying to imagine what experience could have been so shattering as to make even the most painful of life's tricks seem of little consequence. But none of them could puzzle it out.

After he selected more songs on the jukebox, Jack asked a lot of questions of the others, filling the gaps in his knowledge of their various ordeals and putting together a complete picture of their discoveries to date. That done, he guided them through a discussion of strategy, formulating a set of tasks for tomorrow.

Jorja was again intrigued by Jack's leadership skills. By the time the group discussed what steps should be taken next and settled on an agenda, they had agreed to undertake precisely the tasks Jack thought ought to be accomplished, though there was never a sense that he had commanded or manipulated them. When he'd first appeared in the Blocks' apartment, he'd discovered he could take control of a situation and, by sheer force of personality, make people obey him. But now he chose indirection, and the speed with which everyone came around to his purposes was proof this was the right tactic.

Jorja realised that he impressed her for many of the same reasons that Ginger Weiss had impressed her. She saw in him the kind of person she had been struggling to become since her divorce – and the kind of man that Alan could never have been.

The final problem the group dealt with was the danger of an attack by Falkirk's men. Now that there was a real chance their memory blocks would substantially decay – or crumble completely – in the near future, they posed a greater threat to their enemy than at any time since July, the summer before last. Tomorrow, they would be separated most of the day as they carried out their various tasks and researches, but tonight they were in danger if they all stayed at the motel, making one easy target. Therefore, they agreed that most of them would go to bed now, while two or three drove into Elko and spent part of the night circling through town, always on the move, alert. Assuming that the Tranquillity was under observation, the enemy would at once realise they could no longer seize everyone in a clean sweep. At four o'clock in the morning, a second group of outriders could rendezvous with the first team in Elko and relieve them, so they could come back here and get some sleep.

'I'll volunteer for the first team,' Jack said. 'I just have to fetch my Cherokee from the hills, where I left it. Who'll go with me?'

'I will,' Jorja said at once, then became aware of the weight of her daughter in her lap. 'Uh, that is, if someone'll let Marcie sleep in their room tonight.'

'No problem,' Faye said. 'She can stay with Ernie and me.'

Jack said they ought to divide their numbers further, and Brendan Cronin volunteered to join him and Jorja on the first team. The priest's response triggered a peculiar feeling in Jorja, a pang she would not identify as disappointment until much later.

Because everyone else had errands to run early tomorrow,

the second team was composed of only Ned and Sandy. A rendezvous between the teams was set for four o'clock in the morning at the Arco Mini-Mart.

'If you get there first,' Jack said, 'for God's sake don't buy a Hamwich. Okay, I guess that's it. We should get moving.'

'Not quite yet,' Ginger said. The physician folded her hands and looked down at her interlaced fingers, collecting her thoughts. 'Since this afternoon, when Brendan first arrived, when the rings appeared on his and Dom's hands, when the motel office was filled with that strange noise and the light . . . I've been chewing over everything we've been able to learn, trying to make those bizarre phenomena fit in somehow. I've hit on an explanation for some of it; not all, but some of it.'

Everyone expressed an eagerness to hear the theory, half-formed though it might be.

Ginger said, 'As different as our dreams are, one element links all of them: the moon. Okay. Our other dreams – decon suits, IV needles, beds with restraining straps – proved to be based on real experiences, real threats. In fact, they weren't dreams but memories surfacing in the form of dreams. So it seems reasonable to suppose the moon also featured prominently in whatever happened to us, that the moon, too, is a memory trying to surface in our dreams. Agreed?'

'Agreed,' Dom said, and everyone else nodded.

'We've seen how Marcie's lunar obsession changed to a fascination with a *scarlet* moon,' Ginger continued. 'And Jack's told us that, a couple nights ago, the ordinary moonlight in his own nightmare turned into a bloody glow. None of the rest of us has dreamed of a red moon yet, but I submit that the appearance of this scarlet image in Marcie's and Jack's dreams is proof that it's also a memory. In other words, on the night of July 6, we saw something that made the moon turn red. And the apparitional light, which sometimes fills Brendan's bedroom, which some of us witnessed today in the motel office, is a strange sort of re-enactment of what happened to the real moon on the night in July. The apparitional light is a message meant to nudge our memories.'

'Message,' Jack said. 'All right. But who the devil's *sending* the message? What's the light come from? How is it generated?'

491

'I've got an idea about that,' Ginger said. 'But let me take this one step at a time. First, let's consider what might've happened to make the moon turn red that night.'

Jorja listened, as did the others, with interest at first and then with growing uneasiness, while Ginger got up from her chair and, pacing, outlined an unnerving explanation.

*   *   *

Ginger Weiss whole-heartedly embraced the scientific world-view. To her, the universe unfailingly operated by the rules of logic and reason, and no mystery could long endure once attacked in a logical fashion. But unlike some in the scientific community – and *many* in the medical community – she did not believe that a vivid imagination was necessarily a hindrance to logic and reason. Otherwise, she might not have devised the theory she now conveyed to the others in the Tranquillity Grille.

It was a pretty strange theory, and she was nervous about how the others would receive it. So she paced to the jukebox, over to the service counter, back to the table, moving constantly as she talked:

'The men who dealt with us in the first day or two of imprisonment were wearing decontamination suits designed to handle biological risks. They must've been worried we were infected with something. So perhaps part of what we saw was a scarlet cloud of biological contaminant. When it passed overhead, it turned the moon red.'

'And we were all infected with some strange disease,' Jorja said.

Ginger said, 'That may be why, yesterday at that special place along the highway, I had the memory-flash of Dom shouting, "It's inside me. It's inside me." That would have been a logical thing for him to shout if, that night, he had found himself caught up in a red cloud of some contaminant and realised he was breathing it in. And Brendan's told us that the same words – "It's inside me" – came spontaneously to his lips last night in Reno, when the apparitional light filled his room.'

'Bacteria? Disease? Then why didn't we get sick?' Brendan asked.

'Because they treated us immediately,' Dom said. 'We've

492

already worked that one out, Brendan – yesterday, before you got here. But, Ginger, the light that filled the office this afternoon was too bright to represent moonlight filtered through a red cloud.'

'I know,' Ginger said, pacing. 'Underdeveloped as it is, my idea doesn't explain everything – like the rings on your hands. So maybe it's not the right idea. On the other hand, it does explain some things, and maybe if we think about it long enough, we'll see how it explains these other puzzles, as well. And as a theory, it has one big plus.'

'What's that?' Ned asked.

'It could explain why Brendan was involved in two miracle-cures in Chicago. It could explain the whirling paper moons in Zebediah's house. And the destruction here at the diner on Saturday night, when Dom was trying to recall what had happened the summer before last. It could explain the source of the apprational light.'

On the jukebox, the last of a series of songs had faded to its end as Ginger began to speak. But no one got up to choose more music, for they were riveted by her promise to explain the inexplicable.

'To this point,' Ginger said, 'the theory's pretty mundane. A red cloud of contaminant. Nothing hard to accept in that. But now . . . you've got to take a big leap of imagination with me. We've been assuming that the miraculous healing and certainly the poltergeist phenomena have some mysterious external source. Father Wycazik, Brendan's rector, thinks the external source is God. The rest of us don't feel it's exactly divine. We don't know what the hell it is, but we all assume that its an external power, something out there somewhere that's taunting us or trying to reach us with a message or threatening us. But what if these wonders have an *internal* source. Suppose Brendan and Dom really possess some power, and suppose that they possess it *because of what happened during the night of the red moon*. Suppose they have telekinesis – which is the power to move objects without touching them, which would explain the whirling paper moons and the destruction in the diner.'

Everyone looked at Dom and Brendan in amazement, but no one was more startled than those two men, who gaped at Ginger, shocked.

Dom said, 'But that's ridiculous! I'm no psychic, no sorcerer.'

'Me neither,' Brendan said.

Ginger shook her head. 'Not consciously, no. I'm saying maybe the power is in you, and you're just not aware of it. Bear with me. Think about it. The first time the rings appeared on Brendan's hands, the first time he exercised his healing power, was when he was combing the hair of the little girl in the hospital. He's said he was overwhelmed with pity for her and filled with frustration and anger that he couldn't help her. Maybe it was his intense frustration and anger that freed the power in him, even though he wasn't aware of it. He *couldn't* be aware of it because the acquisition of this power is part of what he's been made to forget. Okay, the second time, with the wounded policeman, Brendan found himself in an extreme crisis, which might trigger these powers.' She began pacing and talking more rapidly to prevent debate until she'd finished. 'Now think about Dom's experiences. The first one, in Reno, at Lomack's house. The way you told it to us, Dom . . . as you wandered through the house, you became so frustrated by the ever-deepening nature of the mystery that you wanted to rush through those rooms *and tear those paper moons off the walls*. Those were your very words. And of course, that's what happened: you pulled those moons off the walls, not with your hands but with this power. And remember, the pictures only fell to the floor when you shouted, 'Stop it, stop it!' When it did stop, you thought something had heard you and obeyed or relented, but in fact you stopped it yourself.'

Brendan, Dom, and a couple of the others still looked sceptical.

But Ginger had captured Sandy Sarver's imagination. 'It makes sense! It makes even more sense if you think about what happened here on Saturday night, right in this very room. Dom was trying to remember back to that Friday in July, trying to remember what happened right up to the second where his memory block took effect. And while he was struggling to remember . . . all of a sudden this strange noise, this thunder, started to rumble through the diner, and everything started to shake. He could've been unconsciously using this power of his to recreate the *effects* of whatever happened back then.'

494

'Good!' Ginger said encouragingly. 'See? The more you think about it, the more it hangs together.'

'But the strange light,' Dom said. 'You're saying Brendan and I somehow maufactured that?'

'Yes, possibly,' Ginger said, returning to the table, leaning on her empty chair. 'Pyrokinesis. The ability to spontaneously generate heat or fire with the power of the mind alone.'

'This wasn't fire,' Dom said. 'It was light.'

'So . . . call it "photokinesis,"' Ginger said. 'But I think when you and Brendan met, you subconsciously recognised the power in each other. On a deep level, you were both reminded of what happened to you that July night, the thing you've been forced to forget. And both of you wanted to blast those memories into view. So unwittingly you generated that weird light, which was a re-creation of the way the moon changed from white to red on the night of July 6. It was your subconscious trying to jolt the memory through the block.'

Ginger could see that their minds were spinning with all these odd ideas, and she wanted to keep them unsettled a while longer, because when they were unsettled they were more likely to absorb what she was saying. Given time for quiet reflection, the heavy armour of scepticism would fall back into place, and her ideas would bounce off.

Ernie Block shook his head. 'Wait a minute. You're losing me now. You started all this by suggesting that what turned the moon red was a scarlet cloud of some biological contaminant. Then you jumped way the hell to one side and started talking about how the thing that happened to us was responsible for Dom and Brendan developing these supposed powers. Where's the connection? What does biological contamination have to do with all this psychic stuff, anyway?'

Ginger took a deep breath because they had come to the core of her theory, the wildest part of it. 'What if . . . *what if* we were contaminated by some virus or bacterium that, as a side-effect, causes profound chemical or genetic or hormonal changes in its host, changes in the host's brain? And what if those changes leave the host with something very like psychic powers, even once the infection is gone?'

They stared at her with a variety of expressions, though not as if they thought her mad, and not as if she was too imagina-

495

tive for her own good. Rather, they seemed impressed by the complex chain of logic which she had forged and by the inevitability of the final link.

'Good God,' Dom said, 'I doubt that it's the right answer, but it's sure the prettiest most neatly constructed theory I ever expected to hear. What a concept for a novel! A genetically engineered virus that, as a surprise side-effect, causes a sort of forced evolution of the human brain, resulting in psychic powers. For the first time in weeks, I have a terrific urge to rush to a typewriter. Ginger, if we get out of this alive, I'll have to give you a piece of the royalties on the book that's sure to grow out of that idea.'

Gently rocking her slumbering daughter, Jorja Monatella said, 'But why *couldn't* it be the right answer? Why does it just have to be a terrific concept for a novel?'

'For one thing,' Jack Twist said, 'if it were true, if we'd been contaminated with a virus like that, we'd all have developed psychic powers. Right?'

'Well,' Ginger said, 'maybe we weren't all contaminated. Or maybe we were contaminated, but the virus didn't get a foothold in all of us.'

Faye said, 'Or maybe this special side-effect isn't manifested in everyone who's infected by the bug.'

'Good thought,' Ginger said. She began to pace again, this time, not because she was nervous but because she was excited.

Ned Sarver pushed one hand through his receding hair and said, 'Are you saying the Army knew about this side-effect of the virus, knew that it might cause these changes in some of us?'

'I don't know,' Ginger said. 'Maybe they knew. Maybe not.'

'I think not,' Ernie said. 'Definitely not. From what you found in the *Sentinel*, we know they closed the interstate shortly before the "accident" happened, which means it was no accident. So . . . first of all, I find it hard to believe our own military would intentionally subject us to contamination with a biological-warfare micro-organism in a hare-brained scheme to test its effectiveness in the field. But even if such an atrocity was possible, they wouldn't expose us to a virus that could transform us in the way Ginger has suggested. Because, my

496

friends, people with strong psychic powers would be a new species, a *superior* breed of humanity. Formidable psychic power would translate directly into military, economic, and political power. So if the government *knew* it had a virus that conferred these powers, it would not expose a group of ordinary people like us. Not in a million years. That blessing would be reserved for those already in positions of high authority, for the elite. I agree with Dom: I find the red-cloud-of-virus theory quite fascinating . . . though unlikely. However, if we *were* contaminated by such a thing, the side-effect was unknown to the government.'

In light of what Ernie had said, everyone was looking at Brendan and Dom with a new appreciation composed equally of awe, uneasiness, wonder, respect and fear. Ginger saw both the priest and the writer squirm with the exhilarating yet frightening realisation that they might have within them the potential for superhuman power, a potential that, if fulfilled, would forever separate them from the rest of mankind.

'No,' Dom said, starting to get up in protest, then sitting back down as if he did not think his legs would support him. 'No, no. You're not right, Ginger. I'm no superman, no wizard, no damn . . . freak. If you were right, I'd feel it. I'd *know* it, Ginger.'

Brendan Cronin, equally shaken, said, 'I've thought that somehow I've been the *vehicle* for the healing of Emmy and Winton. I've thought that something – not God, perhaps, but something – is working through me. I never thought of *myself* as the actual healer. Listen, I was under the impression we'd already decided the toxic-spill story was entirely a fake, a cover, that what happened to us wasn't an accident of any kind, neither chemical nor biological, but something altogether different.'

Jack and Jorja and Faye and Ned started talking at the same time. The noise level rose so loud that little Marcie frowned in her sleep, and Ginger said, 'Wait, wait, wait a minute. There's no point discussing it because we can't prove there was such a virus any more than we can prove there wasn't one. Not yet. But maybe we can prove the other part.'

'What do you mean?' Sandy Sarver asked.

Ginger said, 'Maybe we can prove Dom and Brendan have

the power. Not how they got it, but just that they have it.'

Dom was incredulous. 'How?'

'We'll set up a test,' Ginger said.

* * *

Dom was absolutely certain that it would not work, that they were wasting time, that the whole idea was foolish.

Yet he was also scared that it *would* work, and that the proof of his power would condemn him to the condition of a freak or at least to a life forever closed to ordinary human relationships. If he possessed godlike power, no one would ever regard him without wonder and fear. In even the most relaxed or intimate moments with friends or lovers, their awareness of his extraordinary gifts would intrude, either overtly or in an unspoken subtext. Others, perhaps most, would envy or hate him.

The unfairness of his predicament grated on him. For most of his thirty-five years, he had been shy and ineffectual, condemned to a drab existence by his timidity. Then he had changed, and for fifteen months, until his sleepwalking began last October, he'd been outgoing. Now, that brief, wonderful season of normality might be passing. If the test that Ginger outlined were to prove Dom had somehow acquired psychic powers, he would be isolated again, not by his own sense of inferiority, as before, but by everyone else's uneasy awareness of his superiority.

The test. Dom hoped to God he failed.

He and Brendan Cronin were sitting by themselves at the long table, one at each end. Jorja Monatella had put her slumbering daughter in a booth, and the girl had not awakened. The adults – all seven, including Jorja – stood in a semi-circle around the table, back a couple of paces, giving Dom and Brendan space to concentrate free of distraction.

A salt shaker stood on the table in front of Dom. Ginger's test required that he concentrate on moving the object without touching it. 'Just an inch,' she had said. 'If you can evoke just the slightest perceptible motion in the shaker, we'll know you've got the power.'

At the far end of the three joined tables, a pepper shaker stood in front of Brendan Cronin. The priest was staring at the small glass cylinder as intently as Dom was staring at his own shaker, and his round freckled face was filled with a foreboding only marginally less grim than Dom's. Although Brendan had denied that the hand of God lay behind the miraculous cures and apparitional lights, it was clear to Dom that the priest secretly and deeply hoped to discover that, in fact, a divine Presence was at work. He wanted to be drawn back into his faith, into the bosom of the Church. If the miracles proved to be his own work, accomplished by the exertion of heretotore unrecognised psychic powers, and if those powers proved to have been conferred by a mere *germ*, as Ginger's crazy-but-canny theory would have it, Brendan's yearning for spiritual elevation and holy guidance would go unfulfilled.

The salt shaker.

He fixed his eyes on it and tried to clear every thought from his mind except the determined intention to move the shaker. Although he did not want to discover that he had these strange talents, he had to make a sincere attempt to employ them. He had to know if it was true.

If the power existed, neither Ginger nor any of the others could suggest techniques for tapping it. 'But,' Ginger had said, 'if it can explode spontaneously and spectacularly in moments of stress, surely you can learn to call upon it and control it whenever and however you desire . . . just as a musician can apply his *musical* talent any time he pleases. Or just as you apply your writing talent to the blank page.'

The salt shaker remained motionless, unaffected.

Dom strove to narrow his attention until that humble glass cylinder – with its perforated stainless-steel cap and grainy white contents – was the only thing in his universe. He brought all his mind to bear upon it, every speck of his will, and tried to push it along the table, strained until he realised he was gritting his teeth, fisting his hands.

Nothing.

He changed tack. Instead of mentally assaulting the shaker as if he were blasting away with a cannon at the mighty walls of a fortress, he relaxed and studied the object to get an intimate sense of its size, shape, and texture. Perhaps the key was to develop an empathy for the shaker. 'Empathy' was the word that seemed right to him, though he was relating to an inanimate and inorganic object; instead of battling it, perhaps he could empathise and somehow . . . induce it to cooperate in a short telekinetic journey. Only an inch. He leaned forward slightly to better examine the functional simplicity of its design: five bevelled facets to make it easy to grip and hold; a thick glass bottom to provide balance and reduce the frequency of spills; a shiny metal cap. . . .

Nothing. Standing unaffected on the table before him, the shaker seemed like the mythical immovable object, heavy beyond weighing, welded forever to this spot in space and time.

But of course, like all forms of matter in the universe, it was not immovable, and in some ways it was *always* moving, never still. After all, it was composed of billions of ceaselessly moving atoms, the outer parts of which orbited, planetlike, around the billions of sunlike nuclei. The salt shaker was engaged in uninterrupted motion on a sub-atomic level, frantically moving *within* its structure, so it should not be difficult to induce it to make one additional movement, one little jaunt on the macrocosmic level of human perception, just one little hop and skip, just one –

Dom felt a sudden buoyancy, almost as if he himself were going to be moved by some arcane force, but instead – and at last – the salt shaker moved. He had become so deeply involved with that homely object that he had actually forgotten Ginger and the others; he was reminded of their presence when, as one, they gasped and exclaimed softly. The shaker did not simply slide one inch along the table – or two or ten or twenty. It rose into the air instead, as if gravity had ceased to have a claim on it. Like a tiny glass balloon, it floated upwards: one foot, two, three, and stopped four feet above the surface on which, only seconds ago, it had appeared immovable. It remained suspended several inches above the eye-level of those who were standing, and they stared up at it in awe.

At the far end of the table, Brendan's pepper shaker rose, too. Mouth open, eyes wide, Brendan stared at the rising cylinder. When it stopped at precisely the same height as the salt shaker, Brendan finally dared to take his eyes from it. He looked at Dom, glanced nervously at the pepper shaker again, as if certain it would crash down the moment he shifted his gaze, then looked at Dom once more when he realised that eye-contact was not required to maintain levitation. Several sentiments were apparent in the priest's eyes: wonder, amazement, puzzlement, fear, and an emotional acknowledgement of the profound brotherhood that existed between him and Dom by virtue of the strange power they shared.

Dom was intrigued that he did not need to strain to keep the salt shaker aloft. In fact, it seemed hard to believe that he was actually responsible for its magical performance. He was not conscious of either possessing or exerting control of the object. He felt no power surging in him. Evidently, his telekinetic ability functioned automatically, in a fashion similar to respiration and heartbeat.

Brendan raised his hands. The red rings had reappeared on them.

Dom looked at his own hands and saw the same inscrutable stigmata burning brightly.

What did they mean?

Looming overhead, the salt and pepper shakers generated a sense of expectancy in Dom even greater than he had felt at the beginning of this test. Apparently, the others felt it as well, for they began to urge Dom and Brendan to perform additional feats.

'Incredible,' Ginger said breathlessly. 'You've shown us vertical movement, levitation. Can you also move them horizontally?'

'Can you lift something heavier?' Sandy Sarver asked.

'The light,' Ernie said. 'Can you generate the red light?'

Seeking first to accomplish a more modest task than any they had proposed, Dom thought about giving the salt shaker a slight spin, and immediately it began to twirl in mid-air, eliciting another gasp from the onlookers. A moment later, Brendan's pepper shaker began to spin, too. Reflections of the overhead lights glimmered liquidly across the shiny metal caps of the spinning dispensers, flashed off the facets of the glass, travelled scintillantly along the edges where one facet met another, so the shakers looked like glittery Christmas-tree ornaments.

Simultaneously, the two small dispensers began drifting towards one another, the horizontal movement Ginger had requested, though Dom was not aware of consciously directing the salt shaker on this course. He supposed Ginger's suggestion was accepted by his subconscious, which now employed psychic energy to accomplish the task, without waiting for him to make a conscious effort. It was eerie – the way he controlled the shaker yet was unaware of how that control was exerted.

Above the centremost point of the three joined tables, the salt and pepper shakers stopped moving horizontally when they were about ten inches apart. They hung side by side, spinning a bit faster than before, throwing off spangles of reflected light. Then they began to revolve around each other in perfectly circular synchronised orbits. But that lasted only a few seconds. Suddenly, the shakers were spinning faster than before, and swinging around each other much faster as well, and in much more complex parabolic counter-orbits.

Captivated and delighted, the onlookers laughed, applauded. Dom looked at Ginger. Her radiant face shone with an expression of pure, spiritual uplift that made her more beautiful than ever. She lowered her gaze from the salt and pepper shakers to Dom, grinned with wild excitement, and gave him a thumbs-up sign. Ernie Block and Jack Twist watched the aerobatics with open-mouthed wonder that made them look not like hard-bitten ex-soldiers but like two small boys seeing fireworks for the first time in their lives. Laughing, Faye stood with her hands raised toward the shakers, as if she were trying to feel the miraculous field of power in which they were suspended. Ned Sarver was laughing, too, but Sandy was crying, a sight that startled Dom until he realised she was also smiling and that the tears on her cheeks were tears of joy.

'Oh,' Sandy said, turning to Dom as if she had sensed that he was looking at her, 'isn't it wonderful? Whatever it means, isn't it just wonderful? The freedom . . . the freedom of it . . . the breaking away of all the bonds . . . the rising up and above and away . . .'

Dom knew precisely what she was feeling and trying to say, because he felt it, too. For the moment, he forgot that possession of these abilities would forever alienate him from people who were without the talent, and he was filled with a rapturous sense of transcendence, with an appreciation for what it might mean to take a giant leap up the ladder of evolution, breaking away from the chains of human limitations. In the Tranquillity Grille tonight, there was a sense of history-being-made, a sense that nothing in the world would ever be the same again.

'Do something else,' Ginger said.

'Yes!' Sandy said. 'Show us more. Show us more.'

In other parts of the room, other salt shakers flew up from the tables on which they had been standing: six, eight, ten in all. They hung motionless for a moment, then began to spin like the first shaker.

Instantly, an equal number of pepper shakers took flight and began spinning as well.

Dom still did not know how he was doing these things; he made no effort to perform each new trick; the thought merely became fact, as if wishes could come true. He suspected that Brendan was equally baffled.

The jukebox had been silent. Now it began to play a Dolly Parton tune, though no one had punched the programming buttons.

Did I do that, Dom wondered, or was it Brendan?

Ginger said, 'My God, I'm so excited I'm going to *plotz*!'

Laughing, Domn said, '*Plotz*? What's *that* one mean?'

'Bust, explode,' Ginger said. 'I'm so excited I'm going to bust!'

Every salt and pepper shaker spun, and the halves of every pair orbited each other, and now all eleven sets began moving around the room in a train, faster, faster, making a soft *whoosh* as they cut the air, casting off sparks of reflected light.

Abruptly, a dozen chairs rose off the floor, not in the controlled and playful manner in which the salt and pepper shakers had risen from the tables, but with such violence and momentum that they shot instantly to the ceiling, smashing against that barrier with a deafening clatter. One of the wagonwheel lighting fixtures was struck by two chairs; its lightbulbs burst, and the room was only three-quarters as brightly illuminated as it had been. That wagonwheel broke loose of its anchor brackets and wires, crashing to the floor a few feet behind Dom. The chairs remained against the ceiling, vibrating as if they were a flock of enormous bats hovering on

503

dark wings. Most of the salt and pepper shakers were still whirling maniacally around the room above everyone's head, though a few had been brought down by the upflung chairs. Now, a few more stopped spinning, swung erratically out of their orbits, out of the train as well, wobbled, and shot to the floor. One of them struck Ernie's shoulder, and he cried out in pain.

Dom and Brendan had lost control. And because they had never known exactly how they had established control in the first place, they did not know how to regain it.

In a blink, the celebratory mood changed to panic. The onlookers scrambled for shelter under the tables, acutely aware that the levitated chairs – rattling ominously against the ceiling – were potentially far more dangerous missiles than the salt and pepper shakers. The noise awakened Marcie. She sat up in the booth where she had been sleeping, crying now and calling for her mother. Jorja pulled the girl off the booth and scrambled under one of the tables with her, hugging her close, and everyone was out of the line of fire except Brendan and Dom.

Dom felt as if this psychic power was a live grenade that had been wired irremovably to his hand.

Overhead, three or four more shakers lost momentum and came down like bullets. The dozen levitated chairs began to bounce against the ceiling more aggressively, shedding small pieces of themselves.

Dom didn't know if he should dive for cover or attempt to regain control. He looked at Brendan, who was equally paralysed.

Overhead, the three remaining wagonwheel lights swayed wildly on their chains, causing goblin shadows to leap across the room.

The battering chairs gouged out small chunks of the ceiling.

A salt shaker dropped in front of Dom, impacting like a tiny meteorite against the table. The glass was too thick to shatter, but the small jar cracked into three or four pieces, flinging up what salt it still contained, and Dom flinched from the white spray.

Remembering the spinning carousel of paper moons in Lomack's house six days ago, Dom raised both hands towards

504

the rattling chairs and whirling shakers. Clenching his hands into fists, shutting the red-ring stigmata out of sight, he said, 'Stop it. Stop it now. *Stop it!*'

Overhead, the chairs ceased vibrating. The salt and pepper shakers halted in mid-whirl and hung motionless in the air.

For a second or two, the diner was preternaturally silent.

Then the twelve chairs and the last of the shakers dropped straight down, bouncing off tables and other chairs that had never taken flight. When everything at last came to rest in tangled rubble, Dom and Brendan were as unscathed as those who had taken refuge under the tables. Dom blinked at the priest, and around them all was graveyard-still. This moment of silence was longer than the first. It seemed as if time had stopped, until Marcie's thin whimpering and her mother's murmured assurances started the engines of reality purring again, drawing the others out from their places of shelter.

Ernie was still massaging his shoulder, where he had been hit by a salt shaker, but he was not seriously hurt. No one else was injured, though everyone was shaken.

Dom saw the way they were looking at him and Brendan. Warily. Just as he had figured they would look at him if he proved to have the power. Just the way he had dreaded being looked at. Damn.

Ginger seemed to be the only one who was not put off by his new status. She enthusiastically embraced Dom and said, 'What matters is that you've got it. You've got it, and eventually you can learn to use it, and that's wonderful.'

'I'm not so sure,' Dom said, looking at the broken chairs, fallen lighting fixtures. Jack Twist was brushing salt and drywall dust off his clothes. Jorja was still comforting her frightened child. Faye and Sandy were picking splinters and other bits of debris out of their hair, and Ned was pondering the danger of the live wires dangling from the ceiling where the chandelier had torn loose. Dom said, 'Ginger, even when I was using the power, I didn't know how I was doing it. And when it ran wild . . . I didn't know how to stop it.'

'But you did stop it,' she said. She kept one arm around his waist as if she knew – God bless her – that he needed the reassurance of human contact. 'You *did* stop it, Dom.'

'Maybe next time I won't be able.' He realised he was shivering. 'Look at this mess. My God, Ginger, someone could've been badly hurt.'

'No one was.'

'Someone could have been killed. Next time –'

'It'll be better,' she said.

Brendan Cronin came around the long table. 'He'll change his mind, Ginger. Give him time. I know *I'm* going to try again. Alone, next time. In a couple of days, when I've had time to think it through, I'll go out somewhere in an open field, away from people, where no one can be hurt except me, and I'll give it another try. I think it's going to be difficult to control the . . . energy. It's going to take a lot of time, a lot of work, maybe years. But I'll explore, practise. And so will Dom. He'll realise as much when he's had a couple of minutes to think about it.'

Dom shook his head. 'I don't want this. I don't want to be so different from other people.'

'But now you are,' Brendan said. 'We both are.'

'That's damn fatalistic.'

Brendan smiled. 'Though I'm having a crisis of faith, I'm still a priest, so I believe in predestination, fate. That's an article of faith. But we priests are a clever bunch, so we can be fatalistic and believe in free will at the same time! *Both* are articles of faith.' For the priest, the psychological effects of these events were far different from the fear raised in Dom. As he talked, he repeatedly rose onto his toes as if he were nearly buoyant enough to float away.

At a loss to understand the priest's good humour, Dom changed the subject. 'Well, Ginger, if we've proved half of your crazy theory, at least we've disproved the other half.'

She frowned. 'What do you mean?'

'In the midst of all that . . . uproar,' Dom said, gesturing toward the battered ceiling, 'when I saw the rings appear on my hands again, I decided the psychic power wasn't a side-effect of any strange viral infection. I know the source of it is something else, something even stranger, though I don't know what it may be.'

'Oh? Well, which is the case?' she asked. 'Have you merely decided, or do you really know?'

'I know,' Dom said. 'Deep inside, I know.'

'Oh, yes, me too,' Brendan said happily, as Ernie and Faye

506

and the others gathered around. 'You were correct, Ginger, when you suggested the power was in Dom and me. And it's been in use since that July night, like you said. However, you're not right about the method by which we acquired the gift. Like Dom said . . . in the middle of all that chaos, I sensed that biological contamination wasn't the right explanation. I haven't the foggiest notion what the answer is, but we can rule out that part of your theory.'

Now Dom understood why Brendan was in such good spirits in spite of the frightening exhibition in which they'd just participated. Though he professed to see no religious aspect to recent events, in his heart of hearts, the priest had retained hope that the miraculous cures and apparitional lights were of divine origin. He had been depressed by the dismayingly secular thought that the gift could have been bestowed on him not by his Lord but simply as the chance side-effect of an exotic infection, by the unwitting office of a mindless virus – and a *man-made* virus, as well. He was relieved to be able to dismiss that possibility. His high spirits and good humour, even amidst the destruction of the diner, arose from the fact that a divine Presence was once again, for Brendan, at least a viable – if still unlikely – explanation.

Dom wished he, too, could find courage and strength in the notion that their troubles were part of a divine scheme. But at the moment, he believed only in danger and death, twin juggernauts that he sensed bearing down on him. The personality changes that had occurred in him during his move from Portland to Mountainview, two summers ago, were laughably minor in comparison to the changes that had begun working in him tonight, with the discovery of this unwanted power. He almost felt as if the power was *alive* in him, a parasite that in time would eat away everything that had been Dominick Corvaisis and, having assumed his identity, would stalk the world in his body, masquerading as human.

Crazy.

Nevertheless, he was worried and scared.

He looked at each of the others who were gathered around him. Some met his eyes for a moment, then quickly looked away, just as one might hesitate to meet the gaze of a dangerous – or intimidating – man. Others – most notably Jack Twist,

507

Ernie, and Jorja – met his eyes forthrightly, but were incapable of concealing the uneasiness and even apprehension with which they now regarded him. Only Ginger and Brendan seemed to have suffered no change in their attitude toward him.

'Well,' Jack said, breaking the spell, 'we should call it a night, I guess. We've got a lot to do tomorrow.'

'Tomorrow,' Ginger said, 'we'll have cleared up even more of these mysteries. We're making progress every day.'

'Tomorrow,' Brendan said softly, happily, 'will be a day of great revelation. I feel it somehow.'

Tomorrow, Dom thought, we might all be dead. Or wish we were.

*   *   *

Colonel Leland Falkirk still had a splitting headache. With his new talent for introspection – acquired gradually since his involvement in the emotionally and intellectually shattering events of two summers ago – he was able to see that, on one level, he was actually glad that the aspirin had been ineffective. He thrived on the headache in the same way he thrived on other kinds of pain, drawing a perverse strength and energy from the relentless throbbing in his brow and temples.

Lieutenant Horner had gone. Leland was alone once more in his temporary, windowless office beneath the testing grounds of Shenkfield, but he was no longer waiting for the call from Chicago. It had come soon after Horner departed, and the news had been all bad.

The siege at Calvin Sharkle's house in Evanston, which had begun earlier today, was still underway, and that volatile situation would probably not be brought to an end within the next twelve hours. If possible, the colonel did not want to commit his men to another closure of I-80 and another quarantine of the Tranquillity Motel until he could be certain the operation would not be compromised by revelations that Sharkle might make either to Illinois authorities or to the news media. Delay made Leland nervous, especially now that the witnesses at the motel were focused on Thunder Hill and were planning their moves beyond the reach of rifle microphones and infinity transmitters. He figured he could afford to wait, at most, one more day. However, if the dangerous stand-off in Illinois was still underway by sunset tomorrow, he would give the order to move on the Tranquillity in spite of the risks.

The other news from Chicago was that operatives had discreetly investigated Emmeline Halbourg and Winton Tolk and had found reasons to believe their amazing recoveries could not be adequately explained by current medical knowledge. And a reconstruction of Father Stefan Wycazik's activities on Christmas Day – including visits to Halbourg and Tolk, and a stop at the Metropolitan Police Laboratory to consult a ballistics expert – confirmed that the priest had been convinced that his curate, Brendan Cronin, had been responsible for those miraculous cures.

Leland had first become aware of Cronin's healing powers just yesterday, Sunday, when he had monitored a telephone call between Dominick Corvaisis at the Tranquillity and Father Wycazik in Chicago. That conversation would have been a real shocker if the events of Saturday night had not prepared him for the unexpected.

Saturday night, when Corvaisis had arrived at the Tranquillity, Leland Falkirk and his surveillance experts had monitored the first conversation between the Blocks and the writer with growing disbelief. The outlandish tale of moon photographs animated by a poltergeist in Lomack's Reno house had sounded like the product of a fevered mind no longer able to distinguish between fiction and reality.

Later, however, after Corvaisis and the Blocks had eaten dinner at the Grille, the writer had attempted to relive the minutes just before the trouble had started on the night of July 6. What happened then was astonishing, confirmed both by the hidden surveillance team watching the Tranquillity from a point south of the interstate and by the infinity transmitter tap on the diner's payphone. Everything in the Grille had begun to shake, and a strange rumble had filled the place, then an eerie electronic ululation, culminating in the implosion of all the windows.

These phenomena came as a total – and nasty – surprise to Leland and to everyone involved in the cover-up, especially the scientists, who were electrified. The following day's discovery of Cronin's healing power added voltage to the

509

excitement. At first, these developments seemed inexplicable. But after only a little thought, Leland arrived at an explanation that made his blood cold. The scientists had come to similar conclusions. Some of them were as scared as Leland was.

Suddenly, no one knew what to expect. Anything might happen now.

We believed we were in control of the situation that night in July, Leland thought sombrely, but perhaps it had escalated beyond our control even before we arrived on the scene.

The single consolation was that, thus far, only Corvaisis and the priest appeared to be . . . infected. Maybe 'infected' wasn't exactly the right word. Maybe 'possessed' was better. Or maybe there wasn't a word for what had happened to them, because what had happened to them had never happened to anyone else in history, so a specific word for it had not heretofore been required.

Even if the siege at Sharkle's house ended tomorrow, even if that possibility of media exposure was eliminated, Leland would not be able to strike at the group at the motel with full confidence. Corvaisis and Cronin – and perhaps the others – might be more difficult to apprehend and incarcerate than they'd been two summers ago. If Corvaisis and Cronin weren't entirely themselves any more, if they were now someone else – or some*thing* else – dealing with them might prove downright impossible.

Leland's headache was worse.

Feed on it, he told himself, getting up from the desk. Feed on the pain. You've been doing that for years, you dumb son of a bitch, so you can feed on it for another day or two, until you've dealt with this mess or until you're dead, whichever comes first.

He left the windowless office, crossed a windowless outer chamber, walked a windowless hall, and entered the windowless communications centre, where Lieutenant Horner and Sergeant Fixx sat at a table in one corner. 'Tell the men they can hit the sack,' Leland said. 'It's off for tonight. I'll risk another day to see if the situation at Sharkle's house gets resolved.'

'I was just coming to you,' Horner said. 'There's a development at the motel. They finally left the diner. After they came

510

out, Twist brought a Jeep Cherokee in from the hills behind the motel. He, Jorja Monatella, and the priest piled in it and drove off toward Elko.'

'Where the hell are they going at this time of night?' Leland asked, uncomfortably aware that those three might have slipped through his fingers if he *had* ordered his men to move against the motel tonight, for he'd been certain the witnesses were settled down until morning.

Horner pointed to Fixx, who was wearing headphones and listening to the Tranquillity. 'From what we've heard, the others are going to bed. Twist, Monatella, and Cronin have gone off as . . . as sort of insurance against us getting our hands on all the witnesses in one quick clean sweep. This had to be Twist's idea.'

'Damn.' Massaging his throbbing temples with his fingertips, Leland sighed. 'All right. We aren't going after them tonight, anyway.'

'But what about tomorrow? What if they split up all day tomorrow?'

'In the morning,' Leland said, 'we'll put tails on all of them.' To this point, he had seen no need to tail the witnesses everywhere they went, for he had known that, in the end, they would all wind up at the same place – the motel – making it easier for him to deal with them. But now, if they were going to be spread out when the time came to take them into custody, he would need to know where they were at all times.

Horner said, 'Depending on where they go tomorrow, they're likely to spot any tails we put on them. In this kind of open country, it's not easy to be discreet.'

'I know,' Leland said. 'So let them see us. I've wanted to stay out of sight, but we're at the end of that approach. Maybe seeing us will throw them off balance until it's too late. Maybe, scared, they'll even get back together for protection and make our job easier again.'

'If we have to take some of them at a place other than the motel, say in Elko, it'll be difficult,' Horner said worriedly.

'If they can't be taken, they've got to be killed.' Leland pulled up a chair, sat down. 'Let's work out surveillance details now and have the tails in position before dawn.'

TUESDAY, JANUARY 14

At seven-thirty Tuesday morning, in response to a telephone call from Brendan Cronin very late the previous night, Father Stefan Wycazik prepared to set out on a drive to Evanston, to the last known address of Calvin Sharkle, the trucker who had been at the Tranquillity Motel that summer but whose telephone was now disconnected. In light of the enormity of last evening's developments in Nevada, everyone was agreed that every possible effort must be made to contact the other victims who had thus far been unreachable. Standing in the warm rectory kitchen, Stefan buttoned his topcoat and put on his fedora.

Father Michael Gerrano, who was just sitting down to oatmeal and toast after celebrating sunrise Mass, said, 'Perhaps I should know more about this whole situation, about what on earth's wrong with Brendan, in case . . . well, in case something happens to you.'

'Nothing's going to happen to me,' Father Wycazik said firmly. 'God hasn't let me spend five decades learning how the world works just to have me killed now that I'm able to do my best work for the Church.'

Michael shook his head. 'You're always so . . .'

'Certain in my faith? Of course I am. Rely on God, and He will never fail you, Michael.'

'Actually,' Michael said, smiling, 'I was going to say: you're always so bullheaded.'

'Such impudence from a curate!' Stefan said, winding a thick white scarf around his neck. 'Attend thee, Father: what is wanted of a curate is humility, self-effacement, the strong back of a mule, the stamina of a plough horse – and an unfailingly adoring attitude toward his rector.'

Michael grinned. 'Oh, yes, I suppose if the rector is a pious old geezer grown vain from the praise of his parishioners –'

The telephone rang.

'If it's for me, I'm gone,' Stefan said.

Stefan pulled on a pair of gloves but was not quite able to

make it to the back door before Michael held the receiver toward him.

'It's Winton Tolk,' Michael said. 'The cop whose life Brendan saved. He sounds almost hysterical, and he wants to talk to Brendan.'

Stefan took the phone and identified himself.

The policeman's voice was haunted and full of urgency. 'Father, I've got to talk to Brendan Cronin right away, it can't wait.'

'I'm afraid he's away,' Stefan said, 'out at the other end of the country. What's the matter?' Can I be of assistance?'

'Cronin,' Tolk said shakily. 'Something . . . something's happened, and I don't understand, it's strange, Jesus, it's the strangest craziest thing, but I knew right away it was somehow related to Brendan.'

'I'm sure I can help. Where are you, Winton?'

'On duty, end of the shift, graveyard shift, Uptown. There's been a knifing, a shooting. Horrible. And then . . . Listen, I want Cronin to come up here, he's got to explain this, he's got to, right away.'

Father Wycazik elicited an address from Tolk, left the rectory at a run, and drove too fast. Less than half an hour later, he arrived in a block of identical, shabby, six-storey, brick tenements in the Uptown district. He was unable to park in front of the address he had been given and settled for a spot near the corner, for the prime space was occupied by police vehicles – marked and unmarked cars, an SID wagon – whose radios filled the cold air with a metallic chorus of dispatchers' codes and jargon. Two officers were watching over the vehicles to prevent vandalism. In answer to Stefan's question, they told him the action was on the third-floor, in 3-B, the Mendoza's apartment.

The glass in the front door was cracked across one corner, and the temporary repair with electrician's tape looked as if it had become a permanent solution. The door opened on a grim foyer. Some floor tiles were missing and others were hidden by grime. The paint was peeling.

As he climbed the stairs, Stefan encountered two beautiful children playing 'dead doll' with a battered Raggedy Ann and an old shoebox.

513

When he walked through the open door and into the Mendoza's third-floor apartment, Father Wycazik saw a beige sofa liberally stained with still-wet blood, so much that in some places the cushions were almost black. Hundreds of drops had sprayed across the pale-yellow wall behind the sofa, a pattern that evidently had resulted when someone in front of the wall had been hit by large-calibre slugs that passed through him. Four bullet holes marred the plaster. Blood was spattered over a lampshade, coffee table, bookshelf, and part of the carpet.

The gore was even more disgusting than it might ordinarily have been because the apartment was otherwise extremely well-kept, which made the areas of bloody chaos more shocking by comparison. The Mendozas could afford to live only in a slum tenement, but like some other poor people, they refused to surrender to – or become part of – the Uptown squalor. The filth of the streets, the grime of public hallways and staircases, stopped at their door, as if their apartment was a fortress against dirt, a shrine to cleanliness and order. Everything gleamed.

Removing his fedora, Stefan took only two steps into the living room – which flowed without interruption into a small dining area, which itself was separated from a half-size kitchen by a serving counter. The place was crowded with detectives, uniformed officers, lab technicians – maybe a dozen men altogether. Most of them were not acting like cops. Their demeanour puzzled Stefan. Apparently, the lab men had completed their work and the others had nothing to do, yet no one was leaving. They were standing in groups of two or three, talking in the subdued manner of people at a funeral parlour – or in church.

Only one detective was working. He was sitting at the dinette table with a Madonna-faced Latino woman of about forty, asking questions of her (Father Wycazik heard him call her Mrs Mendoza), and recording her answers on legal-looking forms. She was trying to cooperate but was distracted as she glanced repeatedly at a man her own age, probably her husband, who was pacing back and forth with a child in his arms. The child was a cute boy of about six. Mr Mendoza held the child in one burly arm, talking constantly to him, patting him, ruffling his thick hair. Obviously, this man had almost lost his son in whatever violence had occurred here, and he needed to touch and hold the child to convince himself that the worst had not actually happened.

One of the patrolmen noticed Stefan and said, 'Father Wycazik?'

The officer's voice was soft, but at the mention of Stefan's name, the entire group fell silent. Stefan could not remember ever seeing expressions quite like those that came over the faces of the people in the Mendozas' small apartment: as if he were expected to deliver unto them a single sentence that would shed light upon all the mysteries of existence and succinctly convey the meaning of life.

What in the world is going on here? Stefan wondered uneasily.

'This way, Father,' said a uniformed officer.

Pulling off his gloves, Stefan followed the officer across the room. The hush prevailed, and everyone made way for the priest and his guide. They went into a pin-neat bedroom, where Winton Tolk and another officer were sitting on the edge of the bed. 'Father Wycazik's here,' Stefan's guide said, then retreated to the living room.

Tolk was sitting bent forward, his elbows on his knees, his face hidden in his hands. He did not look up.

The other officer rose from the edge of the bed and introduced himself as Paul Armes, Winton's partner. 'I . . . I think you'd better get it directly from Win,' Armes said. 'I'll give you some privacy.' He left, closing the door behind him.

The bedroom was small, with space for only the bed, one nightstand, a half-size dresser, one chair. Father Wycazik pulled the chair around to face the foot of the bed and sat down, so he could look directly at Winton Tolk. Their knees were almost touching.

Removing his scarf, Father Wycazik said, 'Winton, what's happened?'

Tolk looked up, and Stefan was startled by the man's expression. He had thought Tolk was upset by whatever had happened in the living room. But his face revealed that he was exhilarated, filled with an excitement he could barely contain. Simultaneously, he seemed fearful – not terrified, not quaking

515

with fear, but troubled by something that prevented him from giving in completely, happily, to his excitement.

'Father, who is Brendan Cronin?' The tremor in the big man's voice was of an odd character that might have betrayed either incipient joy or terror. 'What is Brendan Cronin?'

Stefan hesitated, decided on the full truth. 'He's a priest.'

Winton shook his head. 'But that's not what we were told.'

Stefan sighed, nodded. He explained about Brendan's loss of faith and about the unconventional therapy that had included a week in a police patrol car. 'You and Officer Armes weren't told he was a priest because you might've treated him differently . . . and because I wished to spare him embarrassment.'

'A fallen priest,' Winton said, looking baffled.

'Not fallen,' Father Wycazik said confidently. 'Merely faltering. He'll regain his faith in time.'

The room's inadequate light came from a dim lamp on the nightstand and from a single narrow window, leaving the dark policeman in velvet gloom. The whites of his eyes were twin lamps, very bright by contrast with the darknesses of shadows and genetic heritage. 'How did Brendan heal me when I was shot? How did he perform that . . . miracle? How?'

'Why have you decided it was a miracle?'

'I was shot twice in the chest, point-blank. Three days later I left the hospital. Three days! In ten days, I was ready to go back to work, but they made me stay home two weeks. Doctors kept talking about my hardy physical condition, the extraordinary healing that's possible if a body's in tip-top shape. I started thinking they were trying to explain my recovery not to me but to themselves. But I still figured I was just really lucky. I came back to work a week ago, and then . . . something else happened' Winton unbuttoned his shirt, pulled it open, and lifted his undershirt to reveal his bare chest. 'The scars.'

Father Wycazik shivered. Though he was close to Winton, he leaned closer, staring in amazement. The man's chest was unmarked. Well, not entirely unmarked, but the entry wounds had already healed until they were just discoloured spots as big as dimes. The surgeon's incisions had almost vanished – thin lines visible now only on close inspection. This soon after major trauma, some swelling and inflammation should have been evident, but there was none. The minimal scar tissue was pale pink-brown against dark-brown skin, neither lumpy nor puckered.

'I've seen other guys with old bullet wounds,' Winton said, his excitement still restrained by a rope of fear. 'Lots of them. Gnarly, thick. Ugly. You don't take two .38s in the chest, undergo major surgery, and look like *this* three weeks later – or ever.'

'When's the last time you visited your doctor? Has he seen this?'

Winton rebuttoned his shirt with trembling hands. 'I saw Dr Sonneford a week ago. The sutures hadn't been removed long before, and my chest was still a mess. It's only been the past four days that the scars melted away. I swear, Father, if I stand at a mirror long enough, I can *see* them fading.'

Finishing with his shirt buttons, Winton said, 'Lately, I've been thinking about your visit to the hospital Christmas Day. The more I've gone over it in my mind, the more it seems your behaviour was peculiar. I remember some of what you said, some of the questions you asked about Brendan, and I start wondering. . . . One thing I wonder about – one thing I've got to know – is whether Brendan Cronin ever healed anyone else.'

'Yes. Nothing as dramatic as your case. But there's another. I'm . . . not at liberty to reveal who,' Stefan said. 'But this isn't why you called the rectory, Winton. Not to show Brendan how well you've healed. Your voice was so full of urgency, even panic. And what about all these policemen with the Mendozas. . . ? What's happened here, Winton?'

A mercurial smile appeared on – and quickly faded from – the man's broad face, followed by a transient glimmer of fear. Emotional turmoil was also evident in his voice. 'We're cruising. Me and Paul. We get a call. This address. We get here, find a sixteen-year-old kid high on PCP. You know what they're like on PCP sometimes? Crazy. Animals. Damn stuff eats brain cells. Later, after it's over, we find out his name's Ernesto, son of Mrs Mendoza's sister. He came to live here a week ago because his mother can't control him any more. The Mendozas . . . they're good people. You see how they keep this place?'

Father Wycazik nodded.

Winton said, 'The kind of people take in a nephew when he's gone wrong, try to set him straight. But you can't set a kid like that straight. You break your heart trying, Father. This Ernesto, he's been in trouble since he was in fifth grade. Juvenile arrest record. Six offences. Two of them pretty serious. We get here, he's naked as a jaybird, screaming his head off, eyes bugging out like the pressure in his head's going to blow his skull apart.'

Winton's gaze unfocused, as if he were seeing back into time and had as clear a view of that scene as when he had first encountered it.

'Ernesto's got Hector, the little boy you probably saw when you came in, he's got him down on the sofa, holding him, and he's got a goddamn six-inch switchblade at Hector's throat. Mr Mendoza . . . well, he's going crazy, wanting to rush Ernesto and take the knife, but scared Ernesto will slash Hector. Ernesto's screaming, he was blissed on angel dust. He's PCP-crazy, and you can't talk sense to him. We drew our guns because you don't just walk up to some doped-out freak with a knife and shake hands. But we didn't want to try to shoot him because he had that knife at Hector's throat, Hector was crying, and Ernesto could've killed the kid if we made the wrong move. So we tried to talk him down, talk him away from Hector, and we seemed to make headway, 'cause he started to take the knife off the boy. But then all of a sudden, Jesus, he slashed quick, cut Hector's throat almost from ear to ear, deep' – Winton shuddered – 'deep. Then he raised the knife over his head, so we shot him, I'm not sure how many times, blew him away, and he fell dead on top of Hector. We pulled him off, and there was little Hector, one hand trying to close up the hole in his throat, blood spurting between his fingers, eyes already glazing over. . . .'

The cop took a deep breath and shuddered again. His eyes came back into focus, as if he needed to retreat from the horror of the past. He looked towards the window, beyond which the grey winter daylight sifted like soot over the grey Uptown street.

Stefan's heart had begun to pound, not because of the bloody horror that Winton had described but because he could see where the cop's story had to be leading, and he was eager to hear the miracle described.

Looking at the window, Winton continued. His voice grew

shakier as he spoke: 'There's no first-aid for that kind of wound, Father. Severed arteries, veins. Big arteries in the neck. Blood pumps out like water from a hose, and you can't use a tourniquet, not on a neck, and direct pressure won't seal up a carotid artery. Shit, no. I knelt on the floor beside the sofa, and I saw Hector was dying fast. He looked so little, Father, so little. That kind of wound, they're gone in two minutes, sometimes a lot less, and he was so little. I knew it was useless, but I put my hands on Hector's neck, like somehow I could hold the blood in him, hold the life in him. I was sick, angry, scared, and it just wasn't right that a boy so little should die that way, that hard, not right he should die at all, not right, and then . . . then. . . .'

'And then he healed,' Father Wycazik said softly.

Winton Tolk finally looked away from the grey light at the window and met Stefan's eyes. 'Yes, Father. He healed. He was soaked in his own blood, seconds away from death, but he healed. I didn't even know what was happening, didn't feel it happening, nothing special in my hands. Wouldn't you think I'd feel something special in my hands? But the first I realised that something incredible was happening was when the blood stopped spurting against my fingers, and the boy shut his eyes at the same time, which was when I thought he was dead for sure, and I just . . . I shouted, 'No! God, no!' And I started to take my hands away from Hector's throat, to look at it, and that's when I saw the wound was . . . the wound was closed up. It still had a raw, ugly look to it, an awful line where the knife cut deep, but the flesh was knit together into a bright red scar, a healing scar.'

The big man stopped speaking because shimmery lenses of tears had formed over his eyes. He was overcome once more. If he'd been wracked by grief, he probably would have suppressed it, but this was something even more powerful: joy. Pure wild disbelieving joy. He could not contain several explosive, wrenching sobs.

With hot tears in his own eyes, Father Wycazik held out both hands.

Winton took them, squeezed them tight, and did not let go as he continued: 'Paul, my partner, saw it happen. So did the Mendozas. And two other uniforms arrived just as we shot

519

Ernesto: they saw it, too. And when I looked at that red line across his throat, somehow I knew what I had to do. I put my hands on the boy again, covered up the wound again, and I thought about him being alive, sort of wished him alive. My mind was in high gear, and I made the connection with Brendan and me, the sandwich shop. I thought about how the scars on my chest had been disappearing the last few days, and I knew somehow it's connected. So I kept my hands on his throat, and in a minute or so he opened his eyes, he smiled at me, you should've *seen* that smile, Father, so I took my hands away again, and the scar was there but lighter. The boy sat up and asked for his mother, and that's . . . that's when I went to pieces.' Winton paused and gulped some air. 'Mrs Mendoza took Hector into the bathroom, stripped him out of his bloody clothes, bathed him, and all the time more people from the department kept showing up. Word was getting around. Thank God, the reporters haven't cottoned to it yet.'

For a while the two men sat facing each other in silence, gripping hands. Then Stefan said, 'Did you try to bring Ernesto back?'

'Yes. In spite of what he'd done, I put my hands on his wounds. But it didn't work with him, Father. Maybe because he was already dead. Hector was only dying, not yet gone, but Ernesto was dead.'

'Did you notice odd marks in your hands, on your palms? Red rings of swollen flesh?'

'Nothing like that. What would it've meant if there'd been rings?'

'I don't know,' Father Wycazik said. 'But they appear in Brendan's hands when . . . when these things happen.'

They were silent again, and then Winton said, 'Is Brendan . . . is Father Cronin some kind of saint?'

Father Wycazik smiled. 'He's a good man. But he's no saint.'

'Then how did he heal me?'

'I don't know precisely. But surely it's a manifestation of the power of God. Somehow. For some reason.'

'But how did Brendan pass along this power to heal?'

'I don't know, Winton. If he *did* pass it along. Maybe the power isn't yours. Maybe it's just God acting through you, first through Brendan and then through you.'

At last Winton let go of Father Wycazik's hands. He turned his palms up and stared at them. 'No, the power's still here, still in me. I know that. Somehow. I feel it. And not just . . . not just the power to heal. There's more.'

Father Wycazik raises his eyebrows. 'More? What else?'

Winton frowned. 'I don't know yet. It's all so new. So strange. But I feel . . . more. It'll take time for it to develop.' He looked up from the pale palms of his calloused black hands, awe-stricken and fearful. 'What is Father Cronin, and what has he made of me?'

'Winton, get rid of the notion there's anything evil or dangerous about this. It's entirely a wonderous thing. Think of Hector, the child you saved. Remember what it was like to feel life regaining its hold in his small body. We're players in a divine mystery, Winton. We can't understand the meaning of it until God allows us to understand.'

Father Wycazik said he wanted to have a look at the boy, Hector Mendoza, and Winton said, 'I'm not ready to go out there and face that crowd, even though they're mostly my people. I'll stay here a while. You'll come back?'

'I've got other rather urgent business this morning, Winton. I have to get on with it soon. But I'll be in touch with you. Oh, you can be sure of that! And if you need me, just call St Bette's.'

When Stefan left the bedroom, the waiting crowd of policemen and lab technicians fell silent as before. They parted in his path as he crossed to the dinette table, where little Hector was now perched on his mother's lap, nibbling happily at a Hershey Bar with almonds.

The boy was small, even for a six-year-old, with delicate facial bones. His eyes were bright and full of intelligence, proof that he'd suffered no brain damage in spite of losing most of his blood. But even more astonishing was the fact that his lost blood had evidently been *replaced*, without need for transfusions, which made the boy's recovery even more miraculous than Tolk's. The power in Winton's hands seemed greater than it had been in Brendan's.

When Father Wycazik stooped down to be at eye-level with Hector, the child grinned at him. 'How are you feeling, Hector?'

'Okay,' the boy said shyly.

521

'Do you remember what happened to you, Hector?'

The child licked chocolate from his lips and shook his head: no.

'Is that a good candy bar?'

The boy nodded and offered Father Wycazik a bite.

The priest smiled. 'Thank you, Hector, but that's all yours.'

'Mama might give you one,' Hector said. 'But don't drop any on the carpet. That's big trouble.'

Stefan looked up at Mrs Mendoza. 'He really doesn't remember. . . ?'

'No,' she said. 'God lifted the memory from him, Father.'

'You're Catholic, Mrs Mendoza?'

'Yes, Father,' she said, crossing herself with her free hand.

'Do you attend Our Lady of Sorrow? Yes, well, that's Father Nilo's parish. Have you called him?'

'No, Father. I didn't know if . . .'

Father Wycazik looked up at Mr Mendoza, who stood on the other side of his wife's chair. 'Call Father Nilo. Tell him what's happened, ask him to come. Explain that I'll be gone when he gets here but that I'll talk to him later. Explain that I've much to tell him, that what he sees here isn't the whole story.'

Mr Mendoza hurried to the telephone.

Looking up at one of the detectives who had come close, Stefan said, 'Have you taken pictures of the boy's throat wound?'

The detective nodded. 'Yeah. Standard procedure.' He laughed nervously. 'What am I saying? There's nothing standard about this.'

'Just so you have photographs to prove this happened,' Father Wycazik said. 'Because I think soon there will be little or no scar.'

He turned to the boy again. 'Now, Hector, if it's okay, I'd like to touch your throat. I'd like to feel that mark.'

The boy lowered the candy bar.

Father Wycazik's fingers were trembling when they touched the fiery scar tissue and moved slowly around the boy's neck from one end of the wound to the other. A strong pulse beat in the carotid arteries on each side of the slender young throat, and Stefan's heart leapt when he felt the miracle of life. Death had been defeated here, and Stefan believed he had been privileged to witness a fulfilment of the promise which was at the root of the Church's existence: 'Death shall not last; unto you shall be given life everlasting.' Tears rose in the priest's eyes.

When at last Stefan reluctantly took his hand away from the boy and stood, one of the policemen said, 'What's it mean, Father? I heard you tell Mr Mendoza this wasn't the whole story. What's happening?'

Stefan turned to look upon the assembly, which now numbered twenty. In their faces, he saw a longing to believe, not particularly in the truths of Catholicism or Christianity, for not all were Catholics or Christians, but a deep-seated longing to believe in *something* greater and better and cleaner than humankind, an intense yearning for spiritual transcendence.

'What's it mean, Father?' one of them asked again.

'Something's happening,' he told them. 'Here, elsewhere. A great and wonderful something. This child is part of it. I can't tell you for sure what it means or that we've seen the hand of God here, though I believe we have. Look at Hector on his mother's lap, eating candy, and remember God's promise: "There shall be no more death, neither sorrow nor crying, neither shall there be any more pain; for the former things are passed away." In my heart of hearts, I feel that the former things are about to pass away. Now I must go. I've urgent business.'

Somewhat to his surprise, even though his explanation had been vague, they parted to make way for him and did not detain him further, perhaps because the miracle of Hector Mendoza had *not* been vague – had in fact been emphatically specific – and had already given them more answers than they could handle. But as Stefan went, some reached out to touch him, to squeeze his hand or shoulder, not with religious fervour but with an emotional camaraderie. Stefan was overcome by the need to touch them as well, to share a profound sense of the community of humankind, which had filled everyone in the room, to share the conviction that they were being swept towards some great destiny.

*   *   *

In Boston, at ten o'clock, Alexander Christophson, former United States Senator and Ambassador to Great Britain, former head of the CIA, now retired for a decade, was reading the morning newspaper when he received a telephone call from his brother, Philip, the antique dealer in Greenwich, Connecticut. They spoke for five minutes about nothing important, just two brothers keeping in touch, but the conversation had a secret purpose. At the end Philip said, 'Oh, by the way. I spoke with Diana this morning. Do you remember her?'

'I certainly do,' Alex said. 'How's she doing?'

'Oh, she has her troubles,' Philip said. 'Too boring to discuss. But she says hello.' Then he changed the subject, recommending two new books that Alex might enjoy, as if Diana were of no real importance.

Diana was the code word that meant Ginger Weiss had phoned Philip and needed to speak with Alex. The moment he had seen Ginger at Pablo's funeral, her silver-blonde hair ashimmer as if with a light of its own, she had made him think of Diana, goddess of the moon.

After he said goodbye to Philip, he told his wife, Ellena, that he intended to drive to the mall. 'I want to stop at the bookstore and pick up a couple of novels that Philip recommended.'

He actually went to the mall, but before he bought the books, he found a public phone booth and, using his AT&T credit card, called Philip to get the number that Ginger Weiss had left.

'She says it's a payphone in Elko, Nevada,' Philip told him.

When Alex put the Nevada call through, Ginger Weiss did not answer until the fifth ring. 'Sorry,' she said. 'I was in the car, parked beside the booth. It was just too cold to stand here and wait.'

'What are you doing in Nevada?' Alex asked.

'If I understood you correctly at Pablo's funeral, you really don't want me to answer questions like that.'

'Right. Less I know, the better. What did you want to ask me?'

She explained, with a minimum of detail, that she had found others suffering from memory blocks similar to hers, some with differing false memories covering the same time span. Since Alex was the expert on brainwashing, Ginger wanted to know if implanting fake memories that included threads of reality was more difficult than implanting entirely false recollections, and he was able to assure her that, indeed, it was.

'That's what we figured,' Ginger said. 'But it's good to hear you confirm it. Shows we're on the right track. Now, one more thing: I want you to get some information for us. We need to know whatever you can learn about a Colonel Leland Falkirk, an officer in one of the Army's elite DERO companies. I also need –'

'Wait, wait,' Alex said, looking nervously through the glass door of the booth at shoppers walking past in the mall, as if he was already under observation or even targeted for removal. 'At the cemetery, I said I'd provide advice or background on mind-control techniques. But I warned you I wouldn't dig up information. I *explained* my position.'

'Well, even though you've been retired for years, you must still know people in many of the right places –'

'Didn't you hear me, Doctor?' I will not get actively involved in your problems. I simply can't afford to. I've got too much to lose.'

'Now, don't worry about digging up anything exotic or highly classified. We don't expect that,' she said, as if she had not heard him. 'Just the bare details of Falkirk's service record might help us understand him and form an idea of what to expect from him.'

'Please, I –'

But she was indefatigable: 'I also need to know about the Thunder Hill Depository, an Army facility here in Elko County.'

'No.'

'It's supposed to be an underground storage facility, and maybe that's all it was for a long time, or maybe it's always been something else, but I know it's not just an underground warehouse these days.'

'Doctor, I won't do this for you.'

'Colonel Leland Falkirk and Thunder Hill Depository. It's not so much to ask: no deep snooping, just what details you can glean. Talk to your old friends who're still in the game. Then report to either Dr George Hannaby there in Boston or to Father Stefan Wycazik, a priest in Chicago.' She gave him phone numbers. 'I can get in touch with them, and they won't

525

mention your name when they tell me what you've reported. That way you don't have to call me direct, and you stay in the clear.'

He tried and failed to control the palsied shaking of his hands. 'Doctor, I'm sorry I volunteered even limited assist-. ance. I'm an old man who's afraid to die.'

'You're also worried about sins you might've committed in the name of duty,' she said, repeating what he'd told her at the cemetery. 'And you'd probably like to do something to atone for some of those sins, real or imagined. This would be atonement of a sort, Mr Christophson.' She repeated the telephone numbers for Hannaby and Wycazik.

'No. If you're interrogated, remember I said no, emphatically no.'

With maddening good cheer, she said, 'Oh, and it would help if you had something for me within the next six or eight hours. I know that's a tall order. But then again, I'm only asking for basic information, whatever's in the unclassified files.'

'Goodbye, Doctor,' he said pointedly.

'I'll look forward to hearing from you.'

'You will *not* hear from me.'

'Toodle-oo,' she said, and hung up on him first.

'Christ!' he said, slamming the receiver down.

She was an attractive woman, personable, intelligent, appealing in so many ways. But her absolute conviction that she would always get what she wanted – this was a trait he sometimes admired in a man, seldom or never in a woman. Well, she'd be disappointed this time. This time, she'd not get what she wanted. Damned if she would.

Yet . . . with his Cross pen, he had made note of the telephone numbers for Hannaby and Wycazik, which she had given him.

*　　*.　　*

Dom and Ernie set out early Tuesday morning to reconnoitre at least part of the perimeter of Thunder Hill Depository. They went in Jack Twist's new Jeep Cherokee. Jack himself was sleeping back at the motel, having gone to bed only a few hours ago, after spending half the night driving around Elko, staying on the move with Brendan Cronin and Jorja Mon-atella. Both the Cherokee and the motel's Dodge van had four-wheel drive, but the Jeep was tougher, more manoeuvr-able. The foothill and mountain roads up towards Thunder Hill might be icy in spots, and as the day promised new snow, they wanted the most reliable transport.

Dom did not like the look of the sky. Thick dark clouds hung low over the high plains, lower over the foothills, and obscured the tops of the mountains. The weather forecast called for the first big storm of the year (later than usual this season), as much as fourteen inches of snow in the higher elevations. Not a single flake had fallen yet.

The raised and threatening lash of winter did not induce a pensive mood in Dom or Ernie; they were in high spirits upon setting out from the motel. They were finally *doing* something, acting not just reacting. In addition, there was the pleasant fellowship that exists when men who like each other set out on an adventure together – a fishing trip or an expedition to a ballpark. Or a scouting trip to explore the perimeter defences of a military installation.

In no little measure, their excellent mood grew from the unexpected peacefulness of the night just past. For the first time in weeks, Dom's sleep hadn't been disturbed by night-mares or sleepwalking. He'd dreamed only of an undetailed chamber filled with golden light, evidently the same place that featured in Brendan's dreams. Likewise, instead of lying awake in fear of the shadows beyond the glow of the bedside lamp, Ernie had drifted off to sleep at once. The others also said it was the most restful night in recent memory. Ginger's theory, put forth over a quick cup of coffee this morning, was that their worst dreams had been related not to the mysterious events they'd witnessed on the night of July 6, but to the subsequent brainwashing. Therefore, now that they had an idea of what they'd endured at the hands of the mind-control experts, the subconscious pressure related to those experi-ences was relieved, eliminating the source of those particular bad dreams.

And Dom had a reason of his own to feel good about the day. This morning, no one had looked warily at him or treated him with deference because of his telekinetic power. At first he was baffled by their quick adjustment to his new status. Then he realised what must be going through their minds: since they had shared his experiences of the summer before last, it was logical that they would also share his strange power sooner or later. They must believe their own development of paranormal abilities was merely lagging behind his. Eventually, if they did not acquire the power, they might build the emotional, intellectual, and psychological walls between them and him that would isolate him, as he feared. But for the moment, anyway, they were acting as if no gulf separated them from him, and he was grateful.

Now, humming softly, Ernie drove north on the two-lane county road, leaving the motel and the interstate behind them. They climbed some of the same rugged hills down which Jack Twist had come last night when making his clandestine approach to the Tranquillity (although Jack had travelled overland), and Dom studied the changing terrain with interest. The rising land seemed leaner the higher it rose, revealing less flesh and more rocky bones that poked up everywhere in clavicles and scapulae and sternums of limestone, in fibulae and femurs of crumbling shale, in occasional ribs and spines of formidable granite. As if in awareness of the colder air of higher altitudes, the land wore more clothes: thicker petticoats of grass; more lavish skirts of sage and other bushes; then trees, trees, more trees – mountain mahogany, tall pines, cedar, quaking-aspen, and on eastern slopes, an occasional spruce or fir.

They'd gone only three miles when they reached the snow line. A thin mantle flanked the road at first, but in the next two miles it deepened to eight inches. Although a winter drought had held sway from September until early December, and although no major storm had swept the area yet this season, a few light snows had put down a respectable ground-cover, also frosting the bristled boughs of the evergreens.

But for a few small scattered patches of ice, the county road was cleared for easy travel. 'They always keep it clean as far as Thunder Hill, even in killing weather,' Ernie explained. 'But up beyond the Depository, the road crews don't do as thorough a job.'

In no time they had gone ten miles, always following the

crest of a valley that fell away on the east, and always with rising mountains on the west. They passed several dirt and gravel lanes leading to isolated homes and ranches in the eastward-sloping lands to their right, and at the ten-mile point they reached the guarded entrance to Thunder Hill Depository, also on the right.

Ernie slowed the Cherokee but did not turn into the entrance-way. 'Haven't been this far up here in a long time. They've made changes since I saw the place last. Didn't used to look this formidable.'

A sign announced the Depository. Beside the sign another paved road branched off the county lane, leading away between towering pines of such a dark-green hue they seemed nearly black in the sombre pre-storm light. Fifteen feet in from the turn-off, the lane was blocked by long metal spikes that speared up from the pavement, precisely angled to puncture the tyres of any vehicle that tried to proceed farther, but also large enough to catch on the axle of a hurtling truck or car and instantly arrest its progress. Twenty feet beyond the spikes, there was a massive steel gate, crowned with spikes, painted red. A concrete-block guardhouse – twenty feet by ten – stood inside the gate, and its black metal door looked capable of withstanding a bazooka barrage.

Ernie pulled to the edge of the main road and slowed almost to a full stop as they eased past the entrance to Thunder Hill. He pointed to a yard-square post at the verge of the entrance lane, just this side of the wicked spikes. 'Looks like an intercom to the guardhouse. Not just a voice link, either. One of those systems like they have in drive-in banks, with a video monitor so they can see you in your car. The man in the guardhouse approves a visitor before the road spikes lower and the gate opens. Even then, I'll bet there're permanently emplaced machine guns to take you out if the guard decides he's been duped after he's already opened the gates.'

From each end of the gate, an eight-foot-high chainlink fence with a barbed-wire overhang disappeared into the trees, and Dom noted a white sign with red lettering that warned DANGER – ELECTRIFIED. Although the perimeter fence led into the forest, no trees overhung it; from the small sections that he could see flanking the main gate, there appeared to be a twenty-foot-wide no-man's land on each side.

Dom's good mood faded. He'd thought that the security along the perimeter of the facility would be minimal. After all, once you got onto the grounds, the actual entrance to Thunder Hill was through eight- or ten-foot-thick blast doors set in the hillside. That barrier was so impregnable that it seemed wasteful to install maximum security around the entire outer edge of the property. Yet that was what they had done. Which meant the secret they were guarding was so important that they did not even trust nuclear-proof doors and subterranean limestone vaults to keep it safe.

'The spikes in the road are new,' Ernie said. 'And the gate they had a couple of years ago was pretty flimsy by comparison. The fence was always here, but it wasn't electrified before.'

'We've no hope at all of getting a look inside.'

Although no one had said as much (for fear of sounding foolish), they all hoped they might get as far as the blast doors of the facility, have a look around the newly-expanded grounds that had been taken from ranchers Brust and Dirkson, and be fortunate enough to stumble across another piece of the puzzle they were committed to solve. Dom had never imagined they would actually get *inside* the underground rooms of Thunder Hill. That was an improbable scenario. But from the comfort of the Tranquillity Motel, getting onto the grounds and snooping around had not seemed like an impossible dream. Until now.

Dom wondered if his newly discovered telekinetic powers might be used to circumvent the Depository's fortifications, but he dismissed that thought as quickly as it occurred to him. Until he could control the gift, it was of little use. It scared him. He sensed that the power was sufficient to cause tremendous destruction and death if he lost control of it, and he would not take that chance again – except under very tightly controlled conditions.

'Well,' Ernie said, 'it was never our intention to try waltzing through the front gate. Let's have a look along some of the perimeter fence.' He touched his foot lightly to the accelerator. Looking in the rearview mirror, he said, 'Oh, and by the way, we're being followed.'

Startled, Dom turned and looked through the rear window of the Cherokee. Less than a hundred yards behind was a pick-up truck, an all-terrain job, loftily perched on tyres twice as wide and more than twice as high as ordinary tyres. Spotlights, currently unlit, were mounted on the roof, and a snowplough, currently raised off the road, was fitted to the front. Although Dom was certain that private citizens living in the mountains might own similar trucks, this one had the look of a military vehicle. The windshield was tinted, the driver unrevealed.

He said, 'You sure they're following us? When did they show up?'

Piloting the Cherokee up the county road, Ernie said, 'I noticed them about half a mile after we left the motel. When we slow down, they slow down, too. When we speed up, so do they.'

'You think there's going to be trouble?'

'There will be if they ask for it. They're probably only Army pussies,' Ernie said. He grinned.

Dom laughed. 'Don't get me in a war just to prove Leathernecks are tougher than GIs. I'll happily accept your word for it.'

The road became steeper. The sombre ashen sky grew lower. The dark trees drew closer on both sides. The pick-up stayed behind them.

*   *   *

Mrs Halbourg, Emmy's mother, answered the door, letting a puff of warm air out of the house into the frigid Chicago morning.

Father Wycazik said, 'Sorry to come unannounced like this, but the most extraordinary thing is happening, and I had to find out if Emmy –'

He stopped in mid-sentence when he realised that Mrs Halbourg was in terrible distress. Her eyes were wide with shock, with fear too.

Before he could ask what was wrong, she said, 'My God, it's you, Father. From the hospital, I remember. But how did you know to come? We haven't called anyone yet. How'd you know to come?'

'What's happened?'

Rather than answer, she took him by the arm, ushered him

531

inside, slammed the door, and hurried him upstairs. 'This way. Quickly.'

Coming directly from the Mendoza's apartment Uptown, he expected to find something odd at the Halbourg place, but not this state of crisis. When they reached the second-floor hallway, Mr Halbourg was there with one of Emmy's older sisters. They were standing halfway down the hall at an open door, staring into a room at something that seemed equally to attract and repel them. In the room, something thumped, rattled, then thumped twice again, followed by a musical burst of girlish laughter.

Mr Halbourg turned, a ghastly expression on his face, and blinked in surprise at Stefan. 'Father, thank God you're here, we didn't know what to do, didn't want to make complete fools of ourselves by calling for help and then maybe nothing's happening when help gets here, you know. But now you've come, so it's settled, and I'm relieved.'

Stefan looked warily through the open doorway and saw the usual accoutrements of a bedroom occupied by a girl of ten-going-on-eleven, the changeling age between childhood and adolescence: half a dozen teddy bears; big posters of the current teenage idols, boys utterly unknown to Stefan; a wooden hatrack hung with a collection of exotic chapeaux probably purchased from thrift shops; roller skates; a tape deck; a flute lying in an open case. Emmy's other sister – in a white sweater, tartan-plaid skirt, and kneesocks – was standing a few feet inside the room, pale and half-paralysed. Emmy was standing up in bed, pyjama-clad, looking even healthier than on Christmas Day. She was hugging a pillow, grinning at the same astonishing performance – a poltergeist at play – that riveted her sister and frightened the rest of her family.

As Father Wycazik stepped into the room, Emmy laughed delightedly at the antics of two small teddy bears waltzing in mid-air. Their movements were nearly as precise and formal as those of real dancers.

But the bears were not the only inanimate objects infused with magical life. The roller skates were not standing still in a corner but were moving about on separate courses, this one past the foot of the bed and then to the closet door, that one to the desk, this one to the window, moving fast, then slow. The hats jiggled on the rack. A Care Bear on a bookshelf bounced up and down.

Stefan went to the foot of the bed, careful to avoid the roller skates, and looked up at Emmy, who still stood on the mattress. 'Emmy?'

The girl glanced down at him. 'Pudge's friend! Hello, Father. Isn't it terrific? Isn't it wild?'

'Emmy, is this you?' he asked, gesturing at the capering objects.

'Me?' she said, genuinely surprised. 'No. Not me.'

But he noticed that the flying-waltzing bears faltered when she turned her attention away from them. They did not drop to the floor, but bobbled and turned and bumped against one another in a clumsy and aimless manner quite different from their previous measured grace.

He also saw indications that the previous phenomena had not all been this harmless. A ceramic lamp had been knocked to the floor and broken. One of the posters was torn. The dresser mirror was cracked.

Seeing the direction of his gaze, Emmy said, 'It was scarey at first. But it calmed down, and now it's just . . . fun. Isn't it *fun*?'

As she was speaking, the flute rose out of the open carrying case, up and up, until it was about seven feet off the floor, only a few feet to the left of the floating teddy bears. Out of the corner of her eye, the girl caught a glimpse of the rising instrument. When she turned to look directly at the flute, sweet music began to issue from it, not just random notes but a well-executed tune. Emmy jumped up and down on the bed excitedly. 'That's *Annie's Song*! I used to play that.'

'You're playing it now,' Stefan said.

'Oh, no,' she said, still staring at the flute. 'My hands got so bad, my knuckle joints, that I had to give up the flute a year ago. I'm cured now, but my hands still aren't good enough to play.'

Stefan said, 'But you aren't using your hands to play it, Emmy.'

His meaning finally penetrated. She looked down at him. 'Me?'

Deprived of her focused attention, the flute produced only a few more poorly executed notes and fell silent. It still hung in the air, but now it bobbled and dipped erratically. Emmy returned her attention to the instrument. It steadied in the air and began to play again.

'Me,' she said wonderingly. She turned to her sister, who was still paralysed by fear and amazement. 'Me,' Emmy said, then looked at her parents, who were standing in the doorway. '*Me*!'

Stefan appreciated what the child must be feeling, and his throat was pinched so tightly with emotion that he had difficulty swallowing. A month ago, she'd been a cripple, unable to dress herself, with nothing to look forward to except further deterioration, pain, and death. Now she was not only cured and her damaged bones reknit, but she was also in possession of this spectacular gift.

Father Wycazik wanted to tell her that somehow this gift had been given to her unwittingly by Brendan Cronin, her Pudge, but then he would have to explain where Brendan had got *his* gift, and he could not do that. Besides, he hadn't time even to tell them what he did know. It was 9:15. He should have been in Evanston by now. Time was of the essence, for Stefan was beginning to suspect that he would be catching a flight for Nevada before the day ended. Whatever was happening in Elko County was bound to be even more incredible than what was happening here, and he was determined to be a part of it.

Emmy looked at the floating bears, and they resumed their formal dance once more. She giggled.

Stefan thought about what Winton Tolk had said only a short while ago in the Mendozas' Uptown apartment: *The power's still here, still in me. I know . . . I feel it. And not just . . . not just the power to heal. There's more.* Winton had not known what powers he might possess in addition to the healing touch, but Stefan suspected that the policeman was in for some surprises similar to those that had thrown the Halbourg household into turmoil.

'Father, will you do it yourself?' Mr Halbourg asked from the doorway, where he stood with his wife, his voice sharp with anxiety.

Mrs Halbourg said, 'Please, we want it to be done as soon

534

as possible. Immediately. Can't you begin at once?'

Baffled, Stefan said, 'I'm sorry . . . but what is it you want done?'

Mr Halbourg said, 'An exorcism, of course!'

Stefan stared at them incredulously, only now fully realising why they had been in such distress when he had arrived and why they had greeted him with such relief. He laughed. 'There won't be any need for an exorcism. This isn't Satan at work. Oh, no. My heavens, no!'

From the corner of his eye, Stefan saw movement on the floor. He looked down at a two-foot-high teddy bear that was tottering past him on stiff little stuffed legs.

Winton Tolk had said that he sensed he would need a long time to learn what his powers were and to be able to control them. Either he was wrong or the task was far easier for Emmy than for him. That might be the case. Children were much more adaptable than adults.

Emmy's parents and her other sister edged into the room, fascinated but wary.

Stefan understood their wariness. All *seemed* well, the power benign. But the situation was so awesome, so profoundly affecting on a primitive level, that even an unfaltering optimist like Stefan Wycazik felt a tingle of fear.

*   *   *

After using a pay phone at a Shell service station in Elko to get in touch with Alexander Christophson in Boston, Ginger accompanied Faye to Elroy and Nancy Jamison's ranch in the Lemoille Valley, twenty miles from Elko. The Jamisons were the Blocks' friends who had been visiting on the evening of July 6, the summer before last. They had surely been caught up in the unknown events of that night and had been detained at the motel for brainwashing, with everyone else, though they remembered differently, of course. According to their programme of false memories, they had been allowed to evacuate the danger zone, taking Ernie and Faye with them. They believed they had returned to their small ranch, where they and the Blocks had passed the next few days. That was also what Faye and Ernie had believed – until recently.

Ginger and Faye were paying a visit to the Jamisons not to

inform them of what had actually happened but to determine, as indirectly as possible, if the Jamisons were having troubles of the kind afflicting Ginger, Ernie, Dom, and some of the others. If they were suffering, they would be brought into the mutually supportive community at the motel – the members of which had come to think of themselves as the 'Tranquillity Family' – and would join the search for answers.

But if the brainwashing had been effective, the Jamisons would not be told anything. To tell the Jamisons would be to endanger them.

Besides, given the urgent strategy developed last night with Jack Twist, if the Jamisons were not already suffering, there was no point wasting a lot of time convincing them that they'd been brainwashed. Time was precious, and every passing hour carried the Tranquillity family deeper into danger. Jack believed – and convinced Ginger – that their enemies would soon move against them.

The drive from Elko in the motel's van was quick and scenic. The picturesque Lemoille Valley – fifteen miles long, four miles wide – began at the foot of the Ruby Mountains. Wheat, barley, and potato farms occupied the lowlands – though the fields were unplanted now, slumbering under scattered patches of snow.

Between the valley floor and the mountains, the higher lands and foothills offered lush pasturage, and that was where the Jamisons had their ranch. At one time, they owned hundreds of acres on which they raised cattle, but eventually they sold off much of their property, which had risen substantially in value, and got out of the livestock business. Now, in their early sixties and retired, they owned about fifty acres in the foothills, employed no ranch hands, and kept only three horses and a few chickens.

As Faye turned off the main valley road onto a lane leading into the highlands, she said, 'I think someone's following us.'

The back doors of the van had no windows, so Ginger looked at the side-mounted mirror. A nondescript sedan was about a hundred feet behind them. 'How do you know?'

'Same car's been back there since the Shell in town.'

'Maybe it's coincidence,' Ginger said.

When they had followed the lane over halfway up the valley

wall, they reached the long narrow driveway to the Jamison's ranch, which led half a mile back through deep shadows thrown by flanking rows of big piñons. Faye pulled into the driveway and slowed to see what the other car would do. Instead of going past, farther up into the hills, it pulled to a stop and parked along the outer lane, directly across from the entrance to the Jamison's property.

In the side-view mirror, Ginger could see that the car was a late-model Plymouth, painted a flat ugly brown-green.

'Obviously a government heap,' Faye said.

'Pretty bold, aren't they?'

'Well, if they've been eavesdropping on us the way Jack says, through our own telephones, then they know we're on to them, so maybe they figure there's no point in playing coy with us.' Faye took her foot off the brake and headed up the driveway.

Watching the unmarked Plymouth dwindle in the side mirror, Ginger said, 'Or maybe they're getting in position to take us into custody. Maybe they've put tails on all of us, and maybe they're just waiting for the order to snatch us all at the same time.'

On the narrow, gravel driveway, the interlacing shadows of the over-arching piñons wove a darkness nearly as deep as night.

*   *   *

As they drove up the two-lane road through the broad snow-covered meadow towards the massive blast doors, Colonel Falkirk sat in the front passenger's seat of the Wagoneer, thinking about the catastrophe that would ensue from the revelation of Thunder Hill's secret.

From a political perspective, this would make the Watergate mess look like a tea party. An unprecedented number of competing government institutions were involved in the cover-up, organisations that often operated in jealous opposition to one another – FBI, CIA, National Security Agency, the United States Army, the Air Force, and others. It was a testament to the degree of potential danger that these groups could work together with nary a hitch and without a single leak in more than eighteen months. But if the cover-up were

537

uncovered, the scandal would extend throughout so much of the government that the faith of the American people in their leaders would be severely shaken. Of course, very few in any of those organisations knew what had happened, no more than six in the FBI, fewer in the CIA; most of their men involved in the cover-up didn't know *what* they were covering up, which was why there had been no leaks. But the numero uno of each organisation – the director of the FBI, the director of the CIA, the Chief of Staff of the Army – was completely in the know. Not to mention the Chairman of the Joint Chiefs of Staff. And the Secretary of State. And the President, his closest advisors, the Vice-President. A lot of prominent men might fall from grace if this affair was not kept under lock and key.

The political destruction wrought by the release of the secret would be only a small part of the devastation. The CISG – a think-tank of physicists, biologists, anthropologists, sociologists, theologists, economists, educators, and other learned people – had pondered precisely this crisis at great length and depth, years before it had arisen here in Nevada. The CISG had issued a 1220-page top-secret report on its conclusions, a document that offered some disturbing reading. Leland knew that report by heart, for he was the military representative to the CISG and had helped write several position papers included in the final text. Within the CISG, the opinion was unanimous that the world would never be the same if such an event were to occur. All societies, all cultures would be radically changed forever. Projected deaths over the first two years ranged in the millions.

Lt Horner, who was driving the Wagoneer, braked twenty feet in front of the giant blast doors that were set in the sudden steep upper slope of the meadow. He didn't wait for the huge barriers to open, for he was not driving directly into Thunder Hill. Horner turned right, into a small parking lot, where three minibuses, four Jeep wagons, a Land Rover, and several other vehicles stood side by side.

The twin blast doors, each thirty feet high and twenty feet wide, were so thick they could be opened only at a ponderous pace, producing a rumble that could be heard a mile away and *felt* in the air and in the ground at least half as far. When a truck – loaded with ammunition, weapons or supplies – pulled up in front of the drive-in entrance, the doors required five minutes to roll apart. Opening those hangar-size portals every time a lone man needed to walk in or out was unthinkably inefficient, so a second man-size door – nearly as formidable – was set in the hillside thirty feet to the right of the main entrance.

There was no better vault than Thunder Hill in which to keep the secret of July 6. It was an impregnable fortress.

Leland and Lt Horner hurried through the bitter air to the walk-in entrance. The small steel door, almost as blast-proof as the massive versions to the left, had an electronic lock that could be disengaged only by tapping the proper four numbers on a keyboard. The code changed every two weeks, and those entrusted with it were required to commit it to memory. Leland punched in the code, and the fourteen-inch-thick, lead-core door slid aside with a sudden pneumatic *whoosh*.

They stepped into a twelve-foot-long concrete tunnel about nine feet in diameter and brightly lit. It angled to the left. At the end was another door identical to the first, but it could not be opened until the outer door was closed. Leland touched a heat-sensitive switch just inside the tunnel entrance, and the outer door hissed shut behind him and Lt Horner.

Immediately, a pair of video cameras, mounted on the ceiling at opposite ends of the chamber, clicked on. The cameras tracked the two men as they walked to the inner door.

No human eyes were watching the colonel and lieutenant on any video display, for the system was operated entirely by VIGILANT, the security computer, as a precaution against the possibility that a traitor within Thunder Hill's own guard unit might open the facility to hostile forces. VIGILANT was not linked to the installation's main computer or to the outside world; therefore, it was invulnerable to saboteurs seeking to take control of it by means of a modem or other electronic tap.

The guard at the perimeter fence had notified VIGILANT that Colonel Leland Falkirk and Lt Thomas Horner would be arriving. Now, as they approached the inner door under the gazes of video cameras, the computer compared their appearance to stored holographic images of them, rapidly matching forty-two points of facial resemblance. It was impossible to deceive VIGILANT either with make-up or with a look-alike for an approved visitor. If Leland or Horner had been an imposter or unauthorised visitor, VIGILANT would have sounded an alarm, simultaneously filling the entrance tunnel with a sedative gas.

The lock on the inner door had no keyboard; no code would open it. Instead, a one-foot-square panel of glass was set in the wall beside the door. Leland almost pressed his right hand palm-down against the panel, hesitated, then used his left, and the glass lit, and a faint humming arose. VIGILANT scanned his palmprint and fingerprints, comparing them to the prints in its files.

Lt Horner said, 'Almost as hard to get in here as into heaven.'

'Harder,' Leland said.

The light behind the milky glass winked out, and Leland took his hand away. The inner door opened.

They stepped into a huge natural tunnel that had been improved by human hands. The domed rock overhead was lost in darkness because the lighting fixtures were suspended from black metal scaffolding, creating the illusion of a ceiling perhaps twenty or thirty feet below the true ceiling. The tunnel was sixty feet across and led into the mountain about a hundred and twenty yards. In some places the rock walls had natural contours, but in other places they carried the imprints of dynamite blasts and jackhammers and other tools that had been used to widen the narrow portions of the passageway. Incoming trucks could drive along the concrete floor to unloading bays inside immense cargo elevators that went down into deeper regions of the facility.

A guard sat at a table beyond the door by which Leland and Horner entered. Considering the remoteness of Thunder Hill, the extent of sophisticated defences, and the thoroughness with which VIGILANT examined all visitors, a lone sentry seemed superfluous to Leland.

Evidently, the sentry was of that same opinion, for he was not prepared for trouble. His revolver was holstered. He was eating a candy bar. Reluctantly, he looked up from an old novel by Jack Finney.

He wore a coat because the open areas of the Depository were never heated; only the enclosed living quarters and work areas were kept warm. An enormous power supply was provided by a mini hydro-electric plant that harnessed an underground river, plus back-up diesel generators, but there was not enough to warm the mammoth caverns. The subterannean temperature was a stable fifty-five degrees, quite bearable if one dressed for long work periods in the chilly air, as the guard had done.

He saluted. 'Colonel Falkirk, Lieutenant Horner, you're cleared to see Dr Bennell. You know how to find him, of course.'

'Of course,' Falkirk said.

Ten feet to the left, the burnished steel surface of the giant blast doors glimmered softly in the fluorescent light, looking rather like the sheer face of a great glacier. Leland and Lt Horner turned right, away from the big doors, and walked deeper into the mountain, toward the elevators.

Thunder Hill Depository was equipped with hydraulic lifts of three sizes, the largest of which rivalled the enormous elevators on aircraft carriers. A carrier's lifts were used to bring planes from the ship's hold onto the flight deck, and Thunder Hill's also lowered and raised planes, among other things. In addition to 2.4 billion dollars of equipment and material – freeze-dried food, medicine, portable field hospitals, clothing, blankets, tents, handguns, rifles, mortars, field artillery, ammunition, light military vehicles such as Jeeps and armoured personnel carriers, and a twenty backpack nukes – the vast storage dump contained a variety of useful aircraft. First, the helicopters: thirty Sikorsky S-67 Blackhawk anti-tank gunships; twenty Bell Kingcobras; eight Anglo-French Westland Pumas, general purpose transports; and three big Medevac choppers. No conventional aircraft were stored at Thunder Hill, but there were twelve vehicle take-off jets of the type manufactured in England and known there as Hawker Siddeley Harriers, but which were called AV-8As when in US service. Because the Harriers were equipped with powerful vectored-thrust engines, the craft could land and take-off vertically, without need of a runway. In a grave crisis – for example, subsequent to a limited nuclear strike and a land invasion by enemy troops – the aircraft of Thunder Hill, both choppers and Harriers, could be lifted to the top level, rolled out through the massive blast doors, and sent hurtling into the sky.

However, the current crisis did not involve war or require the unleashing of the Depository's aircraft, so Leland and the lieutenant by-passed the two immense elevators. They also passed the two smaller but still over-size cargo elevators, their footsteps echoing off the stone walls, and took one of the three smallest cabs – about the size of a standard lift in a hotel – down into the bowels of Thunder Hill.

Medical supplies, food, guns, and all ammunition were stored on the third level, the bottom floor of the complex, in a network of chambers which had been caulked, equipped with pressure-release bores, and fitted with doors for the purposes of blast-containment. On the second – the middle – level, all the vehicles and aircraft were kept in other huge caverns, and it was there, too, that the staff lived and worked.

Leland and Lt Horner got off the lift at the second level. They stepped into a lighted, circular, rock-wall chamber three hundred feet in diameter. It served as a hub – in fact, personnel called it The Hub – from which four other caverns opened; and still more rooms lay beyond those four. The larger of those deep vaults contained – among other things – the aircraft, Jeeps, and armoured personnel carriers.

There were no doors on three of the four caverns which led off The Hub, for there was no serious danger of fire or explosion on that level. But the fourth chamber did, indeed, have doors, for it contained the secret of July 6, which Leland and many others had conspired to conceal. He stopped now, a few steps out of the elevator, to study those portals, which were twenty-six feet high and sixty-four feet wide. They were made of cross-braced two-by-fours rather than steel, because they had been jerry-built to meet an emergency situation; there had been no time to order a fabricated metal door to close off the cavern. They reminded the colonel of the enormous wooden doors in the wall that had protected the frightened natives from the beast on the other half of their island in the original *King Kong*. Considering what lay behind these doors, that horror-movie image did not inspire confidence. Leland shuddered.

Lt Horner said, 'Still gives you the creeps, huh?'

'You mean you're comfortable with it now?'

'Hell no, sir. Hell, no.'

Inset in the bottom of one of those huge wooden barriers

was a much smaller, man-size door through which researchers entered and exited the room beyond. An armed guard was positioned there to allow entrance only to those with the proper pass. The activities in that forbidden chamber had nothing to do with the other – primary – functions of the Depository, and ninety per cent of the personnel were not permitted access to the area. Indeed, ninety percent did not know what was in that cavern.

Around the circumference of The Hub, between the four openings to other caverns, buildings had been erected along the walls and anchored to the rock. The structures dated to the first year of the Depository's construction, back in the early 1960s. Then, they had served as offices for engineers, superintendents, and the Army's project officers. Over the years, an entire subterranean town had been erected in other caverns – sleeping quarters, cafeteria, recreation rooms, laboratories, machine shops, vehicle service centre, computer rooms, even a PX, among other things. They were now occupied by the military and government personnel who were doing one- and two-year tours of duty at Thunder Hill. In the buildings, there was heat, better lighting, inside and outside telephone lines, kitchens, bathrooms, and all the myriad comforts of home. They were constructed of metal panels coated with baked blue or white or grey enamel, with only small windows and narrow metal doors. Though they had no wheels, they somewhat resembled motor homes or house trailers drawn in a circle, as if they were the property of a modern-day encampment of gypsies who had found their way to this snug haven, 240 feet below the winter snows.

Now, turning from the forbidden chamber with the wooden doors, Leland walked across The Hub towards a white metal structure – Dr Miles Bennell's offices. Lt Horner fell in dutifully at his side.

The summer before last, Miles Bennell (whom Leland Falkirk loathed) had moved into Thunder Hill to head all scientific inquiry into the events of that fateful July night. He'd only been out of the Depository on three occasions since then, never for longer than two weeks. He was obsessed with his assignment. Or something worse than obsessed.

A dozen officers, enlisted men, and civilians were in sight

within The Hub, some crossing from one adjoining cavern to another, some just standing in conversation with one another. Leland looked them over as he passed them, unable to understand what kind of person would volunteer to work underground for weeks and months at a stretch. They were paid a thirty per cent hardship bonus, but to Leland's way of thinking, that was inadequate compensation. The Depository was less oppressive than Shenkfield's small, windowless warrens, but not by much.

Leland supposed he was slightly claustrophobic. Being underground made him feel as if he were buried alive. As an admitted masochist, he should have relished his discomfort, but this was one kind of pain he did not seek or enjoy.

Dr Miles Bennell looked ill. Like nearly everyone in Thunder Hill, he was pasty-faced from being too long beyond the reach of sunlight. His curly black hair and beard only made his pallor more pronounced. In the fluorescent glare of his office, he looked almost like a ghost. He greeted Leland and Lt Horner curtly, and he did not offer to shake hands with either of them.

That suited the colonel fine. He was no friend of Bennell's. A handshake would have been sheer hypocrisy. Besides, Leland was half-afraid that Miles Bennell had been compromised, that the scientist was no longer who or what he appeared to be . . . was no longer entirely human. And if that crazy, paranoid possibility was in fact true, he wanted no physical contact with Bennell, not even a quick handshake.

'Dr Bennell,' Leland said coldly, using the hard tone of voice and icy demeanour that always elicited quaverous obedience, 'your handling of this security breach has been criminally inept, or *you're* the traitor we're looking for. Now, hear me loud and clear: this time, we're going to find the bastard who sent those Polaroid snapshots – no more broken lie detectors, no more botched interrogations – and we're going to find out if he's the one who teased Jack Twist into returning, and we're going to come down on him so hard he'll wish he'd been born a fly and spent his life in a stable sucking up horseshit.'

Utterly unruffled, Miles Bennell smiled and said, 'Colonel, that was the best Richard Jaeckel impression I've ever seen, but entirely unnecessary. I'm as anxious as you to find the leak and plug it.'